Dear Reader,

In this trio of classic novels, the incomparable Nora Roberts shows her mastery of romantic suspense. *Suspicious* features three thrilling tales full of mystery, intrigue and—of course—love.

Rival reporters Laurel Armand and Matthew Bates prove to be unwilling *Partners* when they're assigned to investigate a murder case. But can they blame it on the sultry New Orleans heat when their rivalry turns to romance?

While visiting the home of an eccentric sculptor, Adam Haines is drawn to his host's beautiful daughter, Kirby Fairchild. But what secret is he hiding from her? Is Adam well versed in *The Art of Deception* as well as passion?

Maggie Fitzgerald left California seeking peace and solitude in the Maryland hills. She never expected to find a skeleton in her backyard—or love in the arms of irresistible Cliff Delaney. Can Cliff keep Maggie safe until the mystery of the skeleton is solved, in *Night Moves?*

We hope you enjoy these reader favorites, available again for the first time in several years.

The Editors
Silhouette Books

NORA ROBERTS

SUSPICIOUS

Silhouette® Books

Published by Silhouette Books

America's Publisher of Contemporary Romance

SILHOUETTE BOOKS

SUSPICIOUS

Copyright © 2003 by Harlequin Books S.A.

ISBN 0-373-21873-7

The publisher acknowledges the copyright holder
of the individual works as follows:

PARTNERS
Copyright © 1985 by Nora Roberts

THE ART OF DECEPTION
Copyright © 1986 by Nora Roberts

NIGHT MOVES
Copyright © 1985 by Nora Roberts

This edition published by arrangement with Harlequin Books S.A.

® and TM are trademarks of Harlequin Books S.A., used under license.
Trademarks indicated with ® are registered in the United States Patent
and Trademark Office, the Canadian Trade Marks Office and in other
countries.

Visit Silhouette at www.eHarlequin.com

Printed in U.S.A.

CONTENTS

PARTNERS   9

THE ART OF DECEPTION   199

NIGHT MOVES   393

PARTNERS

For Bruce, who changed my plans.

Chapter 1

Bedlam. Phones rang continuously. People shouted, muttered or swore, sitting or on the run. Typewriter keys clattered at varying paces from every direction. There was the scent of old coffee, fresh bread, tobacco smoke and human sweat. An insane asylum? Several of the inmates would have agreed with that description of the city room of the *New Orleans Herald,* especially at deadline.

For most of the staff the chaos went unnoticed, as the inhaling and exhaling of air went unnoticed. There were times when each one of them was too involved with their own daily crises or triumphs to be aware of the dozens of others springing up around them. Not that teamwork was ignored. All were bound, by love for, or obsession with, their jobs, in the exclusive community of journalists. Still each would concentrate on, and greedily guard, his or her own story, own sources and own style. A successful print reporter thrives on pressure and confusion and a hot lead.

Matthew Bates had cut his teeth on newsprint. He'd worked it from every angle from newsboy on the Lower East Side of Manhattan to feature reporter. He'd carried coffee, run copy, written obituaries and covered flower shows.

The ability to scent out a story and draw the meat from it wasn't something he'd learned in his journalism courses; he'd been born with it. His years of structured classes, study and practice had honed the style and technique of a talent that was as inherent as the color of his eyes.

At the age of thirty, Matt was casually cynical but not without humor for life's twists and turns. He liked people without having illusions about them. He understood and accepted that humans were basically ridiculous. How else could he work in a room full of crazy people in a profession that constantly exposed and exploited the human race?

Finishing a story, he called out for a copy boy, then leaned back to let his mind rest for the first time in three hours. A year ago, he'd left New York to accept the position on the *Herald,* wanting, perhaps needing, a change. Restless, he thought now. He'd been restless for…something. And New Orleans was as hard and demanding a town as New York, with more elegant edges.

He worked the police beat and liked it. It was a tough world, and murder and desperation were parts of it that couldn't be ignored. The homicide he'd just covered had been senseless and cruel. It had been life; it had been news. Now, he wiped the death of the eighteen-year-old girl out of his mind. Objectivity came first, unless he wanted to try a new profession. Yet it took a concentrated effort to erase her image and her ending from his mind.

He hadn't the looks of a seasoned, hard-boiled reporter, and he knew it. It had exasperated him in his twenties that he looked more like a carefree surfer than a newsman. Now, it amused him.

He had a lean, subtly muscled body that was more at home in jeans than a three-piece suit, with a height that only added a feeling of ranginess. His dark blond hair curled as it chose, over his ears, down to the collar of his shirt. It merely added to the image of a laid-back, easygoing male who'd rather be sitting on the beach than pounding the pavement. More than one source had talked freely to the façade without fully comprehending the man beneath the image. When and if they did, Matt already had the story.

When he chose, he could be charming, even elegant. But the good-humored blue eyes could turn to fire or, more dan-

gerous, ice. Beneath the easy exterior was a cold, hard determination and a smoldering temper. Matt accepted this with a
shrug. He was human, and entitled to be ridiculous.

With a half smile lingering around his mouth, he turned to
the woman seated across from him. Laurel Armand—with a
face as romantic as her name. She had an aura of delicacy
that came from fine bones and an ivory skin that made a man
want to touch, and touch gently. Her hair fell in clouds of
misty black, swept back from her face, spilling onto her shoulders. Hair made for a man to dive his fingers into, bury his
face in. Her eyes were the color of emeralds, dark and rich.

It was the face of a nineteenth-century belle whose life
revolved around gracious indolence and quiet gentility. And
her voice was just as feminine, Matt mused. It turned vowels
into liquid and smoothed consonants. It never flattened, never
twanged, but flowed like a leisurely stream.

The voice, he reflected as his smile widened, was just as
deceptive as the face. The lady was a sharp, ambitious reporter
with a stubborn streak and a flaring temper. One of his favorite pastimes was setting a match to it.

Her brows were drawn together as she finished the last line
of her copy. Satisfied, Laurel whipped the sheet from her typewriter, called for a copy boy, then focused on the man across
from her. Automatically, her spine straightened. She already
knew he was going to bait her, and that—damn it—she would
bite.

"Do you have a problem, Matthew?" Her tone was soft
and faintly bored.

"No problem, Laurellie." He watched the annoyance flare
into her eyes at his use of her full name.

"Don't you have a murder or armed robbery to go play
with?"

His mouth curved, charmingly, deepening the creases in his
face. "Not at the moment. Off your soapbox for the day?"

She gritted her teeth on a spate of furious words. He never
failed to dig for the emotion that seeped into her work, and
she never failed to defend it. Not this time, Laurel told herself
as she balled her hands into fists under her desk. "I leave the

cynicism to you, Matthew," she returned with a sweetness belied by the daggers in her eyes. "You're so good at it."

"Yeah. How about a bet on whose story makes page one?"

She lifted one fragile, arched brow—a gesture he particularly admired. "I wouldn't want to take your money, Matthew."

"I don't mind taking yours." Grinning, he rose to walk around their desk and bend down to her ear. "Five bucks, magnolia blossom. Even though your papa owns the paper, our editors know the difference between reporting and crusading."

He felt the heat rise, heard the soft hiss of breath. It was tempting, very tempting, to crush his mouth onto those soft, pouting lips and taste the fury. Even as the need worked into him, Matt reminded himself that wasn't the way to outwit her.

"You're on, Bates, but make it ten." Laurel stood. It infuriated her that she had to tilt her head back to meet his eyes. It infuriated her more that the eyes were confident, amused and beautiful. Laurel fell back on the habit of imagining him short, rotund and balding. "Unless that's too rich for your blood," she added.

"Anything to oblige, love." He curled the tips of her hair around his finger. "And to prove even Yankees have chivalry, I'll buy you lunch with my winnings."

She smiled at him, leaning a bit closer so that their bodies just brushed. Matt felt the surprising jolt of heat shoot straight through his system. "When hell freezes over," Laurel told him, then shoved him aside.

Matt watched her storm away; then, dipping his hands into his pockets, he laughed. In the confusion of the city room, no one noticed.

"Damn!" Laurel swore as she maneuvered her car through the choking downtown traffic. Matthew Bates was the most irritating man she'd ever known. Squeezing through on an amber light, she cursed fate. If her brother Curt hadn't met him in college, Matthew would never have accepted the position on the *Herald*. Then he'd be insufferable in New York instead of being insufferable two feet away from her day after day.

Honesty forced her to admit, even when it hurt, that he was the best reporter on the staff. He was thorough and insightful and had the instincts of a bloodhound. But that didn't make him any easier to swallow. Laurel hit the brakes and swerved as a Buick cut her off. She was too annoyed with Matt to be bothered by traffic warfare.

His piece on the homicide had been clean, concise and excellent. She wished she'd stuffed the ten dollars down his throat. That would've made it difficult for him to gloat over it.

In the twelve months she'd known and worked with him, he'd never reacted toward her as other men did. There was no deference in him, no admiration in his eyes. The fact that she despised being deferred to didn't make her resent him any less.

He'd never asked her out—not that she wanted him to, Laurel reminded herself firmly. Except for missing the pure pleasure of turning him down. Even though he'd moved into her apartment building, virtually next door to her, he'd never come knocking at her door on the smallest of pretenses. For a year she'd been hoping he would—so she could slam the door in his face.

What he did, she thought as she gritted her teeth, was make a nuisance of himself in a dozen other ways. He made cute little observations on her dates—all the more irritating because they were invariably true. These days his favorite target was Jerry Cartier, an ultraconservative, somewhat dense city councilman. Laurel saw him because she was too kindhearted not to, and he occasionally gave her a lead. But Matt put her in the intolerable position of having to defend Jerry against her own opinion.

Life would be simpler, she thought, if Matthew Bates were still hustling newsprint in Manhattan. And if he weren't so impossibly attractive. Laurel blocked Matt, and her ten dollars, out of her mind as she left the traffic behind.

Though the sun was hanging low, the sky was still brilliant. Warmth and light filtered through the cypresses and streamed onto the road. Deep in the trees were shadows and the musical sound of insects and birds, creatures of the marsh. She'd always known there were secrets in the marshes. Secrets, shadows, dangers. They only added to the beauty. There was something exciting in knowing another way of life thrived— primitive, predatory—so near civilization.

As she turned into the lane that led to her ancestral home, Laurel felt the familiar mix of pride and tranquility. Cedars guarded each side of the drive, arching overhead to transform the lane into a cool, dim tunnel. The sun filtered through sporadically, throwing patches of light on the ground. Spanish moss dripped from the branches to add that timeless grace so peculiar to the South. As she traveled down the drive of Promesse d'Amour, the clock turned back. Life was easy.

At the end of the drive, Laurel stopped to look at the house. There were two rambling stories of white-washed brick surrounded by a profusion of azaleas, camellias and magnolias. The colors, vivid and delicate, the scents, exotic and gentle, added to the sense of antebellum style and indolence. With the window down, she could smell the mix of heat and fragrance.

There were twenty-eight Doric columns that added dignity rather than ostentation. Ivy clung to each corner post. The grillwork on the encircling balcony was as delicate as black lace and French doors led to it from every room. The effect of the house was one of durability, security and grace. Laurel saw it as a woman who had coped with the years and emerged with character and gentility. If the house had been flesh and blood, she couldn't have loved it more.

She took the side steps to the porch and entered without knocking. Her childhood had been spent there, her girlhood, her adolescence. A wide hallway split the building in two, running from front door to back. Lingering in the air was the scent of beeswax and lemon, to mix with the fragrance from a bowl of camellia blossoms. The hall would have held the same scent a century before. Laurel paused only briefly in front of a cheval glass to brush the hair away from her face before she walked into the front parlor.

"Hello, Papa." She went to him, rising on her toes to kiss

a cheek rough from a day's growth of beard. William Armand
was lanky and handsome with dark hair just hinting at gray.
While he ran his daily paper with verve, temper and tenacity,
he chose an easier pace for his personal life. He smelled of
good whiskey and tobacco. In an old habit, he mussed the
hair Laurel had just straightened.

"Hello, princess. Good story on the mayor." He lifted a
brow in puzzlement as he saw the quick flash of irritation in
her eyes.

"Thanks." She smiled so quickly, her father thought he'd
imagined that dangerous light. Turning, she studied the
woman who sat in a royal-blue tufted chair.

The hair was pure white, but as full and thick as Laurel's.
It surrounded a face layered and lined with wrinkles and un-
ashamedly rouged. Olivia Armand wasn't ashamed of anything. Eyes as sharp and green as the emeralds in her ears
studied Laurel in turn.

"Grandma." With a sigh, Laurel bent to kiss her. "Will
you never grow old?"

"Not if I have anything to say about it." Her voice was
raspy with age and stunningly sensual. "You're the same,"
she continued, taking Laurel's hand in her strong, dry one.
"It's good Creole blood." After giving Laurel's hand a quick
squeeze, she sat back in her chair. "William, fix the child a
drink and top mine off while you're at it. How's your love
life these days, Laurellie?"

Grinning, Laurel dropped down on the hassock at her
grandmother's feet. "Not as varied as yours." She caught her
father's wink as he handed her a glass.

"Hogwash!" Olivia tossed back her bourbon. "I'll tell you
what's wrong with the world today, too much business and
not enough romance. Your problem, Laurellie—" she paused
to jab a finger at her granddaughter "—is wasting time on
that spineless Cartier. Not enough blood in him to warm a
woman's bed."

"Thank God," Laurel said with a grateful look at the ceiling. "That's the last place I want him."

"Time you had someone there," Olivia retorted.

Laurel lifted a brow while her father tried not to choke on

his drink. "Not all of us," Laurel said smoothly, "have your, shall we say, bawdy turn of mind."

Olivia gave a hoot of laughter and smacked the arm of her chair. "Not everyone admits it, that's the difference."

Unable to resist her grandmother's outrageousness, Laurel grinned. "Curt should be here soon, shouldn't he?"

"Any minute." William eased his tall, angular frame into a chair. "He called just before you came in. He's bringing a friend with him."

"A woman, I hope," Olivia said irrepressibly before she polished off her bourbon. "Boy's got his nose stuck in too many law books. Between the two of you," she added, rounding on Laurel again, "I'll never be a great-grandmother. The pair of you're too wrapped up in law and newspapers to find a lover."

"I'm not ready to get married," Laurel said tranquilly as she held her glass up to the light.

"Who said anything about marriage?" Olivia wanted to know. Heaving a sigh, she looked at her son. "Children nowadays don't know anything."

Laurel was laughing when she heard the sound of the front door closing. "That'll be Curt. I believe I'll warn him about the frame of mind you're in."

"Damned pretty girl," Olivia muttered when Laurel strolled out.

"She's the image of you," her son commented as he lit one of his cigars.

Olivia cackled. "Damned pretty."

The moment she entered the hall, Laurel's smile faded and her jaw tensed. Her eyes flicked over her brother to the man beside him. "Oh, it's you."

Matt took her hand, raising it to his lips before Laurel could jerk it away. "Ah, southern hospitality." Good God, he thought as his gaze roamed over her, she's beautiful. All that passion, all that fire, under ivory and roses. One day, Laurellie, he promised silently, we're going to set it all loose. My way.

Ignoring the warmth that lingered on her knuckles from his lips, Laurel turned to her brother. He had the angularity and aristocratic features of their father, and the eyes of a dreamer. As Matt watched, the restrained temper on her face softened with affection.

"Hi." She put her hands on her brother's shoulders, leaving them there after she'd kissed him. "How are you?"

"Fine. Busy." He gave her an absent smile, as if he'd just remembered where he was.

"The busy might be an issue tonight," she told him with a chuckle. "Grandma's in one of her moods."

He gave her such a pained look that Laurel laughed and kissed him again. Poor Curt, she thought, so shy and sweet. Turning her head, she looked directly into Matt's eyes. He was watching her coolly, with something undefinable flickering behind the aloof expression. A tremble skidded up her spine, but she kept her eyes level. Who is he really? she wondered, not for the first time. And why, after an entire year, am I still not sure? It always puzzled her how a man with his energy, wit and cynicism should remain such good friends with her gentle, dreamy brother. It puzzled her, too, that she couldn't pin him down to a type. Perhaps that was why he invaded her thoughts so often. Involuntarily, her gaze slipped down to his mouth. It curved. Silently, she swore.

"I guess we'd better go in," Curt said, oblivious to the undercurrents around him. He smiled in a quick, boyish way that animated his soft eyes. "Having Matt along should distract her. Distracting women's one of his best talents."

Laurel gave an unladylike snort. "I'll bet."

As Curt started into the parlor, Matt took Laurel's hand and tucked it into his arm. "Another wager, Laurellie?" he murmured. "Name the stakes."

There was something insolent in the softly spoken words. She tossed her head back in an angry gesture that pleased him enormously. "If you don't let go of my hand, I'm going to—"

"Embarrass yourself," Matt finished as they crossed the threshold into the parlor.

He'd always liked the room—the faded colors and polished old wood. There were times when he was here that Matt forgot the years he'd spent in a cramped third-floor walk-up with a radiator that let off more noise than heat. That part of his life was over; he'd seen to it. Yet snatches of it crept up on him in spite of success. Shoes that were too small, a belly never quite full—an ambition that threatened to outdistance opportunity. No, he'd never take success for granted. He'd spent too many years fighting for it.

"So, you've brought the Yankee, have you?" Olivia sent Matt a sparkling look and prepared to enjoy herself.

Curt greeted his father, dutifully kissed Olivia's cheek, then busied himself mixing drinks. Grandma had that look in her eye.

"Miss Olivia." Matt took the offered hand and lifted it to his lips. "More beautiful than ever."

"Rascal," she accused, but the pleasure came through. "You haven't been to see me for a month—a dangerous amount of time at my age."

Matt kissed her hand again while his eyes laughed into hers. "I only stay away because you won't marry me."

Laurel struggled not to smile as she chose a chair across the room. Did he have to be so damned charming?

Olivia's laugh was a sound of pure, feminine appreciation. "Thirty years ago, you scoundrel, I'd have given you a chase, even if you are a Yankee."

Matt took the offered glass, and the grateful look, Curt gave him before he turned back to Olivia. "Miss Olivia, I wouldn't have run." He perched on the arm of her chair, much, Laurel thought resentfully, like a favored nephew.

"Well, the time's passed for that," she decided with a sigh before she aimed a look at Laurel. "Why haven't you taken up with this devil, Laurellie? He's a man to keep a woman's blood moving."

Color, as much from annoyance as embarrassment, rose in Laurel's cheeks as Matt sent her a wolfish grin. She sat in stony silence, cursing the fairness of her skin.

"Now that's a fine, feminine trick," her grandmother observed, tapping Matt on the thigh. "Good for the complexion, too. Why, I could still call out a blush on demand after I'd had a husband and three lovers under my belt." Pleased with the deadly stare her granddaughter aimed at her, Olivia lifted her face to Matt's. "Good-looking girl, isn't she?"

"Lovely," Matt agreed, enjoying himself almost as much as Olivia was.

"Breed fine sons."

"Have another drink, Mother," William suggested, observing the war signals in his daughter's eyes.

"Fine idea." She handed over her empty glass. "You haven't seen the gardens, Matthew. They're at their peak. Laurellie, take this Yankee out and show him what a proper garden looks like."

Laurel shot her grandmother an icy glare. "I'm sure Matthew—"

"Would love to," he finished for her, rising.

She switched the glare to him without any effort. "I don't—"

"Want to be rude," he supplied quietly as he helped her out of her chair.

Oh, yes, she did, Laurel thought as she swung through the garden doors. She wanted very badly to be rude. But not in front of her family, and he knew it. "You really enjoy this, don't you?" she hissed at him the moment the door closed behind them.

"Enjoy what?" Matt countered.

"Infuriating me."

"It's impossible not to enjoy something one's so good at."

She chuckled, then despised herself. "All right, here's the garden." She made a wide gesture. "And you don't want to see it any more than I want to show it to you."

"Wrong," Matt said simply, and took her hand again.

"Will you stop that!" Exasperated, Laurel shook her hand but failed to free it. "That's a new habit you've picked up."

"I just found out I like it." He drew her off the terrace onto one of the narrow paths that wound through the flowers. "Besides, if you don't make a good showing at this, Olivia'll just think of something else."

Too true, Laurel admitted. She'd tolerate the man beside her. After all, the sun was splashing red on the horizon and the garden smelled like paradise. It'd been too long since she'd taken the time to see it at dusk. They walked under an arched trellis with wisteria dripping like rain. The birds of the sunlight were beginning to quiet, and those of the night had yet to wake.

"I've always loved it best at this time of day," Laurel said without thinking. "You can almost see the women with their hooped skirts swishing along the edges of the paths. There'd have been musicians in the gazebo and strings of colored lanterns."

He'd known she had a streak of romance, a touch of her brother's dreaminess, but she'd been so careful not to show either to him before. Instinctively, he knew she hadn't meant to now, but the garden had weakened her. He wondered, as he trailed his thumb lightly over her knuckles, what other weaknesses she might have.

"It would've smelled the same then as it does tonight," Matt murmured, discovering just how exquisite her skin looked in the golden light of sunset. "Hot and sweet and secret."

"When I was a girl, I'd come out here sometimes at dusk and pretend I was meeting someone." The memory made her smile, a little dreamy, a little wistful. "Sometimes he'd be dark and dashing—or he'd be tall and blond, but always dangerous and unsuitable. The kind of man a young girl's papa would've whisked her away from." She laughed, letting her fingers trail over a waxy, white camellia. "Strange that I would've had those kinds of fancies when my papa knew I was much too ambitious and practical to fall for a..."

Laurel trailed off when she turned her head and found him close—so close it was his scent that aroused her senses rather than the blossom's; his breath she felt on her skin rather than the sultry evening air. The light was touched with gold, blushed with rose. Hazy, magical. In it, he looked too much like someone she might have dreamed of.

Matt let his fingers play lightly with the pulse at her wrist. It wasn't steady, but this time it wasn't anger that unsettled it. "A what?"

"A rogue," Laurel managed after a moment.

They were talking softly, as if they were telling secrets. The sun slipped lower, and the shadows lengthened.

His face was so lean, she thought suddenly. Not predatory,

but the face of a man who wouldn't step aside if trouble got in his way. His eyes were guarded, but she'd noticed before how easily he concealed his thoughts. Perhaps that was why he nudged information from people without appearing to nudge at all. And his mouth—how was it she'd never realized how tempting, how sensual his mouth was? Or had she simply pretended not to? It wouldn't be soft, she thought as her gaze lingered on it. It would be hard, and the taste essentially male. She could lean just a bit closer and...

Laurel's eyes widened at the drift of her own thoughts. Beneath Matt's fingers, her pulse scrambled before she yanked her hand away. Good Lord, *what* had gotten into her? He'd tease her for months if he had any idea how close she'd come to making a fool of herself.

"We'd better go back in," she said coolly. "It's nearly time for dinner."

Matt had an urge to grab her and take the kiss she'd very nearly given him. And if he did that, he'd lose whatever inching progress he'd made. He'd wanted her for a long time— too long—and was shrewd enough to know she would have refused ordinary advances from the first. Matt had chosen the out of the ordinary, finding it had its amusements.

Patience, Matt reminded himself, was a crucial element of success—but she deserved one small dig for making him pound with desire and frustration.

"So soon?" His voice was mild, his expression ironic. "If Olivia had sent you out here with Cartier I doubt you'd have cut the tour so short."

"She'd never have sent me out here with Jerry," Laurel said before the meaning of her statement sank in.

"Ah." It was a sound designed to infuriate.

"Don't start on Jerry," Laurel snapped.

Matt gave her an innocent grin. "Was I?"

"He's a very nice man," she began, goaded. "He's well mannered and—and harmless."

Matt threw back his head and roared. "God save me from being labeled harmless."

Her eyes frosted and narrowed. "I'll tell you what you

are," she said in a low, vibrating voice. "You're insufferable."

"Much better." Unable to resist, he stepped closer and
gathered her hair in one hand. "I have no desire to be nice,
well mannered or harmless."

She wished his fingers hadn't brushed her neck. They'd left
an odd little trail of shivers. "You've gotten your wish," she
said, not quite evenly. "You're annoying, rude and..."

"Dangerous?" he supplied, lowering his head so that their
lips were only inches apart.

"Don't put words in my mouth, Bates." Why did she feel
as though she were running the last leg of a very long race?
Struggling to even her breathing, Laurel took a step back and
found herself against the wall of the trellis. She would have
sidestepped if he hadn't moved so quickly, blocking her.

"Retreating, Laurellie?" No, it wasn't just temper, he
thought, watching the pulse hammer at the base of her throat.
Not this time.

Something warm moved through her, like a lazy river. Her
spine snapped straight. Her chin jutted up. "I don't have to
retreat from you. It's bad enough that I have to tolerate you
day after day at the *Herald,* but I'll be damned if I'll stand
here and waste my *own* time. I'm going in," she finished on
a near shout, "because I'm hungry."

Shoving him out of her way, Laurel stormed back toward
the house. Matt stayed where he was a moment, looking after
her—the swinging hair, the long, graceful strides, the simmering fury. That, he thought, was one hell of a woman. Making love to her would be a fascinating experience. He intended
to have it, and her, very soon.

Chapter 2

Because she was still seething from the night before, Laurel decided to walk to the paper. Half an hour in the warm air, shifting her way through people, pausing by store windows, listening to snatches of casual conversation from other pedestrians would go a long way toward soothing her agitation. The city, like the plantation house outside it, was an old, consistent love. Laurel didn't consider it a contradiction that she could be drawn to the elegant timelessness of Promesse d'Amour and the bustling rush of downtown traffic. For as long as she could remember, she'd straddled both worlds, feeling equally at home in each. She was ambitious—she was romantic. Practicality and dreaminess were both a part of her nature, but she'd never minded the tug-of-war. At the moment, she felt more comfortable with the noise and hustle around her than with the memory of a twilight garden.

What had he been up to? she asked herself again, jamming her hands in her pockets. Laurel felt she knew Matt well enough to understand that he rarely did anything without an underlying purpose. He'd never touched her quite like that before. Scowling into a shop window, Laurel recalled that Matthew Bates had rarely touched her at all in an entire year. And last night...last night, Laurel remembered, there had been something almost casual about the way his fingers had brushed the back of her neck and skimmed over her wrist. *Almost* casual, she repeated. But there'd been nothing casual about her response to it.

Obviously, he had caught her off-balance—intentionally, Laurel added with a deeper scowl. What she'd felt hadn't been excitement or anticipation, but simply surprise. She was fully recovered now. The garden had been moody, romantic. She'd always been susceptible to moods, that was why she'd found herself telling him foolish things. And why, just for a minute, she'd wanted to feel what it would be like to be held against him.

Blossoms and sunsets. A woman might find the devil himself attractive in that kind of a setting. Temporarily. She'd pulled herself back before she'd done anything humiliating, Laurel reminded herself.

Then there was her grandmother. Laurel gritted her teeth and waited for the light to change. Normally, Olivia's outlandish remarks didn't bother her in the least, but she was going too far when she insinuated that Matthew Bates was exactly what her granddaughter needed.

Oh, he'd lapped that up, Laurel remembered, glaring straight ahead. He was easily as impossible as the old girl herself—without her charm, Laurel added loyally. She took a deep breath of the city—exhaust, humanity, heat. Right now, she appreciated it for what it was: genuine. She wasn't going to let an absurd incident in a fantasy world spoil her day. Determined to forget it, and the man who'd caused it, she started to step off the curb.

"Good morning, Laurellie."

Surprised, she nearly stumbled when a hand shot and grabbed her arm. Good God, wasn't there anywhere in New Orleans she could get away from him? Turning her head, she gave Matt a long, cool look. "Car break down?"

Haughtiness suited her, he mused, as well as temper did. "Nice day for a walk," he countered smoothly, keeping her arm as they started to cross the street. He wasn't fool enough to tell her he'd seen her start out on foot and followed the impulse to go after her.

Laurel made a point of disengaging her arm when they

reached the sidewalk. Why the hell hadn't she just gotten into her car as she would have any other morning? Short of making a scene on the street, she was stuck with him. When she gave him another glance, she caught the amused look in his eye that meant he'd read her thoughts perfectly. After rejecting the idea of knocking him over the head with her purse, Laurel gave him a cold smile.

"Well, Matthew, you seemed to enjoy yourself last night."

"I like your grandmother, she's beautiful," he said so simply, she stopped short. When her brows drew together, he smiled and ran a finger down her nose. "Isn't that allowed?"

With a shrug, Laurel began to walk again. How was she supposed to detest him when he was being sweet and sincere? Laurel made another stab at it. "You encourage her."

"She doesn't need any encouragement," he stated all too accurately. "But I like to anyway."

Laurel wasn't quite successful in smothering a laugh. The sidewalk was crowded enough to make it necessary for their arms to brush as they walked. "You don't seem to mind that she's setting you up as my...."

"Lover?" he suggested, with the annoying habit of finishing her thoughts. "I think Olivia, for all her, ah, liberated ideas, has something more permanent in mind. She threw in the house for good measure."

Stunned, Laurel gaped at him. He grinned, and her sense of the ridiculous took over. "You'd better be sure she tosses in some cash; it's the devil to maintain."

"I admit, it's tempting." He caught the ends of Laurel's hair in his fingers. "The...house," he said when her gaze lifted to his, "isn't something a man turns down lightly."

She slanted a look at him, one she'd never aimed in his direction before. Under the lashes, sultry, amused and irresistible. "Matthew," Laurel said in a soft drawl, "you'll put me in the position of considering Jerry more seriously."

Then, he thought as desire crawled into his stomach, I'd have to quietly kill him. "Olivia'd disown you."

Laurel laughed and, without thinking, linked her arm through his. "Ah, the choices a woman must make. My inheritance or my sensibilities. I guess it's just too bad for both of us that you're not my type.''

Matt put his hand on the glass door of the Herald Building before Laurel could pull it open. ''You put *me* in the position, Laurellie,'' he said quietly, ''of having to change your mind.''

She lifted a brow, not quite as sure of herself as she'd been a moment before. Why hadn't she noticed these rapid mood swings in him before? The truth was, she admitted, she'd dedicated herself to noticing as little about him as possible. From the first moment he'd walked into the city room, she had decided that was the safest course. Determined not to lose the upper hand this time, she smiled as she pushed through the door. ''Not a chance, Bates.''

Matt let her go, but his gaze followed her progress through the crowded lobby. If he hadn't already been attracted to her, her words would have forced his hand. He'd always liked going up against the odds. As far as he was concerned, Laurel had just issued the first challenge. With an odd sort of smile, he moved toward the bank of elevators.

Laurel's entire morning involved interviewing the director of a highway research agency. A story on road repair and detour signs wasn't exactly loaded with fire and flash, she mused, but news was news. Her job was to assimilate the facts, however dry they might be, and report. With luck she could get the story under the fold on page two. Perhaps the afternoon would yield something with a bit more meat.

The hallways, rarely deserted, were quiet in the late-morning lull. Other reporters returned from, or were on their way to, assignments, but most were already in the field or at their desks. Giving a perfunctory wave to a colleague hurrying by with an on-the-run lunch of a candy bar, she began to structure her lead paragraph. Preoccupied, she turned toward the city room and jolted another woman. The contents of the woman's purse scattered onto the floor.

''Damn!'' Without glancing over, Laurel crouched down and began to gather things up. ''Sorry, I wasn't looking where I was going.''

''It's all right.''

Laurel saw a very small hand reach out for a plain manila envelope. The hand was shaking badly. Concerned, she looked over at a pale blonde with pretty features and red-rimmed eyes. Her lips were trembling as badly as her hands.

"Did I hurt you?" Laurel took the hands in hers instinctively. A stray, an injured bird, a troubled stranger—she'd never been able to resist anything or anyone with a problem.

The woman opened her mouth, then closed it again to shake her head violently. The fingers Laurel gripped quivered helplessly. When the first tears rolled down the pale face, Laurel forgot the noise and demands of the city room, the notes scrawled in the book in her bag. Helping the woman up, Laurel led her through the maze of desks and into the glass-walled office of the city editor.

"Sit down," she ordered, nudging the blonde into a faded leather chair. "I'll get you some water." Without waiting for an agreement, Laurel strode out again. When she came back, she noted that the woman had swallowed her tears, but her face hadn't lost that wounded, bewildered expression. "Come on, sip this." After offering the paper cup, Laurel sat on the arm of the chair and waited.

Inside the office, she could hear the muted echo of activity from the city room. It was early enough in the day that desperation hadn't struck yet. Deadline panic was hours away. What desperation there was came from the blonde's efforts to steady her breathing. Hundreds of questions buzzed in Laurel's mind, but she gave the woman silence.

"I'm sorry." She crushed the now empty paper cup in her fingers before she looked up at Laurel. "I don't usually fall apart that way."

"It's all right." Laurel noticed the woman was slowly, systematically tearing the paper cup to shreds. "I'm Laurel Armand."

"Susan Fisher." Blankly, she looked down at the scraps of paper in her lap.

"Can I help, Susan?"

That almost started the tears again. Such simple words, Susan thought as she closed her eyes against them. Why should they make her feel all the more hopeless? "I don't know why

I came here," she began jerkily. "I just couldn't think of anything else. The police..."

Laurel's reporter's drive rose to tangle with her protective instincts. Both were too natural to her for her to even notice them. She laid a hand on Susan's shoulder. "I work here; you can talk to me. Would you like to start at the beginning?"

Susan stared up at her. She no longer knew whom to trust, or if indeed *trust* was a word to believe in. This woman looked so confident, so sure of herself. She'd never had her life shattered. Why would this poised, vibrant-looking woman listen, or believe?

Susan's eyes were blue, soft and light and vulnerable. Laurel didn't know why they made her think of Matt, a man she thought had no sensitivity at all, yet they did. She put her hand over Susan's. "I'll help you if I can."

"My sister." The words tumbled out, then stopped with a jerk. With an effort, Susan swallowed and began again. "My sister, Anne, met Louis Trulane a year ago."

Louis? The name shot through Laurel's mind so that the hand over Susan's stiffened. Bittersweet memories, loyalties, growing pains. What could this tearful, frightened woman have to do with Louis? "Go on," Laurel managed, making her fingers relax.

"They were married less than a month after they met. Anne was so much in love. We had—we were sharing an apartment at the time, and all she could talk about was Louis, and moving here to live in the fabulous old house he owned. Heritage Oak. Do you know it?"

Laurel nodded, staring off into nothing more than her own memories. "Yes, I know it."

"She sent me pictures of it. I just couldn't imagine Anne living there, being mistress of it. Her letters were full of it, and of Louis, of course." Susan paused as her breath came out in a shudder. "She was so happy. They were already talking about starting a family. I'd finally made arrangements to take some time off. I was coming to visit her when I got Louis's letter."

Laurel turned to take Susan's hand in a firmer grip. "Susan, I know—"

"She was dead." The statement was flat and dull, with shock still lingering around the edges. "Anne was dead. Louis wrote—he wrote that she'd gone out alone, after dark, wandered into the swamp. A copperhead bite, he said. If they'd found her sooner...but it wasn't until the next morning, and it was too late." Susan pressed her lips together, telling herself she had to get beyond the tears. The time for them was over. "She was only twenty-one, and so lovely."

"Susan, it must've been dreadful for you to hear that way. It was a terrible accident."

"Murder," Susan said in a deadly calm voice. "It was murder."

Laurel stared at her for a full ten seconds. Her first inclination to soothe and comfort vanished, replaced by a whiff of doubt, a tingle of interest. "Anne Trulane died of a snakebite and exposure. Why do you call it murder?"

Susan rose and paced to the window. Laurel hadn't patted her hand, hadn't made inane comments. She was still listening, and Susan felt a faint flicker of hope. "I'll tell you what I told Louis, what I told the police." She took an extra moment to let the air go in and out of her lungs slowly. "Anne and I were very close. She was always gentle, sensitive. She had a childlike sweetness without being childish. I want you to understand that I knew Anne as well as I know myself."

Laurel thought of Curt and nodded. "I do."

Susan responded to this sign of acceptance with a sigh. "Ever since she was little, Anne had a phobia about dark places. If she had to go into a room at night, she'd reach in and hit the light switch first. It was more than just habit, it was one of those small fears some of us never outgrow. Do you know what I mean?"

Thinking of her own phobia, she nodded again. "Yes, I know."

Susan stepped away from the window. "As much as Anne loved that house, having the swamp so near bothered her. She'd written me that it was like a dark closet—something she avoided even in the daytime. She loved Louis, wanted to please him, but she wouldn't go through it with him."

She whirled back to Laurel with eyes no longer calm, but

pleading. "You have to understand, she adored him, but she wouldn't, couldn't do that for him. It was like an obsession. Anne believed it was haunted—she'd even worked herself up to the point where she thought she saw lights out there. Anne would never have gone in there alone, at night."

Laurel waited a moment, while facts and ideas raced through her mind. "But she was found there."

"Because someone took her."

In silence, Laurel measured the woman who now stood across from her. Gone was the defenseless look. Though the eyes were still puffy and red-rimmed, there was a determination in them, and a demand to be believed. An older sister's shock and loyalty perhaps, Laurel mused, but she let bits and pieces of the story run through her mind, along with what she knew of Anne Trulane's death.

It had never been clear why the young bride had wandered into the swamp alone. Though Laurel had grown up with swamps and bayous, she knew they could be treacherous places, especially at night, for someone who didn't know them. Insects, bogs...snakes.

She remembered too how Louis Trulane had closed out the press after the tragedy—no interviews, no comment. As soon as the inquest had been over, he'd retreated to Heritage Oak.

Laurel thought of Louis, then looked at Susan. Loyalties tugged. And pulling from both sides was a reporter's instinct she'd been born with. The whys in life always demanded an answer.

"Why did you come to the *Herald,* Susan?"

"I went to see Louis last night as soon as I got into town. He wouldn't listen to me. This morning I went to the police." She lifted her hands in a gesture of futility. "Case closed. Before I had a chance to think about it, I was here. Maybe I should hire a private investigator, but..." Trailing off, she shook her head. "Even if that were the right way to go, I don't have the money. I know the Trulanes are a powerful, respected family, but there has to be a way of getting at the truth. My sister was murdered." This time her voice quivered on the statement and the color that had risen to her cheeks from agitation faded.

Not as strong as she wants to be, Laurel realized as she rose. "Susan, would you trust me to look into this?"

Susan dragged a hand through her hair. She didn't want to fall apart now, not now, when someone was offering the help she needed so badly. "I have to trust someone."

"There're a few things I have to do." Abruptly, Laurel became brisk. If there was a story, and she smelled one, she couldn't think of old ties, old memories. "There's a coffee machine in the lobby. Get a cup and wait for me there. When I've finished, we'll get something to eat—talk some more."

Asking no questions, Susan gathered up her purse, watching the torn bits of the paper cup drift to the floor. "Thank you."

"Don't thank me yet," Laurel advised. "I haven't done anything."

Susan paused at the door to glance over her shoulder. "Yes, you have."

Mouth pursed in thought, Laurel watched Susan wind her way through the desks in the city room. Anne Trulane, she thought, and let out a sigh. Louis. Good God, what kind of wasp's nest was she poking into?

Before she could formulate an answer, the city editor came in, his thin face creased into a scowl, his tired eyes annoyed. "Damn it, Laurel, this is a newspaper, not a Miss Lonely-hearts service. When one of your friends has a fight with her boyfriend, find someone else's office to flood. Now move it." He flopped down behind his cluttered desk. "You've got a story to write."

Laurel walked over to the desk and perched on the corner. Don Ballinger was her godfather, a man who had often bounced her on his knee. If it came to a toss-up between personal affection and news copy, the copy'd win hands down. Laurel expected no less. "That was Anne Trulane's sister," she said mildly when he opened his mouth to swear at her.

"Trulane," he repeated as his wispy brows drew together. "What'd she want?"

Laurel picked up a hunk of fool's gold Don used as a paperweight and shifted it from hand to hand. "To prove her sister was murdered."

He gave a short bark that might have been a laugh or a sound of derision. Don took a cigarette out of the desk drawer and ran it lovingly through his fingers. He stroked it, caressed it, but didn't light it. He hadn't lit one in sixteen days, ten hours...twenty-two minutes. "Snakebite," Don said simply, "and a night's exposure don't add up to murder. What about the story on the highway agency?"

"The sister tells me that Anne had a phobia about the dark," Laurel continued. "Anne supposedly mentioned the swamp where she died in her letters. She hadn't set foot in it, and didn't intend to."

"Obviously she changed her mind."

"Or someone changed it for her."

"Laurel—"

"Don, let me do some poking around." Laurel studied the glittering paperweight as she spoke. Things weren't always as they seemed, she mused. Not nearly always. "It couldn't hurt. If nothing else, I could work up a human interest piece."

Don scowled down at his cigarette, running a finger from filter to tip. "Trulane won't like it."

"I can deal with Louis," she said with more confidence than she felt. "There's something in this, Don. There was never any clear reason why Anne Trulane went out there alone. She was already dressed for bed."

They both knew the rumors—that she'd been meeting a lover, that Louis had bracketed her to the house until she'd simply gone out blindly, then lost herself. Don put the cigarette in his mouth and gnawed on the filter. The Trulanes were always good copy. "Nose around," he said at length. "It's still fresh news." Before Laurel could be too pleased that she'd won the first round, he dropped the bomb. "Bates covered the story, work with him."

"Work with Bates?" she repeated. "I don't need him. It's my lead, my story."

"His beat," Don countered, "and no one's story until there is one."

"Damn it, Don, the man's insufferable. I'm not some junior reporter who needs a proctor, and—"

"And he has the contacts, the sources and knows the background." He rose while Laurel simmered. "We don't play personality games on the *Herald,* Laurel. You work together." After shooting her a last look, he stuck his head out the door. "Bates!"

"You can't play personality games with someone who has none," Laurel muttered. "I'm the one who knows the Trulanes. He'll just get in my way."

"Sulking always was a bad habit of yours," Don commented as he rounded his desk again.

"I am not sulking!" she protested as Matt sauntered into the room.

He took one look at Laurel's furious face, lifted a brow and grinned. "Problem?"

Laurel controlled the urge to hiss at him, and sank into a chair. With Matthew Bates around, there was always a problem.

"Cheer up," Matt advised a few minutes later. "Before this is over, you might learn something."

"I don't need to learn anything from you." Laurel swung toward the elevator.

"That," he murmured, enjoying the way her lips formed into a pout, "remains to be seen."

"You're not taking on an apprentice, Bates, but a partner." She jammed her fists into her pockets. "Don insisted on it because you'd covered the investigation and the inquest. You could make it easy on both of us by just giving me your notes."

"The last thing I do," Matt said mildly, "is give anyone my notes."

"And the last thing I need is to have you breathing down my neck on this. It's *my* story."

"That really stuck where it hurts, didn't it?" Casually, he pushed the button on the elevator, then turned to her. "Didn't your papa ever tell you that sharing's good for the soul?"

Fuming, Laurel stepped into the car and pushed for lobby. "Go to hell."

She didn't know he could move quickly. Perhaps this was her first lesson. Before she had an inkling what he was doing,

Matt punched a button and stopped the car between floors. Even as her mouth fell open in surprise, he had her backed up against the side wall. "Watch how far you push," he warned softly, "unless you're willing to take a few hard shoves yourself."

Her throat was so dry it hurt. She'd never seen his eyes frost over like this. It was frightening. Fascinating. Odd, she thought she'd convinced herself he didn't have a temper, but now that it was about to grab her by the throat, she wasn't surprised. No, it wasn't surprise that had the chill racing over her skin.

She was frightened, Matt observed. But she wasn't cringing. Common sense told him to back off now that his point had been made. But a year was a very long time. "I think I'll just get this out of my system now, before we get started."

He saw her eyes widen, stunned as he lowered his mouth toward hers. A twist of amusement curved his lips as he allowed them to hover a breath from hers. "Surprised, Laurellie?"

Why wasn't she moving? Her body simply wouldn't respond to the commands of her brain. She was almost certain she was telling her arms to push him away. Good God, he had beautiful eyes. Incredibly beautiful eyes. His breath whispered over her skin, trailing into her mouth through lips that had parted without her knowledge. He smelled of no more than soap—basic, simple. Wonderful.

In an effort to clear her senses, Laurel straightened against the wall. "Don't you dare—"

The words ended with a strangled sound of pleasure as his lips skimmed over hers. It wasn't a kiss. No one would consider such a thing a kiss: a breath of a touch without pressure. It was more of a hint—or a threat. Laurel wondered if someone had cut the cables on the elevator.

She didn't move, not a muscle. Her eyes were wide open, her mind wiped clean as he stepped fractionally closer so that his body made full contact with hers—firm, lean, strong. Even as her system jolted, she didn't move. His mouth was still whispering on hers, so subtly, so impossibly light she might have imagined it. When she felt the moist tip of his tongue trace her lips, then dip inside to touch, just touch, the tip of hers, the breath she'd been holding shuddered out.

It was that quiet, involuntary sound of surrender that nearly broke his control. If she'd spit and snarled at him, he could have dealt with it easily. He'd been angry enough to. He hadn't expected stunned submission, not from her. Over the anger came a tempting sense of power, then an ache—gnawing and sweet—of need. Even as he nipped his teeth into her soft bottom lip he wondered if he'd ever have her at quite such a disadvantage again.

God, he wanted to touch her, to slip that neat little blouse off her shoulders and let his hands mold slowly, very, very slowly, every inch of her. That skin of hers, pale as a magnolia, soft as rainwater, had driven him mad for months. He could have her now, Matt thought as he nibbled ever so gently at her lips. He was skilled enough, she off guard enough that he could take her there on the floor of the elevator before either of them had regained their senses. It would be crazy, wonderfully crazy. Even as she stood still, he could all but taste that passion fighting to overcome her surprise and reach out for him. But he had different plans for the seduction of Laurel Armand.

So he didn't touch her, but lazily backed away. Not once during those shivering two minutes had she taken her eyes off his. Laurel watched that clever, tortuous mouth curve as he again pressed the button for the lobby. The elevator started with a rumble and jerk.

"A pity we're pressed for time," Matt commented easily, then gave the elevator car a careless glance. "And space."

Layer by layer the mists that had covered her brain cleared until she could think with perfect clarity. Her eyes were glimmering green slits, her ivory skin flushed with rage as she let out a stream of curses in a fluid, effortless style he had to admire.

"Did you know you completely drop your *r*s when your temper's loose?" Matt asked pleasantly. "It's an education in regional cadence. Truce, Laurel." He held up his hand, palm out as she drew breath to start again. "At least a professional one until we run down this lead. We can take up the private war when we're off duty.''

She bit back a retort and smoldered as the elevator came gently to a stop. It wouldn't instill much confidence in Susan Fisher if the two of them were taking potshots at each other. ''An armed truce, Bates,'' she compromised as they stepped into the lobby. ''Try anything like that again, and you'll be missing some teeth.''

Matt ran his tongue over them experimentally. ''Sounds reasonable.'' He offered his hand, and though she didn't trust that sober expression on his face, Laurel accepted. ''Looks like I buy you lunch after all.''

Removing her hand, Laurel straightened the purse on her shoulder. ''Big talk on an expense account.''

Grinning, he swung a friendly arm around her as they moved toward the rear of the lobby. ''Don't be cranky, Laurellie, it's our first date.''

She snorted, and tossed her head—but she didn't push his arm away.

Chapter 3

Matt chose a noisy restaurant in the French Quarter because he always found it easier to make people talk if they weren't sure they could be heard. He'd sensed, from the introduction, that while Susan Fisher had given her trust to Laurel, she was withholding judgment on him. For the moment, he'd decided to let Laurel lead the way.

He was amiable, sympathetic, as he filed away Susan's every word and gesture. She was a woman, Matt decided, who had buckled under pressure and was fighting her way back up. She still had a long way to go, but on one point she wouldn't be swayed. She'd known her sister. Susan wasn't going to let Anne's death rest until all the facts were laid bare. Perhaps Matt admired her for it all the more because her hands weren't quite steady.

He glanced at Laurel and nearly smiled. She'll take in any stray, he mused, though he didn't doubt she'd bite his head off if he suggested it. She didn't want to be considered soft or vulnerable, particularly by him. They were colleagues or, more accurately, competitors. He'd always enjoyed going head to head with her, reporter to reporter. And after that two minutes between floors on the elevator, he didn't think she'd forget he was a man. He wasn't going to give her the chance to.

Pouring more coffee into Susan's cup, Matt sent Laurel a silent signal that it was his turn. Her slight shrug showed him that the truce was still on. "Your sister died nearly a month ago, Susan." He said it softly, watching her face. "Why did you wait so long before bringing all this up?"

She dropped her gaze to her plate, where she'd been pushing food around for twenty minutes. Over her head, Laurel's eyes met Matt's, brows raised. He could almost hear the question in them. *What the hell's this?* But she knew her job. He felt they were already partners without having stated the ground rules. I question. You soothe.

"Susan." Laurel touched her arm. "We want to help you."

"I know." Setting down her fork, she looked up again, skimming over Matt to settle on Laurel. "It's hard to admit it, but I didn't cope with Anne's death well. The truth is, I just fell apart. I stopped answering my phone—didn't leave my apartment. Lost my job." She pressed her lips together. When she spoke again they had to strain to hear her over the cheerful din in the restaurant. "The worst is, I didn't even come down for the funeral. I suppose I was pretending it wasn't happening. I was the only family she had left, and I wasn't here."

"That isn't important. No, it's not," Laurel insisted when Susan began to speak. "You loved her. In the end, love's all that really matters." Looking over, she saw Matt watching her steadily. For a moment, Laurel forgot Susan, suspicions, the noise and scents of the restaurant. She'd expected to see cynicism in his eyes, perhaps a very faint, very mocking smile. Instead, she saw understanding, and a question she didn't know how to answer. Without speaking, he lifted her hand to his lips, then set it down again.

Oh no, she thought, panicking. *Not him.* That wasn't just impossible, it was ludicrous. Dazed, she picked up her coffee, then set it back down when she saw her hand wasn't quite steady. That one long look had scattered her wits more effectively than the odd kiss that wasn't a kiss, on the elevator. As from a distance, she heard Susan's voice and forced herself to tune into it.

"It all hit me last week. I guess the first shock had passed and I started to think about her letters. It didn't fit.'' This time she looked up at Matt, demanding he understand. ''Whenever she'd mention that swamp it was with a kind of loathing. If you'd understand just how much she hated the dark, you'd see that she would never have gone into the place alone, at night. Never. Someone took her there, Mr. Bates. Someone made her go.''

''Why?'' He leaned forward, and while his voice wasn't hard, it was direct. ''Why would someone want to kill your sister?''

''I don't know.'' Her knuckles went white on the edge of the table as she fought the urge to just lay down her head and weep. ''I just don't know.''

''I covered the inquest.'' Taking out a cigarette, Matt reached for the pack of restaurant matches. He didn't want to be tough on her, but if she was going to fold it would be better if she did it now, before they got too deep. ''Your sister'd been here less than a year and knew almost no one, as she and her husband rarely socialized. According to the servants, she doted on him, there was rarely a cross word between them. The basic motives for murder—jealousy, greed—don't apply. What else is there?''

''That doesn't matter.'' Susan turned back to Laurel again. ''None of that matters.''

''Let's take it a step at a time,'' Laurel suggested. ''Do you still have your sister's letters?''

''Yes.'' Susan let out an unsteady breath. ''Back at my hotel.''

Matt crushed out his cigarette. ''Let's go take a look at them.''

When Susan was out of earshot, Laurel brushed close to Matt. ''The shock may be over,'' she murmured, ''but she's still not too sturdy. Matthew, I have a feeling about this.''

''You've got too many feelings, Laurel.''

She frowned at him as they skirted between tables. ''Just what does that mean?''

''We have to deal with facts. If you want to play Girl Scout, you're going to cloud the issue.''

''I should've known better,'' she said between her teeth.

"For a minute back there, I thought I saw some small spark of sensitivity."

He grinned. "I'm loaded with sensitivity. We can talk about it over drinks later."

"In a pig's eye." Laurel swung out the door behind Susan and made a point of ignoring Matt through the cab ride to the hotel.

It was seedy—the streets were narrow, the concrete was chipped, the banisters were peeling. Condensation gathered and dripped from the rusting balconies. The paint on the buildings was cracked and coated with layers of grime and moisture from the constant humidity. All the colors seemed to have faded into one—a steamy gray.

The alleyways were shadowed and dank. At night, Laurel knew, the street would be mean—the kind of street you avoided, or walked on quickly while glancing over your shoulder. From the open window across the street the sounds of an argument overpowered a scratchy jazz recording. A bony cat lay over the stoop and made a low, unfriendly sound in his throat when Susan opened the door.

When Laurel cautiously stepped around it, Susan offered an apologetic smile. "This place has its own...atmosphere."

Matt grinned as he cast a look around the dim lobby. "You should've seen the apartment where I grew up in New York."

The strained smile relaxed as Susan turned toward the stairs. "Well, it was here, and it was cheap."

Following them, Laurel frowned at Matt's back. She'd caught another glimpse of sensitivity. Odd. And, though she hated to admit it, the careless comment about his youth piqued her interest. Who had he been? How had he lived? She'd always been very careful not to allow herself to speculate.

The place was so quiet, so empty, that their footsteps echoed on the uncarpeted steps. Cracked paint and graffiti. Laurel studied Susan's profile as she unlocked the door. I'm going to get her out of here, she promised herself, by this afternoon. Catching the amused, knowing look Matt sent her, Laurel glared at him.

"After another merit badge, Laurellie?" he murmured.

"Shut up, Bates." While he chuckled, Laurel stepped into

Susan's cramped, shadowy room. It had a narrow bed, a scarred dresser and no charm.

"That's funny, I know I left the shades up." Crossing the room, Susan jerked the cord so that the dusty white shade flapped up and the sun poured into the room. She flicked a switch that had a squeaky ceiling fan stirring the hot air. "I'll get the letters."

Laurel sat on the edge of the bed and looked up at Matt. "What part of New York did you come from?"

His brow lifted, as it did when he was amused—or evasive. "You wouldn't know it." His lips curved as he moved to sit beside her. "Ever been north of the Mason-Dixon line, Laurel?"

"I've been to New York several times," she began testily, then made a sound of frustration when his smile only widened. "Twice," she amended.

"The Empire State Building, Ellis Island, the U.N., tea at the Plaza and a Broadway show."

"You love being smug and superior, don't you?"

He ran a fingertip down her jaw. "Yeah."

She fought back a smile. "Did you know you become even more insufferable with prolonged contact?"

"Be careful," Matt warned. "I've a weakness for flattery."

With his eyes on her laughing ones, Matt lifted her hand, palm up, and pressed his lips to the center. He watched, pleased, when confusion replaced the humor in her eyes. Behind them, Susan began to pull out drawers frantically. They didn't notice.

"They're gone!" Susan swept a handful of clothes onto the floor and stared at the empty drawer. "They're gone, all of them."

"What?" A little dazed, Laurel turned to her. "What's gone?"

"The letters. All of Anne's letters."

Immediately Laurel was on her feet and sorting through Susan's jumbled clothing. "Maybe you put them somewhere else."

"No—there is nowhere else," she said with a dangerous

edge of hysteria in her voice. "I put them all in this drawer. There were twelve of them."

"Susan." Matt's voice was cool enough to stiffen her spine. "Are you sure you brought them with you?"

She took long, deep breaths as her gaze shifted from Laurel to Matt. "I had every one of Anne's letters with me when I checked into this hotel. When I unpacked, I put them in that drawer. They were there when I dressed this morning."

Her hands weren't steady, Matt noticed, but her eyes were. He nodded. "I'll go check with the desk clerk."

As the door closed, Susan stared down at the crumpled blouse she held. "Someone was in this room," she said unsteadily. "I know it."

Laurel glanced at the shade Susan had lifted. "Are you missing anything else?"

"No." With a sigh, Susan let the blouse fall. "There isn't anything in here worth stealing. I suppose they realized that. It doesn't make any sense that they'd take Anne's letters."

"Matthew and I'll sort it out," Laurel told her, then was annoyed with herself for linking herself with Matt so easily. "In the meantime..." Bending, she began to gather Susan's clothes. "Can you type?"

Distracted, Susan stared at her. "Well, yes. I work—I worked," she corrected, "as a receptionist in a doctor's office."

"Good. Where's your suitcase?" she asked as she folded Susan's clothes on the bed.

"It's in the closet, but—"

"I have a place for you to stay, and a job—of sorts. Oh, this is lovely." She shook out the blouse Susan had crumpled.

"A job? I don't understand."

"My grandmother lives outside of town. Since my brother and I moved out, she's been lonely." The lie came out too easily to be questioned.

"But I couldn't just stay there."

"You'd pay for it." Laurel grinned as she turned back. "Grandma's been threatening to write her memoirs and I've just about run out of excuses for not typing them up for her. You won't be bored. She's eighty-two and didn't give up men until... Actually, she hasn't given them up at all. If I weren't so busy, I'd love to do it myself. As it is, you'd be doing me quite a favor."

"Why are you doing this for me?" Susan asked. "You don't know me."

"You're in trouble," Laurel said simply. "I can help."

"Just that easy?"

"Does help have to be complicated? Get your suitcase," Laurel ordered before Susan could work out an answer. "You can pack while I see what Matthew's come up with." As she slipped into the hall, Laurel bumped into him. She let the door click shut behind her. "Well?"

"The clerk didn't see anyone." Matt leaned against the wall and lit a cigarette. "But then he's more interested in cheating at solitaire in the back room than covering the desk." He blew out a stream of smoke that rose to the ceiling and hung there. "I spoke to the woman who does the rooms. She didn't pull the shades."

"Then someone was in there."

"Maybe."

Laurel ignored this and stared at the opposite wall. "Susan thinks it was just a break-in. In her state of mind, that's all for the best." '

"You're playing mama, Laurel."

"I am not." Angry, she looked back at him. "It'll be a lot easier to sort through this if she doesn't start thinking someone's deliberately trying to stop her."

"There's no reason for her to think that at this point," Matt said dampeningly. "What's she doing?"

"Packing," Laurel muttered.

He nodded. It wasn't wise for her to stay where she was. "Where's she going?"

Laurel angled her chin. "To my grandmother."

Not quite suppressing a smile, Matt studied the tip of his cigarette. "I see."

"You couldn't see through barbed wire. And don't start spouting off about my getting too personally involved, or—"

"All right." He crushed out the cigarette on the dusty,

scarred floor. "And I won't comment that you're a very sweet, classy lady. I'll get a cab," he added when Laurel only stared at him.

Just when I think I understand him, she mused, he throws me a curve. If I'm not careful, Laurel added as his footsteps echoed off the stairs. If I'm not very, very careful, I'm going to start liking him. On that uncomfortable thought, she went back in to hurry Susan along.

In under ten minutes, Laurel was in the back of a cab with Matt, glancing behind her at the taxi that would take Susan to her grandmother.

"Stop worrying about her," Matt ordered. "Olivia'll keep her mind off her sister, and everything else."

With a shrug, Laurel turned back around. "I don't doubt that. But I'm beginning to doubt that Anne Trulane walked into that swamp alone."

"Let's stick with the facts. Motive." Absently, he wound a lock of Laurel's hair around his finger—a habit he'd recently developed and rather enjoyed. "There doesn't seem to be any. Women aren't lured into swamps for no reason."

"Then there was one."

"No sexual assault," Matt continued, half to himself. "She didn't have any money on her own—and her only heir would've been Susan in any case...or her husband. He has a sister, but I can't see any benefit there."

"The last people I'd consider as murder suspects would be Louis or Marion Trulane. And there are other motives for murder than sex and money."

He lifted a brow at her tone but continued to toy with her hair. "True, but those always spring to mind. Most of us are fond of both."

"Some think beyond your scope, Matthew. There's jealousy, if we go back to your two favorites. Louis is rich and attractive. Someone might have pictured herself in Anne's place."

He caught something—the drift of something he didn't quite understand. And didn't like. "Do you know him well?"

"Louis?" A smile touched her mouth, a gentle one. It reminded him that Laurel had never once looked at him that way. "As well as anyone, I suppose—or I did. He taught me to ride when I was a girl, let me tag along after him when I was ten and he was, oh, twenty-one or -two. He was a beautiful man—and very patient with a girl's infatuation."

When he discovered his fingers were no longer relaxed, Matt released the tendril of hair. "You got over it, I suppose."

Hearing the cynicism in his voice, Laurel turned, the half smile still on her face. "Weren't you ever in love, Matthew?"

The look he gave her was long and guarded while several uncomfortable emotions moved through him. Her eyes were soft; so was her mouth, her skin. If they'd been alone, he might not have answered the question at all, but would simply have taken what he found he needed so badly. "No," he said at length.

"It softens something in you, something that never quite goes away for that particular person." With a sigh, she sat back against the seat. It had been a long time since she'd let herself remember how sweet it had been, and how hurtful. She'd only been a child, and though her dreams had been fairy tales, she'd believed them. "Louis was very important to me. I wanted a knight, and I think he understood that well enough not to laugh at me. And when he married..." She lifted her hands and let them fall. "It broke my heart. Do you know about his first wife?"

Matt was staring down at the hands in her lap; small, elegant hands with the nails painted in the palest of corals and a smoky emerald in an intricate old setting on her finger. An heirloom, he thought. She would have heirlooms, and genteel ancestors—and memories of riding lessons from a tall young man, dashing enough to be a knight.

"Bits and pieces," Matt mumbled as the cab pulled to the curb. "Fill me in later."

Laurel climbed out of the cab, then meticulously brushed off her skirt. "That's perilously close to an order, Bates. Since Don didn't lay down any ground rules, maybe you and I should take care of that ourselves."

"Fine." He didn't know why he was angry. He studied her with eyes narrowed against the glare of the sun. "This is my beat."

With an effort, Laurel smothered the flare of temper. "And it's my lead."

"If you want to get anywhere with it," he said evenly, "you'll leave certain areas to me. When's the last time you fought your way through the red tape in there?" Matt jerked his head toward the station house beside them.

"I've untangled red tape before."

"Not in there," he countered before he took her arm.

"Just a minute, Bates." Laurel pushed his hand away and faced him. "The one thing you're going to understand, is that I may have no choice but to work with you on this story, but the operative word is *with,* not *for.* For the moment, however much it galls me, we're partners."

This seemed to amuse him as the temper turned into an odd little smile. "A nice ring to that. Partners," he agreed, taking her hand. "It might become a habit."

"The danger of that's slim to none. Would you stop touching me?"

"No," he said amiably as they climbed the steps.

Voices boomed off the walls of the station house. Disgruntled voices, insolent voices, irate voices. It smelled dankly, stalely of humanity. Sweat, coffee, cigarettes, alcohol. Five members of opposing street gangs leaned against a wall and eyed each other. A woman with a badly bruised face huddled in a chair and spoke in undertones to a harassed-looking officer who nodded and typed out her statement with two fingers. A young girl in snug shorts snapped her gum and looked bored.

He'd seen it all before—and more. After a cursory glance around, Matt moved through the people and desks. The officers, the victims, the accused, paid no more attention to him than he to them.

A slim brunette in a wilting uniform cupped a phone on her shoulder and lifted a hand in salute. Matt perched on the corner of her desk. Laurel stood beside him, watching as two elderly men nearly came to blows before they were pulled apart.

"Well, Matt, what brings you to paradise?" The brunette set down the phone and smiled at him.

"How you doing, Sarge?"

The brunette tipped back in her chair to give him a long, thorough look. "I haven't changed my phone number here— or at home."

"The city keeps us both pretty tied up, doesn't it? Been to the Nugget lately?"

She picked up a pen and tapped it lightly against her mouth. "Not since last month. Want to buy me a drink?"

"You read my mind, but I have a little business."

Letting out a quick laugh, the sergeant dropped her pen onto a blotter crisscrossed with scrawled names and numbers. "Sure. What do you want, Matt?"

"A quick glimpse at the file on a case—a closed case," he added. "Need to do a little backtracking on a story I did, maybe a follow-up."

Her eyes narrowed. "What case?"

"Anne Trulane."

"Sensitive ground, Matt." Her eyes drifted past his to Laurel's.

"Laurel Armand, Sergeant Carolyn Baker. Laurel and I are on assignment together," Matt said smoothly. "She's an old family friend of the Trulanes. Thought maybe we'd do something a little more in depth. Case is closed, Sarge, and hell, I covered the thing from start to finish."

"You've already seen the report."

"Then it can't hurt for me to see it again." He gave her a charming smile. "You know I play it straight, Carolyn, no printing privileged information, no hints in a story that messes up an investigation."

"Yeah, you play it straight, Matt." She shot him a look that Laurel thought had more to do with personal feelings than professional ones, then shrugged. "It was all public knowledge at the inquest." Rising, she walked away to disappear into a side room. Beside them, the two old men hurled insults at each other.

"You always work that way, Matthew?"

Matt turned to give Laurel a bland smile. "What way?" When she remained silent and staring, he grinned. "Jealous, love? You've got my heart in your hand."

"I'd rather have it under my foot."

"Vicious," he murmured, then pushed off the desk when Carolyn came back in.

"You can look at the file, take it in the first holding room. It's empty." She gave a quick glance around at the cramped room. "For now," she added dryly. Opening a book, she turned it to face him. "Sign for it."

"I owe you one, Sarge."

She waited until he'd scrawled his signature. "I'll collect."

Chuckling, Matt turned to work his way through to the holding room. An interesting woman, Sergeant Baker. Strange that it was never she who crept into his mind at odd moments. Not her, nor any of the other...interesting women he knew. Just one woman.

"Have a seat," Matt invited, closing the door and shutting out most of the din. The chair he chose scraped over the floor as he pulled it away from a long, battered table.

"Cheerful place," Laurel muttered, glancing around at the dull white walls and dingy linoleum.

"Stick with City Hall if you want tidy offices and white collars." Opening the file, he began to scan it briskly.

He fits here, Laurel realized with a grudging kind of respect. For all his easygoing manner, there was a hard, tough edge underneath she'd only glimpsed briefly. The man on the elevator. Yes, she mused, he'd shown her that ruthless, searing temper there. And more. Laurel didn't want to think of that just yet.

But there was no getting around the fact that there were more facets to him than she'd wanted to believe. It was safer to consider him a shallow, inconsequential man who just happened to be a hell of a reporter. Seeing him now, completely at ease in the grim little room, made her wonder just how much he'd seen, how much he'd experienced. He dealt with the troubles, the griefs, the viciousness of people day after day, yet he didn't seem hard or cold, or overwhelmed by it. What made Matthew Bates tick? she wondered. And what made her suddenly so sure she had to find out?

"Nothing much here," he muttered, skimming the papers. "Autopsy report...no sexual abuse, contusions, lacerations attributed to her wandering through the swamp. Copperhead got her on the left calf. Cause of death snakebite, complicated by exposure. Time of death between 12:00 and 4:00 A.M.'' He handed the sheet to Laurel before going on to the investigator's report.

"Trulane was working late in his study. According to him, he thought his wife was upstairs in bed. He went up around two, found the bed empty. He searched the house, then woke his sister and the staff, searched the house again and the grounds.''

Absently, he reached for a cigarette, found the pack empty and swore without heat. "None of her clothes were missing, all the cars were there. His call to the station came through at 2:57 A.M.'' He glanced over at Laurel. "Nearly an hour.''

Her fingers were a bit damp on the autopsy report. "It's a big house. A sensible person doesn't call the police until he's sure he needs them.''

After a slow nod, Matt looked back down at the report. "The police arrived at 3:15. The house was searched again, the staff questioned...'' He mumbled for a moment, skimming the words. "Anne Trulane's body was found at approximately 6:00 A.M., in the southeast section of the swamp.''

He'd been there. Matt remembered the gray light, the hot, humid smells, the nasty feel of the swamp even before they'd come across death.

"No one could account for her being out there. According to Marion Trulane, the sister-in-law, Anne had a phobia about the place. That fits with Susan's claim,'' he murmured. "Trulane stuck with his story about working late, and wouldn't elaborate.''

"Have you ever found your wife dead?'' Laurel demanded as she took the report from Matt. "It's just possible that he was upset.''

He let the scathing words slip off him. "The conclusion is she felt compelled to go in—maybe to face her fears, got lost, bitten, and wandered around until she lost consciousness.'' He glanced over at Laurel. Her brows were drawn together as she read the report for herself. "You still buddies enough to get us into the house, ask some questions?''

"Hmm? Oh, yes, I suppose so. They'll talk to me. You too," she added, "if you spread some of your charm around."

His mouth twisted into a grin. "I didn't think you'd noticed."

"I noticed that you can pull it out rather successfully when you put your mind to it. It's a bit deliberate for my tastes, but effective enough."

"Please, Laurellie, compliments are so embarrassing."

Ignoring him, Laurel set the investigator's report aside. "Louis hasn't had an easy time. He's closed himself in since his first marriage failed, but I think he'll talk to me."

Idly, Matt twisted the empty pack of cigarettes into a mass of foil and cellophane. "His wife ran off with his brother?"

"It was horrible for Louis." She slipped the next paper from the file as Matt gazed up at the ceiling, lost in thought.

Her skin went to ice, her stomach knotted, but she couldn't look away. The police photo was black and white and grim. She'd seen death before, but not like this. Never like this. Appalled, transfixed, she stared down at Anne Fisher Trulane. Or what she had come to.

Oh, God, Laurel thought as her head went light and her stomach rolled. It's not real. It's a gruesome joke. Just someone's twisted idea of a joke.

"How long ago did—" Matt broke off as he shifted his gaze to Laurel. Her skin was dead white, her eyes full of horror. Even as he swore, he whipped the photo away from her, then pushed her head down between her knees. "Breathe deep," he ordered sharply, but his hand was abruptly gentle on the back of her head. Hearing her breath shudder in and out, he cursed himself more savagely. What the hell had he been thinking of? "Easy, love," he murmured, kneading the tension at the base of her neck.

"I'm all right." But she wasn't so sure. Laurel took an extra moment before she tried to straighten in the chair. When Matt's arms came around her, she let her head rest on his shoulder. "I'm sorry, that was stupid."

"No." He tilted her head back. "I'm sorry." Very slowly, very carefully, he brushed the hair away from her face.

She swallowed, hard. "I guess you're used to it."

"God, I hope not." He drew her close again so that her face was pressed against his neck.

She felt safe there. The chill was passing. Laurel relaxed, letting him stroke her hair, allowing the warm, real scent of him to block out the institutional smell of the waiting room. She could feel the steady beat of his heart against her. Life. When his lips brushed her ear, she didn't move. It was comfort he offered and comfort she felt. She told herself that was all, as she held on to him as if she'd just discovered him.

"Matthew..."

"Hmmm?"

"Don't be too nice to me."

With her eyes closed, her face buried at his throat, she felt the smile. "Why not?"

"Just don't." A bit more steady, she drew away because it was much too easy to stay.

He cupped her face in his hand. "You're beautiful," he murmured. "Have I told you that before?"

Cautiously she moved out of reach. Treat it light, she warned herself. And think about it later. "No." She smiled and rose. "I always jot things like that down."

"Beautiful," he repeated. "Even if your chin is just a bit pointed."

"It is not." Automatically, she tilted it.

"Especially from that angle."

"I have very delicate features," Laurel told him decisively as she picked up her purse. No, damn it, her fingers were not steady yet. God, she had to get out of this place, get out and breathe again.

With his back to her, Matt slipped the photo back in the file folder, closing the cover before he turned around. "Except for the chin," he agreed, putting an arm around her shoulders as he started for the door.

With her hand on the knob, Laurel stopped and looked up at him. Her eyes were dark and more aware than they'd been before they'd come into that room. "Matthew." She leaned against him for a moment, just for a moment. "No one deserves to die that way."

He tightened his grip on her for a moment, just for a moment. "No."

Chapter 4

The bar was dim and cool. It was too early for the evening rush, too late for the afternoon regulars. With his mind still on Anne Trulane's file, Matt steered Laurel inside. No, no one deserved to die that way, but then life, and death, didn't always play according to the rules. He'd learned to accept that a long time ago.

Matt had been as quiet as Laurel since they'd walked out of the station house. He was thinking, analyzing. Remembering.

The phone had rung in the early hours of the morning— his source at the station house tipping him on Anne Trulane's disappearance. He'd arrived at Heritage Oak moments after the police. There'd been a mist, he recalled, thinner and nastier than a rain, and an air of silence. He'd sensed Louis Trulane hadn't wanted to call the outside for help. His answers had been clipped, his expression remote. No, he hadn't looked like a harried, concerned husband, but like a man who'd had his evening interrupted.

His sister, and the entourage of servants, had gathered around him a few paces back, in a move that had seemed like a defense before the search had spread into the marsh. It was a winding, humid place with shadows and small, secret sounds. Matt had felt a distaste for it without knowing why.

He'd only known he'd rather have been searching the streets and alleyways than that steamy, dripping maze of shadow and bog.

They'd found her, too late, curled on the ground near a sluggish stream when dawn was just breaking. Mist, gray light, wet pungent smells. He'd heard a bird, a lark perhaps, calling in the distance. And he'd heard the crows. Matt remembered Louis Trulane's reaction. He'd been pale, cold and silent. If there'd been anger, grief or despair, he'd closed it inside. His sister had fainted, the servants had wept, but he'd simply stood....

"I'm going to call Louis."

"What?" Matt glanced over to find Laurel watching him.

"I'm going to call Louis, ask if he'll see us."

Slowly, he tore the wrapper from a fresh pack of cigarettes. "All right." He looked after her as she weaved her way through tables to the pay phone in the corner. It wasn't easy for her, Matt thought, and struck a match with more force than necessary. She was too close, too open. Whatever childhood feelings she'd had for Louis Trulane were still too important to her to allow her to see him objectively.

What about you, Bates? he asked himself as he blew out a stream of smoke. You detest him because of the way Laurel says his name. It was time, he told himself, that they both remembered their priorities. The story came first. It had to. If Laurel's relationship with the Trulanes got them in, so much the better. He'd been in the game too long to be under any illusions. People like the Trulanes could toss obstacles in a reporter's way until getting through them was like walking through a minefield.

Not that it would stop him from getting the story—it would only add to the time and the legwork. Either way, Matt mused, either way he was going to poke some holes into that sanctified wall the Trulanes had around themselves and their name.

He saw Laurel coming back, the sadness lingering in her eyes, the color only a hint in her cheeks. She'd get over it, he told himself as something seemed to tear inside him. Because she had to. He waited until she slid into the booth across from him.

"Well?"

"He'll see us at ten tomorrow."

Matt crushed out his cigarette, warning himself not to touch her. "You don't sound too thrilled about it."

"I used the pressure of an old friendship." She looked up then, meeting his eyes with a kind of weary defiance. "I hated it."

"You've got a job to do," he muttered, and found he'd reached for her hand before he could stop himself.

"I know. I haven't forgotten." Instinctively she tightened her fingers on his. "I don't have to like it to do it well." She knew she'd never be able to back off now, not after seeing that picture—not after imagining what Susan Fisher would have felt if she had seen it.

When the waitress stopped beside her, Laurel glanced up. She had to dull the image. Maybe it was weak, but she had to. "Martini," she said on impulse. "A dry martini with an illusion of vermouth."

"Two," Matt ordered, sending Laurel an off-center smile. "It only helps temporarily, Laurellie."

"That's good enough for now." Resting her elbows on the table, she leaned forward. "Matthew, I'm going to consume great quantities of alcohol. This is totally preplanned and I offer no excuses. I will promise, however, not to get sloppy. Naturally, I'll regret this tomorrow, but I think it'll be a lesson well learned."

He nodded, grinning because he saw she needed it. "Since I'm joining you, I'll try to maintain your high standards. In any case..." He leaned a bit closer. "I've often wondered what it would be like to get you drunk and have my way with you."

She laughed for the first time in hours. "There isn't enough gin in this place for that, Matthew."

"We'll see how you feel in a couple hours." Leaning back, he lit another cigarette. "Why don't you tell me about the Trulanes?"

"What about them?"

"Everything."

She sighed, then, picking up the glass the waitress set in front of her, sipped. "This might just be the only thing in New Orleans completely lacking in humidity."

Matt acknowledged this by tapping the rim of his glass against hers. "The Trulanes, Laurellie."

"All right—and don't call me that. Ancient history first," she began. "Heritage Oak was built in the early nineteenth century. The plantation was vast and rich. The Trulanes still own more land than anyone else in this part of Louisiana. Besides cotton and cattle, they were shipbuilders. The profits from that kept the plantation alive after the war. As far back as anyone would remember, the Trulanes've been an important part of New Orleans, socially, financially and politically. I'm sure Grandma has a large repertoire of stories."

"Undoubtedly," Matt agreed. "Let's just speed up the passage of time a bit. Something in this century."

"Just laying the groundwork." Laurel took a sip from her glass, then toyed with the stem. "Beauregard Trulane—"

"Come on."

"There's always a Beauregard," she said loftily. "Inherited Heritage Oak right after his marriage. He had three children: Marion, Louis and Charles." Her eyes smiled over the rim of her glass. "He was an enormous man, bellowing, dramatic. Grandma loved him. In fact, I've sometimes wondered... well." She grinned and shrugged. "His wife was beautiful, a very quiet, serene sort of woman. Marion looks a great deal like her. Aunt Ellen—I called her that—died less than six months after my mother. I was around six...I've always mixed them a bit in my mind."

With a shrug, she emptied her glass, not noticing that Matt signaled for another round. "In any case, after she died, old Beau went into a steady decline. Louis began to take over the business. Really, he was too young to face those kinds of pressures, but there wasn't much choice. He would've been about eighteen or nineteen at the time, and I suppose I already worshiped him. To me, he was a cross between Prince Charming and Robin Hood. He was kind to me, always laughing and full of fun. That's how I like to remember him," she murmured, and stared into her fresh drink.

"Things change," Matt said briefly. How did a man compete with a childhood memory? he asked himself, frustrated by the look on Laurel's face. Damned if he would. "You're not a child anymore, Laurel."

She shifted her gaze to his and held it steady. "No, but a good deal of my perspective on Louis is that of a child."

He inclined his head and told himself to relax. "Tell me about Marion."

"She's a couple years older than Louis, and as I said, has her mother's looks. When I was young I thought of her as my personal fairy godmother. She was always so poised, and so beautiful."

A picture of dark elegance and flawless skin ran through his mind. "Yes, I noticed."

"She's too old for you," Laurel said without thinking, then looked over with a frown when Matt burst out laughing. "Shut up, Bates, and let me finish."

"I beg your pardon," he said with his tongue in his cheek.

"Marion used to have me over," Laurel continued, rashly finishing off her second martini. "She'd give me tea and cakes in the parlor. She knew I adored Louis and used to tell me to hurry and grow up so Louis could marry me. I adored her too."

"She never married?"

"No. Grandma said she was too choosy, but I think she had a love affair that didn't work out. Once I was there on a gray, gloomy day and she told me if a woman had one great love in her life, it was enough. Of course, at the time I thought she was talking about Louis and me, but when I got older and remembered how she'd looked..." On a sigh, Laurel reached for her glass. "Women like Marion are easily hurt."

He looked at her, the soft skin, soft mouth, soft eyes. "Is that so?"

"Charles was different." Shaking off the mood, Laurel leaned back with her drink. "I suppose he was a bit like Curt, and I thought of him as an extra brother. He was dreamy and abstracted. He was going to be an artist, and when he wasn't sketching, he was studying or hanging around Jackson Square. They'd hung some of his paintings in the main hall—until he left.''

"With the first Mrs. Trulane," Matt finished.

"Yes, twelve years ago. It was a nasty scandal, the sort that causes a lot of pain and fabulous headlines.'' She shook her head over the opposing loyalties and sighed. The martinis were taking the edge off. "Grandma could tell you a great deal more, but from what I remember, Louis came back from a business trip to find Elise and Charles gone. The rumor that buzzed from servants' wing to servants' wing was that there was a note. Most of their clothes and all of Charles's painting gear were gone.''

Laurel looked beyond him, unaware that the bar was filling up with people and noise. Someone was playing on the piano in the rear. "That's when Louis changed. He closed himself off from everyone. The few times I did see him, all the laughter was gone. As far as I know, he's never heard from Charles or Elise. About four years ago, he finally filed for divorce. Marion told me he'd done it strictly as a legality, that he was bitter, very bitter. She worried about him. His second marriage was a surprise to everyone.''

Idly, she watched the smoke from Matt's cigarette curl toward the ceiling. The fans spun gently, slicing at the smoke, stirring the air. He hadn't spoken in some time, but she didn't realize it was the quality of his listening that made it so easy to speak. "I called him, first because I really hoped he was happy, and second, because Louis Trulane's remarriage meant a good story. He sounded almost like his old self—older, certainly, but some of the spark was back. He wouldn't give me an interview, he said...'' She frowned as she searched back for his words. "He said he'd married a child and he needed to keep spring to himself for a little while.''

God, did she know what she did to him when her eyes took on that vulnerable, young look? He wanted to take her away somewhere, anywhere, so that nothing could hurt her. And if he tried, she'd think he was out of his mind. Matt crushed out his cigarette with deliberate care. "What do you know about the first Mrs. Trulane?"

"Nothing really." Looking up again, she smiled wryly. "Except I was horribly jealous of her. She was lovely in that soft, kind of misty style that no one can emulate. I do remember the wedding—pink and white magnolias, a huge, frothy wedding cake and beautiful dresses. Elise wore silk and lace with miles of train. She looked like a porcelain doll—gold and white and tiny. She looked like..." She trailed off, eyes wide, with her glass halfway to her lips. "Oh God, she looked like—"

"Like the second Mrs. Trulane," Matt finished. Leaning back, he signaled the waitress again. "Well, well."

"It doesn't mean anything," she began in a rush. "Only that Louis was attracted to a certain type of woman. The resemblance to his first wife doesn't add up to a motive for murder."

"It's the closest we've got. And we're still a long way from being certain Anne Trulane was murdered." Matt lifted a brow as he studied Laurel's face. "You're quick to rush to his defense, Laurellie. It's going to be difficult for you to think clearly if you don't let go of your childhood infatuation."

"That's ridiculous."

"Is it?" His lips curved without humor.

"Listen, Bates, I always think clearly, and whatever my feelings for Louis, they won't interfere with my work." She looked down at her empty glass. "I finished my drink."

"So I see." This time the amusement leaked through. Indignation was one of her most appealing expressions. She'd had enough of the Trulanes for the day, Matt decided. So had he. Unobtrusively, the waitress replaced empty glasses with fresh ones. "Well, that's for tomorrow. Why don't you bring me up to date on our favorite city councilman? I'm keeping a scrapbook."

"Why don't you leave Jerry alone?" Laurel demanded, starting on the next drink.

"Everyone's entitled to a hobby."

"Don't be so smug and superior," she mumbled into her glass. "Jerry's a very—very..."

"Pompous ass?" Matt suggested blandly, then grinned when she burst into a fit of giggles.

"Damn you, Matthew, if my brain weren't numb, I'd have thought of something." Blowing the hair out of her eyes, she set down her drink and folded her hands. "I find your continually rude comments on Jerry's personality annoying."

"Because I'm right?"

"Yes. I really hate it when you're right."

He grinned, then, tossing a few bills on the table, rose. "I'll walk you home, Laurel. Let's hope the fresh air doesn't clear your brain—you might just be receptive to a few of my baser instincts."

"It'd take more than three martinis to do that." She stood, letting out a long breath when the floor tilted gently under her feet.

"Four," he murmured as he took her arm. "But who's counting?"

"I'm only holding on to you because I have to," Laurel told him as they stepped outside. "After a couple blocks, I'll get my rhythm back."

"Just let me know when you want to go solo."

"How many did you have?"

"The same as you."

Laurel tilted her head back to study him and found the martinis spun not too unpleasantly in her head. "Well, you're taller, and heavier," she added with a smirk. "I have a very delicate build."

"So I've noticed."

She lifted a brow as they passed a sidewalk trumpeter. The sound of jazz was mellow and sad. "Have you really?"

"You could say I've made a study of it—journalistically speaking."

"What's that supposed to mean?"

He paused long enough to touch his lips to hers. "Don't press your luck."

"You have a funny way of kissing," she muttered as her head tilted onto his shoulder. "I don't know if I like it."

To his credit, Matt didn't slip a hand around her throat and squeeze. "We can have a debate on that subject later."

"I really thought you'd have a different technique," she went on. "You know, more...aggressive."

"Been spending time thinking about my technique?" he countered.

"I've given it some thought—journalistically speaking."

"It'd be safer to table this discussion until you can walk a straight line." He turned into the courtyard of the building they shared.

"You know, Matthew..." Laurel gripped the banister as they climbed the stairs. The steps weren't as steady as they'd been that morning. "You're not really so bad after three martinis."

"Four," he mumbled.

"Don't nitpick now that I've decided to tolerate you." Unzipping her purse, she began to fish for her keys. "Here, hold this."

Matt found himself holding a wallet, compact, notebook, broken earrings and several ticket stubs. "Anything else?" he said dryly.

"No, here they are—they always sink to the bottom."

Unceremoniously, he dumped the contents back in her purse and took the keys from her. "Are you going to let me in?" A pot of coffee, he mused as she leaned back against the door. A couple of aspirins and a dark room. He wasn't at all certain she could manage any of the three by herself. "We've been neighbors for nearly a year and I haven't had an invitation."

"What appalling manners." Giving him a misty smile, Laurel gestured him inside.

The room, like the woman, had soft edges, elegance and wit. There was the scent of potpourri with a touch of lavender. The colors were creams and roses. Lace at the curtains, velvet on the sofa. On the wall above a gleaming tea cart was a framed burlesque poster from the 1890s.

"It suits you."

"Really?" Laurel glanced around, unaccountably pleased
with herself. "'S funny, even if I'd seen your place I wouldn't
know if it suited you." Laurel dragged a hand through her
hair as she tried to focus on him. She held it there as she
swayed, only a little. "I don't really understand you at all.
Framed newsprints or Picassos. In an odd sort of way, you're
a fascinating man."

She was smiling at him, only an arm's length away. At the
moment, Matt wasn't certain if she was being deliberately
provocative or if the martinis were doing it for her. Either
way, it wasn't any easier on him. He didn't have many rules,
but one of them dealt strictly with making a move on a woman
who might not remember it the next morning.

"Coffee," he said briefly and took her arm.

"Oh, did you want some?"

"You do," he said between clenched teeth. "Black."

"Okay." In the kitchen, she stared at the automatic coffeemaker, brows knit. She'd have sworn she knew what to do
with it.

"I'll make it," Matt told her, grinning again. "Can you
handle the cups?"

"Certainly." Laurel rummaged in a cupboard, and though
she rattled them dangerously, managed to set violet-trimmed
china cups in their saucers on the counter. "I don't have any
beignets."

"Coffee's fine."

"Guess if you *really* wanted some I could make 'em."

"I'll take a rain check."

"You're a good sport, Matthew." Laughing, she turned and
tumbled into his arms. With a smile, she curled her arms
around his neck. "You've got fabulous eyes," she said on a
sigh. "I bet just everyone tells you that."

"Constantly." He put his hands on her waist, intending to
draw her away. Somehow, she was pressed against him with
his fingers spread over the thin material of her blouse. Desire
curled inside him like a fist. "Laurel..."

"Maybe you should kiss me again, so I can figure out why I always think I don't want you to."

"Tomorrow," he murmured as he lowered his mouth toward hers, "if you remember, you're going to hate yourself for saying that."

"Mmmm, I know." Her lashes lowered as his lips brushed over hers. "That's not a kiss." She drew a long sigh as her nerve ends began to tingle. "It's fabulous." Her fingers crept into his hair to tangle and explore. "More…"

The hell with rules, Matt thought savagely. If he had to pay for what he took now, then he'd pay. And by God, it would be worth it. On an oath, he dragged her against him and crushed her mouth with his.

Instant fire. It flared from her into him—or him into her. The source didn't matter, only the results. She moaned. The sound had nothing to do with pain or with wonder, and everything to do with raw desire. Her body strained into his with a certainty. This is right, this had always been right. She found his tongue with hers and let passion and intimacy merge blindingly, then struggled for more.

At that moment, with her head spinning and her body humming, it no longer mattered that it should be he who touched off all the sparks, all the secrets raging in her. No one else ever had. No one else ever could. Again, above all the whirling thoughts in her mind was one simple demand: more.

He was losing. Perhaps he'd been losing since he'd first seen that face. Bits and pieces of himself were being absorbed and he no longer cared. She could have whatever she wanted as long as he could have her like this. Heated, melting, hungry.

Her taste wasn't delicate like her looks, but wild and daring. Her scent was airy, romantic, her mouth ripe with passion. Though he could feel her breasts yield against him, her hands demanded and took. Muttering threats, promises, pleas, he pressed his mouth to her throat and began to please himself.

Her pulse hammered. He could feel it beneath his lips, strong, fast. With a nip of his teeth it scrambled and raced to war with the low sound she made. Then his hands were on her, hard, rushing, urgent until the sound became his name. There was nothing casual about him now, not a trace of the easygoing, faintly amused man who sat across from her day after day. There was the aggression he'd carefully glossed over. The ruthlessness. The excitement.

He wanted her—too much for comfort. Too much for sanity. Perhaps she was all he'd ever wanted, the silkiness, the fire. When she was pressed against him like this, there was no past, no future, only now. Now was enough for a lifetime.

How could her mind be so clouded and her body so alive? Laurel thought she could feel her own blood racing through her veins. Is this what she'd been waiting for? This mindless freedom? It was enough—it was more than she'd ever dreamed of, more than she'd ever understood. She was far from understanding now, but her body was so busy controlling her mind, she didn't care. With a sound of possession and the strength of greed, she dragged Matt's mouth back to hers. It seemed as though her legs dissolved from the knees down.

She heard him swear against her mouth before he clutched her closer. Then he drew her away while she gripped his shoulders in protest, and for support. "Matthew…"

"The door." His voice wasn't any more steady than the rest of him. No, he wasn't steady, Matt realized as he held Laurel away from him. And maybe not quite sane. "Someone's at the door, Laurel. You'd better answer it."

"The door? Whose door?" She stared up at him, aroused, dazed.

"Your door." A faint smile touched his lips.

"Oh." She looked around the sun-washed kitchen as though she'd never seen it before. "I should answer it?"

He nearly dragged her back. Her flushed, bemused expression had his fingers tightening convulsively on her arms. Carefully, he released her. "Yeah." Disoriented, Laurel walked away. He'd come too close, Matt thought, too damn close to yanking her to the kitchen floor and taking her like a maniac. He turned to the hissing coffeepot, not sure whether to be grateful to whoever was banging on the door, or to murder them.

Laurel felt as though she'd been swimming underwater and had come up much too quickly. Drunk? She pressed her fingers to her temple as she reached for the doorknob. Whatever the martinis had started, Matt had finished. She shook her head, hard, and when it didn't clear, gave up and opened the door.

"Laurel, you took so long answering I nearly went away." Jerry Cartier, three-piece-suited and vaguely annoyed, stared at her.

"Oh." Her blood was cooling, but the alcohol still swam in her head. "Hello, Jerry."

Because she stepped back, swinging the door wider, he came in. "What were you up to?"

"Up to?" she repeated…and remembered. Laurel let out a long breath. "Coffee," she murmured. "I was making coffee."

"You drink too much coffee, Laurel." He turned as she closed the door and leaned back on it. "It isn't good for your nerves."

"No." She thought of Matt. She hadn't realized she had so many nerves until a few moments ago. "No, you're probably right about that." She straightened as it occurred to her what Jerry would have to say if he realized just what she'd been drinking, and how much. The last thing she wanted was a twenty-minute lecture on the evils of alcohol. "Sit down, Jerry," she invited, thinking just how much she wanted to lie down—in a dark room—in silence. If she were lucky, very lucky, she could cross the room and get to the sofa without weaving. She took one hesitant step.

"You're not ready."

Laurel stopped dead. He was right, of course, but crawling wasn't such a good idea. Neither was standing still. "Ready?"

"For dinner," Jerry told her as his brows drew together.

"Hello, Jerry." Carrying a tray of steaming coffee and cups, Matt strolled in.

Jerry crossed one leg over the other. "Matthew."

After setting down the tray, Matt walked casually to where Laurel still stood. "Condemn any good buildings lately?" In an unobtrusive move, he took Laurel's arm and led her to the couch. As she sank down, she shot him a grateful look.

"That's not my jurisdiction," Jerry stated, lacing his fingers together. "The mayor did tell me just the other day about a building on the other side of town. Appalling plumbing."

"Is that so?"

"Coffee?" Laurel interrupted. Martinis or not, she couldn't sit there and let Matt calmly execute an unarmed man. Besides, if she didn't have some coffee, she was going to quietly lay her head on the arm of the sofa and doze off.

"Only a half cup," Jerry told her. "Are you sure you should have any more?"

She made a grab for the handle of the pot and prayed she could pour it. "I haven't had any for hours."

"So, how was your day, Jerry?" Matt asked him as he closed his hand over Laurel's on the handle. Hearing her small sigh of relief, he nearly grinned.

"Busy, busy. There never seems to be enough hours to get everything done."

Matt's gaze slid down to Laurel's, brushing over her mouth. "No, there doesn't."

Jerry reached for the cup Laurel passed him and had to lean to the right when she missed his hand. "Laurel," he began, giving her an oddly intent look. "Have you been…drinking?"

"Drinking?" She set her heel down hard on Matt's foot when he chuckled. "Jerry, I just poured." Lifting the cup to her lips, she drank half the contents. "Why did you say you'd dropped by?"

"Dropped by?" He shook his head as Laurel leaned back, clutching her cup in both hands. "Laurel, we're supposed to go out to dinner."

"Oh." He was probably right, she thought vaguely. If Jerry said they had a dinner date, they had a dinner date. He kept a very precise appointment book.

"Laurel and I are working on a story," Matt put in more for his own amusement than to rescue Laurel. "We've run into some overtime on it. As a matter of fact, we were, ah, covering ground when you knocked on the door." Not by the slightest flicker did he betray the fact that Laurel's heel was digging into his foot. "Reporting really does interfere with a social life."

"Yes, but—"

"You know what it's like to be on deadline, I'm sure." Matt gave him an easy smile. "Laurel and I probably won't have time for anything more than a cold sandwich. We could be tied up on this for…weeks. You'll give Jerry a call when things calm down, won't you, Laurel?"

"What? Yes, yes, of course." She drained her coffee and wished he'd go so that she could pour another. "I'm awfully sorry, Jerry."

"I understand. Business before pleasure." Matt stopped himself before he choked over his coffee. Jerry rose, setting down his cup before he straightened his tie. "Just ring my office when things are clear, Laurel. And try to cut down on that coffee."

"Mmm-hmmm" was the best she could manage as her teeth were digging into her bottom lip. The door closed quietly behind him. "Oh, God!" Not sure whether she wanted to laugh or scream, Laurel covered her face with her hands.

"Tacky, Laurellie," Matt murmured, pouring out more coffee. "Leaving it to me to untangle you."

It would be satisfying to throw the coffee in his face, but she needed it too much. "With everything that happened to-day—the story," she emphasized firmly when his grin broke out, "I simply forgot about dinner. And I didn't ask you to untangle me."

"That's gratitude." He tugged on her hair until she looked at him. "Not only do I let you break three of my toes, but I help you cover up your…impaired condition from your boy-friend."

"He's not." Laurel drank cup number two without a pause, then set down the cup with a snap.

"You're stringing him along."

"That's not true." She started to rise, found it took too much effort and stayed where she was. "We have a perfect understanding. We're friends. Damn it, he's a very nice man, really, just a little…''

"Don't say harmless again, the poor guy doesn't deserve it. Then again, he doesn't seem to be in danger of having his heart broken."

"Jerry doesn't see me that way," Laurel began.

Looking at her, sulky-mouthed and sleepy-eyed, Matt leaned closer. "In that case, you can leave the pompous off of my earlier description of him."

Laurel put her hand firmly on his chest. She wasn't about to risk letting the room spin around her again. "I'm going to bed."

The corner of his mouth tilted. "I love aggressive women."

"Alone," Laurel told him, fighting back a laugh.

"Terrible waste," he murmured, taking the hand she held against him to his lips. Turning it over, he brushed them over her wrist and felt the wild beat below the skin.

"Matthew, don't."

He looked at her. It would be easy, so very easy. He had only to draw her to him and kiss her once; they both knew it. She wanted, he wanted, yet neither of them was quite sure how it had come to this. "Years from now, I'm going to hate myself for handling it this way," he murmured as he rose. "I'd take some aspirin now, Laurellie. You're going to need all the help you can get with that hangover in the morning."

Cursing himself all the way, Matt walked to the door, then shut it firmly behind him.

Chapter 5

"Damn you, Bates."

Laurel stared at the pale, wan reflection in her bathroom mirror while hammers pounded dully in her head. Why did he have to be right?

Grabbing a bottle of aspirin, she slammed the door of the medicine cabinet closed. This was followed by a pitiful moan as she clutched her head. Laurel knew it wasn't going to fall off; she only wished it would.

She deserved it. Laurel downed the two aspirins and shuddered. Anyone who drank four martinis in an afternoon deserved what she got. She might have accepted it with some grace if he just hadn't been right.

It didn't help her mood that she could remember what had happened after the drinking. She'd practically thrown herself at him. God, what a fool! He wasn't going to let her forget it. Oh, no, he'd tease and torment her for months. Maybe she deserved that, too, but... Oh, Lord, did she have to remember how wonderful it had been, how unique? Did she have to stand here knowing she wanted it to happen again?

Well, it wasn't. Dragging both hands through her hair, she willed the pounding in her head to stop. She wasn't going to fall for Matthew Bates and make an idiot out of herself. She might be stuck with him on the story, but personally it was going to be hands off and keep your distance. She'd chalk up her reaction to him to an excess of liquor. Even if it wasn't true.

With a sigh, Laurel turned toward the shower. She'd do the intelligent thing. She'd soak her head. As she reached for the tap, the pounding started again—at the front door and inside her temples. Whoever it was deserved a slow, torturous death, she decided as she trudged out to answer.

"Good morning, Laurellie." Matt leaned against the doorjamb and grinned at her. His gaze slid down her short, flimsy robe. "I like your dress."

He was casually dressed, as always, but fresh and obviously clearheaded. She felt as though she'd walked through a desert, eating a few acres along the way. "I overslept," she muttered, then folded her arms and waited for him to gloat.

"Had any coffee yet?"

She eyed him warily as he closed the door. Maybe he was just waiting for the perfect moment to gloat. "No."

"I'll fix it," he said easily and strolled into the kitchen.

Laurel stared after him. No smart remark, no smirk? How the hell was she supposed to keep up with him? she demanded as she dragged herself back to the shower.

She'd been ready to battle, Matt thought as he reached for the glass container of coffee. And all she really wanted to do was crawl back into bed and shut down. A hell of a woman, he thought again. A great deal like her grandmother.

His thoughts traveled back to the evening before. Because he'd known better than to stay in his apartment, one thin wall away from Laurel, Matt had gotten in his car. A little legwork to take his mind off the woman. Olivia Armand would be a fount of information, and her opinion of the Trulanes was bound to be less biased than Laurel's.

Olivia greeted him on her terrace with a look that held both speculation and pleasure. "Well, well, now the evening has possibilities."

"Miss Olivia." Matt took the gnarled, ringed hand in his and kissed it. It smelled of fresh jasmine. "I'm mad about you."

"They all were," she said with a lusty laugh. "Sit down and have a drink, Matthew. Have you softened that grand-daughter of mine up yet?"

Matt thought of the fiery woman he'd held only an hour before. "A bit," he murmured.

"You're slow, boy."

"I've always thought a man's more successful if he covers all the angles first." He handed her a drink before he sat down beside her.

"Not joining me?"

"It's hard enough to keep a clear head around you." While she laughed, he sat back and lit a cigarette. "Where's Susan?"

"Upstairs, being shocked by my journals."

"What'd you think of her?"

Olivia took a slow sip. Little fingers of moonlight danced over the diamonds on her hands. Insects buzzed around the hanging lantern by the door, tapping against the glass. The scents from the garden beyond rose up lazily. "Bright girl. Well-bred, a bit shaky and sad, but strong enough."

"She claims her sister was murdered."

The thin white brows rose, more, Matt observed, in thoughtfulness than surprise. "So that's what this is all about. Interesting." She took another sip, then tapped her finger against the glass. "The poor girl was bitten by a snake in the swamps behind Heritage Oak. Tell me why Susan's thinking murder."

In the brisk, concise style he used in his reporting, Matt ran through the entire events of the day. He saw a bat swoop low over the trees, then disappear. The air was full of the sounds of crickets and the occasional croak of a frog. Palm fronds rustled overhead. The breeze carried a teasing scent of magnolia. A long way from New York, he mused.

"Not as cut and dried as the Trulanes like to keep things," Olivia commented. "Well, Matthew, murder and mystery keep the blood moving, but you're not telling me this to keep my arteries from hardening."

He grinned. She could always make him grin. Leaning

back, he listened to the sounds of the night. "I know the general background on the Trulanes, and Laurel gave me a few more details—through rose-colored glasses," he added.

"A touch of jealousy's a healthy thing," Olivia decided. "Might get you on your horse."

"The point is," Matthew said dryly, "I'd like you to tell me about them."

"All right. We'll walk in the garden. I get stiff sitting so long."

Matt took the hand she held out and helped her up. She was tiny; it always surprised him. She walked lightly. If there was any pain or discomfort in her joints, she gave no sign of it. He hadn't lied when he'd said he was mad about her. Within five minutes of their first meeting, he'd fallen for her, and had had no trouble understanding why she'd been the most sought-after girl, then woman, then widow, of the parish.

"Marion was finished in France," Olivia began. "There were rumors of an ill-fated love affair, but she'd never talk about it. She's quiet, but she's sharp, always was. For all her good works and elegant airs, she's also a snob. I'm fond enough of the girl, but she's not her mother, as some would like to think."

Matt laughed, patting the hand tucked through his arm. "I knew I could count on you for a straight shot, Miss Olivia."

"Can't stand pussyfooting around. Now Charles was like his mother," she continued. "Good-looking boy, head in the clouds. But he had talent. He was shy about it, but he had talent. One of his watercolors hangs in my sitting room."

Then he was good, Matt mused. Olivia might buy the attempt of a poor neighbor, but she wouldn't hang it in Promesse d'Amour unless it deserved it.

"I was disappointed in him for running off with his brother's wife." Catching the ironic look in Matt's eye, she wagged a finger at him. "I have my standards, Yankee. If Louis's wife and brother wanted each other, they should have been honest about it instead of sneaking off like thieves in the night. Louis would have dealt with it better."

"Tell me about him."

"Laurel's first love." She cackled at Matt's expression. "Simmer down, Matthew, every woman's entitled to one fairy tale. When he was young, he was a vibrant, exciting man. He was devoted to his family, and his family's business, but he wasn't serious or stuffy. I'd never have abided that. I believed he loved his first wife deeply and the betrayal destroyed him. It didn't help when the rumors started that she'd been carrying Charles's baby."

"Did you ever meet Anne Trulane?"

"No, Louis was selfish with her, and I felt he was entitled." She sighed and broke a blossom from an azalea. "They were planning a party in September. Marion told me it was going to be a huge, splashy affair, introducing Anne to New Orleans society. She said the poor child was torn between excitement and terror at the idea. I admit, I was looking forward to getting a close look at her. They said she resembled Elise."

"They?" Matt prompted.

"The servants. Bless them." She turned back toward the house, fleetingly remembering a time when she could have walked and run in the garden for hours. "If I want to know what's going on at Heritage Oak, I ask my cook. She'll tell me what their cook told her." She gave a gusty sigh. "I love espionage."

"You remember what Elise Trulane looked like?"

"My memory's twice as old as you are." She laughed, relishing rather than regretting the years. "More."

Despite the lines time had etched, her face was beautiful in the moonlight. The hand under his was dry with age. And strong. "Miss Olivia, where can I find another like you?"

"You've got one under your nose, you slow-witted Yankee." She settled back in her chair with a little sound of pleasure. "Ah, Susan, come out." She gestured to the woman hesitating at the garden doors. "Poor child," she said to Matt, "she's still blushing. How did you like my journals?"

"They're very—colorful. You've had a…." How did one put it? "A full life, Mrs. Armand."

Olivia gave a hoot of laughter. "Don't water it down, child. I've sinned and loved every minute of it."

"A drink, Susan?" Matt steered her to a chair.

"No, thanks. Laurel's not with you?"

"I don't like to bring her when I'm courting Olivia," he said easily, pleased to see that she could smile. "Since I'm here, I wonder if you can remember any names Anne might have mentioned in her letters, anything unusual or out of place she might have written about."

Susan lifted her hands, then let them fall. "She wrote mostly of Louis and the house…and Marion, of course. She'd grown fond of Marion. The servants…a Binney, a Cajun woman Anne said ran the place." Susan thought back, trying to find the details he wanted. "I got the impression she hadn't really taken over as mistress yet. Anne was a bit overwhelmed by having servants."

"Anyone outside the family?"

"She didn't really know anyone else. Oh, there was one of Louis's accountants, Nathan Brewster. She mentioned him a couple of times. I think he'd come to the house to go over papers with Louis. He made Anne nervous." Susan smiled again, this time with sadness. "Anne was very shy of men. Other than that it was all Louis. He was teaching her to ride…."

"Nathan Brewster," Olivia murmured. "I've heard of him. Sharp boy. Your age, Matthew. Supposed to have a nasty temper, nearly killed a man a couple years back. Seems the man was too friendly with Brewster's sister."

"Anything you don't know, Miss Olivia?"

"Not a damn thing." She grinned and gestured for a fresh drink.

He turned to pour it for her. "Susan, do you have a picture of Anne?"

"Yes, do you want it?"

"I'd like to see it."

When she'd risen to go inside, Matt handed Olivia her drink. "Know anything about the Heritage Oak swamp being haunted?"

"Don't be smug, Matthew," she advised. "We Creoles understand the supernatural more than you Yankees. Most of the swamps are haunted,'' she said with perfect calm as she swirled her bourbon. ''The ghosts in Heritage Oak's date back to before the war.''

Matthew settled back down, knowing there was only one war Olivia would feel worth mentioning. He remembered Laurel had done precisely the same thing. ''Tell me.''

''One of the Trulane women used to meet her lover there. Damned uncomfortable place for adultery,'' she added practically. When Matthew only laughed, she went on blandly. ''When her husband found them, he shot them both—the gun's under glass in their library—and dumped the bodies in quicksand. Since then, occasional lights've been seen or someone'll hear a woman sobbing. Very romantic.''

''And terrifying to someone like Anne Trulane,'' he added thoughtfully.

''It's only a wallet-size,'' Susan said as she came back out. ''But it was taken less than a year ago.''

''Thanks.'' Matt studied the picture. Young, sweet, shy. Those were the words that came to his mind. And alive. He could remember how she'd looked the morning they'd found her. Swearing under his breath, he handed the picture to Olivia.

''I'll be damned,'' she muttered, tapping the photo against her palm. ''She could be Elise Trulane's twin.''

The sound of Laurel rummaging in the bedroom brought him back to the present. Matt shifted his thoughts. There was another interview that day. Louis Trulane. He took the coffee out on the gallery and waited for Laurel.

She liked pink begonias, he mused. Pinching off one of the blossoms that trailed over the railing, Matt let the fragrance envelop him. Pink begonias, he thought again. Lace curtains. Where did a man who'd grown up with holes in his shoes fit into that? Strange, he thought more about his beginnings since he'd gotten involved with Laurel than he had in years.

He was staring down into the courtyard when she came out, but Laurel didn't think he was seeing the ferns and flowers. She'd only seen that expression on his face a few times when she'd happen to glance up and see him at his typewriter, immersed in a story. Intense, brooding.

"Matthew?" It was an encompassing question. She wanted to ask what troubled him, what he was thinking of, or remembering. But the look stayed in his eyes when he turned to her, and she couldn't. Then it cleared, as though it had never been.

"Coffee's hot," he said simply.

She went to it, dressed in a sheer cotton skirt and blouse that made him hope the heat wave continued. "No I-told-you-so?" she asked before she sat on one of the white wrought-iron chairs.

"People in glass houses," he returned, leaning back against the railing. "I've had my share of mornings after. Feeling better?"

"Some. I'm going to call the house before we leave. I want to make sure Susan's settling in all right."

"She's fine." Matt speculated on what a woman like Laurel would wear under a summer dress. Silk—very thin silk, perhaps. "I saw her and your grandmother last night."

The cup paused on its way to Laurel's lips. "You went out there last night?"

"I can't keep away from your grandmother."

"Damn it, Matthew, this is my story."

"Our story," he reminded her mildly.

"Either way, you had no business going out there without me."

Walking over, he helped himself to a cup of coffee. "As I recall, you weren't in the mood to socialize last night. If you had been," he added smoothly, "we wouldn't have found ourselves at your grandmother's."

Her eyes narrowed at that, and she rose. "Just because my mind was fuzzy yesterday, Bates, don't get the idea in your head that you attract me in the least." Because he only smiled, she plunged on. "*Any* man might look good after four martinis. Even you."

He set down his cup very carefully. "Mind clear this morning, Laurellie?"

"Perfectly, and—" She broke off when he pulled her against him.

"Yes, I'd say your mind was clear." He lowered his mouth to her jawline and nibbled. "You're a woman who knows exactly what she wants, and what she doesn't."

Of course she was, Laurel thought as she melted against him. "I don't want—oh." Her breath shuddered out as he nuzzled her ear.

"What?" Matt moistened the lobe with his tongue, then nipped it. "What don't you want?"

"You to—to confuse me."

She felt the brush of his lashes against her cheek as he made a teasing journey toward her mouth. "Do I?"

"Yes." His lips hovered just above hers. Laurel knew exactly what would happen if they met. She took a step back and waited for her system to level. "You're doing this to take my mind off the story."

"We both know—" he caught her hair in his hand "—this has nothing to do with any story."

"Well, the story's what we have to concentrate on." She spoke quickly, had to speak quickly until she was certain the ground was steady again. "I don't want you digging without me. I found Susan in the first place, and—"

"Damn it, if and when there's a story you'll get your half of the byline."

It was easier to be angry than aroused so she let her temper rise with his. "It has nothing to do with the byline. I don't like you probing Grandma and Susan for leads without me. If you'd told me what you wanted to do, I'd have had some more coffee, a cold shower and pulled myself together."

"Maybe you could have." Sticking his hands in his pockets, he rocked back gently on his heels. "The point is, I wanted to talk to someone about the Trulanes, someone who has a little objectivity."

She flared at that, then subsided, hating him for being right. "Let's just go," she muttered, whirling away.

"Laurel." Matt took her arm, stopping her at the doorway.

"It's not a matter of the story," he said quietly. "I don't want you to be hurt."

She stared at him while her guards began to shift on their foundations. Trouble, she thought. I'm really going to be in trouble. "I asked you before not to be nice to me," she murmured.

"I'll give you a hard time later to make up for it. The way you feel about Louis—"

"Has nothing to do with any of this," she insisted, no longer certain either of them were speaking of the story. "Let me deal with it myself, Matthew. I can."

He wanted to press her, for himself, for what he needed from her. The time would come when he would have to. "Okay," he said simply. "Let's go."

The breeze helped. It whispered soothingly through the windows as they drove out of town. With her head back and her eyes shut, Laurel listened to Matt's accounting of his visit to her grandmother the evening before.

"I take it from that scornful tone in your Yankee voice that you don't believe in the Trulane ghosts?"

"And you do?" Grinning, he sent her a sidelong look. When she didn't answer right away, he slowed down to look at her more carefully. "Laurel?"

She shrugged, then made a business out of smoothing her skirts. "Let's just say I've got Creole blood, Matthew."

He couldn't stop the smile, on his lips or in his voice. "Ghosts, Laurel?"

"Atmosphere," she corrected, goaded into admitting something she'd just as soon have kept to herself. "I've been in that swamp. There're flowers where you least expect them, small patches of prairie, blue herons, quiet water." She turned in her seat so that the breeze caught the tips of her hair and carried them out the window. "There's also quicksand, nasty little insects and snakes. Shadows." Frustrated, she turned to stare through the windshield. "I never liked it there. It's brooding. There're places the sun never reaches."

"Laurel." Matt stopped the car at the entrance to Heritage

Oak. "You're going by childhood impressions again. It's a place, that's all."

"I can only tell you how I feel." She turned her head to meet his eyes. "And apparently how Anne Trulane felt."

"All right." Shifting into first, he maneuvered the car be-. tween the high brick pillars. "But for now, let's concentrate on human beings."

The oaks lining the drive were tall and old, the Spanish moss draping them gray green and tenacious. It hadn't changed. And, Laurel realized at the first sighting, neither had the house.

The brick had aged before she'd been born. There were subtle marks of time, but they'd been there as long as she could remember. The lines of the house were sharp and clean, not fluid like Promesse d'Amour's, but no less beautiful. The brick was a dusky rose, the balconies were soft black. Their delicacy didn't detract from the arrogance of the house. If Laurel saw her own ancestral home as a woman, she saw Heritage Oak as a man, bold and ageless.

"It's been a long time," she murmured. Emotions raced through her—memories. Knights and tea parties, filmy dresses and pink cakes. She'd been a child the last time she'd seen it, daydreamed in it.

With a sigh, Laurel turned and found her eyes locked with Matt's. There were new emotions now, not so soft, not so tender. This was reality, with all its pain and pleasure. This was real. Too real. Giving in to the panic of the moment, Laurel fumbled with the door handle and got out of the car.

What was happening to her? she asked herself as she took three long, deep breaths. It was getting to the point where she couldn't even look at him without wanting to run—or to reach out. A physical attraction was no problem. She'd managed to submerge that feeling for a year. This was something else again and it promised not to be so easily dealt with. She was going to have to, Laurel told herself, just as she was going to have to deal with her feelings for the Trulanes.

"Matthew, let me handle this." Calmer, she walked with him to the wide, white porch. "I know Louis and Marion."

"Knew," he corrected. He hadn't missed the way she'd looked at the house. Or the way she'd looked at him. "People have the inconsiderate habit of changing. I won't make you any promises, Laurel, but I won't interfere until I have to."

"You're a hard man, Bates."

"Yeah." He lifted the knocker and let it fall against a door of Honduras mahogany.

A tall, angular woman answered the door. After a brief glance at Matt, her nut-colored eyes fastened on Laurel. "Little Miss Laurel," she murmured, and held out both thin hands.

"Binney. It's so good to see you again."

Josephine Binneford, housekeeper, had weathered the decade since Laurel had last seen her with little change. Her hair was grayer but still worn in the same no-nonsense knot at the back of her neck. Perhaps there were more lines in her face, but Laurel didn't see them.

"Little Miss Laurel," Binney repeated. "Such a fine, beautiful lady now. No more scraped knees?"

"Not lately." With a grin, Laurel leaned over to brush her cheek. She smelled of starch and lilac. "You look the same, Binney."

"You're still too young to know how fast time goes." Stepping back, she gestured them inside before she closed out the brilliant sunshine and heat. "I'll tell Miss Marion you're here." With a gait stiffened by arthritis, she led them to the parlor. *"Revenez bientôt,"* she murmured, turning to Laurel again. *"Cette maison a besoin de jeunesse."* Turning, she headed up the stairs.

"What did she say?" Matt asked as Laurel stared after her.

"Just to come back again." She cradled her elbows in her hands as if suddenly cold. "She says the house needs youth." She crossed into the parlor.

If people change, she thought, this remains constant. The room could have been transported back a century; it would look the same in the century to come.

The sun gleamed through high windows framed with royal-blue portieres. It shone on mahogany tables, drawing out the rich red tints. It sparkled on a cut-glass vase that a long-dead

Trulane bride had received on her wedding day. It lay like a
lover on a porcelain woman who'd been captured for eternity
in the swirl of a partnerless waltz.

Matt watched Laurel's long, silent survey of the room. The
play of emotions on her face had him dealing with frustration,
jealousy, need. How could he get her to turn to him, when so
much of her life was bound up in what had been, who had
been?

"Memories are nice little possessions, Laurel," he said
coolly. "As long as you don't ignore the present when you
take them out to play."

He'd wanted to make her angry, because her anger was the
easier thing for him to deal with. Instead, she turned to him,
her eyes soft, her face stunning. "Do you have any, Matthew?" she asked quietly. "Any of those nice little possessions?"

He thought of a roof that leaked and icy floors and a plate
that never had enough on it. He remembered a woman hacking, always hacking, in her bed at night, weakening already-
weak lungs. And he remembered the promise he'd made to
get out, and to take the woman with him. He'd only been able
to keep the first part of the promise.

"I have them," he said grimly. "I prefer today."

She'd heard something there, under the bitterness. Vulnerability. Automatically, Laurel reached out to him. "Matthew…"

Not that way, he told himself. He'd be damned if he'd get
to her through sympathy. He took the hand she held out, but
brought it to his lips. "Life's a ridiculous cycle to be involved
in, Laurellie. I've always thought making memories has more
going for it than reliving them."

She dropped her hand back to her side. "You're not going
to let me in, are you?"

"Today." He ran his fingers through her hair. "Let's concentrate on today."

Unaccountably hurt, she turned from him. "There isn't any
without a yesterday."

"Damn it, Laurel—"

"Laurel, I'm sorry to keep you waiting." Marion glided in as only a woman taught to walk can do. She wore filmy dresses in pastels that always seemed to float around her. As Laurel took her hands, soft and small, she wondered how anyone could be so coolly beautiful. Marion was nearing forty, but her complexion was flawless, with a bone structure that spoke of breeding. Her scent was soft, like her hands, like her hair, like her eyes.

"Marion, you look lovely."

"Sweet." Marion squeezed her hands before releasing them. "I haven't seen you since that charity function two months ago. It was odd seeing you there with your pad and pencil. Are you happy with your career?"

"Yes, it's what I've always wanted. This is a colleague of mine, Matthew Bates."

"Nice to meet you, Mr. Bates." Marion held his hand an extra moment, hesitating while her eyes searched his face. "Have we met?"

"Not formally, Miss Trulane. I was here when your sister-in-law was found last month."

"I see." Briefly, her eyes clouded with pain. "I'm afraid I don't remember too much of that day clearly. Please sit down. Binney is seeing to some refreshments. Louis will be along in a moment." She chose a Hepplewhite for herself, straight-backed and dully gleaming. "He's tied up on the phone. Actually, I'm glad to have a moment with you before he comes." Marion folded her hands on her lap. "Laurel, you haven't seen Louis in a very long time."

"Ten years."

"Yes, ten years." Marion gazed out of the window a moment, then sighed. "One loses track of time here. I had to stop having you over after Charles and Elise...went away. Louis wasn't in a proper state for an impressionable young girl."

Ten years, Laurel thought, and it still hurts her. What has it done to him? "I understand that, Marion. I'm not a girl anymore."

"No, you're not." Her gaze shifted back, away from the

trim lawn and oaks. "Laurel, you saw only the beginnings of
a change in him, but as the months passed, as the years passed,
he became bitter," she said briskly. "Given to flashes of temper, of absentmindedness. There were times he wouldn't remember—" She stopped herself again, unlacing her hands.
"He didn't forget," she corrected with a wistful smile. "He
simply chose not to remember. He and Charles were—well,
that's done."

"Marion, I know how difficult it must've been for him."
Laurel reached out to lay a hand on hers. "I always knew.
The truth is, I didn't stay away because you didn't ask me to
come, but because I knew Louis wouldn't want me here."

"You always understood a great deal," Marion murmured.
With a sigh, she tried to shake off the mood. "When he
brought Anne home, no one was more surprised, more pleased
than I. She'd taken that hard edge away."

"I felt that, too." She smiled when Marion sent her a questioning look. "I phoned him a few weeks after he was married."

Nodding, Marion laced her hands again. Her nails were
oval, unpainted and buffed. "Perhaps he was overprotective,
possessive, but Anne was so young, and he'd been hurt so
badly. I'm telling you this now because I want you—" her
gaze shifted to Matt "—both of you to understand the state
Louis is in now. There's been so much pain in his life. If he
seems cold and remote, it's only his way of dealing with
grief." She turned her head as Binney wheeled in a tea tray.
"Ah, iced tea. Do you still take too many sugars, Laurel?"

She smiled. "Yes. Oh." She glimpsed the tiny pink cakes
arranged on the tray. "How sweet of you, Binney."

"I only told the cook Miss Laurel was coming for tea."
She gave Laurel a quick wink. "Don't eat more than three,
or your grandmother will scold me."

Laughing, Laurel bit into one as the housekeeper left the
room. The light, sweet taste brought back a new flood of
memories. She heard ice tinkle in the glasses as Marion
poured. "Binney hasn't changed. The house, either," she
added with a smile for Marion. "I'm so glad."

"The house never changes," Marion told her as she offered Laurel fresh, cold tea in a Waterford glass. "Only the people in it."

Laurel didn't hear him, but sensed him. Carefully, she set down the glass she held. Turning her head, she looked into Louis's eyes.

Chapter 6

Can ten years be so long? she thought with a jolt. She'd thought she was prepared. She'd hoped she was. There was gray in his hair now, near the temples. That she would have accepted. There were lines in his face going deep around his mouth and eyes. She could have accepted them too. But the eyes had none of the warmth, none of the humor she'd loved so much.

He was thin, too thin. It made him look older than thirty-six. She rose, and with a mixture of pain and pity, went to him. "Louis."

He took her hand and the ghost of a smile touched his mouth. "Grown up, Laurel? Why did I expect to find a child?" Very lightly, he touched a fingertip to the underside of her chin. She wanted to weep for him. "You always promised to be a beauty."

Laurel smiled, willing the warmth to come to his eyes. "I've missed seeing you." But the warmth didn't come, and his hand dropped away. She felt his tension even before she felt her own. "Louis, this is my associate, Matthew Bates."

Louis's eyes flicked over Matt and grew colder. "I believe we've met."

"Some tea, Louis?" Marion reached for the pitcher.

"No." His voice was curt, but Marion made no sign other

than a quick compression of lips. Neither man noticed, as their eyes were on Laurel. "We're not here for tea and cakes this time, are we, Laurel?" Louis murmured before he crossed the room to stand in front of the empty hearth. Over it was an oil of his mother. Laurel remembered it well. It had been there for years, except for a brief period when Elise Trulane's portrait had replaced it. "Why don't we get on with this?" Louis suggested. "I agreed to see you and Mr. Bates to put an end to this rumor Susan started." He gave Laurel a long look. "Ask your questions. I used to have all the answers for you."

"Louis..." She wanted to go to him, soothe him somehow, but the look in Matt's eyes stopped her. "I'm sorry to intrude this way. Very sorry."

"It isn't necessary to be sorry." Louis drew out a thin cigar, eyeing it for a moment before lighting it. "Nothing ever remains as it was. Do what you came to do."

She felt her stomach tighten. The power in him was still there, a power she'd recognized even as a child. It had driven him to take up the reins of a multimillion-dollar firm before he'd finished college. It had enabled him to enchant a young girl so that the woman could never forget him. But it was so cold now. Laurel stood where she was in the center of the parlor while the gap between memory and today grew wider.

"Susan is certain that Anne would never have gone out into the swamp alone," she began, knowing she began badly. "Susan claims that Anne had a terror of dark places, and that the letters she'd written expressed a specific fear of the place."

"And she believes Anne was forced to go in there," Louis finished. "I know all of that already, Laurel."

She was a journalist, she had an assignment. She had to remember it. "Was Anne afraid of the swamp, Louis?"

He drew on his cigar and watched her through the cloud of smoke. "Yes. But she went in," he added, "because she died there."

"Why would she have gone in?"

"Perhaps to please me." Carelessly he flicked cigar ash into the scrubbed hearth. "She'd begun to feel foolish about this fear she'd dragged along since childhood. When I was with her," he murmured, "she wouldn't need a light on in the hallway at night." Abruptly, his head lifted again, to the arrogant angle Laurel remembered in a young man. "The story about the ghosts in the swamp had her imagining all sorts of things. I was impatient." He drew on the cigar again, harder. "She had a...need for my approval."

"You think she might have gotten up in the middle of the night and gone out there to please you?" Laurel asked him, taking a step closer.

"It makes more sense than believing someone broke in, dragged her out and left her without myself or any of the servants hearing a sound." He gave her another cool, uncompromising look. "You read the police report, I imagine."

"Yes." She moistened her lips as she remembered the photograph. "Yes, I did."

"Then there's no need for me to go over that."

"Did your wife often have trouble sleeping?" Matt put in, watching as a very small muscle worked in Louis's jaw.

"Occasionally. Particularly when I was working." He glanced over Matt's head, out the long windows. "She thought she'd seen lights in the swamp."

"Did anyone else see them?"

Louis's mouth twisted into something like a smile. "Over the years, dozens of people have claimed to—usually when they've kept company with a bottle of bourbon."

"Mr. Bates," Marion broke in. "Anne was afraid of the swamp, but she was also fascinated with it. It's not unusual for someone to be fascinated by something they fear. She'd become obsessed by the legend. The problem...the blame," she amended slowly, "comes from none of us taking her seriously enough. She was so young. Perhaps if we'd insisted she go in during the daylight, she wouldn't have felt compelled to go in at night."

"Do you think she was capable of going in there alone, at night?" Laurel asked her.

"It's the only explanation. Laurel, we all loved her." She sent Louis a quick, misty look. "She was sweet and soft, but she was also highly strung. I thought her nerves came from the plans we were making for the party.''

"What difference does it make now?'' Louis demanded and tossed his cigar into the hearth. It bounced, then lay, smoldering. "Anne's gone, and neither Susan nor her letters can change it.''

"The letters were stolen from Susan's room,'' Laurel said quietly.

"That's ridiculous. Who would steal letters? She misplaced them.'' Louis dismissed them with an angry shrug.

"You were married for nearly a year,'' Matt said casually. "Yet none of your closest neighbors had met your wife. Why?''

"That's my business.''

"Louis, please.'' Laurel took another step toward him. "If we could just understand.''

"Understand?'' he repeated, and stopped her with a look. "How can you? She was hardly more than a child, the child you were when I last saw you. But she didn't have your confidence, your boldness. I kept her to myself because I wanted to. I had to. There was a generation between us.''

"You didn't trust her,'' Laurel murmured.

"Trust is for fools.''

"Isn't it odd,'' Matt commented, drawing Louis's fury from Laurel to himself, "how much Anne resembled your first wife?''

The only sound was Marion's sharp intake of breath. Though his hands clenched into fists, Louis stood very still. Without another word, another look, he strode out.

"Please, Louis just isn't himself.'' Marion fiddled nervously with the glasses. "He's very sensitive about comparisons between Anne and Elise.''

"People are bound to make them,'' Matt returned, "when the physical resemblance is so striking.''

"More than physical,'' Marion murmured, then went on in a rush. "It was a natural observation, Mr. Bates, but Louis won't discuss Elise and Charles. If there's nothing else...?''

"Do you know Nathan Brewster?'' Laurel asked abruptly.

Marion's eyes widened before her lashes swept down. "Yes, of course, he's one of Louis's accountants."

Matt's brow lifted before he exchanged a look with Laurel. "His was one of the few names Anne mentioned in her letters."

"Oh, that's natural, I suppose. He came to the house a few times on business. It's true Anne didn't meet many people. Well." She rose, sending them both an apologetic smile. "I'm sorry I couldn't be of more help, but perhaps you can put Susan's doubts to rest now." She held out her hands to Laurel again. "Come back soon, please, just to talk like we used to."

"I will. Tell Louis..." Laurel sighed as she released Marion's hands. "Tell him I'm sorry."

They walked out of the house in silence, drove away in silence. As the frustration, the anger built, Matt swore to himself he'd say nothing. Whatever Laurel was feeling was her own business. If she let her emotions get in the way, let herself grieve, there was nothing he could do about it.

On an oath, he yanked the wheel, skidded to the side of the road and stopped.

"Damn it, Laurel, stop."

She kept her hands very still in her lap and stared straight ahead. "Stop what?"

"Mourning."

She turned her head then, and though her eyes were dry, they were eloquent. "Oh, Matthew," she whispered, "he looked so lost."

"Laurel—"

"No, you don't have to say it. He's changed. I expected it, but I wasn't ready for it." She drew a deep breath that came out trembling. "I wasn't ready to see him hurting so much."

Cursing Louis Trulane and all he stood for, Matt gathered Laurel close. She didn't protest when he cradled her against him, but held on. The sun streamed into the car. She could hear birds calling and chattering in the trees beyond the car. As he stroked her hair, she closed her eyes, letting herself draw from the comfort he offered.

"I am mourning," she murmured. "I don't know if you

can understand just how important Louis was to my childhood, my adolescence. Seeing him like this today…'' With a
sigh, she kept her head on his shoulder and watched the pat-
terns sun and shade made on the road.

"You're thinking of him as a victim, Laurel. We're all
victims of what life deals out. It's how we handle it that's
important.''

"When you love someone, and you lose them, it kills something in you too.''

"No.'' He let himself breathe in the scent of her hair.
"Damages. We all have to deal with being damaged one way
or the other.''

He was right, of course he was right. But it still hurt. She
said nothing, but sat quietly with her cheek on his shoulder
while his hand trailed through her hair. His body was so firm,
his heartbeat so steady. She could lose herself here, Laurel
realized, in the front seat of his car with the sun pouring
through and the sound of birds calling lazily from tree to tree.

"I keep telling you not to be nice to me,'' she murmured.

He tilted his head back to look at her. His eyes were intense
again, seeing too much. His fingers spread to cup her face.
When her mouth opened, he tightened them. "Shut up,'' he
told her before he pressed his lips to hers.

Not so light this time, not so gentle. She tasted frustration
and didn't understand it. But she also tasted desire, simmering, waiting, and couldn't resist it. Her body went fluid, every
bone, every muscle, as she surrendered to whatever it was
they needed from each other. The need was there, she knew.
Had always been there. The more she had resisted it, fought
it, ignored it, the stronger it had become, until it threatened
to overpower every other. Food, air, warmth, those were in-
significant needs compared to this. If she was seduced, it
wasn't by soft words or skilled kisses, but by the emotions
that had escaped before she'd been able to confine them.

"Matthew.'' She dropped her head on his shoulder and
tried to steady her breathing. "This isn't—I'm not ready for
this.''

Smoldering with impatience and desire, he forced her head back. "You will be."

"I don't know." She pressed her hands to his chest, wishing he could understand—wishing she could. "I told you that you confuse me. You do. I've never wanted a man before, and I never expected it to be you."

"It is me." He drew her closer. "You'll just have to get used to it." His expression changed slowly from barely restrained temper to intentness. "Never wanted a man," he repeated. "Any man? You haven't—been with any man?"

Her chin came up. "I said I never wanted one. I don't do anything I don't want to."

Innocent? Dear God, he thought, shouldn't he have seen it? Sensed it? Gradually, he loosened his grip until he'd released her. "Changes the rules, doesn't it?" he said softly. Matt took out a cigarette while she sat frowning at him. "Changes the rules," he repeated in a whisper. "I'm going to be your lover, Laurellie. Take some time to think about it."

"Of all the arrogant—"

"Yeah, we'll get into that in depth later." He blew out a stream of smoke. She was steadier now, he thought ruefully. He was wired. He'd better give them both some time to think about it. "Let me throw a couple of theories at you on Anne Trulane."

He started the car again while Laurel struggled to control her temper and to remember priorities. The story, she told herself, and forced her jaw to unclench. They'd deal with this…personal business later. "Go ahead."

He drove smoothly, ignoring the knot of need in his stomach. "Louis married Anne Fisher because she looked like his first wife."

"Oh, really, Matthew."

"Let me finish. Whether he cared for her or not isn't the issue. Once they were married he brought her back to Heritage Oak and kept her there, away from outsiders. Men. He didn't trust her."

"He'd been hurt before, in the cruelest possible way."

"Exactly." Matt pitched his cigarette out the window. "He

was obsessed with the idea that she might find a younger man. He was possessive, jealous. What if Anne rebelled? What if she gave him a reason to doubt her loyalty?''

"You're suggesting that Louis killed her because he thought she'd violated his trust.'' She didn't like the chill that brought to her skin, and turned on him. "That's ridiculous. He isn't capable of killing anyone.''

"How do you know what he's capable of?'' he tossed back. "You didn't know that man in the parlor today.''

No, she didn't, and the truth stung. "Your theory's weak,'' she retorted. "Look at the timetable. Anne died between 12:00 and 4:00 A.M. Louis woke the household sometime between two and three.''

"He could've taken her in before two,'' Matt said mildly. "Maybe he never intended for her to die. He might've wanted to frighten her, taken her in and left her there.''

"Then why would he call out a search party?''

Matt turned his head, letting his gaze skim over her face before he shifted it back to the road. "He could've forgotten he'd done it.''

Laurel opened her mouth and closed it again. Absentminded, Marion had said. He'd been absentminded, angry, bitter. She didn't like the picture it was drawing in her mind.

Laurel remained silent as he drove through downtown traffic. No man forgot he'd left his wife alone and lost. No sane man. Matt swung over to the curb and stopped. "Where are we going?''

"To see Nathan Brewster.''

Laurel glanced up at Trulane's, one of the oldest, most prestigious buildings in the city. Perhaps they'd find something in there that would shift the focus from Louis. "Marion didn't want to talk about Nathan Brewster.''

"I noticed.'' Matt stepped out of the car. "Let's find out why.''

"I know what you're thinking,'' she murmured as they walked toward the front doors.

"Mmmm. That could be embarrassing.''

She shot him a look as they walked inside. "Anne was

attracted to Nathan Brewster, acted on it and Louis found out. Rather than dealing with it or divorcing her, he drags her into the swamp in the middle of the night and dumps her.''

Matt checked the board on the wall and located Accounting. ''It crossed my mind,'' he agreed.

''You've got your own prejudices against Louis.''

''You're damned right,'' he muttered, and took her hand to pull her to the elevator. ''Look,'' Matt began before she could retort. ''Let's talk to the man and see what happens. Maybe he's just been embezzling or having an affair with Marion.''

''Your ideas get more and more ludicrous.'' She stepped into the elevator and crossed her arms.

''You're sulking.''

''I am not!'' Letting out an exasperated breath, she glared at him. ''I don't agree with your theory, that's all.''

''Give me yours,'' Matt suggested.

She watched the numbers flash over the elevator door. ''After we talk to Brewster.''

They stepped out on carpet, thick and plush. Without giving Matt a glance, Laurel crossed to the receptionist. ''Laurel Armand, Matthew Bates, with the *Herald*,'' she said briskly. ''We'd like to see Nathan Brewster.''

The receptionist flicked open her book. ''Do you have an appointment?''

''No. Tell Mr. Brewster we'd like to speak with him about Anne Trulane.''

''If you'll have a seat, I'll see if Mr. Brewster's available.''

''Nice touch, Laurellie,'' Matt told her as they crossed the reception area. ''Ever think about the military?''

''It's gotten me into a lot of city officials.'' She took a seat under a potted palm and crossed her legs.

He grinned down at her. There wasn't a trace of the sad, vulnerable woman who'd rested her head on his shoulder. ''You've got style,'' he decided, then let his gaze sweep down. ''And great legs.''

Laurel slanted him a look. ''Yeah.''

''Mr. Brewster will see you now.'' The receptionist led

them down a hallway, past an army of doors. After opening one, she went silently back to her desk.

Laurel's first impression of Nathan Brewster was of sex. He exuded it, ripe, physical. He was dark, and though he wasn't tall, he had a blatant virility no woman could miss. Good looks, though he had them, didn't matter. It was his primitive masculinity that would either draw or repel.

"Ms. Armand, Mr. Bates." He gestured toward two small leather chairs before taking a seat behind his desk. "You wanted to talk to me about Anne Trulane."

"That's right." Laurel settled herself beside Matt as she tried to reason out what kind of reaction a woman like Anne would have had to Nathan Brewster.

"She's dead," Brewster said flatly. "What does the press have to do with it?"

"You met Anne at Heritage Oak," Laurel began. "Not many people did."

"I went there on business." He picked up a pencil and ran it through his fingers.

"Could you give us your impression of her?"

"She was young, shy. My business was with Mr. Trulane; I barely spoke to her."

"Strange." Matt watched Brewster pull the pencil through his fingers again and again. "Yours was one of the few names that came up in Anne's letters." The pencil broke with a quiet snap.

"I don't know what you're talking about."

"Anne wrote to her sister about you." Matt kept his eyes on Brewster's now, waiting, measuring. "Her sister doesn't believe Anne's death was an accident."

Matt watched the little ripple of Brewster's throat as he swallowed. "She died of a snakebite."

"In the swamp," Laurel put in, fascinated by the waves of frustration and passion pouring out of him. "Did you know she was frightened of the swamp, Mr. Brewster?"

He shot Laurel a look, molten, enraged. Matt's muscles tensed. "How would I?" he demanded. "How would I know?"

"Why would you suppose she'd go into a place that terrified her?"

"Maybe she couldn't stand being locked up anymore!" he exploded. "Maybe she had to get out, no matter where, or how."

"Locked up?" Laurel repeated, ignoring the tremor in her stomach. "Are you saying Louis kept her a prisoner?"

"What else can you call it?" he shot back at her. His hands clenched and unclenched on the two jagged pieces of pencil. "Day after day, month after month, never seeing anyone but servants and a man who watched every move she made. She never did anything without asking him first. She never stepped a foot beyond the gates of that place without him."

"Was she unhappy?" Laurel asked. "Did she tell you she was unhappy?"

"She should've been," Nathan tossed back. "Trulane treated her more like a daughter than a wife. She needed someone who'd treat her like a woman."

"You?" Matt said softly. Laurel swallowed.

Brewster's breathing was labored. The temper Matt had been told of was fighting to get free. He'd have to struggle to control it. And, Matt mused, he wouldn't often win.

"I wanted her," Brewster said roughly. "From the first time I saw her out on the lawn, in the sunlight. She belonged in the sunlight. I wanted her, loved her, in a way Trulane couldn't possibly understand."

"Was she in love with you?"

Matt's quiet question drew the blood to Brewster's cheeks. "She would have left him. She wouldn't have stayed in that— monument forever."

"And come to you?" Laurel murmured.

"Sooner or later." The eyes he turned on Laurel were penetrating, filled with passion and feeling. "I told her she didn't have to stay locked up there, I'd help her get away. I told her she'd be better off dead than—"

"Better off dead than living with Louis," Laurel finished as his harsh breathing filled the room.

"It must've been frustrating," Matt continued when Brew-

ster didn't answer. "Loving your employer's wife, rarely being able to see her or tell her how you felt."

"Anne knew how I felt," Brewster bit off. "What difference does it make now? She's dead. That place killed her. He
killed her." Brewster sent them both a heated look. "Print
that in your paper."

"You believe Louis Trulane killed his wife?" Matt
watched Brewster sweep the remains of the pencil from his
desk.

"He might as well have held a gun to her head. She got
away," he murmured as he stared down at his empty hands.
"She finally got away, but she didn't come to me." The hands
curled into fists again. "Now leave me alone."

Laurel's muscles didn't relax until they'd walked out into
the sunlight. "That was a sad, bitter man," she murmured.

"And one who takes little trouble to hide it."

She shivered, then leaned against the side of his car. "I can
understand why he made Anne nervous."

Matt cupped his hands around a match as he lit a cigarette.
"Give me a basic feminine reaction."

"Passion, virility, primitive enough to fascinate." She
shook her head as she stared up at the ribbons of windows.
"For some women, that would be irresistible simply because
it's rather frightening. A woman like Anne Trulane would've
seen him as one of her dark closets and stayed away." With
a short laugh, she dragged a hand through her hair. "I'm not
a psychiatrist, Matthew, but I think a certain kind of woman
would be drawn to a man like Brewster. I don't believe Anne
Trulane would've been."

Letting out a long breath, she turned to him. "It's my turn
to write a scenario."

"Let's hear it."

"Brewster's in love with her—or thinks he is, it wouldn't
matter with a man like him. He tells Anne, asks her to leave
Louis for him. How would she feel? Frightened, appalled. A
little flattered perhaps."

He cocked a brow, intrigued. "Flattered?"

"She was a woman," Laurel said flatly. "Young, unsophisticated.'' She glanced back up at the windows, thinking of Brewster. ''Yes, I believe she might have felt all three emotions. It confuses her, he pressures her. He's very intense, dramatic. She loves her husband, but this is something she doesn't know how to cope with. She can't even write her sister about it.''

Matt nodded, watching her. ''Go on.''

''Suppose Brewster contacts her, demands to see her. Maybe he even threatens to confront Louis. She wouldn't have wanted that. Louis's approval and trust are important to her. Anne had to know about his first wife. So...''

Laurel's eyes narrowed as she tried to picture it. ''She agrees to see him, meets him outside, late, while Louis is working. They argue because she won't leave Louis. He's a physical man.'' She remembered his strong fingers on the pencil. ''He's convinced himself she wants him but is afraid to leave. He drags her away from the house, away from the light. She's terrified now, of him, of the dark. She breaks away and runs, but it's dark and she's in the swamp before she realizes it. She's lost. Brewster either can't find her or doesn't try. And then...''

''Interesting,'' Matt murmured before he flicked his cigarette away. ''And, I suppose, as plausible as anything else. I wish we had those damn letters,'' he said suddenly. ''There must be something there or they wouldn't've been taken.''

''Whatever it was, we won't find it there now.''

Matt nodded, staring past her. ''I want to get into that swamp, look around.''

Laurel felt the shudder and repressed it. ''Tonight?''

''Mmmm.''

She supposed she'd known it was bound to come down to this. Resigned, she blew the hair out of her eyes. ''Let's go get some mosquito repellent.''

He grinned and ran a finger down her nose. ''Only one of us has to go. You stay home and keep a light burning in the window.''

The brow went up, arrogant, haughty. ''My story, Bates. I'm going; you can tag along if you want.''

"Our story," he corrected. "God knows if there'll be anything in there but a bunch of filthy insects and soggy ground."

And snakes, Laurel thought. She swallowed, tasting copper. "We'll have to see, won't we? Matthew, we're running out of angles."

They stared at each other, frowning. Dead end—for now.

"Let's get some lunch," Laurel suggested as she swung around to get into the car. "And get back to the paper before we're both out of a job."

Chapter 7

Laurel spent over an hour with Matt in the newspaper morgue, going through files and crosschecking until her neck ached. With luck, the *Herald* would be on computers within the year. Laurel might miss the ambience of the cavernous morgue with the smell of dust and old paper, but she wouldn't miss the inconvenience. Some of the staff might grumble about having to learn the tricks of a terminal, the codes, the ways and means of putting in and taking out information at the punch of a button. She promised herself, as she rubbed at a crick in the back of her neck, she wouldn't be one of them.

"Brewster made page two with his fists," Laurel murmured as she scanned the story. "Two years ago last April." She glanced up briefly. "No one's memory's quite like Grandma's."

"She mentioned a sister."

"That's right. His sister'd been seeing a man who apparently liked his bourbon a bit too well. He'd seen her in a bar with another man and made a scene—tried to drag her out. Brewster was there. It took roughly ten men to pull him off, and before they did, he'd broken a couple of tables, a mirror, three of the guy's ribs, his nose and jaw and his own hand."

Matt lifted a brow at her cool recital of the violence. "Charged?"

"Assault headed the list," Laurel told him. "Ended up paying a fine when his...ah...opponent wouldn't press charges." She scrawled a note on her pad. "Apparently once Brewster's temper is lost, it's lost. I think I'll see if I can trace the sister. He might have talked to her about Anne."

"Mmm-hmm."

She glanced over to see Matt scribbling quickly in his own book. "What've you got?"

"Speculation," he murmured, then rose. "I have a few calls to make myself."

"Matthew," Laurel began as they started down the corridor, "weren't you the one who had all the big talk about sharing?"

He smiled at her, then pushed the button for the elevator. "After I make the calls."

"Make up your own rules as you go along?" she muttered when they stepped inside the car.

He looked down at her, remembering her passion in his arms, the vulnerability in her eyes. Her innocence. "I might just have to."

Laurel felt the quick chill race up her spine and stared straight ahead. "Let's stick with the story, Bates."

"Absolutely." Grinning, he took her arm as the elevator opened. They walked into the city room and separated.

Reporters have to get used to rude replies, no replies, run-arounds. Laurel dealt with all three as she dialed number after number in an attempt to trace Kate Brewster. When she finally reached her, Laurel had to deal with all three again.

Brewster's sister flatly refused to discuss the barroom brawl and had little to say about her brother. At the mention of Anne Trulane, Laurel sensed a hesitation and caught a slight inflection—fear?—in Kate's voice as she claimed she didn't know anyone by that name.

Laurel found herself dealing with another hazard reporters face. An abrupt dial tone in the ear. Glancing up, she saw Matt cradling his own phone between his shoulder and ear as he made notes. At least one of us is getting somewhere, she thought in disgust as she rose to perch on the corner of his desk. Though she tried, it wasn't possible to read his peculiar type of shorthand upside down. Idly, she picked up the foam cup that held his cooling coffee and sipped. When she heard him mention the name Elise Trulane, she frowned.

What the hell's he up to? Laurel wondered as he easily ignored her and continued to take notes. Checking up on Elise…he's hung up on the similarity in looks, she decided. What does a runaway first wife have to do with a dead second one? As an uncomfortable thought raced into her mind, Laurel's eyes darted to Matt's. *Revenge?* But that would be madness. Louis wasn't—Louis couldn't… From the way he returned the look, she realized Matt read her thoughts while she wasn't able to penetrate his. Deliberately, she turned away to stare into Don Ballinger's office. The information they'd given their editor might have been sketchy, but it had been enough to give them the go-ahead.

Matt hung up and tapped his pencil on the edge of his desk. "What you get?"

"Zero, unless you count the impression that Anne Trulane's name made Brewster's sister very nervous. And another impression that she treads very carefully where her brother's concerned. What're you up to, Matthew?"

He ran the pencil through his hands, but the gesture had none of the nervous passion and energy that Brewster's had. His hands were lean, not elegant like Louis's, she thought, or violent like Brewster's. They were capable and clever and strong—just as he was. Disturbed, she shifted her gaze to his face. It was becoming a habit for thoughts of him to get in the way of what they had to do.

"Matthew?" she repeated as he looked beyond her.

"It seems the two Mrs. Trulanes had one or two things more in common than looks," he began. He dropped the pencil on his desk and drew out a cigarette. "They each had only one relative. In Elise's case, it's an aunt. I just spoke with her."

"Why?"

"Curiosity." He blew out a stream of smoke as a reporter behind them swore and hung up his own phone. "She describes her niece as a shy, quiet girl. Apparently Elise loved Heritage Oak, and unlike Anne, had already begun to take over the position of lady of the manor. She enjoyed the planning, the entertaining, had ideas for redecorating. The aunt was astonished when Elise ran off with Louis's brother—hasn't seen or heard from her since. She thought Elise was devoted to her husband.''

"So did everyone else," Laurel commented. "Things like that do happen, Matthew, without anyone on the outside being aware. I don't imagine Elise would've told her aunt or anyone else that she was having an affair with Charles.''

"Maybe not. There is something I find interesting," he murmured, keeping his eyes on Laurel's. "Elise inherited fifty thousand dollars on her twenty-first birthday. She turned twenty-one the month after she left Heritage Oak. The money," he said slowly, "was never claimed.''

Laurel stared at him while ideas, answers, spun through her mind. "Maybe she—she might've been afraid to claim it thinking Louis could trace her.''

"Fifty thousand buys a lot of courage.''

"I don't see what digging into Elise's business has to do with Anne.''

His eyes were very calm, very direct. "Yes, you do." She looked pale again, drained as she had that morning. Smothering an oath, Matt rose. "It's something to think about," he said briskly. "For now, we'd better concentrate on what we have to do tonight. Let's go home. We can catch a couple of hours' rest before we have to get ready.''

"All right." She didn't want to argue, and though it was cowardly, she didn't want to think about what he'd just told her. There'd been enough that day. If she was to win out over her emotions, she needed the time to do it.

Matt didn't press her, but made easy, innocuous conversation on the drive home. He was good at falling back on a relaxed style to conceal his inner thoughts and feelings. It was one of his greatest professional weapons, and personal defenses. If he was furious with Laurel's automatic and unflagging defense of Louis Trulane, it wasn't apparent. If he harbored frustrating, near-violent urges to take her to some dark, private place until she forgot Louis Trulane existed, he didn't show it. His voice was calm, his driving smooth. His muscles were tight.

"A nap," Laurel said as they left his car to cross the courtyard, "sounds like heaven. It's been a long two days."

A long year, he thought as needs crawled in him. "And it's going to be a long night," he said easily.

She smiled at him for the first time since they'd left the *Herald.* "What time do we go on safari?"

"Midnight's the accepted hour, I believe." He touched the tips of her hair, then started up the steps.

"Garlic doesn't work against ghosts, does it?" Laurel mused. "No silver bullets, wooden stakes. What does?"

"Common sense."

She gave a windy sigh. "No romance."

At the top of the steps, he grinned at her. "Wanna bet?"

Laughing, she bent to pick up a wrapped box at the base of her door. "I don't remember ordering anything."

"From Jerry, no doubt—a box of number-two pencils."

She tried to glare at him and failed. "Midnight, Bates." After a brief search, she found her keys and unlocked the door. With a final arch look, she closed the door in his face.

His grin faded as he started down to his own apartment. The woman was driving him crazy. She had to be blind not to see it, he thought as he jabbed his key into the lock. Maybe he'd been too cautious. As he walked into the kitchen, Matt stripped his shirt over his head and tossed it aside. Then again, it had taken him weeks to get used to the fact that he'd been struck by lightning the first time she'd lifted those dark green eyes and looked at him.

At that point, he'd told himself it was impossible, the same way he'd told himself it was impossible for him to lose his head over the neatly framed photograph Curt had put on their shared desk in their college dorm.

"My sister," Curt had said in his abstracted way. "Runs copy at my father's paper during the summer. Guess you'd know about things like that."

The words hadn't registered because Matt had to concentrate on just breathing. There he'd been—a senior in college, a man who'd already seen and worked his way through more than many men do in a lifetime—rooted to the spot with one of the shirts he'd been unpacking dangling from his hand, head swimming over a girl who couldn't have been more than fifteen. Impossible.

Matt grabbed some orange juice from the refrigerator and chugged straight from the bottle. He'd gotten over that first...whatever it had been quickly enough. Or he'd told himself he had. But when William Armand had written him, all those years later, mentioning his relationship to Matt's senior-year college roommate and offering a position on the *Herald,* Matt hadn't hesitated. And he hadn't asked himself why.

It would've helped, he thought as he tossed the empty bottle in the trash, if he'd found a slow brain underneath that fabulous face. Or a bland or too-sweet personality. It would've helped if he hadn't sat next to her for a full year knowing she was everything he'd ever wanted.

He intended to have her, though her innocence urged him toward a traditional courtship—quiet dinners, candlelight, a gentle touch. Matt felt the stir of desire, and swore. He hoped he had the control he was going to need.

He intended to have her, though the difference in their backgrounds sometimes reared up to mock him. He'd already pushed his way through a lot of doors; now he had to make sure his luck held.

He was going to have her.

Matt stuck his hands in his pockets and headed for the shower. And he heard her scream.

Later, he wouldn't remember bursting out of his own apartment and rushing to hers. He'd remember hearing her scream again, and again, but he wouldn't remember beating on her door and finally, in desperation, knocking it in. What he would remember, always, was the way she'd looked, standing frozen with her hands at her own throat, her face like parchment and her eyes terrified.

"Laurel!" He grabbed her, spinning her around and into

him where she stood in his arms, rigid as a stone. "What? What is it?"

He could feel the beat of her heart. Was it possible for a heart to beat that fast? Her skin was like ice, dampened by a sheen of sweat, but she didn't tremble. Not yet. "The box," she whispered. "In the box."

With one hand still on her arm, he turned and looked into the box on the table. The oath ripped out under his breath, pungent. "It's all right, Laurel. It's dead, it can't hurt you." His body trembled with fury as he lifted a portion of the copperhead from the box. "It can't hurt you now," he repeated, turning back to see her staring, transfixed at what he held in his hand. Sweat pearled on her forehead. Through her parted lips, her breath came harsh and quick.

"Matthew...please."

Without a word, he covered the box and carried it from the apartment. He returned—twenty, thirty seconds later—to find her leaning, palms down on the table, head lowered, weeping. He still didn't speak as he picked her up to carry her to the sofa and cradle her like a baby. Then the trembling started.

Five minutes...ten, and he said nothing, only holding her as she wept into his bare shoulder and shuddered. She seemed so small. Even when he'd seen those flashes of vulnerability he would never have imagined her like this—totally helpless, without the slimmest defense against anything or anyone. As he held her close, Matt promised himself when he found out who'd sent the box, he'd make them pay for it.

Safe. She knew she was safe now, though the fear kept threatening to bubble up again—that awful, strangling fear that couldn't be described but felt only. She could feel his heartbeat under her hand, and the warm flesh. He was holding her, and the world would settle again.

"I'm sorry," she managed, but continued to cling to him.

"No, don't." He kissed her hair, then stroked it.

"It's always been like that. I was bitten once. I can't remember it, or being sick, but I can't, I just can't handle—"

"It's all right. It's gone now, don't think about it anymore." The trembling had nearly stopped, but he could feel the occasional spasm that passed through her. Her breath still came in hitches. His skin was damp from her tears. He wanted to make her forget—he wanted to get his hands on whoever had done this to her. "Let me get you a brandy."

"No." She said it too quickly, and the hands against his chest balled into fists. "Just hold me," she murmured, hating the weakness, needing his strength.

"As long as you want." He heard her sigh, felt her fingers relax. The minutes passed again, long and silent so that he thought she slept. Her breathing had evened, her heartbeat slowed and she was warm again. He knew if she'd needed it, he could have held her just so for days.

"Matthew…" His name came on a sigh as she tilted her head back to look at his face. Her eyes were still puffy, her skin was still pale. He had to fight the wave of emotion to keep his fingers from tightening on her. "Don't go."

"No." He smiled and traced a finger down her cheek. Her skin was still damp, still warm from her weeping. "I won't go."

Laurel caught his hand in hers and pressed it to her lips. Matt felt something wash over him, warm and sweet, that he didn't yet recognize as tenderness. She saw it move in his eyes.

This was what she'd been waiting for, Laurel realized. This was what she'd needed, wanted, refused to consider. If he would ask her now—but he wouldn't, she knew it. The asking would have to come from her.

"Make love with me," she whispered.

"Laurel…" Her words stirred him, impossibly. How could he take her now, when she was utterly without defense? Another time, oh, God, another time, he'd have given anything to hear her say those words. "You should rest," he said inadequately.

He's not sure of himself, she realized. Strange, she'd thought he was always so sure. Perhaps his feelings for her were as confusing as hers for him. "Matthew, I know what I'm asking." Her voice wasn't strong, but it was clear. "I want you. I've wanted you for a long time." She slipped her hand up over his chest and neck to touch his cheek. "Love me—now." She brought her lips to his as if quietly coming home.

Perhaps he could have resisted his own need. Perhaps. But he couldn't resist hers. He drew her closer with a moan, gathering her against him as his mouth told her everything in silence. She was boneless, so pliant it seemed she might simply melt out of his arms like a mirage he'd traveled to over endless, impossible days and nights only to find it vanished. He deepened the kiss with something like panic, but she remained, warm and real against him.

Her mouth tasted of woman, not of visions, so warm and sweet he had to fight the urge to devour it. Her tastes, that small hand that remained on his cheek, the airy scent, merged together to make his senses swim. He couldn't afford the luxury now, not this first time.

Matt buried his face at her throat, struggling to hold on to some slim thread of control, but his lips wouldn't be still. He had to taste her. His hands roamed up and over subtle curves. He had to touch her.

"Laurel..." He slipped her loosened blouse off one shoulder so that his lips could wander there. "I want you—I ache with it."

Even as he told himself to move slowly, he was drawing the blouse from her. She shifted to help him, murmuring, then only sighed.

"Not here." He closed his eyes as her lips brushed his throat. "Not here," he said again, and rose with her still in his arms. This time she'd let herself be led. She rested her head on his shoulder as he carried her into the bedroom.

The lights slanted through wooden shutters. It highlighted his eyes, so suddenly intense, as he laid her on the bed. "I won't hurt you."

She smiled and reached for him. "I know."

The mattress sighed as he lay beside her. With her eyes just open, she could see the play of light while his lips traced over her face. It was so easy. She should have known that with him it would be so easy. Running her palms, then her fingertips over his back, she felt the ripple of muscle, the taut skin, the strength. This had attracted her from the beginning, and she had struggled to ignore it. Now, she could take her fill.

He caressed her with his lips. Caressed. She hadn't known such a thing was possible with lips alone. He showed her. Her skin softened, then tingled from it.

Lazily…thoroughly…

His mouth moved over her throat and shoulders while his hands tarried nowhere but in her hair. A gentle nip, a soft flick of tongue and she was floating.

She heard the bluesy sound of a trumpet from outside. The sound drifted into the room to mix in her mind with Matt's murmurs. He nuzzled into her throat so that she turned her head to give him more freedom and breathed in the sweet scent of vanilla from her bedside candle. She made some sound, a long, low sigh, but had no way of knowing that this alone had his pulses hammering.

His lips pressed onto hers with the edge of desperation under the gentleness. She felt it, yielded to it, as she drew him yet closer.

When he touched her, a lean, hard hand over the silk of her camisole, her sigh became a moan. She arched, feeling the aching fullness in her breasts she'd never experienced. Needs sprang up from everywhere, all at once, to pulse under her skin. But he wouldn't be rushed—by her or himself. His fingers trailed, aroused, but stopped just short of demand. He wanted the demand to come from her own needs, not his.

Slowly, inch by inch, he drew the swatch of silk down to her waist, finding her skin no less luxurious. With open-mouthed kisses he explored it, listening to the shuddering sound of her breathing that meant the loss of control. He wanted that from her, for her, while he desperately hung on to his own. When his mouth closed over her breast, the muscles in his back relaxed. God, she was sweet.

While Laurel went wild beneath him, he lingered, drawing out their mutual pleasure, drinking in her tastes and textures.

He caught her nipple between his teeth, holding it prisoner, tormenting it with the play of his tongue until he knew she was utterly steeped in passion, in the dark, mindless pleasures. Then he went on.

She knew only sensations now—there were no thoughts, no sane thoughts, as flames leaped inside her and fire shivered along her skin. The movements of her body were instinctive, offering, pleading. His lips continued to roam over her as he slipped the rest of her clothes from her. The feel of hot flesh against hot flesh had her gasping. With each trembling breath she took, the scent they made together overwhelmed her. Intimate, earthy. Glorious.

Her body was molten—fluid, fiery—but she was helpless. Whatever he wanted from her he could have taken in whatever way he chose. The choices she had made—first to resist him, then to accept him—no longer applied. There were no choices in this world of dazzling light and radiant heat. Her body craved. Her spirit hungered. She was his.

He knew it. And, knowing, fought to remember her innocence when her passion was tearing at his control. She was agile and slim, and at the moment as abandoned as a sleek young animal. Her hands sought him without hesitation, her lips raced to take whatever he'd allow. With his breath rasping, his blood pounding, he struggled to keep the pace as he'd begun. Easy.

When he touched her, she jolted beneath him, shuddering and shuddering with the first peak. Through his own desire, Matt could feel her stunned, helpless delight. No one else had given her this, no one else had taken this from her. No one.

He buried his face at her throat, groaning. So moist, so warm. So ready. He shifted onto her. "Laurel..."

Suspended on shaft after shaft of sensation, she opened her eyes and looked into his. If her body was fluid, his was tight as a bowstring. Over the waves of passion came one clear certainty. He thought only of her. She couldn't speak, drowned by needs and the sharply sweet newness of love just discovered. Laurel drew his mouth down to hers.

At the touch of her lips, she gave up her innocence as easily, as gently, as sliding down a long, cool bank toward a warm river.

She slept. Matt lay beside her and watched the light through the window slats go from white to rose to gray before the moonlight drifted thinly in. His body was exhausted, from the strain of control, from the ultimate loss of it, but his mind wouldn't rest.

There'd been times over the last months when he'd nearly convinced himself that once he'd had her, the lingering need would pass. Now, as he lay in her bed, with moonlight slanting across her body, with her head nestled against his shoulder, he knew the need would remain as basic and essential as the need for air.

Physically, he knew, she was his. He could touch off her passion, exploit her needs and keep her. It wasn't enough. He wondered if he could draw out her emotions, her love, with the same deliberate care with which he'd drawn out her desire. He wondered if he had the patience he'd need.

Turning his head, he looked down at her as she slept against him. Her skin was like porcelain with the dusky lashes shadowing her cheeks. Delicate... He traced a finger down her cheekbone. Yes, she had delicacy, which at times made him feel like an awkward boy staring at pastries in a bakery window. But she had verve, and energy and ambition. These he understood, as they matched his own.

Partners, he thought, and his eyes glinted with something between amusement and determination. Damn right they were. Bending down, he crushed his mouth to hers.

Head swimming, body throbbing, Laurel came awake on a wave of passion. Her skin leaped under his hands as they raced over her, taking and demanding with a speed that left her giddy. She moaned against his mouth, tossed so quickly from gentle sleep to ruthless desire that she could only cling. He set the pace again, but it was nothing like the first time. She catapulted from peak to peak, swept along, driven, until he took her with all the urgency he'd blocked out before.

Spent, stunned, she waited for her breath to return as he lay over her, his face buried in her hair. Should she have known it would be like this? Could she? More than anything, that quick, desperate loving showed her just how careful he'd been with her the first time.

I love him, she thought as she tightened her arms around him. Wouldn't that knock him off his feet? With a wry smile, she toyed with the hair that curled over his neck. Matthew Bates, I'm going to play a very careful hand with you—and I'm going to win.

She gave a long, luxurious sigh. Did loving make the body feel so wonderfully lazy? "Were you trying to tell me it's time to get up?" she murmured.

Lifting his head, he grinned at her. "I don't think so."

"This wasn't supposed to happen."

"Yes, it was." He kissed her brow lightly, lingeringly. "We're just a little ahead of schedule."

Her brow arched, but the haughty gesture had to compete with the soft, just-loved flush of her skin. "Whose schedule?"

"Ours," he said easily. "Ours, Laurel."

It was difficult to argue with something that seemed so reasonable. Laurel linked her hands at the base of his neck and tilted her head. "You look good, Bates."

Amusement flickered in his eyes. "Yeah?"

"Yeah." She ran her tongue over her teeth. "I guess I'm getting used to those beachboy looks and that Yankee speech pattern. Or maybe—" she caught her bottom lip between her teeth, but the laughter shone in her eyes "—maybe I just like your body. You work out?"

He braced himself comfortably on his elbows. "Now and again."

Experimentally, Laurel pinched his bicep. "Weights?"

"No."

"Well, I've never cared for obvious muscles." She ran a hand down to his wrist, then back again. "You seem to be in good enough shape to handle our plans for the evening."

He nipped at her bottom lip. "Which are?"

"A little hike through the swamp."

He rubbed his lips over hers easily, while his mind did some quick calculations. He could distract her, wait until she slept again, then go without her. "I was thinking we could...postpone that."

"Were you?" Though her body began to soften, her mind was much too sharp. "Until you could sneak out there on your own?"

He should've known better. "Laurel..." He slid a hand up to her breast.

"Oh, no." She shifted quickly until she lay on top of him. "You can forget the idea of going out there without me, Bates. We're a team."

"Listen." He took her firmly by the shoulders while her hair dipped down to brush his. "There isn't any need for you to go. It's just a matter of poking around anyway. It'll be faster and easier with only one of us."

"Then you stay here." She kissed him briskly and sat up.

"Damn it, Laurel. Think."

"About what?" she tossed back as she rose, naked, to rummage through her drawers.

"No one left a nasty little box at my door."

She bit down hard on her lip, then turned with a T-shirt and a pair of panties in her hand. "No, they didn't," she said calmly enough. "They left it at mine, obviously for a reason. We're making someone nervous, Matthew. And that someone is damn well going to have to deal with me."

He looked at her, small and straight with her naked skin glowing in the moonlight. At the moment, she looked perfectly capable of avenging herself. "Okay, tough guy," he drawled as he swung his legs out of bed. "When we find out who it was, you can go a few rounds. In the meantime, you might remember there're snakes in that swamp—and they're not dead in a box."

He knew he'd been deliberately cruel, he'd meant to be. But when he saw her fingers tighten on the shirt she held, he cursed himself.

"I won't look." Jaw set, she wriggled into the panties. "You'd better get dressed."

"Stubborn, hardheaded, obstinate," he began furiously.

"Yeah." Jerking the shirt over her head, Laurel glared at him. "But not stupid. Whoever dropped that thing at my door wanted me to back off. That points to Brewster or—or the Trulanes," she managed after a moment. "If they wanted us to back off, there's a reason, and the reason might just be in that swamp."

"You won't get any argument on that from me," he said evenly. "But it doesn't follow that you have to go."

"If I let that kind of threat steer me away, I'll have to turn in my press badge. Nobody's going to put me in that position." She gave him a long, level look. "Nobody."

Matt's temper struggled toward the surface, then subsided. She was right—that was one point he couldn't get around. In silence, he pulled on his jeans. "I've got to get a shirt, and a flashlight," he said briefly. "Be ready in ten minutes."

"All right." She made a business of searching through her drawers until she was sure he'd gone.

Laurel pressed her fingers to her eyes and let the fear out. It was a sticky, cloying sensation that rolled over her and left her light-headed. As it ebbed, she rested her hands against the dresser and just concentrated on breathing. She had to go— now more than before she'd looked in that box. If a threat wasn't answered, then it was buckled in to. If there was a threat, it meant someone was afraid.

Anne Trulane had been afraid of the swamp. Laurel pulled on worn jeans with hands that were almost steady again. She understood that kind of fear, the kind that has no true explanation but simply is. Laurel didn't believe Anne had voluntarily walked into that dark, secret place any more than she herself would voluntarily walk into a snake exhibit. The full certainty of it hadn't struck until tonight, with the burgeoning of her own fear. And, by God, she was going to prove it.

Matt... Laurel switched on the bedroom light and began to search through the disorder of her closet for boots. He was only being unreasonable because he was concerned for her. While she could appreciate it, she couldn't allow it. Love might urge her to give in to him on this one thing—but then how many other things might she give in to once she started?

However he felt about her, she mused as she located one boot, he felt about her because of the way she was. The best thing she could do for both of them was to stay that way.

Swearing at her own disorganization, Laurel shouldered her way into the closet for the other boot.

When he returned, Matt found her sitting on the floor of her room, fighting with knotted laces. He was wearing an outfit very similar to hers, and his more customary amiable expression. He'd calmed down considerably by rationalizing that she'd be safer with him in any case—and by promising himself he'd watch Laurel like a hawk every moment they were in the swamps of Heritage Oak.

"Having a problem?"

"I don't know how this happened," she muttered, tugging on the laces. "It's like somebody crawled in there, tied these in knots, then buried the boot under a pile of junk."

He glanced at her littered floor. "I'm disillusioned. I always thought you were very precise and organized."

"I am—at work. Damn!" She scowled at a broken nail, then fought with the laces again. "There—now I just need a flashlight." Springing lightly to her feet, she dashed past him and into the kitchen.

"You know, Laurellie," Matt commented as he followed her. "A few more molecules missing and you wouldn't have a seat in those pants."

"It'll be dark."

He patted her bottom. "Not that dark."

Grinning, she pulled a flashlight from the kitchen drawer and tested it. "Then you'll have to walk in front and keep your mind off my anatomy."

"I'd rather watch your back pockets jiggle." Swinging an arm around her, he walked to the door.

"They don't jiggle." She stopped, frowning at the splintered wood. "How did that—"

"You were too busy screaming to open the door," Matt said easily, nudging her outside. "I called the super about it."

"You broke it down?" Laurel turned to stare at him.

He grinned at her expression before he tugged her down the stairs. "Don't make doors like they used to."

He broke it down. The thought of it stunned her, sweetly. At the foot of the stairs she stopped and wrapped her arms around his waist. "You know, Matthew, I've always had a soft spot for knights on white chargers."

He framed her face with his hands before he kissed her. "Even tarnished ones?"

"Especially."

Chapter 8

Matt parked his car in the shadow of the wall that encircled the Trulane estate. The moment he cut the engine, silence fell. He could sense, though she climbed from the car as he did, Laurel's regret over the one thing they'd carefully not talked about. Trespassing, in secret, on what belonged to Louis. He also knew it was something that would continue to remain unsaid. He slipped his flashlight, base first, into his back pocket.

"I'll give you a leg up first."

Nodding, Laurel placed a foot in his cupped hands and reached for the top of the wall. She shinnied up nimbly, then, bracing herself on her stomach, reached a hand down for his. The grip was firm and dry, holding briefly until they lowered themselves on the other side.

"Somehow, I think you've done this sort of thing before," she murmured, dusting her hands on the back of her jeans.

He grinned. "Let's just say I've had to scale a few walls in my career."

"And not all metaphorical," she concluded.

"You'll force me to mention that you went up and over like a veteran yourself."

Laurel took one brief look around, letting her gaze linger

on the shadow of the house in the distance. "I don't suppose you've considered the legal repercussions if we're caught."

It was as close as she'd come, he knew, to speaking of Louis. Matt took her hand, drawing her away from the wall. "Let's not get caught," he said simply.

They moved, as quietly as shadows themselves, over the north lawn. Flashlights weren't needed here. The light of the half-moon was thin, but clear enough to guide the way. The air was still, but far from silent. Night birds rustled in the trees, their whisperings punctuated now and again by the hoot of an owl. Overlaying all was the incessant music of crickets.

Fireflies glimmered with their sporadic gold-toned light. It smelled thickly of summer blossoms and green grass.

Already Laurel could see the gloomy silhouette of the edge of the swamp. The aversion was so ingrained she had to force herself not to hesitate. But her fingers curled tightly around Matt's. His palm was cool and dry against hers.

Doesn't he feel it? she wondered as the chill raced over her skin. Doesn't he feel the *darkness* of the place? It held secrets best left alone—secrets that bred in the soggy grasses. She shuddered as the lawn gave way to it.

"It's a place," Matt said quietly. "It's just a place, Laurel."

"It's evil," she said, so simply he felt a tremor of unease. Then she stepped under the first overhang of trees.

Determination made her force back the fear. Though her fingers remained in his, their grip lightened. "Hard to believe," she began in an easier voice, "even driven by love—or lust—that one of the Trulane women would have picked this place to cheat on her husband. I think her name was Druscilla."

Matt gave a choked laugh as he pulled out his light. "Maybe Druscilla had a thing for humidity and mosquitoes. Now…" He didn't switch the light on, but looked behind him where the outline of the house could just be glimpsed through the trees. "I'd say this is about the most direct spot where someone would enter the swamp if they were coming from the house."

Laurel followed his gaze. "Agreed."

"Then it follows that Anne would most likely have come in somewhere around this point."

"It follows."

"Okay, let's go see what we can find. Stick close."

"An unnecessary warning, Matthew," Laurel said loftily as she unpocketed her flashlight. "If you feel something crawling up your back, it's just me."

They hadn't gone more than three yards when the thick, fat leaves dimmed the moonlight. The shadow of the house was lost behind the tangled hedge of other shadows. Already the wild cane sprang up to block what was within, and what was outside, the swamp. The twin beams of their flashlights cut a path through the dark.

It was a world of clinging dampness, of shadows and whispering sounds that made the flesh creep. Even the smell was damp, with the ripe odor of rotting vegetation. Matt began to understand why Anne Trulane might have been terrorized in there. He wouldn't care to lose his way, alone, in the dark. But he wondered why she'd only gone deeper rather than turning back. Blind panic? He scowled at the crude, overgrown path. Maybe.

She should've gotten the hell out.

"Doesn't make sense," he muttered.

Laurel shone her light off the path where something rustled. Her fingers closed over Matt's wrist and let the light, steady pulsebeat soothe her. "What doesn't?"

"Why didn't she get out?"

Carefully, Laurel turned her light back to the path. It was probably only a possum, not every sound meant snakes. She remembered, uncomfortably, that black bears had often been seen in the northern, forested part of the swamp. "Whatever theory we go by, Matthew, Anne was frightened in here. She panicked, lost her sense of perspective."

"Are you frightened?" He glanced down to where her fingers dug into his wrist.

"No." Sending him a rueful smile, Laurel loosened her hold. "No, I'm way past fear, closing in on terror."

"Could you get out of here?"

"Well, I—" She broke off, seizing his hand again. There was a time and place for dignity—and this wasn't it. "You're not leaving me in here, Bates."

"What would you do if I did?"

"I'd murder you the minute I got out."

Grinning, he took her arm as they began to walk again. "How?"

"Poison, I imagine, it's the slowest, most painful way."

"No, how would you get out?"

"I'd—" She swallowed on the notion of having to find her way out alone, then turned around. Shadows, rustling, and the cloying smell of wet earth and rotted grass were all around. There was quicksand, she knew, to the east and to the southwest. "I'd head that way in a dead run," she said, pointing, "hang a right at that stump and keep on going."

"And you'd be out in five minutes," he murmured. He turned his face back to hers. The moonlight caught in his eyes, glinting. "Why did she keep going deeper?"

If she tried to think like Anne, Laurel realized, she'd end up losing what courage she had and bolting. Dragging a hand through her hair, she tried to think coolly instead. "She'd been bitten—maybe she was sick, delirious."

"How fast does the poison work, I wonder." He shrugged, making a note to check on it if it became necessary. "It seems she'd've had time to get out, or at least get closer to the edge."

"They found her by the river, didn't they?"

"Yeah." He looked down at her again. "Dead center. When we were searching the place, we'd come across her tracks now and again where the ground was wet enough to hold them. There didn't seem to be any pattern."

Blind panic, he thought again. Yet she hadn't been as frozen as Laurel had been that afternoon. She'd been running, in what had appeared to be a random flight, deeper into what she feared most...or running away from something she found more terrifying.

Laurel jolted as the bushes beside them rustled. Matt aimed his light and sent a raccoon scurrying back into the shadows.

"I hate making an ass of myself," she mumbled as her heart slipped back out of her throat. "Let's go on." Annoyed at the blow to her pride, she started ahead of him.

They moved in silence, going deeper. Laurel kept her flashlight trained on the uneven ground to guide their way while Matt shone his from side to side, searching for something neither of them could have named. But they'd both followed hunches before.

"Don't laugh," Laurel ordered, coming to an abrupt halt.

"Okay," he said amiably.

She hesitated, gnawing at her lip. "I mean it, Bates, don't laugh."

"Cross my heart?" he ventured.

"I feel like—something's watching."

"Another raccoon?"

"Matthew—"

"Relax." He cupped the base of her neck in his hand and rubbed, deliberately treating it lightly because he'd felt that trickle between his shoulder blades, as well. Ghost stories, he told himself. He was letting Laurel's feelings about the place get to him.

If he'd believed such things he'd have said there was something evil in the twisting shadows, something that would shrink from the sunlight. But he didn't believe in such things. Evil, when it came, came from the human element.

"Too many people have died here," she said, and shuddered.

He touched her neck again, and his hand, his voice were gentle. "Do you want to go back?"

Oh, God, yes, she thought, but squared her shoulders. "No, let's go on. You can smell the river now."

As they came near the banks, she could smell the wet leaves, vegetation, but the river made no sound as it flowed slowly. Cypress trees made lumpy shadows. A few slivers of moonlight worked through the overhanging trees and fell palely on the water, but only made it seem darker. A frog plopped into the river as they approached.

There were alligators in there, Laurel thought, wrinkling her nose. Big ones.

"It was here." Matt shone his light on the ground. "Laurel, could you still get out of this place if you had to?"

As she followed the play of his light, she was remembering the picture from the police file. Clamping down on her lip, she forced the image from her mind. "Yes, the way we came's the easiest, I imagine, but almost any direction from here would get you out eventually."

"Yeah." He moved around, playing his light on the ground. "Strange that she picked the core of the swamp to give up." He swore in frustration. Nothing here, he thought, nothing here. What the hell had he expected to find? "I'd like to get my hands on those letters."

"Whoever took them would've destroyed them by now if there was anything in them to work with."

"I wonder if Susan—" He broke off as the beam of his light picked up a glimmer. Bending, Matt worked a small piece of metal from the ground.

"What is it?"

"Looks like a broken piece of jewelry. Seen better days." Rising, he turned it over in his hands. "Anne's?"

Laurel took it from him, wiping away some of the caked-on dirt. "I don't know, a month in this place..." She shone her light on it as some nagging memory teased the back of her mind. "It looks like the front of a locket—expensive, look how intricate the carving is." The memory lunged toward the front of her mind, then retreated. Laurel shook her head in exasperation. "It's familiar," she murmured. "Maybe it was Aunt Ellen's—Louis could've given it to Anne after they were married."

"We might be able to check it out, for what it's worth." Taking it from her, he slipped it into his pocket. Frustrated, he shone his light to the right and down the bank of the river. "Stay here a minute, I want to get a closer look down there."

"For what?"

"If I knew, I wouldn't feel like I was chasing wild geese."

"I'll go with you."

"Laurel, it's a bog down there. You've been lucky avoiding snakes this far. Don't press your luck."

She remembered the water moccasins that swam in the river. With a gesture of indifference, she shrugged. "You've got two minutes, Bates. Any longer and I'm coming after you."

"Two minutes." He kissed her lightly. "Stay here."

"I'm not moving."

She watched the beam of his light as he walked away, then made his slippery way down the bank. He didn't know what he was looking for, but she understood his need to do something. All they'd found so far were more questions, and a broken piece of jewelry.

She frowned again, thinking of it. A childhood memory? she wondered, pushing the hair away from her face. Had she seen that locket when it had been bright and clean—against a white dress? Laurel pressed her fingers to her temple as she tried to bring the image into focus. One of Aunt Ellen's lacy party dresses? Frustrated, she dropped her hand.

Another minute, Bates, she told him silently. Why was it the small night noises seemed to grow louder now that he wasn't standing beside her? She shifted uncomfortably as a bead of sweat trickled down her back, leaving a chill in its wake.

It's just this place, she told herself, refusing the urge to look over her shoulder. In an hour we'll be back home and I'll be able to laugh at how I stood here shivering in the heat and imagining goblins at my back. In an hour...

The soft rustle at her back had her stiffening. Damn raccoons, Laurel thought on a wave of self-disgust. She opened her mouth to call for Matt when an arm locked around her throat.

Shock registered first, seconds before her body reacted to it, or the abrupt lack of air. In an instinctive move of self-preservation, Laurel jabbed back with her elbow, only to meet empty space as she was shoved away. Her flashlight spun out of her hand as her body whooshed through wild cane. She landed hard, her head slamming back into the base of a cypress.

At the edge of the river, Matt saw the arch of light, then darkness where he'd left Laurel. He plunged up the bank, cursing the slick grass and shouting her name. When he saw her sprawled, his heart stopped—with the vivid picture of Anne Trulane leaping in his mind's eye. He grabbed her, not gently, and hauled her against him. At her moan, he began to breathe again.

"What the hell're you doing!" he demanded, rolling with the fury fear had given him.

"I'm having a concussion," she managed, and shook her head to clear it—a mistake as the ground tilted under her. "Someone pushed me—came up from behind." She reached gingerly to test the bump at the back of her head, then gripped Matt's shirtfront with sudden strength as he started to rise. "Oh, no, you're not leaving me here again."

Simmering with rage, straining at impotence, he settled beside her again. "All right, just sit a minute." He ran his fingers through her hair to lift her face to his. "Are you hurt?"

She saw the anger, the concern, the frustration in his eyes. "Not really." She smiled—her head was throbbing, but that was all. "Just a bump. It didn't knock me out; I just saw stars—not unlike the ones I saw the first time you kissed me."

That helped, she thought, feeling the grip of his fingers on her arm relax slightly. But that brooding look was still in his eyes as he searched her face.

"I shouldn't have left you alone."

"Matthew, if you're going to start being macho and guilty, I'll get cranky." Leaning forward, she kissed him. "Let's see if I can stand up."

With his hands cupping her armpits, he pulled her gently to her feet. No dizziness, she thought, waiting a moment. The throbbing was subsiding to an ache.

"It's okay, really," she said when he continued to study her face. "I've had worse bumps."

You won't have any more while I'm around, he swore to

himself viciously, but smiled. "I won't make any remarks about hard heads. Now, what did you see—besides stars?"

"Nothing." She let out a frustrated breath. "I was so busy telling myself I wasn't going to be a fool that I wouldn't look around when I heard something rustling in the bushes. The next thing I knew someone had an arm around my throat. I hadn't even started defensive move 21-A when they pushed me into that tree. By the time the stars stopped exploding, you were here and they were gone."

Whatever grim thoughts of revenge worked in his mind, his touch was gentle as he felt the back of her head. "You'll have a bump," he said easily as he forced his jaw to unclench, "but the skin's not broken."

"There's good news."

Tilting her head back to his, he gave her one long, hard kiss. His hands were steady again, but his temper wasn't. "Sure you can walk?"

"If you mean as in out of here, absolutely. I lost my flashlight."

"Buy a new one," he advised as he picked up his own. "It went in the river."

"Oh, that's just great. I only bought it a month ago." She scowled over this as they started back the way they'd come. "Well, I guess we found something after all," she murmured.

"Yeah. Someone who knows what we're up to doesn't like it one damn bit. Lovelorn ghosts don't shove people into trees, do they, Laurel?"

"No." And she was thinking, as he was, that the house was close. The people in it knew the swamp.

They walked back in silence, each of them more cautious than before, listening to every sound, second-guessing the shadows. Matt kept Laurel at his side, his hand on hers until they walked into the clear. There wasn't the faintest glimmer of light from the house in the distance.

The lingering distaste for where they'd been clung to him even after they'd dropped on the other side of the wall. He wanted a shower—a long one.

Laurel didn't speak again until Heritage Oak was miles behind them.

"We'll have to talk to Louis and Marion again."

"I know." Matt punched in the car lighter. Maybe if he filled his lungs with smoke he'd stop tasting the air of the swamp. "Tomorrow."

Leaning back, Laurel closed her eyes. And tomorrow was soon enough to think about it. "I don't know about you, but I'm starving."

He turned his head to look at her. She was still a bit pale—but even that could've been the moonlight. Her voice was steady, her breathing calm. He hadn't sensed fear in her, not even when she'd been half-dazed and sprawled on the ground. Frustration, yes, annoyance with herself for being caught unaware. But no fear.

With her head back and the shadows dancing over her face, she reminded him forcibly of Olivia. Unique, indomitable, fascinating. Laughing, Matt grabbed her hand and pressed it to his lips.

"We'll order a pizza and take it back home."

Though she hadn't a clue what had lightened his mood so abruptly, Laurel went with it. "With everything," she demanded.

It was after two when Laurel pushed away from Matt's smoked-glass table, stuffed. She couldn't say his apartment wasn't what she'd expected because she'd had no idea just what to expect. She did know it showed an easy mode of living—deep, plump cushions, thick carpet, soothing colors all mixed together with a flair for style and a penchant for comfort.

There were neither framed newspapers on his walls nor Picassos, but a set of oils done by an artist she didn't recognize. Both were of New York, one a cityscape showing its elegance and glitz, the other a street scene with crumbling buildings and cracked sidewalks. Both were excellent in their way, and the contrasts intrigued her. She supposed, in his career there, he'd have seen both sides.

"I've reached my limit," she said when Matt started to slide another piece onto her plate.

"Big talk about eating it, box and all." Matt bit into the slice he'd offered her.

Picking up her wineglass, Laurel rose to wander the room. Her feet sank into the carpet. "I like your place. You like—" she wiggled her bare toes "—to be comfortable."

"Most people do." He watched as she wandered to his stereo to sort through his album collection.

"Mmmm. But not everyone makes an art out of it." Laurel set a record aside to study the paintings more closely. "These are very good," she commented. "I don't recognize the artist, but I have a feeling I'll be seeing his work again."

"He'd be glad to hear it." Matt picked up his own glass, studying her over the rim. The wine was heavy and sweet. "We grew up in the same neighborhood."

"Really?" Laurel tilted her head, even more interested. "Do you miss it? New York?"

Matt's gaze flicked up to the painting, then back to the wine in his glass. "No."

"But you carry it with you."

"We all carry our baggage around," he murmured, then got up to stick what remained of the pizza in the refrigerator.

Laurel frowned after him. What brought that on? she wondered, then looked back at the paintings. The same neighborhood, she mused, seeing the soiled streets and tired buildings. When he came out of the kitchen, she was still facing them. "You grew up here."

He didn't have to see which painting she was looking at to know what she meant. "Yeah." He pulled his shirt over his head as he walked. "I need a shower."

"Matthew." Laurel went after him, catching his arm outside the bathroom door. She recognized impatience and ignored it. "It was hard, wasn't it?"

"I survived," he said indifferently. "Not everyone does."

Her sympathy was automatic and reflected in her eyes, the touch of her hand on his arm, her voice. "Tell me about it."

"Just leave it."

She stared at him, the hurt unexpected and brutally sharp. Her step back was a retreat from it before she straightened her shoulders. "All right, I'm sorry. Thanks for the pizza, Bates. I'll see you in the morning."

He took her arm to stop her. "Laurel, you know you can't stay in your place until the door's fixed."

She met his eyes calmly. "Not all of us needs locks and bolts, Matthew."

"Damn it—" He broke off, making a savage effort to keep his temper. He knew he was wound up, still tense from what had happened to her in the swamp, still dazed by what had happened between them in her bed. Emotions were crowding him, and he wasn't dealing with them well. "Listen, I grew up in a tough little neighborhood on the East Side. It has nothing to do with you. Nothing."

A dash of salt for the wound, Laurel thought as she stared up at him. "That's clear enough," she said evenly. "Let's just call it professional curiosity and leave it at that."

"Damn it, Laurel." He grabbed her by the shoulders when she started to leave again. "You're not staying in that place alone tonight."

"Don't you tell me what I'm going to do."

"I *am* telling you," he tossed back. "And for once you're going to *do* what you're told."

She gave him a cold, neutral look. "Take your hands off me."

He started to get angry, but even through his own anger he could see beneath hers to the hurt. On a sigh, he dropped his forehead to hers. "I'm sorry."

"You don't owe me an apology," she said carefully.

"I do." When he lifted his head, his eyes were dark and thoughtful. "I hurt you, I didn't mean to."

"No, it's all right." Without fuel, her temper vanished, leaving only a faint echo of the hurt. "I was prying."

"No, I—" Matt hesitated, then let it go. He wasn't ready to drag it all out and look at it again, not with Laurel. "I don't want to argue with you, Laurel. Look, it's late, we've both had enough to deal with today. I can't dig back there tonight."

Her arms went around him. Even if the anger had still lashed at her, she couldn't have stopped them. "No more questions tonight."

"Laurel..." He covered her offered mouth with his. The tension began to drain, degree by degree, as he filled himself with her. "Stay here," he murmured. "Stay with me."

With a sigh, content, accepting, she rested her head on his shoulder. "Do I get shower privileges?"

She heard his low laugh as he nuzzled at her throat. "Sure. But we have to double up. You've heard about the water shortage."

"No, not a word."

"Really?" He tugged her into the bathroom. "It's at a crisis stage. Let me tell you about it."

She was laughing as he drew her shirt over her head.

When she got out of the shower, Laurel was flushed and tingling. Clutching a towel at her breasts, she looked up at Matt. "I'm so impressed." When his grin tilted, she went on blandly, "With the fact that you're such a conservationist."

"Conservation is my life." He tugged the towel from her, smiling easily when she gasped. "Gotta cut back on the laundry too. You know how many gallons of water a washing machine uses?" His eyes swept down her, then up again. "Better get you into bed, you'll catch a chill."

Regally, she walked away, leaving Matt to admire the view. "I suppose turning on a light would go against your values."

"Civic duty," he corrected, then surprised her by grabbing her around the waist and tumbling onto the bed with her.

Winded, she glared up at him. "Now listen, Bates—"

He silenced her quickly, completely and effectively. He'd meant to tease her, continue the half torturous, half pleasurable game they'd begun under the cool spray of the shower. But her legs were tangled with his, her body yielding, and her mouth...

"Oh, God, Laurel, I need you." His mouth crushed back on hers with a savagery the night seemed to have worked on him.

He forgot patience, and she, the need for it. He forgot gentleness, and she, the need for it. His tongue dived deep into her mouth as if there were some taste, some hint of flavor he might be denied. But she would have denied him nothing. Her passion raced from tingling arousal to raging desire, and her mouth was as greedy, as insistent, as his. She was not to be seduced this time, or to be swept helplessly along, but to take as much as she gave.

She hadn't known passion could strip every remnant of civilization away, but she learned. Glorying in the abandon, she touched and tasted where she would with hands and lips that moved quickly, with no more patience than his. He smelled of the soap she'd lathered on him herself. The sharp, clean scent played with her senses, swam in her head while her needs delved in darker places.

They were only shadows in the bed, tangling, clinging, but their passion had substance and form. Perhaps the whispering threats of the past hours drove them both to take, and take hungrily, all that could be found between man and woman. Damp skin, thundering pulses, breathless moans. For both of them it was the moment, the heady present, that mattered. Yesterday and tomorrow were forgotten.

He knew he was rough, but control had vanished. Heat seemed to pour out of her, drawing him deeper and deeper into his own furious passion. Her body was as it had been when he'd first taken her hours—oh, God, had it only been hours?—before. Sleek and smooth and agile. But the change came from within. There was no pliancy in her now, but an urgency and demand that raced with his.

His lips rushed over her, running low on her stomach with hungry kisses. But his need to taste wasn't any stronger than her need to experience. She wanted all there was to have this time, everything he'd already given her and whatever secrets were left. She wanted to learn whatever desire had left to teach.

She opened for both of them, eager, urging him down until he found her. She arched, stunned and only more desperate at the play of his tongue. He whipped her up and over the first crest, never pausing, relentless, as she shuddered with her nails digging into his shoulders.

Wave after wave of heavy, molten pleasure swept her, but he continued as if he would keep her, keep them both, spinning on the very verge of fulfillment. There couldn't be so much. But even as the thought raced through her mind there was more. And still more. She should have been sated from it, but she pulsed with energy. She should have been overwhelmed, but it was as if, somehow, she'd always known it would be like this. His heart raced with hers, beat matching beat. Passion poured out of her, but as it poured it was replenished.

"Matthew." His name was a moan, a gasp. "I want you."

As his mouth hurried back, skimming over her, she felt his tremors and the hammer-thrust beat of his heart. Each rasping breath seemed to merge with her. She saw his eyes glimmer once in the pale light of the moon, then tasted the mixture of soap and salt on his flesh.

"I need you...." They spoke together. She arched to meet him.

Chapter 9

The sky hung low. Thick pewter clouds trapped the heat and humidity so that rain wouldn't have been a threat, but a blessed relief. The leaves didn't stir, or turn their pale undersides up in anticipation, but hung limply.

Laurel leaned back and let the sticky air coming through the car window do what it could. Along the sides of the road the trees stood, casting shade that could offer only slight relief to the throbbing heat. Glancing at them, she wished she were sitting under one, near a cool river on soft, damp grass.

She was traveling the road to Heritage Oak for the third time in two days. Each time, it was just a bit more difficult to face the kind of answers she might find there.

Louis would be angry, she had no doubt of it. The man she'd seen yesterday would be furious at being disturbed again—if he spoke to them at all. And Marion...Marion would be hurt, Laurel thought with a flash of guilt. Hurt that she persisted in pursuing something Marion found distasteful and distressing to both herself and her brother.

I won't think about it, Laurel told herself, and turned her head to stare, brooding, out the window. What choice do I have? Questions have to be asked, things have to be said. It's gone too far to turn back now. If anything, it should be easier to have the questions come from me. But it wasn't, she thought miserably. Not for any of us.

She knew why Matt was silent. He was giving her time to pull herself together, sort out her emotions for herself before they arrived at Heritage Oak. Considerate. Strange, she thought with a small smile, a week before she'd have sworn Matthew Bates hadn't a considerate bone in his body. She'd learned quite a bit about him in the last few days. Not quite all, Laurel mused, thinking of the paintings in his apartment. But still, a great many important things—the most important of which was that she loved him.

They'd yet to speak seriously about what had happened between them. In an odd way, she felt they'd both been reluctant to probe the other's emotions. Treat it light—don't press. Those were the words that ran around in her head. She wondered if they ran in his as well.

It had all happened so fast. A year? That's fast? she thought with a faint smile. But it had. Whatever had been building between them over the months had been so cleverly ignored that the sudden blaze of passion had been totally unexpected. And that much more exciting. But was that all it was for him? Laurel wished she had the confidence, or the courage, to ask.

Turning back, she studied his profile. Strong, casually handsome, with an easygoing smile and amused eyes. Yet he wasn't quite all those things. From his writing she'd already known him to be savvy, ironic, insightful. She'd also discovered that he was only laid-back when he chose to be. That wasn't his true nature. He was an impatient, restless man who simply played the game his own way. Over and above the love that had crept up on her, Laurel had discovered to her own amusement, that quite simply she liked his style.

Partners, she thought as her smile widened. You'd better get used to it, Bates, because we're going to stay that way for a long, long time.

"See something you like?" he asked dryly.

Laurel tilted her head and continued to study him. *Play it light.* The words ran through her mind yet again. "As a matter of fact, I do—and it still surprises me."

He chuckled, and with his eyes on the road reached over and tugged on her hair. "I'm crazy about your compliments, Laurellie. A man never knows if he's been pumped up or slapped down."

"Keeps you on your toes, Bates."

"You did tell me once I had fabulous eyes."

Her brow lifted. "I did?"

"Well, you'd had four martinis at the time."

She laughed as he swung between the pillars of Heritage Oak. "Oh, well, who knows what a person might say in that condition? What color are they, anyway?"

He narrowed them as he turned toward her.

"Blue," she said, catching her tongue between her teeth. "Blond hair, blue eyes—rather an ordinary combination, but you do the best you can with it."

"Yeah. And it is a pity about your chin."

Laurel lifted it automatically. "My chin," she said as he stopped the car, "is not pointed."

"I hardly notice it." Matt jingled the keys in his hand as he stepped from the car. He'd lightened her mood, he noticed, but only temporarily. Already, as she glanced up at the house, he could see the struggle between her emotions and her profession. Laurel being Laurel, the profession won, but not without cost.

"Matthew, Marion will see us because her upbringing wouldn't allow her not to, but..." She hesitated as they climbed the porch. "I doubt if Louis will talk to us."

"We'll have to convince him otherwise," he said flatly, and let the knocker fall heavily on the door.

"I don't want to push him too hard right now. If—"

It was the way his head whipped around, the way his eyes flared, that stopped her. "When?" he demanded.

She opened her mouth, but the annoyance and impatience on his face had her biting back the first reckless words. "All right," she murmured, turning to face the door again. "All right."

Guilt. He felt the sting and wasn't quite sure what to do about it. "Laurel—"

The door opened, cutting off whatever he might have said. Binney glanced at both of them while a flicker of surprise— and something else—came and went in her eyes. "Miss Laurel, we didn't expect to see you again so soon."

"Hello, Binney. I hope it's not inconvenient, but we'd like to speak to Louis and Marion."

Her eyes darted to Matt, then came back to Laurel. "Mr. Louis has a black mood. It's not a good time."

"Black mood?" Laurel repeated. "Is he ill?"

"No." She shook her head, but hesitated as if the denial had come too quickly. "He is…" Binney stopped as if searching for a phrase. "Not well," she finished, lacing her long, bony fingers together.

"I'm sorry." Laurel gave her an easy smile and hated herself. "We won't keep him long. It's important Binney." Without invitation, she stepped into the hall.

"Very well." Laurel caught the quick, accusing glance before the housekeeper shut the door. "Come into the parlor, I'll tell Miss Marion you're here."

"Thank you, Binney." Laurel caught her hand at the entrance to the parlor. "Is Louis often…not well?"

"It comes and goes."

She closed her other hand over the thin, hard one as if willing Binney to understand. "Did he have these black moods when Anne was—when he was married to Anne?"

Binney's lips compressed until there was nothing but a tight line. In the way of a woman well used to the house she lived in, and the people she lived with, Binney let her gaze sweep down the hall and up the stairs in a gesture so quick it was hardly noticeable. When she spoke, her words were hurried, low and French.

"You knew him, Miss Laurel, but there have been so many changes, so much pain. Nothing as it was when you came for your tea parties and riding lessons."

"I understand that, Binney. I'd like to help him."

Binney's gaze swept the hall again. "Before," she began, "during the time between when Mr. Charles left and when Mr. Louis brought the girl home, he had many…hard moods.

He might roam the house and speak to no one, or lock himself in his study for hours. We worried but..." Her shrug was eloquent. "Later, he began to go away on business and it would be better. The years, they weren't easy, but they were...quiet. Then he brought the girl back, his wife."

"And things changed again?" Laurel prompted.

"Only better." The housekeeper hesitated. Laurel thought she understood perfectly the tug-of-war her loyalties were waging. "We were surprised. She had the look of the first one," Binney said so quietly Laurel strained to hear. "It was strange to see her, even her voice.... But Mr. Louis was happy with her, young again. Sometimes, only sometimes, he would brood and lock himself away."

Ignoring the knot in her stomach, Laurel pressed on. "Binney, was Anne afraid when Louis would...brood?"

Her mouth became prim again. "Perhaps she was puzzled."

"Was she happy here?"

The nut-brown eyes clouded. Her mouth worked before her face became still again. "She said the house was like a fairy tale."

"And the swamp?"

"She feared it. She should have stayed away. What's there," she said in a low voice, "is best left alone."

"What's there?" Laurel repeated.

"Spirits," Binney said, so simply Laurel shivered. There was no arguing with old beliefs, old legends. She let it pass.

"Did Anne see Nathan Brewster often?"

"She was a loyal wife." Her tone changed subtly, but enough that Laurel knew the automatic defense of the estate and all in it had been thrown up. Laurel took what she knew might be the final step.

"Did Louis know that Brewster was in love with Anne?"

"It is not my place to say," Binney replied stiffly and with disapproval. *Or yours to ask.* Laurel heard the unspoken words very clearly. "I'll tell Miss Marion you're here." Coolly, she turned her back on them both and walked away.

"Damn," Laurel breathed. "I've lost her, too."

"Sit down," Matt ordered, steering her to a chair. "And tell me what that was all about."

Sitting, Laurel began to speak in the flat tone of recital. "She told me that Louis was prone to black moods and brooding after Charles and Elise left. Understandable enough," she added automatically—too automatically for Matt's liking. "The servants worried about him. Then he apparently pulled out of it a bit when he began to travel on business. They weren't expecting him to bring Anne back and obviously her resemblance to Elise caused some talk, but Binney seemed fond of her. She said Louis was happy, less moody, that Anne was happy too."

She sighed, leaning back in the chair, but her fingers drummed on the arms. "She holds to the local feeling about the swamp."

"Ghosts again?"

"Don't be so literal-minded," Laurel snapped. "It's the...essence of the place," she finished lamely.

As Laurel had with the housekeeper, Matt let it pass. "Didn't I hear Brewster's name mentioned?"

"She'd only say that Anne was a loyal wife. I tried to press." She lifted her eyes to his. "That's when I lost her."

"Forget your feelings for a minute and use your head." He spoke sharply because he'd rather face her annoyance than her vulnerability. "If the housekeeper knew about Brewster—and from the way she clammed up she must have—who else knew?"

"You don't hide things from servants, Matthew. They'd all know."

"Yet not one of them mentioned his name when they were questioned by the police."

Laurel linked her hands in her lap to stop her fingers from drumming. "To have mentioned it would've cast a shadow on Anne's reputation and therefore Louis's. Remember, too, the investigation led to nothing more than a verdict of accidental death. It would've seemed pointless to stir all that up then."

"And now?"

"The servants are loyal to Louis," she said wearily. "They're not going to gossip to outsiders about something that would bring him more pain."

"I have connections downtown," Matt mused. "I could probably get someone out here to ask a few questions."

"Not yet, Matthew, a few more days." Laurel caught Matt's hand in hers as he stood next to her chair. "I don't want to push the police on Louis until there's no other choice. We don't have enough to justify reopening the investigation in any case. You know it."

"Maybe, maybe not." He frowned down at her and bit back a sigh. "A few days, Laurel. That's all."

"Laurel, Mr. Bates." Marion came in with her hands already extended for Laurel's. "Please, sit down, Mr. Bates. I'm sorry I've kept you waiting, but we weren't expecting you."

Laurel caught the faint disapproval and acknowledged it. "I'm sorry, Marion, I hope we didn't catch you at a bad time."

"Well, I'm a bit pressed, but..." She squeezed Laurel's hands before choosing the brocade love seat across from her. "Would you like some coffee? A cold drink, perhaps. It's such a dismal day."

"No, thank you, Marion, and we won't keep you long." Party talk, she thought in disgust. How easy it is to cover ugliness with party talk. "It's important that we speak to you and Louis again."

"Oh." Marion's gaze swept from Laurel to Matt and back again. "Louis is out, I'm afraid."

"Will he be back?" Matt asked her, without accepting her invitation to sit.

"I can't say. That is, I can't say when. I'm sorry." Her expression altered subtly, brow creasing as if she were forced to say something unpleasant. "The truth is, Laurel, I'm not sure he'll agree to talk to you again."

That hurt, but she'd expected it. Laurel kept her eyes level. "Marion, Matthew and I went to see Nathan Brewster yesterday."

They both saw, and registered, each flicker of expression on Marion's face. Distress, agitation, annoyance, doubt; all came quickly and were as quickly gone. "Did you? Why?"

"He was in love with Anne," Laurel returned. "And apparently made little secret of it."

Marion's eyes cooled, the only hint of annoyance now. "Laurel, Anne was a lovely child. Any man might be attracted to her."

"I didn't say he was attracted," Laurel corrected. "I said he was in love with her, in his way. He wanted her to leave Louis."

Laurel saw Marion's throat work before she spoke. The thin gold chain she wore around it glittered with the movement. "What Mr. Brewster may have wanted doesn't mean anything. Anne loved Louis."

"You knew about this." Laurel watched Marion's eyes, pale gray like her brother's.

For a moment Marion said nothing, then the only sound she made was a sigh. "Yes," she said at length. "I knew. It would've been impossible not to see by the way the man looked at her. Anne was confused." Her hands lifted, linked, then fell. "She confided in me because she just didn't know how to deal with it. Anne would never have left Louis," she murmured as her fingers unlinked to knead the material of her skirt. As the nervous gesture continued, her eyes remained level and nearly calm, as if her hands were controlled by something else entirely. "She loved him."

"Did Louis know?"

"There was nothing for him to know," Marion said sharply, then struggled to regain her composure. "Anne only spoke to me because the man upset her. She told her sister that he made her nervous. Anne *loved* Louis," Marion repeated. "What difference does it make now?" She looked at both of them with suddenly tormented eyes, her fingers clutching the filmy material of her skirt. "The poor child's dead, and rumors, nasty rumors like this, will only make it more difficult on Louis. Laurel, can't you stop this? You must know what this continued pressure does to Louis."

"If things were just that simple," Matt began, breaking in before Laurel could speak. "Why do you suppose someone sent Laurel a warning?"

"Warning." Marion shook her head as her nervous fingers finally stilled. "What warning?"

"Someone left a box on my doorstep," Laurel said with studied, surface calm. "There was a dead copperhead inside."

"Oh, my God! Oh, Laurel." She stretched her hands out to grip Laurel's. They trembled ever so slightly. "Why would anyone have done something so nasty? When? When did this happen?"

"Late yesterday afternoon. A few hours after we'd left Heritage Oak."

"Oh, my dear, you must have... Anne was bitten by a copperhead," she murmured, as if she'd just remembered. "You think—Laurel, you don't believe that Louis would do such a thing to you. You can't!"

"I can't—I don't want to believe it of Louis," Laurel corrected. "We thought it best if both of you knew about it."

With a steadying breath, Marion released Laurel's hands. "It must have been dreadful for you. My own nerves— Louis's..." She broke off with a shake of her head. "Of course I'll tell him, you know I will, but—"

"Miss Marion?"

Distracted, Marion looked over her shoulder to the doorway. "Yes, Binney."

"Excuse me, but Mrs. Hollister's on the phone, about the hospital charity drive. She's insistent."

"Yes, yes, all right, tell her I'll just be a moment." She turned back, playing with the collar of her dress. "I'm sorry, Laurel, about everything. If you'd like to wait here, I'll take care of this and come back. But I don't know what else I can say."

"It's all right, Marion, go ahead. We'll just let ourselves out."

"Once you put your teeth into it," Matt commented when he was alone with Laurel, "you chomp down nicely."

"Yes, didn't I?" Without looking at him, she picked up her bag and rose. "Professional hazard, I suppose."

"Laurel." Matt took her shoulders until she looked up at him. "Stop doing this to yourself."

"I would if I could," she murmured, then turned away to stare out the window. "I didn't like the way Marion came apart when I mentioned Brewster."

"She knows more than she's saying." He touched her hair, and would have drawn her back against him.

"Louis is outside," Laurel said quietly. "I want to talk to him alone, Matthew."

He took a step back, surprised that such an ordinary request would hurt so much. "All right." When she walked out the French doors, he stuffed his hands in his pockets and moved closer to the window. Without the least compunction, he wished Louis Trulane to hell.

The heat outdoors was only more stifling after the coolness of the parlor. The air tasted of rain, but the rain wouldn't come. What birds bothered to sing, sang gloomily. She smelled the roses as she passed them, and the scent was hot and overripe. As she came closer to him, Laurel could see the damp patches on Louis's shirt.

"Louis."

His head jerked up when she called him, and he stopped. There wasn't any welcome in his face or in his stance, nor was there the cool indifference she'd seen the day before. He was furious. "What're you doing here?"

"I have to talk to you."

"There's nothing to say."

"Louis." She took his arm when he started to go on without her. Though he stopped again, he spun back to her with a look that made her drop the hand.

"Leave us both with a few decent memories, Laurel, and stay away from me."

"I still have the memories, Louis, but I have a job to do." She searched his face, wishing there was something she could do, something she could say, to prevent what she knew could be the final breach between them. "I don't believe Anne went into that swamp freely."

"I don't give a damn what you believe. She's dead." He looked over her head, out to the edge of the north lawn, where the marsh took over. "Anne's dead," he said again, shutting his eyes. "That's the end of it."

"Is it?" she countered, hardening herself. "If there's the slightest possibility that someone lured or frightened her into that place, don't you want to know?"

He broke off a thin branch of crape myrtle. Laurel was reminded forcibly of Brewster's hands on a pencil. "What you're saying's absurd. No one did—no one would have a reason to."

"No?" She heard the quiet snap of wood between his fingers. "Someone doesn't appreciate our probing into it."

"*I* don't appreciate your probing into it," Louis exploded, tossing down the mangled wood and blossoms. "Does it follow that I murdered my wife?" He spun away from her to stare at the edge of the north lawn. "For God's sake, Laurel. Why do you interfere in this? It's over. Nothing can bring her back."

"Does my interference bother you enough that you'd leave a dead snake on my doorstep?"

"What?" He shook his head as if to clear it. "What did you say?"

"Someone sent me a dead copperhead, all done up nicely in a box."

"A copperhead—the same as…" His words trailed off as he slowly turned back to her. "A nasty joke," he said, tossing the hair back from his face in a gesture she remembered. "I'm afraid I haven't been up to jokes of any kind lately, though I hardly see…" He broke off again, staring down at her. His expression altered into something she couldn't quite read. "I remember. Poor little Laurel, you were always terrified of them. I nearly strangled that cousin of mine the day he stuck a garter snake under your nose at one of Marion's garden parties. What were you? Nine, ten? Do you remember?"

"I remember."

His face softened, just a little. "Have you outgrown it?"
She swallowed. "No."

"I'm sorry." He touched her face in the first gesture of friendship. She found it hurt more than his angry words. "You never liked the swamp because of them."

"I never liked the swamp, Louis."

"Anne hated it." His eyes drifted back. "I used to try to tease her out of it—just as I used to tease you. Oh, God, she was sweet."

"You never let me meet her," Laurel murmured. "Why didn't you let anyone meet her?"

"She looked like Elise." His hand was still on her face, but she knew he'd forgotten it. "It stunned me the first time I saw her. But she wasn't like Elise." His eyes hardened, as slate gray as the sky. "People would've said differently just by looking at her. I wouldn't tolerate it—the comparisons, the whispers."

"Did you marry her because she reminded you of Elise?"
The fury came back at that, so sudden and fierce Laurel would've backed away if his hand hadn't tightened. "I married her because I loved her—needed her. I married her because she was young and malleable and would depend on me. She wasn't a woman who'd look elsewhere. I stayed with her through the year we had so that she wouldn't grow bored and discontent, as Elise claimed she had in that damned note."

"Louis, I know how you must feel—"

"Do you?" he interrupted softly, so softly the words hung on the stagnant air. "Do you understand loss, Laurel? Betrayal? No," he said before she could speak. "You have to live it first."

"If there had been someone else." Laurel moistened her lips when she found her mouth was dry. "If there'd been another man, Louis, what would you've done?"

He looked back at her, cool again, icy. "I'd have killed him. One Judas is enough for any man." He turned, walking away from her and the house again. Laurel shivered in the sticky heat.

He'd seen enough. Matt crossed to the French doors and,

fighting the urge to go after Louis and vent some of his frustration, went to where Laurel still stood, looking after him.

"Let's go," he said briefly.

She nodded. The mood—hers, Louis's, Matt's—seemed to match the tightness in the air. A storm was brewing in all of them. It wouldn't take much to set it off. In silence, they walked across the neatly trimmed lawn to Matt's car, then drove away from Heritage Oak.

"Well?" Matt touched the car lighter to the tip of a cigarette and waited.

"Binney was right about his mood," Laurel said after a moment. "He's on edge, angry, with nothing to strike out at. He still dismisses Anne's death as an accident. The way he looked out at the swamp..." Laurel glanced up at Matt, seeing the hard, set profile that wasn't so very different from the expression Louis had worn. "Matthew, I'd swear he loved her. He might've gotten involved with her because of her resemblance to Elise, even married her with some sort of idea about having a second chance, but Louis loved Anne."

"Do you think he always kept them separated in his mind?"

"I told you before, I'm not a psychiatrist." Her answer was sharp, and she set her teeth. Nothing would be accomplished if she and Matt started sniping at each other again. "I can only give you my own observations," she said more calmly, "and that is that Louis loved Anne, and he's still grieving for her. Part of the grief might be guilt—that he'd teased her about being afraid of the swamp," she told him when he sent her a quick look. "That he didn't take it seriously enough."

"You told him about the box?"

"Yes." Why doesn't it rain? she thought as she pulled her sticky blouse away from her shoulder blades. Maybe the rain would wash everything clean again. "He didn't put it together at first, then when he did, I'd say he was more disgusted than anything else. Then...then he remembered I'd always been terrified of snakes. For a couple of minutes, he was just like he used to be. Kind, warm." Swallowing, Laurel looked out the side window while Matt swore, silently, savagely.

"I asked him why he hadn't let Anne meet anyone. He said he didn't want the comparisons to Elise he knew would crop up. He kept close to her because he didn't want her to grow bored and—"

"Look elsewhere," Matt finished.

"All right, yes." Laurel's head whipped back around. "Aren't you forgetting about those glass houses now, Matthew? Haven't you any compassion at all? Any understanding as to what it's been like for him?"

He met her heated look briefly. "You've got enough for both of us."

"Damn you, Matthew," she whispered. "You're so smug, so quick to judge. Isn't it lucky you never lost anyone you loved?"

He hurled his cigarette out the window. "We're talking about Trulane, not me. If you're going to start crusading again, Laurel, do it on your own time. Not when you're my partner. I deal in facts."

She felt the rage bubble up and barely, just barely, suppressed it. Her voice was frigid. "All right, then here's another one for you. Louis said he would've killed any man that Anne was involved with. He said it with a cold-bloodedness I'm sure you'd admire. Yet Nathan Brewster still works for him."

"And here's another one." Matt pulled into a parking space at the *Herald* and turned on her. "You're so hung up on Trulane you've made some kind of Brontë hero out of him. You refuse to see him any other way. He's a ruthless, bitter man capable of cold violence. His first wife chose his younger brother. Haven't you ever asked yourself why?"

She jerked her arm out of his hold. "You know nothing about love and loyalty, Matthew."

"And you do?" he tossed back. "If you'd grow up, you'd see that you don't love Trulane, you're obsessed with him."

She paled, and as the blood drained from her face, her eyes grew darker, colder. "I do love him," she said in a low, vibrating voice. "You haven't the capacity to understand that.

You want things black-and-white, Matthew. Fine, you stick with that and leave me the hell alone.''

She was out of the car quickly, but he had her by the shoulders before she could dash into the building. "Don't you walk away from me.'' The anger spilled out, with something very close to panic at the edges. "I've had enough of Louis Trulane. I'll be damned if I'm going to have him breathing down my neck every time I touch you.''

Laurel stared up at him, eyes dry. "You're a fool. Maybe you'd better take a good look at the facts again, Matthew. Now leave me alone.'' When her voice broke, they both swore. "Just stay away from me for a while.''

This time when she turned from him, Matt didn't stop her. He waited until she'd disappeared inside the building before he leaned against the hood of his car. With the heat shimmering in waves around him, he drew out a cigarette and tried to pull himself together.

What the hell had gotten into him? He'd attacked her. Matt dragged a hand through his hair. An emotional attack wasn't any prettier than a physical one. The heat? He shifted his shoulders beneath his damp, sticky shirt. That might be part of it, it was enough to set anyone's nerves on edge.

Who was he trying to kid—himself? Matt blew out a long breath and watched the smoke hang in the thick, still air. The crux of it was, she'd spent the night with him, giving herself to him, bringing him all the things he'd needed, wanted...then he'd seen Louis put a hand to her cheek.

Idiot. Laurel couldn't have cursed him more accurately than he did himself. He'd let jealousy claw at him until he'd clawed at her. He hadn't been able to stop it. No, he corrected, he hadn't tried to stop it. It'd been easier to be angry than to let the fear take over. The fear that he'd had for her since he'd looked in the box on her table—the fear that he had of her since he'd discovered he was hopelessly in love with her. He didn't want to lose her. He wouldn't survive.

Maybe he'd sniped at her hoping she'd back off and let him take over the investigation. If he'd found a way to prevent her going with him into the swamp, she wouldn't have been hurt.

Maybe he'd used Louis as an obstacle because he'd been afraid to risk telling Laurel how he felt about her. He'd planned things so carefully—he always had. Yet things had gotten out of hand from the moment he'd started to work with Laurel on this story. How was he supposed to tell her that he loved her—perhaps on some level had loved her from the moment he'd seen that picture propped against Curt's books? She'd think he was crazy. Matt crushed the cigarette under his heel. Maybe he was.

But he was still a reporter, and reporters knew how to follow through, step by step. The first thing was to give Laurel the space she'd demanded. He owed her that. In giving it to her, he could do a little digging on his own. The next thing was to find a way to apologize without bringing Trulane into the picture again.

The last thing, Matt thought as he crossed the parking lot, the last thing was to get it into her thick head that he loved her. Whether she liked the idea or not.

Chapter 10

Laurel considered it fortunate that she'd been sent back out on an assignment almost immediately after coming into the city room. She was able to grab a fresh pad, hook up with a photographer and dash out again before Matt was even halfway up on the elevator.

She didn't want to see him, not until the anger and the hurt had faded a bit. The three-car pileup at a main intersection downtown, with all the heat, noise and confusion it would generate, should distract her from her personal problems. Temporarily.

He was being unreasonable, she told herself with gritted teeth while the photographer cruised through a yellow light and joined a stream of traffic. Unreasonable and unyielding. How could anyone be so utterly lacking in compassion or empathy? How could a man who had shown her such unquestioning support and comfort when she'd been frightened feel nothing for someone who'd been through what Louis Trulane had? Didn't he recognize pain? How could she love someone who... That's where she stopped, because no matter how or why, she loved Matt. It was as simple as that.

Because she loved him, his lack of feeling and his words had cut that much deeper. To accuse her of being obsessed by Louis. Oh, that grated. Any rational person would understand that Louis Trulane had been her childhood hero. She'd loved him freely, with a child's heart and in a child's way. In the course of time, the love had changed, not because Louis had changed but because she had.

She still loved Louis, perhaps not quite objectively. She loved Louis the way a woman loves the memory of the first boy who kissed her, the first boy who brought her a bouquet. It was soft and safe and passionless, but it was so very sweet. Matt was asking her to turn her back on that memory. Or to dim it, darken it with suspicion.

To a woman like Laurel, the memory of a young man who'd treated a child and her infatuation gently should have no shadows. But Matt was using it to swipe at her for something she couldn't understand. He'd even implied that she might be thinking of Louis when they were together. How could he possibly believe...

Here, her thoughts broke off again as a new idea crept in. A fascinating one. Matt was plain and simply jealous.

"Ha!" Laurel uttered the syllable out loud and flopped back against the car seat. Her photographer sent her a sidelong look and said nothing.

Jealous...well, that was certainly interesting, even if it was still unreasonable and asinine. But if he was jealous, didn't it follow that his feelings for her were more involved than she'd let herself believe? Maybe. Or maybe he was just being typically insufferable—as she'd almost forgotten in the first heady waves of love that he was. Still, it was something to think about.

They had to stop the car in a thick tangle of traffic and bad-tempered blasting of horns. "I'll get out here and go up on foot," Laurel told her photographer absently. "Pull over as soon as you can." Stepping out, Laurel went to work.

Matt was out on the street as well. The noise in the Vieux Carré might have been a great deal more pleasant than what Laurel was dealing with, but the heat was only slightly less intense. He could smell the river and the flowers, a combination that had come to mean New Orleans to him. At the moment, he hardly thought of them. For the past hour, he'd been very busy.

A trip to the police station and a few carefully placed questions had earned him the information that no official search had ever been issued for Elise or Charles Trulane. A missing-persons report had never been filed on either of them. The note, the missing clothes and painting gear had been enough to satisfy everyone. Matt wasn't satisfied.

When he'd questioned further, he'd hit a blank wall of indifference. What did it matter how they'd left town or if anyone had seen them? They *had* left, and ten years was a long time. There was plenty of other business in New Orleans to keep the force busy other than an adultery that was a decade old. Sure, the lab boys would play with his little chunk of metal when they had the time, and what was he up to?

Matt had evaded and left with fewer answers than he'd had when he'd gone in. Maybe he'd draw a few out of Curt.

Turning a corner, Matt strolled into a dim little bar where a trio was playing a cool, brassy rendition of "The Entertainer." He spotted Curt immediately, huddled in a corner booth with papers spread all over the table. There was a glass of untouched beer at his elbow. Matt had a quick flashback of seeing Curt exactly the same way during their college days. The smile—the first one in hours—felt good.

"How's it going, Counselor?"

"What?" Distracted, Curt looked up. "Hi." He tipped the papers together in one neat, economical movement and slid them into a folder. "What's up, Matt?"

"The same," he told the waitress, indicating Curt's beer. "A little legal advice," he said when he turned back to Curt.

"Oh-oh." Grinning, Curt stroked his chin, the only resemblance to his sister Matt could see.

"Advice, not representation," Matt countered.

"Oh, well." When the waitress put Matt's beer on the table, Curt remembered his own.

"If I decided to add to my portfolio, would you consider Trulane Shipping a wise investment?"

Curt looked up from his drink, his abstracted expression

sharpening. "I'd say that was more a question for your broker than your lawyer. In any case, we both know your portfolio's solid. You're the one who gives me tips, remember?"

"A hypothetical question then," Matt said easily. "If I were interested in speculating with a New Orleans-based company, would Trulane be a wise place to sink my money?"

"All right. Then I'd say that Trulane is one of the most solid companies in the country."

"Okay," Matt muttered. He'd figured that one was a blind alley. "Why do you think no one's touched Elise Trulane's inheritance?"

Curt set down his beer and gave Matt a long, level look. "How do you know about that?"

"You know I can't reveal a source, Curt. Fifty thousand," he mused, running a finger down the condensation on his glass. "A hefty amount. Interest over ten years would be a tidy little sum. I'd think even a man like Trulane would find some use for it."

"He doesn't have any claim on the money. It's a straight inheritance in Elise's name." He shrugged at Matt's unspoken question. "The firm handled it."

"And the lady just lets it sit." Matt's brow rose at his own statement. "Strange. Hasn't your firm tried to track her down?"

"You know I can't get into that," Curt countered.

"Okay, let's take it hypothetically again. When someone inherits a large amount of money and makes no claim, what steps're taken by the executors to locate the beneficiary?"

"Basic steps," Curt began, not sure he liked the drift. "Ads in newspapers. In all likelihood an investigator would be hired."

"Say the beneficiary had a husband she wanted to avoid."

"The investigation, any correspondence pertaining to it, would be confidential."

"Mmm-hmm." Matt toyed with his beer as the piano player did a quick, hot rip over the keys. "Did Elise Trulane have a will?"

"Matt—"

"Off the record, Curt. It may be important."

If it had been anyone else, Curt would have brushed it off and found some handy legal jargon to evade the question. He'd known Matt too long and too well. "No," he said simply. "Both she and Louis had wills drawn up, but Elise took off before they were signed."

"I see. And the beneficiaries?"

"Standard wills for husband and wife without issue. Marion and Charles have their own money."

"Substantial?"

"Putting it mildly. Marion's a very wealthy woman." Then, because he anticipated the question before it was spoken, he added, "Charles's investments and his savings sit collecting interest as Elise's do."

"Interesting."

Curt kept his eyes level—not emerald like his sister's, but sea green and calm. "Are you going to tell me what all this is about?"

"Just covering all the angles."

"It has something to do with what you and Laurel are working on—for Susan."

"Yeah." Matt swirled his beer as he studied his friend. "You've met Susan?"

"I was out at the house." A faint color rose under Curt's skin, bringing Matt a picture of the time, years before, when Curt had fallen hard for a premed student. "She told me about Anne, and the letters." Curt's gaze came back to Matt's, reminding him that Curt wasn't an impressionable college student any longer, but a man with a sharp legal mind and a quiet strength, despite his dreaminess. "Are you going to be able to help her?"

"We're doing what we can on this end. Since you know her, and she's confided in you, maybe you can keep her calm, and out of it, until something breaks."

"I'd already planned on that," Curt said simply. "You taking care of Laurel?"

Matt grimaced, remembering how they'd parted a few hours before. "Nobody takes care of Laurel," he muttered.

"No, I guess not." Distracted again, Curt slipped his folder into his briefcase. "I've got an appointment, but when there's more time, I'd like a few more details on this."

"Okay. And thanks."

Alone, Matt brooded into his beer. Too many loose ends, he mused. Too many pieces that just don't fit. Two people might turn their backs on friends and relatives, especially in the first impetus of love, but not on more money than most people see in a lifetime. Not for ten years.

Either love made them delirious, he concluded, or they're dead. Dead, to him, made a lot more sense.

Leaning back, he lit a cigarette. If they'd had an accident after leaving Heritage Oak, didn't it follow that they'd have been identified? He shook his head as theories formed and unformed in his mind. It all tied together, somehow, with Anne Trulane. And if one of his theories was right, the one he kept coming back to, then someone had killed not once, but three times.

He studied the thin blue wisp of smoke and swore. It was too late in the day to allow a thorough check of Louis's whereabouts on the day of Elise and Charles's disappearance. And tomorrow was Sunday, which meant he probably couldn't get his hands on the information he needed until after the weekend. Monday then, he thought, and crushed out his cigarette. On Monday, no matter how reluctant Laurel was, they would start digging back, and digging thoroughly.

Rising, he tossed bills on the table and strode out. Maybe it was time they had a talk.

Laurel was totally involved with her story when Matt walked into the city room. He started toward her, glanced at the clock, then went to his own desk. Deadline was sacred. When he sat down across from her, he noticed the expression on her face. Unholy glee was the closest he could come.

Laurel nearly chuckled out loud as she dashed off the story. A three-car pileup, a lot of bent metal. Not normally anything she'd have found amusing, but no one had been hurt. And the mayor's wife had been in the second car.

Better than a sideshow, Laurel thought again as she typed swiftly. The mayor's wife had dropped all dignity and decorum and very nearly belted the hapless driver who'd plowed into her from behind, sandwiching her between him and the car stopped at a light in front of her.

The air, already steaming, had been blue before it was over. Maybe it was the heat, or the pressure she'd been under for the last few days, but Laurel found this a much-needed comic relief. It would've taken a stronger person than she not to be amused watching a prim, nattily dressed woman with a wilted corsage grab a man built like a truck driver by his lapels and threaten to break his nose. And that had been before her radiator had blown, spewing water up like a fountain.

Ah, well, she thought as she finished up the report, it would do everyman good to read that people in high places get their fenders dented and their tempers scraped too. Page one, oh, yes indeed.

"Copy," she shouted, glancing at the clock. Just under deadline. Her smile was smug as she turned back and found her gaze linked with Matt's. A dozen conflicting emotions hit her all at once, with one fighting to push aside all the others. She loved him.

"I didn't see you come in," she said carefully and began to tidy the disorder of her desk.

"Just a few minutes ago. You were working." The bedlam of the city room went on around them with shouts of *"Copy!"* and rushing feet and clicking typewriter keys. "Are you finished?"

"Soon as the copy's approved."

"I need to talk to you. Can we have dinner?"

She hadn't expected that cautious, slightly formal tone from him, and wasn't sure how to deal with it. "All right. Matthew—" The phone on her desk rang. Still thinking about what she would say to him, Laurel answered, "City room, Laurel Armand."

Matt watched her expression change, the color fluctuate before her gaze jerked back to him. "I'm sorry," she began, indicating the phone on his desk a split second after he'd already started to reach for it. "You'll have to speak up, it's very noisy in here." She heard the faint click as Matt picked up her extension.

"You've been warned twice." It was a whisper of a voice, sexless, but Laurel didn't think it was her imagination that she sensed fear in it. "Stop prying into Anne Trulane's death."

"Did you send me the snake?" Laurel watched Matt punch another extension on the phone and dial rapidly.

"A warning. The next one won't be dead."

She couldn't control the silver shot of panic up her spine, but she could control her voice. "Last night, you were in the swamp."

"You have no business there. If you go in again, you won't come out."

Laurel heard someone across the room yell out a request for coffee, no sugar. She wondered if she was dreaming. "What are you afraid I'll find?"

"Anne should've stayed out of the swamp. Remember that."

There was a click, then the drone of the dial tone. Seconds later, Matt swore and hung up his own phone. "Not enough time for the trace. Any impressions on the voice? Anything you recognized?"

"Nothing."

He picked up her pad, where Laurel had automatically recorded the conversation in shorthand. "To the point," he muttered. "We're making someone very nervous." Someone, he thought as his own theory played back in his head, who may have killed three times.

"You're thinking about the police again," Laurel decided.

"You're damn right."

Laurel dragged a hand through her hair as she rose. "Listen, Matthew, I'm not saying you're wrong, I just want some time to think it through. Listen," she repeated when he started to speak. "Whoever that was wants us to back off. Well, for all intents and purposes we will be for the weekend. I want some time to go over my notes, to put them together with yours, hash it out. If we do go to the police, on *Monday,*" she added with emphasis, "we'd better go with all the guns we have."

She was right, but he didn't like it. Several ideas for nudging her out of the investigation ran through his mind. He'd have the weekend to choose the best of them. "All right, check in with Don. I'll get my notes together."

Instead of the rare steak and candlelight Matt had planned on, they ate take-out burgers and chili fries at Laurel's drop-leaf table. Their notes were spread out—Matt's made up of scribbles Laurel thought resembled hieroglyphics while her own were sketched in precise Gregg shorthand. They hadn't taken the time—and both of them separately agreed it was just as well—to touch on their earlier argument or the reasons for it. For now they were professionals covering every angle of a story.

"I'd say it's safe to assume we have enough circumstantial evidence to conclude that Anne Trulane's death was something more than an unfortunate accident." Laurel wrote in a composition notebook, a valiant attempt to organize their snatches of words and phrases into coherency.

"Very good," Matt murmured. "That sounded like something Curt would say to the jury."

"Don't be a smart aleck, Bates," she said mildly. "Pass me that soda." Taking it, she sipped straight from the bottle and frowned. "We have Susan's claim that Anne was afraid of dark places—the swamp in particular—which has since been corroborated by Louis, Marion and Binney. We have the stolen letters from Susan's hotel room, my nasty little box, a hefty shove in the swamp and an anonymous phone call."

Because she was writing, Laurel didn't notice that Matt snapped the filter clean off his cigarette when he crushed it out. "The first interview with Louis and Marion...nothing much to go on there but emotion, which you don't like to deal with."

"It can be useful enough," Matt said evenly, "when you look at it with some objectivity."

She opened her mouth to hurl something back at him, then stopped. "I'm sorry. I didn't mean to snipe. Brewster," she went on briskly. "We know he thought he was in love with Anne, wanted her to leave Louis. No conjecture there, since he said so himself." She underlined Brewster's name heavily and continued. "We also have Marion's corroboration of the first part of that, and Anne's reaction to it. My second interview with Louis leads me to believe that he either didn't know about Brewster's feelings or didn't think they were important enough to worry about, as Brewster's still employed by his company."

Laurel rubbed a hand over the back of her neck, the first and only outward sign that she was tired. "The gist of it is that we agree it seems unlikely Anne would've gone into the swamp without some kind of outside pressure—and that it's less likely she would have continued to head deeper unless she had no choice. In my opinion, Brewster's still the obvious candidate."

Matt flipped over his pad to a new set of notes. "I spoke with Curt today."

"Huh?" Laurel looked up at him, trying to tie his statement with hers.

"I wanted some corroboration on a theory I had."

"What does Curt have to do with this?"

"He's a lawyer." With a shrug, Matt lit a cigarette. "As it turns out, I was luckier than I expected, as he works for the firm that handles Elise Trulane's inheritance."

Laurel put down the bottle she'd lifted. "What does that have to do with any of this?"

"I'm beginning to think quite a lot. Listen." He skimmed through his notes. "Fifty thousand dollars, plus ten years' interest, has never been touched. Charles Trulane's money sits moldering. Untouched. There would've been a very discreet, and I'm sure very thorough investigation on behalf of the bank to locate them." He flipped back a few pages, then lifted his eyes to Laurel's. "No missing-persons report was ever filed on either Elise or Charles Trulane."

"What're you getting at?"

Very carefully, he set down his pad. "You know what I'm getting at, Laurel."

Needing to move, she rose from the table. "You think they're dead," she said flatly. "Maybe they are. They could've had an accident, and—" She broke off, and he knew her thoughts had followed the same train his had. Laurel turned back to him, her eyes very steady. "You think they were dead before they left Heritage Oak."

"It's more than a possibility, isn't it?"

"I don't know." Pressing her fingers to her temples, she tried to think logically. "They could've taken off, changed their names, gone to Europe or the Orient or God knows where."

"Could've," he agreed. "But there's enough room to doubt that, isn't there?"

"All right, yes." She took a deep breath. "And if we go that route, figuring they were tied with Anne's death somehow, it'd put Brewster in the clear. But why?" Laurel demanded. "Who'd have had a motive but Louis, and he was out of town."

"Was he?" Matt rose, knowing they had to tread carefully around Louis Trulane. "He has his own plane, doesn't he? Flies himself—or did. You know what the possibilities are there, Laurel."

She did. An unexpected arrival, the lovers caught, unaware. A moment's madness. In a small private plane the bodies could've been taken anywhere. Pale, she turned back to face Matt. He was expecting her to argue, or to back out. Of course, she could do neither now.

"It won't be easy—maybe impossible," she added in a calm, professional voice, "to check the incoming and outgoing flights on a night ten years ago."

"I'll get started on it Monday."

She nodded. "I'll work on Curt. We might be able to get the name of the firm that looked for Elise and Charles."

"No."

"No?" she repeated blankly. "But it makes sense to try that angle if we're going at it this way."

"I want you to back off." He spaced his words very evenly as he rose. "I don't want you asking any more questions."

"What the hell are you talking about? You don't get a story without asking questions."

"Whatever we get out of this, whatever the outcome as far as the paper is concerned, we'll split down the middle. But from now on I take over."

Laurel tilted her head. "You're out of your mind."

Maybe it was the very calm, very mild way she said it that tripped the last button. Every reasonable argument, every carefully thought-out method of persuasion, deserted him. "I'm out of *my* mind!" he threw back. "That's rich." He paced, deliberately walking away from her so that he wouldn't just grab her by the collar and shake. "It's not a game, damn it. We're not playing who can hit page one."

"I've never considered my profession a game."

"I don't want you in my way."

Her eyes narrowed. "Then I'll stay out of it. You stay out of mine."

"It's dangerous!" he shouted. "Use your head. You're the one who's been threatened, not once, but three times. Whoever's behind Anne's death isn't going to hesitate to kill again."

Her brow lifted—that damned, beautiful, haughty black brow. "Then I'll have to watch my step, won't I?"

"You idiot, no one called me and told me to back off. No one threatened me." There was panic in his voice now, raw panic, but she was too busy fuming to notice.

"You want to know why, Bates?" she hurled out at him. "Because I'm a woman and obviously would buckle under. The same way you figure if you shout enough and throw your weight around I'll do the same thing."

"Don't be any more stupid than you have to."

"But the one thing they forgot," she continued furiously, "the one thing *you* forgot, is that I'm a reporter. And to get a story, to get the truth, a reporter does what's necessary. Most of us deal with being in jeopardy in one form or another. That's the business."

"I'm not in love with most reporters," Matt tossed back.

"I'm in love with you!" He stormed right past her as he said it, not stopping until he'd reached the table and his cigarettes.

Laurel stared at him while he pushed aside papers in search of a match. She was winded, as though she'd raced up flight after flight of stairs two at a time. Now that she'd reached the top, she simply forgot why she was in such a hurry in the first place. It wasn't until he'd stopped swearing and muttering to turn to her that she felt the glow, the warmth, the pleasure.

Matt set down the unlit cigarette and stared at her. What the hell had he said? Oh, God, had he just blown everything by laying his cards on the table before he'd covered his bet? And just how was he going to handle this one? He decided to give her a way out if she wanted one.

"Did I...just say what I think I said?"

Laurel didn't smile, but folded her hands neatly in front of her. "Yes, I have a witness."

His brow lifted. "There's no one here."

"I'll bribe someone."

He hooked his hands in his pockets because he wanted so badly to touch her. "Is it what you want?"

She gave him an odd look, then took a step closer. "I wonder why I thought you were insightful and observant. It's a general sort of rule, Matthew, that when a woman's in love with a man she likes it better if he's in love with her too."

His heartbeat was very light and fast. He couldn't remember ever feeling like that before. "Tell me," he murmured. "Don't make me beg you."

"Matthew..." A little dazed that he couldn't see what must have been glowing on her face, she reached for him. "You're the only man I've made love to because you're the only man I've been in love with. Neither of those things is ever going to change."

"Laurel." But he couldn't say more because her mouth was on his, giving, just giving. His arms came around her to draw her closer as thoughts spun in his head. So long—it's been so long. He could hardly remember a time when he hadn't wanted it to be like this. A time when he hadn't wanted to have those words still lingering on the air. "Again," he demanded. "Tell me again."

"I love you. Only you." Her arms curved up his back until she could grip his shoulders. "I thought if I told you before, even an hour ago, you'd think I was crazy. When?" Giddy, she clung to him. "When did it start?"

"You wouldn't believe me." Before she could disagree, his lips were on hers again.

He took her deep, and still deeper, quickly. If he'd thought he'd loved her to the point of madness before, it was nothing compared to what stormed through him now. His love was met, and matched. Everything was washed from his mind but Laurel.

She could lose herself in a kiss from him, lose herself in that soft, velvet-edged darkness he'd first taken her to. To know that he wanted her was exciting. To know that he loved her was glory. Words, there were so many words she wanted to say. But they would wait until this first overriding need was satisfied. As she felt her bones melting, she drew him with her to the floor.

Quickly, quickly. Neither spoke, but each knew the other's mind. Hurry. Just to feel one another's flesh. Clothes tangled, untangled, then were discarded. Oh, the sweetness of it, the sweetness that came from only a touch. She could smell the hot muskiness of the day on him with the lingering scent of soap. She wallowed in it with her lips pressed against his throat. His pulse beat there, fast and light.

He murmured against her ear, only her name, but the sound of it drifted through her softly. The slow, liquefying pleasure made everything she'd ever felt before seem hollow. Then his tongue dipped inside to follow her name.

A long, lingering stroke, a whispering caress. There was no need to hurry now. Passion was filled with wonder. I'm loved, I'm wanted. Spirits are fed on this alone. She could feel it pouring from him—contentment—even as his heartbeat hammered against hers. Desire, when mixed with such emotions, has more power. And at times, more patience. They'd woo each other.

His lips moved over her shoulder, down, lazily down, to linger on the pulse point at the inside of her elbow. She felt the answering beat from a hundred others. Her hand ran through his hair, the curling thickness of it, before she let her fingers stroke beneath to his neck. He lifted his head to look at her and the look held—long, silent—until, smiling, their lips joined again.

The change happened so slowly, perhaps neither of them noticed. Not yet urgent, not yet desperate, but desire grew sharper. Gradually, quiet sighs became quiet moans. With his mouth at her breast he heard her breathing quicken. His senses were clouded—her scent, her taste, the satin that was her skin. Hunger seeped into them, and the excitement that came from knowing the hunger would be satisfied. His hands journeyed down.

The inside of her thighs was as warm and alluring as velvet. He let his fingers linger there, then his mouth. Though she shuddered, the first crest came easily, a gentle lifting up and up, a quiet settling. Her body throbbed with anticipation of the next while her mind was filled with him. Head whirling, she shifted to lie over him, to give to him all the pleasures he'd given to her.

How warm his flesh was, how firm his body. Her hands wandered down to his hips, skimmed over his thighs. She felt the quiver of muscle beneath her.

She was floating, but the air was thick and syrupy. Her limbs were weighted, but her head was light and spinning. She felt him grasp her, heard him hoarsely mutter her name. Then he was inside her and the explosion went on and on and on. She had only enough sanity left to pray it would never stop.

He watched her. He struggled to hold back that seductive darkness so that he would always have this image of her. The light fell over her brilliantly. With her head thrown back, her hair streamed down her back. She knew only pleasure now— his pleasure. He held her there for an instant with perfect clarity. Then the darkness, and all its savage delights, overcame him.

Chapter 11

It was dark. Matt had no idea of the time, and cared less. They were snuggled close in Laurel's bed, naked and warm. Like careless children, they'd left their clothes in heaps in the living room. It was pleasant to imagine they could stay just as they were for the whole weekend—dozing, making love, saturating themselves with each other.

He knew all there was to know about her, what pleased her, what annoyed, what made her laugh. He knew where she'd come from, how she'd grown up, snatches of her childhood that he'd drawn out of Olivia or her father and Curt. She'd broken her ankle when she was nine, and she'd worked on her high school paper. She'd slept with a one-eared stuffed dog until she was seven.

It made him smile to think of it, though he wasn't certain she'd be pleased to learn he knew.

There was so much he hadn't told her. Matt could remember the hurt on her face when he'd pushed her questions away. There was so much he hadn't told her—but she loved him anyway.

Laurel shifted against him, her eyes open and adjusted to the dark, her body quietly content. "What're you thinking?"

He was silent for a moment, then lifted a hand to touch her hair. "I grew up in that painting." Laurel put her hand in his and said nothing. "Old people stayed off the street at night and anyone else traveled in groups. Too many alleys and broken streetlights. Cops patrolled in pairs, in cars. I can't remember a night when I didn't hear the sirens."

She was so warm and soft beside him. The room was so quiet. Why was he bringing it all back? Because it never really goes away, he answered himself. And I need to tell her.

"I worked for a guy who ran a newsstand. One summer we were robbed six times. The last time he was fed up enough to put up a fight. I was out of the hospital in two days, but it took him two weeks. He was sixty-four."

"Oh, Matthew." Laurel pressed her face into his shoulder. "You don't have to talk about it."

"I want you to know where I came from." But he fell silent again as two long minutes passed. "In the apartment where I lived, the halls smelled of old cooking and sweat. It never went away. In the winter it was cold, drafts through the windows, icy floors. In the summer it was a furnace. You could smell the garbage from the alley three floors down. At night you could hear the street—dealers, prostitutes, the kids who looked for both. I stayed away from the dealers because I wanted to stay healthy and used the prostitutes when I could scrape up the extra money."

He waited, wondering if he'd sense her withdrawal. Her hand stayed in his. Laurel was remembering her impression of his apartment. He'd made an art out of comfort. How much he must have hated growing up without the basic rights of warmth and security. And yet…he'd brought the painting with him. He hadn't forgotten his roots, nor was he ignoring that part they'd had in forming him. Neither would she ignore them.

"I lived with my aunt. She took me in when my mother died and my father took off. She didn't have to." He linked his fingers with Laurel's. "She was the most unselfish person I've ever known."

"She loved you," Laurel murmured, grateful.

"Yes. There was never enough money, even though she worked too hard and when I was old enough I brought in more. The rent would go up in that filthy place or..." He broke off and shrugged. "Life," he said simply. "I swore I was going to get us out of there. One way or the other I was going to get us the hell out. I knew what I wanted to do, but it was like pie in the sky. A reporter, a job on one of the big New York papers and a salary that would move her out to some nice little place in Brooklyn Heights or New Rochelle.

"So I ran copy and studied until my eyes hurt. There were other ways," he murmured, "quicker ways, to get the kind of money I wanted, but that would've destroyed her. So when the scholarship came I took it, and I got out. When I'd come back during the summer, it was so hot I'd forget what it was like to live in that place in January. By the middle of my senior year I had nearly enough saved to move her out—not to a house in Brooklyn Heights, but to a decent apartment. By that summer I'd have gotten her out. She died in March."

Laurel turned her head so that her lips could brush over his skin, lightly, easily. "She would've been proud of you."

"If I'd have taken another way, she might still be alive."

"If you'd have taken another way," Laurel said slowly, rising on her elbows to look at him, "you'd have killed her yourself."

His eyes glinted in the filtered light of the moon. "I've told myself that, but other times I think I might've given her even six months of comfort." He caught Laurel's hair in his hand, feeling the fine silk of it. "She used to laugh. Somehow, she'd always find a way to laugh. I owe her just for that."

"Then so do I." Lowering her head, she kissed him. "I love you, Matthew."

"When I've thought of you, and me, I've wondered how the hell I was going to work it." He cupped the back of her neck. "We couldn't have had more different beginnings. There were times I thought I wanted you just because of that."

When she lifted her head, he was surprised to see her smiling. "You ass," she said lovingly.

"So beautiful," Matt murmured. "I'll never forget that picture Curt had of you, the one he kept on his desk in our room.''

Surprised, Laurel started to speak, then stopped. He'd said she wouldn't believe it; now, with emotions swamping her, she didn't want to tell him he'd been wrong. She wanted to show him.

''I could see you at one of those long, lazy garden parties in a silk dress and picture hat,'' Matt said softly. ''It made my mouth water. And I could see you with someone bred for the same things.''

''I hate to repeat myself,'' she began, but he didn't smile. ''You're thinking of Louis,'' Laurel said flatly.

''No.'' He started to draw her back to him. ''Not tonight.''

''You listen to me.'' The humor and the softness had fled from her eyes as she pulled away. ''The way I feel about you has nothing, *nothing,* to do with the way I feel about Louis. I've loved him since I was a child and in almost exactly the same way. Both he and Marion were an integral, vital part of my childhood. The fairy-tale part. Every girl's entitled to one.''

He remembered her grandmother saying essentially the same thing. The muscles in his shoulders began to relax. ''I think I understand that, Laurel. It's today that concerns me.''

''Today my heart aches for him, for both of them. Today I wish I could help, knowing, at the same time, that what I have to do might hurt them beyond repair. If my feelings had been different, don't you think that sometime over the last ten years, I'd have gone to him? I wonder why,'' she said heatedly before he could answer, ''when I waited all these years to fall in love, I had to fall in love with an idiot.''

''The luck of the draw, I guess.''

''Well, I'll tell you one thing, Bates, I'm not going to explain myself to you on this again. Take it or leave it.''

He let out a deep breath and paused as if weighing the pros and cons of the ultimatum. In the dim light he could see the angry glare in her eyes, the agitated rise and fall of her shoulders. She might've been molded in a softer manner than he, but no one matched wits or wills so well.

"Will you marry me, Laurel?" he asked simply.

He heard the quick hitch of her breath, saw the surprise rush into her eyes. For a moment, there was quiet. "It took you long enough," she said just as simply, then dived onto him.

Laurel awoke with the sun streaming over her face and Matt nibbling on her ear. She didn't have to open her eyes to know it was a beautiful day. Sometime during the night the rain had come to wash the heaviness from the air. Without opening her eyes, she stretched and sighed. Matt's lips moved to her jawline.

"I love the way you wake up," he murmured. He slid a hand down to cradle her hip.

"Mmmm...what time is it?"

"Morning." His lips finally found hers.

With another lazy stretch, she linked her arms around his neck. "Have I ever told you how much I like you to kiss me just like that?"

"No." Lowering his head, he did so again while she lay boneless beneath him. "Why don't you?"

"If I tell you...mmmm...you'll know how to win every argument."

Laughing, he pressed his lips to the curve of her shoulder. "I'm crazy about you, Laurellie. When're we getting married?"

"Soon," she said definitely. "Although the minute we tell Grandma she'll—" Laurel broke off, eyes flying open. "Oh, God, *brunch!*"

"I wasn't thinking of food just yet," Matt murmured, going back to nibble on her ear.

"Oh, no, no, you don't understand. What time is it?" Shoving him aside, Laurel grabbed the bedside clock. "Oh, boy, we'd better get moving or we'll be in serious trouble."

Matt grabbed her around the waist as she started to hop out of bed. "If we stay right here," he began, pinning her beneath him again, "we can get into serious trouble by ourselves."

"Matthew." Laurel avoided the kiss, but it landed on the

vulnerable hollow of her throat. "Sunday brunch at Promesse d'Amour is sacred," she said unsteadily.

"Can you cook?"

"What? Oh, well, yes, that is, if your stomach's very broad-minded you could almost call it that. Matthew, don't." Breathless, she caught his wandering hand in hers.

"Why don't we have a private brunch here, somewhere around dinnertime?"

"Matthew—" she shook her head to clear it, then put both hands firmly on his shoulders. "Since you're going to join the family, you might as well get used to certain ironclad rules and traditions. Sunday brunch," she continued when he grinned, "is nothing to play around with."

"I'm an iconoclast."

"Bite your tongue," she told him, and struggled with a grin of her own. "Grandma would forgive me if I took up exotic dancing. She'll even overlook the fact that I'm marrying a Yankee, but she'd never, never let me get away with missing Sunday brunch. Even being late clouds the reputation, and we're pushing that."

Matt gave a long, exaggerated sigh. "For Miss Olivia, then," he agreed, and let Laurel wiggle out from under him.

"I'm going to get a shower," she said, dashing toward the bathroom. "If we move fast, we'll make it before deadline."

"Two can shower as quick as one," he commented as he stepped in with her.

"Matthew!" Laughing, Laurel lifted a hand to his chest. "If we're in here together we're definitely going to be late for brunch."

He drew her against him. "I'll risk it."

"Matthew—"

"You forget." He lowered his mouth to nibble on hers. "I know how to win arguments."

"Oh, damn," she sighed, and melted against him.

They were late.

"We're really in for it," Laurel muttered as Matt turned the car under the arched cedars.

Matt sent her a quick wolfish grin. "It was worth it."

"Just get that cat-ate-the-canary look off your face, Matthew," Laurel warned. "Try to look suitably humble."

"We could use the one about the flat tire," he suggested.

"No less than a five-car pileup equals pardon," she said grimly. "And you don't have a dent in this car." She shot him a look.

"No," he said positively, "not even for you."

"It's that practical Yankee streak," she said under her breath as the house came into view. "Okay, it probably won't work, but we'll go for it. Turn your watch back."

"Do what?"

"Turn your watch back, fifteen minutes." She fussed rapidly with her own. "Go on!"

"What's she going to do?" he demanded as he parked his car beside Curt's. "Take you to the woodshed?"

"You'd be surprised," Laurel muttered. "Oh-oh, here she comes. Listen, I know this might be almost impossible for you, Matthew, but look innocent."

"Maybe I'll just drop you off here and see you back in town."

"You do and I'll break your arm," she promised as she stepped from the car. "Grandma!" Laurel went forward with smiles and open arms. She kissed both lined cheeks and pretended she didn't notice the coolness in the sharp emerald eyes. "You look wonderful."

"You're late," Olivia said flatly.

"Oh, no, minutes to spare. I've brought Matthew with me," she added quickly. With luck, a lot of it, it would be enough to distract Olivia.

"Miss Olivia." He took the haughtily offered hand and lifted it to his lips. "I hope I'm not intruding."

"You're late," she repeated while her gaze raked over both of them.

"Why, how could we be?" Laurel countered, glancing down at her watch. "It's only just eleven now."

"That trick's older than I am." Olivia lifted her chin in the manner her granddaughter had inherited. "*Why* are you late?" she demanded, daring either of them to make an excuse.

Laurel moistened her lips. If she had a few more minutes, she could probably come up with a great lie. "Well, you see, Grandma—"

"It's my fault, Miss Olivia," Matt put in, earning a grateful glance from Laurel.

"What," Olivia began regally, "does my granddaughter being late have to do with you?"

"I distracted her in the shower," he said easily.

"Matthew!" Laurel cast him a horrified look that altered into one that promised swift and lethal revenge. His name echoed off into silence.

"I see." Olivia nodded. "That's a reasonable excuse," she decreed as Laurel's mouth dropped open. "Close your mouth, girl," she said absently as she continued to study Matt. "Took your own sweet time about it, but that's worked out for the best. You'll be marrying her soon."

It wasn't a question. Matt could only grin as Laurel began to sputter. "Very soon," he told Olivia.

"Welcome to the family—" she grinned and offered her cheek "—Yankee." With a wink for her granddaughter, she held out a hand for Matt to formally escort her around the house to the terrace.

No one's like her, Laurel thought with a fierce flurry of love and pride. Absolutely no one.

With her usual panache, Olivia dominated the table, with her son at the opposite end and the younger generation between them. As always, she'd made the most out of the Sunday tradition. White linen, gleaming silver and crystal, fresh flowers in bowls that had been treasured before the war.

The talk was quiet, general, easy. Laurel could see that Susan was a much different woman from the one who had fallen apart outside the city room. No more trembling fingers. If there was a sadness in her eyes, it was fading. She cast Laurel one look that spoke of complete trust. With it, Laurel felt the burden grow.

Not now, she told herself as she sipped at cool, dry champagne. Tomorrow was soon enough to bring all that back. For today, she needed to absorb the magic and the timelessness. Where else, she wondered, could six people be sitting with the sun gleaming on silver that was more than a century old? There was birdsong and a precious breeze that might only last a moment. It was too rare to crowd with sorrows and suspicions. And she was in love.

She glanced over at Matt, and her eyes told him everything.

"This will be your job one day, Laurellie," Olivia stated, cutting delicately into the crepe on her plate. "Traditions like this are important—more for the children than their parents. You and Matthew are welcome to the west wing when you're married. Permanently or whenever you feel the need to come. The house is big enough so that we won't bump into each other."

"Have some more coffee, Mother," William interrupted, sending her a telling look that expressed his feelings about matchmaking. "I want to talk to both of you." He nodded to his daughter and to Matt. His glance barely skimmed over Susan, but it was enough to tell Laurel he was referring to Anne Trulane. "Monday morning, my office."

"Business is for Monday." Olivia sent her son back a look every bit as stubborn. "I want to talk about the wedding. The garden couldn't be better suited to a summer wedding. You're welcome to have it here on the terrace."

"How about next weekend?" Matt put in, reaching for his coffee.

"Matt, don't encourage her," William advised. "She'll have Curt suing you for breach of promise."

"Damn right!" The thought made Olivia give a hoot of laughter as her hand came down on Laurel's. "We've got him now, Laurellie. William!" She caught him in the act of smothering a laugh with a cough. "Aren't you going to ask this boy all the rude questions a father's supposed to ask? A father can't be too careful when a man wants his daughter—especially a Yankee."

"The truth is," Laurel began before her father could speak,

"Matthew's marrying me for the house, and as a cover so he can dangle after Grandma."

Her father's grin altered into blank astonishment. "Are you joking?"

"No," Laurel said lightly as she dipped a strawberry into cream. "Matthew's crazy about Grandma."

"Laurel—" William began with a half laugh, only to break off without any idea what to say.

"She's not joking," Curt murmured, studying his sister. He glanced over at Matt as he remembered his roommate's fascination with a photograph, the questions. "All this time?" he said softly.

"Yes." Matt looked over at Laurel and smiled. "All this time."

"Well, it's been a cleverly kept secret," her father stated. "And from a veteran bloodhound like me."

Smiling, Laurel reached out a hand to him. "Do you mind?"

He gripped her hand. "Nothing could please me more." His gaze shifted to Matt. "Nothing. The point is—" his fingers relaxed with his smile "—I didn't think the two of you even liked each other. You had one particular adjective for Matt, as I recall."

"Insufferable," Laurel supplied. "It still holds."

"That's what adds spice to a relationship," Olivia declared as she pushed back from the table, a signal that meant the formality of the brunch was over. "Susan, be a sweet child and run up to my room. There's a small locket in my jewelry case, gold, encrusted with pearls."

The moment she'd gone, Olivia turned to Curt. "Going to let this Yankee show you up, Curtis?"

Rising, Curt made a great to-do over removing a piece of lint from his jacket. "Ma'am?"

"*He* lollygagged around for a year. I expect you should be able to snatch that girl up in half the time."

"Mother." William strolled over to place a hand on her shoulder. "Be satisfied with one victory."

"After I'm through with Curtis," she continued irrepressibly, "I'm getting started on you."

He acknowledged that with a nod before he turned to his son. "Every man for himself. Ah, Matt, there's something I've been meaning to talk to you about."

"Coward," Olivia murmured as her son drew Matt away.

"Is this it, Miss Olivia?"

"Yes, thank you." She smiled as Susan handed her the locket. "Curtis, why don't you take Susan through the garden. You like the garden, don't you, Susan?"

"Yes." Susan looked down at her hands, then lifted her eyes to Curt's. "Yes, I do."

"There, you see, she likes the garden. Run along. Now then." Without pausing for breath, she turned to Laurel.

"Grandma." Laurel gave her a long, hard hug. "I adore you."

Olivia let herself enjoy the warmth and scent of youth before she drew Laurel away. In her own masterly way, she studied her granddaughter. "You're happy."

"Yes." With a laugh, Laurel tossed back her hair. "If you'd have asked me a month ago—good God, a week ago—how I'd feel about marrying Matthew Bates on the terrace, I'd've said..." She broke off, laughing again. "I'd better not repeat what I'd've said."

"You pretended you weren't attracted to him right from the beginning."

"I did a good job of it."

Olivia gave a hoot. "Ah, but you're like me, child!"

"The highest of compliments."

Olivia dropped the locket into her lap and took Laurel's hands. "When we love, really love, it's with everything we have, so we don't give it easily. Your grandfather..." She looked misty for a moment, young. "God, but I loved that man. Fifteen years with him wasn't enough. When he died, I grieved and grieved hard, but then life—you have to live it as it comes. The others, after him, they were..." She shook her head and smiled again. "They were for fun. I cared about

every man I've been with, but only one had all of me. You'd
understand that,'' she murmured. ''So would your Yankee.''

''Yes.'' Laurel felt the tears swim into her eyes and blinked
them back. ''I love you, Grandma.''

''You'll lead each other a dance,'' Olivia said after giving
Laurel's hands a quick squeeze. ''There's nothing better I
could wish for you. This is for you now.'' Olivia lifted the
locket from her lap, cupping it in her hand a moment as if
warming it. ''Your grandfather gave it to me when we were
engaged. I wore it when I married him. It would mean a great
deal to me if you wore it when you marry Matthew.''

''Oh, Grandma, it's lovely.'' Laurel took the gold, gleaming dully and still warm from her grandmother's hands. It was
studded with tiny pearls that carried just a hint of blue under
the white. ''I've never seen you wear it.''

''I haven't since he died. It's time it was worn again and
worn by a bride.''

''Thank you.'' Leaning over, Laurel kissed Olivia's cheek,
then with a smile turned the locket over in her palm. So
lovely, she thought, and it would look so perfect against a
floaty, romantic white dress. Maybe something with lace
and...

As memory jarred, she pressed a hand to her temple.

''Laurellie?''

''No.'' Absently she patted her grandmother's hand. ''I'm
all right, I've just remembered something. Or think I have. I
have to use the phone.''

Jumping up, she dashed into the house with the locket
clutched in her hand. From memory, she dialed Heritage Oak.
With her eyes on the locket in her hand and her mind on
another, she barely heard the answering voice.

''Oh, Binney,'' she said quickly. ''It's Laurel Armand.''
When there was silence, she leaped into it. ''Please, Binney,
I know you're angry with me for questioning you. I under-
stand. I'm sorry, truly sorry if I pressed too hard.''

''It isn't my place to be angry with you, Miss Laurel,'' she
said quietly. ''It isn't my place to answer questions.''

''Please, there's something I have to know. It could be very important. A locket.'' She plowed on into the unreceptive silence. "The locket Louis gave Elise before they were married. She wore it on her wedding day, and, I think, always after that. I can remember that I never saw her when she wasn't wearing it. The gold locket with the etching on the front. Do you remember it, Binney? You must,'' she went on before there could be an answer. "She kept Louis's picture in it.''

"I remember the locket.''

Something—not excitement, not fear—began to pound in her chest. Laurel recognized it as disillusionment. "She always wore it, didn't she? It was very small and elegant, something she could wear every day and still wear with evening clothes.''

"It was her habit to wear it.''

Laurel swallowed and fought to keep her voice steady. "Binney, was Elise afraid of the swamp?'' She knew the answer herself, but wouldn't go with childhood memories now. It was time for facts, no matter how they hurt.

"It was a long time ago.''

"Please, Binney. You knew her, you were there.''

"She did not like it,'' Binney said flatly. "She knew the legend.''

"But sometimes—sometimes—she went in there,'' Laurel whispered.

"Yes, sometimes she went in, but only with Mr. Louis.''

"Yes, yes, I know.'' Laurel let out a long breath. "Only with Louis. Thank you, Binney.''

Hanging up, Laurel stared down at the locket in her hand. She slipped it gently in her pocket and went to find Matt.

He saw her, crossing the lawn. With a brief word to her father, Matt went to meet her. Even from the distance, he'd recognized the look in her eyes. "What is it, Laurel?''

Her arms went around him, her cheek to his chest. For a moment, she just needed that—the strength, the promise. The tug-of-war inside her was almost over. It didn't surprise her that she still loved Louis, or the Louis she'd known. "Matthew, where's the piece of locket you found in the swamp?''

"I took it to the police lab. They're going to run some

tests.'' He drew her away far enough so that he could see her face. ''Why?''

Quietly, she drew a breath. Then she straightened and stood on her own. ''They're going to find that it was out in the weather, perhaps covered and uncovered by rain and dirt over and over—for ten years.''

''Ten—'' He broke off as understanding came. ''It was Elise's.''

''I remembered where I'd seen it. I just called Heritage Oak and spoke to Binney to be sure. Elise wore that locket every day.''

Because she was pale, because he loved her, Matt chose to play devil's advocate. ''All right, but it's still not proof. She could've lost it in there any time.''

''No, it's not proof,'' Laurel agreed. ''But I don't think there's a chance that Elise simply lost it there. First, it was too important to her. And second, she didn't go in there often. She wasn't afraid the same way Anne was, but she had a healthy respect for the legend. The only times she went in, she went in with Louis. Binney just corroborated.''

He could see the struggle, the emotion, in her eyes. This time he felt none of the frustration, the jealousy, that had plagued him. Gently, he cupped her face in his hands. ''I'm sorry, Laurel.''

She caught his wrists in her hands and held tight. ''Oh, God, Matthew, so am I.''

''I think we should fill in your father before we leave,'' he said carefully. ''But we might want to keep it away from Susan for a while. We still don't have anything solid for the police.''

''No.'' Laurel glanced over as she heard Susan's laugh drift from the garden. ''Let's leave her out of it for now. My father can probably put on enough pressure to reopen the investigation on Anne, and stir one up on Elise and Charles.''

''We've got enough,'' Matt agreed, watching the struggle on her face, ''to start putting pressure in the right places.''

''Oh, God, Matthew, do you realize, if what we're thinking is fact...Louis must be terribly ill. With Charles and Elise it might have been a moment of blind fury, but all these years it would've eaten at him. And then to meet Anne.'' She pressed her fingers to her eyes. Would she ever be able to separate the emotion from the necessity? "He needs help, Matthew. Can you imagine what a dark place he's been living in all this time?"

"He'll get help. But, Laurel..." He took her shoulders until she dropped her hands and looked at him. "First we have to prove it. I think if we concentrate on the first—on Charles and Elise," he said carefully, "it'll lead to Anne. It's not going to be easy for you."

"No," she agreed, "not easy, but necessary." Watching his eyes, she thought she could almost see the idea forming. "What're you thinking, Matthew?"

"Pressure," he murmured. "The right pressure in the right place." He brought his attention back to her. "Louis must already be on the edge, Laurel, ready to go over. He's warned you off three times. Just what do you think his reaction would be if he saw that piece of locket?"

"I think—" Laurel's hand reached automatically for the one in her pocket—"it would break him."

"So do I." He slipped an arm around her shoulders. "We'll have to make another trip to Heritage Oak tomorrow."

Chapter 12

The clutter of notes was still spread over Laurel's drop-leaf table with the wrappers and cardboard of their take-out meal. Clothes—hers and some of his—were scattered over the floor. Laurel closed the door behind them and jiggled her keys in her palm.

"You're a slob, Matthew."

"Me? It's your place. Besides—" he nudged his shirt out of his way with his foot and sat down "—you were the one who dragged me to the floor, crazy for my body. And," he continued when she snorted, "you were the one who pulled me out of here this morning like the building was on fire."

He was distracting her—she was distracting him—from what hovered around the verges of both their thoughts: Louis Trulane and what to do about him.

"Well, since I've already had your body, and brunch," she added sweetly, "you can help me clean up this mess."

"Better idea." Rising, he yanked her into his arms. "Let's add to it."

"Matthew!" But his mouth crushed down on hers. His fingers were making quick work of the zipper at the back of her dress. "Stop it!" Half laughing, half in earnest, she struggled against him. "You're crazy. Don't you ever think about anything else?"

"Sometimes I think about eating," he confessed, then nipped, none too gently, at her collarbone.

"Matthew, this is ridiculous." But the quick heating of her blood told her otherwise. "It was only a few hours ago that— oh."

"I'm hungry again," he murmured, then devoured her mouth.

God, he was making her head spin. With her dress already down to her waist, Laurel tried to pull away. "Stop. There's things we have to talk about, and—"

"Mmm, a reluctant woman." He dragged her against him again. "That gets my lust cells moving."

"Your what?" she demanded, choking on a laugh.

"Just watch." Before she realized what he was up to, she was slung over his shoulder.

"Bates! Have you lost your mind?"

"Yeah." He pulled the dress the rest of the way off as he headed for the bedroom. Carelessly, he dropped it at the doorway, sending her shoes to follow. "Blame it on the lust cells."

"I'll tell you what I think about your lust cells," she began, but the wind rushed out of her as she landed on the bed beneath him.

Then he was taking her back to places she'd been, but so swiftly, so immediately, she couldn't keep up. Relentless, he wouldn't allow her to fall behind. Bright streams of color seemed to burst inside her head while her body was consumed with pleasure, such hot, liquid, throbbing pleasure.

No thought. No words. She could only feel and feel and feel. The rest of her clothes were gone. Had she heard something rip? Did it matter? Her body was wild to be touched, tasted, to experience all the mad things he seemed determined to do.

Emotions exploded in her, poured out of her. Oh, God, she was so free, so wonderfully free. Pleasure was an absence of pain, and she felt only pleasure in his hands, his lips, the taste of his tongue inside her mouth, the feel of his flesh beneath her fingers.

Excitement, heady, steamy excitement. Liberation. Soaring, half crazy with delight. The knowledge that her life would be splashed with moments like this made her laugh aloud. The next moment he had her gasping. She locked her arms around him as her world rocked and spun.

He took her on a roller coaster of sensations, plummeting down, climbing, climbing, only to whip blindly around a turn to fall again. Weightless, helpless, with the air rushing in her lungs and her heart thundering in her ears.

Then he plunged into her, driving her over that last, giddy hill.

When she could breathe again without gasping, when she could think without pooling all her concentration onto one word, Laurel slid a hand across his chest. He was lying on his back, possibly, she thought, just possibly, as enervated as she.

Laurel turned her face into his shoulder. "You did that more for me than yourself."

Matt gave a weak laugh. "I'm a real Samaritan. No lengths I won't go to to serve my fellow man."

"Matthew." Laurel shifted, so that she lay over him, her head supported just under his by her folded arms. "You knew I was tense, trying not to be. You knew I didn't want to think about what's going to happen, even though I have to. I was being a coward."

"No." He brushed the hair back from her face. "You were being human. You needed to wipe it away for a little while, blank it out. I did, too." He smiled, with the touch of irony in the lifted brow. "This was better than an aspirin."

She managed to match the smile. "You'll have to keep yourself available every time I have a headache." She lowered her face to kiss his chest, then lifted it again. "Matthew, I can handle this. I can."

Maybe, he thought. Maybe not. But he'd give her the first test. "Okay. I want to run over to the lab and get the locket back whether it's been tested yet or not. I'd feel better if I had it."

Laurel nodded, accepting. "And in the morning, we take it out to see Louis."

I take it out, he corrected silently, but merely nodded. That was something he'd deal with when the time came. "If he doesn't just fall apart at that, we'll have a lot of legwork to do, but we bring the uniforms in."

"Agreed," she said simply. Her heart was already numb.

He sat up, wondering just where he'd tossed his clothes. "Do you want to come with me now?"

"No." She let out a deep breath. What had her grandmother said? Life—you have to live it. "I'll tell you what I'm going to do for you, Bates, and believe me, you're the first man I've offered this to."

He was standing, pulling on his slacks. The grin tilted. "Fascinating."

"I'm going to cook you dinner."

"Laurel, I'm—overwhelmed."

"You might be a great deal more than that after you eat it," she murmured.

"We could always eat out."

"Don't be a coward," she said absently, wondering just what she had in the freezer that could be used. "Better pick up some wine." Kneeling, she buttoned up the rest of his shirt for him herself. "And some bicarbonate," she added, laughing up at him.

"Bicarbonate," he murmured. "That doesn't inspire confidence."

"No, but it'd be a smart move."

"I shouldn't be long."

"Take my door key in case I'm involved in the kitchen. And, Matthew," she murmured, sliding her arms around his neck, "make sure you control those lust cells until you get back."

He kissed her, then gave her a friendly pat on the bottom. "An hour," he promised before he strolled out.

An hour, Laurel mused, and stretched her arms to the ceiling as she heard the front door close. That should give her time enough to try her hand at being domestic.

It didn't take her long to deal with the disorder of the apartment, or to realize just how smoothly Matt had eased out of helping. She decided that having to eat her cooking would be punishment enough for him. Going to the kitchen, she poked in the refrigerator.

A little juice, less milk, two pounds of butter. *Two* pounds, Laurel mused. How had that happened? Still, there was the makings for a salad in the vegetable bin. A start. Maybe a casserole, she decided. She was almost sure she had a cookbook around somewhere.

Fifteen minutes later, she was elbows deep in the beginnings of a tuna-and-macaroni dish that the cookbook promised was foolproof. With a glance around the now cluttered and disarranged kitchen, she smirked. Whoever wrote the book didn't know Laurel. She was going over the next step when the phone rang.

Matt, she thought, dusting off her hands as she went to answer. He probably wants to know if I'd like him to pick up some take-out Chinese. You're not getting off that easy, Bates. Grinning, she answered.

"Hello."

"Oh, Laurel, thank God you're home."

Tension banded the back of her neck immediately. "Marion? What is it?"

"Laurel, I didn't know what to do. Who else to call. It's Louis."

"Is he hurt?" Laurel asked quickly. "Has he been hurt?"

"No—I don't know. Laurel..." Her voice broke and she began to weep.

"Marion, calm down and tell me what's happened."

Her breathing rasped into the phone. "I've never seen him this bad before. All day, he wouldn't speak to anyone, but that happens sometimes. Oh, God, Laurel," she said on a sudden burst of emotion, "it's been such a strain, worse since Anne... Laurel," she began again, nerves quivering in her voice. "I need help."

"I'm going to help," Laurel said as calmly as she could. "What's happened?"

"Just now, a few minutes ago." Laurel heard her take a steadying breath. "He flew into a rage. He wasn't—wasn't making any sense. He was saying things about Elise, and about Anne. I don't know—it was as though he'd gotten them mixed up in his mind."

Laurel pressed her lips together. She had to be calm, had to think straight. "Where is he now?"

"He's locked himself in his room. He's raging up there, I can hear the furniture... Laurel, he won't let me in."

"Marion, call a doctor."

"Oh, God, Laurel, don't you think I've tried that before? He won't see one, and he's never been as—as out of control as this. Please, come. You were always our friend. Louis was so close to you before—before all of this. You might be able to calm him down, and then if I could just figure out what to do so that he'd—he'd get help," she finished in a whisper. "Laurel, please, I just can't expose him to strangers the way he is now. I don't know who else to trust."

"All right, Marion." She pictured Louis locked in his room, on the edge of madness. "I'll be there as quickly as I can."

"Laurel...as a friend, not as a reporter, please."

"As a friend, Marion." After hanging up the receiver, Laurel pressed the heels of her hands to her eyes.

Matt shifted the bag he carried and slipped Laurel's key into the lock. "I got red and white," he called out. "You didn't say what we were having." A glance at the living room showed him that Laurel had already tidied up. He was going to hear about that, Matt mused, grinning. "I don't smell anything burning."

He swung into the kitchen and lifted a brow. Whatever she was making, it apparently required every inch of counter space. Matt set the wine in the sink—the only place left for it—and shook his head. This was the woman whose notes were always in perfect order? Whose desk was clear and ordered at the end of each day? Dipping his hand into a bowl he drew out a cold, spongy elbow of macaroni.

"Ah, Laurel," he began, dropping it again. "There's this little place on Canal Street, great seafood. Why don't we…" He paused at the entrance to the bedroom. Empty. He felt the first prickles of unease. "Laurel?" Matt repeated, pushing open the bathroom door. Empty. Fear washed over him; he pushed it back. She'd just gone out for something she was missing for the recipe. She probably left a note.

When he hurried back into the living room, he found it by the phone. But even before he read it, he didn't feel relief, only more fear.

Matthew—Marion phoned, very upset. Louis is losing control, talking about Elise and Anne. He's locked himself in the bedroom. She needs help. I couldn't say no. Laurel.

"Damn it!" Matt tossed down the note and raced for the door. The fear was still with him.

Shadows were lengthening as Laurel turned down the drive toward Heritage Oak. The air was still again in the late-afternoon hush. A bird called out, as if testing the silence, then was quiet again. Even as she stopped the car at the end of the drive, Marion was running down the front steps toward her.

Her hair was loose, her face pale and tear-stained. It ran through Laurel's mind quickly that she'd never seen Marion so totally lacking in composure.

"Oh, God, Laurel." Marion grabbed her as if she were a lifeline. "I couldn't stop him. I couldn't stop him!"

Laurel's head whipped up, her eyes fixing on the window of Louis's room. She had a sickening picture of him lying dead by his own hand. "From what? Marion, what has he done?"

"The swamp. He's gone in the swamp." She covered her face with her hands and sobbed. "I think he's lost his mind. The things he was saying—he pushed me."

Not dead, Laurel told herself. Not dead. You have to be calm. "What did he say?"

Marion lowered her hands. Her eyes were wide, stricken. "He said," she began in a whisper, "he said he was going to find Elise."

"Elise," Laurel repeated, forcing herself not to give in to the horror of it.

"We have to do something!" Marion grabbed her again. "Laurel, we have to do something, go after him—*find* him. He's having a breakdown or—"

"Marion, how can we find him in there? We should call the police."

"*No!* Not the police. It's Louis." She seemed to come to grips with herself as she released Laurel. "I can find him. I know the swamp as well as he does. You don't have to come with me—I asked too much."

Laurel dragged both hands through her hair as Marion started across the lawn. He'd put her up on her first pony, she remembered. Played patient games of chess, listened to her rambling stories. Whatever he'd done, how could she walk away without trying to help?

"Marion, wait. I'm coming with you."

Marion stopped and held out a hand.

They moved quickly toward the swamp. The instant revulsion came as she stood at the edge of it, but she forced it back. It was just a place, she told herself. And Louis was in it.

The shadows were long on the ground now. Daylight was thinning. They'd have an hour, maybe a bit longer, Laurel reassured herself, before it was too dark to see. By then, they'd have found him. She moved into the swamp without hesitation.

"I think he might have gone to the river—to where Anne was found." How much did Marion know or suspect, Laurel wondered. At the moment, she didn't think Marion was in any shape for questions or theories. "Are you going to be all right?" she asked, looking at Marion's flowing pastel skirts and elegant pumps. "It's hard going through here."

"It doesn't matter," Marion said impatiently. "Louis is my brother."

"It's going to work out for the best," Laurel told her, almost believing it herself.

"I know." Marion managed a smile.

They moved slowly, side by side, and then with Laurel just ahead as the path narrowed. The place was alive with noise—birds, insects. Once she saw a blue heron rise up gracefully and glide. They were coming to the river.

"Maybe we should call to him, let him know we're here," Laurel suggested. "It might frighten him if we're too quiet."

"He won't hear you."

"Not if he's gone the other way, but if he's anywhere near the river, then—" Laurel broke off as she turned around.

Marion held a gleaming old gun in her hand. A sliver of sunlight dashed against the chrome. For a moment, as her gaze rested on it, Laurel's mind went blank. Then, slowly, she looked up into Marion's face. Despite the red-rimmed eyes, the tracks of tears and disordered hair, her expression was calm and composed. There was something buzzing in her ears that Laurel didn't yet recognize as terror. She kept her eyes on Marion's face.

"Marion." The name came out calmly enough. Calmly and very soft. "What are you doing?"

"What I have to do," she said mildly.

Was the gun for Louis? Laurel thought frantically. If it was for Louis, then why was it pointed at her? She wouldn't look at it—not yet—she'd look only into Marion's clear gray eyes. "Where's Louis, Marion? Do you know?"

"Of course, he's working in his study. He's been working all afternoon."

"All afternoon," Laurel repeated, trying to hold back the trickle of fear that was eating at her wall of control. "Why did you call me?"

"I had to." Marion smiled. It was a gentle one. "After I spoke to you this morning about Elise's locket, I knew it had gone too far. You'd gone too far."

"Spoke to me? But I talked to Binney..." She trailed off. "It was you?"

"I'm surprised you didn't remember that Binney spends her Sundays with her sister. You made it terribly simple, Laurel. You expected Binney, so I was Binney." The smile faded. Marion's brows drew together, delicately, as they did when she was annoyed. "I'm very disappointed in you, Laurel. I warned you to stay out of this. Can you imagine the trouble you'd have caused if it had been Binney? Questioning a servant about family matters." She shook her head as a flicker of irritation darkened her eyes. "You've been raised better than that."

Raised better? Laurel thought giddily. Was she mad? Oh, God, she thought as fear washed over her. Of course she was mad. "Marion, what are you going to do?"

"You'll have to be punished," Marion told her calmly. "Just like the others."

Matt's car skidded to a halt next to Laurel's. He hadn't stopped cursing since he'd tossed her note aside. Cursing helped hold off the fear. If he's hurt her, Matt thought as he sprinted up the steps. By God, if he's touched her... Lifting a fist, he pounded on the door.

"Trulane!" He pounded again, sick with fear. When the door opened, he was through it in seconds, with his hands gripping hard on Louis's shirt. "Where's Laurel?"

"What the hell do you think you're doing?" Louis stood rigid, his eyes burning with fury.

"What have you done with Laurel?" Matt demanded.

"I've done nothing with Laurel. I haven't seen her." He looked down at the hands gripping his shirt. "Get your hands off me, Bates." He'd like a fight, Matt realized. He'd like the simple release of a purely physical explosion—fist against flesh. Matt saw it in his eyes.

"We'll go a few rounds, Trulane," Matt promised grimly. "There's nothing I'd like better—after you tell me what you've done with Laurel."

Louis felt something bubbling inside of him. The emotion, for the first time in weeks, had nothing to do with grief. It was pure fury. Somehow it was cleansing. "I told you I haven't seen her. She isn't here."

"You can do better." Matt flung a hand toward the open door. "Her car's out front."

Louis followed the gesture and frowned. Some of the pent-up anger gave way to puzzlement. "She must've come to see Marion."

"Marion called her." Matt shoved him back against the wall, catching him off-balance. "She told her to come because you were out of control, locked in your room."

"Are you crazy?" Louis pushed him away, and they stood eyeing each other, both tall men, both ready, anxious, for blood. "Marion would hardly call Laurel if I were locked in my room. As it happens, I've been working all afternoon."

Matt stood, breathing fast, trying to hold on. If he hit Trulane, even once, he might never stop. He could feel the violence bubbling up inside him. Not until he saw Laurel, he promised himself. And after that...

"Laurel left me a note that she was coming here after a phone call from Marion concerning your unstable condition."

"I don't know what the hell you're talking about."

"Laurel's car's out front," Matt said between his teeth. "And you're here."

Louis gave him a cold stare. "Perhaps you'd care to search the house."

"I'll do just that," Matt tossed back. "While I'm at it," he continued as he reached in his pocket, "why don't you take a look at this and see what explanation you can come up with?"

Opening his palm, he held out the piece of locket. Louis gripped his wrist, fingers biting into flesh. "Elise—where did you get that?" His eyes whipped up to Matt's, dark, tormented. "Where in hell did you get that?"

"In the swamp." Matt closed his hand over it. "Laurel recognized it too, then confirmed it with your housekeeper on the phone this morning."

"Binney?" Louis stared down at Matt's closed hand. "No, Binney isn't here. The swamp? In the swamp?" Again Louis lifted his head. His face was white. "Elise never went in there without me. She always wore that, always. She had it on the day I left for New York, before she—" He shook his head, color rushing back to his face. "What the hell are you trying to do?"

Matt tried to take it step by step. A new fear was crawling in. "Laurel told me she called here—around noon—and spoke with your housekeeper."

"I tell you Binney isn't here, hasn't been here all day! She goes to her sister's. All the servants are free on Sundays. There's only Marion and I."

"Only Marion?" Matt murmured. Marion who had called—Marion who had, by her nervous distress, sent them after Brewster. And Marion, Matt remembered all at once, who had said Anne had told Susan that Brewster made her nervous. How would she have known that unless—unless she'd seen the letters. "Where is she?" Matt demanded, already halfway down the hall. "Where's your sister?"

"You just wait a damned minute." Louis grabbed Matt by the arm. "What are you getting at? Where did you get that locket?"

"In the swamp!" Matt exploded. "Damn you, don't you understand Marion's got her!" His face became very still and very pale. "In the swamp," he repeated. "She has her in the swamp, just like the others."

"What others?" Louis was on him before Matt could move. *"What others?"*

"Your sister's a murderer," Matt flung back at him. "She's killed three times, and now she has Laurel."

"You're crazy!"

"I'm not crazy." He opened his fist again so that the locket sat dully in the center of his palm. "We were in the swamp the other night—someone attacked her. The same person who sent her the dead snake, and the one who threatened her over the phone yesterday. The same person," he said evenly, "who called her here now. Laurel came here for you," Matt told Louis, watching his eyes. "Are you going to help me?"

Louis stared down at the locket, his breath unsteady. "We'll go in. Wait here."

Turning, he walked into a room across from the parlor. Seconds later, he came back with a small pistol. The color had drained from his face again. In silence, he handed it to

Matt. "She's taken the gun." His eyes met Matt's. "The an-
tique we've kept under glass."

Don't panic, don't try to run. Laurel ran the words over
and over in her mind as she watched Marion. She looks so
calm now, as if any minute she'd smile and offer me tea and
cakes. How long has she been mad? Laurel swallowed slowly,
careful to make no movement at all. Talk—she wants to talk
about it.

"Punish," Laurel repeated. "You punished the others,
Marion?"

"I had to."

"Why?"

"You were always a clever child, Laurel, but not clever
enough." She smiled again, old friend to old friend. "After
all, look how easily I threw your attention onto Brewster, just
by telling the truth. Anne would never have left Louis. She
adored him."

"Then why did you punish her, Marion?"

"She shouldn't have come back." Marion let out a little,
shuddering sigh. "She should never have come back."

"Come back?" Laurel repeated, allowing herself a quick
glimpse over Marion's head. If she could distract her, get just
a few seconds' head start, could she lose herself in the brush?

"She didn't fool me," Marion said, smiling again. "Oh,
she fooled the rest of them—especially Louis—but I knew.
Of course, I pretended I didn't. I'm very good at pretending.
She was afraid of the swamp," Marion said absently. "I knew
why, of course I knew why. She died here before, she had to
die here again."

Laurel stared as the horror of what was in Marion's mind
washed over her. Keep talking, keep talking, keep talking, she
told herself as a thrush began to sing in the cypress behind
her. "Why did you kill Elise the first time?"

"She had no right!" Marion exploded so that Laurel gave
a quick, involuntary jerk back. "She had no right to the house.
It was mine, always it's been mine. Louis was going to will
it to her. To *her!* She didn't have Trulane blood, wasn't one

of us. *I'm* the oldest," she raged. "By rights, the house was mine. Father was wrong to leave it to Louis."

Her chest began to shudder, but when Laurel looked down, she saw the gun was still steady. "It's always been mine. I love it. All of this." Her eyes skimmed the swamp and softened. "It's the only thing I've ever loved."

"But why Elise?" Laurel interrupted. A house, she thought frantically. Did someone kill for a house, a plot of grass and dirt? It had been done before, she reminded herself. Over and over again, since the caves. "Why didn't you kill Louis, Marion? Then you'd have inherited."

"Laurel." Her voice was soft. "Louis is my brother."

"But—but Charles," she began.

"I never wanted to hurt Charles." Tears sprang and swam in her eyes. "I loved him. But he saw us, he interfered." A single tear drifted down her cheek. "I didn't have a choice. Elise and I went for a walk—she was lonely without Louis. When we were far enough away from the house, I took out the gun. This gun," she said, lifting it higher. "Do you recognize it, Laurel?"

She did. She'd seen it under glass in the library. The same gun another Trulane had used to kill—to punish. "Yes."

"I knew I had to use this." She ran a fingertip down the barrel. "It was as if it was waiting for me, as if someone was telling me that it was right that I punish Elise with this. Do you understand?"

"I'm trying to."

"Poor Laurel," Marion murmured. "Always so understanding, so caring. That's how I knew you'd come today when I called."

Laurel felt her knees start to shake. "You were telling me about Charles."

"Yes, yes. He saw us, you see. Saw me leading Elise into the swamp at gunpoint. At least, he must have—I didn't have time to ask, everything happened so quickly. We were here when he found us. Just here."

She glanced around as if they might not be alone after all. Laurel took a very slow, very small step to the right. "Don't,

Laurel," Marion murmured, lifting the gun a fraction higher. Laurel stood still. "Elise went wild—that must be when her locket was broken. I should've been more careful. I had to shoot her. Then Charles was pushing me down. My own brother—shouting at me. The gun seemed to go off again, all by itself. Then he was dead."

Her tears were dry now, her eyes clear. "I didn't know what to do at first, and then, it just came. They'd been lovers, like the other two who'd died here. I'd have to forge another note. This time Elise would tell Louis she'd left him for Charles. It was better," she muttered. "Really, it was better that way. I had to drag them to the quicksand."

"Oh, God." Laurel closed her eyes, but Marion didn't notice.

"I packed some of their clothes. All the servants were gone because it was Sunday. Charles's paints, too—I nearly forgot them. Of course, he'd never have left without his paints. They went in the quicksand too. Then it was done. It was simple. Of course, Louis was hurt. He suffered." Her eyes clouded for a moment. "I know he blamed himself, but I could hardly tell him it was all for the best. The house was mine again, he was busy with his work. But sometimes," she whispered. "Sometimes I'd hear them in here. At night."

Laurel swallowed the metallic taste of horror. "Charles and Elise?"

"I'd hear them—it would wake me up and I'd have to come out, come look. I never saw them—" Again, she looked around as if expecting someone. "But I heard."

It's driven her mad, Laurel thought. How is it no one saw, no one suspected? She remembered Marion at a charity function only months before—delicate, elegant, with a spray of violets pinned to her lapel. She looked down at the gun again.

"Then she came back," Marion said flatly. "She said her name was Anne, and Louis believed her. I knew. She'd look at me with those soft, shy eyes, and she was laughing! I let her think she'd fooled me."

"And you brought her in here again."

"I had to be more careful this time. Louis hardly let her

out of his sight, and she'd never, never go near the swamp. That night, he was working late. I heard her in the study with him. He told her he'd probably be a couple hours more, to go up to bed without him. I knew it was time. I went into her room, put a pillow over her face. Oh, I had to be careful, I couldn't kill her then. It had to look like an accident this time. She was very small, and not strong. It only took a minute until she was unconscious. Then I carried her out here.''

Marion smiled, remembering. "I had the gun, but she didn't know I couldn't afford to use it. When she came to, she was terrified. Elise knew she was going to die again. She begged me to let her go, but I made her get up. I thought it best if she drowned in the river. When she started to run, I let her. It would be simpler if she exhausted herself first and I kept close. Then I heard her scream. The snake, a young one, Elise had walked right over the nest. You see, it was meant,'' Marion told her. "It was right. All I needed then was enough time for the poison to work—and a night, a whole night out in that damp air. I waited until she stopped running, until she was unconscious, here, right here where she'd died before. Then I went home.'' Marion smiled, but now her eyes were blank. "She won't come back this time.''

"No," Laurel said quietly. "She won't come back.''

"I've always been fond of you, Laurel. If you'd only listened, this wouldn't have happened.''

Laurel moistened her lips and prayed her voice would be steady. "If you shoot me, Marion, they'll take you away from Heritage Oak.''

"No!'' Her hand tightened on the gun, then relaxed. "No, I'm not going to shoot you, unless I have to. If I do, I'll have to place the blame on Louis. I'll have to, you'll be responsible for that.''

It was so hard to breathe, Laurel discovered. So hard to make the air come in and go out. If she concentrated on it, she'd keep herself from screaming until Marion made her stop. "I won't walk into the river, or the quicksand for you.''

"No," Marion agreed. "You're not like the others, not so easily frightened. But there's one thing...'' Holding the gun level, she sidestepped toward the wild cane. "You came in here to snoop around, you couldn't leave it alone. And you met with a tragic accident. Just like Elise—Anne." She drew a wicker hamper out of the bush. "This one," she said quietly, "isn't dead."

She knew, and the fear wrapped around her. Tight. With a long, smooth stick, Marion pushed the hamper closer, then flicked off the lid. Laurel froze, feeling the weightlessness in her head, the ice in her stomach as the snake slithered out. Then another one.

"I didn't want to take any chances," Marion murmured. Setting down the gun, she held the stick with both hands. She looked up at Laurel and smiled. "You've always been terrified of them, haven't you? How well I remember you fainting dead away over a little garter snake. Harmless creatures." She poked her stick at the copperheads until they coiled and hissed. "These aren't."

She wanted to run, to scream. The gun would've been better. But her voice was trapped by the fear, her legs imprisoned by it. As if her consciousness had floated off, she felt her skin spring damp and clammy.

"It won't matter if you don't move," Marion told her easily. "They're angry. I can make them angrier." She prodded them again, nudging them closer to Laurel. One lashed out at the stick, and Marion laughed.

It was the laugh Matt heard. It chilled him to the bone. When he saw them, the snakes were less than a foot away from Laurel, hissing, coiling, enraged, as Marion continued to prod at them. Matt gripped the gun in both hands, prayed, and fired.

"No!" Marion's scream was long and wild as the body of one snake jerked, then lay still. She spun around, stumbling, not even feeling the fangs that sank into her ankle before Matt pulled the trigger again. And she ran, bursting through the wild cane like an animal, hunted.

"Laurel!" Matt had his arms around her, dragging her against him. "You're all right." Desperate, he closed his mouth over hers. "It's over. I'm getting you out."

"Matthew." The sobs were heaving in her chest and she fought against them. "She's mad. She killed them all—all of them. My God, Matthew. The snakes—"

"Gone," he said quickly, pulling her closer. "They're gone. You're all right."

"For the house," Laurel said into his chest. "Dear God, she killed them for the house. Louis—"

Matt turned his head. Only a few yards away, Louis stood staring at them. There was no color in his face. Only his eyes seemed alive. "She's been bitten," Louis said, so quietly Matt barely heard. "I'll go after her."

"Louis—" Matt looked back at him, finding there was nothing, absolutely nothing, that could be said. "I'm sorry," he murmured.

Nodding, Louis walked into the cane. "Just get Laurel out of here."

"Come on." Matt pressed his lips to her temple. "Can you walk?"

"Yes." The tears were streaming down her face, but she found them a relief. "Yes, I'm all right."

"When I'm sure of that," he said as he held her close by his side, "I'm going to strangle you."

He waited until they were in the clear, then drew Laurel down on the grass. Her head sank to her knees. "I'll be all right in a minute, really. We'll have to call the police."

"Louis took care of it before he left the house. They'll be here any minute. Can you tell me now?"

At first, she kept her head on her knees as she spoke. Gradually, as the horror and the dizziness faded, she lifted it. When she heard the sirens, her hand slipped into Matt's and held tight.

So much confusion—with the police in the swamp, all the questions. A hell of a story, Laurel thought on a bright bubble of hysteria. Though she swallowed it, she gave in to the need to press her face into Matt's shoulder. Just a few more minutes, she told herself. I'll be all right in just a few more minutes. She let Matt lead her back to the house, then drank the brandy he urged on her.

"I'm better," she told him. "Please, stop looking at me as though I were going to dissolve."

He stared at her a minute, then, pulling her into his arms, buried his face in her hair. "Damn you, Laurel." And his voice trembled. "Don't ever do that to me again. I thought I was too late. Another five minutes—"

"No more," she murmured, soothing him. "No more, Matthew. Oh, I love you." She drew his face back. "I love you so much."

She met the aggressive kiss, feeling all the fears drain. He was here, holding her. Nothing else mattered. She lifted a hand to his face as the front door closed. "It's Louis," she said quietly.

He came in slowly. His hair and clothes were streaked and disheveled. His eyes, Laurel saw, were not cold, were not remote, but weary and vulnerable. Without hesitation, she rose and went to him. "Oh, Louis."

He slipped his arms around her, holding on. His face dropped to the top of her head. "We found her. She's— they're taking her to the hospital, but I don't know if... She's delirious," he managed, and drew away. "Did she hurt you, Laurel?"

"No, no, I'm fine."

His gaze shifted to Matt. "I owe you much more than an apology."

"No, you don't."

Louis accepted this with a nod and walked to the brandy. "Are you up to telling me the whole story now?"

He kept his back to them as Laurel related everything Marion had said. Once, when she saw his shoulders shudder, she faltered. He shook his head and gestured for her to finish.

"I need to talk to Susan," he said when Laurel fell silent.

"She's with my grandmother."

Pouring another brandy, Louis nodded. "If she'll see me, I'll go out tomorrow."

"She'll see you, Louis," Laurel murmured. "Please, please, don't take the blame for this."

He turned around slowly. "Do something for me?"

"Of course, you know I will."

"Yes," he said with a faint laugh. "Yes, I know you will. Write your story," he said in a stronger voice. "And make it good. Everything, I want everything out. Maybe then I can live with it."

"Matthew and I'll write it," Laurel told him, and rose to take his hand. "And you'll live with it, Louis. I'm coming back and see that you do." She touched his cheek. "I love you."

With a ghost of a smile, he kissed her. "You're well matched with him, Laurel," he murmured, looking over at Matt. "You're as stubborn as he is. Come back," he agreed, squeezing her hands. "I'm going to need you."

When they walked from the house a few minutes later, Laurel breathed deep. Just the scent of night. The scent of life. "It's beautiful, isn't it?" She threw her face up to the stars. "We'd better call my father, let him know we have one hell of an exclusive on the way."

"Next time you decide to go for one," he said dryly, "remember we're partners. No more solo meets."

"You got it," she agreed. "Let's take your car," she decided, too keyed up to drive. "I can get mine tomorrow. Oh, God, Matthew!" Dropping down inside, she leaned back against the seat. "I never want to go through another night like this, even for a Pulitzer."

"That's what you get for taking off before you fixed dinner." His hands were finally steady, he noted as he turned the key. "Makes a man wonder what kind of wife he's getting."

"A gem," she assured him. "You're getting a gem, Bates." Leaning over, she kissed him. "I haven't thanked you for saving my life."

"No." He smiled, cupping the back of her neck so he could linger over the kiss. "What'd you have in mind?"

"Doing the same for you." She grinned at him. "We're eating out."

*   *   *   *   *

THE ART OF DECEPTION

For the Romance Writers of America.
In gratitude for the friends I've made
and the friends still to come.

Chapter 1

It was more like a castle than a house. The stone was gray, but beveled at the edges, Herodian-style, so that it shimmered with underlying colors. Towers and turrets jutted toward the sky, joined together by a crenellated roof. Windows were mullioned, long and narrow with diamond-shaped panes.

The structure—Adam would never think of it as anything so ordinary as a house—loomed over the Hudson, audacious and eccentric and, if such things were possible, pleased with itself. If the stories were true, it suited its owner perfectly.

All it required, Adam decided as he crossed the flagstone courtyard, was a dragon and a moat.

Two grinning gargoyles sat on either side of the wide stone steps. He passed by them with a reservation natural to a practical man. Gargoyles and turrets could be accepted in their proper place—but not in rural New York, a few hours' drive out of Manhattan.

Deciding to reserve judgment, he lifted the heavy brass knocker and let it fall against a door of thick Honduras mahogany. After a third pounding, the door creaked open. With strained patience, Adam looked down at a small woman with huge gray eyes, black braids and a soot-streaked face. She wore a rumpled sweatshirt and jeans that had seen better days.

Lazily, she rubbed her nose with the back of her hand and stared back.

"Hullo."

He bit back a sigh, thinking that if the staff ran to half-witted maids, the next few weeks were going to be very tedious. "I'm Adam Haines. Mr. Fairchild is expecting me," he enunciated.

Her eyes narrowed with curiosity or suspicion, he couldn't be sure. "Expecting you?" Her accent was broad New England. After another moment of staring, she frowned, shrugged, then moved aside to let him in.

The hall was wide and seemingly endless. The paneling gleamed a dull deep brown in the diffused light. Streaks of sun poured out of a high angled window and fell over the small woman, but he barely noticed. Paintings. For the moment, Adam forgot the fatigue of the journey and his annoyance. He forgot everything else but the paintings.

Van Gogh, Renoir, Monet. A museum could claim no finer exhibition. The power pulled at him. The hues, the tints, the brush strokes, and the overall magnificence they combined to create, tugged at his senses. Perhaps, in some strange way, Fairchild had been right to house them in something like a fortress. Turning, Adam saw the maid with her hands loosely folded, her huge gray eyes on his face. Impatience sprang back.

"Run along, will you? Tell Mr. Fairchild I'm here."

"And who might you be?" Obviously impatience didn't affect her.

"Adam Haines," he repeated. He was a man accustomed to servants—and one who expected efficiency.

"Ayah, so you said."

How could her eyes be smoky and clear at the same time? he wondered fleetingly. He gave a moment's thought to the fact that they reflected a maturity and intelligence at odds with her braids and smeared face. "Young lady..." He paced the words, slowly and distinctly. "Mr. Fairchild is expecting me. Just tell him I'm here. Can you handle that?"

A sudden dazzling smile lit her face. "Ayah."

The smile threw him off. He noticed for the first time that she had an exquisite mouth, full and sculpted. And there was something…something under the soot. Without thinking, he lifted a hand, intending to brush some off. The tempest hit.

"I can't do it! I tell you it's impossible. A travesty!" A man barreled down the long, curved stairs at an alarming rate. His face was shrouded in tragedy, his voice croaked with doom. "This is all your fault." Coming to a breathless stop, he pointed a long, thin finger at the little maid. "It's on your head, make no mistake."

Robin Goodfellow, Adam thought instantly. The man was the picture of Puck, short with a spritely build, a face molded on cherubic lines. The spare thatch of light hair nearly stood on end. He seemed to dance. His thin legs lifted and fell on the landing as he waved the long finger at the dark-haired woman. She remained serenely undisturbed.

"Your blood pressure's rising every second, Mr. Fairchild. You'd better take a deep breath or two before you have a spell."

"Spell!" Insulted, he danced faster. His face glowed pink with the effort. "I don't have spells, girl. I've never had a spell in my life."

"There's always a first time." She nodded, keeping her fingers lightly linked. "Mr. Adam Haines is here to see you."

"Haines? What the devil does Haines have to do with it? It's the end, I tell you. The climax." He placed a hand dramatically over his heart. The pale blue eyes watered so that for one awful moment, Adam thought he'd weep. "Haines?" he repeated. Abruptly he focused on Adam with a brilliant smile. "I'm expecting you, aren't I?"

Cautiously Adam offered his hand. "Yes."

"Glad you could come, I've been looking forward to it." Still showing his teeth, he pumped Adam's hand. "Into the parlor," he said, moving his grip from Adam's hand to his arm. "We'll have a drink." He walked with the quick bouncing stride of a man who hadn't a worry in the world.

In the parlor Adam had a quick impression of antiques and old magazines. At a wave of Fairchild's hand he sat on a

horsehair sofa that was remarkably uncomfortable. The maid
went to an enormous stone fireplace and began to scrub out
the hearth with quick, tuneful little whistles.

"I'm having scotch," Fairchild decided, and reached for a
decanter of Chivas Regal.

"That'll be fine."

"I admire your work, Adam Haines." Fairchild offered the
scotch with a steady hand. His face was calm, his voice mod-
erate. Adam wondered if he'd imagined the scene on the
stairs.

"Thank you." Sipping scotch, Adam studied the little genius across from him.

Small networks of lines crept out from Fairchild's eyes and
mouth. Without them and the thinning hair, he might have
been taken for a very young man. His aura of youth seemed
to spring from an inner vitality, a feverish energy. The eyes
were pure, unfaded blue. Adam knew they could see beyond
what others saw.

Philip Fairchild was, indisputably, one of the greatest living
artists of the twentieth century. His style ranged from the
flamboyant to the elegant, with a touch of everything in between. For more than thirty years, he'd enjoyed a position of
fame, wealth and respect in artistic and popular circles, something very few people in his profession achieved during their
lifetime.

Enjoy it he did, with a temperament that ranged from pompous to irascible to generous. From time to time he invited
other artists to his house on the Hudson, to spend weeks or
months working, absorbing or simply relaxing. At other times,
he barred everyone from the door and went into total seclusion.

"I appreciate the opportunity to work here for a few weeks,
Mr. Fairchild."

"My pleasure." The artist sipped scotch and sat, gesturing
with a regal wave of his hand—the king granting benediction.

Adam successfully hid a smirk. "I'm looking forward to
studying some of your paintings up close. There's such incredible variety in your work."

"I live for variety," Fairchild said with a giggle. From the hearth came a distinct snort. "Disrespectful brat," Fairchild muttered into his drink. When he scowled at her, the maid tossed a braid over her shoulder and plopped her rag noisily into the bucket. "Cards!" Fairchild bellowed, so suddenly Adam nearly dumped the scotch in his lap.

"I beg your pardon?"

"No need for that," Fairchild said graciously and shouted again. At the second bellow the epitome of butlers walked into the parlor.

"Yes, Mr. Fairchild." His voice was grave, lightly British. The dark suit he wore was a discreet contrast to the white hair and pale skin. He held himself like a soldier.

"See to Mr. Haines's car, Cards, and his luggage. The Wedgwood guest room."

"Very good, sir," the butler agreed after a slight nod from the woman at the hearth.

"And put his equipment in Kirby's studio," Fairchild added, grinning as the hearth scrubber choked. "Plenty of room for both of you," he told Adam before he scowled. "My daughter, you know. She's doing sculpture, up to her elbows in clay or chipping at wood and marble. I can't cope with it." Gripping his glass in both hands, Fairchild bowed his head. "God knows I try. I've put my soul into it. And for what?" he demanded, jerking his head up again. "For what?"

"I'm afraid I—"

"Failure!" Fairchild moaned, interrupting him. "To have to deal with failure at my age. It's on your head," he told the little brunette again. "You have to live with it—if you can."

Turning, she sat on the hearth, folded her legs under her and rubbed more soot on her nose. "You can hardly blame me if you have four thumbs and your soul's lost." The accent was gone. Her voice was low and smooth, hinting of European finishing schools. Adam's eyes narrowed. "You're determined to be better than I," she went on. "Therefore, you were doomed to fail before you began."

"Doomed to fail! Doomed to fail, am I?" He was up and dancing again, scotch sloshing around in his glass. "Philip

Fairchild will overcome, you heartless brat. He shall triumph! You'll eat your words.''

"Nonsense." Deliberately, she yawned. "You have your medium, Papa, and I have mine. Learn to live with it."

"Never." He slammed a hand against his heart again. "Defeat is a four-letter word."

"Six," she corrected, and, rising, commandeered the rest of his scotch.

He scowled at her, then at his empty glass. "I was speaking metaphorically."

"How clever." She kissed his cheek, transferring soot.

"Your face is filthy," Fairchild grumbled.

Lifting a brow, she ran a finger down his cheek. "So's yours."

They grinned at each other. For a flash, the resemblance was so striking, Adam wondered how he'd missed it. Kirby Fairchild, Philip's only child, a well-respected artist and eccentric in her own right. Just what, Adam wondered, was the darling of the jet set doing scrubbing out hearths?

"Come along, Adam." Kirby turned to him with a casual smile. "I'll show you to your room. You look tired. Oh, Papa," she added as she moved to the door, "this week's issue of *People* came. It's on the server. That'll keep him entertained," she said to Adam as she led him up the stairs.

He followed her slowly, noting that she walked with the faultless grace of a woman who'd been taught how to move. The pigtails swung at her back. Jeans, worn white at the stress points, had no designer label on the back pocket. Her canvas Nikes had broken shoelaces.

Kirby glided along the second floor, passing half a dozen doors before she stopped. She glanced at her hands, then at Adam. "You'd better open it. I'll get the knob filthy."

He pushed open the door and felt like he was stepping back in time. Wedgwood blue dominated the color scheme. The furniture was all Middle Georgian—carved armchairs, ornately worked tables. Again there were paintings, but this time, it was the woman behind him who held his attention.

"Why did you do that?"

"Do what?"

"Put on that act at the door." He walked back to where she stood at the threshold. Looking down, he calculated that she barely topped five feet. For the second time he had the urge to brush the soot from her face to discover what lay beneath.

"You looked so polished, and you positively glowered." She leaned a shoulder against the doorjamb. There was an elegance about him that intrigued her, because his eyes were sharp and arrogant. Though she didn't smile, the amusement in her expression was soft and ripe. "You were expecting a dimwitted parlor maid, so I made it easy for you. Cocktails at seven. Can you find your way back, or shall I come for you?"

He'd make do with that for now. "I'll find it."

"All right. *Ciao*, Adam."

Unwillingly fascinated, he watched her until she'd turned the corner at the end of the hall. Perhaps Kirby Fairchild would be as interesting a nut to crack as her father. But that was for later.

Adam closed the door and locked it. His bags were already set neatly beside the rosewood wardrobe. Taking the brief-case, Adam spun the combination lock and drew up the lid. He pulled out a small transmitter and flicked a switch.

"I'm in."

"Password," came the reply.

He swore, softly and distinctly. "Seagull. And that is, with-out a doubt, the most ridiculous password on record."

"Routine, Adam. We've got to follow routine."

"Sure." There'd been nothing routine since he'd stopped his car at the end of the winding uphill drive. "I'm in, Mc-Intyre, and I want you to know how much I appreciate your dumping me in this madhouse." With a flick of his thumb, he cut McIntyre off.

Without stopping to wash, Kirby jogged up the steps to her father's studio. She opened the door, then slammed it so that jars and tubes of paint shuddered on their shelves.

"What have you done this time?" she demanded.

"I'm starting over." Wispy brows knit, he huddled over a moist lump of clay. "Fresh start. Rebirth."

"I'm not talking about your futile attempts with clay. Adam Haines," she said before he could retort. Like a small tank, she advanced on him. Years before, Kirby had learned size was of no consequence if you had a knack for intimidation. She'd developed it meticulously. Slamming her palms down on his worktable, she stood nose to nose with him. "What the hell do you mean by asking him here and not even telling me?"

"Now, now, Kirby." Fairchild hadn't lived six decades without knowing when to dodge and weave. "It simply slipped my mind."

Better than anyone else, Kirby knew nothing slipped his mind. "What're you up to now, Papa?"

"Up to?" He smiled guilelessly.

"Why did you ask him here now, of all times?"

"I've admired his work. So've you," he pointed out when her mouth thinned. "He wrote such a nice letter about *Scarlet Moon* when it was exhibited at the Metropolitan last month."

Her brow lifted, an elegant movement under a layer of soot. "You don't invite everyone who compliments your work."

"Of course not, my sweet. That would be impossible. One must be...selective. Now I must get back to my work while the mood's flowing."

"Something's going to flow," she promised. "Papa, if you've a new scheme after you promised—"

"Kirby!" His round, smooth face quivered with emotion. His lips trembled. It was only one of his talents. "You'd doubt the word of your own father? The seed that spawned you?"

"That makes me sound like a gardenia, and it won't work." She crossed her arms over her chest. Frowning, Fairchild poked at the unformed clay.

"My motives are completely altruistic."

"Hah."

"Adam Haines is a brilliant young artist. You've said so yourself."

"Yes, he is, and I'm sure he'd be delightful company under different circumstances." She leaned forward, grabbing her father's chin in her hand. "Not now."

"Ungracious," Fairchild said with disapproval. "Your mother, rest her soul, would be very disappointed in you."

Kirby ground her teeth. "Papa, the Van Gogh!"

"Coming along nicely," he assured her. "Just a few more days."

Knowing she was in danger of tearing out her hair, she stalked to the tower window. "Oh, bloody murder."

Senility, she decided. It had to be senility. How could he consider having that man here now? Next week, next month, but now? That man, Kirby thought ruthlessly, was nobody's fool.

At first glance she'd decided he wasn't just attractive—very attractive—but sharp. Those big camel's eyes gleamed with intelligence. The long, thin mouth equaled determination. Perhaps he was a bit pompous in his bearing and manner, but he wasn't soft. No, she was certain instinctively that Adam Haines would be hard as nails.

She'd like to do him in bronze, she mused. The straight nose, the sharp angles and planes in his face. His hair was nearly the color of deep, polished bronze, and just a tad too long for convention. She'd want to capture his air of arrogance and authority. But not now!

Sighing, she moved her shoulders. Behind her back, Fairchild grinned. When she turned back to him, he was studiously intent on his clay.

"He'll want to come up here, you know." Despite the soot, she dipped her hands in her pockets. They had a problem; now it had to be dealt with. For the better part of her life, Kirby had sorted through the confusion her father gleefully created. The truth was, she'd have had it no other way. "It would seem odd if we didn't show him your studio."

"We'll show him tomorrow."

"He mustn't see the Van Gogh." Kirby planted her feet, prepared to do battle on this one point, if not the others.

"You're not going to make this more complicated than you already have."

"He won't see it. Why should he?" Fairchild glanced up briefly, eyes wide. "It has nothing to do with him."

Though she realized it was foolish, Kirby was reassured. No, he wouldn't see it, she thought. Her father might be a little...unique, she decided, but he wasn't careless. Neither was she. "Thank God it's nearly finished."

"Another few days and off it goes, high into the mountains of South America." He made a vague, sweeping gesture with his hands.

Moving over, Kirby uncovered the canvas that stood on an easel in the far corner. She studied it as an artist, as a lover of art and as a daughter.

The pastoral scene was not peaceful but vibrant. The brush strokes were jagged, almost fierce, so that the simple setting had a frenzied kind of motion. No, it didn't sit still waiting for admiration. It reached out and grabbed by the throat. It spoke of pain, of triumph, of agonies and joys. Her lips tilted because she had no choice. Van Gogh, she knew, could have done no better.

"Papa." When she turned her head, their eyes met in perfect understanding. "You are incomparable."

By seven, Kirby had not only resigned herself to their house guest, but was prepared to enjoy him. It was a basic trait of her character to enjoy what she had to put up with. As she poured vermouth into a glass, she realized she was looking forward to seeing him again, and to getting beneath the surface gloss. She had a feeling there might be some fascinating layers in Adam Haines.

She dropped into a high-backed chair, crossed her legs and tuned back in to her father's rantings.

"It hates me, fails me at every turn. Why, Kirby?" He spread his hands in an impassioned plea. "I'm a good man, loving father, faithful friend."

"It's your attitude, Papa." She shrugged a shoulder as she drank. "Your emotional plane's faulty."

"There's nothing wrong with my emotional plane." Sniffing, Fairchild lifted his glass. "Not a damn thing wrong with it. It's the clay that's the problem, not me."

"You're cocky," she said simply. Fairchild made a sound like a train straining up a long hill.

"Cocky? *Cocky?* What the devil kind of word is that?"

"Adjective. Two syllables, five letters."

Adam heard the byplay as he walked toward the parlor. After a peaceful afternoon, he wondered if he was ready to cope with another bout of madness. Fairchild's voice was rising steadily, and as Adam paused in the doorway, he saw that the artist was up and shuffling again.

McIntyre was going to pay for this, Adam decided. He'd see to it that revenge was slow and thorough. When Fairchild pointed an accusing finger, Adam followed its direction. For an instant he was totally and uncharacteristically stunned.

The woman in the chair was so completely removed from the grimy, pigtailed chimney sweep, he found it nearly impossible to associate the two. She wore a thin silk dress as dark as her hair, draped at the bodice and slit up the side to show off one smooth thigh. He studied her profile as she watched her father rant. It was gently molded, classically oval with a very subtle sweep of cheekbones. Her lips were full, curved now in just a hint of a smile. Without the soot, her skin was somewhere between gold and honey with a look of luxurious softness. Only the eyes reminded him this was the same woman—gray and large and amused. Lifting one hand, she tossed back the dark hair that covered her shoulders.

There was something more than beauty here. Adam knew he'd seen women with more beauty than Kirby Fairchild. But there was something... He groped for the word, but it eluded him.

As if sensing him, she turned—just her head. Again she stared at him, openly and with curiosity, as her father continued his ravings. Slowly, very slowly, she smiled. Adam felt the power slam into him.

Sex, he realized abruptly. Kirby Fairchild exuded sex the way other women exuded perfume. Raw, unapologetic sex.

With a quick assessment typical of him, Adam decided she wouldn't be easy to deceive. However he handled Fairchild, he'd have to tread carefully with Fairchild's daughter. He decided as well that he already wanted to make love to her. He'd have to tread *very* carefully.

"Adam." She spoke in a soft voice that nonetheless carried over her father's shouting. "You seem to have found us. Come in, Papa's nearly done."

"Done? I'm undone. And by my own child." Fairchild moved toward Adam as he entered the room. "Cocky, she says. I ask you, is that a word for a daughter to use?"

"An aperitif?" Kirby asked. She rose with a fluid motion that Adam had always associated with tall, willowy women.

"Yes, thank you."

"Your room's agreeable?" His face wreathed in smiles again, Fairchild plopped down on the sofa.

"Very agreeable." The best way to handle it, Adam decided, was to pretend everything was normal. Pretenses were, after all, part of the game. "You have an...exceptional house."

"I'm fond of it." Content, Fairchild leaned back. "It was built near the turn of the century by a wealthy and insane English lord. You'll take Adam on a tour tomorrow, won't you, Kirby?"

"Of course." As she handed Adam a glass, she smiled into his eyes. Diamonds, cold as ice, glittered at her ears. He could feel the heat rise.

"I'm looking forward to it." Style, he concluded. Whether natural or developed, Miss Fairchild had style.

She smiled over the rim of her own glass, thinking precisely the same thing about Adam. "We aim to please."

A cautious man, Adam turned to Fairchild again. "Your art collection rivals a museum's. The Titian in my room is fabulous."

The Titian, Kirby thought in quick panic. How could she have forgotten it? What in God's name could she do about it? No difference. It made no difference, she reassured herself. It couldn't, because there was nothing to be done.

"The Hudson scene on the west wall—" Adam turned to her just as Kirby was telling herself to relax "—is that your work?"

"My... Oh, yes." She smiled as she remembered. She'd deal with the Titian at the first opportunity. "I'd forgotten that. It's sentimental, I'm afraid. I was home from school and had a crush on the chauffeur's son. We used to neck down there."

"He had buck teeth," Fairchild reminded her with a snort.

"Love conquers all," Kirby decided.

"The Hudson River bank is a hell of a place to lose your virginity," her father stated, suddenly severe. He swirled his drink, then downed it.

Enjoying the abrupt paternal disapproval, she decided to poke at it. "I didn't lose my virginity on the Hudson River bank." Amusement glimmered in her eyes. "I lost it in a Renault in Paris."

Love conquers all, Adam repeated silently.

"Dinner is served," Cards announced with dignity from the doorway.

"And about time, too." Fairchild leaped up. "A man could starve in his own home."

With a smile at her father's retreating back, Kirby offered Adam her hand. "Shall we go in?"

In the dining room, Fairchild's paintings dominated. An enormous Waterford chandelier showered light over mahogany and crystal. A massive stone fireplace thundered with flame and light. There were scents of burning wood, candles and roasted meat. There was Breton lace and silver. Still, his paintings dominated.

It appeared he had no distinct style. Art was his style, whether he depicted a sprawling, light-filled landscape or a gentle, shadowy portrait. Bold brush strokes or delicate ones, oils streaked on with a pallet knife or misty watercolors, he'd done them all. Magnificently.

As varied as his paintings were his opinions on other artists. While they sat at the long, laden table, Fairchild spoke of each artist personally, as if he'd been transported back in time and had developed relationships with Raphael, Goya, Manet.

His theories were intriguing, his knowledge was impressive. The artist in Adam responded to him. The practical part, the part that had come to do a job, remained cautious. The opposing forces made him uncomfortable. His attraction to the woman across from him made him itchy.

He cursed McIntyre.

Adam decided the weeks with the Fairchilds might be interesting despite their eccentricities. He didn't care for the complications, but he'd allowed himself to be pulled in. For now, he'd sit back and observe, waiting for the time to act.

The information he had on them was sketchy. Fairchild was just past sixty, a widower of nearly twenty years. His art and his talent were no secrets, but his personal life was veiled. Perhaps due to temperament. Perhaps, Adam mused, due to necessity.

About Kirby, he knew almost nothing. Professionally, she'd kept a low profile until her first showing the year before. Though it had been an unprecedented success, both she and her father rarely sought publicity for their work. Personally, she was often written up in the glossies and tabloids as she jetted to Saint Moritz with this year's tennis champion or to Martinique with the current Hollywood golden boy. He knew she was twenty-seven and unmarried. Not for lack of opportunity, he concluded. She was the type of woman men would constantly pursue. In another century, duels would have been fought over her. Adam thought she'd have enjoyed the melodrama.

From their viewpoint, the Fairchilds knew of Adam only what was public knowledge. He'd been born under comfortable circumstances, giving him both the time and means to develop his talent. At the age of twenty, his reputation as an artist had begun to take root. A dozen years later, he was well established. He'd lived in Paris, then in Switzerland, before settling back in the States.

Still, during his twenties, he'd traveled often while painting. With Adam, his art had always come first. However, under the poised exterior, under the practicality and sophistication, there was a taste for adventure and a streak of cunning. So there had been McIntyre.

He'd just have to learn control, Adam told himself as he thought of McIntyre. He'd just have to learn how to say no, absolutely no. The next time Mac had an inspiration, he could go to hell with it.

When they settled back in the parlor with coffee and brandy, Adam calculated that he could finish the job in a couple of weeks. True, the place was immense, but there were only a handful of people in it. After his tour he'd know his way around well enough. Then it would be routine.

Satisfied, he concentrated on Kirby. At the moment she was the perfect hostess—charming, personable. All class and sophistication. She was, momentarily, precisely the type of woman who'd always appealed to him—well-groomed, well-mannered, intelligent, lovely. The room smelled of hothouse roses, wood smoke and her own tenuous scent, which seemed to blend the two. Adam began to relax with it.

"Why don't you play, Kirby?" Fairchild poured a second brandy for himself and Adam. "It helps clear my mind."

"All right." With a quick smile for Adam, Kirby moved to the far end of the room, running a finger over a wing-shaped instrument he'd taken for a small piano.

It took only a few notes for him to realize he'd been wrong. A harpsichord, he thought, astonished. The tinny music floated up. Bach. Adam recognized the composer and wondered if he'd fallen down the rabbit hole. No one—no one normal—played Bach on a harpsichord in a castle in the twentieth century.

Fairchild sat, his eyes half closed, one thin finger tapping, while Kirby continued to play. Her eyes were grave, her mouth was faintly moist and sober. Suddenly, without missing a note or moving another muscle, she sent Adam a slow wink. The notes flowed into Brahms. In that instant, Adam knew he was not only going to take her to bed. He was going to paint her.

"I've got it!" Fairchild leaped up and scrambled around the room. "I've got it. Inspiration. The golden light!"

"Amen," Kirby murmured.

"I'll show you, you wicked child." Grinning like one of his gargoyles, Fairchild leaned over the harpsichord. "By the end of the week, I'll have a piece that'll make anything you've ever done look like a doorstop."

Kirby raised her brows and kissed him on the mouth. "Goat droppings."

"You'll eat your words," he warned as he dashed out of the room.

"I sincerely hope not." Rising, she picked up her drink. "Papa has a nasty competitive streak." Which constantly pleased her. "More brandy?"

"Your father has a...unique personality." An emerald flashed on her hand as she filled her glass again. He saw her hands were narrow, delicate against the hard glitter of the stone. But there'd be strength in them, he reminded himself as he moved to the bar to join her. Strength was indispensable to an artist.

"You're diplomatic." She turned and looked up at him. There was the faintest hint of rose on her lips. "You're a very diplomatic person, aren't you, Adam?"

He'd already learned not to trust the nunlike expression. "Under some circumstances."

"Under most circumstances. Too bad."

"Is it?"

Because she enjoyed personal contact during any kind of confrontation, she kept her eyes on his while she drank. Her irises were the purest gray he'd ever seen, with no hint of other colors. "I think you'd be a very interesting man if you didn't bind yourself up. I believe you think everything through very carefully."

"You see that as a problem?" His voice had cooled. "It's a remarkable observation after such a short time."

No, he wouldn't be a bore, she decided, pleased with his annoyance. It was lack of emotion Kirby found tedious. "I could've come by it easily enough after an hour, but I'd already seen your work. Besides talent, you have self-control, dignity and a strong sense of the conventional.''

"Why do I feel as though I've been insulted?''

"Perceptive, too.'' She smiled, that slow curving of lips that was fascinating to watch. When he answered it, she made up her mind quickly. She'd always found it the best way. Still watching him, she set down her brandy. "I'm impulsive,'' she explained. "I want to see what it feels like.''

Her arms were around him, her lips on his, in a move that caught him completely off balance. He had a very brief impression of wood smoke and roses, of incredible softness and strength, before she drew back. The hint of a smile remained as she picked up her brandy and finished it off. She'd enjoyed the brief kiss, but she'd enjoyed shocking him a great deal more.

"Very nice,'' she said with borderline approval. "Breakfast is from seven on. Just ring for Cards if you need anything. Good night.''

She turned to leave, but he took her arm. Kirby found herself whirled around. When their bodies collided, the surprise was hers.

"You caught me off guard,'' he said softly. "I can do much better than nice.''

He took her mouth swiftly, molding her to him. Soft to hard, thin silk to crisp linen. There was something primitive in her taste, something...ageless. She brought to his mind the woods on an autumn evening—dark, pungent and full of small mysteries.

The kiss lengthened, deepened without plan on either side. Her response was instant, as her responses often were. It was boundless as they often were. She moved her hands from his shoulders, to his neck, to his face, as if she were already sculpting. Something vibrated between them.

For the moment, blood ruled. She was accustomed to it; he wasn't. He was accustomed to reason, but he found none here. Here was heat and passion, needs and desires without questions or answers.

Ultimately, reluctantly, he drew back. Caution, because he was used to winning, was his way.

She could still taste him. Kirby wondered, as she felt his breath feather over her lips, how she'd misjudged him. Her head was spinning, something new for her. She understood heated blood, a fast pulse, but not the clouding of her mind.

Not certain how long he'd have the advantage, Adam smiled at her. "Better?"

"Yes." She waited until the floor became solid under her feet again. "That was quite an improvement." Like her father, she knew when to dodge and weave. She eased herself away and moved to the doorway. She'd have to do some thinking, and some reevaluating. "How long are you here, Adam?"

"Four weeks," he told her, finding it odd she didn't know.

"Do you intend to sleep with me before you go?"

Torn between amusement and admiration, he stared at her. He respected candor, but he wasn't used to it in quite so blunt a form. In this case, he decided to follow suit. "Yes."

She nodded, ignoring the little thrill that raced up her spine. Games—she liked to play them. To win them. Kirby sensed one was just beginning between her and Adam. "I'll have to think about that, won't I? Good night."

Chapter 2

Shafts of morning light streamed in the long windows of the dining room and tossed their diamond pattern on the floor. Outside the trees were touched with September. Leaves blushed from salmon to crimson, the colors mixed with golds and rusts and the last stubborn greens. The lawn was alive with fall flowers and shrubs that seemed caught on fire. Adam had his back to the view as he studied Fairchild's paintings.

Again, Adam was struck with the incredible variety of styles Fairchild cultivated. There was a still life with the light and shadows of a Goya, a landscape with the frantic colors of a Van Gogh, a portrait with the sensitivity and grace of a Raphael. Because of its subject, it was the portrait that drew him.

A frail, dark-haired woman looked out from the canvas. There was an air of serenity, of patience, about her. The eyes were the same pure gray as Kirby's, but the features were gentler, more even. Kirby's mother had been a rare beauty, a rare woman who looked like she'd had both strength and understanding. While she wouldn't have scrubbed at a hearth, she would have understood the daughter who did. That Adam could see this, be certain of it, without ever having met Rachel Fairchild, was only proof of Fairchild's genius. He created life with oil and brush.

The next painting, executed in the style of Gainsborough, was a full-length portrait of a young girl. Glossy black curls fell over the shoulders of a white muslin dress, tucked at the bodice, belled at the skirt. She wore white stockings and neat black buckle shoes. Touches of color came from the wide pink sash around her waist and the dusky roses she carried in a basket. But this was no demure *Pinky*.

The girl held her head high, tilting it with youthful arrogance. The half smile spoke of devilment while the huge gray eyes danced with both. No more than eleven or twelve, Adam calculated. Even then, Kirby must have been a handful.

"An adorable child, isn't she?" Kirby stood at the doorway as she had for five full minutes. She'd enjoyed watching and dissecting him as much as Adam had enjoyed dissecting the painting.

He stood very straight—prep school training, Kirby decided. Yet his hands were dipped comfortably in his pockets. Even in a casual sweater and jeans, there was an air of formality about him. Contrasts intrigued her, as a woman and as an artist.

Turning, Adam studied her as meticulously as he had her portrait. The day before, he'd seen her go from grubby urchin to sleek sophisticate. Today she was the picture of the bohemian artist. Her face was free of cosmetics and unframed as her hair hung in a ponytail down her back. She wore a shapeless black sweater, baggy, paint-streaked jeans and no shoes. To his annoyance, she continued to attract him.

She turned her head and, by accident or design, the sunlight fell over her profile. In that instant, she was breathtaking. Kirby sighed as she studied her own face. "A veritable angel."

"Apparently her father knew better."

She laughed, low and rich. His calm, dry voice pleased her enormously. "He did at that, but not everyone sees it." She was glad he had, simply because she appreciated a sharp eye and a clever mind. "Have you had breakfast?"

He relaxed. She'd turned again so that the light no longer

illuminated her face. She was just an attractive, friendly woman. "No, I've been busy being awed."

"Oh, well, one should never be awed on an empty stomach. It's murder on the digestion." After pressing a button, she linked her arm through his and led him to the table. "After we've eaten, I'll take you through the house."

"I'd like that." Adam took the seat opposite her. She wore no fragrance this morning but soap—clean and sexless. It aroused nonetheless.

A woman clumped into the room. She had a long bony face, small mud-brown eyes and an unfortunate nose. Her graying hair was scraped back and bundled at the nape of her neck. The deep furrows in her brow indicated her pessimistic nature. Glancing over, Kirby smiled.

"Good morning, Tulip. You'll have to send a tray up to Papa, he won't budge out of the tower." She drew a linen napkin from its ring. "Just toast and coffee for me, and don't lecture. I'm not getting any taller."

After a grumbling disapproval, Tulip turned to Adam. His order of bacon and eggs received the same grumble before she clumped back out again.

"Tulip?" Adam cocked a brow as he turned to Kirby.

"Fits beautifully, doesn't it?" Lips sober, eyes amused, she propped her elbows on the table and dropped her face in her hands. "She's really a marvel as far as organizing. We've had a running battle over food for fifteen years. Tulip insists that if I eat, I'll grow. After I hit twenty, I figured I'd proved her wrong. I wonder why adults insist on making such absurd statements to children."

The robust young maid who'd served dinner the night before brought in coffee. She showered sunbeam smiles over Adam.

"Thank you, Polly." Kirby's voice was gentle, but Adam caught the warning glance and the maid's quick blush.

"Yes, ma'am." Without a backward glance, Polly scurried from the room. Kirby poured the coffee herself.

"Our Polly is very sweet," she began. "But she has a habit of becoming, ah, a bit too matey with two-thirds of the male population." Setting down the silver coffee urn, Kirby smiled across the table. "If you've a taste for slap and tickle, Polly's your girl. Otherwise, I wouldn't encourage her. I've even had to warn her off Papa."

The picture of the lusty young Polly with the Pucklike Fairchild zipped into Adam's mind. It lingered there a moment with perfect clarity until he roared with laughter.

Well, well, well, Kirby mused, watching him. A man who could laugh like that had tremendous potential. She wondered what other surprises he had tucked away. Hopefully she'd discover quite a few during his stay.

Picking up the cream pitcher, he added a stream to his coffee. "You have my word, I'll resist temptation."

"She's built stupendously," Kirby observed as she sipped her coffee black.

"Really?" It was the first time she'd seen his grin—quick, crooked and wicked. "I hadn't noticed."

Kirby studied him while the grin did odd things to her nervous system. Surprise again, she told herself, then reached for her coffee. "I've misjudged you, Adam," she murmured. "A definite miscalculation. You're not precisely what you seem."

He thought of the small transmitter locked in his dignified briefcase. "Is anyone?"

"Yes." She gave him a long and completely guileless look. "Yes, some people are precisely what they seem, for better or worse."

"You?" He asked because he suddenly wanted to know badly who and what she was. Not for McIntyre, not for the job, but for himself.

She was silent a moment as a quick, ironic smile moved over her face. He guessed, correctly, that she was laughing at herself. "What I seem to be today is what I am—today." With one of her lightning changes, she threw off the mood. "Here's breakfast."

They talked a little as they ate, inconsequential things, polite things that two relative strangers speak about over a meal. They'd both been raised to handle such situations—small talk, intelligent give-and-take that skimmed over the surface and meant absolutely nothing.

But Kirby found herself aware of him, more aware than she should have been. More aware than she wanted to be.

Just what kind of man was he, she wondered as he sprinkled salt on his eggs. She'd already concluded he wasn't nearly as conventional as he appeared to be—or perhaps as he thought himself to be. There was an adventurer in there, she was certain. Her only annoyance stemmed from the fact that it had taken her so long to see it.

She remembered the strength and turbulence of the kiss they'd shared. He'd be a demanding lover. And a fascinating one. Which meant she'd have to be a great deal more careful. She no longer believed he'd be easily managed. Something in his eyes...

Quickly she backed off from that line of thought. The point was, she had to manage him. Finishing off her coffee, she sent up a quick prayer that her father had the Van Gogh well concealed.

"The tour begins from bottom to top," she said brightly. Rising, she held out her hand. "The dungeons are marvelously morbid and damp, but I think we'll postpone that in respect of your cashmere sweater."

"Dungeons?" He accepted her offered arm and walked from the room with her.

"We don't use them now, I'm afraid, but if the vibrations are right, you can still hear a few moans and rattles." She said it so casually, he nearly believed her. That, he realized, was one of her biggest talents. Making the ridiculous sound plausible. "Lord Wickerton, the original owner, was quite dastardly."

"You approve?"

"Approve?" She weighed this as they walked. "Perhaps not, but it's easy to be intrigued by things that happened nearly a hundred years ago. Evil can become romantic after a certain period of time, don't you think?"

"I've never looked at it quite that way."

"That's because you have a very firm grip on what's right and what's wrong."

He stopped and, because their arms were linked, Kirby stopped beside him. He looked down at her with an intensity that put her on guard. "And you?"

She opened her mouth, then closed it again before she could say something foolish. "Let's just say I'm flexible. You'll enjoy this room," she said, pushing open a door. "It's rather sturdy and staid."

Taking the insult in stride, Adam walked through with her. For nearly an hour they wandered from room to room. It occurred to him that he'd underestimated the sheer size of the place. Halls snaked and angled, rooms popped up where they were least expected, some tiny, some enormous. Unless he got very, very lucky, Adam concluded, the job would take him a great deal of time.

Pushing open two heavy, carved doors, Kirby led him into the library. It had two levels and was the size of an average two-bedroom apartment. Faded Persian rugs were scattered over the floor. The far wall was glassed in the small diamond panes that graced most of the windows in the house. The rest of the walls were lined floor to ceiling with books. A glance showed Chaucer standing beside D. H. Lawrence. Stephen King leaned against Milton. There wasn't even the pretense of organization, but there was the rich smell of leather, dust and lemon oil.

The books dominated the room and left no space for paintings. But there was sculpture.

Adam crossed the room and lifted a figure of a stallion carved in walnut. Freedom, grace, movement, seemed to vibrate in his hands. He could almost hear the steady heartbeat against his palm.

There was a bronze bust of Fairchild on a high, round stand. The artist had captured the puckishness, the energy, but more, she'd captured a gentleness and generosity Adam had yet to see.

In silence, he wandered the room, examining each piece as Kirby looked on. He made her nervous, and she struggled against it. Nerves were something she felt rarely, and never acknowledged. Her work had been looked at before, she reminded herself. What else did an artist want but recognition? She linked her fingers and remained silent. His opinion hardly mattered, she told herself, then moistened her lips.

He picked up a piece of marble shaped into a roaring mass of flames. Though the marble was white, the fire was real. Like every other piece he'd examined, the mass of marble flames was physical. Kirby had inherited her father's gift for creating life.

For a moment, Adam forgot all the reasons he was there and thought only of the woman and the artist. "Where did you study?"

The flip remark she'd been prepared to make vanished from her mind the moment he turned and looked at her with those calm brown eyes. "École des Beaux-Arts formally. But Papa taught me always."

He turned the marble in his hands. Even a pedestrian imagination would've felt the heat. Adam could all but smell it. "How long have you been sculpting?"

"Seriously? About four years."

"Why the hell have you only had one exhibition? Why are you burying it here?"

Anger. She lifted her brow at it. She'd wondered just what sort of a temper he'd have, but she hadn't expected to see it break through over her work. "I'm having another in the spring," she said evenly. "Charles Larson's handling it." Abruptly uncomfortable, she shrugged. "Actually, I was pressured into having the other. I wasn't ready."

"That's ridiculous." He held up the marble as if she hadn't seen it before. "Absolutely ridiculous."

Why should it make her feel vulnerable to have her work in the palm of his hand? Turning away, Kirby ran a finger down her father's bronze nose. "I wasn't ready," she repeated, not sure why, when she never explained herself to anyone, she was explaining such things to him. "I had to be sure, you see. There are those who say—who'll always say— that I rode on Papa's coattails. That's to be expected." She blew out a breath, but her hand remained on the bust of her father. "I had to know differently. *I* had to know."

He hadn't expected sensitivity, sweetness, vulnerability. Not from her. But he'd seen it in her work, and he'd heard it in her voice. It moved him, every bit as much as her passion had. "Now you do."

She turned again, and her chin tilted. "Now I do." With an odd smile, she crossed over and took the marble from him. "I've never told anyone that before—not even Papa." When she looked up, her eyes were quiet, soft and curious. "I wonder why it should be you."

He touched her hair, something he'd wanted to do since he'd seen the morning sun slant on it. "I wonder why I'm glad it was."

She took a step back. There was no ignoring a longing so quick and so strong. There was no forgetting caution. "Well, we'll have to think about it, I suppose. This concludes the first part of our tour." She set the marble down and smiled easily. "All comments and questions are welcome."

He'd dipped below the surface, Adam realized, and she didn't care for it. That he understood. "Your home's… overwhelming," he decided, and made her smile broaden into a grin. "I'm disappointed there isn't a moat and dragon."

"Just try leaving your vegetables on your plate and you'll see what a dragon Tulip can be. As to the moat…" She started to shrug an apology, then remembered. "Toadstools, how could I have forgotten?"

Without waiting for an answer, she grabbed his hand and dashed back to the parlor. "No moat," she told him as she went directly to the fireplace. "But there are secret passageways."

"I should've known."

"It's been quite a while since I—" She broke off and began to mutter to herself as she pushed and tugged at the carved oak mantel. "I swear it's one of the flowers along here—there's a button, but you have to catch it just right." With an annoyed gesture, she flicked the ponytail back over her shoulder. Adam watched her long, elegant fingers push and prod. He saw that her nails were short, rounded and unpainted. A schoolgirl's nails, or a nun's. Yet the impression of sexual vitality remained. "I know it's here, but I can't quite... *Et voilà.*" Pleased with herself, Kirby stepped back as a section of paneling slid creakily aside. "Needs some oil," she decided.

"Impressive," Adam murmured, already wondering if he'd gotten lucky. "Does it lead to the dungeons?"

"It spreads out all over the house in a maze of twists and turns." Moving to the entrance with him, she peered into the dark. "There's an entrance in nearly every room. A button on the other side opens or closes the panel. The passages are horribly dark and moldy." With a shudder, she stepped back. "Perhaps that's why I forgot about them." Suddenly cold, she rubbed her hands together. "I used to haunt them as a child, drove the servants mad."

"I can imagine." But he saw the quick dread in her eyes as she looked back into the dark.

"I paid for it, I suppose. One day my flashlight went out on me and I couldn't find my way out. There're spiders down there as big as schnauzers." She laughed, but took another step back. "I don't know how long I was in there, but when Papa found me I was hysterical. Needless to say, I found other ways to terrorize the staff."

"It still frightens you."

She glanced up, prepared to brush it off. For the second time the quiet look in his eyes had her telling the simple truth. "Yes. Yes, apparently it does. Well, now that I've confessed my neurosis, let's move on."

The panel closed, grumbling in protest as she pushed the control. Adam felt rather than heard her sigh of relief. When he took her hand, he found it cold. He wanted to warm it, and her. Instead he concentrated on just what the passages could mean to him. With them he'd have access to every room without the risk of running into one of the staff or one of the Fairchilds. When an opportunity was tossed in your lap, you took it for what it was worth. He'd begin tonight.

"A delivery for you, Miss Fairchild."

Both Kirby and Adam paused on the bottom landing of the stairs. Kirby eyed the long white box the butler held in his hands. "Not again, Cards."

"It would appear so, miss."

"Galoshes." Kirby sniffed, scratched a point just under her jaw and studied the box. "I'll just have to be more firm."

"Just as you say, miss."

"Cards..." She smiled at him, and though his face remained inscrutable, Adam would have sworn he came to attention. "I know it's rude, but give them to Polly. I can't bear to look at another red rose."

"As you wish, miss. And the card?"

"Details," she muttered, then sighed. "Leave it on my desk, I'll deal with it. Sorry, Adam." Turning, she started up the stairs again. "I've been bombarded with roses for the last three weeks. I've refused to become Jared's mistress, but he's persistent." More exasperated than annoyed, she shook her head as they rounded the first curve. "I suppose I'll have to threaten to tell his wife."

"Might work," Adam murmured.

"I ask you, shouldn't a man know better by the time he hits sixty?" Rolling her eyes, she bounced up the next three steps. "I can't imagine what he's thinking of."

She smelled of soap and was shapeless in the sweater and jeans. Moving behind her to the second story, Adam could imagine very well.

The second floor was lined with bedrooms. Each was unique, each furnished in a different style. The more Adam saw of the house, the more he was charmed. And the more he realized how complicated his task was going to be.

"The last room, my boudoir." She gave him the slow, lazy smile that made his palms itchy. "I'll promise not to compromise you as long as you're aware my promises aren't known for being kept." With a light laugh, she pushed open the door and stepped inside. "Fish fins."

"I beg your pardon?"

"Whatever for?" Ignoring him, Kirby marched into the

room. "Do you see that?" she demanded. In a gesture remarkably like her father's, she pointed at the bed. A scruffy dog lay like a lump in the center of a wedding ring quilt. Frowning, Adam walked a little closer.

"What is it?"

"A dog, of course."

He looked at the gray ball of hair, which seemed to have no front or back. "It's possible."

A stubby tail began to thump on the quilt.

"This is no laughing matter, Montique. I take the heat, you know."

Adam watched the bundle shift until he could make out a head. The eyes were still hidden behind the mop of fur, but there was a little black nose and a lolling tongue. "Somehow I'd've pictured you with a brace of Afghan hounds."

"What? Oh." Giving the mop on the bed a quick pat, she turned back to Adam. "Montique doesn't belong to me, he belongs to Isabelle." She sent the dog an annoyed glance. "She's going to be very put out."

Adam frowned at the unfamiliar name. Had McIntyre missed someone? "Is she one of the staff?"

"Good grief, no." Kirby let out a peal of laughter that had Montique squirming in delight. "Isabelle serves no one. She's... Well, here she is now. There'll be the devil to pay," she added under her breath.

Shifting his head, Adam looked toward the doorway. He started to tell Kirby there was no one there when a movement caught his eye. He looked down on a large buff-colored Siamese. Her eyes were angled, icily blue and, though he hadn't considered such things before, regally annoyed. The cat crossed the threshold, sat and stared up at Kirby.

"Don't look at me like that," Kirby tossed out. "I had nothing to do with it. If he wanders in here, it has nothing to do with me." Isabelle flicked her tail and made a low, dangerous sound in her throat. "I won't tolerate your threats, and I will not keep my door locked." Kirby folded her arms and tapped a foot on the Aubusson carpet. "I refuse to change a habit of a lifetime for your convenience. You'll just have to keep a closer eye on him."

As he watched silently, Adam was certain he saw genuine temper in Kirby's eyes—the kind of temper one person aims toward another person. Gently he placed a hand on her arm and waited for her to look at him. "Kirby, you're arguing with a cat."

"Adam." Just as gently, she patted his hand. "Don't worry. I can handle it." With a lift of her brow, she turned back to Isabelle. "Take him, then, and put him on a leash if you don't want him wandering. And the next time, I'd appreciate it if you'd knock before you come into my room."

With a flick of her tail, Isabelle moved to the bed and stared up at Montique. He thumped his tail, tongue lolling, before he leaped clumsily to the floor. With a kind of jiggling trot, he followed the gliding cat from the room.

"He went with her," Adam murmured.

"Of course he did," Kirby retorted. "She has a beastly temper."

Refusing to be taken for a fool, Adam gave Kirby a long, uncompromising look. "Are you trying to tell me that the dog belongs to that cat?"

"Do you have a cigarette?" she countered. "I rarely smoke, but Isabelle affects me that way." She noted that his eyes never lost their cool, mildly annoyed expression as he took one out and lit it for her. Kirby had to swallow a chuckle. Adam was, she decided, remarkable. She drew on the cigarette and blew out the smoke without inhaling. "Isabelle maintains that Montique followed her home. I think she kidnapped him. It would be just like her."

Games, he thought again. Two could play. "And to whom does Isabelle belong?"

"Belong?" Kirby's eyes widened. "Isabelle belongs to no one but herself. Who'd want to lay claim to such a wicked creature?"

And he could play as well as anyone. Taking the cigarette from her, Adam drew in smoke. "If you dislike her, why don't you just get rid of her?"

She nipped the cigarette from his fingers again. "I can hardly do that as long as she pays the rent, can I? There, that's enough," she decided after another drag. "I'm quite calm again." She handed him back the cigarette before she walked to the door. "I'll take you up to Papa's studio. We'll just skip over the third floor, everything's draped with dustcovers."

Adam opened his mouth, then decided that some things were best left alone. Dismissing odd cats and ugly dogs, he followed Kirby back into the hall again. The stairs continued up in a lazy arch to the third floor, then veered sharply and became straight and narrow. Kirby stopped at the transition point and gestured down the hall.

"The floor plan is the same as the second floor. There's a set of stairs at the opposite side that lead to my studio. The rest of these rooms are rarely used." She gave him the slow smile as she linked hands. "Of course, the entire floor's haunted."

"Of course." He found it only natural. Without a word, he followed her to the tower.

Chapter 3

Normalcy. Tubes of paint were scattered everywhere, brushes stood in jars. The scent of oil and turpentine hung in the air. This Adam understood—the debris and the sensuality of art.

The room was rounded with arching windows and a lofty ceiling. The floor might have been beautiful at one time, but now the wood was dull and splattered and smeared with paints and stains. Canvases were in the corners, against the walls, stacked on the floor.

Kirby gave the room a swift, thorough study. When she saw all was as it should be, the tension eased from her shoulders. Moving across the room, she went to her father.

He sat, motionless and unblinking, staring down at a partially formed mound of clay. Without speaking, Kirby walked around the worktable, scrutinizing the clay from all angles. Fairchild's eyes remained riveted on his work. After a few moments, Kirby straightened, rubbed her nose with the back of her hand and pursed her lips.

"Mmm."

"That's only your opinion," Fairchild snapped.

"It certainly is." For a moment, she nibbled on her thumbnail. "You're entitled to another. Adam, come have a look."

He sent her a killing glance that caused her to grin. Trapped by manners, he crossed the studio and looked down at the clay.

It was, he supposed, an adequate attempt—a partially formed hawk, talons exposed, beak just parted. The power, the life, that sung in his paints, and in his daughter's sculptures, just wasn't there. In vain, Adam searched for a way out.

"Hmm," he began, only to have Kirby pounce on the syllable.

"There, he agrees with me." Kirby patted her father's head and looked smug.

"What does he know?" Fairchild demanded. "He's a painter."

"And so, darling Papa, are you. A brilliant one."

He struggled not to be pleased and poked a finger into the clay. "Soon, you hateful brat, I'll be a brilliant sculptor as well."

"I'll get you some Play-Doh for your birthday," she offered, then let out a shriek as Fairchild grabbed her ear and twisted. "Fiend." With a sniff, she rubbed at the lobe.

"Mind your tongue or I'll make a Van Gogh of you."

As Adam watched, the little man cackled; Kirby, however, froze—face, shoulders, hands. The fluidity he'd noticed in her even when she was still vanished. It wasn't annoyance, he thought, but...fear? Not of Fairchild. Kirby, he was certain, would never be afraid of a man, particularly her father. *For* Fairchild was more feasible, and just as baffling.

She recovered quickly enough and tilted her chin. "I'm going to show Adam my studio. He can settle in."

"Good, good." Because he recognized the edge to her voice, Fairchild patted her hand. "Damn pretty girl, isn't she, Adam?"

"Yes, she is."

As Kirby heaved a gusty sigh, Fairchild patted her hand again. The clay on his smeared onto hers. "See, my sweet, aren't you grateful for those braces now?"

"Papa." With a reluctant grin, Kirby laid her cheek against his balding head. "I never wore braces."

"Of course not. You inherited your teeth from me." He

gave Adam a flashing smile and a wink. "Come back when you've got settled, Adam. I need some masculine company." He pinched Kirby's cheek lightly. "And don't think Adam's going to sniff around your ankles like Rick Potts."

"Adam's nothing like Rick," Kirby murmured as she picked up a rag and wiped the traces of clay from her hands. "Rick is sweet."

"She inherited her manners from the milkman," Fairchild observed.

She shot a look at Adam. "I'm sure Adam can be sweet, too." But there was no confidence in her voice. "Rick's forte is watercolor. He's the sort of man women want to mother. I'm afraid he stutters a bit when he gets excited."

"He's madly in love with our little Kirby." Fairchild would've cackled again, but for the look his daughter sent him.

"He just thinks he is. I don't encourage him."

"What about the clinch I happened in on in the library?" Pleased with himself, Fairchild turned back to Adam. "I ask you, when a man's glasses are steamed, isn't there a reason for it?"

"Invariably." He liked them, damn it, whether they were harmless lunatics or something more than harmless. He liked them both.

"You know very well that was totally one-sided." Barely shifting her stance, she became suddenly regal and dignified. "Rick lost control, temporarily. Like blowing a fuse, I suppose." She brushed at the sleeve of her sweater. "Now that's quite enough on the subject."

"He's coming to stay for a few days next week." Fairchild dropped the bombshell as Kirby walked to the door. To her credit, she barely broke stride. Adam wondered if he was watching a well-plotted game of chess or a wild version of Chinese checkers.

"Very well," Kirby said coolly. "I'll tell Rick that Adam and I are lovers and that Adam's viciously jealous, and keeps a stiletto in his left sock."

"Good God," Adam murmured as Kirby swept out of the door. "She'll do it, too."

"You can bank on it," Fairchild agreed, without disguising the glee in his voice. He loved confusion. A man of sixty was entitled to create as much as he possibly could.

The structure of the second tower studio was identical to the first. Only the contents differed. In addition to paints and brushes and canvases, there were knives, chisels and mallets. There were slabs of limestone and marble and lumps of wood. Adam's equipment was the only spot of order in the room. Cards had stacked his gear personally.

A long wooden table was cluttered with tools, wood shavings, rags and a crumpled ball of material that might've been a paint smock. In a corner was a high-tech stereo component system. An ancient gas heater was set into one wall with an empty easel in front of it.

As with Fairchild's tower, Adam understood this kind of chaos. The room was drenched with sun. It was quiet, spacious and instantly appealing.

"There's plenty of room," Kirby told him with a sweeping gesture. "Set up where you're comfortable. I don't imagine we'll get in each other's way," she said doubtfully, then shrugged. She had to make the best of it. Better for him to be here, in her way, than sharing her father's studio with the Van Gogh. "Are you temperamental?"

"I wouldn't say so," Adam answered absently as he began to unpack his equipment. "Others might. And you?"

"Oh, yes." Kirby plopped down behind the worktable and lifted a piece of wood. "I have tantrums and fits of melancholia. I hope it won't bother you." He turned to answer, but she was staring down at the wood in her hands, as if searching for something hidden inside. "I'm doing my emotions now. I can't be held responsible."

Curious, Adam left his unpacking to walk to the shelf behind her. On it were a dozen pieces in various stages. He chose a carved piece of fruitwood that had been polished. "Emotions," he murmured, running his fingers over the wood.

"Yes, that's—"

"*Grief*," he supplied. He could see the anguish, feel the pain.

"Yes." She wasn't sure if it pleased her or not to have him so in tune—particularly with that one piece that had cost her so much. "I've done *Joy* and *Doubt* as well. I thought to save *Passion* for last." She spread her hands under the wood she held and brought it to eye level. "This is to be *Anger*." As if to annoy it, she tapped the wood with her fingers. "One of the seven deadly sins, though I've always thought it mislabeled. We need anger."

He saw the change in her eyes as she stared into the wood. Secrets, he thought. She was riddled with them. Yet as she sat, the sun pouring around her, the unformed wood held aloft in her hands, she seemed to be utterly, utterly open, completely readable, washed with emotion. Even as he began to see it, she shifted and broke the mood. Her smile when she looked up at him was teasing.

"Since I'm doing *Anger*, you'll have to tolerate a few bouts of temper."

"I'll try to be objective."

Kirby grinned, liking the gloss of politeness over the sarcasm. "I bet you have bundles of objectivity."

"No more than my share."

"You can have mine, too, if you like. It's very small." Still moving the wood in her hands, she glanced toward his equipment. "Are you working on anything?"

"I was." He walked around to stand in front of her. "I've something else in mind now. I want to paint you."

Her gaze shifted from the wood in her hands to his face. With some puzzlement, he saw her eyes were wary. "Why?"

He took a step closer and closed his hand over her chin. Kirby sat passively as he examined her from different angles. But she felt his fingers, each individual finger, as it lay on her skin. Soft skin, and Adam didn't bother to resist the urge to run his thumb over her cheek. The bones seemed fragile under his hands, but her eyes were steady and direct.

"Because," he said at length, "your face is fascinating. I want to paint that, the translucence, and your sexuality."

Her mouth heated under the careless brush of his fingers. Her hands tightened on the fruitwood, but her voice was even. "And if I said no?"

That was another thing that intrigued him, the trace of hauteur she used sparingly—and very successfully. She'd bring men to their knees with that look, he thought. Deliberately he leaned over and kissed her. He felt her stiffen, resist, then remain still. She was, in her own way, in her own defense, absorbing the feelings he brought to her. Her knuckles had whitened on the wood, but he didn't see. When he lifted his head, all Adam saw was the deep, pure gray of her eyes.

"I'd paint you anyway," he murmured. He left the room, giving them both time to think about it.

She did think about it. For nearly thirty minutes, Kirby sat perfectly still and let her mind work. It was a curious part of her nature that such a vibrant, restless woman could have such a capacity for stillness. When it was necessary, Kirby could do absolutely nothing while she thought through problems and looked for answers. Adam made it necessary.

He stirred something in her that she'd never felt before. Kirby believed that one of the most precious things in life was the original and the fresh. This time, however, she wondered if she should skirt around it.

She appreciated a man who took the satisfaction of his own desires for granted, just as she did. Nor was she averse to pitting herself against him. But... She couldn't quite get past the *but* in Adam's case.

It might be safer—smarter, she amended—if she concentrated on the awkwardness of Adam's presence with respect to the Van Gogh and her father's hobby. The attraction she felt was ill-timed. She touched her tongue to her top lip and thought she could taste him. Ill-timed, she thought again. And inconvenient.

Her father had better be prudent, she thought, then imme-

diately sighed. Calling Philip Fairchild prudent was like calling Huck Finn studious. The blasted, brilliant Van Gogh was
going to have to make a speedy exit. And the Titian, she
remembered, gnawing on her lip. She still had to handle that.

Adam was huddled with her father, and there was nothing
she could do at the moment. Just a few more days, she reminded herself. There'd be nothing more to worry about. The
smile crept back to her mouth. The rest of Adam's visit might
be fun. She thought of him, the serious brown eyes, the strong,
sober mouth.

Dangerous fun, she conceded. But then, what was life without a bit of danger? Still smiling, she picked up her tools.

She worked in silence, in total concentration. Adam, her
father, the Van Gogh were forgotten. The wood in her hand
was the center of the universe. There was life there; she could
feel it. It only waited for her to find the key to release it. She
would find it, and the soaring satisfaction that went hand in
hand with the discovery.

Painting had never given her that. She'd played at it, enjoyed it, but she'd never possessed it. She'd never been possessed by it. Art was a lover that demanded complete alle-
giance. Kirby understood that.

As she worked, the wood seemed to take a tentative breath.
She felt suddenly, clearly, the temper she sought pushing
against the confinement. Nearly—nearly free.

At the sound of her name, she jerked her head up. "Bloody
murder!"

"Kirby, I'm so sorry."

"Melanie." She swallowed the abuse, barely. "I didn't
hear you come up." Though she set down her tools, she continued to hold the wood. She couldn't lose it now. "Come in.
I won't shout at you."

"I'm sure you should." Melanie hesitated at the doorway.
"I'm disturbing you."

"Yes, you are, but I forgive you. How was New York?"
Kirby gestured to a chair as she smiled at her oldest friend.

Pale blond hair was elegantly styled around a heart-shaped

face. Cheekbones, more prominent than Kirby's, were tinted expertly. The Cupid's-bow mouth was carefully glossed in deep rose. Kirby decided, as she did regularly, that Melanie Burgess had the most perfect profile ever created.

"You look wonderful, Melly. Did you have fun?"

Melanie wrinkled her nose as she brushed off the seat of her chair. "Business. But my spring designs were well received."

Kirby brought up her legs and crossed them under her. "I'll never understand how you can decide in August what we should be wearing next April." She was losing the power of the wood. Telling herself it would come back, she set it on the table, within reach. "Have you done something nasty to the hemlines again?"

"You never pay any attention anyway." She gave Kirby's sweater a look of despair.

"I like to think of my wardrobe as timeless rather than trendy." She grinned, knowing which buttons to push. "This sweater's barely twelve years old."

"And looks every day of it." Knowing the game and Kirby's skill, Melanie switched tactics. "I ran into Ellen Parker at 21."

"Did you?" After lacing her hands, Kirby rested her chin on them. She never considered gossiping rude, particularly if it was interesting. "I haven't seen her for months. Is she still spouting French when she wants to be confidential?"

"You won't believe it." Melanie shuddered as she pulled a long, slender cigarette from an enameled case. "I didn't believe it myself until I saw it with my own eyes. Jerry told me. You remember Jerry Turner, don't you?"

"Designs women's underwear."

"Intimate apparel," Melanie corrected with a sigh. "Really, Kirby."

"Whatever. I appreciate nice underwear. So what did he tell you?"

Melanie pulled out a monogrammed lighter and flicked it on. She took a delicate puff. "He told me that Ellen was having an affair."

"There's news," Kirby returned dryly. With a yawn, she stretched her arms to the ceiling and relieved the stiffness in her shoulder blades. "Is this number two hundred and three, or have I missed one?"

"But, Kirby—" Melanie tapped her cigarette for emphasis as she leaned forward "—she's having this one with her son's orthodontist."

It was the sound of Kirby's laughter that caused Adam to pause on his way up the tower steps. It rang against the stone walls, rich, real and arousing. He stood as it echoed and faded. Moving quietly, he continued up.

"Kirby, really. An orthodontist." Even knowing Kirby as well as she did, Melanie was stunned by her reaction. "It's so—so middle-class."

"Oh, Melanie, you're such a wonderful snob." She smothered another chuckle as Melanie gave an indignant huff. When Kirby smiled, it was irresistible. "It's perfectly acceptable for Ellen to have any number of affairs, as long as she keeps her choice socially prominent but an orthodontist goes beyond good taste?"

"It's not acceptable, of course," Melanie muttered, finding herself caught in the trap of Kirby's logic. "But if one is discreet, and…"

"Selective?" Kirby supplied good-naturedly. "Actually, it is rather nasty. Here's Ellen carrying on with her son's orthodontist, while poor Harold shells out a fortune for the kid's overbite. Where's the justice?"

"You say the most astonishing things."

"Orthodonture work is frightfully expensive."

With an exasperated sigh, Melanie tried another change of subject. "How's Stuart?"

Though he'd been about to enter, Adam stopped in the doorway and kept his silence. Kirby's smile had vanished. The eyes that had been alive with humor were frigid. Something hard, strong and unpleasant came into them. Seeing the change, Adam realized she'd make a formidable enemy. There was grit behind the careless wit, the raw sexuality and the eccentric-rich-girl polish. He wouldn't forget it.

"Stuart," Kirby said in a brittle voice. "I really wouldn't know."

"Oh, dear." At the arctic tone, Melanie caught her bottom lip between her teeth. "Have you two had a row?"

"A row?" The smile remained unpleasant. "One might put it that way." Something flared—the temper she'd been prodding out of the wood. With an effort, Kirby shrugged it aside. "As soon as I'd agreed to marry him, I knew I'd made a mistake. I should've dealt with it right away."

"You'd told me you were having doubts." After stubbing out her cigarette, Melanie leaned forward to take Kirby's hands. "I thought it was nerves. You'd never let any relationship get as far as an engagement before."

"It was an error in judgment." No, she'd never let a relationship get as far as an engagement. Engagements equaled commitment. Commitments were a lock, perhaps the only lock, Kirby considered sacred. "I corrected it."

"And Stuart? I suppose he was furious."

The smile that came back to Kirby's lips held no humor. "He gave me the perfect escape hatch. You know he'd been pressuring me to set a date?"

"And I know that you'd been putting him off."

"Thank God," Kirby murmured. "In any case, I'd finally drummed up the courage to renege. I think it was the first time in my life I've felt genuine guilt." Moving her shoulders restlessly, she picked up the wood again. It helped to steady her, helped her to concentrate on temper. "I went by his place, unannounced. It was a now-or-never sort of gesture. I should've seen what was up as soon as he answered the door, but I was already into my neat little speech when I noticed a few—let's say articles of intimate apparel tossed around the room."

"Oh, Kirby."

Letting out a long breath, Kirby went on. "That part of it was my fault, I suppose. I wouldn't sleep with him. There was just no driving urge to be intimate with him. No..." She searched for a word. "Heat," she decided, for lack of anything better. "I guess that's why I knew I'd never marry him.

But, I was faithful." The fury whipped through her again. "I was faithful, Melly."

"I don't know what to say." Distress vibrated in her voice. "I'm so sorry, Kirby."

Kirby shook her head at the sympathy. She never looked for it. "I wouldn't have been so angry if he hadn't stood there, telling me how much he loved me, when he had another woman keeping the sheets warm. I found it humiliating."

"You have nothing to be humiliated about," Melanie returned with some heat. "He was a fool."

"Perhaps. It would've been bad enough if we'd stuck to the point, but we got off the track of love and fidelity. Things got nasty."

Her voice trailed off. Her eyes clouded over. It was time for secrets again. "I found out quite a bit that night," she murmured. "I've never thought of myself as a fool, but it seems I'd been one."

Again, Melanie reached for her hand. "It must have been a dreadful shock to learn Stuart was unfaithful even before you were married."

"What?" Blinking, Kirby brought herself back. "Oh, that. Yes, that, too."

"Too? What else?"

"Nothing." With a shake of her head, Kirby swept it all aside. "It's all dead and buried now."

"I feel terrible. Damn it, I introduced you."

"Perhaps you should shave your head in restitution, but I'd advise you to forget it."

"Can you?"

Kirby's lips curved up, her brow lifted. "Tell me, Melly, do you still hold André Fayette against me?"

Melanie folded her hands primly. "It's been five years."

"Six, but who's counting?" Grinning, Kirby leaned forward. "Besides, who expects an oversexed French art student to have any taste?"

Melanie's pretty mouth pouted. "He was very attractive."

"But base." Kirby struggled with a new grin. "No class,

Melly. You should thank me for luring him away, however unintentionally.''

Deciding it was time to make his presence known, Adam stepped inside. Kirby glanced up and smiled without a trace of the ice or the fury. "Hello, Adam. Did you have a nice chat with Papa?"

"Yes."

Melanie, he decided as he glanced in her direction, was even more stunning at close quarters. Classic face, classic figure draped in a pale rose dress cut with style and simplicity. "Am I interrupting?"

"Just gossip. Melanie Burgess, Adam Haines. Adam's our guest for a few weeks."

Adam accepted the slim rose-tipped hand. It was soft and pampered, without the slight ridge of callus that Kirby's had just under the fingers. He wondered what had happened in the past twenty-four hours to make him prefer the untidy artist to the perfectly groomed woman smiling up at him. Maybe he was coming down with something.

"*The* Adam Haines?" Melanie's smile warmed. She knew of him, the irreproachable lineage and education. "Of course you are," she continued before he could comment. "This place attracts artists like a magnet. I have one of your paintings."

"Do you?" Adam lit her cigarette, then one of his own. "Which one?"

"*A Study in Blue.*" Melanie tilted her face to smile into his eyes, a neat little feminine trick she'd learned soon after she'd learned to walk.

From across the table, Kirby studied them both. Two extraordinary faces, she decided. The tips of her fingers itched to capture Adam in bronze. A year before, she'd done Melanie in ivory—smooth, cool and perfect. With Adam, she'd strive for the undercurrents.

"I wanted the painting because it was so strong," Melanie continued. "But I nearly let it go because it made me sad. You remember, Kirby. You were there."

"Yes, I remember." When she looked up at him, her eyes were candid and amused, without the traces of flirtation that flitted in Melanie's. "I was afraid she'd break down and disgrace herself, so I threatened to buy it myself. Papa was furious that I didn't."

"Uncle Philip could practically stock the Louvre already," Melanie said with a casual shrug.

"Some people collect stamps," Kirby returned, then smiled again. "The still life in my room is Melanie's work, Adam. We studied together in France."

"No, don't ask," Melanie said quickly, holding up her hand. "I'm not an artist. I'm a designer who dabbles."

"Only because you refuse to dig your toes in."

Melanie inclined her head, but didn't agree or refute. "I must go. Tell Uncle Philip I said hello. I won't risk disturbing him, as well."

"Stay for lunch, Melly. We haven't seen you in two months."

"Another time." She rose with the grace of one who'd been taught to sit and stand and walk. Adam stood with her, catching the drift of Chanel. "I'll see you this weekend at the party." With another smile, she offered Adam her hand. "You'll come, too, won't you?"

"I'd like that."

"Wonderful." Snapping open her bag, Melanie drew out thin leather gloves. "Nine o'clock, Kirby. Don't forget. Oh!" On her way to the door, she stopped, whirling back. "Oh, God, the invitations were sent out before I... Kirby, Stuart's going to be there."

"I won't pack my derringer, Melly." She laughed, but it wasn't quite as rich or quite as free. "You look as though someone's just spilled caviar on your Saint Laurent. Don't worry about it." She paused, and the chill passed quickly in and out of her eyes. "I promise you, I won't."

"If you're sure..." Melanie frowned. It was, however, not possible to discuss such a thing in depth in front of a guest. "As long as you won't be uncomfortable."

"I won't be the one who suffers discomfort." The careless arrogance was back.

"Saturday, then." Melanie gave Adam a final smile before she slipped from the room.

"A beautiful woman," Adam commented, coming back to the table.

"Yes, exceptional." The simple agreement had no undertones of envy or spite.

"How do two women, two exceptional women, of totally different types, remain friends?"

"By not attempting to change one another." She picked up the wood again and began to roll it around in her hands. "I overlook what I see as Melanie's faults, and she overlooks mine." She saw the pad and pencil in his hand and lifted a brow. "What're you doing?"

"Some preliminary sketches. What are your faults?"

"Too numerous to mention." Setting the wood down again, she leaned back.

"Any good points?"

"Dozens." Perhaps it was time to test him a bit, to see what button worked what switch. "Loyalty," she began breezily. "Sporadic patience and honesty."

"Sporadic?"

"I'd hate to be perfect." She ran her tongue over her teeth. "And I'm terrific in bed."

His gaze shifted to her bland smile. Just what game was Kirby Fairchild playing? His lips curved as easily as hers. "I bet you are."

Laughing, she leaned forward again, chin cupped in her hands. "You don't rattle easily, Adam. It makes me all the more determined to keep trying."

"Telling me something I'd already concluded isn't likely to rattle me. Who's Stuart?"

The question had her stiffening. She'd challenged him, Kirby conceded, now she had to meet one of his. "A former fiancé," she said evenly. "Stuart Hiller."

The name clicked, but Adam continued to sketch. "The same Hiller who runs the Merrick Gallery?"

"The same." He heard the tightening in her voice. For a moment he wanted to drop it, to leave her to her privacy and her anger. The job came first.

"I know him by reputation," Adam continued. "I'd planned to see the gallery. It's about twenty miles from here, isn't it?"

She paled a bit, which confused him, but when she spoke her voice was steady. "Yes, it's not far. Under the circumstances, I'm afraid I can't take you."

"You may mend your differences over the weekend." Prying wasn't his style. He had a distaste for it, particularly when it involved someone he was beginning to care about. When he lifted his gaze, however, he didn't see discomfort. She was livid.

"I think not." She made a conscious effort to relax her hands. Noting the gesture, Adam wondered how much it cost her. "It occurred to me that my name would be Fairchild-Hiller." She gave a slow, rolling shrug. "That would never do."

"The Merrick Gallery has quite a reputation."

"Yes. As a matter of fact, Melanie's mother owns it, and managed it until a couple of years ago."

"Melanie? Didn't you say her name was Burgess?"

"She was married to Carlyse Burgess—Burgess Enterprises. They're divorced."

"So, she's Harriet Merrick's daughter." The cast of players was increasing. "Mrs. Merrick's given the running of the gallery over to Hiller?"

"For the most part. She dips her hand in now and then."

Adam saw that she'd relaxed again, and concentrated on the shape of her eyes. Round? Not quite, he decided. They were nearly almond shaped, but again, not quite. Like Kirby, they were simply unique.

"Whatever my personal feelings, Stuart's a knowledgeable dealer." She gave a quick, short laugh. "Since she hired him, she's had time to travel. Harriet's just back from an African safari. When I phoned her the other day, she told me she'd brought back a necklace of crocodile teeth."

To his credit, Adam closed his eyes only briefly. "Your families are close, then. I imagine your father's done a lot of dealing through the Merrick Gallery."

"Over the years. Papa had his first exhibition there, more than thirty years ago. It sort of lifted his and Harriet's careers off at the same time." Straightening in her chair, Kirby frowned across the table. "Let me see what you've done."

"In a minute," he muttered, ignoring her outstretched hand.

"Your manners sink to my level when it's convenient, I see." Kirby plopped back in her chair. When he didn't comment, she screwed her face into unnatural lines.

"I wouldn't do that for long," Adam advised. "You'll hurt yourself. When I start in oil, you'll have to behave or I'll beat you."

Kirby relaxed her face because her jaw was stiffening. "Corkscrews, you wouldn't beat me. You have the disadvantage of being a gentleman, inside and out."

Lifting his head, he pinned her with a look. "Don't bank on it."

The look alone stopped whatever sassy rejoinder she might have made. It wasn't the look of a gentleman, but of a man who made his own way however he chose. Before she could think of a proper response, the sound of shouting and wailing drifted up the tower steps and through the open door. Kirby made no move to spring up and investigate. She merely smiled.

"I'm going to ask two questions," Adam decided. "First, what the hell is that?"

"Which that is that, Adam?" Her eyes were dove gray and guileless.

"The sound of mourning."

"Oh, that." Grinning, she reached over and snatched his sketch pad. "That's Papa's latest tantrum because his sculpture's not going well—which of course it never will. Does my nose really tilt that way?" Experimentally she ran her finger down it. "Yes, I guess it does. What was your other question?"

"Why do you say 'corkscrews' or something equally ridiculous when a simple 'hell' or 'damn' would do?"

"It has to do with cigars. You really must show these sketches to Papa. He'll want to see them."

"Cigars." Determined to have her full attention, Adam grabbed the pad away from her.

"Those big, nasty, fat ones. Papa used to smoke them by the carload. You needed a gas mask just to come in the door. I begged, threatened, even tried smoking them myself." She swallowed on that unfortunate memory. "Then I came up with the solution. Papa is a sucker."

"Is that so?"

"That is, he just can't resist a bet, no matter what the odds." She touched the wood again, knowing she'd have to come back to it later. "My language was, let's say, colorful. I can swear eloquently in seven languages."

"Quite an accomplishment."

"It has its uses, believe me. I bet Papa ten thousand dollars that I could go longer without swearing than he could without smoking. Both my language and the ozone layer have been clean for three months." Rising, Kirby circled the table. "I have the gratitude of the entire staff." Abruptly she dropped in his lap. Letting her head fall back, she wound her arms around his neck. "Kiss me again, will you? I can't resist."

There can't be another like her, Adam thought as he closed his mouth over hers. With a low sound of pleasure, Kirby melted against him, all soft demand.

Then neither of them thought, but felt only.

Desire was swift and sharp. It built and expanded so that they could wallow in it. She allowed herself the luxury, for such things were too often brief, too often hollow. She wanted the speed, the heat, the current. A risk, but life was nothing without them. A challenge, but each day brought its own. He made her feel soft, giddy, senseless. No one else had. If she could be swept away, why shouldn't she be? It had never happened before.

She needed what she'd never realized she needed from a man before: strength, solidity.

Adam felt the initial stir turn to an ache—something deep and dull and constant. It wasn't something he could resist, but something he found he needed. Desire had always been basic and simple and painless. Hadn't he known she was a woman who would make a man suffer? Knowing it, shouldn't he have been able to avoid it? But he hurt. Holding her soft and pliant in his arms, he hurt. From wanting more.

"Can't you two wait until after lunch?" Fairchild demanded from the doorway.

With a quiet sigh, Kirby drew her lips from Adam's. The taste lingered as she knew now it would. Like the wood behind her, it would be something that pulled her back again and again.

"We're coming," she murmured, then brushed Adam's mouth again, as if in promise. She turned and rested her cheek against his in a gesture he found impossibly sweet. "Adam's been sketching me," she told her father.

"Yes, I can see that." Fairchild gave a quick snort. "He can sketch you all he chooses after lunch. I'm hungry."

Chapter 4

Food seemed to soothe Fairchild's temperament. As he plowed his way through poached salmon, he went off on a long, technical diatribe on surrealism. It appeared breaking conventional thought to release the imagination had appealed to him to the extent that he'd given nearly a year of his time in study and application. With a good-humored shrug, he confessed that his attempts at surrealistic painting had been poor, and his plunge into abstraction little better.

"He's banished those canvases to the attic," Kirby told Adam as she poked at her salad. "There's one in shades of blue and yellow, with clocks of all sizes and shapes sort of melting and drooping everywhere and two left shoes tucked in a corner. He called it *Absence of Time*."

"Experimental," Fairchild grumbled, eyeing Kirby's uneaten portion of fish.

"He refused an obscene amount of money for it and locked it, like a mad relation, in the attic." Smoothly she transferred her fish to her father's plate. "He'll be sending his sculpture to join it before long."

Fairchild swallowed a bite of fish, then ground his teeth. "Heartless brat." In the blink of an eye he changed from amiable cherub to gnome. "By this time next year, Philip Fairchild's name will be synonymous with sculpture."

"Horse dust," Kirby concluded, and speared a cucumber. "That shade of pink becomes you, Papa." Leaning over, she placed a loud kiss on his cheek. "It's very close to fuchsia."

"You're not too old to forget my ability to bring out the same tone on your bottom."

"Child abuser." As Adam watched, she stood and wrapped her arms around Fairchild's neck. In the matter of love for her father, the enigma of Kirby Fairchild was easily solvable. "I'm going out for a walk before I turn yellow and dry up. Will you come?"

"No, no, I've a little project to finish." He patted her hand as she tensed. Adam saw something pass between them before Fairchild turned to him. "Take her for a walk and get on with your...sketching," he said with a cackle. "Have you asked Kirby if you can paint her yet? They all do." He stabbed at the salmon again. "She never lets them."

Adam lifted his wine. "I told Kirby I was going to paint her."

The new cackle was full of delight. Pale blue eyes lit with the pleasure of trouble brewing. "A firm hand, eh? She's always needed one. Don't know where she got such a miserable temper." He smiled artlessly. "Must've come from her mother's side."

Adam glanced up at the serene, mild-eyed woman in the portrait. "Undoubtedly."

"See that painting there?" Fairchild pointed to the portrait of Kirby as a girl. "That's the one and only time she modeled for me. I had to pay the brat scale." He gave a huff and a puff before he attacked the fish again. "Twelve years old and already mercenary."

"If you're going to discuss me as if I weren't here, I'll go fetch my shoes." Without a backward glance, Kirby glided from the room.

"Hasn't changed much, has she?" Adam commented as he drained his wine.

"Not a damn bit," Fairchild agreed proudly. "She'll lead you a merry chase, Adam, my boy. I hope you're in condition."

"I ran track in college."

Fairchild's laugh was infectious. Damn it, Adam thought again, I like him. It complicated things. From the other room he heard Kirby in a heated discussion with Isabelle. He was beginning to realize complication was the lady's middle name. What should've been a very simple job was developing layers he didn't care for.

"Come on, Adam." Kirby poked her head around the doorway. "I've told Isabelle she can come, but she and Montique have to keep a distance of five yards at all times. Papa—" she tossed her ponytail back "—I really think we ought to try raising the rent. She might look for an apartment in town."

"We should never have agreed to a long-term lease," Fairchild grumbled, then gave his full attention to Kirby's salmon.

Deciding not to comment, Adam rose and went outside.

It was warm for September, and breezy. The grounds around the house were alive with fall. Beds of zinnias and mums spread out helter-skelter, flowing over their borders and adding a tang to the air. Near a flaming maple, Adam saw an old man in patched overalls. With a whimsical lack of dedication, he raked at the scattered leaves. As they neared him, he grinned toothlessly.

"You'll never get them all, Jamie."

He made a faint wheezing sound that must've been a laugh. "Sooner or later, missy. There be plenty of time."

"I'll help you tomorrow."

"Ayah, and you'll be piling them up and jumping in 'em like always." He wheezed again and rubbed a frail hand over his chin. "Stick to your whittling and could be I'll leave a pile for you."

With her hands hooked in her back pockets, she scuffed at a leaf. "A nice big one?"

"Could be. If you're a good girl."

"There's always a catch." Grabbing Adam's hand, she pulled him away.

"Is that little old man responsible for the grounds?" Three acres, he calculated. Three acres if it was a foot.

"Since he retired."

"Retired?"

"Jamie retired when he was sixty-five. That was before I was born." The breeze blew strands of hair into her face and she pushed at them. "He claims to be ninety-two, but of course he's ninety-five and won't admit it." She shook her head. "Vanity."

Kirby pulled him along until they stood at a dizzying height above the river. Far below, the ribbon of water seemed still. Small dots of houses were scattered along the view. There was a splash of hues rather than distinct tones, a melding of textures.

On the ridge where they stood there was only wind, river and sky. Kirby threw her head back. She looked primitive, wild, invincible. Turning, he looked at the house. It looked the same.

"Why do you stay here?" Blunt questions weren't typical of him. Kirby had already changed that.

"I have my family, my home, my work."

"And isolation."

Her shoulders moved. Though her lashes were lowered, her eyes weren't closed. "People come here. That's not isolation."

"Don't you want to travel? To see Florence, Rome, Venice?"

From her stance on a rock, she was nearly eye level with him. When she turned to him, it was without her usual arrogance. "I'd been to Europe five times before I was twelve. I spent four years in Paris on my own when I was studying."

She looked over his shoulder a moment, at nothing or at everything, he couldn't be sure. "I slept with a Breton count in a chateau, skied in the Swiss Alps and hiked the moors in Cornwall. I've traveled, and I'll travel again. But..." He knew she looked at the house now, because her lips curved. "I always come home."

"What brings you back?"

"Papa." She stopped and smiled fully. "Memories, familiarity. Insanity."

"You love him very much." She could make things impossibly complicated or perfectly simple. The job he'd come to do was becoming more and more of a burden.

"More than anything or anyone." She spoke quietly, so that her voice seemed a part of the breeze. "He's given me everything of importance: security, independence, loyalty, friendship, love—and the capability to give them back. I'd like to think someday I'll find someone who wants that from me. My home would be with him then."

How could he resist the sweetness, the simplicity, she could show so unexpectedly? It wasn't in the script, he reminded himself, but reached a hand to her face, just to touch. When she brought her hand to his, something stirred in him that wasn't desire, but was just as potent.

She felt the strength in him, and sensed a confusion that might have been equal to her own. Another time, she thought. Another time, it might have worked. But now, just now, there were too many other things. Deliberately she dropped her hand and turned back to the river. "I don't know why I tell you these things," she murmured. "It's not in character. Do people usually let you in on their personal thoughts?"

"No. Or maybe I haven't been listening."

She smiled and, in one of her lightning changes of mood, leaped from the rock. "You're not the type people would confide in." Casually she linked her arm through his. "Though you seem to have strong, sturdy shoulders. You're a little aloof," she decided. "And just a tad pompous."

"Pompous?" How could she allure him one instant and infuriate him the next? "What do you mean, pompous?"

Because he sounded dangerously like her father, she swallowed. "Just a tad," she reminded him, nearly choking on a laugh. "Don't be offended, Adam. Pomposity certainly has its place in the world." When he continued to scowl down at her, she cleared her throat of another laugh. "I like the way your left brow lifts when you're annoyed."

"I'm not pompous." He spoke very precisely and watched her lips tremble with fresh amusement.

"Perhaps that was a bad choice of words."

"It was a completely incorrect choice." Just barely, he

caught himself before his brow lifted. Damn the woman, he thought, and swore he wouldn't smile.

"Conventional." Kirby patted his cheek. "I'm sure that's what I meant."

"I'm sure those two words mean the same thing to you. I won't be categorized by either."

Tilting her head, she studied him. "Maybe I'm wrong," she said, to herself as much as him. "I've been wrong before. Give me a piggyback ride."

"*What?*"

"A piggyback ride," Kirby repeated.

"You're crazy." She might be sharp, she might be talented, he'd already conceded that, but part of her brain was permanently on holiday.

With a shrug, she started back toward the house. "I knew you wouldn't. Pompous people never give or receive piggyback rides. It's the law."

"Damn." She was doing it to him, and he was letting her. For a moment, he stuck his hands in his pockets and stood firm. Let her play her games with her father, Adam told himself. He wasn't biting. With another oath, he caught up to her. "You're an exasperating woman."

"Why, thank you."

They stared at each other, him in frustration, her in amusement, until he turned his back. "Get on."

"If you insist." Nimbly she jumped on his back, blew the hair out of her eyes and looked down. "Wombats, you're tall."

"You're short," he corrected, and hitched her to a more comfortable position.

"I'm going to be five-seven in my next life."

"You'd better add pounds as well as inches to your fantasy." Her hands were light on his shoulders, her thighs firm around his waist. Ridiculous, he thought. Ridiculous to want her now, when she's making a fool of both of you. "What do you weigh?"

"An even hundred." She sent a careless wave to Jamie.

"And when you take the ball bearings out of your pocket?"

"Ninety-six, if you want to be technical." With a laugh, she gave him a quick hug. Her laughter was warm and distracting at his ear. "You might do something daring, like not wearing socks."

"The next spontaneous act might be dropping you on your very attractive bottom."

"Is it attractive?" Idly she swung her feet back and forth. "I see so little of it myself." She held him for a moment longer because it felt so right, so good. Keep it light, she reminded herself. And watch your step. As long as she could keep him off balance, things would run smoothly. Leaning forward, she caught the lobe of his ear between her teeth. "Thanks for the lift, sailor."

Before he could respond, she'd jumped down and dashed into the house.

It was night, late, dark and quiet, when Adam sat alone in his room. He held the transmitter in his hand and found he wanted to smash it into little pieces and forget it had ever existed. No personal involvements. That was rule number one, and he'd always followed it. He'd never been tempted not to.

He'd wanted to follow it this time, he reminded himself. It just wasn't working that way. Involvement, emotion, conscience; he couldn't let any of it interfere. Staring at Kirby's painting of the Hudson, he flicked the switch.

"McIntyre?"

"Password."

"Damn it, this isn't a chapter of Ian Fleming."

"Procedure," McIntyre reminded him briskly. After twenty seconds of dead air, he relented. "Okay, okay, what've you found out?"

I've found out I'm becoming dangerously close to being crazy about a woman who makes absolutely no sense to me, he thought. "I've found out that the next time you have a brainstorm, you can go to hell with it."

"Trouble?" McIntyre's voice snapped into the receiver. "You were supposed to call in if there was trouble."

"The trouble is I like the old man and the daughter's...

unsettling.'' An apt word, Adam mused. His system hadn't settled since he'd set eyes on her.

"It's too late for that now. We're committed.''

"Yeah.'' He let out a breath between his teeth and blocked Kirby from his mind. "Melanie Merrick Burgess is a close family friend and Harriet Merrick's daughter. She's a very elegant designer who doesn't seem to have any deep interest in painting. At a guess I'd say she'd be very supportive of the Fairchilds. Kirby recently broke off her engagement to Stuart Hiller.''

"Interesting. When?''

"I don't have a date,'' Adam retorted. "And I didn't like pumping her about something that sensitive.'' He struggled with himself as McIntyre remained silent. "Sometime during the last couple months, I'd say, no longer. She's still smoldering.'' And hurting, he said to himself. He hadn't forgotten the look in her eyes. "I've been invited to a party this weekend. I should meet both Harriet Merrick and Hiller. In the meantime, I've had a break here. The place is riddled with secret passages.''

"With what?''

"You heard me. With some luck, I'll have easy access throughout the house.''

McIntyre grunted in approval. "You won't have any trouble recognizing it?''

"If he's got it, and if it's in the house, *and* if by some miracle I can find it in this anachronism, I'll recognize it.'' He switched off and, resisting the urge to throw the transmitter against the wall, dropped it back in the briefcase.

Clearing his mind, Adam rose and began to search the fireplace for the mechanism.

It took him nearly ten minutes, but he was rewarded with a groaning as a panel slid halfway open. He squeezed inside with a flashlight. It was both dank and musty, but he played the light against the wall until he found the inside switch. The panel squeaked closed and left him in the dark.

His footsteps echoed and he heard the scuttering sound of rodents. He ignored both. For a moment he stopped at the wall of Kirby's room. Telling himself he was only doing his job, he took the time to find the switch. But he wondered if she was already sleeping in the big four-poster bed, under the wedding ring quilt.

He could press the button and join her. The hell with McIntyre and the job. The hell with everything but what lay beyond the wall. Procedure, he thought on an oath. He was sick to death of procedure. But Kirby had been right. Adam had a very firm grip on what was right and what was wrong.

He turned and continued down the passage.

Abruptly the corridor snaked off, with steep stone steps forking to the left. Mounting them, he found himself in another corridor. A spider scrambled on the wall as he played his light over it. Kirby hadn't exaggerated much about the size. The third story, he decided, was as good a place to start as any.

He turned the first mechanism he found and slipped through the opening. Dust and dustcovers. Moving quietly, he began a slow, methodical search.

Kirby was restless. While Adam had been standing on the other side of the wall, fighting back the urge to open the panel, she'd been pacing her room. She'd considered going up to her studio. Work might calm her—but any work she did in this frame of mind would be trash. Frustrated, she sank down on the window seat. She could see the faint reflection of her own face and stared at it.

She wasn't completely in control. Almost any other flaw would've been easier to admit. Control was essential and, under the current circumstances, vital. The problem was getting it back.

The problem was, she corrected, Adam Haines.

Attraction? Yes, but that was simple and easily dealt with. There was something more twisted into it that was anything but simple. He could involve her, and once involved, nothing would be easily dealt with.

Laying her hands on the sill, she rested her head on them. He could hurt her. That was a first—a frightening first. Not a superficial blow to the pride or ego, Kirby admitted, but a hurt down deep where it counted; where it wouldn't heal.

Obviously, she told herself, forewarned was forearmed. She just wouldn't let him involve her, therefore she wouldn't let him hurt her. And that little piece of logic brought her right back to the control she didn't have. While she struggled to methodically untangle her thoughts, the beam of headlights distracted her.

Who'd be coming by at this time of night? she wondered without too much surprise. Fairchild had a habit of asking people over at odd hours. Kirby pressed her nose to the glass. A sound, not unlike Isabelle's growl, came from her throat.

"Of all the nerve," she muttered. "Of all the bloody nerve."

Springing up, she paced the floor three times before she grabbed a robe and left the room.

Above her head, Adam was about to reenter the passageway when he, too, saw the beams. Automatically he switched off his flashlight and stepped beside the window. He watched the man step from a late-model Mercedes and walk toward the house. Interesting, Adam decided. Abandoning the passageway, he slipped silently into the hall.

The sound of voices drifted up as he eased himself into the cover of a doorway and waited. Footsteps drew nearer. From his concealment, Adam watched Cards lead a slim, dark man up to Fairchild's tower studio.

"Mr. Hiller to see you, sir." Cards gave the information as if it were four in the afternoon rather than after midnight.

"Stuart, so nice of you to come." Fairchild's voice boomed through the doorway. "Come in, come in."

After counting to ten, Adam started to move toward the door Cards had shut, but just then a flurry of white scrambled up the stairs. Swearing, he pressed back into the wall as Kirby passed, close enough to touch.

What the hell is this? he demanded, torn between frustration and the urge to laugh. Here he was, trapped in a doorway, while people crept up tower steps in the middle of the night.

While he watched, Kirby gathered the skirt of her robe around her knees and tiptoed up to the tower.

It was a nightmare, he decided. Women with floating hair sneaking around drafty corridors in filmy white. Secret passages. Clandestine meetings. A normal, sensible man wouldn't be involved in it for a minute. Then again, he'd stopped being completely sensible when he'd walked in the front door.

After Kirby reached the top landing, Adam moved closer. Her attention was focused on the studio door. Making a quick calculation, Adam moved up the steps behind her, then melted into the shadows in the corner. With his eyes on her, he joined Kirby in the eavesdropping.

"What kind of fool do you think I am?" Stuart demanded. He stood beside Adam with only the wall separating them.

"Whatever kind you prefer. Makes no difference to me. Have a seat, my boy."

"Listen to me, we had a deal. How long did you think it would take before I found out you'd double-crossed me?"

"Actually I didn't think it would take you quite so long." Smiling, Fairchild rubbed a thumb over his clay hawk. "Not as clever as I thought you were, Stuart. You should've discovered the switch weeks ago. Not that it wasn't superb," he added with a touch of pride. "But a smart man would've had the painting authenticated."

Because the conversation confused her, Kirby pressed even closer to the door. She tucked her hair behind her ear as if to hear more clearly. Untended, her robe fell open, revealing a thin excuse for a nightgown and a great deal of smooth golden skin. In his corner, Adam shifted and swore to himself.

"We had a deal—" Stuart's voice rose, but Fairchild cut him off with no more than a wave of his hand.

"Don't tell me you believe in that nonsense about honor among thieves? Time to grow up if you want to play in the big leagues."

"I want the Rembrandt, Fairchild."

Kirby stiffened. Because his attention was now fully focused on the battle in the tower, Adam didn't notice. By God, he thought grimly, the old bastard did have it.

"Sue me," Fairchild invited. Kirby could hear the shrug in his voice.

"Hand it over, or I'll break your scrawny neck."

For a full ten seconds, Fairchild watched calmly as Stuart's face turned a deep, dull red. "You won't get it that way. And I should warn you that threats make me irritable. You see..." Slowly he picked up a rag and began to wipe some excess clay from his hands. "I didn't care for your treatment of Kirby. No, I didn't care for it at all."

Abruptly he was no longer the harmless eccentric. He was neither cherub nor gnome, but a man. A dangerous one. "I knew she'd never go as far as marrying you. She's far too bright. But your threats, once she told you off, annoyed me. When I'm annoyed, I tend to be vindictive. A flaw," he said amiably. "But that's just the way I'm made." The pale eyes were cold and calm on Stuart's. "I'm still annoyed, Stuart. I'll let you know when I'm ready to deal. In the meantime, stay away from Kirby."

"You're not going to get away with this."

"I hold all the cards." In an impatient gesture, he brushed Stuart aside. "I have the Rembrandt, and only I know where it is. If you become a nuisance, which you're dangerously close to becoming, I may decide to keep it. Unlike you, I have no pressing need for money." He smiled, but the chill remained in his eyes. "One should never live above one's means, Stuart. That's my advice."

Impotent, intimidated, Stuart loomed over the little man at the worktable. He was strong enough, and furious enough, to have snapped Fairchild's neck with his hands. But he wouldn't have the Rembrandt, or the money he so desperately needed. "Before we're done, you'll pay," Stuart promised. "I won't be made a fool of."

"Too late," Fairchild told him easily. "Run along now. You can find your way out without disturbing Cards, can't you?"

As if he were already alone, Fairchild went back to his hawk.

Swiftly, Kirby looked around for a hiding place. For one

ridiculous moment, Adam thought she'd try to ease herself into the corner he occupied. The moment she started to cross the hall toward him, the handle of the door turned. She'd left her move too late. With her back pressed against the wall, Kirby closed her eyes and pretended to be invisible.

Stuart wrenched open the door and stalked from the room, blind with rage. Without a backward glance he plunged down the steps. His face, Adam noted as he passed, was murderous. At the moment, he lacked a weapon. But if he found one, he wouldn't hesitate.

Kirby stood, still and silent, as the footsteps receded. She sucked in a deep breath, then let it out on a huff. What now? *What now?* she thought, and wanted to just bury her face in her hands and surrender. Instead, she straightened her shoulders and went in to confront her father.

"Papa." The word was quiet and accusing. Fairchild's head jerked up, but his surprise was quickly masked by a genial smile.

"Hello, love. My hawk's beginning to breathe. Come have a look."

She took another deep breath. All of her life she'd loved him, stood by him. Adored him. None of that had ever stopped her from being angry with him. Slowly, keeping her eyes on him, she crossed the front panels of her robe and tied the sash. As she approached, Fairchild thought she looked like a gunslinger buckling on his six-gun. She wouldn't, he thought with a surge of pride, intimidate like Hiller.

"Apparently you haven't kept me up to date," she began. "A riddle, Papa. What do Philip Fairchild, Stuart Hiller and Rembrandt have in common?"

"You've always been clever at riddles, my sweet."

"*Now,* Papa."

"Just business." He gave her a quick, hearty smile as he wondered just how much he'd have to tell her.

"Let's be specific, shall we?" She moved so that only the table separated them. "And don't give me that blank, foolish look. It won't work." Bending over, she stared directly into his eyes. "I heard quite a bit while I was outside. Tell me the rest."

"Eavesdropping." He made a disapproving tsk-tsk. "Rude."

"I come by it honestly. Now tell me or I'll annihilate your hawk." Sweeping up her arm, she held her palm three inches above his clay.

"Vicious brat." With his bony fingers, he grabbed her wrist, each knowing who'd win if it came down to it. He gave a windy sigh. "All right."

With a nod, Kirby removed her hand then folded her arms under her breasts. The habitual gesture had him sighing again.

"Stuart came to me with a little proposition some time ago. You know, of course, he hasn't a cent to his name, no matter what he pretends."

"Yes, I know he wanted to marry me for my money." No one but her father would've detected the slight tightening in her voice.

"I didn't bring that up to hurt you." His hand reached for hers in the bond that had been formed when she'd taken her first breath.

"I know, Papa." She squeezed his hand, then stuck both of hers in the pockets of her robe. "My pride suffered. It has to happen now and again, I suppose. But I don't care for humiliation," she said with sudden fierceness. "I don't care for it one bloody bit." With a toss of her head, she looked down at him. "The rest."

"Well." Fairchild puffed out his cheeks, then blew out the breath. "Among his other faults, Stuart's greedy. He needed a large sum of money, and didn't see why he had to work for it. He decided to help himself to the Rembrandt self-portrait from Harriet's gallery."

"He *stole* it?" Kirby's eyes grew huge. "Great buckets of bedbugs! I wouldn't have given him credit for that much nerve."

"He thought himself clever." Rising, Fairchild walked to the little sink in the corner to wash off his hands. "Harriet was going on her safari, and there'd be no one to question the disappearance for several weeks. Stuart's a bit dictatorial with the staff at the gallery.''

"It's such a treat to flog underlings."

"In any case—" lovingly, Fairchild draped his hawk for the night "—he came to me with an offer—a rather paltry offer, too—if I'd do the forgery for the Rembrandt's replacement."

She hadn't thought he could do anything to surprise her. Certainly nothing to hurt her. "Papa, it's Harriet's Rembrandt," she said in shock.

"Now, Kirby, you know I'm fond of Harriet. Very fond." He put a comforting arm around her shoulders. "Our Stuart has a very small brain. He handed over the Rembrandt when I said I needed it to do the copy." Fairchild shook his head. "There wasn't any challenge to it, Kirby. Hardly any fun at all."

"Pity," she said dryly and dropped into a chair.

"Then I told him I didn't need the original any longer, and gave him the copy instead. He never suspected." Fairchild linked his hands behind his back and stared up at the ceiling. "I wish you'd seen it. It was superlative. It was one of Rembrandt's later works, you know. Rough textures, such luminous depth—"

"Papa!" Kirby interrupted what would've become a lecture.

"Oh, yes, yes." With an effort, Fairchild controlled himself. "I told him it'd take just a little more time to complete the copy and treat it for the illusion of age. He bought it. Gullibility," Fairchild added and clucked his tongue. "It's been almost three weeks, and he just got around to having the painting tested. I made certain it wouldn't stand up to the most basic of tests, of course."

"Of course," Kirby murmured.

"Now he has to leave the copy in the gallery. And I have the original."

She gave herself a moment to absorb all he'd told her. It didn't make any difference in how she felt. Furious. "Why,

Papa? Why did you do this! It isn't like all the others. It's Harriet."

"Now, Kirby, don't lose control. You've such a nasty temper." He did his best to look small and helpless. "I'm much too old to cope with it. Remember my blood pressure."

"Blood pressure be hanged." She glared up at him with fury surging into her eyes. "Don't think you're going to get around me with that. Old?" she tossed back. "You're still your youngest child."

"I feel a spell coming on," he said, inspired by Kirby's own warning two days before. He pressed a trembling hand to his heart and staggered. "I'll end up a useless heap of cold spaghetti. Ah, the paintings I might have done. The world's losing a genius."

Clenching her fists, Kirby beat them on his worktable. Tools bounced and clattered while she let out a long wail. Protective, Fairchild placed his hands around his hawk and waited for the crisis to pass. At length, she slumped back in the chair, breathless.

"You used to do better than that," he observed. "I think you're mellowing."

"Papa." Kirby clamped her teeth to keep from grinding them. "I know I'll be forced to beat you about the head and ears, then I'll be arrested for patricide. You know I've a terror of closed-in places. I'd go mad in prison. Do you want that on your conscience?"

"Kirby, have I ever given you cause for one moment's worry?"

"Don't force me into a recital, Papa, it's after midnight. What have you done with the Rembrandt?"

"Done with it?" He frowned and fiddled with the cover of his hawk. "What do you mean, done with it?"

"Where is it?" she asked, carefully spacing the words. "You can't leave a painting like that lying around the house, particularly when you've chosen to have company."

"Company? Oh, you mean Adam. Fine boy. I'm fond of him already." His eyebrows wiggled twice. "You seem to be finding him agreeable."

Kirby narrowed her eyes. "Leave Adam out of this."

"Dear, dear, dear." Fairchild grinned lavishly. "And I thought you'd brought him up."

"Where *is* the Rembrandt?" All claim to patience disintegrated. Briefly, she considered banging her head on the table, but she'd given up that particular ploy at ten.

"Safe and secure, my sweet." Fairchild's voice was calm and pleased. "Safe and secure."

"Here? In the house?"

"Of course." He gave her an astonished look. "You don't think I'd keep it anywhere else?"

"*Where?*"

"You don't need to know everything." With a flourish, he whipped off his painting smock and tossed it over a chair. "Just content yourself that it's safe, hidden with appropriate respect and affection."

"Papa."

"Kirby." He smiled—a gentle father's smile. "A child must trust her parent, must abide by the wisdom of his years. You do trust me, don't you?"

"Yes, of course, but—"

He cut her off with the first bars of "Daddy's Little Girl" in a wavering falsetto.

Kirby moaned and lowered her head to the table. When would she learn? And how was she going to deal with him this time? He continued to sing until the giggles welled up and escaped. "You're incorrigible." She lifted her head and took a deep breath. "I have this terrible feeling that you're leaving out a mountain of details and that I'm going to go along with you anyway."

"Details, Kirby." His hand swept them aside. "The world's too full of details, they clutter things up. Remember, art reflects life, and life's an illusion. Come now, I'm tired." He walked to her and held out his hand. "Walk your old Papa to bed."

Defeated, she accepted his hand and stood. Never, never would she learn. And always, always would she adore him. Together they walked from the room.

Adam watched as they started down the steps, arm in arm.

"Papa..." Only feet away from Adam's hiding place, Kirby stopped. "There is, of course, a logical reason for all this?"

"Kirby." Adam could see the mobile face move into calm, sober lines. "Have I ever done anything without a sensible, logical reason?"

She started with a near-soundless chuckle. In moments, her laughter rang out, rich and musical. It echoed back, faint and ghostly, until she rested her head against her father's shoulder. In the half-light, with her eyes shining, Adam thought she'd never looked more alluring. "Oh, my papa," she began in a clear contralto. "To me he is so wonderful." Linking her arm through Fairchild's, she continued down the steps.

Rather pleased with himself, and with his offspring, Fairchild joined her in his wavery falsetto. Their mixed voices drifted over Adam until the distance swallowed them.

Leaving the shadows, he stood at the head of the stairway. Once he heard Kirby's laugh, then there was silence.

"Curiouser and curiouser," he murmured.

Both Fairchilds were probably mad. They fascinated him.

Chapter 5

In the morning the sky was gray and the rain sluggish. Adam was tempted to roll over, close his eyes and pretend he was in his own well-organized home, where a housekeeper tended to the basics and there wasn't a gargoyle in sight. Partly from curiosity, partly from courage, he rose and prepared to deal with the day.

From what he'd overheard the night before, he didn't count on learning much from Kirby. Apparently she'd known less about the matter of the Rembrandt than he. Adam was equally sure that no matter how much he prodded and poked, Fairchild would let nothing slip. He might look innocent and harmless, but he was as shrewd as they came. And potentially dangerous, Adam mused, remembering how cleanly Fairchild had dealt with Hiller.

The best course of action remained the nightly searches with the aid of the passages. The days he determined for his own sanity to spend painting.

I shouldn't be here in the first place, Adam told himself as he stood in the shower under a strong cold spray of water. If it hadn't been for the fact that Mac tantalized me with the Rembrandt, I *wouldn't* be here. The last time, he promised himself as he toweled off. The very last time.

Once the Fairchild hassle was over, painting would not only be his first order of business, it would be his only business.

Dressed, and content with the idea of ending his secondary career in a few more weeks, Adam walked down the hallway thinking of coffee. Kirby's door was wide open. As he passed, he glanced in. Frowning, he stopped, walked back and stood in the doorway.

"Good morning, Adam. Isn't it a lovely day?" She smiled, upside down, as she stood on her head in the corner.

Deliberately he glanced at the window to make sure he was on solid ground. "It's raining."

"Don't you like the rain? I do." She rubbed her nose with the back of her hand. "Look at it this way, there must be dozens of places where the sun's shining. It's all relative. Did you sleep well?"

"Yes." Even in her current position, Adam could see that her face glowed, showing no signs of a restless night.

"Come in and wait a minute, I'll go down to breakfast with you."

He walked over to stand directly in front of her. "Why are you standing on your head?"

"It's a theory of mine." She crossed her ankles against the wall while her hair pooled onto the carpet. "Could you sit down a minute? It's hard for me to talk to you when your head's up there and mine's down here."

Knowing he'd regret it, Adam crouched. Her sweater had slipped up, showing a thin line of smooth midriff.

"Thanks. My theory is that all night I've been horizontal, and most of the day I'll be right side up. So..." Somehow she managed to shrug. "I stand on my head in the morning and before bed. That way the blood can slosh around a bit."

Adam rubbed his nose between his thumb and forefinger. "I think I understand. That terrifies me."

"You should try it."

"I'll just let my blood stagnate, thanks."

"Suit yourself. You'd better stand back, I'm coming up."

She dropped her feet and righted herself with a quick athletic agility that surprised him. Facing him, she pushed at the hair that floated into her eyes. As she tossed it back she gave him a long, slow smile.

"Your face is red," he murmured, more in his own defense than for any other reason.

"Can't be helped, it's part of the process." She'd spent a good many hours arguing with herself the night before. This morning she'd decided to let things happen as they happened. "It's the only time I blush," she told him. "So, if you'd like to say something embarrassing…or flattering…?"

Against his better judgment, he touched her, circling her waist with his hands. She didn't move back, didn't move forward, but simply waited. "Your blush is already fading, so it seems I've missed my chance."

"You can give it another try tomorrow. Hungry?"

"Yes." Her lips made him hungry, but he wasn't ready to test himself quite yet. "I want to go through your clothes after breakfast."

"Oh, really?" She drew out the word, catching her tongue between her teeth.

His brow lifted, but only she was aware of the gesture. "For the painting."

"You don't want to do a nude." The humor in her eyes faded into boredom as she drew away. "That's the usual line."

"I don't waste my time with lines." He studied her—the cool gray eyes that could warm with laughter, the haughty mouth that could invite and promise with no more than a smile. "I'm going to paint you because you were meant to be painted. I'm going to make love with you for exactly the same reason."

Her expression didn't change, but her pulse rate did. Kirby wasn't foolish enough to pretend even to herself it was anger. Anger and excitement were two different things. "How decisive and arrogant of you," she drawled. Strolling over to her dresser, she picked up her brush and ran it quickly through her hair. "I haven't agreed to pose for you, Adam, nor have I agreed to sleep with you." She flicked the brush through a last time then set it down. "In fact, I've serious doubts that I'll do either. Shall we go?"

Before she could get to the door, he had her. The speed surprised her, if the strength didn't. She'd hoped to annoy him, but when she tossed her head back to look at him, she didn't see temper. She saw cool, patient determination. Nothing could have been more unnerving.

Then he had her close, so that his face was a blur and his mouth was dominant. She didn't resist. Kirby rarely resisted what she wanted. Instead she let the heat wind through her in a slow continuous stream that was somehow both terrifying and peaceful.

Desire. Wasn't that how she'd always imagined it would be with the right man? Wasn't that what she'd been waiting for since the first moment she'd discovered herself a woman? It was here now. Kirby opened her arms to it.

His heartbeat wasn't steady, and it should have been. His mind wasn't clear, and it had to be. How could he win with her when he lost ground every time he was around her? If he followed through on his promise—or threat—that they'd be lovers, how much more would he lose? And gain, he thought as he let himself become steeped in her. The risk was worth taking.

"You'll pose for me," he said against her mouth. "And you'll make love with me. There's no choice."

That was the word that stopped her. That was the phrase that forced her to resist. She'd always have a choice. "I don't—"

"For either of us," Adam finished as he released her. "We'll decide on the clothes after breakfast." Because he didn't want to give either of them a chance to speak, he propelled her from the room.

An hour later, he propelled her back.

She'd been serene during the meal. But he hadn't been fooled. Livid was what she was, and livid was exactly how he wanted her. She didn't like to be outmaneuvered, even on a small point. It gave him a surge of satisfaction to be able to do so. The defiant, sulky look in her eyes was exactly what he wanted for the portrait.

"Red, I think," he stated. "It would suit you best."

Kirby waved a hand at her closet and flopped backward onto her bed. Staring up at the ceiling, she thought through her position. It was true she'd always refused to be painted, except by her father. She hadn't wanted anyone else to get that close to her. As an artist, she knew just how intimate the relationship was between painter and subject, be the subject a person or a bowl of fruit. She'd never been willing to share herself with anyone to that extent.

But Adam was different. She could, if she chose, tell herself it was because of his talent, and because he wanted to paint her, not flatter her. It wasn't a lie, but it wasn't quite the truth. Still, Kirby was comfortable with partial truths in certain cases. If she was honest, she had to admit that she was curious to see just how she'd look from his perspective, and yet she wasn't entirely comfortable with that.

Moving only her eyes, she watched him as he rummaged through her closet.

He didn't have to know what was going on in her head. Certainly she was skilled in keeping her thoughts to herself. It might be a challenge to do so under the sharp eyes of an artist. It might be interesting to see just how difficult she could make it for him. She folded her hands demurely on her stomach.

While Kirby was busy with her self-debate, Adam looked through an incredible variety of clothes. Some were perfect for an orphan, others for an eccentric teenager. He wondered if she'd actually worn the purple miniskirt and just how she'd looked in it. Elegant gowns from Paris and New York hung haphazardly with army surplus. If clothes reflected the person, there was more than one Kirby Fairchild. He wondered just how many she'd show him.

He discarded one outfit after another. This one was too drab, that one too chic. He found a pair of baggy overalls thrown over the same hanger with a slinky sequin dress with a two-thousand-dollar label. Pushing aside a three-piece suit perfect for an assistant D.A., he found it.

Scarlet silk. It was undoubtedly expensive, but not chic in the way he imagined Melanie Burgess would design. The square-necked bodice tapered to a narrow waist before the material flared into a full skirt. There were flounces at the hem and underskirts of white and black and fuchsia. The sleeves were short and puffed, running with stripes of the same colors. It was made for a wealthy gypsy. It was perfect.

"This." Adam carried it to the bed and stood over Kirby. With a frown, she continued to stare up at the ceiling. "Put it on and come up to the studio. I'll do some sketches."

She spoke without looking at him. "Do you realize that not once have you asked me to pose for you? You told me you wanted to paint me, you told me you were going to paint me, but you've never *asked* if you could paint me." With her hands still folded, one finger began to tap. "Instinct tells me you're basically a gentleman, Adam. Perhaps you've just forgotten to say please."

"I haven't forgotten." He tossed the dress across the bottom of the bed. "But I think you hear far too many pleases from men. You're a woman who brings men to their knees with the bat of an eye. I'm not partial to kneeling." No, he wasn't partial to kneeling, and it was becoming imperative that he handle the controls, for both of them. Bending over, he put his hands on either side of her head then sat beside her. "And I'm just as used to getting my own way as you are."

She studied him, thinking over his words and her position. "Then again, I haven't batted my eyes at you yet."

"Haven't you?" he murmured.

He could smell her, that wild, untamed fragrance that was suited to isolated winter nights. Her lips pouted, not by design, but mood. It was that that tempted him. He had to taste them. He did so lightly, as he'd intended. Just a touch, just a taste, then he'd go about his business. But her mouth yielded to him as the whole woman hadn't. Or perhaps it conquered.

Desire scorched him. Fire was all he could relate to. Flames and heat and smoke. That was her taste. Smoke and temptation and a promise of unreasonable delights.

He tasted, but it was no longer enough. He had to touch.

Her body was small, delicate, something a man might fear to take. He did, but no longer for her sake. For his own. Small and delicate she might be, but she could slice a man in two. Of that he was certain. But as he touched, as he tasted, he didn't give a damn.

Never had he wanted a woman more. She made him feel like a teenager in the back seat of a car, like a man paying for the best whore in a French bordello, like a husband nuzzling into the security of a wife. Her complexities were more erotic than satin and lace and smoky light—the soft, agile mouth, the strong, determined hands. He wasn't certain he'd ever escape from either. In possessing her, he'd invite an endless cycle of complications, of struggles, of excitement. She was an opiate. She was a dive from a cliff. If he wasn't careful, he was going to overdose and hit the rocks.

It cost him more than he would have believed to draw back. She lay with her eyes half closed, her mouth just parted. Don't get involved, he told himself frantically. Get the Rembrandt and walk away. That's what you came to do.

"Adam..." She whispered his name as if she'd never said it before. It felt so beautiful on her tongue. The only thought that stayed with her was that no one had ever made her feel like this. No one else ever would. Something was opening inside her, but she wouldn't fight it. She'd give. The innocence in her eyes was real, emotional not physical. Seeing it, Adam felt desire flare again.

She's a witch, he told himself. Circe. Lorelei. He had to pull back before he forgot that. "You'll have to change."

"Adam..." Still swimming, she reached up and touched his face.

"Emphasize your eyes." He stood before he could take the dive.

"My eyes?" Mind blank, body throbbing, she stared up at him.

"And leave your hair loose." He strode to the door as she struggled up to her elbows. "Twenty minutes."

She wouldn't let him see the hurt. She wouldn't allow herself to feel the rejection. "You're a cool one, aren't you?" she said softly. "And as smooth as any I've ever run across. You might find yourself on your knees yet."

She was right—he could've strangled her for it. "That's a risk I'll have to take." With a nod, he walked through the door. "Twenty minutes," he called back.

Kirby clenched her fists together then slowly relaxed them. "On your knees," she promised herself. "I swear it."

Alone in Kirby's studio, Adam searched for the mechanism to the passageway. He looked mainly from curiosity. It was doubtful he'd need to rummage through a room that he'd been given free run in, but he was satisfied when he located the control. The panel creaked open, as noisily as all the others he'd found. After a quick look inside, he shut it again and went back to the first order of business—painting.

It was never a job, but it wasn't always a pleasure. The need to paint was a demand that could be soft and gentle, or sharp and cutting. Not a job, but work certainly, sometimes every bit as exhausting as digging a trench with a pick and shovel.

Adam was a meticulous artist, as he was a meticulous man. Conventional, as Kirby had termed him, perhaps. But he wasn't rigid. He was as orderly as she wasn't, but his creative process was remarkably similar to hers. She might stare at a piece of wood for an hour until she saw the life in it. He would do the same with a canvas. She would feel a jolt, a physical release the moment she saw what she'd been searching for. He'd feel that same jolt when something would leap out at him from one of his dozens of sketches.

Now he was only preparing, and he was as calm and ordered as his equipment. On an easel he set the canvas, blank and waiting. Carefully, he selected three pieces of charcoal. He'd begin with them. He was going over his first informal sketches when he heard her footsteps.

She paused in the doorway, tossed her head and stared at him. With deliberate care, he set his pad back on the worktable.

Her hair fell loose and rich over the striped silk shoulders. At a movement, the gold hoops at her ears and the half-dozen gold bracelets on her arm jangled. Her eyes, darkened and sooty, still smoldered with temper. Without effort, he could picture her whirling around an open fire to the sound of violins and tambourines.

Aware of the image she projected, Kirby put both hands on her hips and walked into the room. The full scarlet skirt flowed around her legs. Standing in front of him, she whirled around twice, turning her head each time so that she watched him over her shoulder. The scent of wood smoke and roses flowed into the room.

"You want to paint Katrina's picture, eh?" Her voice lowered into a sultry Slavic accent as she ran a fingertip down his cheek. Insolence, challenge, and then a laugh that skidded warm and dangerous over his skin. "First you cross her palm with silver."

He'd have given her anything. What man wouldn't? Fighting her, fighting himself, he pulled out a cigarette. "Over by the east window," he said easily. "The light's better there."

No, he wouldn't get off so easy. Behind the challenge and the insolence, her body still trembled for him. She wouldn't let him know it. "How much you pay?" she demanded, swirling away in a flurry of scarlet and silk. "Katrina not come free."

"Scale." He barely resisted the urge to grab her by the hair and drag her back. "And you won't get a dime until I'm finished."

In an abrupt change, Kirby brushed and smoothed her skirts. "Is something wrong?" she asked mildly. "Perhaps you don't like the dress after all."

He crushed out his cigarette in one grinding motion. "Let's get started."

"I thought we already had," she murmured. Her eyes were luminous and amused. He wanted to choke her every bit as much as he wanted to crawl for her. "You insisted on painting."

"Don't push me too far, Kirby. You have a tendency to bring out my baser side."

"I don't think I can be blamed for that. Maybe you've locked it up too long." Because she'd gotten precisely the reaction she'd wanted, she became completely cooperative. "Now, where do you want me to stand?"

"By the east window."

Tie score, she thought with satisfaction as she obliged him.

He spoke only when he had to—tilt your chin higher, turn your head. Within moments he was able to turn the anger and the desire into concentration. The rain fell, but its sound was muffled against the thick glass windows. With the tower door nearly closed, there wasn't another sound.

He watched her, studied her, absorbed her, but the man and the artist were working together. Perhaps by putting her on canvas, he'd understand her...and himself. Adam swept the charcoal over the canvas and began.

Now she could watch him, knowing that he was turned inward. She'd seen dozens of artists work; the old, the young, the talented, the amateur. Adam was, as she'd suspected, different.

He wore a sweater, one he was obviously at home in, but no smock. Even as he sketched he stood straight, as though his nature demanded that he remain always alert. That was one of the things she'd noticed about him first. He was always watching. A true artist did, she knew, but there seemed to be something more.

She called him conventional, knowing it wasn't quite true. Not quite. What was it about him that didn't fit into the mold he'd been fashioned for? Tall, lean, attractive, aristocratic, wealthy, successful, and...daring? That was the word that came to mind, though she wasn't completely sure why.

There was something reckless about him that appealed to her. It balanced the maturity, the dependability she hadn't known she'd wanted in a man. He'd be a rock to hold on to during an earthquake. And he'd be the earthquake. She was,

Kirby realized, sinking fast. The trick would be to keep him from realizing it and making a fool of herself. Still, beneath it all, she liked him. That simple.

Adam glanced up to see her smiling at him. It was disarming, sweet and uncomplicated. Something warned him that Kirby without guards was far more dangerous than Kirby with them. When she let hers drop, he put his in place.

"Doesn't Hiller paint a bit?"

He saw her smile fade and tried not to regret it. "A bit."

"Haven't you posed for him?"

"No."

"Why not?"

The ice that came into her eyes wasn't what he wanted for the painting. The man and artist warred as he continued to sketch. "Let's say I didn't care much for his work."

"I suppose I can take that as a compliment to mine."

She gave him a long, neutral look. "If you like."

Deceit was part of the job, he reminded himself. What he'd heard in Fairchild's studio left him no choice. "I'm surprised he didn't make an issue of it, being in love with you."

"He wasn't." She bit off the words, and ice turned to heat.

"He asked you to marry him."

"One hasn't anything to do with the other."

He looked up and saw she said exactly what she meant. "Doesn't it?"

"I agreed to marry him without loving him."

He held the charcoal an inch from the canvas, forgetting the painting. "Why?"

While she stared at him, he saw the anger fade. For a moment she was simply a woman at her most vulnerable. "Timing," she murmured. "It's probably the most important factor governing our lives. If it hadn't been for timing, Romeo and Juliet would've raised a half-dozen children."

He was beginning to understand, and understanding only made him more uncomfortable. "You thought it was time to get married?"

"Stuart's attractive, very polished, charming, and I'd thought harmless. I realized the last thing I wanted was a polished, charming, harmless husband. Still, I thought he loved me. I didn't break the engagement for a long time because I thought he'd make a convenient husband, and one who wouldn't demand too much." It sounded empty. It had been empty. "One who'd give me children."

"You want children?"

The anger was back, quickly. "Is there something wrong with that?" she demanded. "Do you think it strange that I'd want a family?" She made a quick, furious movement that had the gold jangling again. "This might come as a shock, but I have needs and feelings almost like a real person. And I don't have to justify myself to you."

She was halfway to the door before he could stop her. "Kirby, I'm sorry." When she tried to jerk out of his hold, he tightened it. "I *am* sorry."

"For what?" she tossed back.

"For hurting you," he murmured. "With stupidity."

Her shoulders relaxed under his hands, slowly, so that he knew it cost her. Guilt flared again. "All right. You hit a nerve, that's all." Deliberately she removed his hands from her shoulders and stepped back. He'd rather she'd slapped him. "Give me a cigarette, will you?"

She took one from him and let him light it before she turned away again. "When I accepted Stuart's proposal—"

"You don't have to tell me anything."

"I don't leave things half done." Some of the insolence was back when she whirled back to him. For some reason it eased Adam's guilt. "When I accepted, I told Stuart I wasn't in love with him. It didn't seem fair otherwise. If two people are going to have a relationship that means anything, it has to start out honestly, don't you think?"

He thought of the transmitter tucked into his briefcase. He thought of McIntyre waiting for the next report. "Yes."

She nodded. It was one area where she wasn't flexible. "I told him that what I wanted from him was fidelity and children, and in return I'd give him those things and as much affection as I could." She toyed with the cigarette, taking one of her quick, nervous drags. "When I realized things just wouldn't work for either of us that way, I went to see him. I didn't do it carelessly, casually. It was very difficult for me. Can you understand that?''

''Yes, I understand that.''

It helped, she realized. More than Melanie's sympathy, more even than her father's unspoken support, Adam's simple understanding helped. ''It didn't go well. I'd known there'd be an argument, but I hadn't counted on it getting so out of hand. He made a few choice remarks on my maternal abilities and my track record. Anyway, with all the blood and bone being strewn about, the real reason for him wanting to marry me came out.''

She took a last puff on the cigarette and crushed it out before she dropped into a chair. ''He never loved me. He'd been unfaithful all along. I don't suppose it mattered.'' But she fell silent, knowing it did. ''All the time he was pretending to care for me, he was using me.'' When she looked up again, the hurt was back in her eyes. She didn't know it—she'd have hated it. ''Can you imagine how it feels to find out that all the time someone was holding you, talking with you, he was thinking of how you could be useful?'' She picked up the piece of half-formed wood that would be her anger. ''Useful,'' she repeated. ''What a nasty word. I haven't bounced back from it as well as I should have.''

He forgot McIntyre, the Rembrandt and the job he still had to do. Walking over, he sat beside her and closed his hand over hers. Under them was her anger. ''I can't imagine any man thinking of you as useful.''

When she looked up, her smile was already spreading. ''What a nice thing to say. The perfect thing.'' Too perfect for her rapidly crumbling defenses. Because she knew it would take so little to have her turning to him now and later, she lightened the mood. ''I'm glad you're going to be there Saturday.''

''At the party?''

''You can send me long, smoldering looks and everyone'll think I jilted Stuart for you. I'm fond of petty revenge.''

He laughed and brought her hands to his lips. ''Don't

change,'' he told her with a sudden intenseness that had her uncertain again.

''I don't plan on it. Adam, I— Oh, chicken fat, what're you doing here? This is a private conversation.''

Wary, Adam turned his head and watched Montique bounce into the room. ''He won't spread gossip.''

''That isn't the point. I've told you you're not allowed in here.''

Ignoring her, Montique scurried over and with an awkward leap plopped into Adam's lap. ''Cute little devil,'' Adam decided as he scratched the floppy ears.

''Ah, Adam, I wouldn't do that.''

''Why?''

''You're only asking for trouble.''

''Don't be absurd. He's harmless.''

''Oh, yes, he is. *She* isn't.'' Kirby nodded her head toward the doorway as Isabelle slinked through. ''Now you're in for it. I warned you.'' Tossing back her head, Kirby met Isabelle's cool look equally. ''I had nothing to do with it.''

Isabelle blinked twice, then shifted her gaze to Adam. Deciding her responsibility had ended, Kirby sighed and rose. ''There's nothing I can do,'' she told Adam and patted his shoulder. ''You asked for it.'' With this, she swept out of the room, giving the cat a wide berth.

''I didn't ask him to come up here,'' Adam began, scowling down at Isabelle. ''And there can't be any harm in— Oh, God,'' he murmured. ''She's got me doing it.''

Chapter 6

"Let's walk," Kirby demanded when the afternoon grew late and Fairchild had yet to budge from his studio. Nor would he budge, she knew, until the Van Gogh was completed down to the smallest detail. If she didn't get out and forget about her father's pet project for a while, she knew she'd go mad.

"It's raining," Adam pointed out as he lingered over coffee.

"You mentioned that before." Kirby pushed away her own coffee and rose. "All right then, I'll have Cards bring you a lap robe and a nice cup of tea."

"Is that a psychological attack?"

"Did it work?"

"I'll get a jacket." He strode from the room, ignoring her quiet chuckle.

When they walked outside, the fine misting rain fell over them. Leaves streamed with it. Thin fingers of fog twisted along the ground. Adam hunched inside his jacket, thinking it was miserable weather for a walk. Kirby strolled along with her face lifted to the sky.

He'd planned to spend the afternoon on the painting, but perhaps this was better. If he was going to capture her with colors and brush strokes, he should get to know her better. No easy task, Adam mused, but a strangely appealing one.

The air was heavy with the fragrance of fall, the sky gloomy. For the first time since he'd met her, Adam sensed a serenity in Kirby. They walked in silence, with the rain flowing over them.

She was content. It was an odd feeling for her to identify as she felt it so rarely. With her hand in his, she was content to walk along as the fog moved along the ground and the chilly drizzle fell over them. She was glad of the rain, of the chill and the gloom. Later, there would be time for a roaring fire and warm brandy.

"Adam, do you see the bed of mums over there?"

"Hmm?"

"The mums, I want to pick some. You'll have to be the lookout."

"Lookout for what?" He shook wet hair out of his eyes.

"For Jamie, of course. He doesn't like anyone messing with his flowers."

"They're your flowers."

"No, they're Jamie's."

"He works for you."

"What does that have to do with it?" She put a hand on his shoulder as she scanned the area. "If he catches me, he'll get mad, then he won't save me any leaves. I'll be quick—I've done this before."

"But if you—"

"There's no time to argue. Now, you watch that window there. He's probably in the kitchen having coffee with Tulip. Give me a signal when you see him."

Whether he went along with her because it was simpler, or because he was getting into the spirit of things despite himself, Adam wasn't sure. But he walked over to the window and peeked inside. Jamie sat at a huge round table with a mug of coffee in both frail hands. Turning, he nodded a go-ahead to Kirby.

She moved like lightning, dashing to the flower bed and plucking at stems. Dark and wet, her hair fell forward to curtain her face as she loaded her arms with autumn flowers. She should be painted like this, as well, Adam mused. In the fog, with her arms full of wet flowers. Perhaps it would be possible to capture those odd little snatches of innocence in the portrait.

Idly he glanced back in the window. With a ridiculous jolt of panic, he saw Jamie rise and head for the kitchen door. Forgetting logic, Adam dashed toward her.

"He's coming."

Surprisingly swift, Kirby leaped over the bed of flowers and kept on going. Even though he was running full stride, Adam didn't catch her until they'd rounded the side of the house. Giggling and out of breath, she collapsed against him.

"We made it!"

"Just," he agreed. His own heart was thudding—from the race? Maybe. He was breathless—from the game? Perhaps. But they were wet and close and the fog was rising. It didn't seem he had a choice any longer.

With his eyes on hers, he brushed the dripping hair back from her face. Her cheeks were cool, wet and smooth. Yet her mouth, when his lowered to it, was warm and waiting.

She hadn't planned it this way. If she'd had the time to think, she'd have said she didn't want it this way. She didn't want to be weak. She didn't want her mind muddled. It didn't seem she had a choice any longer.

He could taste the rain on her, fresh and innocent. He could smell the sharp tang of the flowers that were crushed between them. He couldn't keep his hands out of her hair, the soft, heavy tangle of it. He wanted her closer. He wanted all of her, not in the way he'd first wanted her, but in every way. The need was no longer the simple need of a man for woman, but of him for her. Exclusive, imperative, impossible.

She'd wanted to fall in love, but she'd wanted to plan it out in her own way, in her own time. It wasn't supposed to happen in a crash and a roar that left her trembling. It wasn't supposed to happen without her permission. Shaken, Kirby drew back. It wasn't going to happen until she was ready. That was that. Nerves taut again, she made herself smile.

"It looks like we've done a good job of squashing them." When he would've drawn her back, Kirby thrust the flowers at him. "They're for you."

"For me?" Adam looked down at the mums they held between them.

"Yes, don't you like flowers?"

"I like flowers," he murmured. However unintentionally, she'd moved him as much with the gift as with the kiss. "I don't think anyone's given me flowers before."

"No?" She gave him a long, considering look. She'd been given floods of them over the years, orchids, lilies, roses and more roses, until they'd meant little more than nothing. Her smile came slowly as she touched a hand to his chest. "I'd've picked more if I'd known."

Behind them a window was thrown open. "Don't you know better than to stand in the rain and neck?" Fairchild demanded. "If you want to nuzzle, come inside. I can't stand sneezing and sniffling!" The window shut with a bang.

"You're terribly wet," Kirby commented, as if she hadn't noticed the steadily falling rain. She linked her arm with his and walked to the door that was opened by the ever-efficient Cards.

"Thank you." Kirby peeled off her soaking jacket. "We'll need a vase for the flowers, Cards. They're for Mr. Haines's room. Make sure Jamie's not about, will you?"

"Naturally, miss." Cards took both the dripping jackets and the dripping flowers and headed back down the hall.

"Where'd you find him?" Adam wondered aloud. "He's incredible."

"Cards?" Like a wet dog, Kirby shook her head. "Papa brought him back from England. I think he was a spy, or maybe it was a bouncer. In either case, it's obvious he's seen everything."

"Well, children, have you had a nice holiday?" Fairchild bounced out of the parlor. He wore a paint-streaked shirt and a smug smile. "My work's complete, and now I'm free to give my full attention to my sculpting. It's time I called Victor Alvarez," he murmured. "I've kept him dangling long enough."

"He'll dangle until after coffee, Papa." She sent her father a quick warning glance Adam might've missed if he hadn't been watching so closely. "Take Adam in the parlor and I'll see to it."

She kept him occupied for the rest of the day. Deliberately, Adam realized. Something was going on that she didn't want him getting an inkling of. Over dinner, she was again the perfect hostess. Over coffee and brandy in the parlor, she kept him entertained with an in-depth discussion on baroque art. Though her conversations and charm were effortless, Adam was certain there was an underlying reason. It was one more thing for him to discover.

She couldn't have set the scene better, he mused. A quiet parlor, a crackling fire, intelligent conversation. And she was watching Fairchild like a hawk.

When Montique entered, the scene changed. Once again, the scruffy puppy leaped into Adam's lap and settled down.

"How the hell did he get in here?" Fairchild demanded.

"Adam encourages him," Kirby stated as she sipped at her brandy. "We can't be held responsible."

"I should say not!" Fairchild gave both Adam and Montique a steely look. "And if that—that creature threatens to sue again, Adam will have to retain his own attorney. I won't be involved in a legal battle, particularly when I have my business with Senhor Alvarez to complete. What time is it in Brazil?"

"Some time or other," Kirby murmured.

"I'll call him immediately and close the deal before we find ourselves slapped with a summons."

Adam sat back with his brandy and scratched Montique's ears. "You two don't seriously expect me to believe you're worried about being sued by a cat?"

Kirby ran a fingertip around the rim of her snifter. "I don't think we'd better tell him about what happened last year when we tried to have her evicted."

"No!" Fairchild leaped up and shuffled before he darted to the door. "I won't discuss it. I won't remember it. I'm going to call Brazil."

"Ah, Adam..." Kirby trailed off with a meaningful glance at the doorway.

Adam didn't have to look to know that Isabelle was making an entrance.

"I won't be intimidated by a cat."

"I'm sure that's very stalwart of you." Kirby downed the rest of her drink then rose. "Just as I'm sure you'll understand if I leave you to your courage. I really have to reline my dresser drawers."

For the second time that day, Adam found himself alone with a dog and cat.

A half hour later, after he'd lost a staring match with Isabelle, Adam locked his door and contacted McIntyre. In the brief, concise tones that McIntyre had always admired, Adam relayed the conversation he'd overheard the night before.

"It fits," McIntyre stated. Adam could almost see him rubbing his hands together. "You've learned quite a bit in a short time. The check on Hiller reveals he's living on credit and reputation. Both are running thin. No idea where Fairchild's keeping it?"

"I'm surprised he doesn't have it hanging in full view." Adam lit a cigarette and frowned at the Titian across the room. "It would be just like him. He mentioned a Victor Alvarez from Brazil a couple of times. Some kind of deal he's cooking."

"I'll see what I can dig up. Maybe he's selling the Rembrandt."

"He hardly needs the money."

"Some people never have enough."

"Yeah." But it didn't fit. It just didn't fit. "I'll get back to you."

Adam brooded, but only for a few moments. The sooner he had something tangible, the sooner he could untangle himself. He opened the panel and went to work.

In the morning, Kirby posed for Adam for more than two hours without the slightest argument. If he thought her cooperation and her sunny disposition were designed to confuse him, he was absolutely right. She was also keeping him occupied while Fairchild made the final arrangements for the disposal of the Van Gogh.

Adam had worked the night before until after midnight, but had found nothing. Wherever Fairchild had hidden the Rembrandt, he'd hidden it well. Adam's search of the third floor was almost complete. It was time to look elsewhere.

"Hidden with respect and affection," he remembered. In all probability that would rule out the dungeons and the attic. Chances were he'd have to give them some time, but he intended to concentrate on the main portion of the house first. His main objective would be Fairchild's private rooms, but when and how he'd do them he had yet to determine.

After the painting session was over and Kirby went back to her own work, Adam wandered around the first floor. There was no one to question his presence. He was a guest and he was trusted. He was supposed to be, he reminded himself when he became uncomfortable. One of the reasons McIntyre had drafted him for this particular job was because he would have easy access to the Fairchilds and the house. He was, socially and professionally, one of them. They'd have no reason to be suspicious of a well-bred, successful artist whom they'd welcomed into their own home. And the more Adam tried to justify his actions, the more the guilt ate at him.

Enough, he told himself as he stared out at the darkening sky. He'd had enough for one day. It was time he went up and changed for Melanie Burgess's party. There he'd meet Stuart Hiller and Harriet Merrick. There was no emotional ties there to make him feel like a spy and a thief. Swearing at himself, he started up the stairs.

"Excuse me, Mr. Haines." Impatient, Adam turned and looked down at Tulip. "Were you going up?"

"Yes." Because he stood on the bottom landing blocking her way, he stood aside to let her pass.

"You take this up to her then, and see she drinks it." Tulip shoved a tall glass of milky white liquid into his hand. "All," she added tersely before she clomped back toward the kitchen.

Where did they get their servants? Adam wondered, frowning down at the glass in his hands. And why, for the love of

God, had he let himself be ordered around by one? When in Rome, he supposed, and started up the steps again.

The *she* obviously meant Kirby. Adam sniffed doubtfully at the glass as he knocked on her door.

"You can bring it in," she called out, "but I won't drink it. Threaten all you like."

All right, he decided, and pushed her door open. The bedroom was empty, but he could smell her.

"Do your worst," she invited. "You can't intimidate me with stories of intestinal disorders and vitamin deficiencies. I'm healthy as a horse."

The warm, sultry scent flowed over him. Glass in hand, he walked through and into the bathroom where the steam rose up, fragrant and misty as a rain forest. With her hair pinned on top of her head, Kirby lounged in a huge sunken tub. Overhead, hanging plants dripped down, green and moist. White frothy bubbles floated in heaps on the surface of the water.

"So she sent you, did she?" Unconcerned, Kirby rubbed a loofah sponge over one shoulder. The bubbles, she concluded, covered her with more modesty than most women at the party that night would claim. "Well, come in then, and stop scowling at me. I won't ask you to scrub my back."

He thought of Cleopatra, floating on her barge. Just how many men other than Caesar and Antony had she driven mad? He glanced at the long mirrored wall behind the sink. It was fogged with the steam that rose in visible columns from her bath. "Got the water hot enough?"

"Do you know what that is?" she demanded, and plucked her soap from the dish. The cake was a pale, pale pink and left a creamy lather on her skin. "It's a filthy-tasting mixture Tulip tries to force on me periodically. It has raw eggs in it and other vile things." Making a face she lifted one surprisingly long leg out of the bath and soaped it. "Tell me the truth, Adam, would you voluntarily drink raw eggs?"

He watched her run soap and fingertips down her calf. "I can't say I would."

"Well, then." Satisfied, she switched legs. "Down the drain with it."

"She told me to see that you drank it. All," he added, beginning to enjoy himself.

Her lower lip moved forward a bit as she considered. "Puts you in an awkward position, doesn't it?"

"A position in any case."

"Tell you what, I'll have a sip. Then when she asks if I drank it I can say I did. I'm trying to cut down on my lying."

Adam handed her the glass, watching as she sipped and grimaced. "I'm not sure you're being truthful this way."

"I said cutting down, not eliminating. Into the sink," she added. "Unless you'd care for the rest."

"I'll pass." He poured it out then sat on the lip of the tub.

Surprised by the move, she tightened her fingers on the soap. It plopped into the water. "Hydrophobia," she muttered. "No, don't bother, I'll find it." Dipping her hand in, she began to search. "You'd think they could make a soap that wasn't forever leaping out of your hands." Grateful for the distraction, she gripped the soap again. "Aha. I appreciate your bringing me that revolting stuff, Adam. Now if you'd like to run along..."

"I'm in no hurry." Idly he picked up her loofah. "You mentioned something about scrubbing your back."

"Robbery!" Fairchild's voice boomed into the room just ahead of him. "Call the police. Call the FBI. Adam, you'll be a witness." He nodded, finding nothing odd in the audience to his daughter's bath.

"I'm so glad I have a large bathroom," she murmured. "Pity I didn't think to serve refreshments." Relieved by the interruption, she ran the soap down her arm. "What's been stolen, Papa? The Monet street scene, the Renoir portrait? I know, your sweat socks."

"My black dinner suit!" Dramatically he pointed a finger to the ceiling. "We'll have to take fingerprints."

"Obviously stolen by a psychotic with a fetish for formal attire," Kirby concluded. "I love a mystery. Let's list the suspects." She pushed a lock of hair out of her eyes and leaned back—a naked, erotic Sherlock Holmes. "Adam, have you an alibi?"

With a half smile, he ran the damp abrasive sponge through his hands. "I've been seducing Polly all afternoon."

Her eyes lit with amusement. She'd known he had potential. "That won't do," she said soberly. "It wouldn't take above fifteen minutes to seduce Polly. You have a black dinner suit, I suppose."

"Circumstantial evidence."

"A search warrant," Fairchild chimed in, inspired. "We'll get a search warrant and go through the entire house."

"Time-consuming," Kirby decided. "Actually, Papa, I think we'd best look to Cards."

"The butler did it." Fairchild cackled with glee, then immediately sobered. "No, no, my suit would never fit Cards."

"True. Still, as much as I hate to be an informer, I overheard Cards telling Tulip he intended to take your suit."

"Trust," Fairchild mumbled to Adam. "Can't trust anyone."

"His motive was sponging and pressing, I believe." She sunk down to her neck and examined her toes. "He'll crumble like a wall if you accuse him. I'm sure of it."

"Very well." Fairchild rubbed his thin, clever hands together. "I'll handle it myself and avoid the publicity."

"A brave man," Kirby decided as her father strode out of the room. Relaxed and amused, she smiled at Adam. "Well, my bubbles seem to be melting, so we'd better continue this discussion some other time."

Reaching over, Adam yanked the chain and drew the old-fashioned plug out of the stupendous tub. "The time's coming when we're going to start—and finish—much more than a conversation."

Wary, Kirby watched her water level and last defense recede. When cornered, she determined, it was best to be nonchalant. She tried a smile that didn't quite conceal the nerves. "Let me know when you're ready."

"I intend to," he said softly. Without another word, he rose and left her alone.

Later, when he descended the stairs, Adam grinned when he heard her voice.

"Yes, Tulip, I drank the horrid stuff. I won't disgrace you by fainting in the Merrick living room from malnutrition." The low rumble of response that followed was dissatisfied. "Cricket wings, I've been walking in heels for half my life. They're not six inches, they're three. And I'll still have to look up at everyone over twelve. Go bake a cake, will you?"

He heard Tulip's mutter and sniff before she stomped out of the room and passed him.

"Adam, thank God. Let's go before she finds something else to nag me about."

Her dress was pure, unadorned white, thin and floaty. It covered her arms, rose high at the throat, as modest as a nun's habit, as sultry as a tropical night. Her hair fell, black and straight over the shoulders.

Tossing it back, she picked up a black cape and swirled it around her. For a moment she stood, adjusting it while the light from the lamps flitted over the absence of color. She looked like a Manet portrait—strong, romantic and timeless.

"You're a fabulous-looking creature, Kirby."

They both stopped, staring. He'd given compliments before, with more style, more finesse, but he'd never meant one more. She'd been flattered by princes, in foreign tongues and with smooth deliveries. It had never made her stomach flutter.

"Thank you," she managed. "So're you." No longer sure it was wise, she offered her hand. "Are you ready?"

"Yes. Your father?"

"He's already gone," she told him as she walked toward the door. And the sooner they were, the better. She needed a little more time before she was alone with him again. "We don't drive to parties together, especially to Harriet's. He likes to get there early and usually stays longer, trying to talk Harriet into bed. I've had my car brought around." She shut the door and led him to a silver Porsche. "I'd rather drive than navigate, if you don't mind."

But she didn't wait for his response as she dropped into the driver's seat. "Fine," Adam agreed.

"It's a marvelous night." She turned the key in the ignition. The power vibrated under their feet. "Full moon, lots of stars." Smoothly she released the brake, engaged the clutch and pressed the accelerator. Adam was tossed against the seat as they roared down the drive.

"You'll like Harriet," Kirby continued, switching gears as Adam stared at the blurring landscape. "She's like a mother to me." When they came to the main road, Kirby downshifted and swung to the left, tires squealing. "You met Melly, of course. I hope you won't desert me completely tonight after seeing her again."

Adam braced his feet against the floor. "Does anyone notice her when you're around?" And would they make it to the Merrick home alive?

"Of course." Surprised by the question, she turned to look at him.

"Good God, watch where you're going!" None too gently, he pushed her head around.

"Melly's the most perfectly beautiful woman I've ever known." Downshifting again, Kirby squealed around a right turn then accelerated. "She's a very clever designer and very, very proper. Wouldn't even take a settlement from her husband when they divorced. Pride, I suppose, but then she wouldn't need the money. There's a marvelous view of the Hudson coming up on your side, Adam." Kirby leaned over to point it out. The car swerved.

"I prefer seeing it from up here, thanks," Adam told her as he shoved her back in her seat. "Do you always drive this way?"

"Yes. There's the road you take to the gallery," she continued. She waved her hand vaguely as the car whizzed by an intersection. Adam glanced down at the speedometer.

"You're doing ninety."

"I always drive slower at night."

"There's good news." Muttering, he flicked on the lighter.

"There's the house up ahead." She raced around an ess curve. "Fabulous when it's all lit up this way."

The house was white and stately, the type you expected to

see high above the riverbank. It glowed with elegance from dozens of windows. Without slackening pace, Kirby sped up the circular drive. With a squeal of brakes, and a muttered curse from Adam, she stopped the Porsche at the front entrance.

Reaching over, Adam pulled the keys from the ignition and pocketed them. "I'm driving back."

"How thoughtful." Offering her hand to the valet, Kirby stepped out. "Now I won't have to limit myself to one drink. Champagne," she decided, moving up the steps beside him. "It seems like a night for it."

The moment the door opened, Kirby was enveloped by a flurry of dazzling, trailing silks. "Harriet." Kirby squeezed the statuesque woman with flaming red hair. "It's wonderful to see you, but I think I'm being gnawed by the denture work of your crocodile."

"Sorry, darling." Harriet held her necklace and drew back to press a kiss to each of Kirby's cheeks. She was an impressive woman, full-bodied in the style Rubens had immortalized. Her face was wide and smooth, dominated by deep green eyes that glittered with silver on the lids. Harriet didn't believe in subtlety. "And this must be your houseguest," she continued with a quick sizing up of Adam.

"Harriet Merrick, Adam Haines." Kirby grinned and pinched Harriet's cheek. "And behave yourself, or Papa'll have him choosing weapons."

"Wonderful idea." With one arm still linked with Kirby's, Harriet twined her other through Adam's. "I'm sure you have a fascinating life story to tell me, Adam."

"I'll make one up."

"Perfect." She liked the look of him. "We've a crowd already, though they're mostly Melanie's stuffy friends."

"Harriet, you've got to be more tolerant."

"No, I don't." She tossed back her outrageous hair. "I've been excruciatingly polite. Now that you're here, I don't have to be."

"Kirby." Melanie swept into the hall in an ice-blue sheath. "What a picture you make. Take her cloak, Ellen, though it's a pity to spoil that effect.'' Smiling, she held out a hand to Adam as the maid slipped Kirby's cloak off her shoulders. ''I'm so glad you came. We've some mutual acquaintances here, it seems. The Birminghams and Michael Towers from New York. You remember Michael, Kirby?''

''The adman who clicks his teeth?''

Harriet let out a roar of laughter while Adam struggled to control his. With a sigh, Melanie led them toward the party. ''Try to behave, will you?'' But Adam wasn't certain whether she spoke to Kirby or her mother.

This was the world he was used to—elegant people in elegant clothes having rational conversations. He'd been raised in the world of restrained wealth where champagne fizzed quietly and dignity was as essential as the proper alma mater. He understood it, he fit in.

After fifteen minutes, he was separated from Kirby and bored to death.

''I've decided to take a trek through the Australian bush,'' Harriet told Kirby. She fingered her necklace of crocodile teeth. ''I'd love you to come with me. We'd have such fun brewing a billy cup over the fire.''

''Camping?'' Kirby asked, mulling it over. Maybe what she needed was a change of scene, after her father settled down.

''Give it some thought,'' Harriet suggested. ''I'm not planning on leaving for another six weeks. Ah, Adam.'' Reaching out, she grabbed his arm. ''Did Agnes Birmingham drive you to drink? No, don't answer. It's written all over your face, but you're much too polite.''

He allowed himself to be drawn between her and Kirby, where he wanted to be. ''Let's just say I was looking for more stimulating conversation. I've found it.''

''Charming.'' She decided she liked him, but would reserve judgment a bit longer as to whether he'd suit her Kirby. ''I admire your work, Adam. I'd like to put the first bid in on your next painting.''

He took glasses from a passing waiter. ''I'm doing a portrait of Kirby.''

"She's posing for you?" Harriet nearly choked on her champagne. "Did you chain her?"

"Not yet." He gave Kirby a lazy glance. "It's still a possibility."

"You have to let me display it when it's finished." She might've been a woman who ran on emotion on many levels, but the bottom line was art, and the business of it. "I can promise to cause a nasty scene if you refuse."

"No one does it better," Kirby toasted her.

"You'll have to see the portrait of Kirby that Philip painted for me. She wouldn't sit for it, but it's brilliant." She toyed with the stem of her glass. "He painted it when she returned from Paris—three years ago, I suppose."

"I'd like to see it. I'd planned on coming by the gallery."

"Oh, it's here, in the library."

"Why don't you two just toddle along then?" Kirby suggested. "You've been talking around me, you might as well desert me physically, as well."

"Don't be snotty," Harriet told her. "You can come, too. And I... Well, well," she murmured in a voice suddenly lacking in warmth. "Some people have no sense of propriety."

Kirby turned her head, just slightly, and watched Stuart walk into the room. Her fingers tightened on the glass, but she shrugged. Before the movement was complete, Melanie was at her side.

"I'm sorry, Kirby. I'd hoped he wouldn't come after all."

In a slow, somehow insolent gesture, Kirby pushed her hair behind her back. "If it had mattered, I wouldn't have come."

"I don't want you to be embarrassed," Melanie began, only to be cut off by a quick and very genuine laugh.

"When have you ever known me to be embarrassed?"

"Well, I'll greet him, or it'll make matters worse." Still, Melanie hesitated, obviously torn between loyalty and manners.

"I'll fire him, of course," Harriet mused when her daughter went to do her duty. "But I want to be subtle about it."

"Fire him if you like, Harriet, but not on my account." Kirby drained her champagne.

"It appears we're in for a show, Adam." Harriet tapped a coral fingertip against her glass. "Much to Melanie's distress, Stuart's coming over."

Without saying a word, Kirby took Adam's cigarette.

"Harriet, you look marvelous." The smooth, cultured voice wasn't at all like the tone Adam had heard in Fairchild's studio. "Africa agreed with you."

Harriet gave him a bland smile. "We didn't expect to see you."

"I was tied up for a bit." Charming, elegant, he turned to Kirby. "You're looking lovely."

"So are you," she said evenly. "It seems your nose is back in joint." Without missing a beat, she turned to Adam. "I don't believe you've met. Adam, this is Stuart Hiller. I'm sure you know Adam Haines's work, Stuart."

"Yes, indeed." The handshake was polite and meaningless. "Are you staying in our part of New York long?"

"Until I finish Kirby's portrait," Adam told him and had the dual satisfaction of seeing Kirby grin and Stuart frown. "I've agreed to let Harriet display it in the gallery."

With that simple strategy, Adam won Harriet over.

"I'm sure it'll be a tremendous addition to our collection." Even a man with little sensitivity wouldn't have missed the waves of resentment. For the moment, Stuart ignored them. "I wasn't able to reach you in Africa, Harriet, and things have been hectic since your return. The Titian woman has been sold to Ernest Myerling."

As he lifted his glass, Adam's attention focused on Kirby. Her color drained, slowly, degree by degree until her face was as white as the silk she wore.

"I don't recall discussing selling the Titian," Harriet countered. Her voice was as colorless as Kirby's skin.

"As I said, I couldn't reach you. As the Titian isn't listed under your personal collection, it falls among the saleable paintings. I think you'll be pleased with the price." He lit a cigarette with a slim silver lighter. "Myerling did insist on having it tested. He's more interested in investment than art,

I'm afraid. I thought you'd want to be there tomorrow for the procedure.''

Oh, God, oh, my God! Panic, very real and very strong, whirled through Kirby's mind. In silence, Adam watched the fear grow in her eyes.

"Tested!" Obviously insulted, Harriet seethed. "Of all the gall, doubting the authenticity of a painting from my gallery. The Titian should not have been sold without my permission, and certainly not to a peasant."

"Testing isn't unheard-of, Harriet." Seeing a hefty commission wavering, Stuart soothed, "Myerling's a businessman, not an art expert. He wants facts." Taking a long drag, he blew out smoke. "In any case, the paperwork's already completed and there's nothing to be done about it. The deal's a fait accompli, hinging on the test results."

"We'll discuss this in the morning." Harriet's voice lowered as she finished off her drink. "This isn't the time or place."

"I—I have to freshen my drink," Kirby said suddenly. Without another word, she spun away to work her way through the crowd. The nausea, she realized, was a direct result of panic, and the panic was a long way from over. "Papa." She latched on to his arm and pulled him out of a discussion on Dali's versatility. "I have to talk to you. Now."

Hearing the edge in her voice, he let her drag him from the room.

Chapter 7

Kirby closed the doors of Harriet's library behind her and leaned back against them. She didn't waste any time. "The Titian's being tested in the morning. Stuart sold it."

"Sold it!" Fairchild's eyes grew wide, his face pink. "Impossible. Harriet wouldn't sell the Titian."

"She didn't. She was off playing with lions, remember?" Dragging both hands through her hair, she tried to speak calmly. "Stuart closed the deal, he just told her."

"I told you he was a fool, didn't I? Didn't I?" Fairchild repeated as he started dancing in place. "I told Harriet, too. Would anyone listen? No, not Harriet." He whirled around, plucked up a pencil from her desk and broke it in two. "She hires the idiot anyway and goes off to roam the jungle."

"There's no use going over that again!" Kirby snapped at him. "We've got to deal with the results."

"There wouldn't be any results if I'd been listened to. Stubborn woman falling for a pretty face. That's all it was." Pausing, he took a deep breath and folded his hands. "Well," he said in a mild voice, "this is a problem."

"Papa, this isn't an error in your checkbook."

"But it can be handled, probably with less effort. Any way out of the deal?"

"Stuart said the paperwork had been finalized. And it's Myerling," she added.

"That old pirate." He scowled a moment and gave Harriet's desk a quick kick. "No way out of it," Fairchild concluded. "On to the next step. We exchange them." He saw by Kirby's nod that she'd already thought of it. There was a quick flash of pride before anger set in. The round, cherubic face tightened. "By God, Stuart's going to pay for making me give up that painting."

"Very easily said, Papa." Kirby walked into the room until she stood toe to toe with him. "But who was it who settled Adam in the same room with the painting? Now we're going to have to get it out of his room, then get the copy from the gallery in without him knowing there's been a switch. I'm sure you've noticed Adam's not a fool."

Fairchild's eyebrows wiggled. His lips curved. He rubbed his palms together. "A plan."

Knowing it was too late for regrets, Kirby flopped into a chair. "We'll phone Cards and have him put the painting in my room before we get back."

He approved this with a brief nod. "You have a marvelous criminal mind, Kirby."

She had to smile. A sense of adventure was already spearing through the panic. "Heredity," she told her father. "Now, here's my idea...." Lowering her voice, she began the outline.

"It'll work," Fairchild decided a few moments later.

"That has yet to be seen." It sounded plausible enough, but she didn't underestimate Adam Haines. "So there's nothing to be done but to do it."

"And do it well."

Her agreement was a careless shrug of her shoulders. "Adam should be too tired to notice that the Titian's gone, and after I make the exchange at the gallery, I'll slip it back into his room. Sleeping pills are the only way." She stared down at her hands, dissatisfied, but knowing it was the only way out. "I don't like doing this to Adam."

"He'll just get a good night's sleep." Fairchild sat on the arm of her chair. "We all need a good night's sleep now and again. Now we'd better go back or Melanie'll send out search parties.''

"You go first." Kirby let out a deep breath. "I'll phone Cards and tell him to get started.''

Kirby waited until Fairchild had closed the doors again before she went to the phone on Harriet's desk. She didn't mind the job she had to do, in fact she looked forward to it. Except for Adam's part. It couldn't be helped, she reminded herself, and gave Cards brief instructions.

Now, she thought as she replaced the receiver, it was too late to turn back. The die, so to speak, had been cast. The truth was, the hastily made plans for the evening would prove a great deal more interesting than a party. While she hesitated a moment longer, Stuart opened the door, then closed it softly behind him.

"Kirby." He crossed to her with a half smile on his face. His patience had paid off now that he'd found her alone. "We have to talk.''

Not now, she thought on a moment's panic. Didn't she have enough to deal with? Then she thought of the way he'd humiliated her. The way he'd lied. Perhaps it was better to get everything over with at once.

"I think we said everything we had to say at our last meeting.''

"Not nearly everything.''

"Redundancy bores me," she said mildly. "But if you insist, I'll say this. It's a pity you haven't the money to suit your looks. Your mistake, Stuart, was in not making me want you—not the way you wanted me." Deliberately her voice dropped, low and seductive. She hadn't nearly finished paying him back. "You could deceive me about love, but not about lust. If you'd concentrated on that instead of greed, you might've had a chance. You are," she continued softly, "a liar and a cheat, and while that might've been an interesting diversion for a short time, I thank God you never got your hands on me or my money.''

Before she could sweep around him, he grabbed her arm.

"You'd better remember your father's habits before you sling mud."

She dropped her gaze to his hand, then slowly raised it again. It was a look designed to infuriate. "Do you honestly compare yourself with my father?" Her fury came out on a laugh, and the laugh was insult itself. "You'll never have his style, Stuart. You're second-rate, and you'll always be second-rate."

He brought the back of his hand across her face hard enough to make her stagger. She didn't make a sound. When she stared up at him, her eyes were slits, very dark, very dangerous slits. The pain meant nothing, only that he'd caused it and she had no way to pay him back in kind. Yet.

"You prove my point," Kirby said evenly as she brushed her fingers over her cheek. "Second-rate."

He wanted to hit her again, but balled his hands into fists. He needed her, for the moment. "I'm through playing games, Kirby. I want the Rembrandt."

"I'd take a knife to it before I saw Papa hand it over to you. You're out of your class, Stuart." She didn't bother to struggle when he grabbed her arms.

"Two days, Kirby. You tell the old man he has two days or it's you who'll pay."

"Threats and physical abuse are your only weapons." Abruptly, with more effort that she allowed him to see, Kirby turned her anger to ice. "I've weapons of my own, Stuart, infinitely more effective. And if I chose to drop to gutter tactics, you haven't the finesse to deal with me." She kept her eyes on his, her body still. He might curse her, but Stuart knew the truth when he heard it. "You're a snake," she added quietly. "And you can't stay off your belly for long. The fact that you're stronger than I is only a temporary advantage."

"Very temporary," Adam said as he closed the door at his back. His voice matched Kirby's chill for chill. "Take your hands off her."

Kirby felt the painful grip on her arms relax and watched Stuart struggle with composure. Carefully he straightened his tie. "Remember what I said, Kirby. It could be important to you."

"You remember how Byron described a woman's revenge," she countered as she rubbed the circulation back into her arm. "'Like a tiger's spring—deadly, quick and crushing.'" She dropped her arms to her sides. "It could be important to you." Turning, she walked to the window and stared out at nothing.

Adam kept his hand on the knob as Stuart walked to the door. "Touch her again and you'll have to deal with me." Slowly Adam turned the knob and opened the door. "That's something else for you to remember." The sounds of the party flowed in, then silenced again as he shut the door at Stuart's back.

"Well," he began, struggling with his own fury. "I guess I should be grateful I don't have an ex-fiancée hanging around." He'd heard enough to know that the Rembrandt had been at the bottom of it, but he pushed that aside and went to her. "He's a poor loser, and you're amazing. Most women would have been weeping or pleading. You stood there flinging insults."

"I don't believe in pleading," she said as lightly as she could. "And Stuart would never reduce me to tears."

"But you're trembling," he murmured as he put his hands on her shoulders.

"Anger." She drew in a deep breath and let it out slowly. She didn't care to show a weakness, not to anyone. "I appreciate the white-knight routine."

He grinned and kissed the top of her head. "Any time. Why don't we..." He trailed off as he turned her to face him. The mark of Stuart's hand had faded to a dull, angry red, but it was unmistakable. When Adam touched his fingers to her cheek, his eyes were cold. Colder and more dangerous than she'd ever seen them. Without a word, he spun around and headed for the door.

"*No!*" Desperation wasn't characteristic, but she felt it now as she grabbed his arm. "No, Adam, don't. Don't get involved." He shook her off, but she sprinted to the door ahead of him and stood with her back pressed against it. The tears she'd been able to control with Stuart now swam in her eyes. "Please, I've enough on my conscience without dragging you into this. I live my life as I choose, and what I get from it is of my own making."

He wanted to brush her aside and push through the crowd outside the door until he had his hands on Stuart. He wanted, more than he'd ever wanted anything, the pleasure of smelling the other man's blood. But she was standing in front of him, small and delicate, with tears in her eyes. She wasn't the kind of woman tears came easily to.

"All right." He brushed one from her cheek and made a promise on it. Before it was over, he would indeed smell Stuart Hiller's blood. "You're only postponing the inevitable."

Relieved, she closed her eyes a moment. When she opened them again, they were still damp, but no longer desperate. "I don't believe in the inevitable." She took his hand and brought it to her cheek, holding it there a moment until she felt the tension drain from both of them. "You must've come in to see my portrait. It's there, above the desk."

She gestured, but he didn't take his eyes from hers. "I'll have to give it a thorough study, right after I give my attention to the original." He gathered her close and just held her. It was, though neither one of them had known it, the perfect gesture of support. Resting her head against his shoulder, she thought of peace, and she thought of the plans that had already been put into motion.

"I'm sorry, Adam."

He heard the regret in her voice and brushed his lips over her hair. "What for?"

"I can't tell you." She tightened her arms around his waist and clung to him as she had never clung to anyone. "But I am sorry."

The drive away from the Merrick estate was more sedate than the approach. Kirby sat in the passenger seat. Under most circumstances, Adam would've attributed her silence and unease to her scene with Hiller. But he remembered her reaction at the mention of the sale of a Titian.

What was going on in that kaleidoscope brain of hers? he wondered. And how was he going to find out? The direct approach, Adam decided, and thought fleetingly that it was a shame to waste the moonlight. "The Titian that's been sold," he began, pretending he didn't see Kirby jolt. "Has Harriet had it long?"

"The Titian." She folded her hands in her lap. "Oh, years and years. Your Mrs. Birmingham's shaped like a zucchini, don't you think?"

"She's not my Mrs. Birmingham." A new game, he concluded, and relaxed against the seat. "It's too bad it was sold before I could see it. I'm a great admirer of Titian. The painting in my room's exquisite."

Kirby let out a sound that might have been a nervous giggle. "The one at the gallery is just as exquisite," she told him. "Ah, here we are, home again. Just leave the car out front," she said, half relieved, half annoyed, that the next steps were being put into play. "Cards will see to it. I hope you don't mind coming back early, Adam. There's Papa," she added as she stepped from the car. "He must've struck out with Harriet. Let's have a nightcap, shall we?"

She started up the steps without waiting for his agreement. Knowing he was about to become a part of some hastily conceived plan, he went along. It's all too pat, he mused as Fairchild waited at the door with a genial smile.

"Too many people," Fairchild announced. "I much prefer small parties. Let's have a drink in the parlor and gossip."

Don't look so bloody anxious, Kirby thought, and nearly scowled at him. "I'll go tell Cards to see to the Rolls and my car." Still, she hesitated as the men walked toward the parlor. Adam caught the indecision in her eyes before Fairchild cackled and slapped him on the back.

"And don't hurry back," he told Kirby. "I've had enough of women for a while."

"How sweet." The irony and strength came back into her

voice. "I'll just go in and eat Tulip's lemon trifle. All," she added as she swept past.

Fairchild thought of his midnight snack with regret. "Brat," he muttered. "Well, we'll have scotch instead."

Adam dipped his hands casually in his pockets and watched every move Fairchild made. "I had a chance to see Kirby's portrait in Harriet's library. It's marvelous."

"One of my best, if I say so myself." Fairchild lifted the decanter of Chivas Regal. "Harriet's fond of my brat, you know." In a deft move, Fairchild slipped two pills from his pocket and dropped them into the scotch.

Under normal circumstances Adam would've missed it. Clever hands, he thought as intrigued as he was amused. Very quick, very agile. Apparently they wanted him out of the way. He was going to find it a challenge to pit himself against both of them. With a smile, he accepted the drink, then turned to the Corot landscape behind him.

"Corot's treatment of light," Adam began, taking a small sip. "It gives all of his work such deep perspective."

No ploy could've worked better. Fairchild was ready to roll. "I'm very partial to Corot. He had such a fine hand with details without being finicky and obscuring the overall painting. Now the leaves," he began, and set down his drink to point them out. While the lecture went on, Adam set down his own drink, picked up Fairchild's and enjoyed the scotch.

Upstairs Kirby found the Titian already wrapped in heavy paper. "Bless you, Cards," she murmured. She checked her watch and made herself wait a full ten minutes before she picked up the painting and left the room. Quietly she moved down the back stairs and out to where her car waited.

In the parlor, Adam studied Fairchild as he sat in the corner of the sofa, snoring. Deciding the least he could do was to make his host more comfortable, Adam started to swing Fairchild's legs onto the couch. The sound of a car engine stopped him. Adam was at the window in time to see Kirby's Porsche race down the drive.

"You're going to have company," he promised her. Within moments, he was behind the wheel of the Rolls.

The surge of speed added to Kirby's sense of adventure. She drove instinctively while she concentrated on her task for the evening. It helped ease the guilt over Adam, a bit.

A quarter mile from the gallery, she stopped and parked on the side of the road. Grateful that the Titian was relatively small, though the frame added weight, she gathered it up again and began to walk. Her heels echoed on the asphalt.

Clouds drifted across the moon, obscuring the light then freeing it again. With her cape swirling around her, Kirby walked into the cover of trees that bordered the gallery. The light was dim, all shadows and secrets. Up ahead came the low moan of an owl. Tossing back her hair, she laughed.

"Perfect," she decided. "All we need is a rumble of thunder and a few streaks of lightning. Skulking through the woods on a desperate mission," she mused. "Surrounded by the sounds of night." She shifted the bundle in her arms and continued on. "What one does for those one loves."

She could see the stately red brick of the gallery through the trees. Moonlight slanted over it. Almost there, she thought with a quick glance at her watch. In an hour she'd be back home—and perhaps she'd have the lemon trifle after all.

A hand fell heavily on her shoulder. Her cape spread out like wings as she whirled. Great buckets of blood, she thought as she stared up at Adam.

"Out for a stroll?" he asked her.

"Why, hello, Adam." Since she couldn't disappear, she had to face him down. She tried a friendly smile. "What are you doing out here?"

"Following you."

"Flattering. But wasn't Papa entertaining you?"

"He dozed off."

She stared up at him a moment, then let out a breath. A wry smile followed it. "I suppose he deserved it. I hope you left him comfortable."

"Enough. Now what's in the package?"

Though she knew it was useless, she fluttered her lashes. "Package?"

He tapped his finger on the wrapping.

"Oh, this package. Just a little errand I have to run. It's getting late, shouldn't you be starting back?"

"Not a chance."

"No." She moved her shoulders. "I thought not."

"What's in the package, Kirby, and what do you intend to do with it?"

"All right." She thrust the painting into his arms because hers were tiring. When the jig was up, you had to make the best of it. "I suppose you deserve an explanation, and you won't leave until you have one anyway. It has to be the condensed version, Adam, I'm running behind schedule." She laid a hand on the package he held. "This is the Titian woman, and I'm going to put it in the gallery."

He lifted a brow. He didn't need Kirby to tell him that he held a painting. "I was under the impression that the Titian woman was in the gallery."

"No..." She drew out the word. If she could have thought of a lie, a half-truth, a fable, she'd have used it. She could only think of the truth. "This is a Titian," she told him with a nod to the package. "The painting in the gallery is a Fairchild."

He let the silence hang a moment while the moonlight filtered over her face. She looked like an angel...or a witch. "Your father forged a Titian and palmed it off on the gallery as an original?"

"Certainly not!" Indignation wasn't feigned. Kirby bit back on it and tried to be patient. "I won't tell you any more if you insult my father."

"I don't know what came over me."

"All right then." She leaned back against a tree. "Perhaps I should start at the beginning."

"Good choice."

"Years ago, Papa and Harriet were vacationing in Europe. They came across the Titian, each one swearing they'd seen it first. Neither one would give way, and it would've been criminal to let the painting go altogether. They compromised." She gestured at the package. "Each paid half, and Papa painted a copy. They rotate ownership of the original every six months, alternating with the copy, if you get the drift. The stipulation was that neither of them could claim ownership. Harriet kept hers in the gallery—not listing it as part of her private collection. Papa kept it in a guest room.''

He considered for a moment. ''That's too ridiculous for you to have made up.''

''Of course I didn't make it up.'' As it could, effectively, her bottom lip pouted. ''Don't you trust me?''

''No. You're going to do a lot more explaining when we get back.''

Perhaps, Kirby thought. And perhaps not.

''Now just how do you intend to get into the gallery?''

''With Harriet's keys.''

''She gave you her keys?''

Kirby let out a frustrated breath. ''Pay attention, Adam. Harriet's furious about Stuart selling the painting, but until she studies the contracts there's no way to know how binding the sale is. It doesn't look good, and we can't take a chance on having the painting tested—my father's painting, that is. If the procedure were sophisticated enough, it might prove that the painting's not sixteenth-century.''

''Harriet's aware that a forgery's hanging in her gallery?''

''An emulation, Adam.''

''And are there any other...emulations in the Merrick Gallery?''

She gave him a long, cool look. ''I'm trying not to be annoyed. All of Harriet's paintings are authentic, as is her half of the Titian.''

''Why didn't she replace it herself?''

''Because,'' Kirby began and checked her watch. Time was slipping away from her. ''Not only would it have been difficult for her to disappear from the party early as we did, but it would've been awkward altogether. The night watchman could report to Stuart that she came to the gallery in the middle of the night carrying a package. He might put two and two together. Yes, even he might add it up.''

''So what'll the night watchman have to say about Kirby Fairchild coming into the gallery in the middle of the night?''

"He won't see us." Her smile was quick and very, very smug.
"Us?"

"Since you're here." She smiled at him again, and meant
it. "I've told you everything, and being a gentleman you'll
help me make the switch. We'll have to work quickly. If we're
caught, we'll just brazen it out. You won't have to do anything, I'll handle it."

"You'll handle it." He nodded at the drifting clouds. "We
can all sleep easy now. One condition." He stopped her before she could speak. "When we're done, if we're not in jail
or hospitalized, I want to know it all. If we are in jail, I'll
murder you as slowly as possible."

"That's two conditions," she muttered. "But all right."

They watched each other a moment, one wondering how
much would have to be divulged, one wondering how much
could be learned. Both found the deceit unpleasant.

"Let's get it done." Adam gestured for her to go first.

Kirby walked across the grass and went directly to the main
door. From the deep pocket of her cloak, she drew out keys.

"These two switch off the main alarm," she explained as
she turned keys in a series of locks. "And these unbolt the
door." She smiled at the faint click of tumblers. Turning, she
studied Adam, standing behind her in his elegant dinner suit.
"I'm so glad we dressed for it."

"Seems right to dress formally when you're breaking into
a distinguished institution."

"True." Kirby dropped the keys back in her pocket. "And
we do make a rather stunning couple. The Titian hangs in the
west room on the second floor. The watchman has a little
room in the back, here on the main floor. I assume he drinks
black coffee laced with rum and reads pornographic magazines. I would. He's supposed to make rounds hourly, though
there's no way to be certain he's diligent."

"And what time does he make them, if he does?"

"On the hour—which gives us twenty minutes." She
glanced at her watch and shrugged. "That's adequate, though
if you hadn't pressed me for details we'd've had more time."

Don't scowl," she added. She pressed her finger to her lips and slipped through the door.

From out of the depths of her pocket came a flashlight. They followed the narrow beam over the carpet. Together they moved up the staircase.

Obviously she knew the gallery well. Without hesitation, she moved through the dark, turning on the second floor and marching down the corridor without breaking rhythm. Her cape swirled out as she pivoted into a room. In silence she played her light over paintings until it stopped on the copy of the Titian that had hung in Adam's room.

"There," Kirby whispered as the light shone on the sunset hair Titian had immortalized. The light was too poor for Adam to be certain of the quality, but he promised himself he'd examine it minutes later.

"It's not possible to tell them apart—not even an expert." She knew what he was thinking. "Harriet's a respected authority, and she couldn't. I'm not sure the tests wouldn't bear it out as authentic. Papa has a way of treating the paints." She moved closer so that her light illuminated the entire painting. "Papa put a red circle on the back of the copy's frame so they could be told apart. I'll take the package now," she told him briskly. "You can get the painting down." She knelt and began to unwrap the painting they'd brought with them. "I'm glad you happened along," she decided. "Your height's going to be an advantage when it comes to taking down and putting up again."

Adam paused with the forgery in his hands. Throttling her would be too noisy at the moment, he decided. But later... "Let's have it then."

In silence they exchanged paintings. Adam replaced his on the wall, while Kirby wrapped the other. After she'd tied the string, she played the light on the wall again. "It's a bit crooked," she decided. "A little to the left."

"Look, I—" Adam broke off at the sound of a faint, tuneless whistle.

"He's early!" Kirby whispered as she gripped the painting. "Who expects efficiency from hired help these days?"

In a quick move, Adam had the woman, the painting and himself pressed against the wall by the archway. Finding herself neatly sandwiched, and partially smothered, Kirby held back a desperate urge to giggle. Certain it would annoy Adam, she held her breath and swallowed.

The whistle grew louder.

In her mind's eye, Kirby's pictured the watchman strolling down the corridor, pausing to shine his light here and there as he walked. She hoped, for the watchman's peace of mind and Adam's disposition, the search was cursory.

Adam felt her trembling and held her tighter. Somehow he'd manage to protect her. He forgot that she'd gotten him into the mess in the first place. Now his only thought was to get her out of it.

A beam of light streamed passed the doorway, with the whistle close behind. Kirby shook like a leaf. The light bounced into the room, sweeping over the walls in a curving arch. Adam tensed, knowing discovery was inches away. The light halted, rested a moment, then streaked away over its original route. And there was darkness.

They didn't move, though Kirby wanted to badly, with the frame digging into her back. They waited, still and silent, until the whistling receded.

Because her light trembling had become shudder after shudder, Adam drew her away to whisper reassurance. "It's all right. He's gone."

"You were wonderful." She covered her mouth to muffle the laughter. "Ever thought about making breaking and entering a hobby?"

He slid the painting under one arm, then took a firm grip on hers. When the time was right, he'd pay her back for this one. "Let's go."

"Okay, since it's probably a bad time to show you around. Pity," she decided. "There are some excellent engravings in the next room, and a really marvelous still life Papa painted."

"Under his own name?"

"Really, Adam." They paused at the hallway to make certain it was clear. "That's tacky."

They didn't speak again until they were hidden by the trees. Then Adam turned to her. "I'll take the painting and follow you back. If you go over fifty, I'll murder you."

She stopped when they reached the cars, then threw him off balance with suddenly serious eyes. "I appreciate everything, Adam. I hope you don't think too badly of us. It matters."

He ran a finger down her cheek. "I've yet to decide what I think of you."

Her lips curved up at the corners. "That's all right then. Take your time."

"Get in and drive," he ordered before he could forget what had to be resolved. She had a way of making a man forget a lot of things. Too many things.

The trip back took nearly twice the time, as Kirby stayed well below the speed limit. Again she left the Porsche out front, knowing Cards would handle the details. Once inside, she went straight to the parlor.

"Well," she mused as she looked at her father. "He seems comfortable enough, but I think I'll just stretch him out."

Adam leaned against the doorjamb and waited as she settled her father for the night. After loosening his tie and pulling off his shoes, she tossed her cape over him and kissed his balding head. "Papa," she murmured. "You've been outmaneuvered."

"We'll talk upstairs, Kirby. Now."

Straightening, Kirby gave Adam a long, mild look. "Since you ask so nicely." She plucked a decanter of brandy and two glasses from the bar. "We may as well be sociable during the inquisition." She swept by him and up the stairs.

Chapter 8

Kirby switched on the rose-tinted bedside lamp before she poured brandy. After handing Adam a snifter, she kicked off her shoes and sat cross-legged on the bed. She watched as he ripped off the wrapping and examined the painting.

Frowning, he studied the brush strokes, the use of color, the Venetian technique that had been Titian's. Fascinating, he thought. Absolutely fascinating. "This is a copy?"

She had to smile. She warmed the brandy between her hands but didn't drink. "Papa's mark's on the frame."

Adam saw the red circle but didn't find it conclusive. "I'd swear it was authentic."

"So would anyone."

He propped the painting against the wall and turned to her. She looked like an Indian priestess—the nightfall of hair against the virgin white silk. With an enigmatic smile, she continued to sit in the lotus position, the brandy cupped in both hands.

"How many other paintings in your father's collection are copies?"

Slowly she lifted the snifter and sipped. She had to work at not being annoyed by the question, telling herself he was entitled to ask. "All of the paintings in Papa's collection are authentic. Excepting now this Titian.'' She moved her shoulders carelessly. It hardly mattered at this point.

''When you spoke of his technique in treating paints for age, you didn't give the impression he'd only used it on one painting.''

What had given her the idea he wouldn't catch on to a chance remark like that one? she wondered. The fat's in the fire in any case, she reminded herself. And she was tired of trying to dance around it. She swirled her drink and red and amber lights glinted against the glass.

''I trust you,'' she murmured, surprising them both. ''But I don't want to involve you, Adam, in something you'll regret knowing about. I really want you to understand that. Once I tell you, it'll be too late for regrets.''

He didn't care for the surge of guilt. Who was deceiving whom now? his conscience demanded of him. And who'd pay the price in the end? ''Let me worry about that,'' he stated, dealing with Kirby now and saving his conscience for later. He swallowed brandy and let the heat ease through him. ''How many copies has your father done?''

''Ten—no, eleven,'' she corrected, and ignored his quick oath. ''Eleven, not counting the Titian, which falls into a different category.''

''A different category,'' he murmured. Crossing the room, he splashed more brandy into his glass. He was certain to need it. ''How is this different?''

''The Titian was a personal agreement between Harriet and Papa. Merely a way to avoid bad feelings.''

''And the others?'' He sat on a fussily elegant Queen Anne chair. ''What sort of arrangements did they entail?''

''Each is individual, naturally.'' She hesitated as she studied him. If they'd met a month from now, would things have been different? Perhaps. Timing again, she mused and sipped the warming brandy. ''To simplify matters, Papa painted them, then sold them to interested parties.''

''Sold them?'' He stood because he couldn't be still. Wishing it had been possible to stop her before she'd begun, he started to pace the room. ''Good God, Kirby. Don't you understand what he's done? What he's doing? It's fraud, plain and simple.''

"I wouldn't call it fraud," she countered, giving her brandy a contemplative study. It was, after all, something she'd given a great deal of thought to. "And certainly not plain or simple.''

"What then?" If he'd had a choice, he'd have taken her away then and there—left the Titian, the Rembrandt and her crazy father in the ridiculous castle and taken off. Somewhere. Anywhere.

"Fudging," Kirby decided with a half smile.

"Fudging," he repeated in a quiet voice. He'd forgotten she was mad as well. "Fudging. Selling counterfeit paintings for large sums of money to the unsuspecting is fudging? Fixing a parking ticket's fudging." He paced another moment, looking for answers. "Damn it, his work's worth a fortune. Why does he do it?"

"Because he can," she said simply. She spread one hand, palm out. "Papa's a genius, Adam. I don't say that just as his daughter, but as a fellow artist. With the genius comes a bit of eccentricity, perhaps." Ignoring the sharp sound of derision, she went on. "To Papa, painting's not just a vocation. Art and life are one, interchangeable.''

"I'll go along with all that, Kirby, but it doesn't explain why—''

"Let me finish." She had both hands on the snifter again, resting it in her lap. "One thing Papa can't tolerate is greed, in any form. To him greed isn't just the worship of money, but the hoarding of art. You must know his collection's constantly being lent out to museums and art schools. Though he has strong feelings that art belongs in the private sector, as well as public institutions, he hates the idea of the wealthy buying up great art for investment purposes.''

"Admirable, Kirby. But he's made a business out of selling fraudulent paintings.''

"Not a business. He's never benefited financially." She set her glass aside and clasped her hands together. "Each prospective buyer of one of Papa's emulations is first researched thoroughly.'' She waited a beat. ''By Harriet.''

He nearly sat back down again. ''Harriet Merrick's in on all of this?''

''All of this,'' she said mildly, ''has been their joint hobby for the last fifteen years.''

''Hobby,'' he murmured and did sit.

''Harriet has very good connections, you see. She makes certain the buyer is very wealthy and that he or she lives in a remote location. Two years ago, Papa sold an Arabian sheik a fabulous Renoir. It was one of my favorites. Anyway—'' she continued, getting up to freshen Adam's drink, then her own ''—each buyer would also be known for his or her attachment to money, and/or a complete lack of any sense of community spirit or obligation. Through Harriet, they'd learn of Papa's ownership of a rare, officially undiscovered artwork.''

Taking her own snifter, she returned to her position on the bed while Adam remained silent. ''At the first contact, Papa is always uncooperative without being completely dismissive. Gradually he allows himself to be worn down until the deal's made. The price, naturally, is exorbitant, otherwise the art fanciers would be insulted.'' She took a small sip and enjoyed the warm flow of the brandy. ''He deals only in cash, so there's no record. Then the paintings float off to the Himalayas or Siberia or somewhere to be kept in seclusion. Papa then donates the money anonymously to charity.''

Taking a deep breath at the end of her speech, Kirby rewarded herself with more brandy.

''You're telling me that he goes through all that, all the work, all the intrigue, for nothing?''

''I certainly am not.'' Kirby shook her head and leaned forward. ''He gets a great deal. He gets satisfaction, Adam. What else is necessary after all?''

He struggled to remember the code of right and wrong. ''Kirby, he's stealing!''

Kirby tilted her head and considered. ''Who caught your

support and admiration, Adam? The Sheriff of Nottingham or Robin Hood?''

"It's not the same." He dragged a hand through his hair as he tried to convince them both. "Damn it, Kirby, it's not the same."

"There's a newly modernized pediatric wing at the local hospital," she began quietly. "A little town in Appalachia has a new fire engine and modern equipment. Another, in the dust bowl, has a wonderful new library."

"All right." He rose again to cut her off. "In fifteen years I'm sure there's quite a list. Maybe in some strange way it's commendable, but it's also illegal, Kirby. It has to stop."

"I know." Her simple agreement broke his rhythm. With a half smile, Kirby moved her shoulders. "It was fun while it lasted, but I've known for some time it had to stop before something went wrong. Papa has a project in mind for a series of paintings, and I've convinced him to begin soon. It should take him about five years and give us a breathing space. But in the meantime, he's done something I don't know how to cope with."

She was about to give him more. Even before she spoke, Adam knew Kirby was going to give him all her trust. He sat in silence, despising himself, as she told him everything she knew about the Rembrandt.

"I imagine part of it's revenge on Stuart," she continued, while Adam smoked in silence and she again swirled her brandy without drinking. "Somehow Stuart found out about Papa's hobby and threatened exposure the night I broke our engagement. Papa told me not to worry, that Stuart wasn't in a position to make waves. At the time I had no idea about the Rembrandt business."

She was opening up to him, no questions, no hesitation. He was going to probe, God help him, he hadn't a choice. "Do you have any idea where he might've hidden it?"

"No, but I haven't looked." When she looked at him, she wasn't the sultry gypsy or the exotic princess. She was only a daughter concerned about an adored father. "He's a good man, Adam. No one knows that better than I. I know there's

a reason for what he's done, and for the time being, I have
to accept that. I don't expect you to share my loyalty, just my
confidence." He didn't speak, and she took his silence for
agreement. "My main concern now is that Papa's underesti-
mating Stuart's ruthlessness."

"He won't when you tell him about the scene in the library."

"I'm not going to tell him. Because," she continued before
Adam could argue, "I have no way of predicting his reaction.
You may have noticed, Papa's a very volatile man." Tilting
her glass, she met his gaze with a quick change of mood. "I
don't want you to worry about all this, Adam. Talk to Papa
about it if you like. Have a chat with Harriet, too. Personally,
I find it helpful to tuck the whole business away from time
to time and let it hibernate. Like a grizzly bear."

"Grizzly bear."

She laughed and rose. "Let me get you some more
brandy."

He stopped her with a hand on her wrist. "Have you told
me everything?"

With a frown, she brushed at a speck of lint on the bed-
spread. "Did I mention the Van Gogh?"

"Oh, God." He pressed his fingers to his eyes. Somehow
he'd hoped there'd be an end without really believing it.
"What Van Gogh?"

Kirby pursed her lips. "Not exactly a Van Gogh."

"Your father?"

"His latest. He's sold it to Victor Alvarez, a coffee baron
in South America." She smiled as Adam said nothing and
stared straight ahead. "The working conditions on his farm
are deplorable. Of course, there's nothing we can do to rem-
edy that, but Papa's already allocated the purchase price for
a school somewhere in the area. It's his last for several years,
Adam," she added as he sat with his fingers pressed against
his eyes. "And really, I think he'll be pleased that you know
all about everything. He'd love to show this painting to you.
He's particularly pleased with it."

Adam rubbed his hands over his face. It didn't surprise him

to hear himself laughing. "I suppose I should be grateful he hasn't decided to do the ceiling in the Sistine Chapel."

"Only after he retires," Kirby put in cheerfully. "And that's years off yet."

Not certain whether she was joking or not, he let it pass. "I've got to give all this a little time to settle."

"Fair enough."

He wasn't going back to his room to report to McIntyre, he decided as he set his brandy aside. He wasn't ready for that yet, so soon after Kirby shared it all with him without questions, without limitations. It wasn't possible to think about his job, or remember outside obligations, when she looked at him with all her trust. No, he'd find a way, somehow, to justify what he chose to do in the end. Right and wrong weren't so well defined now.

Looking at her, he needed to give, to soothe, to show her she'd been right to give him that most precious of gifts— unqualified trust. Perhaps he didn't deserve it, but he needed it. He needed her.

Without a word, he pulled her into his arms and crushed his mouth to hers, no patience, no requests. Before either of them could think, he drew down the zipper at the back of her dress.

She wanted to give to him—anything, everything he wanted. She didn't want to question him but to forget all the reasons why they shouldn't be together. It would be so easy to drown in the flood of feeling that was so new and so unique. And yet, anything real, anything strong, was never easy. She'd been taught from an early age that the things that mattered most were the hardest to obtain. Drawing back, she determined to put things back on a level she could deal with.

"You surprise me," she said with a smile she had to work at.

He pulled her back. She wouldn't slip away from him this time. "Good."

"You know, most women expect a seduction, no matter how perfunctory."

The amusement might be in her eyes, but he could feel the

thunder of her heart against his. "Most women aren't Kirby Fairchild." If she wanted to play it lightly, he'd do his damnedest to oblige her—as long as the result was the same. "Why don't we call this my next spontaneous act?" he suggested, and slipped her dress down her shoulders. "I wouldn't want to bore you with a conventional pursuit."

How could she resist him? The hands light on her skin, the mouth that smiled and tempted? She'd never hesitated about taking what she wanted...until now. Perhaps the time had come for the chess game to stop at a stalemate, with neither winning all and neither losing anything.

Slowly she smiled and let her dress whisper almost soundlessly to the floor.

He found her a treasure of cool satin and warm flesh. She was as seductive, as alluring, as he'd known she'd be. Once she'd decided to give, there were no restrictions. In a simple gesture she opened her arms to him and they came together.

Soft sighs, low murmurs, skin against skin. Moonlight and the rose tint from the lamp competed, then merged, as the mattress yielded under their weight. Her mouth was hot and open, her arms were strong. As she moved under him, inviting, taunting, he forgot how small she was.

Everything. All. Now. Needs drove them both to take without patience, and yet... Somehow, beneath the passion, under the heat, was a tenderness neither had expected from the other.

He touched. She trembled. She tasted. He throbbed. They wanted until the air seemed to spark with it. With each second both of them found more of what they'd needed, but the findings brought more greed. Take, she seemed to say, then give and give and give.

She had no time to float, only to throb. For him. From him. Her body craved—*yearn* was too soft a word. She required him, something unique for her. And he, with a kiss, with a touch of his hand, could raise her up to planes she'd only dreamed existed. Here was the completion, here was the delight, she'd hoped for without truly believing in. This was what she'd wanted so desperately in her life but had never found. Here and now. Him. There was and needed to be nothing else.

He edged toward madness. She held him, hard and tight, as they swung toward the edge together. Together was all she could think. Together.

Quiet. It was so quiet there might never have been such a thing as sound. Her hair brushed against his cheek. Her hand, balled into a loose fist, lay over his heart. Adam lay in the silence and hurt as he'd never expected to hurt.

How had he let it happen? Control? What had made him think he had control when it came to Kirby? Somehow she'd wrapped herself around him, body and mind, while he'd been pretending he'd known exactly what he'd been doing.

He'd come to do a job, he reminded himself. He still had to do it, no matter what had passed between them. Could he go on with what he'd come to do, and protect her? Was it possible to split himself in two when his road had always been so straight? He wasn't certain of anything now, but the tug-of-war he'd lose whichever way the game ended. He had to think, create the distance he needed to do so. Better for both of them if he started now.

But when he shifted away, she held him tighter. Kirby lifted her head so that moonlight caught in her eyes and mesmerized him. "Don't go," she murmured. "Stay and sleep with me. I don't want it to end yet."

He couldn't resist her now. Perhaps he never would. Saying nothing, Adam drew her close again and closed his eyes. For a little while he could pretend tomorrow would take care of itself.

Sunlight woke her, but Kirby tried to ignore it by piling pillows on top of her head. It didn't work for long. Resigned, she tossed them on the floor and lay quietly, alone.

She hadn't heard Adam leave, nor had she expected him to stay until morning. As it was, she was grateful to have woken alone. Now she could think.

How was it she'd given her complete trust to a man she hardly knew? No answer. Why hadn't she evaded his questions, skirted her way around certain facts as she was well capable of doing? No answer.

It wasn't true. Kirby closed her eyes a moment, knowing she'd been more honest with Adam than she was being with herself. She knew the answer.

She'd given him more than she'd ever given to any man. It had been more than a physical alliance, more than a few hours of pleasure in the night. The essence of self had been shared with him. There was no taking it back now, even if both of them would have preferred it.

Unknowingly, he'd taken her innocence. Emotional virginity was just as real, just as vital, as the physical. And it was just as impossible to reclaim. She, thinking of the night, knew that she had no desire to go back. Now they would both move forward to whatever waited for them.

Rising, she prepared to face the day.

Upstairs in Fairchild's studio, Adam studied the rural landscape. He could feel the agitation and drama. The serene scene leaped with frantic life. Vivid, real, disturbing. Its creator stood beside him, not the Vincent van Gogh who Adam would've sworn had wielded the brush and pallette, but Philip Fairchild.

"It's magnificent," Adam murmured. The compliment was out before he could stop it.

"Thank you, Adam. I'm fond of it." Fairchild spoke as a man who'd long before accepted his own superiority and the responsibility that came with it.

"Mr. Fairchild—"

"Philip," Fairchild interrupted genially. "No reason for formality between us."

Somehow Adam felt even the casual intimacy could complicate an already hopelessly tangled situation. "Philip," he began again, "this is fraud. Your motives might be sterling, but the result remains fraud."

"Absolutely." Fairchild bobbed his head in agreement. "Fraud, misrepresentation, a bald-faced lie without a doubt." He lifted his arms and let them fall. "I'm stripped of defenses."

Like hell, Adam thought grimly. Unless he was very much mistaken, he was about to be treated to the biggest bag of pure, classic bull on record.

"Adam..." Fairchild drew out the name and steepled his hands. "You're an astute man, a rational man. I pride myself on being a good judge of character." As if he were very old and frail, Fairchild lowered himself into a chair. "Then, again, you're imaginative and open-minded—that shows in your work."

Adam reached for the coffee Cards had brought up. "So?"

"Your help with our little problem last night—and your skill in turning my own plot against me—leads me to believe you have the ability to adapt to what some might term the unusual."

"Some might."

"Now." Accepting the cup Adam handed him, Fairchild leaned back. "You tell me Kirby filled you in on everything. Odd, but we'll leave that for now." He'd already drawn his own conclusions there and found them to his liking. He wasn't about to lose on other points. "After what you've been told, can you find one iota of selfishness in my enterprise? Can you see my motive as anything but humanitarian?" On a roll, Fairchild set down his cup and let his hands fall between his bony knees. "Small, sick children, and those less fortunate than ourselves, have benefited from my hobby. Not one dollar have I kept, not a dollar, a franc, a sou. Never, never have I asked for credit or honor that, naturally, society would be anxious to bestow on me."

"You haven't asked for the jail sentence they'd bestow on you, either."

Fairchild tilted his head in acknowledgment but didn't miss a beat. "It's my gift to mankind, Adam. My payment for the talent awarded to me by a higher power. These hands..." He held them up, narrow, gaunt and oddly beautiful. "These hands hold a skill I'm obliged to pay for in my own way. This I've done." Bowing his head, Fairchild dropped them into his lap. "However, if you must condemn me, I understand."

Fairchild looked, Adam mused, like a stalwart Christian faced by pagan lions: firm in his belief, resigned to his fate. "One day," Adam murmured, "your halo's going to slip and strangle you."

"A possibility." Grinning, he lifted his head again. "But in the meantime, we enjoy what we can. Let's have one of those Danishes, my boy."

Wordlessly, Adam handed him the tray. "Have you considered the repercussions to Kirby if your...hobby is discovered?"

"Ah." Fairchild swallowed pastry. "A straight shot to my Achilles' heel. Naturally both of us know that Kirby can meet any obstacle and find a way over, around or through it." He bit off more Danish, enjoying the tang of raspberry. "Still, merely by being, Kirby demands emotion of one kind or another. You'd agree?"

Adam thought of the night, and what it had changed in him. "Yes."

The brief, concise answer was exactly what Fairchild had expected. "I'm taking a hiatus from this business for various reasons, the first of which is Kirby's position."

"And her position as concerns the Merrick Rembrandt?"

"A different kettle of fish." Fairchild dusted his fingers on a napkin and considered another pastry. "I'd like to share the ins and outs of that business with you, Adam, but I'm not free to just yet." He smiled and gazed over Adam's head. "One could say I've involved Kirby figuratively, but until things are resolved, she's a minor player in the game."

"Are you casting as well as directing this performance, Papa?" Kirby walked into the room and picked up the Danish Fairchild had been eyeing. "Did you sleep well, darling?"

"Like a rock, brat," he muttered, remembering the confusion of waking up on the sofa under her cape. He didn't care to be outwitted, but was a man who acknowledged a quick mind. "I'm told your evening activities went well."

"The deed's done." She glanced at Adam before resting her hands on her father's shoulders. The bond was there, unbreakable. "Maybe I should leave the two of you alone for a while. Adam has a way of digging out information. You might tell him what you won't tell me."

"All in good time." He patted her hands. "I'm devoting the morning to my hawk." Rising, he went to uncover his clay, an obvious dismissal. "You might give Harriet a call and tell her all's well before you two amuse yourselves."

Kirby held out her hand. "Have you any amusements in mind, Adam?"

"As a matter of fact..." He went with the impulse and kissed her as her father watched and speculated. "I had a session of oils and canvas in mind. You'll have to change."

"If that's the best you can do. Two hours only," she warned as they walked from the room. "Otherwise my rates go up. I have my own work, you know."

"Three."

"Two and a half." She paused at the second-floor landing.

"You looked like a child this morning," he murmured, and touched her cheek. "I couldn't bring myself to wake you." He left his hand there only a moment, then moved away. "I'll meet you upstairs."

Kirby went to her room and tossed the red dress on the bed. While she undressed with one hand, she dialed the phone with the other.

"Harriet, it's Kirby to set your mind at rest."

"Clever child. Was there any trouble?"

"No." She wiggled out of her jeans. "We managed."

"We? Did Philip go with you?"

"Papa was snoozing on the couch after Adam switched drinks."

"Oh, dear." Amused, Harriet settled back. "Was he very angry?"

"Papa or Adam?" Kirby countered, then shrugged. "No matter, in the end they were both very reasonable. Adam was a great help."

"The test isn't for a half hour. Give me the details."

Struggling in and out of clothes, Kirby told her everything.

"Marvelous!" Pleased with the drama, Harriet beamed at the phone. "I wish I'd done it. I'll have to get to know your

Adam better and find some spectacular way of showing him my gratitude. Do you think he'd like the crocodile teeth?''

"Nothing would please him more.''

"Kirby, you know how grateful I am to you.'' Harriet's voice was abruptly serious and maternal. "The situation's awkward to say the least.''

"The contract's binding?''

"Yes.'' She let out a sigh at the thought of losing the Titian. "My fault. I should've explained to Stuart that the painting wasn't to be sold. Philip must be furious with me.''

"You can handle him. You always do.''

"Yes, yes. Lord knows what I'd do without you, though. Poor Melly just can't understand me as you do.''

"She's just made differently.'' Kirby stared down at the floor and tried not to think about the Rembrandt and the guilt it brought her. "Come to dinner tonight, Harriet, you and Melanie.''

"Oh, I'd love to, darling, but I've a meeting. Tomorrow?''

"Fine. Shall I call Melly, or will you speak with her?''

"I'll see her this afternoon. Take care and do thank Adam for me. Damn shame I'm too old to give him anything but crocodile teeth.''

With a laugh, Kirby hung up.

The sun swept over her dress, shooting it with flames or darkening it to blood. It glinted from the rings at her ears, the bracelets on her arms. Knowing the light was as perfect as it would ever be, Adam worked feverishly.

He was an artist of subtle details, one who used light and shadow for mood. In his portraits he strove for an inner reality, the truth beneath the surface of the model. In Kirby he saw the essence of woman—power and frailty and that elusive, mystical quality of sex. Aloof, alluring. She was both. Now, more than ever, he understood it.

Hours passed without him giving them a thought. His model, however, had a different frame of mind.

"Adam, if you'll consult your watch, you'll see I've given you more than the allotted time already.''

He ignored her and continued to paint.

"I can't stand here another moment." She let her arms drop from their posed position, then wiggled them from the shoulders down. "As it is, I'll probably never pole-vault again."

"I can work on the background awhile," he muttered. "I need another three hours in the morning. The light's best then."

Kirby bit off a retort. Rudeness was something to be expected when an artist was taken over by his art. Stretching her muscles, she went to look over his shoulder.

"You've a good hand with light," she decided as she studied the emerging painting. "It's very flattering, certainly, rather fiery and defiant with the colors you've chosen." She looked carefully at the vague lines of her face, the tints and hues he was using to create her on canvas. "Still, there's a fragility here I don't quite understand."

"Maybe I know you better than you know yourself." He never looked at her, but continued to paint. In not looking, he didn't see the stunned expression or the gradual acceptance.

Linking her hands together, Kirby wandered away. She'd have to do it quickly, she decided. It needed to be done, to be said. "Adam…"

An inarticulate mutter. His back remained to her.

Kirby took a deep breath. "I love you."

"Umm-hmm."

Some women might've been crushed. Others would've been furious. Kirby laughed and tossed back her hair. Life was never what you expected. "Adam, I'd like just a moment of your attention." Though she continued to smile, her knuckles turned white. "I'm in love with you."

It got through on the second try. His brush, tipped in coral, stopped in midair. Very slowly, he set it down and turned. She was looking at him, the half smile on her face, her hands linked together so tightly they hurt. She hadn't expected a response, nor would she demand one.

"I don't tell you that to put pressure on you, or to embarrass you." Nerves showed only briefly as she moistened her lips. "It's just that I think you have a right to know." Her words began to spill out quickly. "We haven't known each other for long, I know, but I suppose it just happens this way sometimes. I couldn't do anything about it. I don't expect anything from you, permanently or temporarily." When he still didn't speak, she felt a jolt of panic she didn't know how to deal with. Had she ruined it? Now the smile didn't reach her eyes. "I've got to change," she said lightly. "You've made me miss lunch as it is."

She was nearly to the door before he stopped her. As he took her shoulders, he felt her tense. And as he felt it, he understood she'd given him everything that was in her heart. Something he knew instinctively had never been given to any other man.

"Kirby, you're the most exceptional woman I've ever known."

"Yes, someone's always pointing that out." She had to get through the door and quickly. "Are you coming down, or shall I have a tray sent up?"

He lowered his head to the top of hers and wondered how things had happened so quickly, so finally. "How many people could make such a simple and unselfish declaration of love, then walk away without asking for anything? From the beginning you haven't done one thing I'd've expected." He brushed his lips over her hair, lightly, so that she hardly felt it. "Don't I get a chance to say anything?"

"It's not necessary."

"Yes, it is." Turning her, he framed her face with his hands. "And I'd rather have my hands on you when I tell you I love you."

She stood very straight and spoke very calmly. "Don't feel sorry for me, Adam. I couldn't bear it."

He started to say all the sweet, romantic things a woman wanted to hear when love was declared. All the traditional, normal words a man offered when he offered himself. They weren't for Kirby. Instead he lifted a brow. "If you hadn't counted on being loved back, you'll have to adjust."

She waited a moment because she had to be certain. She'd take the risk, take any risk, if she was certain. As she looked into his eyes, she began to smile. The tension in her shoulders vanished. "You've brought it on yourself."

"Yeah. I guess I have to live with it."

The smile faded as she pressed against him. "Oh, God, Adam, I need you. You've no idea how much."

He held her just as tightly, just as desperately. "Yes, I do."

Chapter 9

To love and to be loved in return. It was bewildering to Kirby, frightening, exhilarating. She wanted time to experience it, absorb it. Understanding it didn't matter, not now, in the first rush of emotion. She only knew that although she'd always been happy in her life, she was being offered more. She was being offered laughter at midnight, soft words at dawn, a hand to hold and a life to share. The price would be a portion of her independence and the loyalty that had belonged only to her father.

To Kirby, love meant sharing, and sharing had no restrictions. Whatever she had, whatever she felt, belonged to Adam as much as to herself. Whatever happened between them now, she'd never be able to change that. No longer able to work, she went down from her studio to find him.

The house was quiet in the early-evening lull with the staff downstairs making the dinner preparations and gossiping. Kirby had always liked this time of day—after a long, productive session in her studio, before the evening meal. These were the hours to sit in front of a roaring fire, or walk along the cliffs. Now there was someone she needed to share those hours with. Stopping in front of Adam's door, she raised a hand to knock.

The murmur of voices stopped her. If Adam had her father

in another discussion, he might learn something more about the Rembrandt that would put her mind at ease. While she hesitated, the thumping of the front door knocker vibrated throughout the house. With a shrug, she turned away to answer.

Inside his room, Adam shifted the transmitter to his other hand. "This is the first chance I've had to call in. Besides, there's nothing new."

"You're supposed to check in every night." Annoyed, McIntyre barked into the receiver. "Damn it, Adam, I was beginning to think something had happened to you."

"If you knew these people, you'd realize how ridiculous that is."

"They don't suspect anything?"

"No." Adam swore at the existence of this job.

"Tell me about Mrs. Merrick and Hiller."

"Harriet's charming and flamboyant." He wouldn't say harmless. Though he thought of what he and Kirby had done the night before, he left it alone. Adam had already rationalized the entire business as having nothing to do with his job. Not specifically. That was enough to justify his keeping it from McIntyre. Instead, Adam would tell him what Adam felt applied and nothing more. "Hiller's very smooth and a complete phony. I walked in on him and Kirby in time to keep him from shoving her around."

"What was his reason?"

"The Rembrandt. He doesn't believe her father's keeping her in the dark about it. He's the kind of man who thinks you can always get what you want by knocking the other person around—if they're smaller."

"Sounds like a gem." But he'd heard the change in tone. If Adam was getting involved with the Fairchild woman... No. McIntyre let it go. That they didn't need. "I've got a line on Victor Alvarez."

"Drop it." Adam kept his voice casual, knowing full well just how perceptive Mac could be. "It's a wild-goose chase. I've already dug it up and it doesn't have anything to do with the Rembrandt."

"You know best."

"Yeah." McIntyre, he knew, would never understand Fairchild's hobby. "Since we agree about that, I've got a stipulation."

"Stipulation?"

"When I find the Rembrandt, I handle the rest my own way."

"What do you mean your own way? Listen, Adam—"

"My way," Adam cut him off. "Or you find someone else. I'll get it back for you, Mac, but after I do, the Fairchilds are kept out of it."

"Kept out?" McIntyre exploded so that the receiver crackled with static. "How the hell do you expect me to keep them out?"

"That's your problem. Just do it."

"The place is full of crazies," McIntyre muttered. "Must be contagious."

"Yeah. I'll get back to you." With a grin, Adam switched off the transmitter.

Downstairs, Kirby opened the door and looked into the myopic, dark-framed eyes of Rick Potts. Knowing his hand would be damp with nerves, she held hers out. "Hello, Rick. Papa told me you were coming to visit."

"Kirby." He swallowed and squeezed her hand. Just the sight of her played havoc with his glands. "You look mar-marvelous." He thrust drooping carnations into her face.

"Thank you." Kirby took the flowers Rick had partially strangled and smiled. "Come, let me fix you a drink. You've had a long drive, haven't you? Cards, see to Mr. Potts's luggage, please," she continued without giving Rick a chance to speak. He'd need a little time, she knew, to draw words together. "Papa should be down soon." She found a club soda and poured it over ice. "He's been giving a lot of time to his new project; I'm sure he'll want to discuss it with you." After handing him his drink, she gestured to a chair. "So, how've you been?"

He drank first, to separate his tongue from the roof of his mouth. "Fine. That is, I had a bit of a cold last week, but I'm much better now. I'd never come to see you if I had any germs.''

She turned in time to hide a grin and poured herself a glass of Perrier. ''That's very considerate of you, Rick.''

''Have you—have you been working?''

''Yes, I've nearly done enough for my spring showing.''

''It'll be wonderful,'' he told her with blind loyalty. Though he recognized the quality of her work, the more powerful pieces intimidated him. ''You'll be staying in New York?''

''Yes.'' She walked over to sit beside him. ''For a week.''

''Then maybe—that is, I'd love to, if you had the time, of course, I'd like to take you to dinner.'' He gulped down club soda. ''If you had an evening free.''

''That's very sweet of you.''

Astonished, he gaped, pupils dilating. From the doorway, Adam watched the puppylike adulation of the lanky, somewhat untidy man. In another ten seconds, Adam estimated, Kirby would have him at her feet whether she wanted him there or not.

Kirby glanced up, and her expression changed so subtly Adam wouldn't have noticed if he hadn't been so completely tuned in to her. ''Adam.'' If there'd been relief in her eyes, her voice was casual. ''I was hoping you'd come down. Rick, this is Adam Haines. Adam, I think Papa mentioned Rick Potts to you the other day.''

The message came across loud and clear. Be kind. With an easy smile, Adam accepted the damp handshake. ''Yes, Philip said you were coming for a few days. Kirby tells me you work in watercolors.''

''She did?'' Nearly undone by the fact that Kirby would speak of him at all, Rick simply stood there a moment.

''We'll have to have a long discussion after dinner.'' Rising, Kirby began to lead Rick gently toward the door. ''I'm sure you'd like to rest a bit after your drive. You can find the way to your room, can't you?''

''Yes, yes, of course.''

Kirby watched him wander down the hall before she turned

back. She walked back to Adam and wrapped her arms around him. "I hate to repeat myself, but I love you."

He framed her face with his hands and kissed her softly, lightly, with the promise of more. "Repeat yourself as often as you like." He stared down at her, suddenly and completely aroused by no more than her smile. He pressed his mouth into her palm with a restraint that left her weak. "You take my breath away," he murmured. "It's no wonder you turn Rick Potts to jelly."

"I'd rather turn you to jelly."

She did. It wasn't an easy thing to admit. With a half smile, Adam drew her away. "Are you really going to tell him I'm a jealous lover with a stiletto?"

"It's for his own good." Kirby picked up her glass of Perrier. "He's always so embarrassed after he loses control. Did you learn any more from Papa?"

"No." Puzzled, he frowned. "Why?"

"I was coming to see you right before Rick arrived. I heard you talking."

She slipped a hand into his and he fought to keep the tension from being noticeable. "I don't want to press things now." That much was the truth, he thought fiercely. That much wasn't a lie.

"No, you're probably right about that. Papa tends to get obstinate easily. Let's sit in front of the fire for a little while," she said as she drew him over to it. "And do nothing."

He sat beside her, holding her close, and wished things were as simple as they seemed.

Hours went by before they sat in the parlor again, but they were no longer alone. After an enormous meal, Fairchild and Rick settled down with them to continue the ongoing discussion of art and technique. Assisted by two glasses of wine and half a glass of brandy, Rick began to heap praise on Kirby's work. Adam recognized the warning signals of battle—Fairchild's pink ears and Kirby's guileless eyes.

"Thank you, Rick." With a smile, Kirby lifted her brandy.

"I'm sure you'd like to see Papa's latest work. It's an attempt in clay. A bird or something, isn't it, Papa?"

"A bird? A bird?" In a quick circle, he danced around the table. "It's a hawk, you horrid girl. A bird of prey, a creature of cunning."

A veteran, Rick tried to soothe. "I'd love to see it, Mr. Fairchild."

"And so you will." In one dramatic gulp, Fairchild finished off his drink. "I intend to donate it to the Metropolitan."

Whether Kirby's snort was involuntary or contrived, it produced results.

"Do you mock your father?" Fairchild demanded. "Have you no faith in these hands?" He held them out, fingers spread. "The same hands that held you fresh from your mother's womb?"

"Your hands are the eighth wonder of the world," Kirby told him. "However…" She set down her glass, sat back and crossed her legs. Meticulously she brought her fingers together and looked over them. "From my observations, you have difficulty with your structure. Perhaps with a few years of practice, you'll develop the knack of construction."

"Structure?" he sputtered. "Construction?" His eyes narrowed, his jaw clenched. "Cards!" Kirby sent him an easy smile and picked up her glass again. "Cards!"

"Yes, Mr. Fairchild."

"Cards," Fairchild repeated, glaring at the dignified butler, who stood waiting in the doorway.

"Yes, Mr. Fairchild."

"Cards!" He bellowed and pranced.

"I believe Papa wants a deck of cards—Cards," Kirby explained. "Playing cards."

"Yes, miss." With a slight bow, Cards went to get some.

"What's the matter with that man?" Fairchild muttered. In hurried motions, he began to clear off a small table. Exquisite Wedgwood and delicate Venetian glass were dumped unceremoniously on the floor. "You'd think I didn't make myself clear."

"It's so hard to get good help these days," Adam said into his glass.

"Your cards, Mr. Fairchild." The butler placed two sealed decks on the table before gliding from the room.

"Now I'll show you about construction." Fairchild pulled up a chair and wrapped his skinny legs around its legs. Breaking the seal on the first deck, he poured the cards on the table. With meticulous care, he leaned one card against another and formed an arch. "A steady hand and a discerning eye," Fairchild mumbled as he began slowly, and with total intensity, to build a house of cards.

"That should keep him out of trouble for a while," Kirby declared. Sending Adam a wink, she turned to Rick and drew him into a discussion on mutual friends.

An hour drifted by over brandy and quiet conversation. Occasionally there was a mutter or a grumble from the architect in the corner. The fire crackled. When Montique entered and jumped into Adam's lap, Rick paled and sprang up.

"You shouldn't do that. She'll be here any second." He set down his glass with a clatter. "Kirby, I think I'll go up. I want to start work early."

"Of course." She watched his retreat before turning to Adam. "He's terrified of Isabelle. Montique got into his room when he was sleeping and curled on his pillow. Isabelle woke Rick with some rather rude comments while she stood on his chest. I'd better go up and make sure everything's in order." She rose, then bent over and kissed him lightly.

"That's not enough."

"No?" The slow smile curved her lips. "Perhaps we'll fix that later. Come on, Montique, let's go find your wretched keeper."

"Kirby…" Adam waited until both she and the puppy were at the doorway. "Just how much rent does Isabelle pay?"

"Ten mice a month," she told him soberly. "But I'm going to raise it to fifteen in November. Maybe she'll be out by Christmas." Pleased with the thought, she led Montique away.

"A fascinating creature, my Kirby," Fairchild commented. Adam crossed the room and stared down at the huge, erratic card structure Fairchild continued to construct. "Fascinating."

"She's a woman with much below the surface. Kirby can be cruel when she feels justified. I've seen her squash a six-foot man like a bug." He held a card between the index fingers of both hands, then slowly lowered it into place. "You'll notice, however, that her attitude toward Rick is invariably kind."

Though Fairchild continued to give his full attention to his cards, Adam knew it was more than idle conversation. "Obviously she doesn't want to hurt him."

"Exactly." Fairchild began to patiently build another wing. Unless Adam was very much mistaken, the cards were slowly taking on the lines of the house they were in. "She'll take great care not to because she knows his devotion to her is sincere. Kirby's a strong, independent woman. Where her heart's involved, however, she's a marshmallow. There are a handful of people on this earth she'd sacrifice anything she could for. Rick's one of them—Melanie and Harriet are others. And myself." He held a card on the tops of his fingers as if weighing it. "Yes, myself," he repeated softly. "Because of this, the circumstances of the Rembrandt are very difficult for her. She's torn between separate loyalties. Her father, and the woman who's been her mother most of her life."

"You do nothing to change it," Adam accused. Irrationally he wanted to sweep the cards aside, flatten the meticulously formed construction. He pushed his hands into his pockets, where they balled into fists. Just how much could he berate Fairchild, when he was deceiving Kirby in nearly the same way? "Why don't you give her some explanation? Something she could understand?"

"Ignorance is bliss," Fairchild stated calmly. "In this case, the less Kirby knows, the simpler things are for her."

"You've a hell of a nerve, Philip."

"Yes, yes, that's quite true." He balanced more cards, then went back to the subject foremost in his mind. "There've been dozens of men in Kirby's life. She could choose and discard them as other women do clothing. Yet, in her own way, she was always cautious. I think Kirby believed she wasn't capable of loving a man and had decided to settle for much, much less by agreeing to marry Stuart. Nonsense, of course.'' Fairchild picked up his drink and studied his rambling card house. "Kirby has a great capacity for love. When she loves a man, she'll love with unswerving devotion and loyalty. And when she does, she'll be vulnerable. She loves intensely, Adam.''

For the first time, he raised his eyes and met Adam's. "When her mother died, she was devastated. I wouldn't want to live to see her go through anything like that again.''

What could he say? Less than he wanted to, but still only the truth. "I don't want to hurt Kirby. I'll do everything I can to keep from hurting her.''

Fairchild studied him a moment with the pale blue eyes that saw deep and saw much. "I believe you, and hope you find a way to avoid it. Still, if you love her, you'll find a way to mend whatever damage is done. The game's on, Adam, the rules set. They can't be altered now, can they?''

Adam stared down at the round face. "You know why I'm here, don't you?''

With a cackle, Fairchild turned back to his cards. Yes, indeed, Adam Haines was sharp, he thought, pleased. Kirby had called it from the beginning. "Let's just say for now that you're here to paint and to…observe. Yes, to observe.'' He placed another card. "Go up to her now, you've my blessing if you feel the need for it. The game's nearly over, Adam. Soon enough we'll have to pick up the pieces. Love's tenuous when it's new, my boy. If you want to keep her, be as stubborn as she is. That's my advice.''

In long, methodical strokes, Kirby pulled the brush through her hair. She'd turned the radio on low so that the hot jazz was hardly more than a pulse beat. At the sound of a knock, she sighed. "Rick, you really must go to bed. You'll hate yourself in the morning.''

Adam pushed open the door. He took a long look at the

woman in front of the mirror, dressed in wisps of beige silk and ivory lace. Without a word, he closed and latched the door behind him.

"Oh, my." Setting the brush on her dresser, Kirby turned around with a little shudder. "A woman simply isn't safe these days. Have you come to have your way with me—I hope?"

Adam crossed to her. Letting his hands slide along the silk, he wrapped his arms around her. "I was just passing through." When she smiled, he lowered his mouth to hers. "I love you, Kirby. More than anyone, more than anything." Suddenly his mouth was fierce, his arms were tight. "Don't ever forget it."

"I won't." But her words were muffled against his mouth. "Just don't stop reminding me. Now..." She drew away, inches only, and slowly began to loosen his tie. "Maybe I should remind you."

He watched his tie slip to the floor just before she began to ease his jacket from his shoulders. "It might be a good idea."

"You've been working hard," she told him as she tossed his jacket in the general direction of a chair. "I think you should be pampered a bit."

"Pampered?"

"Mmm." Nudging him onto the bed, she knelt to take off his shoes. Carelessly she let them drop, followed by his socks, before she began to massage his feet. "Pampering's good for you in small doses."

He felt the pleasure spread through him at the touch that could almost be described as motherly. Her hands were soft, with that ridge of callus that proved they weren't idle. They were strong and clever, belonging both to artist and to woman. Slowly she slid them up his legs, then down—teasing, promising, until he wasn't certain whether to lay back and enjoy, or to grab and take. Before he could do either, Kirby stood and began to unbutton his shirt.

"I like everything about you," she murmured as she tugged

the shirt from the waistband of his slacks. "Have I mentioned that?"

"No." He let her loosen the cuffs and slip the shirt from him. Taking her time, Kirby ran her hands up his rib cage to his shoulders. "The way you look." Softly she pressed a kiss to his cheek. "The way you feel." Then the other. "The way you think." Her lips brushed over his chin. "The way you taste." Unhooking his slacks, she drew them off, inch by slow inch. "There's nothing about you I'd change."

She straddled him and began to trace long, lingering kisses over his face and neck. "Once when I wondered about falling in love, I decided there simply wasn't a man I'd like well enough to make it possible." Her mouth paused just above his. "I was wrong."

Soft, warm and exquisitely tender, her lips met his. Pampering...the word drifted through his mind as she gave him more than any man could expect and only a few might dream of. The strength of her body and her mind, the delicacy of both. They were his, and he didn't have to ask. They'd be his as long as his arms could hold her and open wide enough to give her room.

Knowing only that she loved, Kirby gave. His body heated beneath hers, lean and hard. Disciplined. Somehow the word excited her. He knew who he was and what he wanted. He'd work for both. And he wouldn't demand that she lose any part of what she was to suit that.

His shoulders were firm. Not so broad they would overwhelm her, but wide enough to offer security when she needed it. She brushed her lips over them. There were muscles in his arms, but subtle, not something he'd flex to show her his superiority, but there to protect if she chose to be protected. She ran her fingers over them. His hands were clever, elegantly masculine. They wouldn't hold her back from the places she had to go, but they would be there, held out, when she returned. She pressed her mouth to one, then the other.

No one had ever loved him just like this—patiently, devotedly. He wanted nothing more than to go on feeling those long, slow strokes of her fingers, those moist, lingering traces of her lips. He felt each in every pore. A total experience. He could see the glossy black fall of her hair as it tumbled over his skin and hear the murmur of her approval as she touched him.

The house was quiet again, but for the low, simmering sound of the music. The quilt was soft under his back. The light was dim and gentle—the best light for lovers. And while he lay, she loved him until he was buried under layer upon layer of pleasure. This he would give back to her.

He could touch the silk, and her flesh, knowing that both were exquisite. He could taste her lips and know that he'd never go hungry as long as she was there. When he heard her sigh, he knew he'd be content with no other sound. The need for him was in her eyes, clouding them, so that he knew he could live with little else as long as he could see her face.

Patience began to fade in each of them. He could feel her body spring to frantic life wherever he touched. He could feel his own strain from the need only she brought to him. Desperate, urgent, exclusive. If he'd had only a day left to live, he'd have spent every moment of it there, with Kirby in his arms.

She smelled of wood smoke and musky flowers, of woman and of sex, ripe and ready. If he'd had the power, he'd have frozen time just then, as she loomed above him in the moonlight, eyes dark with need, skin flashing against silk.

Then he drew the silk up and over her head so that he could see her as he swore no man would ever see her again. Her hair tumbled down, streaking night against her flesh. Naked and eager, she was every primitive fantasy, every midnight dream. Everything.

Her lips were parted as the breath hurried between them. Passion swamped her so that she shuddered and rushed to take what she needed from him—for him. Everything. Everything and more. With a low sound of triumph, Kirby took him inside her and led the way. Fast, furious.

Her body urged her on relentlessly while her mind exploded with images. Such color, such sound. Such frenzy. Arched back, she moved like lightning, hardly aware of how tightly his hands gripped her hips. But she heard him say her name. She felt him fill her.

The first crest swamped her, shocking her system then thrusting her along to more, and more and more. There was nothing she couldn't have and nothing she wouldn't give. Senseless, she let herself go.

With his hands on her, with the taste of her still on his lips, Adam felt his system shudder on the edge of release. For a moment, only a moment, he held back. He could see her above him, poised like a goddess, flesh damp and glowing, hair streaming back as she lifted her hands to it in ecstasy. This he would remember always.

The moon was no longer full, but its light was soft and white. They were still on top of the quilt, tangled close as their breathing settled. As she lay over him, Adam thought of everything Fairchild had said. And everything he could and couldn't do about it.

Slowly their systems settled, but he could find none of the answers he needed so badly. What answers would there be based on lies and half-truths?

Time. Perhaps time was all he had now. But how much or how little was no longer up to him. With a sigh, he shifted and ran a hand down her back.

Kirby rose on an elbow. Her eyes were no longer clouded, but saucy and clear. She smiled, touched a fingertip to her own lips and then to his. "Next time you're in town, cowboy," she drawled as she tossed her hair over her shoulder, "don't forget to ask for Lulu."

She'd expected him to grin, but he grabbed her hair and held her just as she was. There was no humor in his eyes, but the intensity she'd seen when he held a paintbrush. His muscles had tensed, she could feel it.

"Adam?"

"No, don't." He forced his hand to relax, then stroked her cheek. It wouldn't be spoiled by the wrong word, the wrong move. "I want to remember you just like this. Fresh from loving, with moonlight on your hair."

He was afraid, unreasonably, that he'd never see her like that again—with that half smile inches away from his face. He'd never feel the warmth of her flesh spread over his with nothing, nothing to separate them.

The panic came fast and was very real. Unable to stop it, Adam pulled her against him and held her as if he'd never let her go.

Chapter 10

After thirty minutes of posing, Kirby ordered herself not to be impatient. She'd agreed to give Adam two hours, and a bargain was a bargain. She didn't want to think about the time she had left to stand idle, so instead tried to concentrate on her plans for sculpting once her obligation was over. Her *Anger* was nearly finished.

But the sun seemed too warm and too bright. Every so often her mind would go oddly blank until she pulled herself back just to remember where she was.

"Kirby." Adam called her name for the third time and watched as she blinked and focused on him. "Could you wait until the session's over before you take a nap?"

"Sorry." With an effort, she cleared her head and smiled at him. "I was thinking of something else."

"Don't think at all if it puts you to sleep," he muttered, and slashed scarlet across the canvas. It was right, so right. Nothing he'd ever done had been as right as this painting. The need to finish it was becoming obsessive. "Tilt your head to the right again. You keep breaking the pose."

"Slave driver." But she obeyed and tried to concentrate.

"Cracking the whip's the only way to work with you." With care, he began to perfect the folds in the skirt of her dress. He wanted them soft, flowing, but clearly defined.

"You'd better get used to posing for me. I've already several other studies in mind that I'll start after we're married."

Giddiness washed over her. She felt it in waves—physical, emotional—she couldn't tell one from the other. Without thinking, she dropped her arms.

"Damn it, Kirby." He started to swear at her again when he saw how wide and dark her eyes were. "What is it?"

"I hadn't thought...I didn't realize that you..." Lifting a hand to her spinning head, she walked around the room. The bracelets slid down to her elbow with a musical jingle. "I need a minute," she murmured. Should she feel as though someone had cut off her air? As if her head was three feet above her shoulders?

Adam watched her for a moment. She didn't seem quite steady, he realized. And there was an unnaturally high color in her cheeks. Standing, he took her hand and held her still. "Are you ill?"

"No." She shook her head. She was never ill, Kirby reminded herself. Just a bit tired—and, perhaps for the first time in her life, completely overwhelmed. She took a deep breath, telling herself she'd be all right in a moment. "I didn't know you wanted to marry me, Adam."

Was that it? he wondered as he ran the back of his hand over her cheek. Shouldn't she have known? And yet, he remembered, everything had happened so fast. "I love you." It was simple for him. Love led to marriage and marriage to family. But how could he have forgotten Kirby wasn't an ordinary woman and was anything but simple? "You accused me of being conventional," he reminded her, and ran his hands down her hair to her shoulders. "Marriage is a very conventional institution." And one she might not be ready for, he thought with a quick twinge of panic. He'd have to give her room if he wanted to keep her. But how much room did she need, and how much could he give?

"I want to spend my life with you." Adam waited until her gaze had lifted to his again. She looked stunned by his words—a woman like her, Adam thought. Beautiful, sensuous, strong. How was it a woman like Kirby would be surprised to be wanted? Perhaps he'd moved too quickly, and too clumsily. "Any way you choose, Kirby. Maybe I should've chosen a better time, a better place, to ask rather than assume."

"It's not that." Shaky, she lifted a hand to his face. It was so solid, so strong. "I don't need that." His face blurred a moment, and, shaking her head, she moved away again until she stood where she'd been posing. "I've had marriage proposals before—and a good many less binding requests." She managed a smile. He wanted her, not just for today, but for the tomorrows, as well. He wanted her just as she was. She felt the tears well up, of love, of gratitude, but blinked them back. When wishes came true it was no time for tears. "This is the one I've been waiting for all of my life, I just didn't expect to be so flustered."

Relieved, he started to cross to her. "I'll take that as a good sign. Still, I wouldn't mind a simple yes."

"I hate to do anything simple."

She felt the room lurch and fade, then his hands on her shoulders.

"Kirby— Good God, there's gas leaking!" As he stood holding her up, the strong, sweet odor rushed over him. "Get out! Get some air! It must be the heater." Giving her a shove toward the door, he bent over the antiquated unit.

She stumbled across the room. The door seemed miles away, so that when she finally reached it she had only the strength to lean against the heavy wood and catch her breath. The air was cleaner there. Gulping it in, Kirby willed herself to reach for the knob. She tugged, but it held firm.

"Damn it, I told you to get out!" He was already choking on the fumes when he reached her. "The gas is pouring out of that thing!"

"I can't open the door!" Furious with herself, Kirby pulled again. Adam pushed her hands away and yanked himself. "Is it jammed?" she murmured, leaning against him. "Cards will see to it."

Locked, he realized. From the outside. "Stay here." After propping her against the door, Adam picked up a chair and smashed it against the window. The glass cracked, but held. Again, he rammed the chair, and again, until with a final heave, the glass shattered. Moving quickly, he went back for Kirby and held her head near the jagged opening.

"Breathe," he ordered.

For the moment she could do nothing else but gulp fresh air into her lungs and cough it out again. "Someone's locked us in, haven't they?"

He'd known it wouldn't take her long once her head had cleared. Just as he knew better than to try to evade. "Yes."

"We could shout for hours." She closed her eyes and concentrated. "No one would hear us, we're too isolated up here." With her legs unsteady, she leaned against the wall. "We'll have to wait until someone comes to look for us."

"Where's the main valve for that heater?"

"Main valve?" She pressed her fingers to her eyes and forced herself to think. "I just turn the thing on when it's cold up here.... Wait. Tanks—there are tanks out in back of the kitchen." She turned back to the broken window again, telling herself she couldn't be sick. "One for each tower and for each floor."

Adam glanced at the small, old-fashioned heater again. It wouldn't take much longer, even with the broken window. "We're getting out of here."

"How?" If she could just lie down—just for a minute... "The door's locked. I don't think we'd survive a jump into Jamie's zinnias," she added, looking down to where the chair had landed. But he wasn't listening to her. When Kirby turned, she saw Adam running his hand over the ornate trim. The panel yawned open. "How'd you find that one?"

He grabbed her by the elbow and pulled her forward. "Let's go."

"I can't." With the last of her strength, Kirby braced her hands against the wall. Fear and nausea doubled at the thought of going into the dark, dank hole in the wall. "I can't go in there."

"Don't be ridiculous."

When he would've pulled her through, Kirby jerked away

and backed up. "No, you go. I'll wait for you to come around and open the door."

"Listen to me." Fighting the fumes, he grabbed her shoulders. "I don't know how long it'd take me to find my way through that maze in the dark."

"I'll be patient."

"You could be dead," he countered between his teeth. "That heater's unstable—if there's a short this whole room would go up! You've already taken in too much of the gas."

"I won't go in!" Hysteria bubbled, and she didn't have the strength or the wit to combat it. Her voice rose as she stumbled back from him. "I can't go in, don't you understand?"

"I hope you understand this," he muttered, and clipped her cleanly on the jaw. Without a sound, she collapsed into his arms. Adam didn't hesitate. He tossed her unceremoniously over his shoulder and plunged into the passageway.

With the panel closed to cut off the flow of gas, the passage was in total darkness. With one arm holding Kirby in place, Adam inched along the wall. He had to reach the stairs, and the first mechanism. Groping, testing each step, he hugged the wall, knowing what would happen to both of them if he rushed and plunged them headlong down the steep stone stairway.

He heard the skitter of rodents and brushed spiderwebs out of his face. Perhaps it was best that Kirby was unconscious, he decided. He'd get her through a lot easier carrying her than he would dragging her.

Five minutes, then ten, then at last his foot met empty space.

Cautiously, he shifted Kirby on his shoulder, pressed the other to the wall, and started down. The steps were stone, and treacherous enough with a light. In the dark, with no rail for balance, they were deadly. Fighting the need to rush, Adam checked himself on each step before going on to the next. When he reached the bottom, he went no faster, but began to trace his hand along the wall, feeling for a switch.

The first one stuck. He had to concentrate just to breathe. Kirby swayed on his shoulder as he maneuvered the sharp turn in the passage. Swearing, Adam moved forward blindly until his fingers brushed over a second lever. The panel groaned open just enough for him to squeeze himself and his burden through. Blinking at the sunlight, he dashed around dust-covered furniture and out into the hall.

When he reached the second floor and passed Cards, he didn't break stride. "Turn off the gas to Kirby's studio from the main valve," he ordered, coughing as he moved by. "And keep everyone away from there."

"Yes, Mr. Haines." Cards continued to walk toward the main stairway, carrying his pile of fresh linens.

When Adam reached her room, he laid Kirby on the bed, then opened the windows. He stood there a moment, just breathing, letting the air rush over his face and soothe his eyes. His stomach heaved. Forcing himself to take slow, measured breaths, he leaned out. When the nausea passed, he went back to her.

The high color had faded. Now she was as pale as the quilt. She didn't move. Hadn't moved, he remembered, since he'd hit her. With a tremor, he pressed his fingers to her throat and felt a slow, steady pulse. Quickly he went into the bathroom and soaked a cloth with cold water. As he ran it over her face, he said her name.

She coughed first, violently. Nothing could've relieved him more. When her eyes opened, she stared at him dully.

"You're in your room," he told her. "You're all right now."

"You hit me."

He grinned because there was indignation in her voice. "I thought you'd take a punch better with a chin like that. I barely tapped you."

"So you say." Gingerly she sat up and touched her chin. Her head whirled once, but she closed her eyes and waited for it to pass. "I suppose I had it coming. Sorry I got neurotic on you."

He let his forehead rest against hers. "You scared the hell out of me. I guess you're the only woman who's received a marriage proposal and a right jab within minutes of each other.''

''I hate to do the ordinary.'' Because she needed another minute, she lay back against the pillows. ''Have you turned off the gas?''

''Cards is seeing to it.''

''Of course.'' She said this calmly enough, then began to pluck at the quilt with her fingers. ''As far as I know, no one's tried to kill me before.''

It made it easier, he thought, that she understood and accepted that straight off. With a nod, he touched a hand to her cheek. ''First we call a doctor. Then we call the police.''

''I don't need a doctor. I'm just a little queasy now, it'll pass.'' She took both his hands and held them firmly. ''And we can't call the police.''

He saw something in her eyes that nearly snapped his temper. Stubbornness. ''It's the usual procedure after attempted murder, Kirby.''

She didn't wince. ''They'll ask annoying questions and skulk all over the house. It's in all the movies.''

''This isn't a game.'' His hands tightened on hers. ''You could've been killed—would've been if you'd been in there alone. I'm not giving him another shot at you.''

''You think it was Stuart.'' She let out a long breath. Be objective, she told herself. Then you can make Adam be objective. ''Yes, I suppose it was, though I wouldn't have thought him ingenious enough. There's no one else who'd want to hurt me. Still, we can't prove a thing.''

''That has yet to be seen.'' His eyes flashed a moment as he thought of the satisfaction he'd get from beating a confession out of Hiller. She saw it. She understood it.

''You're more primitive than I'd imagined.'' Touched, she traced her finger down his jaw. ''I didn't know how nice it would be to have someone want to vanquish dragons for me. Who needs a bunch of silly police when I have you?''

''Don't try to outmaneuver me.''

''I'm not.'' The smile left her eyes and her lips. ''We're not in the position to call the police. I couldn't answer the questions they'd ask, don't you see? Papa has to resolve the business of the Rembrandt, Adam. If everything came out now, he'd be hopelessly compromised. He might go to prison. Not for anything," she said softly. "Not for anything would I risk that."

"He won't," Adam said shortly. No matter what strings he'd have to pull, what dance he'd have to perform, he'd see to it that Fairchild stayed clear. "Kirby, do you think your father would continue with whatever he's plotting once he knew of this?"

"I couldn't predict his reaction." Weary, she let out a long breath and tried to make him understand. "He might destroy the Rembrandt in a blind rage. He could go after Stuart single-handed. He's capable of it. What good would any of that do, Adam?" The queasiness was passing, but it had left her weak. Though she didn't know it, the vulnerability was her best weapon. "We have to let it lie for a while longer."

"What do you mean, let it lie?"

"I'll speak to Papa—tell him what happened in my own way, so that he doesn't overreact. Harriet and Melanie are coming to dinner tonight. It has to wait until tomorrow."

"How can he sit down and have dinner with Harriet when he has stolen something from her?" Adam demanded. "How can he do something like this to a friend?"

Pain shot into her eyes. Deliberately she lowered them, but he'd already seen it. "I don't know."

"I'm sorry."

She shook her head. "No, you have no reason to be. You've been wonderful through all of this."

"No, I haven't." He pressed the heels of his hands to his eyes.

"Let me be the judge of that. And give me one more day." She touched his wrists and waited until he lowered his hands. "Just one more day, then I'll talk to Papa. Maybe we'll get everything straightened out."

"That much, Kirby. No more." He had some thinking of his own to do. Perhaps one more night would give him some answers. "Tomorrow you tell Philip everything, no glossing over the details. If he doesn't agree to resolve the Rembrandt business then, I'm taking over."

She hesitated a minute. She'd said she trusted him. It was true. "All right."

"And I'll deal with Hiller."

"You're not going to fight with him."

Amused, he lifted a brow. "No?"

"Adam, I won't have you bruised and bloodied. That's it."

"Your confidence in me is overwhelming."

With a laugh, she sat up again and threw her arms around him. "My hero. He'd never lay a hand on you."

"I beg your pardon, Miss Fairchild."

"Yes, Cards." Shifting her head, Kirby acknowledged the butler in the doorway.

"It seems a chair has somehow found its way through your studio window. Unfortunately, it landed in Jamie's bed of zinnias."

"Yes, I know. I suppose he's quite annoyed."

"Indeed, miss."

"I'll apologize, Cards. Perhaps a new lawn mower... You'll see to having the window repaired?"

"Yes, miss."

"And have that heater replaced by something from the twentieth-century," Adam added. He watched as Cards glanced at him then back at Kirby.

"As soon as possible, please, Cards."

With a nod, the butler backed out of the doorway.

"He takes his orders from you, doesn't he?" Adam commented as the quiet footsteps receded. "I've seen the subtle nods and looks between the two of you."

She brushed a smudge of dirt on the shoulder of his shirt. "I've no idea what you mean."

"A century ago, Cards would've been known as the queen's man." When she laughed at the term, he eased her back on the pillows. "Rest," he ordered.

"Adam, I'm fine."

"Want me to get tough again?" Before she could answer, he covered her mouth with his, lingering. "Turn the batteries down awhile," he murmured. "I might have to call the doctor after all."

"Blackmail." She brought his mouth back to hers again. "But maybe if you rested with me..."

"Rest isn't what would happen then." He drew away as she grumbled a protest.

"A half hour."

"Fine. I'll be back."

She smiled and let her eyes close. "I'll be waiting."

It was too soon for stars, too late for sunbeams. From a window in the parlor, Adam watched the sunset hold off twilight just a few moments longer.

After reporting the attempt on Kirby's life to McIntyre, he'd found himself suddenly weary. Half-lies, half-truths. It had to end. It would end, he decided, tomorrow. Fairchild would have to see reason, and Kirby would be told everything. The hell with McIntyre, the job and anything else. She deserved honesty along with everything else he wanted to give her. Everything else, he realized, would mean nothing to Kirby without it.

The sun lowered further and the horizon exploded with rose-gold light. He thought of the Titian woman. She'd understand, he told himself. She had to understand. He'd make her understand. Thinking to check on her again, Adam turned from the window.

When he reached her room, he heard the sound of running water. The simple, natural sound of her humming along with her bath dissolved his tension. He thought about joining her, then remembered how pale and tired she'd looked. Another time, he promised both of them as he shut the door to her room again. Another time he'd have the pleasure of lounging in the big marble tub with her.

"Where's that wretched girl?" Fairchild demanded from behind him. "She's been hiding out all day."

"Having a bath," Adam told him.

"She'd better have a damn good explanation, that's all I

have to say." Looking grim, Fairchild reached for the door-knob. Adam blocked the door automatically.

"For what?"

Fairchild glared at him. "My shoes."

Adam looked down at Fairchild's small stockinged feet. "I don't think she has them."

"A man tugs himself into a restraining suit, chokes himself with a ridiculous tie, then has no shoes." Fairchild pulled at the knot around his neck. "Is that justice?"

"No. Have you tried Cards?"

"Cards couldn't get his big British feet in my shoes." Then he frowned and pursed his lips. "Then again, he did have my suit."

"I rest my case."

"The man's a kleptomaniac," Fairchild grumbled as he wandered down the hall. "I'd check my shorts if I were you. No telling what he'll pick up next. Cocktails in a half hour, Adam. Hustle along."

Deciding a quiet drink was an excellent idea after the day they'd put in, Adam went to change. He was adjusting the knot in his own tie when Kirby knocked. She opened it without waiting for his answer, then stood a moment, deliberately posed in the doorway—head thrown back, one arm raised high on the jamb, the other at her hip. The slinky jumpsuit clung to every curve, falling in folds from her neck and dispensing with a back altogether. At her ears, emeralds the size of quarters picked up the vivid green shade. Five twisted, gold chains hung past her waist.

"Hello, neighbor." Glittering and gleaming, she crossed to him. Adam put a finger under her chin and studied her face. As an artist, she knew how to make use of the colors of a makeup palette. Her cheeks were tinted with a touch of bronze, her lips just a bit darker. "Well?"

"You look better," he decided.

"That's a poor excuse for a compliment."

"How do you feel?"

"I'd feel a lot better if you'd stop examining me as though I had a rare terminal disease and kiss me as you're supposed to.'' She twisted her arms around his neck and let her lashes lower.

It was them he kissed first, softly, with a tenderness that had her sighing. Then his lips skimmed down, over her cheeks, gently over her jawline.

"Adam..." His name was only a breath on the air as his mouth touched hers. She wanted it all now. Instantly. She wanted the fire and flash, the pleasure and the passion. She wanted that calm, spreading contentment that only he could give to her. "I love you," she murmured. "I love you until there's nothing else but that."

"There is nothing else but that," he said, almost fiercely. "We've a lifetime for it." He drew her away so he could bring both of her hands to his lips. "A lifetime, Kirby, and it isn't long enough."

"Then we'll have to start soon." She felt the giddiness again, the light-headedness, but she wouldn't run from it. "Very soon," she added. "But we have to wait at least until after dinner. Harriet and Melanie should be here any minute."

"If I had my choice, I'd stay with you alone in this room and make love until sunrise."

"Don't tempt me to tarnish your reputation." Because she knew she had to, she stepped back and finished adjusting his tie herself. It was a brisk, womanly gesture he found himself enjoying. "Ever since I told Harriet about your help with the Titian, she's decided you're the greatest thing since peanut butter. I wouldn't want to mess that up by making you late for dinner."

"Then we'd better go now. Five more minutes alone with you and we'd be a lot more than late." When she laughed, he linked her arm through his and led her from the room. "By the way, your father's shoes were stolen."

To the casual observer, the group in the parlor would have seemed a handful of elegant, cosmopolitan people. Secure, friendly, casually wealthy. Looking beyond the sparkle and glitter, a more discerning eye might have seen the pallor of Kirby's skin that her careful application of makeup disguised.

Someone looking closely might have noticed that her friendly
nonsense covered a discomfort that came from battling loyalties.

To someone from the outside, the group might have taken
on a different aspect if the canvas were stretched. Rick's stut-
tering nerves were hardly noticed by those in the parlor. As
was Melanie's subtle disdain for him. Both were the expected.
Fairchild's wolfish grins and Harriet's jolting laughter covered
the rest.

Everyone seemed relaxed, except Adam. The longer it went
on, the more he wished he'd insisted that Kirby postpone the
dinner party. She looked frail. The more energy she poured
out, the more fragile she seemed to him. And touchingly valiant. Her devotion to Harriet hadn't been lip service. Adam
could see it, hear it. When she loved, as Fairchild had said,
she loved completely. Even the thought of the Rembrandt
would be tearing her in two. Tomorrow. By the next day, it
would be over.

"Adam." Harriet took his arm as Kirby poured after-dinner
drinks. "I'd love to see Kirby's portrait."

"As soon as it's finished you'll have a private viewing."
And until the repairs in the tower were complete, he thought,
he was keeping all outsiders away.

"I'll have to be content with that, I suppose." She pouted
a moment, then forgave him. "Sit beside me," Harriet com-
manded and spread the flowing vermilion of her skirt on the
sofa. "Kirby said I could flirt with you."

Adam noticed that Melanie turned a delicate pink at her
mother's flamboyance. Unable to resist, he lifted Harriet's
hand to his lips. "Do I need permission to flirt with you?"

"Guard your heart, Harriet," Kirby warned as she set out
drinks.

"Mind your own business," Harriet tossed back. "By the
way, Adam, I'd like you to have my necklace of crocodile
teeth as a token of my appreciation."

"Good heavens, Mother." Melanie sipped at her black-
berry brandy. "Why would Adam want that hideous thing?"

"Sentiment," she returned without blinking an eye.

"Adam's agreed to let me exhibit Kirby's portrait, and I want to repay him."

The old girl's quick, Adam decided as she sent him a guileless smile, and Melanie's been kept completely in the dark about the hobby her mother shares with Fairchild. Studying Melanie's cool beauty, Adam decided her mother knew best. She'd never react as Kirby did. Melanie could have their love and affection, but secrets were kept within the triangle. No, he realized, oddly pleased. It was now a rectangle.

"He doesn't have to wear it," Harriet went on, breaking into his thoughts.

"I should hope not," Melanie put in, rolling her eyes at Kirby.

"It's for good luck." Harriet sent Kirby a glance, then squeezed Adam's arm. "But perhaps you have all the luck you need."

"Perhaps my luck's just beginning."

"How quaintly they speak in riddles." Kirby sat on the arm of Melanie's chair. "Why don't we ignore them?"

"Your hawk's coming along nicely, Mr. Fairchild," Rich hazarded.

"Aha!" It was all Fairchild needed. Bursting with good feelings, he treated Rick to an in-depth lecture on the use of calipers.

"Rick's done it now," Kirby whispered to Melanie. "Papa has no mercy on a captive audience."

"I didn't know Uncle Philip was sculpting."

"Don't mention it," Kirby said quickly. "You'll never escape." Pursing her lips, she looked down at Melanie's elegant dark rose dress. The lines flowed fluidly with the flash of a studded buckle at the waist. "Melly, I wonder if you'd have time to design a dress for me."

Surprised, Melanie glanced up. "Oh course, I'd love to. But I've been trying to talk you into it for years and you've always refused to go through the fittings."

Kirby shrugged. A wedding dress was a different matter, she mused. Still, she didn't mention her plans with Adam.

Her father would know first. "I usually buy on impulse, whatever appeals at the time."

"From Goodwill to Rive Gauche," Melanie murmured. "So this must be special."

"I'm taking a page from your book," Kirby evaded. "You know I've always admired your talent, I just knew I wouldn't have the patience for all the preliminaries." She laughed. "Do you think you can design a dress that'd make me look demure?"

"Demure?" Harriet cut in, pouncing on the word. "Poor Melanie would have to be a sorceress to pull that off. Even as a child in that sweet little muslin you looked capable of battling a tribe of Comanches. Philip, you must let me borrow that painting of Kirby for the gallery."

"We'll see." His eyes twinkled. "You'll have to soften me up a bit first. I've always had a deep affection for that painting." With a hefty sigh, he leaned back with his drink. "Its value goes below the surface."

"He still begrudges me my sitting fee." Kirby sent her father a sweet smile. "He forgets I never collected for any of the others."

"You never posed for the others," Fairchild reminded her.

"I never signed a release for them, either."

"Melly posed for me out of the goodness of her heart."

"Melly's nicer than I am," Kirby said simply. "I like being selfish."

"Heartless creature," Harriet put in mildly. "It's so selfish of you to teach sculpture in the summer to those handicapped children."

Catching Adam's surprised glance, Kirby shifted uncomfortably. "Harriet, think of my reputation."

"She's sensitive about her good deeds," Harriet told Adam with a squeeze for his knee.

"I simply had nothing else to do." With a shrug, Kirby turned away. "Are you going to Saint Moritz this year, Melly?"

Fraud, Adam thought as he watched her guide the subject

away from herself. A beautiful, sensitive fraud. And finding her so, he loved her more.

By the time Harriet and Melanie rose to leave, Kirby was fighting off a raging headache. Too much strain, she knew, but she wouldn't admit it. She could tell herself she needed only a good night's sleep, and nearly believe it.

"Kirby." Harriet swirled her six-foot shawl over her shoulder before she took Kirby's chin in her hand. "You look tired, and a bit pale. I haven't seen you look pale since you were thirteen and had the flu. I remember you swore you'd never be ill again."

"After that disgusting medicine you poured down my throat, I couldn't afford to. I'm fine." But she threw her arms around Harriet's neck and held on. "I'm fine, really."

"Mmm." Over her head, Harriet frowned at Fairchild. "You might think about Australia. We'll put some color in your cheeks."

"I will. I love you."

"Go to sleep, child," Harriet murmured.

The moment the door was closed, Adam took Kirby's arm. Ignoring her father and Rick, he began to pull her up the stairs. "You belong in bed."

"Shouldn't you be dragging me by the hair instead of the arm?"

"Some other time, when my intentions are less peaceful." He stopped outside her door. "You're going to sleep."

"Tired of me already?"

The words were hardly out of her mouth when his covered it. Holding her close, he let himself go for a moment, releasing the needs, the desires, the love. He could feel her heart thud, her bones melt. "Can't you see how tired I am of you?" He kissed her again with his hands framing her face. "You must see how you bore me."

"Anything I can do?" she murmured, slipping her hands under his jacket.

"Get some rest." He took her by the shoulders. "This is your last opportunity to sleep alone."

"Am I sleeping alone?"

It wasn't easy for him. He wanted to devour her, he wanted to delight her. He wanted, more than anything else, to have a clean slate between them before they made love again. If she hadn't looked so weary, so worn, he'd have told her everything then and there. "This may come as a shock to you," he said lightly. "But you're not Wonder Woman."

"Really?"

"You're going to get a good night's sleep. Tomorrow." He took her hands and the look, the sudden intenseness, confused her. "Tomorrow, Kirby, we have to talk."

"About what?"

"Tomorrow," he repeated before he could change his mind. "Rest now." He gave her a nudge inside. "If you're not feeling any better tomorrow, you're going to stay in bed and be pampered."

She managed one last wicked grin. "Promise?"

Chapter 11

It was clear after Kirby had tossed in bed and fluffed up her pillow for more than an hour that she wasn't going to get the rest everyone seemed to want for her. Her body was dragging, but her mind refused to give in to it.

She tried. For twenty minutes she recited dull poetry. Closing her eyes, she counted five hundred and twenty-seven camels. She turned on her bedside radio and found chamber music. She was, after all of it, wide awake.

It wasn't fear. If Stuart had indeed tried to kill her, he'd failed. She had her own wits, and she had Adam. No, it wasn't fear.

The Rembrandt. She couldn't think of anything else after seeing Harriet laughing, after remembering how Harriet had nursed her through the flu and had given her a sweet and totally unnecessary woman-to-woman talk when she'd been a girl.

Kirby had grieved for her own mother, and though she'd died when Kirby had been a child, the memory remained perfectly clear. Harriet hadn't been a substitute. Harriet had simply been Harriet. Kirby loved her for that alone.

How could she sleep?

Annoyed, Kirby rolled over on her back and stared at the

ceiling. Maybe, just maybe, she could make use of the insomnia and sort it all out and make some sense out of it.

Her father, she was certain, would do nothing to hurt Harriet without cause. Was revenge on Stuart cause enough? After a moment, she decided it didn't follow.

Harriet had gone to Africa—that was first. It had been nearly two weeks after that when Kirby had broken her engagement with Stuart. Afterward she had told her father of Stuart's blackmail threats and he'd been unconcerned. He'd said, Kirby remembered, that Stuart wasn't in any position to make waves.

Then it made sense to assume they'd already begun plans to switch the paintings. Revenge was out.

Then why?

Not for money, Kirby thought. Not for the desire to own the painting himself. That wasn't his way—she knew better than anyone how he felt about greed. But then, stealing from a friend wasn't his way either.

If she couldn't find the reason, perhaps she could find the painting itself.

Still staring at the ceiling, she began to go over everything her father had said. So many ambiguous comments, she mused. But then, that was typical of him. In the house—that much was certain. In the house, hidden with appropriate affection and respect. Just how many hundreds of possibilities could she sort through in one night?

She blew out a disgusted breath and rolled over again. With a last thump for her pillow, she closed her eyes. The yawn, she felt, was a hopeful sign. As she snuggled deeper, a tiny memory probed.

She'd think about it tomorrow.... No, now, she thought, and rolled over again. She'd think about it now. What was it her father had been saying to Adam when she'd walked into his studio the night after the Titian switch? Something... Something...about involving her figuratively.

"Root rot," she muttered, and squeezed her eyes shut in concentration. "What the devil was that supposed to mean?"

Just as she was about to give up, the idea seeped in. Her eyes sprang open as she sprang up. "It'd be just like him!"

Grabbing a robe, she dashed from the room.

For a moment in the hall she hesitated. Perhaps she should wake Adam and tell him of her theory. Then again, it was no more than that, and he hadn't had the easiest day of it, either. If she produced results, then she'd wake him. And if she was wrong, her father would kill her.

She made a quick trip to her father's studio, then went down to the dining room.

On neither trip did she bother with lights. She wanted no one to pop out of their room and ask what she was up to. Carrying a rag, a bottle and a stack of newspapers, she went silently through the dark. Once she'd reached the dining room, she turned on the lights. No one would investigate downstairs except Cards. He'd never question her. She worked quickly.

Kirby spread the newspapers in thick pads on the dining room table. Setting the bottle and the rag on them, she turned to her own portrait.

"You're too clever for your own good, Papa," she murmured as she studied the painting. "I'd never be able to tell if this was a duplicate. There's only one way."

Once she'd taken the portrait from the wall, Kirby laid it on the newspaper. "Its value goes below the surface," she murmured. Isn't that what he'd said to Harriet? And he'd been smug. He'd been smug right from the start. Kirby opened the bottle and tipped the liquid onto the rag. "Forgive me, Papa," she said quietly.

With the lightest touch—an expert's touch—she began to remove layers of paint in the lower corner. Minutes passed. If she was wrong, she wanted the damage to be minimal. If she was right, she had something priceless in her hands. Either way, she couldn't rush.

She dampened the rag and wiped again. Her father's bold signature disappeared, then the bright summer grass beneath it, and the primer.

And there, beneath where there should have been only canvas, was a dark, somber brown. One letter, then another, appeared. It was all that was necessary.

"Great buckets of blood," she murmured. "I was right."

Beneath the feet of the girl she'd been was Rembrandt's signature. She'd go no further. As carefully as she'd unstopped it, Kirby secured the lid of the bottle.

"So, Papa, you put Rembrandt to sleep under a copy of my portrait. Only you would've thought to copy yourself to pull it off."

"Very clever."

Whirling, Kirby looked behind her into the dark outside the dining room. She knew the voice; it didn't frighten her. As her heart pounded, the shadows moved. What now? she asked herself quickly. Just how would she explain it?

"Cleverness runs in the family, doesn't it, Kirby?"

"So I'm told." She tried to smile. "I'd like to explain. You'd better come in out of the dark and sit down. It could take—" She stopped as the first part of the invitation was accepted. She stared at the barrel of a small polished revolver. Lifting her gaze from it, she stared into clear, delicate blue eyes. "Melly, what's going on?"

"You look surprised. I'm glad." With a satisfied smile, Melanie aimed the gun at Kirby's head. "Maybe you're not so clever after all."

"Don't point that at me."

"I intend to point it at you." She lowered the gun to chest level. "And I'll do more than point it if you move."

"Melly." She wasn't afraid, not yet. She was confused, even annoyed, but she wasn't afraid of the woman she'd grown up with. "Put that thing away and sit down. What're you doing here this time of night?"

"Two reasons. First, to see if I could find any trace of the painting you've so conveniently found for me. Second, to finish the job that was unsuccessful this morning."

"This morning?" Kirby took a step forward then froze when she heard the quick, deadly click. Good God, could it actually be loaded? "Melly..."

"I suppose I must have miscalculated a bit or you'd be

dead already." The elegant rose silk whispered as she
shrugged. "I know the passages very well. Remember, you
used to drag me around in them when we were children—
before you went in with a faulty flashlight. I'd changed the
batteries in it, you see. I'd never told you about that, had I?"
She laughed as Kirby remained silent. "I used the passages
this morning. Once I was sure you and Adam were settled in,
I went out and turned on the gas by the main valve—I'd
already broken the switch on the unit."

"You can't be serious." Kirby dragged a hand through her
hair.

"Deadly serious, Kirby."

"Why?"

"Primarily for money, of course."

"Money?" She would've laughed, but her throat was closing. "But you don't need money."

"You're so smug." The venom came through. Kirby wondered that she'd never heard it before. "Yes, I need money."

"You wouldn't take a settlement from your ex-husband."

"He wouldn't give me a dime," Melanie corrected. "He
cut me off, and as he had me cold on adultery, I wasn't in a
position to take him to court. He let me get a quiet, discreet
divorce so that our reputations wouldn't suffer. And except
for one incident, I'd been very discreet. Stuart and I were
always very careful."

"Stuart?" Kirby lifted a hand to rub at her temple. "You
and Stuart?"

"We've been lovers for over three years. Questions are just
buzzing around in your head, aren't they?" Enjoying herself,
Melanie stepped closer. The whiff of Chanel followed her.
"It was more practical for us if we pretended to be just acquaintances. I convinced Stuart to ask you to marry him. My
inheritance has dwindled to next to nothing. Your money
would have met Stuart's and my tastes very nicely. And we'd
have got close to Uncle Philip."

She ignored the rest and homed in on the most important.
"What do you want from my father?"

"I found out about the little game he and Mother indulged

in years ago. Not all the details, but enough to know I could use it if I had to. I thought it was time to use your father's talent for my own benefit.''

"You made plans to steal from your own mother.''

"Don't be so self-righteous.'' Her voice chilled. The gun was steady. "Your father betrayed her without a murmur, then double-crossed us in the bargain. Now you've solved that little problem for me.'' With her free hand, she gestured to the painting. "I should be grateful I failed this morning. I'd still be looking for the painting.''

Somehow, some way, she'd deal with this. Kirby started with the basics. "Melly, how could you hurt me? We've been friends all our lives.''

"Friends?'' The word sounded like an obscenity. "I've hated you for as long as I can remember.''

"No—''

"Hated,'' Melanie repeated, coldly this time and with the ring of truth. "It was always you people flocked around, always you men preferred. My own mother preferred you.''

"That's not true.'' Did it go so deep? Kirby thought with a flood of guilt. Should she have seen it before? "Melly—'' But as she started forward, Melanie gestured with the gun.

"'Melanie, don't be so stiff and formal…. Melanie, where's your sense of humor?''' Her eyes narrowed into slits. "She never came right out and said I should be more like you, but that's what she wanted.''

"Harriet loves you—''

"Love?'' Melanie cut Kirby off with a laugh. "I don't give a damn for love. It won't buy what I need. You may have taken my mother, but that was a minor offense. The men you snatched from under my nose time and time again is a bigger one.''

"I never took a man from you. I've never shown an interest in anyone you were serious about.''

"There have been dozens,'' Melanie corrected. Her voice was as brittle as glass. "You'd smile and say something stupid and I'd be forgotten. You never had my looks, but you'd use that so-called charm and lure them away, or you'd freeze up and do the same thing.''

"I might've been friendly to someone you cared for," Kirby said quickly. "If I froze it was to discourage them. Good God, Melly, I'd never have done anything to hurt you. I love you."

"I've no use for your love any longer. It served its purpose well enough." She smiled slowly as tears swam in Kirby's eyes. "My only regret is that you didn't fall for Stuart. I wanted to see you fawn over him, knowing he preferred me— married you only because I wanted it. When you came to see him that night, I nearly came out of the bedroom just for the pleasure of seeing your face. But…" She shrugged. "We had long-range plans."

"You used me," Kirby said quietly when she could no longer deny it. "You had Stuart use me."

"Of course. Still, it wasn't wise of me to come back from New York for the weekend to be with him."

"Why, Melanie? Why have you pretended all these years?"

"You were useful. Even as a child I knew that. Later, in Paris, you opened doors for me, then again in New York. It was even due to you that I spent a year of luxury with Carlyse. You wouldn't sleep with him and you wouldn't marry him. I did both."

"And that's all?" Kirby murmured. "That's all?"

"That's all. You're not useful any longer, Kirby. In fact, you're an inconvenience. I'd planned your death as a warning to Uncle Philip, now it's just a necessity."

She wanted to turn away, but she needed to face it. "How could I have known you all my life and not seen it? How could you have hated me and not shown it?"

"You let emotions rule your life, I don't. Pick up the painting, Kirby." With the gun, she gestured. "And be careful with it. Stuart and I have been offered a healthy sum for it. If you call out," she added, "I'll shoot you now and be in the passage with the painting before anyone comes down."

"What are you going to do?"

"We're going into the passage. You're going to have a nasty spill, Kirby, and break your neck. I'm going to take the painting home and wait for the call to tell me of your accident."

She'd stall. If only she'd woken Adam... No, if she'd woken him, he, too, would have a gun pointed at him. "Everyone knows how I feel about the passages."

"It'll be a mystery. When they find the empty space on the wall, they'll know the Rembrandt was responsible. Stuart should be the first target, but he's out of town and has been for three days. I'll be devastated by the death of my oldest and dearest friend. It'll take months in Europe to recover from the grief."

"You've thought this out carefully." Kirby rested against the table. "But are you capable of murder, Melly?" Slowly she closed her fingers around the bottle, working off the top with her thumb. "Face-to-face murder, not remote-control like this morning."

"Oh, yes." Melanie smiled beautifully. "I prefer it. I feel better with you knowing who's going to kill you. Now pick up the painting, Kirby. It's time."

With a jerk of her arm, Kirby tossed the turpentine mixture, splattering it on Melanie's neck and dress. When Melanie tossed up her hand in protection, Kirby lunged. Together they fell in a rolling heap onto the floor, the gun pressed between them.

"What do you mean Hiller's been in New York since yesterday?" Adam demanded. "What happened this morning wasn't an accident. He had to have done it."

"No way." In a few words McIntyre broke Adam's theory. "I have a good man on him. I can give you the name of Hiller's hotel. I can give you the name of the restaurant where he had lunch and what he ate while you were throwing chairs through windows. He's got his alibi cold, Adam, but it doesn't mean he didn't arrange it."

"Damn." Adam lowered the transmitter while he rearranged his thinking. "It gives me a bad feeling, Mac. Dealing with Hiller's one thing, but it's a whole new story if he has a partner or he's hired a pro to do his dirty work. Kirby needs protection, official protection. I want her out.''

"I'll work on it. The Rembrandt—"

"I don't give a damn about the Rembrandt," Adam tossed back. "But it'll be in my hands tomorrow if I have to hang Fairchild up by his thumbs."

McIntyre let out a sigh of relief. "That's better. You were making me nervous thinking you were hung up on the Fairchild woman."

"I am hung up on the Fairchild woman," Adam returned mildly. "So you'd better arrange for—" He heard the shot. One, sharp and clean. It echoed and echoed through his head. "*Kirby!*" He thought of nothing else as he dropped the open transmitter on the floor and ran.

He called her name again as he raced downstairs. But his only answer was silence. He called as he rushed like a madman through the maze of rooms downstairs, but she didn't call back. Nearly blind with terror, his own voice echoing back to mock him, he ran on, slamming on lights as he went until the house was lit up like a celebration. Racing headlong into the dining room, he nearly fell over the two figures on the floor.

"Oh, my God!"

"I've killed her! Oh, God, Adam, help me! I think I've killed her!" With tears streaming down her face, Kirby pressed a blood-soaked linen napkin against Melanie's side. The stain spread over the rose silk of the dress and onto Kirby's hand.

"Keep the pressure firm." He didn't ask questions, but grabbed a handful of linen from the buffet behind him. Nudging Kirby aside, he felt for a pulse. "She's alive." He pressed more linen to Melanie's side. "Kirby—"

Before he could speak again, there was chaos. The rest of the household poured into the dining room from every direction. Polly let out one squeal that never ended.

"Call an ambulance," Adam ordered Cards, even as the

butler turned to do so. "Shut her up, or get her out," he told Rick, nodding to Polly.

Recovering quickly, Fairchild knelt beside his daughter and the daughter of his closest friend. "Kirby, what happened here?"

"I tried to take the gun from her." She struggled to breathe as she looked down at the blood on her hands. "We fell. I don't—Papa, I don't even know which one of us pulled the trigger. Oh, God, I don't even know."

"Melanie had a gun?" Steady as a rock, Fairchild took Kirby's shoulders and turned her to face him. "Why?"

"She hates me." Her voice shook, then leveled as she stared into her father's face. "She's always hated me, I never knew. It was the Rembrandt, Papa. She'd planned it all."

"Melanie?" Fairchild glanced beyond Kirby to the unconscious figure on the floor. "She was behind it." He fell silent, only a moment. "How bad, Adam?"

"I don't know, damn it. I'm an artist, not a doctor." There was fury in his eyes and blood on his hands. "It might've been Kirby."

"Yes, you're right." Fairchild's fingers tightened on his daughter's shoulder. "You're right."

"I found the Rembrandt," Kirby murmured. If it was shock that was making her light-headed, she wouldn't give in to it. She forced herself to think and to speak clearly.

Fairchild looked at the empty space on the wall, then at the table where the painting lay. "So you did."

With a cluck of her tongue, Tulip pushed Fairchild aside and took Kirby by the arm. Ignoring everyone else, she pulled Kirby to her feet. "Come with me, lovie. Come along with me now, that's a girl."

Feeling helpless, Adam watched Kirby being led away while he fought to stop the bleeding. "You'd better have a damn good explanation," he said between his teeth as his gaze swept over Fairchild.

"Explanations don't seem to be enough at this point," he murmured. Very slowly he rose. The sound of sirens cut through the quiet. "I'll phone Harriet."

Almost an hour had passed before Adam could wash the blood from his hands. Unconscious still, Melanie was speeding on her way to the hospital. His only thought was for Kirby now, and he left his room to find her. When he reached the bottom landing, he came upon an argument in full gear. Though the shouting was all one-sided, the noise vibrated through the hall.

"I want to see Adam Haines and I want to see him immediately!"

"Gate-crashing, Mac?" Adam moved forward to stand beside Cards.

"Adam, thank God." The small, husky man with the squared-off face and disarming eyes ran a hand through his disheveled mat of hair. "I didn't know what'd happened to you. Tell this wall to move aside, will you?"

"It's all right, Cards." He drew an expressionless stare. "He's not a reporter. I know him."

"Very well, sir."

"What the hell's going on?" McIntyre demanded when Cards walked back down the hall. "Who just got carted out of here in an ambulance? Damn it, Adam, I thought it might be you. Last thing I know, you're shouting and breaking transmission."

"It's been a rough night." Putting a hand on his shoulder, Adam led him into the parlor. "I need a drink." Going directly to the bar, Adam poured, drank and poured again. "Drink up, Mac," he invited. "This has to be better than the stuff you've been buying in that little motel down the road. Philip," he continued as Fairchild walked into the room, "I imagine you could use one of these."

"Yes." With a nod of acknowledgment for McIntyre, and no questions, Fairchild accepted the glass Adam offered.

"We'd better sit down. Philip Fairchild," Adam went on as Fairchild settled himself, "Henry McIntyre, investigator for the Commonwealth Insurance company."

"Ah, Mr. McIntyre." Fairchild drank half his scotch in one gulp. "We have quite a bit to discuss. But first, Adam, satisfy my curiosity. How did you become involved with the investigation?''

''It's not the first time I've worked for Mac, but it's the last.'' He sent McIntyre a quiet look that was lined in steel. ''There's a matter of our being cousins,'' he added. ''Second cousins.''

''Relatives.'' Fairchild smiled knowingly, then gave McIntyre a charming smile.

''You knew why I was here,'' Adam said. ''How?''

''Well, Adam, my boy, it's nothing to do with your cleverness.'' Fairchild tossed off the rest of the scotch, then rose to fill his glass again. ''I was expecting someone to come along. You were the only one who did.'' He sat back down with a sigh. ''Simple as that.''

''Expecting?''

''Would someone tell me who was in that ambulance?'' McIntyre cut in.

''Melanie Burgess.'' Fairchild looked into his scotch. ''Melly.'' It would hurt, he knew, for a long time. For himself, for Harriet and for Kirby. It was best to begin to deal with it. ''She was shot when Kirby tried to take her gun away—the gun she was pointing at my daughter.''

''Melanie Burgess,'' McIntyre mused. ''It fits with the information I got today. Information,'' he added to Adam, ''I was about to give you when you broke transmission. I'd like it from the beginning, Mr. Fairchild. I assume the police are on their way.''

''Yes, no way around that.'' Fairchild sipped at his scotch and deliberated on just how to handle things. Then he saw he no longer had McIntyre's attention. He was staring at the doorway.

Dressed in jeans and a white blouse, Kirby stood just inside the room. She was pale, but her eyes were dark. She was beautiful. It was the first thing McIntyre thought. The second was that she was a woman who could empty a man's mind the way a thirsty man empties a bottle.

''Kirby.'' Adam was up and across the room. He had his

hands on hers. Hers were cold, but steady. "Are you all right?"

"Yes. Melanie?"

"The paramedics handled everything. I got the impression the wound wasn't as bad as it looked. Go lie down," he murmured. "Forget it for a while."

"No." She shook her head and managed a weak smile. "I'm fine, really. I've been washed and patted and plied with liquor, though I wouldn't mind another. The police will want to question me." Her gaze drifted to McIntyre. She didn't ask, but simply assumed he was with the police. "Do you need to talk to me?"

It wasn't until then he realized he'd been staring. Clearing his throat, McIntyre rose. "I'd like to hear your father's story first, Miss Fairchild."

"Wouldn't we all?" Struggling to find some balance, she walked to her father's chair. "Are you going to come clean, Papa, or should I hire a shady lawyer?"

"Unnecessary, my sweet." He took her hand and held it. "The beginning," he continued with a smile for McIntyre. "It started, I suppose, a few days before Harriet flew off to Africa. She's an absentminded woman. She had to return to the gallery one night to pick up some papers she'd forgotten. When she saw the light in Stuart's office, she started to go in and scold him for working late. Instead she eavesdropped on his phone conversation and learned of his plans to steal the Rembrandt. Absentminded but shrewd, Harriet left and let Stuart think his plans were undetected." He grinned and squeezed Kirby's hand. "An intelligent woman, she came directly to a friend known for his loyalty and his sharp mind."

"Papa." With a laugh of relief, she bent over and kissed his head. "You were working together, I should've known."

"We developed a plan. Perhaps unwisely, we decided not to bring Kirby into it." He looked up at her. "Should I apologize?"

"Never."

But the fingers brushing over her hand said it for him. "Kirby's relationship with Stuart helped us along in that decision. And her occasional shortsightedness. That is, when she doesn't agree with my point of view.''

"I might take the apology after all.''

"In any case.'' Rising, Fairchild began to wander around the room, hands clasped behind his back. His version of Sherlock Holmes, Kirby decided, and settled back for the show. ''Harriet and I both knew Stuart wasn't capable of constructing and carrying through on a theft like this alone. Harriet hadn't any idea whom he'd been talking to on the phone, but my name had been mentioned. Stuart had said he'd, ah, 'feel me out on the subject of producing a copy of the painting.''' His face fell easily into annoyed lines. ''I've no idea why he should've thought a man like me would do something so base, so dishonest.''

"Incredible,'' Adam murmured, and earned a blinding smile from father and daughter.

"We decided I'd agree, after some fee haggling. I'd then have the original in my possession while palming the copy off on Stuart. Sooner or later, his accomplice would be forced into the open to try to recover it. Meanwhile, Harriet reported the theft, but refused to file a claim. Instead she demanded that the insurance company act with discretion. Reluctantly she told them of her suspicion that I was involved, thereby ensuring that the investigation would be centered around me, and by association, Stuart and his accomplice. I concealed the Rembrandt behind a copy of a painting of my daughter, the original of which is tucked away in my room. I'm sentimental.''

"Why didn't Mrs. Merrick just tell the police and the insurance company the truth?'' McIntyre demanded after he'd worked his way through the explanation.

"They might have been hasty. No offense,'' Fairchild added indulgently. ''Stuart might've been caught, but his accomplice would probably have gotten away. And, I confess, it was the intrigue that appealed to both of us. It was irresistible. You'll want to corroborate my story, of course.''

"Of course,'' McIntyre agreed, and wondered if he could deal with another loony.

"We'd have done things differently if we'd had any idea that Melanie was involved. It's going to be difficult for Harriet." Pausing, he aimed a long look at McIntyre that was abruptly no-nonsense. "Be careful with her. Very careful. You might find our methods unorthodox, but she's a mother who's had two unspeakable shocks tonight: her daughter's betrayal and the possibility of losing her only child." He ran a hand over Kirby's hair as he stopped by her. "No matter how deep the hurt, the love remains, doesn't it, Kirby?"

"All I feel is the void," she murmured. "She hated me, and I think, I really think, she wanted me dead more than she wanted the painting. I wonder...I wonder just how much I'm to blame for that."

"You can't blame yourself for being, Kirby." Fairchild cupped her chin. "You can't blame a tree for reaching for the sun or another for rotting from within. We make our own choices and we're each responsible for them. Blame and credit belong to the individual. You haven't the right to claim either from someone else."

"You won't let me cover the hurt with guilt." After a long breath she rose and kissed his cheek. "I'll have to deal with it." Without thinking, she held out a hand for Adam before she turned to McIntyre. "Do you need a statement from me?"

"No, the shooting's not my jurisdiction, Miss Fairchild. Just the Rembrandt." Finishing off the rest of his scotch he rose. "I'll have to take it with me, Mr. Fairchild."

All graciousness, Fairchild spread his arms wide. "Perfectly understandable."

"I appreciate your cooperation." If he could call it that. With a weary smile, he turned to Adam. "Don't worry, I haven't forgotten your terms. If everything's as he says, I should be able to keep them out of it officially, as we agreed the other day. Your part of the job's over, and all in all you handled it well. So, I'll be sorry if you're serious about not working for me anymore. You got the Rembrandt back, Adam. Now I've got to get started on untangling the red tape."

"Job?" Going cold, Kirby turned. Her hand was still linked

in Adam's, but she felt it go numb as she drew it slowly away. "Job?" she repeated, pressing the hand to her stomach as if to ward off a blow.

Not now, he thought in frustration, and searched for the words he'd have used only a few hours later. "Kirby—"

With all the strength she had left, all the bitterness she'd felt, she brought her hand across his face. "Bastard," she whispered. She fled at a dead run.

"Damn you, Mac." Adam raced after her.

Chapter 12

Adam caught up to her just as Kirby started to slam her bedroom door. Shoving it open, he pushed his way inside. For a moment, they only stared at each other.

"Kirby, let me explain."

"No." The wounded look had been replaced by glacial anger. "Just get out. All the way out, Adam—of my house and my life."

"I can't." He took her by the shoulders, but her head snapped up, and the look was so cold, so hard, he dropped his hands again. It was too late to explain the way he'd planned. Too late to prevent the hurt. Now he had to find the way around it. "Kirby, I know what you must be thinking. I want—"

"Do you?" It took all of her effort to keep her voice from rising. Instead it was cool and calm. "I'm going to tell you anyway so we can leave everything neat and tidy." She faced him because she refused to turn her back on the pain or on the betrayal. "I'm thinking that I've never detested anyone more than I detest you at this moment. I'm thinking Stuart and Melanie could take lessons on using people from you. I'm thinking how naive I was, how stupid, to have believed there was something special about you, something stable and honest. And I wonder how I could've made love with you and never seen it. Then again, I didn't see it in Melanie, either. I loved and trusted her.'' Tears burned behind her eyes but she ignored them. ''I loved and trusted you.''

''Kirby...''

''Don't touch me.'' She backed away, but it was the tremor in her voice, not the movement, that stopped him from going to her. ''I don't ever want to feel your hands on me again.'' Because she wanted to weep, she laughed, and the sound was as sharp as a knife. ''I've always admired a really good liar, Adam, but you're the best. Every time you touched me, you lied. You prostituted yourself in that bed.'' She gestured toward it and wanted to scream. She wanted to fling herself on it and weep until she was empty. She stood, straight as an arrow. ''You lay beside me and said all the things I wanted to hear. Do you get extra points for that, Adam? Surely that was above and beyond the call of duty.''

''Don't.'' He'd had enough. Enough of her cold, clear look, her cold, clear words. ''You know there was no dishonesty there. What happened between us had nothing to do with the rest.''

''It has everything to do with it.''

''No.'' He'd take everything else she could fling at him, but not that. She'd changed his life with hardly more than a look. She had to know it. ''I should never have put my hands on you, but I couldn't stop myself. I wanted you. I needed you. You have to believe that.''

''I'll tell you what I believe,'' she said quietly, because every word he spoke was another slice into her heart. She'd finished with being used. ''You came here for the Rembrandt, and you meant to find it no matter who or what you had to go through. My father and I were means to an end. Nothing more, nothing less.''

He had to take it, had to let her say it, but there'd be no lies between them any longer. ''I came for the Rembrandt. When I walked through the door I only had one priority, to find it. But I didn't know you when I walked through the door. I wasn't in love with you then.''

''Is this the part where you say everything changed?'' she

demanded, falling back on fury. "Shall we wait for the violins?" She was weakening. She turned away and leaned on the post of the bed. "Do better, Adam."

She could be cruel. He remembered her father's warning. He only wished he believed he had a defense. "I can't do better than the truth."

"Truth? What the hell do you know about truth?" She whirled back around, eyes damp now and shimmering with heat. "I stood here in this room and told you everything, everything I knew about my father. I trusted you with his welfare, the most important thing in my life. Where was your truth then?"

"I had a commitment. Do you think it was easy for me to sit here and listen, knowing I couldn't give you what you were giving me?"

"Yes." Her tone was dead calm, but her eyes were fierce. "Yes, I think it was a matter of routine for you. If you'd told me that night, the next day or the next, I might've believed you. If I'd heard it from you, I might've forgiven you."

Timing. Hadn't she told him how vital timing could be? Now he felt her slipping away from him, but he had nothing but excuses to give her. "I was going to tell you everything, start to finish, tomorrow."

"Tomorrow?" Slowly she nodded. "Tomorrows are very convenient. A pity for us all how rarely they come."

All the warmth, all the fire, that had drawn him to her was gone. He'd only seen this look on her face once before—when Stuart had backed her into a corner and she'd had no escape. Stuart had used physical dominance, but it was no prettier than the emotional pressure Adam knew he used. "I'm sorry, Kirby. If I'd taken the risk and told you this morning, it would've been different for all of us."

"I don't want your apology!" The tears beat her and poured out. She'd sacrificed everything else, now her pride was gone, as well. "I thought I'd found the man I could share my life with. I fell in love with you in the flash of an instant. No questions, no doubts. I believed everything you said to me. I gave you everything I had. In all my life no one's been allowed to know me as you did. I entrusted you with everything I am and you used me.'' Turning, she pressed her face into the bedpost.

He had, he couldn't deny it even to himself. He'd used her, as Stuart had used her. As Melanie had used her. Loving her made no difference, yet he had to hope it made all the difference. "Kirby." It took all the strength he had not to go to her, to comfort her, but he'd only be comforting himself if he put his arms around her now. "There's nothing you can say to me I haven't said to myself. I came here to do a job, but I fell in love with you. There wasn't any warning for me, either. I know I've hurt you. There's nothing I can do to turn back the clock.''

"Do you expect me to fall into your arms? Do you expect me to say nothing else matters but us?'' She turned, and though her cheeks were still damp, her eyes were dry. "It all matters,'' she said flatly. "Your job's finished here, Adam. You've recovered your Rembrandt. Take it, you earned it.''

"You're not going to cut me out of your life.''

"You've done that for me.''

"No.'' The fury and frustration took over so that he grabbed her arm and jerked her against him. "No, you'll have to adjust to the way things are, because I'm coming back.'' He ran his hands down her hair, and they weren't steady. "You can make me suffer. By God, you can do it. I'll give you that, Kirby, but I'll be back.''

Before his anger could push him too far, he whirled around and left her alone.

Fairchild was waiting for him, sitting calmly in the parlor by the fire. "I thought you'd need this.'' Without getting up, he gestured to the glass of scotch on the table beside him. He waited until Adam had tossed it back. He didn't need to be told what had passed between them. "I'm sorry. She's hurt. Perhaps in time the wounds will close and she'll be able to listen.''

Adam's knuckles whitened on the glass. "That's what I told her, but I didn't believe it. I betrayed her.'' His glance lowered and settled on the older man. "And you.''

"You did what you had to do. You had a part to play."
Fairchild spread his hands on his knees and stared at them,
thinking of his own part. "She would've dealt with it, Adam.
She's strong enough. But even Kirby has a breaking point.
Melanie… It was too soon after Melanie."

"She won't let me comfort her." It was that anguish that
had him turning to stare out of the window. "She looks so
wounded, and my being here only makes it harder for her."
Steadying himself, he stared out at nothing. "I'll be out as
soon as I can pack." He turned, his head only, and looked at
the small, balding man in front of the fire. "I love her,
Philip."

In silence Fairchild watched Adam walk away. For the first
time in his six decades he felt old. Old and tired. With a deep,
deep sigh he rose and went to his daughter.

He found her curled on her bed, her head cradled by her
knees and arms. She sat silent and unmoving and, he knew,
utterly, utterly beaten. When he sat beside her, her head jerked
up. Slowly, with his hand stroking her hair, her muscles relaxed.

"Do we ever stop making fools of ourselves, Papa?"

"You've never been a fool."

"Oh, yes, yes, it seems I have." Settling her chin on her
knees, she stared straight ahead. "I lost our bet. I guess you'll
be breaking open that box of cigars you've been saving."

"I think we can consider the extenuating circumstances."

"How generous of you." She tried to smile and failed.
"Aren't you going to the hospital to be with Harriet?"

"Yes, of course."

"You'd better go then. She needs you."

His thin, bony hand continued to stroke her hair. "Don't
you?"

"Oh, Papa." Tears came in a flood as she turned into his
arms.

Kirby followed Cards downstairs as he carried her bags. In
the week since the discovery of the Rembrandt she'd found
it impossible to settle. She found no comfort in her art, no

comfort in her home. Everything here held memories she could no longer deal with. She slept little and ate less. She knew she was losing touch with the person she was, and so she'd made plans to force herself back.

She opened the door for Cards and stared out at the bright, cheery morning. It made her want to weep.

"I don't know why a sensible person would get up at this ridiculous hour to drive to the wilderness."

Kirby forced back the gloom and turned to watch her father stride down the stairs in a ratty bathrobe and bare feet. What hair he had left was standing on end. "The early bird gathers no moss," she told him. "I want to get to the lodge and settle in. Want some coffee?"

"Not while I'm sleeping," he muttered as she nuzzled his cheek. "I don't know what's wrong with you, going off to that shack in the Himalayas."

"It's Harriet's very comfortable cabin in the Adirondacks, twenty miles from Lake Placid."

"Don't nitpick. You'll be alone."

"I've been alone before," she reminded him. "You're annoyed because you won't have anyone but Cards to shout at for a few weeks."

"He never shouts back." But even as he grumbled, Fairchild was studying Kirby's face. The shadows were still under her eyes and the loss of weight was much too apparent. "Tulip should go with you. Someone has to make you eat."

"I'm going to do that. Mountain air should make me ravenous." When he continued to frown at her, she touched his cheek. "Don't worry, Papa."

"I am worried." Taking her shoulders, he held her at arm's length. "For the first time in your life, you're causing me genuine concern."

"A few pounds, Papa."

"Kirby." He cupped her face in his strong, thin hand. "You have to talk to Adam."

"No!" The word came out violently. With an effort, she drew a steadying breath. "I've said all I want to say to Adam. I need time and some solitude, that's all."

"Running away, Kirby?"

"As fast as I can. Papa, Rick proposed to me again before he left."

"What the hell does that have to do with anything?" he demanded. "He always proposes to you before he leaves."

"I nearly said yes." She lifted her hands to his, willing him to understand. "I nearly said yes because it seemed an easy way out. I'd have ruined his life."

"What about yours?"

"I have to glue the pieces back together. Papa, I'll be fine. It's Harriet who needs you now."

He thought of his friend, his oldest and closest friend. He thought of the grief. "Melanie's going to Europe when she's fully recovered."

"I know." Kirby tried not to remember the gun, or the hate. "Harriet told me. She'll need both of us when Melly's gone. If I can't help myself, how can I help Harriet?"

"Melanie won't see Harriet. The girl's destroying herself with hate." He looked at his own daughter, his pride, his treasure. "The sooner Melanie's out of the hospital and thousands of miles away, the better it'll be for everyone."

She knew what he'd done, how he'd fought against his feelings about Melanie to keep from causing either her or Harriet more grief. He'd comforted them both without releasing his own fury. She held him tightly a moment, saying nothing. Needing to say nothing.

"We all need some time," she murmured. When she drew away, she was smiling. She wouldn't leave him with tears in her eyes. "I'll cloister myself in the wilderness and sculpt while you pound on your hawk."

"Such a wicked tongue in such a pretty face."

"Papa..." Absently she checked the contents of her purse. "Whatever painting you do will be done under your own name?" When he didn't answer, she glanced up, narrowing her eyes. "Papa?"

"All my paintings will be Fairchilds. Haven't I given you my word?" He sniffed and looked injured. Kirby began to feel alarmed.

"This obsession with sculpting," she began, eyeing him carefully. "You don't have it in your head to attempt an emulation of a Rodin or Cellini?"

"You ask too many questions," he complained as he nudged her toward the door. "The day's wasting away, better get started. Don't forget to write."

Kirby paused on the porch and turned back to him. "It'll take you years," she decided. "If you ever acquire the talent. Go ahead and play with your hawk." She kissed his forehead. "I love you, Papa."

He watched her dart down the steps and into her car. "One should never interfere in the life of one's child," he murmured. Smiling broadly, he waved goodbye. When she was out of sight, he went directly to the phone.

The forest had always appealed to her. In mid-autumn, it shouted with life. The burst of colors were a last swirling fling before the trees went into the final cycle. It was an order Kirby accepted—birth, growth, decay, rebirth. Still, after three days alone, she hadn't found her serenity.

The stream she walked past rushed and hissed. The air was brisk and tangy. She was miserable.

She'd nearly come to terms with her feelings about Melanie. Her childhood friend was ill, had been ill for a long, long time and might never fully recover. It hadn't been a betrayal any more than cancer was a betrayal. But it was a malignancy Kirby knew she had to cut out of her life. She'd nearly accepted it, for Melanie's sake and her own.

She could come to terms with Melanie, but she had yet to deal with Adam. He'd had no illness, nor a lifetime of resentments to feed it. He'd simply had a job to do. And that was too cold for her to accept.

With her hands in her pockets, she sat down on a log and scowled into the water. Her life, she admitted, was a mess. She was a mess. And she was damn sick of it.

She tried to tell herself she'd put Adam out of her life. She hadn't. Yes, she'd refused to listen to him. She'd made no attempt to contact him. It wasn't enough. It wasn't enough,

Kirby decided, because it left things unfinished. Now she'd never know if he'd had any real feelings for her. She'd never know if, even briefly, he'd belonged to her.

Perhaps it was best that way.

Standing, she began to walk again, scuffling the leaves that danced around her feet. She was tired of herself. Another first. It wasn't going to go on, she determined. Whatever the cost, she was going to whip Kirby Fairchild back into shape. Starting now. At a brisk pace, she started back to the cabin.

She liked the way it looked, set deep in the trees by itself. The roof was pitched high and the glass sparkled. Today, she thought as she went in through the back door, she'd work. After she'd worked, she'd eat until she couldn't move.

Peeling off her coat as she went, she walked directly to the worktable she'd set up in the corner of the living room. Without looking around, she tossed the coat aside and looked at her equipment. She hadn't touched it in days. Now she sat and picked up a formless piece of wood. This was to be her *Passion*. Perhaps now more than ever, she needed to put that emotion into form.

There was silence as she explored the feel and life of the wood in her hands. She thought of Adam, of the nights, the touches, the tastes. It hurt. Passion could. Using it, she began to work.

An hour slipped by. She only noticed when her fingers cramped. With a sigh, she set the wood down and stretched them. The healing had begun. She could be certain of it now. "A start," she murmured to herself. "It's a start."

"It's *Passion*. I can already see it."

The knife slipped out of her hand and clattered on the table as she whirled. Across the room, calmly sitting in a faded wingback chair, was Adam. She'd nearly sprung out of the chair to go to him before she stopped herself. He looked the same, just the same. But nothing was. That she had to remember.

"How did you get in here?"

He heard the ice in her voice. But he'd seen her eyes. In that one instant, she'd told him everything he'd ached for. Still, he knew she couldn't be rushed. "The front door wasn't locked." He rose and crossed to her. "I came inside to wait for you, but when you came in, you looked so intense; then you started right in. I didn't want to disturb your work." When she said nothing, he picked up the wood and turned it over in his hand. He thought it smoldered. "Amazing," he murmured. "Amazing what power you have." Just holding it made him want her more, made him want what she'd put into the wood. Carefully he set it down again, but his eyes were just as intense when he studied her. "What the hell've you been doing? Starving yourself?"

"Don't be ridiculous." She stood and walked away from him, but she didn't know where to go.

"Am I to blame for that, too?"

His voice was quiet, serious. She'd never be able to resist that tone. Gathering her strength, she turned back to him. "Did Tulip send you to check up on me?"

She was too thin. Damn it. Had the pounds melted off her? She was so small. How could she be so small and look so arrogant? He wanted to go to her. Beg. He was nearly certain she'd listen now. Yet she wouldn't want it that way. Instead, he tucked his hands in his pockets and rocked back on his heels. "This is a cozy little place. I wandered around a bit while you were out."

"Glad you made yourself at home."

"It's everything Harriet said it would be." He looked at her again and smiled. "Isolated, cozy, charming."

She lifted a brow. It was easiest with the distance between them. "You've spoken to Harriet?"

"I took your portrait to the gallery."

Emotion came and went again in her eyes. Picking up a small brass pelican, she caressed it absently. "My portrait?"

"I promised her she could exhibit it when I'd finished." He watched her nervous fingers run over the brass. "It wasn't difficult to finish without you. I saw you everywhere I looked."

Quickly she turned to walk to the front wall. It was all glass, open to the woods. No one could feel trapped with that view. Kirby clung to it. "Harriet's having a difficult time."

"The strain shows a bit." In her, he thought, and in you. "I think it's better for her that Melanie won't see her at this point. With Stuart out of the way, the gallery's keeping Harriet busy." He stared at her back, trying to imagine what expression he'd find on her face. "Why aren't you pressing charges, Kirby?"

"For what purpose?" she countered. She set the piece of brass down. A crutch was a crutch, and she was through with them. "Both Stuart and Melanie are disgraced, banished from the elite that means so much to them. The publicity's been horrid. They have no money, no reputation. Isn't that punishment enough?"

"Melanie tried to kill you. Twice." Suddenly furious at the calm, even tone, he went to her and spun her around. "Damn it, Kirby, she wanted you dead!"

"It was she who nearly died." Her voice was still even, but she took a step back, from him. "The police have to accept my story that the gun went off accidentally, even if others don't. I could have sent Melly to jail. Wouldn't I feel avenged watching Harriet suffer?"

Adam forced back the impatience and stared through the glass. "She's worried about you."

"Harriet?" Kirby shrugged. "There's no need. When you see her, tell her I'm well."

"You can tell her yourself when we get back."

"We?" The lightest hint of temper entered her voice. Nothing could have relieved him more. "I'm going to be here for some time yet."

"Fine. I've nothing better to do."

"That wasn't an invitation."

"Harriet already gave me one," he told her easily. He gave the room another sweeping glance while Kirby smoldered. "The place looks big enough for two."

"That's where you're wrong, but don't let me spoil your plans." She spun on her heel and headed for the stairs. Before she'd gotten five feet, his fingers curled around her arm and held her still. When she whirled, he saw that his gypsy was back.

"You don't really think I'd let you leave? Kirby, you disappoint me."

"You don't *let* me do anything, Adam. Nor do you prevent me from doing anything."

"Only when it's necessary." While she stood rigid, he put his hands on her shoulders. "You're going to listen to me this time. And you're going to start listening in just a minute."

He pressed his mouth to hers as he'd needed to for weeks. She didn't resist. Nor did she respond. He could feel her fighting the need to do both. He could press her, he knew, and she'd give in to him. Then he might never really have her. Slowly their gazes locked; he straightened.

"You're nearly through making me suffer," he murmured. "I've paid, Kirby, in every moment I haven't been with you. Through every night you haven't been beside me. When are you going to stop punishing me?"

"I don't want to punish you." It was true. She'd already forgiven him. Yet, her confidence, that strong, thin shield she'd always had, had suffered an enormous blow. This time when she stepped back he didn't try to stop her. "I know we parted badly. Maybe it'd be best if we just admitted we'd both made a mistake and left it at that. I realize you did what you had to do. I've always done the same. It's time I got on with my life and you with yours."

He felt a quick jiggle of panic. She was too calm, much too calm. He wanted emotion from her, any kind she'd give. "What sort of life would either of us have without the other?"

None. But she shook her head. "I said we made a mistake—"

"And now you're going to tell me you don't love me?"

She looked straight at him and opened her mouth. Weakening, she shifted her gaze to just over his shoulder. "No, I don't love you, Adam. I'm sorry."

She'd nearly cut him off at the knees. If she hadn't looked away at the last instant, it would've been over for him.

"I'd've thought you could lie better than that." In one move he closed the distance between them. His arms were around her, firm, secure. The same, she thought. Nothing had changed after all. "I've given you two weeks, Kirby. Maybe I should give you more time, but I can't." He buried his face in her hair while she squeezed her eyes shut. She'd been wrong, she remembered. She'd been wrong about so many things. Could this be right?

"Adam, please..."

"No, no more. I love you." He drew her away, barely resisting the need to shake her. "I love you and you'll have to get used to it. It isn't going to change."

She curled her hand into a fist before she could stroke his cheek. "I think you're getting pompous again."

"Then you'll have to get used to that, too. Kirby..." He framed her face with his hands. "How many ways would you like me to apologize?"

"No." Shaking her head she moved away again. She should be able to think, she warned herself. She had to think. "I don't need apologies, Adam."

"You wouldn't," he murmured. Forgiveness would come as easily to her as every other emotion. "Your father and I had a long talk before I drove up here."

"Did you?" She gave her attention to a bowl of dried flowers. "How nice."

"He's given me his word he'll no longer...emulate paintings."

With her back to him, she smiled. The pain vanished without her realizing it, and with it, the doubts. They loved. There was so little else in life. Still smiling, Kirby decided she wouldn't tell Adam of her father's ambition with sculpting. Not just yet. "I'm glad you convinced him," she said with her tongue in her cheek.

"He decided to concede the point to me, since I'm going to be a member of the family."

With a flutter of her lashes, she turned. "How lovely. Is Papa adopting you?"

"That wasn't precisely the relationship we discussed."

Crossing to her, he took her into his arms again. This time he felt the give and the strength. "Tell me again that you don't love me."

"I don't love you," she murmured, and pulled his mouth to hers. "I don't want you to hold me." Her arms wound around his neck. "I don't want you to kiss me again. Now." Her lips clung to his, opening, giving. As the heat built, he groaned and drew her in.

"Obstinate, aren't you?" he muttered.

"Invariably."

"But are you going to marry me?"

"On my terms."

When her head tilted back, he ran kisses up the length of her throat. "Which are?"

"I may come easy, but I don't come free."

"What do you want, a marriage settlement?" On a half laugh, he drew her away. She was his, whoever, whatever she was. He'd never let her go again. "Can't you think of anything but money?"

"I'm fond of money—and we still have to discuss my sitting fee. However..." She drew a deep breath. "My terms for marriage are four children."

"Four?" Even knowing Kirby, he'd been caught off guard. "Four children?"

She moistened her lips but her voice was strong. "I'm firm on that number, Adam. The point's non-negotiable." Then her eyes were young and full of needs. "I want children. Your children."

Every time he thought he loved her completely, he found he could love her more. Still more. "Four?" he repeated with a slow nod. "Any preference to gender?"

The breath she'd been holding came out on a laugh. No, she hadn't been wrong. They loved. There was very little else. "I'm flexible, though a mix of some sort would be nice." She tossed her head back and smiled up at him. "What do you think?"

He swept her into his arms then headed for the stairs. "I think we'd better get started."

*   *   *   *   *

NIGHT MOVES

To the mountains I live in,
and the people who love them.

Chapter 1

"What the hell are you doing in a place like this?"

Maggie, on her hands and knees, didn't look up. "C.J., you're playing the same old song."

C.J. pulled down the hem of his cashmere sweater. He was a man who made worry an art, and he worried about Maggie. Someone had to. Frustrated, he looked down at the sable-brown hair twisted untidily into a knot on top of her head. Her neck was slender, pale, her shoulders curved slightly forward as she rested her weight on her forearms. She had a delicate build, with the kind of fragility C.J. had always associated with nineteenth-century English aristocratic ladies. Though perhaps they, too, had possessed endless stores of strength and endurance under frail bones and porcelain skin.

She wore a T-shirt and jeans that were both faded and slightly damp from perspiration. When he looked at her hands, fine-boned, elegant hands, and saw they were grimy, he shuddered. He knew the magic they were capable of.

A phase, he thought. She was just going through a phase. After two marriages and a few affairs, C.J. understood that women went through odd moods from time to time. He brushed at his trim, sandy mustache with one finger. It was up to him to guide her back, gently, to the real world.

As he glanced around at nothing but trees and rocks and

isolation, he wondered, fleetingly, if there were bears in the woods. In the real world, such things were kept in zoos. Keeping a nervous lookout for suspicious movements, he tried again.

"Maggie, just how long are you going to go on this way?"

"What way is that, C.J.?" Her voice was low, husky, as if she'd just been awakened. It was a voice that made most men wish they'd awakened her.

The woman was infuriating. C.J. tugged a hand through his carefully styled, blow-dried hair. What was she doing three thousand miles from L.A., wasting herself on this dirty work? He had a responsibility to her and, damn it, to himself. C.J. blew out a long breath, an old habit he had whenever he met with opposition. Negotiations were, after all, his business. It was up to him to talk some sense into her. He shifted his feet, careful to keep his polished loafers out of the dirt. "Babe, I love you. You know I do. Come home."

This time Maggie turned her head, looking up with a flash of a smile that involved every inch of her face—the mouth that stopped just short of being too wide, the chin a bit pointed, the sweep of cheekbones that gave her face a diamond shape. Her eyes, big, round and shades darker than her hair, added that final spark of animation. It wasn't a stunning face. You'd tell yourself that while you tried to focus in on the reason you were stunned. Even now, without makeup, with a long streak of topsoil across one cheek, the face involved you. Maggie Fitzgerald involved you because she was exactly what she seemed. Interesting. Interested.

Now she sat back on her haunches, blowing a wisp of hair out of her eyes as she looked up at the man who was frowning at her. She felt a tug of affection, a tug of amusement. Both had always come easily to her. "C.J., I love you, too. Now stop acting like an old woman."

"You don't belong here," he began, more exasperated than insulted. "You shouldn't be grubbing around on your hands and knees—"

"I like it," she said simply.

It was the very simplicity of the tone that told him he had

a real problem. If she'd shouted, argued, his chances of turning her around would've been all but secured. But when she was like this, calmly stubborn, changing her mind would be like climbing Mount Everest. Treacherous and exhausting. Because he was a clever man, C.J. changed tactics.

"Maggie, I can certainly understand why you might like to get away for a while, rest a bit. No one deserves it more." That was a nice touch, he thought, because it was true. "Why don't you take a couple weeks in Cancún, or go on a shopping spree in Paris?"

"Mmm." Maggie shifted on her knees and fluffed up the petals of the pansies she was planting. They looked, she decided, a bit sick. "Hand me that watering can, will you?"

"You're not listening."

"Yes, I am." Stretching over, she retrieved the can herself. "I've been to Cancún, and I have so many clothes now I left half of them in storage in L.A."

Without breaking stride, C.J. tried a different turn. "It's not just me," he began again, watching as she drenched the pansies. "Everyone who knows you, who knows about this, thinks you've—"

"Slipped a gear?" Maggie supplied. Overdid the water, she decided as the saturated blossoms drooped. She had a lot to learn about the basics of country life. "C.J., instead of nagging me and trying to talk me into doing something I've no intention of doing, why don't you come down here and give me a hand?"

"A hand?" His voice held the slightly appalled note it might have if she'd suggested he dilute prime scotch with tap water. Maggie chuckled.

"Pass me that flat of petunias." She stuck the small spade in the ground again, fighting the rocky soil. "Gardening's good for you. It gets you back in touch with nature."

"I've no desire to touch nature."

This time she laughed and lifted her face to the sky. No, the closest C.J. would come to nature would be a chlorinated pool—solar-heated. Up to a few months ago she'd barely gotten much closer herself. She'd certainly never attempted to.

But now she'd found something—something she hadn't even been looking for. If she hadn't come to the East Coast to collaborate on the score for a new musical, if she hadn't taken an impulsive drive south after the long, grueling sessions had ended, she never would've happened on the sleepy little town tucked into the Blue Ridge.

Do we ever know where we belong, Maggie wondered, unless we're lucky enough to stumble onto our own personal space? She only knew that she'd been heading nowhere in particular and she'd come home.

Maybe it had been fate that had led her into Morganville, a cluster of houses cupped in the foothills that boasted a population of 142. From the town proper, it spread out into farms and isolated mountain homes. If fate had taken her to Morganville, it had again taken her past the sign that listed the sale of a house and twelve acres. There'd been no moment of indecision, no quibbling over the price, no last-minute doubts. Maggie had met the terms and had had the deed in her hand within thirty days.

Looking up at the three-story frame house, with shutters still hanging crooked, Maggie could well imagine her friends and colleagues wondering about her mental state. She'd left her Italian-marble entrance hall and mosaic-tiled pool for rusty hinges and rocks. She'd done it without a backward glance.

Maggie patted the dirt around the petunias, then sat back. They looked a bit more spritely than her pansies. Maybe she was beginning to get the hang of it. "What do you think?"

"I think you should come back to L.A. and finish the score."

"I meant the flowers." She brushed off her jeans as she rose. "In any case, I am finishing the score—right here."

"Maggie, how can you work here?" C.J. exploded. He tossed out both arms in a gesture she'd always admired for its unapologetic theatrics. "How can you live here? This place isn't even civilized."

"Why? Because there's no health club and boutique on every other corner?" Wanting to temper the words, she tucked a hand through C.J.'s arm. "Go ahead, take a deep breath. The clean air won't hurt you."

"Smog's underrated," he mumbled as he shifted his feet again. Professionally he was her agent, but personally C.J. considered himself her friend, perhaps her best friend since Jerry had died. Thinking of that, he changed his tone again. This time it was gentle. "Look, Maggie, I know you've been through some rough times. Maybe L.A. has too many memories for you to deal with right now. But you can't bury yourself."

"I'm not burying myself." She put her hands on his forearms, squeezing for both emphasis and support. "And I buried Jerry nearly two years ago. That was another part of my life, C.J., and has nothing to do with this. This is home. I don't know how else to explain it." She slid her hands down to his, forgetting hers were smeared with earth. "This is my mountain now, and I'm happier here, more settled, than I ever was in Los Angeles."

He knew he was beating his head against a wall, but opted to give it one more shot. "Maggie." He slipped an arm around her shoulder, as if, she thought ruefully, she was a small child needing guidance. "Look at that place." He let the silence hang a moment while they both studied the house on the rise above. He noticed that the porch was missing several boards and that the paint on the trim was peeling badly. Maggie saw the sun reflecting off the window glass in rainbows. "You can't possibly be serious about living there."

"A little paint, a few nails." She shrugged it away. Long ago she'd learned that surface problems were best ignored. It was the problem simmering under the surface, not quite visible, that had to be dealt with. "It has such possibilities, C.J."

"The biggest one is that it'll fall down on your head."

"I had the roof fixed last week—a local man."

"Maggie, I'm not at all convinced there are any local men, or women, within ten miles. This place doesn't look fit for anything but elves and gnomes."

"Well, he might've been a gnome." Her sense of fun spurred her on as she stretched her back muscles. "He was about five foot five, stocky as a bull and somewhere around a hundred and two. His name was Bog.''

"Maggie—"

"He was very helpful," she went on. "He and his boy are coming back to deal with the porch and some of the other major repairs."

"All right, so you've got a gnome to do some hammering and sawing. What about this?" He swept his hand around to take in the surrounding land. It was rocky, uneven and overgrown with weeds and thickets. Not even a dedicated optimist could've considered any part of it a lawn. A burly tree slanted dangerously toward the house itself, while thorny vines and wildflowers scrambled for space. There was a pervading smell of earth and green.

"Like Sleeping Beauty's castle," Maggie murmured. "I'll be sorry in a way to hack it down, but Mr. Bog has that under control, too."

"He does excavation work, too?"

Maggie tilted her head and arched her brows. It was a look that made anyone over forty remember her mother. "He recommended a landscaper. Mr. Bog assures me that Cliff Delaney is the best man in the county. He's coming by this afternoon to take a look at the place."

"If he's a smart man, he'll take one look at that gully you call a road leading up here and keep on going."

"But you brought your rented Mercedes all the way up." Turning, she threw her arms around his neck and kissed him. "Don't think I don't appreciate that or the fact that you flew in from the Coast or that you care enough to be concerned. I appreciate all of it. I appreciate you." She ruffled his hair, something no one else would've gotten away with. "Trust my judgment on this, C.J. I really do know what I'm doing. Professionally, my work can't do anything but improve here."

"That's yet to be seen," he muttered, but lifted a hand to touch her cheek. She was still young enough to have foolish dreams, he thought. Still sweet enough to believe in them. "You know it's not your work I'm worried about."

"I know." Her voice softened, and with it her eyes, her

mouth. She was not a woman who guided her emotions, but one who was guided by them. "I need the peace here. Do you know, this is the first time in my life I've gotten off the merry-go-round? I'm enjoying the solid ground, C.J."

He knew her well and understood that there was no moving her, for the moment, from the position she'd taken. He understood, too, that from birth her life had been ribboned with the stuff of fantasies—and of nightmares. Perhaps she did need to compensate, for a time.

"I've got a plane to catch," he grumbled. "As long as you insist on staying here, I want you to call me every day."

Maggie kissed him again. "Once a week," she countered. "You'll have the completed score for *Heat Dance* in ten days." With her arm around his waist, she led him to the end of the uneven, overgrown path where his Mercedes sat in incongruous splendor. "I love the film, C.J. It's even better than I thought it would be when I first read the script. The music's all but writing itself."

He only grunted and cast one look behind him at the house. "If you get lonely—"

"I won't." With a quick laugh, Maggie nudged him into the car. "It's been enlightening discovering how self-sufficient I can be. Now, have a nice trip back and stop worrying about me."

Fat chance, he thought, automatically reaching in his briefcase to make certain his Dramamine was there. "Send me the score, and if it's sensational, I might stop worrying…a little."

"It is sensational." She backed off from the car to give him room to turn around. "*I'm* sensational!" she shouted as the Mercedes began to inch around. "Tell everyone back on the Coast that I've decided to buy some goats and chickens."

The Mercedes stopped dead. "Maggie…"

Laughing, she waved at him and backed down the path. "Not yet…but maybe in the fall." She decided it was best to reassure him, or else he might get out and start again. "Oh, and send me some Godiva chocolates."

That was more like it, C.J. thought, and put the car in gear again. She'd be back in L.A. in six weeks. He glanced in his rearview mirror as he started to drive away. He could see her, small and slender, still laughing, against the backdrop of the overgrown land, greening trees and dilapidated house. Once again he shuddered, but this time it wasn't from an offense of his sensibilities. This time it was from something like fear. He had a sudden flash of certainty that she wasn't safe there.

Shaking his head, C.J. reached in his pocket for his antacids as the car bumped noisily over a rock. Everyone told him he worried too much.

Lonely, Maggie thought as she watched the Mercedes bump and wind its way down her excuse for a lane. No, she wasn't lonely. She was as certain as she'd ever been about anything that she'd never be lonely here. She felt an unexpected sense of foreboding that she shrugged off as ridiculous.

Wrapping her arms around herself, she turned in two slow circles. Trees rose up out of the rocky hillside. The leaves were hardly more than buds now, but in a few weeks they would grow and spread, turning the woods into a lush cover of green. She liked to imagine it that way and to try to picture it in the dead of winter—white, all white and black with ice clinging to the branches and shimmering on the rocks. In the fall there'd be a tapestry outside every window. She was far from lonely.

For the first time in her life, she had a chance to put her own stamp on a place. It wouldn't be a copy of anything she'd had before or anything that'd been given to her. It was hers, absolutely, and so were any mistakes she made here, any triumphs. There'd be no press to compare this isolated spot in western Maryland with her mother's mansion in Beverly Hills or her father's villa in the south of France. If she was lucky, very, very lucky, Maggie thought with a satisfied sigh, there'd been no press at all. She could make her music and live her life in peace and solitude.

If she stood very still, if she closed her eyes and didn't move, she could hear the music all around her. Not birdsong but the ruffle of air through branches and tiny leaves. If she concentrated, she could hear the faint trickle of the narrow creek that ran along the other side of the lane. The quality of silence was rich, flowing over her like a symphony.

There was a place for glitz, she mused, and for glamour. She simply didn't want that place any longer. The truth was she hadn't wanted that place for a very long time but hadn't known the way out. When your birth had been celebrated by the international press, your first step, your first words, cataloged for the public, it was natural to forget there was another way of life.

Her mother had been one of the greatest blues and ballad singers in America, her father a child actor turned successful film director. Their courtship and marriage had been followed religiously by fans around the world. The birth of their daughter had been an event treated like the birth of royalty. And Maggie had lived the life of a pampered princess. Gold carousels and white fur coats. She'd been lucky because her parents had adored her, and each other. That had compensated for the make-believe, often hard-edged world of show business, with all its demands and inconstancy. Her world had been cushioned by wealth and love, rippled continually with publicity.

The paparazzi haunted her on dates through her teenage years—to her amusement but often to the boys' frustration. Maggie had accepted the fact that her life was public domain. It had never been otherwise.

And when her parents' private plane had crashed into the Swiss Alps, the press had frozen her grief in glossies and newsprint. She hadn't tried to stop it; she'd realized that the world had mourned with her. She'd been eighteen when the fabric of her world had torn.

Then there had been Jerry. First friend, then lover, then husband. With him, her life had drifted into more fantasy, and more tragedy.

She wouldn't think of any of that now, Maggie told herself as she picked up her spade and began to fight the tough soil again. All that was really left of that portion of her life was her music. That she would never give up. She couldn't have if she'd tried. It was part of her the way her eyes and ears were part of her. She composed words and music and twined them together, not effortlessly, as it sometimes seemed from the fluid finished result, but obsessively, wonderingly, constantly. Unlike her mother, she didn't perform but fed other performers with her gift.

At twenty-eight, she had two Oscars, five Grammies and a Tony. She could sit at the piano and play any song she'd ever written from memory. The awards were still in the packing boxes that had been shipped from L.A.

The little flower plot she was planting in a spot perhaps no one would see but herself was a labor of love with no guarantee of success. It was enough that it gave her pleasure to add her own peculiar spot of color to the land she'd claimed as hers. Maggie began to sing as she worked. She'd completely forgotten her former feeling of apprehension.

Normally he didn't do the estimating and initial planning on a job himself. Not anymore. For the past six years Cliff Delaney had been in the position of being able to send one or two of his best men out on the first stage of a project; then he would fine-tune. If the job was interesting enough, he would visit the site while work was in progress, perhaps handle some of the grading and planting himself. He was making an exception.

He knew the old Morgan place. It had been built by a Morgan, even as the tiny community a few miles away had been named after one. For ten years, since William Morgan's car had crashed into the Potomac, the house had stood empty. The house had always been stern, the land formidable. But with the right touch, the right insight, Cliff knew, it could be magnificent. He had his doubts that the lady from L.A. had the right insight.

He knew of her. Naturally he knew of her. Anyone who hadn't spent the last twenty-eight years in a cave knew Maggie Fitzgerald. At the moment, she was the biggest news in Morganville—all but eclipsing the hot gossip of Lloyd Messner's wife running off with the bank manager.

It was a simple town, the kind that moved slowly. The kind

of town where everyone took pride in the acquisition of a new fire engine and the yearly Founder's Day parade. That's why Cliff chose to live there after he'd reached a point where he could live anywhere he chose. He'd grown up there and understood the people, their unity and their possessiveness. He understood their failings. More, perhaps much more, than that, he understood the land. He had serious doubts that the glamorous song writer from California would understand, either.

C.J. had estimated six weeks before she flew back. Cliff, without ever setting eyes on her, cut that in half. But perhaps before Maggie Fitzgerald grew bored with her shot at rural living, he could put his own mark on the land.

He turned off the paved road onto the quarter-mile lane that cut through the Morgan property. It had been years since he'd been on it, and it was worse than he remembered. Rain and neglect had worn ruts in the dirt. From both sides of the lane, branches reached out to whip at the truck. The first order of business would be the lane itself, Cliff thought as his small pickup bounced over ruts. It would be graded, leveled, filled. Drainage ditches would have to be dug, gravel spread.

He went slowly, not for the truck's sake but because the land on either side of the lane appealed to him. It was wild and primitive, timeless. He'd want to work with that, incorporate his own talents with the genius of nature. If Maggie Fitzgerald wanted blacktop and hothouse plants, she'd come to the wrong place. He'd be the first one to let her know.

If he had a distrust of outsiders, Cliff considered he'd come by it honestly. They came, often from the rich suburbs of D.C., and wanted their lawns flat and free of the poplar and oak that had first claim. They wanted neat little flowers in orderly rows. Lawns should be even, so that their mowers could handle the weekly cutting effortlessly. What they wanted, Cliff thought derisively, was to say they lived *in the country* while they brought city attitudes and city tastes with them. By the time he rounded the last bend, he was already out of patience with Maggie Fitzgerald.

Maggie heard the truck coming before it was in sight. That was something else she liked about her new home. It was quiet—so quiet that the sound of a truck, which would have been ignored in the city, brought her to attention. Halfheartedly brushing her hands on the seat of her pants, she rose from her planting, then shielded her eyes against the sun.

While she watched, the truck rounded the curve and parked where the Mercedes had been only an hour before. A bit dusty from the road, with its chrome dull rather than gleaming, the truck looked much more comfortable than the luxury car had. Though she couldn't yet see the driver through the glare of sun on windshield, Maggie smiled and lifted a hand in greeting.

The first thing Cliff thought was that she was smaller than he'd expected, more delicate in build. The Fitzgeralds had always been larger than life. He wondered, with a quick grunt, if she'd want to raise orchids to match her style. He got out of the truck, convinced she was going to annoy him.

Perhaps it was because she'd been expecting another Mr. Bog that Maggie felt a flutter of surprise when Cliff stepped out of the truck. Or perhaps, she thought with her usual penchant for honesty, it was because he was quite simply a magnificent example of manhood. Six-two, Maggie decided, with an impressive breadth of shoulders. Black hair that had been ruffled by the wind through the open truck windows fell over his forehead and ears in loose waves. He didn't smile, but his mouth was sculpted, sensual. She had a fleeting regret that he wore dark glasses so that his eyes were hidden. She judged people from their eyes.

Instead, Maggie summed him up from the way he moved—loosely, confidently. Athletic, she concluded, as he strode over the uneven ground. Definitely self-assured. He was still a yard away when she got the unmistakable impression that he wasn't particularly friendly.

"Miss Fitzgerald?"

"Yes." Giving him a neutral smile, Maggie held out a hand. "You're from Delaney's?"

"That's right." Their hands met, briefly, hers soft, his hard, both of them capable. Without bothering to identify himself,

Cliff scanned the grounds. "You wanted an estimate on some landscaping."

Maggie followed his gaze, and this time her smile held amusement. "Obviously I need something. Does your company perform miracles?"

"We do the job." He glanced down at the splash of color behind her, wilted pansies and soggy petunias. Her effort touched something in him that he ignored, telling himself she'd be bored long before it was time to pull the first weeds. "Why don't you tell me what you have in mind?"

"A glass of iced tea at the moment. Look around while I get some; then we'll talk about it." She'd been giving orders without a second thought all her life. After giving this one, Maggie turned and climbed the rickety steps to the porch. Behind the tinted glasses, Cliff's eyes narrowed.

Designer jeans, he thought with a smirk as he watched the graceful sway of hips before the screen door banged shut at her back. And the solitaire on the thin chain around her neck had been no less than a karat. Just what game was little Miss Hollywood playing? She'd left a trace of her scent behind, something soft and subtle that would nag at a man's senses. Shrugging, he turned his back on the house and looked at the land.

It could be shaped and structured without being tamed. It should never lose its basic unruly sense by being manicured, though he admitted the years of neglect had given the rougher side of nature too much of an advantage. Still, he wouldn't level it for her. Cliff had turned down more than one job because the client had insisted on altering the land's personality. Even with that, he wouldn't have called himself an artist. He was a businessman. His business was the land.

He walked farther away from the house, toward a grove of trees overrun with tangling vines, greedy saplings and thistles. Without effort he could see it cleared of undergrowth, richly mulched, naturalized perhaps with jonquils. That one section would personify peace, as he saw it. Hitching his thumbs in his back pockets, Cliff reflected that from the reams that had been written about Maggie Fitzgerald over the years, she didn't go in much for peace.

Jet-setting, the fast lane, glitter and glitz. What the hell had she moved out here for?

Before he heard her, Cliff caught a fresh whiff of her perfume. When he turned, she was a few paces behind him, two glasses in her hand. She watched him steadily with a curiosity she didn't bother to hide. He learned something more about her then as she stood with her eyes on his face and the sun at her back. She was the most alluring woman he'd ever met, though he'd be damned if he knew why.

Maggie approached him and offered a glass of frosty tea. "Want to hear my ideas?"

The voice had something to do with it, Cliff decided. An innocent question, phrased in that sultry voice, conjured up a dozen dark pleasures. He took a slow sip. "That's what I'm here for," he told her with a curtness he'd never shown any potential client.

Her brow lifted at the tone, the only sign that she'd noticed his rudeness. With that attitude, she thought, he wouldn't have the job for long. Then again, he didn't strike her as a man who'd work for someone else. "Indeed you are, Mr....?"

"Delaney."

"Ah, the man himself." That made more sense, she decided, if his attitude didn't. "Well, Mr. Delaney, I'm told you're the best. I believe in having the best, so..." Thoughtfully, she ran a fingertip down the length of her glass, streaking the film of moisture. "I'll tell you what I want, and you tell me if you can deliver."

"Fair enough." He didn't know why her simple statement should annoy him any more than he could understand why he was just noticing how smooth her skin was and how compelling were those large velvet eyes. Like a doe's, Cliff realized. He wasn't a man who hunted but a man who watched. "I'll tell you up front that my company has a policy against destroying the natural terrain in order to make the land into something it's not. This is rough country, Miss Fitzgerald. It's supposed to be. If you want an acre or two of manicured lawn, you've bought the wrong land and called the wrong land-scaper.''

It took a great deal to fire up her temper. Maggie had worked long and hard to control a natural tendency toward quick fury in order to block the label of temperamental daughter of temperamental artists. "Decent of you to point it out," she managed after three long, quiet breaths.

"I don't know why you bought the place," he began.

"I don't believe I've offered that information."

"And it's none of my business," Cliff finished with an acknowledging nod. "But this—" he indicated the property with a gesture of his hand "—is my business."

"You're a bit premature in condemning me, aren't you, Mr. Delaney?" To keep herself in check, Maggie took a sip of tea. It was cold, with a faint bite of lemon. "I've yet to ask you to bring on the bulldozers and chain saws." She ought to tell him to haul his buns into his truck and take off. Almost before she could wonder why she didn't, the answer came. Instinct. Instinct had brought her to Morganville and to the property she now stood on. It was instinct that told her he was indeed the best. Nothing else would do for her land. To give herself a moment to be sure she didn't do anything rash, Maggie took another sip from her glass.

"That grove there," she began briskly. "I want it cleared of undergrowth. It can't be enjoyed if you have to fight your way through thorns and thickets to walk in it." She shot him a look. "Don't you want to take notes?"

He watched her, consideringly. "No. Go on."

"All right. This stretch right here, in front of the porch—I imagine that was a lawn of sorts at one time." She turned, looking at the knee-high weeds. "It should be again, but I want enough room to plant, I don't know, some pines, maybe, to keep the line between lawn and woods from being too marked. Then there's the way the whole thing just sort of falls away until it reaches the lane below."

Forgetting her annoyance for the moment, Maggie made her way across the relatively flat land to where it sloped steeply down. Weeds, some of them as tall as she, grew in abundance wherever the rocks would permit. "It's certainly too steep for grass to be practical," she said half to herself. "But I can't just let all these weeds have their way. I'd like some color, but I don't want uniformity."

"You'll want some evergreens," he said from behind her. "Some spreading junipers along the bottom edge of the whole slope, a few coming farther up over there, with some forsythia mixed in. Here, where the grade's not so dramatic, you'd want some low ground cover." He could see phlox spilling and bumping over the rocks. "That tree's got to come down," he went on, frowning at the one that leaned precariously toward her roof. "And there's two, maybe three, on the rise behind the house that've got to be taken down before they fall down."

She was frowning now, but she'd always believed in letting an expert set the plan. "Okay, but I don't want you to cut down anything that doesn't have to be cleared."

Maggie could only see her own reflection in his glasses when he faced her. "I never do." He turned and began to walk around the side of the house. "That's another problem," Cliff continued without checking to see if she was following. "The way that dirt wall's eroding down from the cliff here. You're going to end up with a tree or a boulder in your kitchen when you least expect it."

"So?" Maggie tilted her head so she could scan the ridge behind her house. "You're the expert."

"It'll need to be recut, tapered back some. Then I'd put up a retaining wall, three, maybe four, foot high. Crown vetch'd hold the dirt above that. Plant it along the entire slope. It's hardy and fast."

"All right." It sounded reasonable. He sounded more reasonable, Maggie decided, when he was talking about his business. A man of the land, she mused, and wished again she could see beyond the tinted glass to his eyes. "This part behind the house has to be cleared." She began to fight her way through the weeds and briars as she talked. "I think if I had a walkway of some kind from here to the lane, I could have a rockery...here." A vague gesture of her hands indicated the spot she had in mind. "There're plenty of rocks," she muttered, nearly stumbling over one. "Then down here—"

Cliff took her arm before she could start down the slope on the far side of the house. The contact jolted both of them. More surprised than alarmed, Maggie turned her head.

"I wouldn't," Cliff said softly, and she felt a tiny trickle, an odd excitement, sprint up her spine.

"Wouldn't what?" Her chin automatically tilted, her eyes challenged.

"Walk down there." Her skin was soft, Cliff discovered. With his hand wrapped around her arm, he could touch his fingertips to his thumb. Small and soft, he mused, enjoying the feel of his flesh against hers. Too small and soft for land that would fight back at you.

Maggie glanced down to where he held her. She noticed the tan on the back of his hand; she noticed the size and the strength of it. When she noticed her pulse wasn't quite steady, she lifted her gaze again. "Mr. Delaney—"

"Snakes," he said simply, and had the satisfaction of seeing her take two quick steps back. "You're almost sure to have some down in a spot like that. In fact, with the way this place is overgrown, you're likely to have them everywhere."

"Well, then—" Maggie swallowed and made a herculean effort not to shudder "—maybe you can start the job right away."

For the first time, he smiled, a very slight, very cautious, curving of lips. They'd both forgotten he still held her, but they were standing much closer now, within a hand span of touching. She certainly hadn't reacted the way he'd expected. He wouldn't have been surprised if she'd screeched at the mention of snakes, then had dashed into the house, slamming and locking the door. Her skin was soft, Cliff mused, unconsciously moving his thumb over it. But apparently she wasn't.

"I might be able to send a crew out next week, but the first thing that has to be dealt with is your road."

Maggie dismissed this with a shrug. "Do whatever you think best there, excluding asphalt. It's only a means of getting in and out to me. I want to concentrate on the house and grounds.''

''The road's going to run you twelve, maybe fifteen, hundred,'' he began, but she cut him off again.

''Do what you have to,'' she told him with the unconscious arrogance of someone who'd never worried about money. ''This section here—'' She pointed to the steep drop in front of them, making no move this time to go down it. At the base it spread twenty feet wide, perhaps thirty in length, in a wicked maze of thorny vines and weeds as thick at the stem as her thumb. ''I want a pond.''

Cliff brought his attention back to her. ''A pond?''

She gave him a level look and stood her ground. ''Allow me one eccentricity, Mr. Delaney. A small one,'' she continued before he could comment. ''There's certainly enough room, and it seems to me that this section here's the worst. It's hardly more than a hole in the ground in a very awkward place. Do you have an objection to water?''

Instead of answering, he studied the ground below them, running through the possibilities. The truth was, she couldn't have picked a better spot as far as the lay of the land and the angle to the house. It could be done, he mused. It wouldn't be an easy job, but it could be done. And it would be very effective.

''It's going to cost you,'' he said at length. ''You're going to be sinking a lot of cash into this place. If you're weighing that against resale value, I can tell you, this property won't be easy to sell.''

It snapped her patience. She was tired, very tired, of having people suggest she didn't know what she was doing. ''Mr. Delaney, I'm hiring you to do a job, not to advise me on real estate or my finances. If you can't handle it, just say so and I'll get someone else.''

His eyes narrowed. The fingers on her arm tightened fractionally. ''I can handle it, Miss Fitzgerald. I'll draw up an estimate and a contract. They'll be in the mail tomorrow. If you still want the job done after you've looked them over, call my office.'' Slowly, he released her arm, then handed her back the glass of tea. He left her there, near the edge where the slope gave way to gully as he headed back toward his truck. "By the way," he said without turning around, "you overwatered your pansies."

Maggie let out one long, simmering breath and dumped the tepid tea on the ground at her feet.

Chapter 2

When she was alone, Maggie went back inside, through the back door, which creaked ominously on its hinges. She wasn't going to think about Cliff Delaney. In fact, she doubted if she'd see him again. He'd send crews out to deal with the actual work, and whatever they had to discuss would be done via phone or letter. Better that way, Maggie decided. He'd been unfriendly, abrupt and annoying, though his mouth had been attractive, she reflected, even kind.

She was halfway through the kitchen when she remembered the glasses in her hand. Turning back, she crossed the scarred linoleum to set them both in the sink, then leaned on the windowsill to look out at the rise behind her house. Even as she watched, a few loose stones and dirt slid down the wall. A couple of hard rains, she mused, and half that bank would be at her back door. A retaining wall. Maggie nodded. Cliff Delaney obviously knew his business.

There was just enough breeze to carry a hint of spring to her. Far back in the woods a bird she couldn't see sang out as though it would never stop. Listening, she forgot the eroding wall and the exposed roots of trees that were much too close to its edge. She forgot the rudeness, and the attraction, of a stranger. If she looked up, far up, she could see where the tops of the trees met the sky.

She wondered how this view would change with the seasons and found herself impatient to experience them all. Perhaps she'd never realized how badly she'd needed a place to herself, time to herself, until she'd found it.

With a sigh, Maggie moved away from the window. It was time to get down to work if she was to deliver the finished score as promised. She walked down the hall where the wallpaper was peeling and curled and turned into what had once been the back parlor. It was now her music room.

Boxes she hadn't even thought of unpacking stood in a pile against one wall. A few odd pieces of furniture that had come with the house sat hidden under dustcovers. The windows were uncurtained, the floor was uncarpeted. There were pale squares intermittently on the walls where pictures had once hung. In the center of the room, glossy and elegant, stood her baby grand. A single box lay open beside it, and from this Maggie took a sheet of staff paper. Tucking a pencil behind her ear, she sat.

For a moment she did nothing else, just sat in the silence while she let the music come and play in her head. She knew what she wanted for this segment—something dramatic, something strong and full of power. Behind her closed eyelids she could see the scene from the film sweep by. It was up to her to underscore, to accentuate, to take the mood and make it music.

Reaching out, she switched on the reel-to-reel tape and began.

She let the notes build in strength as she continued to visualize the scene her music would amplify. She only worked on films she had a feeling for. Though the Oscars told her she excelled in this area of work, Maggie's true affection was for the single song—words and music.

Maggie had always compared the composing of a score to the building of a bridge. First came the blueprint, the overall plan. Then the construction had to be done, slowly, meticulously, until each end fit snugly on solid ground, a flawless arch in between. It was a labor of precision.

The single song was a painting, to be created as the mood

dictated. The single song could be written from nothing more
than a phrasing of words or notes. It could encapsulate mood,
emotion or a story in a matter of minutes. It was a labor of
love.

When she worked, she forgot the time, forgot everything
but the careful structuring of notes to mood. Her fingers
moved over the piano keys as she repeated the same segment
again and again, changing perhaps no more than one note until
her instincts told her it was right. An hour passed, then two.
She didn't grow weary or bored or impatient with the constant
repetition. Music was her business, but it was also her lover.

She might not have heard the knock if she hadn't paused
to rewind the tape. Disoriented, she ignored it, waiting for the
maid to answer before she recalled where she was.

No maids, Maggie, she reminded herself. *No gardener, no
cook. It's all up to you now.* The thought pleased her. If there
was no one to answer to her, she had no one to answer to.

Rising, she went back into the hall and down to the big
front door. She didn't have to develop the country habit of
leaving the doors unlocked. In L.A., there'd been servants to
deal with bolts and chains and security systems. Maggie never
gave them a thought. Taking the knob in both hands, she
twisted and tugged. She reminded herself to tell Mr. Bog
about the sticking problem as the door swung open.

On the porch stood a tall, prim-looking woman in her early
fifties. Her hair was a soft, uniform gray worn with more
tidiness than style. Faded blue eyes studied Maggie from behind rose-framed glasses. If this was the welcome wagon lady,
Maggie thought after a glance at the unhappy line of the
woman's mouth, she didn't seem thrilled with the job. Much
too used to strangers' approaches to be reserved, Maggie tilted
her head and smiled.

"Hello, can I help you?"

"You are Miss Fitzgerald?" The voice was low and even,
as subdued and inoffensive as her plain, pale coatdress.

"Yes, I am."

"I'm Louella Morgan."

It took Maggie a moment; then the name clicked. Louella

Morgan, widow of William Morgan, former owner of the house that was now hers. For an instant Maggie felt like an intruder; then she shook the feeling away and extended her hand. "Hello, Mrs. Morgan. Won't you come in?"

"I don't want to disturb you."

"No, please." As she spoke, she opened the door a bit wider. "I met your daughter when we settled on the house."

"Yes, Joyce told me." Louella's gaze darted around and behind Maggie as she stepped over the threshold. "She never expected to sell so quickly. The property had only been on the market a week."

"I like to think it was fate." Maggie put her weight against the door and pushed until she managed to close it. Definitely a job for Bog, she decided.

"Fate?" Louella turned back from her study of the long, empty hall.

"It just seemed to be waiting for me." Though she found the woman's direct, unsmiling stare odd, Maggie gestured toward the living room. "Come in and sit down," she invited. "Would you like some coffee? Something cold?"

"No, thank you. I'll stay only a minute." Louella did wander into the living room, and though there was a single sofa piled with soft, inviting pillows, she didn't accept Maggie's invitation to sit. She looked at the crumbling wallpaper, the cracked paint and the windows that glistened from Maggie's diligence with ammonia. "I suppose I wanted to see the house again with someone living in it."

Maggie took a look at the almost-empty room. Maybe she'd start stripping off the wallpaper next week. "I guess it'll be a few weeks more before it looks as though someone is."

Louella didn't seem to hear. "I came here as a newlywed." She smiled then, but Maggie didn't see anything happy in it. The eyes, she thought, looked lost, as if the woman had been lost for years. "But then, my husband wanted something more modern, more convenient to town and his business. So we moved, and he rented it out."

Louella focused on Maggie again. "Such a lovely, quiet

spot," she murmured. "A pity it's been so neglected over the years."

"It is a lovely spot," Maggie agreed, struggling not to sound as uncomfortable as she felt. "I'm having some work done on both the house and the land…" Her voice trailed off when Louella wandered to the front window and stared out. *Heavens,* Maggie thought, searching for something more to say, *what have I got here?* "Ah, of course I plan to do a lot of the painting and papering and such myself."

"The weeds have taken over," Louella said with her back to the room.

Maggie's brows lifted and fell as she wondered what to do next. "Yes, well, Cliff Delaney was out this afternoon to take a look around."

"Cliff." Louella's attention seemed to focus again as she turned back. The light coming through the uncurtained windows made her seem more pale, more insubstantial. "An interesting young man, rather rough-and-ready, but very clever. He'll do well for you here, for the land. He's a cousin of the Morgans, you know." She paused and seemed to laugh, but very softly. "Then, you'll find many Morgans and their kin scattered throughout the county."

A cousin, Maggie mused. Perhaps he'd been unfriendly because he didn't think the property should've been sold to an outsider. Resolutely, she tried to push Cliff Delaney aside. He didn't have to approve. The land was hers.

"The front lawn was lovely once," Louella murmured.

Maggie felt a stirring of pity. "It will be again. The front's going to be cleared and planted. The back, too." Wanting to reassure her, Maggie stepped closer. Both women stood by the window now. "I'm going to have a rock garden, and there'll be a pond where the gully is on the side."

"A pond?" Louella turned and fixed her with another long stare. "You're going to clear out the gully?"

"Yes." Uncomfortable again, Maggie shifted. "It's the perfect place."

Louella ran a hand over the front of her purse as if she were wiping something away. "I used to have a rock garden.

Sweet william and azure Adams. There was wisteria beneath my bedroom window, and roses, red roses, climbing on a trellis.''

"I'd like to have seen it," Maggie said gently. "It must've been beautiful."

"I have pictures."

"Do you?" Struck with an idea, Maggie forgot her discomfort. "Perhaps I could see them. They'd help me decide just what to plant."

"I'll see that you get them. You're very kind to let me come in this way." Louella took one last scan of the room. "The house holds memories." When she walked out into the hall, Maggie went with her to tug open the front door again. "Goodbye, Miss Fitzgerald."

"Goodbye, Mrs. Morgan." Her pity stirred again, and Maggie reached out to touch the woman's shoulder. "Please, come again."

Louella looked back, her smile very slight, her eyes very tired. "Thank you."

While Maggie watched, she walked to an old, well-preserved Lincoln, then drove slowly down the hill. Vaguely disturbed, Maggie went back into the music room. She hadn't met many residents of Morganville yet, she mused, but they were certainly an interesting bunch.

The noise brought Maggie out of a sound sleep into a drowsy, cranky state. For a moment, as she tried to bury her head under the pillow, she thought she was in New York. The groan and roar sounded like a big, nasty garbage truck. But she wasn't in New York, she thought as she surfaced, rubbing her hands over her eyes. She was in Morganville, and there weren't any garbage trucks. Here you piled your trash into the back of your car or pickup and hauled it to the county dump. Maggie had considered this the height of self-sufficiency.

Still, something was out there.

She lay on her back for a full minute, staring up at the ceiling. The sunlight slanted, low and thin, across her newly purchased quilt. She'd never been a morning person, nor did she intend to have country life change that intimate part of her nature. Warily, she turned her head to look at the clock: 7:05. Good heavens.

It was a struggle, but she pushed herself into a sitting position and stared blankly around the room. Here, too, boxes were piled, unopened. There was a precariously stacked pile of books and magazines on decorating and landscaping beside the bed. On the wall were three fresh strips of wallpaper, an ivory background with tiny violets, that she'd hung herself. More rolls and paste were pushed into a corner. The noise outside was a constant, irritating roar.

Resigned, Maggie got out of bed. She stumbled over a pair of shoes, swore, then went to the window. She'd chosen that room as her own because she could see out over the rolling pitch of what would be her front yard, over the tops of the trees on her own property to the valley beyond.

There was a farmhouse in the distance with a red roof and a smoking chimney. Beside it was a long, wide field that had just been plowed and planted. If she looked farther still, she could see the peaks of mountains faintly blue and indistinct in the morning mist. The window on the connecting wall would give her a view of the intended pond and the line of pines that would eventually be planted.

Maggie pushed the window up the rest of the way, struggling as it stuck a bit. The early-spring air had a pleasant chill. She could still hear the constant low sound of a running engine. Curious, she pressed her face against the screen, only to have it topple out of the window frame and fall to the porch below. One more thing for Mr. Bog to see to, Maggie thought with a sigh as she leaned through the opening. Just then the yellow bulk of a bulldozer rounded the bend in her lane and broke into view.

So, she thought, watching it inch its way along, leveling and pushing at rock and dirt, Cliff Delaney was a man of his word. She'd received the promised estimate and contract two days after his visit. When she'd called his office, Maggie had spoken to an efficient-sounding woman who'd told her the work would begin the first of the week.

And it's Monday, she reflected, leaning her elbows on the sill. Very prompt. Narrowing her eyes, she looked more closely at the man on top of the bulldozer. His build was too slight, she decided, his hair not quite dark enough. She didn't have to see his face to know it wasn't Cliff. Shrugging, she turned away from the window. Why should she have thought Cliff Delaney would work his own machines? And why should she have wanted it to be he? Hadn't she already decided she wouldn't see him again? She'd hired his company to do a job; the job would be done, and she'd write out a check. That was all there was to it.

Maggie attributed her crankiness to the early awakening as she snatched up her robe and headed for the shower.

Two hours later, fortified with the coffee she'd made for herself and the bulldozer operator, Maggie was on her knees on the kitchen floor. Since she was up at a barbaric hour, she thought it best to do something physical. On the counter above her sat her reel-to-reel tape player. The sound of her score, nearly completed, all but drowned out the whine of machinery. She let herself flow with it while words to the title song she'd yet to compose flitted in and out of her mind.

While she let her thoughts flow with the music she'd created, Maggie chipped away at the worn tile on the kitchen floor. True, her bedroom had only one wall partially papered, and only the ceiling in the upstairs bath was painted, *and* there were two more steps to be stripped and lacquered before the main stairway was finished, but she worked in her own way, at her own speed. She found herself jumping from project to project, leaving one partially done and leaping headlong into the next. This way, she reasoned, she could watch the house come together piece by piece rather than have one completed, out-of-place room.

Besides, she'd gotten a peek at the flooring beneath the tile when she'd inadvertently knocked an edge off a corner. Curiosity had done the rest.

When Cliff walked to the back door, he was already annoyed. It was ridiculous for him to be wasting time here, with all the other jobs his firm had in progress. Yet he was here. He'd knocked at the front door for almost five minutes. He knew Maggie was inside, her car was in the driveway, and the bulldozer operator had told him she'd brought out coffee an hour or so before. Didn't it occur to her that someone usually knocked when they wanted something?

The music coming through the open windows caught his attention, and his imagination. He'd never heard the melody before. It was compelling, sexy, moody. A lone piano, no backdrop of strings or brass, but it had the power of making the listener want to stop and hear every note. For a moment he did stop, both disturbed and moved.

Shifting the screen he'd found into his other hand, Cliff started to knock. Then he saw her.

She was on her hands and knees, prying up pieces of linoleum with what looked like a putty knife. Her hair was loose, falling over one shoulder so that her face was hidden behind it. The deep, rich sable brown picked up hints of gold from the sunlight that streamed through the open door and window.

Gray corduroys fit snugly over her hips, tapering down to bare ankles and feet. A vivid red suede shirt was tucked into the waist. He recognized the shirt as one sold in exclusive shops for very exclusive prices. Her wrists and hands looked impossibly delicate against it. Cliff was scowling at them when Maggie got too enthusiastic with the putty knife and scraped her knuckle against a corner of the tile.

"What the hell are you doing?" he demanded, swinging the door open and striding in before Maggie had a chance to react. She'd barely put the knuckle to her mouth in an instinctive move when he was crouched beside her and grabbing her hand.

"It's nothing," she said automatically. "Just a scratch."

"You're lucky you didn't slice it, the way you're hacking at that tile." Though his voice was rough and impatient, his hand was gentle. She left hers in it.

Yes, his hand was gentle, though rough-edged, like his

voice, but this time she could see his eyes. They were gray; smoky, secret. Evening mists came to her mind. Mists that were sometimes dangerous but always compelling. That was the sort of mist she'd always believed had cloaked Brigadoon for a hundred years at a time. Maggie decided she could like him, in a cautious sort of way.

"Who'd be stupid enough to put linoleum over this?" With the fingers of her free hand, she skimmed over the hardwood she'd exposed. "Lovely, isn't it? Or it will be when it's sanded and sealed."

"Get Bog to deal with it," Cliff ordered. "You don't know what you're doing."

So everyone said. Maggie withdrew a bit, annoyed by the phrase. "Why should he have all the fun? Besides, I'm being careful."

"I can see that." He turned her hand over so that she saw the scrape over her thumb. It infuriated him to see the delicacy marred. "Doesn't someone in your profession have to be careful with their hands?"

"They're insured," she tossed back. "I think I can probably hit a few chords, even with a wound as serious as this." She pulled her hand out of his. "Did you come here to criticize me, Mr. Delaney, or did you have something else in mind?"

"I came to check on the job." Which wasn't necessary, he admitted. In any case, why should it matter to him if she was careless enough to hurt her hand? She was just a woman who had touched down in his territory and would be gone again before the leaves were full-blown with summer. He was going to have to remember that, and the fact that she didn't interest him personally. Shifting, he picked up the screen he'd dropped when he'd taken her hand. "I found this outside."

It wasn't often her voice took on that regal tone. He seemed to nudge it out of her. "Thank you." She took the screen and leaned it against the stove.

"Your road'll be blocked most of the day. I hope you weren't planning on going anywhere."

Maggie gave him a level look that held a hint of challenge. "I'm not going anywhere, Mr. Delaney."

He inclined his head. "Fine." The music on the tape player changed tempo. It was more hard-driving, more primitive. It seemed something to be played on hot, moonless nights. It drew him, pulled at him. "What is that?" Cliff demanded. "I've never heard it before."

Maggie glanced up at the recorder. "It's a movie score I'm composing. That's the melody for the title song." Because it had given her a great deal of trouble, she frowned at the revolving tape. "Do you like it?"

"Yes."

It was the most simple and most direct answer he'd given her thus far. It wasn't enough for Maggie.

"Why?"

He paused a moment, still listening, hardly aware that they were both still on the floor, close enough to touch. "It goes straight to the blood, straight to the imagination. Isn't that what a song's supposed to do?"

He could have said nothing more perfect. Her smile flashed, a quick, stunning smile that left him staring at her as though he'd been struck by lightning. "Yes. Yes, that's exactly what it's supposed to do." In her enthusiasm she shifted. Their knees brushed. "I'm trying for something very basic with this. It has to set the mood for a film about a passionate relationship—an intensely passionate relationship between two people who seem to have nothing in common but an uncontrollable desire for each other. One of them will kill because of it."

She trailed off, lost in the music and the mood. She could see it in vivid colors—scarlets, purples. She could feel it, like the close, sultry air on a hot summer night. Then she frowned, and as if on cue, the music stopped. From the tape came a sharp, pungent curse, then silence.

"I lost something in those last two bars," she muttered. "It was like—" she gestured with both hands, bringing them up, turning them over, then dropping them again "—something came unmeshed. It has to build to desperation, but it has to be more subtle than that. Passion at the very edge of control.''

''Do you always write like that?'' Cliff was studying her when she focused on him again, studying her as he had her land—thoroughly, with an eye both for detail and an overview.

She sat back on her haunches, comfortable now with a conversation on her own turf. He could hardly frustrate her in a discussion of music. She'd lived with it, in it, all her life. ''Like what?'' she countered.

''With the emphasis on mood and emotions rather than notes and timing.''

Her brows lifted. With one hand, she pushed back the hair that swept across her cheek. She wore an amethyst on her finger, wine-colored, square. It caught the light, holding it until she dropped her hand again. As she thought it over, it occurred to her that no one, not even her closest associates, had ever defined her style so cleanly. It pleased her, though she didn't know why, that he had done so. ''Yes,'' she said simply.

He didn't like what those big, soft eyes could do to him. Cliff rose. ''That's why your music is good.''

Maggie gave a quick laugh, not at the compliment, but at the grudging tone with which he delivered it. ''So, you can say something nice, after all.''

''When it's appropriate.'' He watched her stand, noting that she moved with the sort of fluidity he'd always associated with tall, willowy women. ''I admire your music.''

Again, it was the tone, rather than the words, that spoke to her. This time it touched off annoyance, rather than humor. ''And little else that has to do with me.''

''I don't know you,'' Cliff countered.

''You didn't like me when you drove up that hill the other day.'' With her temper rising, Maggie put her hands on her hips and faced him squarely. ''I get the impression you didn't like me years before we met.''

That was direct, Cliff decided. Maggie Fitzgerald, glamour girl from the Coast, didn't believe in evasions. Neither did he.

"I have a problem with people who live their lives on silver platters. I've too much respect for reality."

"Silver platters," Maggie repeated in a voice that was much, much too quiet. "In other words, I was born into affluence, therefore, I can't understand the real world."

He didn't know why he wanted to smile. Perhaps it was the way color flooded her face. Perhaps it was because she stood nearly a foot beneath him but gave every appearance of being ready to Indian-wrestle and win. Yet he didn't smile. Cliff had the impression that if you gave an inch to this lady, you'd soon be begging to give a mile. "That about sums it up. The gravel for the lane'll be delivered and spread by five."

"Sums it up?" Accustomed to ending a conversation when she chose, Maggie grabbed his arm as he started to turn for the door. "You're a narrow-minded snob, and you know nothing about my life."

Cliff looked down at the delicate hand against his tanned muscled arm. The amethyst glowed up at him. "Miss Fitzgerald, everyone in the country knows about your life."

"That is one of the most unintelligent statements I've ever heard." She made one final attempt to control her temper, then forgot it. "Let me tell you something, Mr. Delaney—" The phone interrupted what would have been a stream of impassioned abuse. Maggie ended up swearing. "You stay there," she ordered as she turned to the wall phone.

Cliff's brows lifted at the command. Slowly, he leaned against the kitchen counter. He'd stay, he decided. Not because she'd told him to, but because he'd discovered he wanted to hear what she had to say.

Maggie yanked the receiver from the wall and barked into it. "Hello."

"Well, it's nice to hear that country life's agreeing with you."

"C.J." She struggled to hold down her temper. She wanted neither questions nor I-told-you-sos. "Sorry, you caught me in the middle of a philosophical discussion." Though she heard Cliff's quick snort of laughter, she ignored it. "Something up, C.J.?"

"Well, I hadn't heard from you in a couple of days—"

"I told you I'd call once a week. Will you stop worrying?"

"You know I can't."

She had to laugh. "No, I know you can't. If it relieves your mind, I'm having the lane fixed even as we speak. The next time you visit, you won't have to worry about your muffler falling off."

"It doesn't relieve my mind," C.J. grumbled. "I have nightmares about that roof caving in on your head. The damn place is falling apart."

"The place is not falling apart." She turned, inadvertently kicking the screen and sending it clattering across the floor. At that moment, her eyes met Cliff's. He was still leaning against the counter, still close enough to the back door to be gone in two strides. But now he was grinning. Maggie looked at the screen, then back at Cliff, and covered her mouth to smother a giggle.

"What was that noise?" C.J. demanded.

"Noise?" Maggie swallowed. "I didn't hear any noise." She covered the mouth of the receiver with her hand when Cliff laughed again. "Shh," she whispered, smiling. "C.J.," she said back into the phone, knowing she needed to distract him, "the score's nearly finished."

"When?" The response was immediate and predictable. She sent Cliff a knowing nod.

"For the most part, it's polished. I'm a little hung up on the title song. If you let me get back to work, the tape'll be in your office next week."

"Why don't you deliver it yourself? We'll have lunch."

"Forget it."

He sighed. "Just thought I'd try. To show you my heart's in the right place, I sent you a present."

"A present? The Godiva?"

"You'll have to wait and see," he said evasively. "It'll be there by tomorrow morning. I expect you to be so touched you'll catch the next plane to L.A. to thank me in person."

"C.J.—"

"Get back to work. And call me," he added, clever enough

to know when to retreat and when to advance. "I keep having visions of you falling off that mountain."

He hung up, leaving her, as he often did, torn between amusement and annoyance. "My agent," Maggie said as she replaced the receiver. "He likes to worry."

"I see."

Cliff remained where he was; so did she. That one silly shared moment seemed to have broken down a barrier between them. Now, in its place, was an awkwardness neither of them fully understood. He was suddenly aware of the allure of her scent, of the slender line of her throat. She was suddenly disturbed by his basic masculinity, by the memory of the firm, rough feel of his palm. Maggie cleared her throat.

"Mr. Delaney—"

"Cliff," he corrected.

She smiled, telling herself to relax. "Cliff. We seem to've gotten off on the wrong foot for some reason. Maybe if we concentrate on something that interests us both—my land— we won't keep rubbing each other the wrong way."

He found it an interesting phrase, particularly since he was imagining what it would feel like to run his hands over her skin. "All right," he agreed as he straightened from the counter. He crossed to her, wondering who he was testing, himself or her. When he stopped, she was trapped between him and the stove.

He didn't touch her, but both of them could sense what it would be like. Hard hands, soft skin. Warmth turning quickly to heat. Mouth meeting mouth with confidence, with knowledge, with passion.

"I consider your land a challenge." He said it quietly, his eyes on hers. She didn't think of mists now but of smoke— of smoke and fire. "Which is why I've decided to give this project quite a bit of my personal attention."

Her nerves were suddenly strung tight. Maggie didn't back away, because she was almost certain that was what he wanted. Instead, she met his gaze. If her eyes weren't calm, if they'd darkened with the first traces of desire, she couldn't prevent it. "I can't argue with that."

"No." He smiled a little. If he stayed, even moments longer, he knew he'd find out how her lips tasted. That might be the biggest mistake he'd ever make. Turning, he went to the back door. "Call Bog." He tossed this over his shoulder as he pushed the screen door open. "Your fingers belong on piano keys, not on putty knives."

Maggie let out a long, tense breath when the screen door slammed. Did he do that on purpose, she wondered as she pressed a hand to her speeding heart. Or was it a natural talent of his to turn women into limp rags? Shaking her head, she told herself to forget it. If there was one thing she had experience in, it was in avoiding and evading the professional lothario. She was definitely uninterested in going a few rounds with Morganville's leading contender.

With a scowl, she dropped back to her knees and picked up the putty knife. She began to hack at the tile with a vengeance. Maggie Fitzgerald could take care of herself.

Chapter 3

For the third morning in a row, Maggie was awakened by the sound of men and machinery outside her windows. It occurred to her that she'd hardly had the chance to become used to the quiet when the chaos had started.

The bulldozer had been replaced by chain saws, industrial weed eaters and trucks. While she was far from getting used to the early risings, she was resigned. By seven-fifteen she had dragged herself out of the shower and was staring at her face in the bathroom mirror.

Not so good, she decided, studying her own sleepy eyes. But then she'd been up until two working on the score. Displeased, she ran a hand over her face. She'd never considered pampering her skin a luxury or a waste of time. It was simply something she did routinely, the same way she'd swim twenty laps every morning in California.

She'd been neglecting the basics lately, Maggie decided, squinting at her reflection. Had it been over two months since she'd been in a salon? Ruefully, she tugged at the bangs that swept over her forehead. It was showing, and it was time to do something about it.

After wrapping her still-damp hair in a towel, she pulled open the mirrored medicine-cabinet door. The nearest Elizabeth Arden's was seventy miles away. There were times,

Maggie told herself as she smeared on a clay mask, that you had to fend for yourself.

She was just rinsing her hands when the sound of quick, high-pitched barking reached her. C.J.'s present, Maggie thought wryly, wanted his breakfast. In her short terry-cloth robe, which was raveled at the hem, her hair wrapped in a checked towel and the clay mask hardening on her face, she started downstairs to tend to the demanding gift her agent had flown out to her. She had just reached the bottom landing when a knock on the door sent the homely bulldog puppy into a frenzy.

"Calm down," she ordered, scooping him up under one arm. "All this excitement and I haven't had my coffee yet. Give me a break." The pup lowered his head and growled when she pulled on the front door. Definitely city-oriented, she thought, trying to calm the pup. She wondered if C.J. had planned it that way. The door resisted, sticking. Swearing, Maggie set down the dog and yanked with both hands.

The door swung open, carrying her a few steps back with the momentum. The pup dashed through the closest doorway, poking his head around the frame and snarling as if he meant business. Cliff stared at Maggie as she stood, panting, in the hall. She blew out a breath, wondering what could happen next. "I thought country life was supposed to be peaceful."

Cliff grinned, tucking his thumbs in the front pockets of his jeans. "Not necessarily. Get you up?"

"I've been up for quite some time," she said loftily.

"Mmm-hmm." His gaze skimmed over her legs, nicely exposed by the brief robe, before it lingered on the puppy crouched in the doorway. Her legs were longer, he mused, than one would think, considering the overall size of her. "Friend of yours?"

Maggie looked at the bulldog, which was making fierce sounds in his throat while keeping a careful distance. "A present from my agent."

"What's his name?"

Maggie sent the cowering puppy a wry look. "Killer."

Cliff watched the pup disappear behind the wall again. "Very apt. You figure to train him as a guard dog?"

"I'm going to teach him to attack music critics." She lifted a hand to push it through her hair—an old habit—and discovered the towel. Just as abruptly, she remembered the rest of her appearance. One hand flew to her face and found the thin layer of hardened clay. "Oh, my God," Maggie murmured as Cliff's grin widened. "Oh, damn." Turning, she raced for the stairs. "Just a minute." He was treated to an intriguing glimpse of bare thighs as she dashed upstairs.

Ten minutes later, she walked back down, perfectly composed. Her hair was swept back at the side with mother-of-pearl combs; her face was lightly touched with makeup. She'd pulled on the first thing she'd come to in her still-unpacked trunk. The tight black jeans proved an interesting contrast to the bulky white sweatshirt. Cliff sat on the bottom landing, sending the cowardly puppy into ecstasy by rubbing his belly. Maggie frowned down at the crown of Cliff's head.

"You weren't going to say a word, were you?"

He continued to rub the puppy, not bothering to look up. "About what?"

Maggie narrowed her eyes and folded her arms under her breasts. "Nothing. Was there something you wanted to discuss this morning?"

He wasn't precisely sure why that frosty, regal tone appealed to him. Perhaps he just liked knowing he had the ability to make her use it. "Still want that pond?"

"Yes, I still want the pond," she snapped, then gritted her teeth to prevent herself from doing so again. "I don't make a habit of changing my mind."

"Fine. We'll be clearing out the gully this afternoon." Rising, he faced her while the puppy sat expectantly at his feet. "You didn't call Bog about the kitchen floor."

Confusion came and went in her eyes. "How do you—"

"It's easy to find things out in Morganville."

"Well, it's none of your—"

"Hard to keep your business to yourself in small towns," Cliff interrupted again. It amused him to hear her breath huff out in frustration. "Fact is, you're about the top news item in town these days. Everybody wonders what the lady from California's doing up on this mountain. The more you keep to yourself," he added, "the more they wonder."

"Is that so?" Maggie tilted her head and stepped closer. "And you?" she countered. "Do you wonder?"

Cliff knew a challenge when he heard one, and knew he'd answer it in his own time. Impulsively, he cupped her chin in his hand and ran his thumb over her jawline. She didn't flinch or draw back, but became very still. "Nice skin," he murmured, sweeping his gaze along the path his thumb took. "Very nice. You take good care of it, Maggie. I'll take care of your land."

With this, he left her precisely as she was—arms folded, head tilted back, eyes astonished.

By ten, Maggie decided it wasn't going to be the quiet, solitary sort of day she'd moved to the country for. The men outside shouted above the machinery to make themselves heard. Trucks came and went down her newly graveled lane. She could comfort herself that in a few weeks that part of the disruption would be over.

She took three calls from the Coast from friends who wondered how and what she was doing. By the third call, she was a bit testy from explaining she was scraping linoleum, papering walls, painting woodwork and enjoying it. She left the phone off the hook and went back to her putty knife and kitchen floor.

More than half of the wood was exposed now. The progress excited her enough that she decided to stick with this one job until it was completed. The floor would be beautiful, and, she added, thinking of Cliff's comments, she'd have done it herself.

Maggie had barely scraped off two more inches when there was a knock behind her. She turned her head, ready to flare if it was Cliff Delaney returned to taunt her. Instead, she saw a tall, slender woman of her own age with soft brown hair and pale blue eyes. As Maggie studied Joyce Morgan Agee, she wondered why she hadn't seen the resemblance to Louella before.

"Mrs. Agee." Maggie rose, brushing at the knees of her jeans. "Please, come in. I'm sorry." Her sneakers squeaked as she stepped on a thin layer of old glue. "The floor's a bit sticky."

"I don't mean to disturb your work." Joyce stood uncertainly in the doorway, eyeing the floor. "I would've called, but I was on my way home from Mother's."

Joyce's pumps were trim and stylish. Maggie felt the glue pull at the bottom of her old sneakers. "We can talk outside, if you don't mind." Taking the initiative, Maggie walked out into the sunshine. "Things are a little confused around here right now."

"Yes." They heard one of the workers call to a companion, punctuating his suggestion with good-natured swearing. Joyce glanced over in their direction before she turned back to Maggie. "You're not wasting any time, I see."

"No." Maggie laughed and eyed the crumbling dirt wall beside them. "I've never been very patient. For some reason, I'm more anxious to have the outside the way I want it than the inside."

"You couldn't have picked a better company," Joyce murmured, glancing over at one of the trucks with *Delaney's* on the side.

Maggie followed her gaze but kept her tone neutral. "So I'm told."

"I want you to know I'm really glad you're doing so much to the place." Joyce began to fiddle with the strap of her shoulder bag. "I can hardly remember living here. I was a child when we moved, but I hate waste." With a little smile, she looked around again and shook her head. "I don't think I could live out here. I like being in town, with neighbors close by and other children for my children to play with. Of course, Stan, my husband, likes being available all the time."

It took Maggie a moment; then she remembered. "Oh, your husband's the sheriff, isn't he?"

"That's right. Morganville's a quiet town, nothing like Los

Angeles, but it keeps him busy." She smiled, but Maggie wondered why she sensed strain. "We're just not city people."

"No." Maggie smiled, too. "I guess I've discovered I'm not, either."

"I don't understand how you could give up—" Joyce seemed to catch herself. "I guess what I meant was, this must be such a change for you after living in a place like Beverly Hills."

"A change," Maggie agreed. Was she sensing undercurrents here, too, as she had with Louella's dreaminess? "It was one I wanted."

"Yes, well, you know I'm glad you bought the place, and so quickly. Stan was a little upset with my putting it on the market when he was out of town, but I couldn't see it just sitting here. Who knows, if you hadn't come along so fast, he might've talked me out of selling it."

"Then we can both be grateful I saw the sign when I did." Mentally, Maggie was trying to figure out the logistics of the situation. It seemed the house had belonged exclusively to Joyce, without her husband or her mother having any claim. Fleetingly, she wondered why Joyce hadn't rented or sold the property before.

"The real reason I came by, Miss Fitzgerald, is my mother. She told me she was here a few days ago."

"Yes, she's a lovely woman."

"Yes." Joyce looked back toward the men working, then took a deep breath. Maggie no longer had to wonder if she was sensing undercurrents. She was sure of it. "It's more than possible she'll drop in on you again. I'd like to ask you a favor, that is, if she begins to bother you, if you'd tell me instead of her."

"Why should she bother me?"

Joyce let out a sound that was somewhere between fatigue and frustration. "Mother often dwells on the past. She's never completely gotten over my father's death. She makes some people uncomfortable."

Maggie remembered the discomfort she'd felt on and off

during Louella's brief visit. Still, she shook her head. "Your mother's welcome to visit me from time to time, Mrs. Agee."

"Thank you, but you will promise to tell me if—well, if you'd like her to stay away. You see, she'd often come here, even when the place was deserted. I don't want her to get in your way. She doesn't know who you are. That is—" Obviously embarrassed, Joyce broke off. "I mean, Mother doesn't understand that someone like you would be busy."

Maggie remembered the lost eyes, the unhappy mouth. Pity stirred again. "All right, if she bothers me, I'll tell you."

The relief in Joyce's face was quick and very plain. "I appreciate it, Miss Fitzgerald."

"Maggie."

"Yes, well..." As if only more uncertain of her ground, Joyce managed a smile. "I understand that someone like you wouldn't want to have people dropping by and getting in the way."

Maggie laughed, thinking how many times the phone calls from California had interrupted her that morning. "I'm not a recluse," she told Joyce, though she was no longer completely sure. "And I'm not really very temperamental. Some people even consider me normal."

"Oh, I didn't mean—"

"I know you didn't. Come back when I've done something with that floor, and we'll have some coffee."

"I'd like to, really. Oh, I nearly forgot." She reached into the big canvas bag on her shoulder and pulled out a manila envelope. "Mother said you wanted to see these. Some pictures of the property."

"Yes." Pleased, Maggie took the envelope. She hadn't thought Louella would remember or bother to put them together for her. "I hoped they might give me some ideas."

"Mother said you could keep them as long as you liked." Joyce hesitated, fiddling again with the strap of her bag. "I have to get back. My youngest gets home from kindergarten at noon, and Stan sometimes comes home for lunch. I haven't done a thing to the house. I hope I see you sometime in town."

"I'm sure you will." Maggie tucked the envelope under her arm. "Give my best to your mother."

Maggie started back into the house, but as she put her hand on the doorknob, she noticed Cliff crossing to Joyce. Curiosity had her stopping to watch as Cliff took both the brunette's hands in his own. Though she couldn't hear the conversation over the din of motors, it was obvious that they knew each other well. There was a gentleness on Cliff's face Maggie hadn't seen before, and something she interpreted as concern. He bent down close, as if Joyce were speaking very softly, then touched her hair. The touch of a brother? Maggie wondered. Or a lover?

As she watched, Joyce shook her head, apparently fumbling with the door handle before she got into the car. Cliff leaned into the window for a moment. Were they arguing? Maggie wondered. Was the tension she sensed real or imaginary? Fascinated with the silent scene being played out in her driveway, Maggie watched as Cliff withdrew from the window and Joyce backed out to drive away. Before she could retreat inside, Cliff turned, and their gazes locked.

There were a hundred feet separating them, and the air was full of the sounds of men and machines. The sun was strong enough to make her almost too warm in the sweatshirt, yet she felt one quick, unexpected chill race up her spine. Perhaps it was hostility she felt. Maggie tried to tell herself it was hostility and not the first dangerous flutters of passion.

There was a temptation to cross those hundred feet and test both of them. Even the thought of it stirred her blood. He didn't move. He didn't take his eyes from her. With fingers gone suddenly numb, Maggie twisted the handle and went inside.

Two hours later, Maggie went out again. She'd never been one to retreat from a challenge, from her emotions or from trouble. Cliff Delaney seemed connected with all three. While she'd scraped linoleum, Maggie had lectured herself on letting Cliff intimidate her for no reason other than his being powerfully male and sexy.

And different, she'd admitted. Different from most of the

men she'd encountered in her profession. He didn't fawn—
far from it. He didn't pour on the charm. He wasn't impressed
with his own physique, looks or sophistication. It must have
been that difference that had made her not quite certain how
to handle him.

A very direct, very frank business approach, she decided
as she circled around the back of the house. Maggie paused
to look at the bank fronting her house.

The vines, briars and thick sumac were gone. Piles of rich,
dark topsoil were being spread over what had been a tangled
jungle of neglect. The tree that had leaned toward her house
was gone, stump and all. Two men, backs glistening with
sweat, were setting stone in a low-spreading wall where the
edge of the slope met the edge of the lawn.

Cliff Delaney ran a tight ship, Maggie concluded, and made
her way through the new dirt toward the side yard. Here, too,
the worst had been cleared out. An enormous bearded man in
bib overalls sat atop a big yellow backhoe as easily as another
might sit in an armchair. At the push of a lever, the digger
went down into the gully, bit into earth and rock and came
up full.

Maggie shaded her eyes and watched the procedure while
the puppy circled her legs and snarled at everything in sight.
Each time the digger would open its claws to drop its load,
the dog would send up a ruckus of barks. Laughing, Maggie
crouched down to scratch his ears and soothe him.

"Don't be a coward, Killer. I won't let it get you."

"I wouldn't get any closer," Cliff said from behind her.

She turned her head, squinting against the sun. "This is
close enough." Disliking the disadvantage of looking up and
into the sun, Maggie stood. "You seem to be making progress."

"We need to get the plants in and the wall of this thing
solid—" he gestured toward the gully "—before the rain hits.
Otherwise, you'll have a real mess on your hands."

"I see." Because he wore the frustrating tinted glasses
again, she turned from him to watch the backhoe work. "You
certainly have a large staff."

Cliff's thumbs went into his pockets. "Large enough." He'd told himself he'd imagined that powerful sexual pull hours before. Now, feeling it again, he couldn't deny it.

She wasn't what he wanted, yet he wanted her. She wasn't what he would have chosen, yet he was choosing her. He could turn away logic until he'd learned what it was like to touch her.

Maggie was very aware of how close they stood. The stirring she'd felt hours before began to build again, slowly, seductively, until she felt her whole body tense with it. She understood that you could want someone you didn't know, someone you passed on the street. It all had to do with chemistry, but her chemistry had never reacted this way before. She had a wild urge to turn into his arms, to demand or offer the fulfillment, or whatever it was, that simmered between them. It was something that offered excitement, and pleasure she had only glimpsed before. So she did turn, completely uncertain as to what she would say.

"I don't think I like what's happening here."

Cliff didn't pretend to misunderstand her. Neither of their minds was on the pond or the machine. "Do you have a choice?"

Maggie frowned, wishing she was more certain of her moves. He wasn't like the men she'd known before; therefore, the standard rules didn't apply. "I think so. I moved here because it was where I wanted to live, where I wanted to work. But I also moved here because I wanted to be on my own. I intend to do all those things."

Cliff studied her a moment, then gave the backhoe driver an absent wave as he shut off the machine to take his lunch break. "I took this job because I wanted to work this land. I intend to do it."

Though she didn't feel the slightest lessening of tension, Maggie nodded. "Then we understand each other."

As she started to turn away, Cliff put a hand on her shoulder, holding her still. "I think we both understand quite a bit."

The muscles in her stomach tightened and loosened like a

nervous fist. With his fingers so light on the bulky sweatshirt, she shouldn't have felt anything. But hundreds of pulses sprang to life in her body. The air seemed to grow closer, hotter, the sounds of men more distant. "I don't know what you mean."

"Yes, you do."

Yes, she did. "I don't know anything about you," Maggie managed.

Cliff caught the tips of her hair in his fingers. "I can't say the same."

Maggie's temper flared, though she knew when she was being baited. "So, you believe everything you read in the tabloids and glossies." She tossed her head to free her hair from his fingers. "I'm surprised that a man who's obviously so successful and talented could be so ignorant."

Cliff acknowledged the hit with a nod. "I'm surprised a woman who's obviously so successful and talented could be so foolish."

"Foolish? What the hell's that supposed to mean?"

"It seems foolish to me to encourage the press to report every area of your life."

She clenched her teeth and tried deep breathing. Neither worked. "I don't encourage the press to do anything."

"You don't discourage them," Cliff countered.

"Discouragement *is* encouragement," she tossed back. Folding her arms under her breasts as she'd done earlier, she stared out over the open gully. "Why am I defending myself?" she muttered. "You don't know anything about it. I don't need you to know anything about it."

"I know you gave an interview about yourself and your husband weeks after his death." He heard her quick intake of breath even as he cursed himself for saying something so personal, and so uncalled-for.

"Do you have any idea how the press hammered at me during those weeks?" Her voice was low and strained, and she no longer looked at him. "Do you know all the garbage they were printing?" Her fingers tightened on her own arms. "I chose a reporter I could trust, and I gave the most honest, most straightforward interview I could manage, knowing it was my only chance to keep things from sinking lower. That interview was for Jerry. It was the only thing I had left to give him.''

He'd wanted to prod, perhaps even to prick, but he hadn't wanted to hurt. "I'm sorry." Cliff put his hand on her shoulder again, but she jerked away.

"Forget it."

This time he took both of her shoulders, turning her firmly to face him. "I don't forget blows below the belt, especially when I'm the one doing the punching.''

She waited to speak until she was certain she had some control again. "I've survived hits before. My advice to you is not to criticize something you have no capacity for understanding.''

"I apologized." He didn't release her shoulders when she tried to draw away. "But I'm not very good at following advice.''

Maggie became still again. Somehow they had gotten closer, so that now their thighs brushed. The combination of anger and desire was becoming too strong to ignore. "Then you and I don't have any more to say to each other.''

"You're wrong." His voice was very quiet, very compelling. "We haven't begun to say all there is to say.''

"You work for me—''

"I work for myself," Cliff corrected.

She understood that kind of pride, admired it. But admiration wouldn't remove his hands from her shoulders. "I'm paying you to do a job.''

"You're paying my company. That's business.''

"It's going to be our only business.''

"Wrong again," he murmured, but released her.

Maggie opened her mouth to hurl something back at him, but the dog began to bark in quick, excited yelps. She decided turning her back on him to investigate her pet was a much grander insult than the verbal one she'd planned. Without a word, she began to make her way around the slope of the gully to the pile of earth and rock and debris the backhoe had dumped.

"All right, Killer." The going was so rough that she swore under her breath as she stumbled over stones. "You'll never find anything worthwhile in that pile, anyway."

Ignoring her, the puppy continued to dig, his barking muffled as his nose went farther in, his backside wriggling with either effort or delight in the new game.

"Cut it out." She bent to pull him out of the heap and ended up sitting down hard. "Damn it, Killer." Staying as she was, she grabbed the dog with one hand, dragging him back and unearthing a small avalanche of rock.

"Will you be careful?" Cliff shouted from above her, knowing she'd been lucky not to have one of the rocks bounce off her shin.

"It's the stupid dog!" Maggie shouted back as she lost her grip on him again. "God knows what he thinks is so fascinating about this mess. Nothing but dirt and rocks," she muttered, pushing at the pile that had landed near her hip.

"Well, grab him and get back up here before you're both hurt."

"Yeah," she muttered under her breath. "You're a big help." Disgusted, she started to struggle up when her fingers slid into the worn, rounded rock her hand had rested on. Hollow, she thought curiously. Her attention torn between the gully and the dog's unrelenting barks, Maggie glanced down.

Then she began to scream, loud and long enough to send the puppy racing for cover.

Cliff's first thought as he raced down the slope to her was snakes. When he reached her, he dragged her up and into his arms in an instinctive move of protection. She'd stopped screaming, and though her breathing was shallow, Maggie grabbed his shirt before he could carry her back up the slope. "Bones," she whispered. Closing her eyes, she dropped her head on his shoulder. "Oh, my God."

Cliff looked down and saw what the machine and dog had unearthed. Mixed with the rock and debris was a pile of what might have been mistaken for long white sticks layered with dirt.

But lying on the bones, inches from where Maggie had sat, was a human skull.

Chapter 4

"I'm all right." Maggie sat at the kitchen table and gripped the glass of water Cliff had handed her. When the pain in her fingers finally registered, she relaxed them a bit. "I feel like an idiot, screaming that way."

She was still pale, he noted. Though the hands on the glass were steady now, they were still white at the knuckles. Her eyes were wide and shocked, suddenly too big for the rest of her face. He started to stroke her hair, then stuck his own hands in his pockets. "A natural enough reaction."

"I guess." She looked up and managed a shaky smile. She was cold, but prayed she wouldn't begin to shiver in front of him. "I've never found myself in that sort of…situation before."

Cliff lifted a brow. "Neither have I."

"No?" Somehow she'd wanted to think it had happened before. If it had, it might make it less horrible—and less personal. She looked down at the floor, not realizing until that moment that the dog lay across her feet, whimpering. "But don't you dig up a lot of—" She hesitated, not sure just how she wanted to phrase it. "Things," Maggie decided weakly, "in your line of work?"

She was reaching, Cliff thought, and whether she knew it or not, those big brown eyes were pleading with him for some sort of easy explanation. He didn't have one to give her. "Not that kind of thing."

Their gazes held for one long, silent moment before Maggie nodded. If there was one thing she'd learned in the hard, competitive business she'd chosen, it was to handle things as they came. "So, neither of us has a tidy explanation." The little expulsion of breath was the last sign of weakness she intended to show him. "I guess the next step is the police."

"Yeah." The more determined she became to be calm, the more difficult it became for him. She was weakening something in him that he was determined to keep objective. His hands were balled into fists inside his pockets in his struggle not to touch her. Distance was the quickest defense. "You'd better call," Cliff said briskly. "I'll go out and make sure the crew keeps clear of the gully."

Again, her answer was a nod. Maggie watched as he crossed to the screen door and pushed it open. There he hesitated. He'd have cursed if he'd understood what it was he wanted to swear at. When he looked back, she saw the concern on his face she'd seen when he'd spoken to Joyce. "Maggie, are you all right?"

The question, and the tone, helped her to settle. Perhaps it had something to do with her knowing just what it was like to be pressured by another's weakness. "I will be. Thanks." She waited until the screen door banged shut behind him before she dropped her head on the table.

Good heavens, what had she walked into here? People didn't find bodies in their front yard. C.J. would've said it was totally uncivilized. Maggie choked back a hysterical giggle and straightened. The one unarguable fact she had to face was that she had found one. Now she had to deal with it. Taking deep breaths, she went to the phone and dialed the operator.

"Get me the police," she said quickly.

A few minutes later, Maggie went outside. Though she'd hoped the practical routine of reporting what she'd found would calm her, it hadn't worked. She didn't go near the gully, but she found she couldn't sit inside, waiting alone.

Circling around the front of the house, she found a convenient rock and sat. The puppy stretched out in the patch of sunlight at her feet and went to sleep.

She could almost believe she'd imagined what she'd seen in that pile of dirt and rock. It was too peaceful here for anything so stark. The air was too soft, the sun too warm. Her land might be unruly, but it held a serenity that blocked out the harsher aspects of life.

Was that why she'd chosen it, Maggie wondered. Because she wanted to pretend there wasn't any real madness in the world? Here she could cocoon herself from so many of the pressures and demands that had threaded through her life for so long. Was this spot the home she'd always wanted, or was it in reality just an escape for her? She squeezed her eyes shut. If that were true, it made her weak and dishonest, two things she couldn't tolerate. Why had it taken this incident to make her question what she hadn't questioned before? As she tried to find her tranquillity again, a shadow fell over her. Opening her eyes, Maggie looked up at Cliff.

For some reason it toughened her. She wouldn't admit to him that she'd begun to doubt herself or her motives. No, not to him.

"Someone should be here soon." She linked her folded hands over one knee and looked back into the woods.

"Good." Several minutes passed while they both remained silent, looking into the trees.

Eventually, Cliff crouched down beside her. Funny, but he thought that she looked more apt to fall apart now than she had when he'd carried her into her kitchen. Reaction, he decided, had different speeds for different people. He wanted to hold her again, hard and close, as he'd done all too briefly before. The contact had made something strong and sultry move through him. Like her music—something like her music.

He wished like hell he'd turned down the job and had walked away the first time he'd seen her. Cliff looked past her to the slope that led to the gully.

"You talked to Stan?"

"Stan?" Blankly, Maggie stared at Cliff's set profile. At that moment, he was close enough to reach but seemed miles away. "Oh, the sheriff." She wished he'd touch her, just for a moment. Just a hand on her. "No, I didn't call him. I called the operator and asked for the police. She connected me with the state police in Hagerstown." She lapsed into silence, waiting for him to make some comment on her typical city response.

"Probably for the best," Cliff murmured. "I let the crew go. It'll be less confusing."

"Oh." She must've been in a daze not to notice that the trucks and men were gone. When she forced herself to look, she saw that the backhoe remained, sitting on the rise above the gully, big and yellow and silent. The sun was warm on her back. Her skin was like ice. Time to snap out of it, Maggie told herself, and straightened her shoulders. "Yes, I'm sure you're right. Should I call your office when the police say it's all right to start work again?" Her voice was businesslike. Her throat was dry with the thought of being left alone, completely alone, with what was down by the gully.

Cliff turned his head. Without speaking, he took off his sunglasses so that their eyes met. "Thought I'd hang around."

Relief washed over her. Maggie knew it must've shown in her face, but she didn't have the will to put pride first. "I'd like you to. It's stupid, but—" She glanced over in the direction of the gully.

"Not stupid."

"Maybe weak's a better word," she mumbled, trying to smile.

"Human." Despite his determination not to, Cliff reached out and took her hand. The touch, one designed to comfort, to reassure her, set off a chain reaction of emotion too swift to stop.

It ran through her head that she should rise swiftly and go inside. He might stop her, or he might let her go. Maggie didn't ask herself which she wanted, nor did she move. Instead, she sat where she was, meeting his gaze and letting the sensation of torrid, liquid heat flow through her. Nothing else existed. Nothing else mattered.

She felt each of his fingers tense individually on her hand. There was a sense of power there; whether it was his or hers, she wasn't sure. Perhaps it was the melding of both. She saw his eyes darken until the irises were only shades lighter than the pupils. It was as if he were looking through her, into her chaotic thoughts. In the quiet of midafternoon, she heard each breath he drew in and expelled. The sound stirred the excitement that vibrated in the air between them.

Together they moved toward each other until mouth molded itself to mouth.

Intensity. She hadn't known anything between two people could be so concentrated, such pure sensation. She understood that if years passed, if she was blind and deaf, she would know this man just by the touch of his lips. In one instant she became intimate with the shape of his mouth, the taste and texture of his tongue. Her mouth was on his, his hand on hers, and they touched nowhere else. In that moment there was no need to.

There was an aggressiveness, even a harshness, to the kiss that Maggie hadn't expected. It held none of the sweetness, the hesitation, that first kisses often do, yet she didn't back away from it. Perhaps it was all part of the attraction that had begun the moment he'd stepped from the truck. Different, yes, he was different from the other men who'd touched her life— different still from the man she'd shared her body with. She'd known that from the first encounter. Now, with his mouth stirring her senses, she found herself grateful for it. She wanted nothing to be the same as it had been, no reminders of what she'd had once and lost. This man wouldn't pamper or worship. He was strong enough to want strength in return. She felt his tongue tangle with hers, probing deeper. Maggie reveled in the demands.

It was easy, almost too easy, to forget her delicate build, her fragile looks, when her mouth was so ardent on his. He should've known there'd be deep, restless passion in a woman who created music with such sexuality. But how could he have known that passion would call to him as though he'd been waiting for years?

It was much too easy to forget she wasn't the kind of woman he wanted in his life when her taste was filling him. Again, he should have known she'd have the power to make a man toss aside all logic, all intellect. Her lips were warm, moist, the taste as pungent as the scent of newly turned earth around them. The urge rose to take her in his arms and fulfill, there under the clear afternoon sun, all the needs that welled inside him. Cliff drew back, resisting that final painful twist of desire.

Breathless, throbbing, Maggie stared at him. Could that one searing meeting of lips have moved him as it had moved her? Were his thoughts swimming as hers were? Was his body pulsing with wild, urgent needs? She could tell nothing from his face. Though his eyes were fixed on hers, their expression was unreadable. If she asked, would he tell her that he, too, had never known a wave of passion so overwhelming or so mesmerizing? She would ask, and would know, as soon as she had the voice to question. As she sat, struggling to catch her breath, the events of the day came flashing back into her mind. Abruptly, Maggie sprang to her feet.

"God, what are we doing?" she demanded. With a hand that shook, she pushed the hair away from her face. "How can we sit here like this when that—that thing's only a few yards away?"

Cliff took her arm, turning her back to face him. "What does one have to do with the other?"

"Nothing. I don't know." With her insides churning, she looked up at him. Her emotions had always been too dominant. Though she knew it, Maggie had never been able to change it. It had been years since she'd really tried. Confusion, distress, passion, radiated from her as tangible things. "What we found, it's dreadful, unbelievably dreadful, and a few moments ago I was sitting there wondering what it would be like to make love with you."

Something flashed in his eyes, quickly controlled. Unlike Maggie, Cliff had learned long ago to channel his emotions and keep them to himself. "You obviously don't believe in evading the issue."

"Evasions take too much time and effort." After letting out a long breath, Maggie managed to match his even, casual tone. "Listen, I didn't expect that sort of—eruption," she decided. "I suppose I'm wound up over all of this, and a bit too susceptible."

"Susceptible." Her choice of words made him smile. Somehow, when she became cool and calm, he became tempted to prod. Deliberately, he lifted a hand and ran his fingertips down her cheek. Her skin was still warm with desire. "I wouldn't have described you that way. You seem to be a woman who knows what she wants and how to get it."

If he'd wanted to fire her up, he'd found the perfect key. "Stop it." In one sharp move, she pushed his hand from her face. "I've said it before—you don't know me. Every time we're together, I become more certain that I don't want you to. You're a very attractive man, Cliff. And very unlikable. I stay away from people I don't like."

It occurred to him that he'd never gone out of his way to argue with anyone before. A lot of things were changing. "In a small community like this, it's hard to stay away from anyone."

"I'll put more effort into it."

"Nearly impossible."

She narrowed her eyes and fought to keep her lips from curving. "I'm very good when I put my mind to something."

"Yeah." He put his sunglasses back on. When he grinned, the deliberate cockiness was almost too appealing to resist. "I bet you are."

"Are you trying to be smart, or are you trying to be charming?"

"I never had to try to be either one."

"Think again." Because she was having trouble controlling the grin, Maggie turned away. As luck would have it, she found herself staring out over the gully. A chill raced up her spine. Swearing, she folded her arms under her breasts. "I can't believe it," she muttered. "I can't believe I'm standing here having a ridiculous conversation when there's a—'' She found she couldn't say it and detested herself. ''I think the whole world must be going mad.''

He wasn't going to let her get shaky on him again. When she was vulnerable, she was much more dangerous. ''What's down there's been there for a long time.'' His voice was brisk, almost hard. ''It doesn't have anything to do with you.''

''It's my land,'' Maggie tossed back. She whirled around, eyes glowing, chin angled. ''So it has everything to do with me.''

''Then you better stop shaking every time you think about it.''

''I'm not shaking.''

Without a word, he drew her hand away from her elbow so they could both see the tremor. Furious, Maggie snatched it away again. ''When I want you to touch me, I'll let you know,'' she said between her teeth.

''You already have.''

Before she could think of an appropriate response, the dog scrambled up and began to bark furiously. Seconds later, they both heard the sound of an approaching car.

''He might make you a decent watchdog, after all,'' Cliff said mildly. The pup bounded around in circles like a mad thing, then hid behind the rock. ''Then again...''

As the official car came into sight, he bent down to pat the dog on the head before he walked toward the end of the drive. Maggie hurried to keep pace. Her land, her problem, her responsibility, she told herself. *She'd* do the talking.

A trooper climbed out of the car, adjusted his hat, then broke into a grin. ''Cliff, didn't expect to see you out here.''

''Bob.'' Because the greeting didn't include a handshake, Maggie assumed the men knew each other well and saw each other often. ''My company's handling the landscaping.''

''The old Morgan place.'' The trooper looked around with interest. ''Been a while since I was back here. You dig up something we should know about?''

''So it seems.''

''It's the Fitzgerald place now,'' Maggie cut in briskly.

The trooper touched the brim of his hat and started to make a polite comment. His eyes widened when he took his first good look at her. "Fitzgerald," he repeated. "Hey, aren't you Maggie Fitzgerald?"

She smiled, though the recognition, with Cliff beside her, made her uncomfortable. "Yes, I am."

"I'll be damned. You look just like your pictures in all the magazines. I guess there isn't a song you've written I can't hum. You bought the Morgan place."

"That's right."

He pushed the hat back on his head in a gesture that made her think of cowboys. "Wait till I tell my wife. We had 'Forever' played at our wedding. You remember, Cliff. Cliff was best man."

Maggie tilted her head to look at the man beside her. "Really?"

"If you've finished being impressed," Cliff said mildly, "you might want to take a look at what's down by the gully."

Bob grinned again, all amiability. "That's why I'm here." They began to walk toward the gully together. "You know, it isn't easy to tell what's from a human and what's from an animal just by looking. Could be, ma'am, that you uncovered a deer."

Maggie glanced over at Cliff. She could still feel the way her hand had slid into the hollow opening of what she'd taken for a rock. "I wish I could think so."

"Down here," Cliff said without acknowledging the look. "The going's rough." In a smooth, calculated move, he blocked Maggie's way before she could start down. It forced her to pull up short and grab his arm for support. "Why don't you wait here?"

It would've been easy to do so. Much too easy. "It's my land," Maggie said, and, brushing by him, led the way down herself. "The dog started digging in this pile." She heard the nerves in her own voice and fought against them. "I came down to pull him away, and that's when I saw..." Trailing off, she pointed.

The trooper crouched down, letting out a low whistle.

"Holy hell," he murmured. He turned his head, but it was Cliff he looked at, not Maggie. "It doesn't look like you dug up any deer."

"No." In a casual move, Cliff shifted so that he blocked Maggie's view. "What now?"

Bob rose. He wasn't smiling now, but Maggie thought she detected a gleam of excitement. "I'll have to call the investigation section. Those boys are going to want to take a look at this."

Maggie didn't speak when they climbed up the slope again. She waited in silence while the trooper went to his car to radio in his report. When she did speak, she deliberately avoided the reason they were all standing outside in the middle of the afternoon.

"So you two know each other," she commented as though it were any normal remark made on any normal day.

"Bob and I went to school together." Cliff watched a big black crow swoop over the trees. He was remembering the look on Maggie's face the moment before she'd begun to scream. "He ended up marrying one of my cousins a couple of years ago."

Bending over, she plucked a wildflower and began to shred it. "You have a lot of cousins."

He shrugged. The crow landed and was still. "Enough."

"A few Morgans."

That caught his attention. "A few," he said slowly. "Why?"

"I wondered if it was your connection with them that made you resent my having this land."

Cliff wondered why, when he normally respected candor, it annoyed him from her. "No."

"But you did resent it," Maggie insisted. "You resented me before you even saw me."

He had, and perhaps the resentment had grown since he'd had a taste of her. "Joyce had the right to sell this property whenever, and to whomever, she wanted."

Maggie nodded, looking down to where the puppy scrambled in the new dirt. "Is Joyce a cousin, too?"

"What are you getting at?"

Lifting her head, Maggie met his impatient look. "I'm just trying to understand small towns. After all, I'm going to be living here."

"Then the first thing you should learn is that people don't like questions. They might volunteer more information than you want to hear, but they don't like to be asked."

Maggie acknowledged this with a lift of a brow. "I'll keep that in mind." Rather pleased that she'd annoyed him, Maggie turned to the trooper as he approached.

"They're sending out a team." He glanced from her to Cliff, then over his friend's shoulder toward the gully. "Probably be here for a while, then take what they find with them."

"What then?"

Bob brought his attention back to Maggie. "Good question." He shifted his feet as he considered it. "To tell you the truth, I've never been in on anything like this before, but my guess would be they'd ship everything off to the medical examiner in Baltimore. He'd have to check the, ah, everything out before they could start an investigation."

"Investigation?" she repeated, and felt something tighten in her throat. "What kind of investigation?"

The trooper ran his thumb and forefinger down his nose. "Well, ma'am, as far as I can see, there's no reason for anything like that to be buried down in that gully unless—"

"Unless someone buried it there," Cliff finished.

Maggie stared out into the peaceful spread of greening wood across the lane. "I think we could all use some coffee," she murmured. Without waiting for an acknowledgment, she went back toward the house.

Bob took off his hat and wiped at the sweat on his forehead. "This is one for the books."

Cliff followed his friend's long look at the woman climbing the rickety front steps. "Which? Her or that?" With one hand he gestured toward the gully.

"Both." Bob took out a pack of gum and carefully unwrapped a piece. "First place, what's a woman like her, a celebrity, doing holed up here in the woods?"

"Maybe she decided she likes trees."

Bob slipped the gum into his mouth. "Must be ten, twelve acres of them here."

"Twelve."

"Looks to me like she bought more than she bargained for. Holy hell, Cliff, we haven't had anything like this down in this end of the county since crazy Mel Stickler set those barn fires. Now, in the city—"

"Taken to the fast pace, have you?"

Bob knew Cliff well enough to catch both the dig and the humor. "I like some action," he said easily. "Speaking of which, the lady songwriter smells like heaven."

"How's Carol Ann?"

Bob grinned at the mention of his wife. "Just fine. Look, Cliff, if a man doesn't look, and appreciate, he better see a doctor. You're not going to tell me you haven't noticed just how nice that lady's put together."

"I've noticed." He glanced down at the rock beside him. She'd sat there when he'd kissed her. It wouldn't take any effort to remember each separate sensation that had run through him in that one moment. "I'm more interested in her land."

Bob let out a quick laugh. "If you are, you've done a lot of changing since high school. Remember when we used to come up here—those blond twins, the cheerleaders whose parents rented the place for a while? That old Chevy of yours lost its muffler right there on that turn."

"I remember."

"We had some interesting walks up there in the woods," Bob reminisced. "They were the prettiest girls in school till their daddy got transferred and they moved away."

"Who moved in after that?" Cliff wondered, half to himself. "That old couple from Harrisburg—the Faradays. They were here a long time, until the old man died and she went to live with her kids." Cliff narrowed his eyes as he tried to remember. "That was a couple months before Morgan ran off the bridge. Nobody's lived here since."

Bob shrugged; then both of them looked toward the gully. "Guess it's been ten years since anybody lived here."

"Ten years," Cliff repeated. "A long time."

They both looked over at the sound of a car. "The investigators," Bob said, adjusting his hat again. "They'll take over now."

From the corner of the porch, Maggie watched the proceedings. She'd decided that if the police crew needed her, they'd let her know. It appeared to her that they knew their business. She would just be in the way down there, Maggie reasoned as she drank another cup of black coffee.

She watched them shovel, sift and systematically bag what they'd come for. Maggie told herself that once it was off her property, she'd forget it. It would no longer concern her. She wished she could believe it. What was now being transferred into plastic bags had once been a living being. A man or a woman who'd had thoughts and feelings had lain, alone, only yards from what was now her home. No, she didn't believe she'd be able to forget that.

Before it was over, she'd have to know who that person had been, why they had died and why their grave had been on her land. She'd have to have the answers if she were to live in the home she'd chosen. She finished the last swallow of coffee as one of the police crew broke away from the group and came toward the porch. Maggie went to the steps to meet him.

"Ma'am." He nodded to her but, to her relief, didn't offer his hand. Instead, he took out a badge, flashing the cover up briefly. "I'm Lieutenant Reiker."

She thought he looked like a middle-aged accountant and wondered if he carried a gun under his jacket. "Yes, Lieutenant."

"We're just about finished up. Sorry for the inconvenience."

"That's all right." She gripped her hands together over the cup and wished she could go inside, to her music.

"I've got the trooper's report, but I wonder if you could tell me how you happened to find the remains."

Remains, Maggie thought with a shudder. It seemed a very cold word. For the second time, she related her story of the puppy's digging. She did so calmly now, without a tremor.

"You just bought the place?"

"Yes, I only moved in a few weeks ago."

"And you hired Delaney to do some landscaping."

"Yes." She looked down to where Cliff stood talking to another of the team. "The handyman I hired recommended him."

"Mmm-hmm." In a very casual way, the investigator took notes. "Delaney tells me you wanted the gully there dug out for a pond."

Maggie moistened her lips. "That's right."

"Nice place for one," he said conversationally. "I'd like to ask you to hold off on that for a while, though. We might need to come back and take another look around."

Maggie's hands twisted on the empty cup. "All right."

"What we'd like to do is block off that area." He hitched at his belt, then settled one foot on the step above the other. "Some chicken wire," he said easily, "to keep your dog and any other stray animal from digging around in there."

And people, Maggie thought, deciding it didn't take a genius to read between the lines. Before the day was over, this would be the biggest news flash in the county. She was learning fast. "Do whatever you need to do."

"We appreciate the cooperation, Miss Fitzgerald." He twirled the pen in his fingers, hesitating.

"Is there something else?"

"I know it's a bad time," he said with a sheepish smile, "but I can't pass it up. Would you mind signing my pad? I was a big fan of your mother's, and I guess I know most all of your songs, too."

Maggie laughed. It was far better to laugh. The day had been a series of one ludicrous event after another. "Of course." She took the offered pad and pen. "Would you like me to say anything special?"

"Maybe you could just write—to my good friend Harvey."

Before she could oblige, she glanced up and caught Cliff's

eyes on her. She saw his lips twist into something between a sneer and a smile. With a silent oath, she signed the pad and handed it back.

"I don't know much about this kind of thing," she began briskly, "but I'd appreciate it if you kept me informed on whatever's being done."

"We'll have the medical examiner's report in a few days." Pocketing his pad, the investigator became solidly professional again. "We'll all know more then. Thanks for your time, Miss Fitzgerald. We'll be out of your way as soon as we can."

Though she felt Cliff's gaze still on her, Maggie didn't look over. Instead, she turned and walked back into the house. Moments later, music could be heard through the open windows.

Cliff remained where he was, though he'd answered all the questions that he could answer. His thoughts were focused on the sounds coming from the music room. It wasn't one of her songs, he concluded, but something from the classics, something that required speed, concentration and passion. Therapy, he wondered, frowning up at the window. With a shrug, he started toward his car. It wasn't his concern if the lady was upset. Hadn't she told him she'd moved back here to be on her own?

Turning his head, he saw the investigators preparing to leave. Within moments, he reflected, she'd be alone. The music pouring out of the windows was tense, almost desperate. Swearing, Cliff stuffed his keys back in his pocket and strode toward the steps.

She didn't answer his knock. The music played on. Without giving it a second thought, he pushed open the front door. The house vibrated with the storm coming from the piano. Following it into the music room, he watched her from the doorway.

Her eyes were dark, her head was bent, though he didn't think she even saw the keys. Talent? There was no denying it, any more than there could be any denying her tension or her vulnerability. Later, he might ask himself why all three made him uncomfortable.

Perhaps he did want to comfort her, he told himself. He'd do the same for anyone, under the circumstances. She didn't have to mean anything to him for him to want to offer a diversion. Strays and wounded birds had always been weaknesses of his. Dissatisfied with his own logic, Cliff waited until she'd finished.

Maggie looked up, startled to see him in the doorway. Damn her nerves, she thought, carefully folding her hands in her lap. "I thought you'd gone."

"No. They have."

She tossed the hair out of her eyes and hoped she looked composed. "Was there something else?"

"Yeah." He walked over to run a finger over the piano keys. No dust, he noted, in a house nearly choked with it. Her work was obviously of first importance.

When he didn't elaborate, Maggie frowned. Cliff preferred the impatience he saw in her eyes now. "What?"

"I had a steak in mind."

"I beg your pardon?"

The cool response made his lips curve. Yes, he definitely preferred her this way. "I haven't eaten."

"Sorry." Maggie began to straighten her sheet music. "I don't happen to have one handy."

"There's a place about ten miles out of town." He took her arm to draw her to her feet. "I have a feeling they'd treat a steak better than you would, anyway."

She pulled away, stood her ground and studied him. "We're going out to dinner?"

"That's right."

"Why?"

He took her arm again, so that he wouldn't ask himself the same question. "Because I'm hungry," Cliff said simply.

Maggie started to resist, though he didn't appear to notice. Then it struck her how much she wanted to get out, to get away, just for a little while. Sooner or later, she'd have to be alone in the house, but right then— No, right then, she didn't want to be alone anywhere.

He knew, understood, and whatever his approach, Cliff was offering her exactly what she needed.

Though their thoughts weren't particularly calm, neither of them spoke as they walked through the door together.

Chapter 5

Maggie set aside the next day to complete the title song for the movie score. She made a conscious effort to forget everything that had happened the day before. Everything. She wouldn't think of what had been buried and unearthed so close to her house, nor would she think of police or investigators or medical examiners.

In exactly the same way, she refused to think of Cliff, of the one wildly exciting kiss or of the oddly civilized dinner they'd shared. It was difficult to believe that she'd experienced both with the same man.

Today, she was Maggie Fitzgerald, writer of songs, creator of music. If she thought of only that, *was* only that, perhaps she could convince herself that everything that had happened yesterday had happened to someone else.

She knew there were men outside spreading seed, planting. There were shrubs going in, mulch being laid, more brush being cleared. If the landscape timbers she'd seen brought in that morning meant what she thought, construction was about to begin on her retaining wall.

None of that concerned her. The score demanded to be completed, and she'd complete it. The one form of discipline she understood perfectly was that a job had to be done no matter what went on around you. She'd seen her father direct a movie when his equipment had broken down and his actors had thrown tantrums. She'd known her mother to perform while running a fever. Much of her life might have been lived in a plush, make-believe world, but she'd learned responsibility.

The score came first today, and the title song would be written. Perhaps she'd even add some clever little aside to C.J. at the end of the tape before she mailed it off.

It certainly wouldn't do to mention what was going on in her side yard, Maggie thought as she meticulously copied notes onto staff paper. C.J. wouldn't be able to find enough antacids in L.A. to handle it for him. Poor man, she mused, he'd been worried about the roof caving in on her. In a totally unexpected way, it certainly had. If he knew there'd been policemen swarming over her land with plastic bags, he'd catch the next plane and drag her back to L.A.

She wondered if Cliff would've dragged her from the house the night before if she hadn't gone voluntarily. Fortunately, it hadn't been an issue, because Maggie thought him perfectly capable of it. Yet he'd been the ideal dinner companion. While she hadn't expected consideration from him, he'd been considerate. She hadn't expected subtle kindness, but it had been there. Finding both had made it difficult to remember she considered him an unlikable man.

They hadn't spoken of what had been found on her property that day, nor had there been any speculation on the whys and hows. They hadn't discussed his work or hers, but had simply talked.

Looking back, Maggie couldn't say precisely what they'd talked about, only that the mood had been easy. So easy, she had almost forgotten the passion they'd pulled from each other in the quiet afternoon sunlight. Almost forgotten. The memory had been there, quietly nagging at her throughout the evening. It had made her blood move a little faster. It had made her wonder if he'd felt it, too.

Maggie swore and erased the last five notes she'd copied down. C.J. wouldn't appreciate the fact that she was mixing her bass and tenor. She was doing exactly what she'd promised herself she wouldn't do, and as she'd known it would, the upheaval of yesterday was affecting her work. Calmly, she took deep breaths until her mind was clear again. The wisest course was to switch the recorder back on to play and start from the beginning. Then the knock on the front door disrupted her thoughts. Quiet country life. She asked herself where she'd ever heard that expression as she went to answer.

The gun on the man's hip made her stomach twist. The little badge pinned to the khaki shirt told her he was the sheriff. When she took her gaze up to his face, she was surprised by his looks. Blond, tanned, with blue eyes fanned by lines that spoke of humor or sun. For a moment, she had the insane notion that C.J. had sent him out from central casting.

"Miss Fitzgerald?"

She moistened her lips as she tried to be rational. C.J. worried too much for practical jokes. Besides, the gun looked very, very real. "Yes."

"I'm Sheriff Agee. Hope you don't mind me dropping by."

"No." She tried a polite smile, but found it strained. Guns and badges and official vehicles. Too many police in too short a time, Maggie told herself.

"If it wouldn't put you out too much, I'd like to come in and talk to you for a few minutes."

It did put her out. She wanted to say it did, then close the door on him and everything he wanted to talk about. *Coward,* she told herself, and stepped back to let him in. "I suppose you're here about what we found yesterday." Maggie put her shoulder to the door to shut it. "I don't know what I can tell you."

"I'm sure it was a nasty experience, Miss Fitzgerald, and one you'd just as soon forget." His voice held just the right trace of sympathy mixed with professionalism. She decided he knew his business. "I wouldn't feel I was doing my duty as sheriff or as a neighbor if I didn't give you whatever help I can."

Maggie looked at him again. This time her smile came a bit more easily. "I appreciate that. I can offer you coffee, if you don't mind the mess in the kitchen."

He smiled and looked so solid, so pleasant, Maggie almost forgot the gun at his hip. "I never turn down coffee."

"The kitchen's down here," she began, then laughed. "I don't have to tell you, do I? You'd know this house as well as I do."

He fell into step beside her. "Tell you the truth, I've been around the outside, hacking at the weeds now and again or hunting, but I've only been inside a handful of times. The Morgans moved out when Joyce was still a kid."

"Yes, she told me."

"Nobody's lived here for more'n ten years. Louella just let it go after the old man died." He glanced up at the cracked ceiling paint. "She held it in trust till Joyce inherited it at twenty-five. You probably heard I held Joyce off from selling."

"Well..." Uncertain how to respond, Maggie busied herself at the stove.

"Guess I thought we'd fix it up eventually, rent it out again." To her, he sounded like a man who knew about dreams but never found the time for them. "But a big old place like this needs a lot of time and money to put right. Joyce probably did the right thing, selling out."

"I'm glad she did." After switching on the coffeemaker, Maggie indicated a chair.

"With Bog handling repairs and Delaney working on the grounds, you picked the right men." When Maggie just looked at him, the sheriff grinned again. "Nothing travels fast in small towns but news."

"No, I suppose not."

"Look, what happened yesterday..." He paused, clearing his throat. "I know it must be rough on you. I gotta tell you, Joyce was worked up about it. A lot of people find something like that a stone's throw from their house would just pull up stakes and take off."

Maggie reached in the cabinets for cups. "I'm not going anywhere."

"Glad to hear it." He was silent a moment, watching her

pour the coffee. Her hands looked steady enough. "I under-stand Cliff was here yesterday, too."

"That's right. He was overseeing some of the work."

"And your dog dug up—"

"Yes." Maggie set both cups on the table before she sat down. "He's just a puppy. Right now he's asleep upstairs. Too much excitement."

The sheriff waved away her offer of cream, sipping the coffee black. "I didn't come to press you for details. The state police filled me in. I just wanted to let you know I was as close as the phone if you needed anything."

"I appreciate that. I'm not really familiar with the proce-dure, but I suppose I should've called you yesterday."

"I like to take care of my own territory," he said slowly, "but with something like this—" He shrugged. "Hell, I'd've had to call in the state, anyway." She watched his wedding ring gleam dully in the sunlight. Joyce had had a matching one, Maggie recalled. Plain and gold and solid. "Looks like you're redoing this floor."

Maggie looked down blankly. "Oh, yes, I took up the old linoleum. I've got to get to the sanding."

"You call George Cooper," the sheriff told her. "He's in the book. He'll get you an electric sander that'll take care of this in no time. Just tell him Stan Agee gave you his name."

"All right." She knew the conversation should've eased her mind, but her nerves were jumping again. "Thank you."

"Anything else you need, you just give us a call. Joyce'll want to have you over for dinner. She bakes the best ham in the county."

"That'd be nice."

"She can't get over someone like you moving here to Mor-ganville." He sipped at his coffee while Maggie's grew cold. While he leaned back in the chair, relaxed, she sat very straight with tension. "I don't keep up with music much, but Joyce knows all of your songs. She reads all those magazines, too, and now somebody's who's in them's living in her old house." He glanced idly at the back door. "You ought to speak to Bog about putting some dead bolts on."

She looked over at the screen, remembering the hinges needed oiling. "Dead bolts?"

With a laugh, he finished off his coffee. "That's what happens when you're sheriff. You're always thinking of security. We've got a nice, quiet community, Miss Fitzgerald. Wouldn't want you to think otherwise. But I'd feel better knowing you had some good solid locks on the doors, since you're back here alone." Rising, he tugged absently at his holster. "Thanks for the coffee. You just remember to call if you need anything."

"Yes, I'll remember."

"I'll go on out this way and let you get back to work. You call George Cooper, now."

"All right." Maggie walked to the back door with him. "Thank you, Sheriff."

For a moment she just stood there by the door, her head resting against the jamb. She hated knowing she could be so easily worked up. The sheriff had come to reassure her, to show her that the community she'd chosen to live in had a concerned, capable law enforcer. Now her nerves were raw from talking to so many police. So many police, Maggie mused, just as it had been when Jerry died. All the police, all the questions. She thought she'd been over it, but now everything was coming back again, much too clearly.

"Your husband drove off the road, Mrs. Browning. We haven't located his body yet, but we're doing everything we can. I'm sorry."

Yes, there'd been sympathy at first, Maggie remembered. She'd had sympathy from the police, from her friends, Jerry's friends. Then questions: "Had your husband been drinking when he left the house?" "Was he upset, angry?" "Were you fighting?"

God, hadn't it been enough that he'd been dead? Why had they picked and pulled at all the reasons? How many reasons could there be for a twenty-eight-year-old man to turn his car toward a cliff and drive over it?

Yes, he'd been drinking. He'd done a lot of drinking since his career had started to skid and hers had kept climbing. Yes, they'd been fighting, because neither of them had understood what had happened to the dreams they'd once had. She'd answered their questions; she'd suffered the press until she had thought she'd go mad.

Maggie squeezed her eyes tight. That was over, she told herself. She couldn't bring Jerry back and solve his problems now. He'd found his own solution. Turning from the door, she went back to the music room.

In her work she found the serenity and the discipline she needed. It had always been that way for her. She could escape into the music so that her emotions found their outlet. She could train her mind on timing and structure. Her drive had always been to release the emotions, hers by the creation of a song and the listener's by hearing it. If she was successful in that, she needed no other ambition.

Talent wasn't enough in itself, she knew. It hadn't been enough for Jerry. Talent had to be harnessed by discipline; discipline, guided by creativity. Maggie used all three now.

As time passed, she became absorbed in the music and in the goal she'd set. The title song had to be passionate, full of movement and sexuality, as the title itself suggested. When it was played, she wanted it to stir the senses, touch off needs, build longings.

No one had been signed to perform it yet, so she was free to use whatever style she chose. She wanted something bluesy, and in her mind she could hear the moan of a sax. Sexy, sultry. She wanted the quiet wail of brass and the smoky throb of bass. Late the night before, when she'd been restless, she'd written down a few phrases. Now she experimented with them, twining words to music.

Almost at once she knew she'd found the key. The key was unexplained passion, barely controlled. It was desire that promised to rip aside anything civilized. It was the fury and heat that a man and woman could bring to each other until both were senseless from it. She had the key now, Maggie thought as her pulse began to pound with the music, because she'd experienced it herself. Yesterday, on the rise, in the sun, with Cliff.

Madness. That was the word that streamed through her mind. Desire was madness. She closed her eyes as words and melody flowed through her. Hadn't she felt that madness, the sweetness and the ache of it, when his mouth had moved on hers? Hadn't she wanted to feel him against her, flesh to flesh? He'd made her think of dark nights, steamy, moonless nights when the air was so thick you'd feel it pulse on your skin. Then she hadn't thought at all, because desire was madness.

She let the words come, passionate, wanton promises that simmered over the heat of the music. Seductive, suggestive, they poured out of her own needs. Lovers' words, desperate words, were whispered out in her low, husky voice until the room was charged with them. No one who heard would be unmoved. That was her ambition.

When she was finished, Maggie was breathless and moved and exhilarated. She reached up to rewind the recorder for playback when, for the second time, she saw Cliff standing in the doorway.

Her hand froze, and her pulse, already fast, went racing. Had she called him with the song, she wondered frantically. Was the magic that strong? When he said nothing, she switched off the recorder and spoke with studied calm. "Is it an accepted habit in the country for people to walk into homes uninvited?"

"You don't seem to hear the door when you're working."

She acknowledged this with an inclination of her head. "That might mean I don't like to be disturbed when I'm working."

"It might." Disturbed. The word almost made him laugh. Perhaps he had disturbed her work, but that was nothing compared to what the song had done to him—to what watching her sing had done to him. It had taken every ounce of his control not to yank her from the piano stool and take her on the littered, dusty floor. He came closer, knowing before it reached him that her scent would be there to add to her allure.

"I lost quite a bit of time yesterday." Maggie swallowed whatever was trying to block her voice. Her body was still throbbing, still much too vulnerable from the passion she'd released. "I have a deadline on this score."

He glanced down at her hands. He wanted to feel them stroke over him with the same skill she'd used on the piano keys. Slowly, he took his gaze up her arms, over the curve of her shoulder to her face. For both of them, it was as if he'd touched her.

Her breath wasn't steady; her eyes weren't calm. That was as he wanted it now. No matter how often or how firmly he told himself to back off from her, Cliff knew he was reaching a point when it would be impossible. She wasn't for him—he could convince himself of that. But they had something that had to be freed and had to be tasted.

"From what I heard," he murmured, "you seem to be finished."

"That's for me to decide."

"Play it back." It was a challenge. He saw from her eyes that she knew it. A challenge could backfire on either of them. "The last song—I want to hear it again."

Dangerous. Maggie understood the danger. As she hesitated, his lips curved. It was enough. Without a word, she punched the rewind button. The song was a fantasy, she told herself as the tape hurried backward. It was a fantasy, just as the film was a fantasy. The song was for the characters in a story and had nothing, absolutely nothing, to do with her. Or with him. She flicked the recorder to play.

She'd listen objectively, Maggie decided as the music began to spill into the room. She'd listen as a musician, as a technician. That was what her job demanded. But she found, as her own voice began to tempt her, that she was listening as a woman. Rising, she walked to the window and faced out. When a hunger was this strong, she thought, distance could mean everything.

Wait for night when the air's hot and there's madness
I'll make your blood swim
Wait for night when passion rises like a flood in the heat
dance
Desire pours over the rim

He listened, as he had before, and felt his system respond to the music and the promises that low voice made. He wanted all that the song hinted at. All that, and more.

When Cliff crossed the room, he saw her tense. He thought he could feel the air snap, hissing with the heat the song had fanned. Before he reached her, Maggie turned. The sun at her back shot a nimbus around her. In contrast, her eyes were dark. Like night, he thought. Like her night music. The words she'd written filled the room around them. It seemed those words were enough.

He didn't speak, but circled the back of her neck with his hand. She didn't speak, but resisted, forcing her body to stiffen. There was anger in her eyes now, as much for herself as for him. She'd taken herself to this point by allowing her own needs and fantasies to clear the path. It wasn't madness she wanted, Maggie told herself as she drew back. It was stability. It wasn't the wild she sought, but serenity. He wouldn't offer those things.

His fingers only tightened as she pulled back. That surprised them both. He'd forgotten the rules of a civilized seduction, just as he'd forgotten he'd only come there to see how she was. The music, the words, made the vulnerability that had concerned him a thing of the past. Now he felt strength as his fingers pressed into her skin. He saw challenge in her stance, and a dare, mixed with the fury in her eyes. Cliff wanted nothing less from her.

He stepped closer. When she lifted a hand in protest, he took her wrist. The pulse throbbed under his hand as intensely as the music throbbed on the air. Their eyes met, clashed, passion against passion. In one move, he pulled her against him and took her mouth.

She saw the vivid colors and lights she'd once imagined. She tasted the flavor of urgent desire. As her arms pulled him yet closer to her, Maggie heard her own moan of shuddering pleasure. The world was suddenly fined down to an instant, and the instant went on and on.

Had she been waiting for this? This mindless, melting pleasure? Were these sensations, these emotions, what she'd poured out into music for so long? She could find no answers, only more needs.

He'd stopped thinking. In some small portion of his brain, Cliff knew he'd lost the capacity to reason. She made him feel, outrageously, so that there was no room for intellect. His hands sought her, skimming under her shirt to find the soft, heated skin he knew he'd dreamed about. She strained against him, offering more. Against his mouth, he felt her lips form his name. Something wild burst inside him.

He wasn't gentle, though as a lover he'd never been rough before. He was too desperate to touch to realize that he might bruise something more fragile than he. The kiss grew savage. He knew he'd never be able to draw enough from her to satisfy him. More, and still more, he wanted, though her mouth was as crazed and demanding as his.

He was driving her mad. No one had ever shown her a need so great. Hunger fueled hunger until she ached with it. She knew it could consume her, perhaps both of them. With a fire so hot, they could burn each other out and be left with nothing. The thought made her moan again, and cling. She wanted more. Yet she feared to take more and find herself empty.

"No." His lips at her throat were turning her knees to water. "No, this is crazy," she managed.

He lifted his head. His eyes were nearly black now, and his breathing was unsteady. For the first time, Maggie felt a twinge of fear. What did she know of this man? "You called it madness," he murmured. "You were right."

Yes, she'd been right, and it had been he she'd thought of when she'd written the words. Yet she told herself it was sanity she needed. "It's not what either of us should want."

"No." His control was threatening to snap completely. Deliberately, he ran a hand down her hair. "But it's already too far along to stop. I want you, Maggie, whether I should or not."

If he hadn't used her name— Until then she hadn't realized

that he could say her name and make her weak. As needs welled up again, she dropped her head on his chest. It was that artless, unplanned gesture that cleared his frenzied thoughts and tugged at something other than desire.

This was the kind of woman who could get inside a man. Once she did, he'd never be free of her. Knowing that, he fought back the overwhelming need to hold her close again. He wanted her, and he intended to have her. That didn't mean he'd get involved. They both knew that what had ignited between them would have to be consummated sooner or later. It was basic; it was simple. And they'd both walk away undamaged.

Whereas the arousal he'd felt hadn't worried him, the tenderness he was feeling now did. They'd better get things back on the right road. He took her by the shoulders and drew her back.

"We want each other." It sounded simple when he said it. Cliff was determined to believe it could be.

"Yes." She nodded, almost composed again. "I'm sure you've learned, as I have, that you can't have everything you want."

"True enough. But there's no reason for either of us not to have what we want this time."

"I can think of a few. The first is that I barely know you."

He frowned as he studied her face. "Does that matter to you?"

Maggie jerked away so quickly his hands fell to his sides. "So, you do believe everything you read." Her voice was brittle now, and her eyes were cold. "Los Angeles, land of sinning and sinners. I'm sorry to disappoint you, Cliff, but I haven't filled my life with nameless, faceless lovers. This fills my life." She slapped her hand down on the piano so that papers slid off onto the floor. "And since you read so much, since you *know* so much about me, you'll know that up to two years ago I was married. I had a husband, and as ridiculous as it sounds, was faithful for six years."

"My question didn't have anything to do with that." His voice was so mild in contrast to hers that she stiffened. Maggie had learned to trust him the least when he used that tone. "It was more personal, as in you and me."

"Then let's just say I have a rule of thumb not to hop into bed with men I don't know. You included."

He crossed the room, then laid his hand over hers on the piano. "Just how well do you have to know me?"

"Better, I think, than I ever will." She had to fight the urge to snatch her hand away. She'd made a fool of herself enough for one day. "I have another rule about steering clear of people who don't like who and what I am."

He looked down at the hand beneath his. It was pale, slender and strong. "Maybe I don't know who and what you are." His gaze lifted to lock on hers. "Maybe I intend to find out for myself."

"You'll have to have my cooperation for that, won't you?"

He lifted a brow, as if amused. "We'll see."

Her voice became only more icy. "I'd like you to leave. I've a lot of work to do."

"Tell me what you were thinking about when you wrote that song."

Something fluttered over her face so quickly he couldn't be certain if it was panic or passion. Either would have suited him.

"I said I want you to leave."

"I will—after you tell me what you were thinking of."

She kept her chin angled and her eyes level. "I was thinking of you."

He smiled. Taking her hand, he brought her palm to his lips. The unexpected gesture had thunderbolts echoing in her head. "Good," he murmured. "Think some more. I'll be back."

She closed her fingers over her palm as he walked away. He'd given her no choice but to do as he'd asked.

It was late, late into the night, when she woke. Groggy, Maggie thought it had been the dream that had disturbed her. She cursed Cliff and rolled onto her back. She didn't want to dream of him. She certainly didn't want to lie awake in the middle of the night, thinking of him.

Staring up at the ceiling, she listened to the quiet. At times like this, it struck her how alone she was. There were no servants sleeping downstairs, as there had been all her life. Her closest neighbor was perhaps a quarter of a mile away through the woods. No all-night clubs or drugstores, she mused. So far, she'd yet to even deal with getting an outside antenna for television. She was on her own, as she'd chosen.

Then why, Maggie wondered, did her bed suddenly seem so empty and the night so long? Rolling to her side, she struggled to shake off the mood and her thoughts of Cliff.

Overhead, a board creaked, but she paid no attention. Old houses made noises at night. Maggie had learned that quickly. Restless, she shifted in bed and lay watching the light of the waning moon.

She didn't want Cliff there, with her. Even allowing herself to think that she did was coming too close to dangerous ground. It was true her body had reacted to him, strongly. A woman couldn't always control the needs of her body, but she could control the direction of her thoughts. Firmly, she set her mind on the list of chores for the next day.

When the sound came again, she frowned, glancing automatically at the ceiling. The creaks and groans rarely disturbed her, but then, she'd always slept soundly in this house. Until Cliff Delaney, she thought, and determinedly shut her eyes. The sound of a door shutting quietly had them flying open again.

Before panic could register or reason overtake it, her heart was lodged in her throat, pounding. She was alone, and someone was in the house. All the nightmares that had ever plagued a woman alone in the dark loomed in her mind. Her fingers curled into the sheets as she lay stiffly, straining to hear.

Was that a footstep on the stairs, or was it all in her imagination? As terror flowed into her, she thought of the gully outside. She bit down on her lip to keep herself from making a sound. Very slowly, Maggie turned her head and made out the puppy sleeping at the foot of the bed. He didn't hear anything. She closed her eyes again and tried to even her breathing.

If the dog heard nothing that disturbed him, she reasoned, there was nothing to worry about. Just boards settling. Even as she tried to convince herself, Maggie heard a movement downstairs. A soft squeak, a gentle scrape. The kitchen door? she asked herself as the panic buzzed in her head. Fighting to move slowly and quietly, she reached for the phone beside the bed. As she held it to her ear, she heard the buzz that reminded her she'd left the kitchen extension off the hook earlier so as not to be disturbed. Her phone was as good as dead. Hysteria bubbled and was swallowed.

Think, she ordered herself. *Stay calm and think.* If she was alone, with no way to reach help, she had to rely on herself. How many times in the past few weeks had she stated that she could do just that?

She pressed a hand against her mouth so that the sound of her own breathing wouldn't disturb her concentrated listening. There was nothing now, no creaks, no soft steps on wood.

Careful to make no sound, she climbed out of bed and found the fireplace poker. Muscles tense, Maggie propped herself in the chair, facing the door. Gripping the poker in both hands, she prayed for morning.

Chapter 6

After a few days, Maggie had all but forgotten about the noises in her house. As early as the morning after the incident, she'd felt like a fool. She'd been awakened by the puppy licking her bare feet while she sat, stiff and sore from the night in the chair. The fireplace poker had lain across her lap like a medieval sword. The bright sunlight and birdsong had convinced her she'd imagined everything, then had magnified every small noise the way a child magnifies shadows in the dark. Perhaps she wasn't quite as acclimated to living alone as she'd thought. At least she could be grateful she'd left the downstairs extension off the hook. If she hadn't, everyone in town would know she was a nervous idiot.

If she had nerves, Maggie told herself, it was certainly understandable under the circumstances. People digging up skeletons beside her house, the local sheriff suggesting she lock her doors, and Cliff Delaney, Maggie added, keeping her up at night. The only good thing to come out of the entire week was the completed score. She imagined that C.J. would be pleased enough with the finished product not to nag her about coming back to L.A., at least for a little while.

Maggie decided the next constructive thing to do was to take the tape and sheet music she'd packaged to the post office and mail it off. Perhaps later she'd celebrate her first songs written in her new home.

She enjoyed the trip to town and took it leisurely. The narrow little roads were flanked by trees that would offer a blanket of shade in a few short weeks. Now the sun streamed through the tiny leaves to pour white onto the road. Here and there the woods were interrupted by fields, brown earth turned up. She could see farmers working with their tractors and wondered what was being planted. Corn, hay, wheat? She knew virtually nothing of that aspect of the home she'd chosen. Maggie thought it would be interesting to watch things grow until the summer or autumn harvest.

She saw cows with small calves nursing frantically. There was a woman carrying a steel bucket to what must have been a chicken coop. A dog raced along a fenced yard, barking furiously at Maggie's car.

Her panic of a few nights before seemed so ridiculous she refused to think of it.

She passed a few houses, some of them hardly more than cabins, others so obviously new and modern they offended the eyes. She found herself resenting the pristine homes on lots where trees had been cleared. Why hadn't they worked with what was there, instead of spoiling it? Then she laughed at herself. She was sounding too much like Cliff Delaney. People had a right to live where and how they chose, didn't they? But she couldn't deny that she preferred the old weathered brick or wood homes surrounded by trees.

As she drove into Morganville, she noted the homes were closer together. That was town life, she decided. There were sidewalks here, and a few cars parked along the curb. People kept their lawns trimmed. Maggie decided that from the look of it, there was quite a bit of pride and competition among the flower gardens. It reminded her to check her own petunias.

The post office was on the corner, a small redbrick building with a two-car parking lot. Beside it, separated by no more than a two-foot strip of grass, was the Morganville bank. Two men stood beside the outside mailbox, smoking and talking. They watched as Maggie pulled into the lot, as she stepped out of the car and as she walked toward the post office. Deciding to try her luck, she turned her head and flashed them a smile.

"Good morning."

"Morning," they said in unison. One of them pushed back his fishing cap. "Nice car."

"Thank you."

She walked inside, pleased that she had had what could pass for a conversation.

There was one woman behind the counter already engaged in what appeared to be casual gossip with a younger woman who toted a baby on her hip. "No telling how long they've been there," the postmistress stated, counting out stamps. "Nobody's lived out there since the Faradays, and that's been ten years last month. Old lady Faraday used to come in for a dollar's worth of stamps once a week, like clockwork. 'Course, they were cheaper then." She pushed the stamps across the counter. "That's five dollars' worth, Amy."

"Well, I think it's spooky." The young mother jiggled the baby on her hip while he busied himself gurgling at Maggie. Gathering up the stamps, she stuffed them into a bag on her other shoulder. "If I found a bunch of old bones in my yard, I'd have a for-sale sign up the next day." Hearing the words, Maggie felt some of her pleasure in the day fade. "Billy said some drifter probably fell in that gully and nobody ever knew about it."

"Could be. Guess the state police'll figure it out before long." The postmistress closed the conversation by turning to Maggie. "Help you?"

"Yes." Maggie stepped up to the counter. The young woman gave her one long, curious look before she took her baby outside. "I'd like to send this registered mail."

"Well, let's see what it weighs." The postmistress took the package and put it on the scale. "You want a return receipt?"

"Yes, please."

"Okay." She took the pencil from behind her ear to run the tip along a chart taped to the scale. "Cost you a bit more, but you'll know it got there. Let's see, it's going to zone—"

She broke off as she caught the return address on the corner of the package. Her gaze lifted, focusing sharply on Maggie, before she began to fill out the form. "You're the songwriter from California. Bought the Morgan place."

"That's right." Because she wasn't sure what to say after the conversation she'd overheard, Maggie left it at that.

"Nice music." The postmistress wrote in meticulously rounded letters. "Lot of that stuff they play I can't even understand. I got some of your mama's records. She was the best. Nobody else comes close."

Maggie's heart warmed, as it always did when someone spoke of her mother. "Yes, I think so, too."

"You sign this here." As she obeyed, Maggie felt the postmistress's eyes on her. It occurred to her that this woman saw every piece of correspondence that came to or from her. Though it was an odd feeling, she found it wasn't unpleasant. "Big old house, the Morgan place." The woman figured the total on a little white pad. "You settling in all right out there?"

"Bit by bit. There's a lot to be done."

"That's the way it is when you move into a place, 'specially one's been empty so long. Must be a lot different for you."

Maggie lifted her head. "Yes. I like it."

Perhaps it was the direct eyes or perhaps it was the simple phrasing, but the postmistress seemed to nod to herself. Maggie felt as though she'd found her first full acceptance. "Bog'll do well by you. So will young Delaney."

Maggie smiled to herself as she reached for her wallet. Small towns, she thought. No secrets.

"You had a shock the other day."

Because she'd been expecting some kind of comment, Maggie took it easily. "I wouldn't care to have another like it."

"Nope, guess nobody would. You just relax and enjoy that old house," the postmistress advised. "It was a showcase in its day. Louella always kept it fine. Let the police worry about the rest of it."

"That's what I'm trying to do." Maggie pocketed her change. "Thank you."

"We'll get this off for you right away. You have a nice day."

Maggie was definitely feeling pleased with herself when she walked back outside. She took a deep breath of soft spring air, smiled again at the two men still talking beside the mailbox, then turned toward her car. The smile faded when she saw Cliff leaning against the hood.

"Out early," he said easily.

He'd told her it was difficult to avoid anyone in a town that size. Maggie decided it was his accuracy that annoyed her. "Shouldn't you be working somewhere?"

He grinned and offered her the bottle of soda he held. "Actually, I just came off a job site and was on my way to another." When she made no move to take the soda, he lifted the bottle to his lips again and drank deeply. "You don't see too many of these in Morganville." He tapped a finger against the side of her Aston Martin.

She started to move around him to the driver's door. "If you'll excuse me," she said coolly, "I'm busy."

He stopped her effortlessly with a hand on her arm. Ignoring her glare, as well as the interested speculation of the two men a few yards away, Cliff studied her face. "You've shadows under your eyes. Haven't you been sleeping?"

"I've been sleeping just fine."

"No." He stopped her again, but this time he lifted a hand to her face, as well. Though she didn't seem to know it, every time her fragile side showed, he lost ground. "I thought you didn't believe in evasions."

"Look, I'm busy."

"You've let that business in the gully get to you."

"Well, what if I have?" Maggie exploded. "I'm human. It's a normal reaction."

"I didn't say it wasn't." The hand on her face tilted her chin back a bit farther. "You fire up easily these days. Is it just that business that has you tense, or is there something else?"

Maggie stopped trying to pull away and stood very still. Maybe he hadn't noticed the men watching them, or the postmistress in the window, but she had. "It's none of your business whether I'm tense or not. Now, if you'll stop making a scene, I have to go home and work."

"Do scenes bother you?" Amused now, he drew her closer. "I wouldn't have thought so, from the amount of times you've had your picture snapped."

"Cliff, cut it out." She put both hands on his chest. "For heaven's sake, we're standing on Main Street."

"Yeah. And we've just become the ten-o'clock bulletin."

A laugh escaped before she even knew it was going to happen. "You get a real kick out of that, don't you?"

"Well..." He took advantage of her slight relaxing and wrapped his arms around her. "Maybe. I've been meaning to talk to you."

A woman walked by with a letter in her hand. Maggie noticed that she took her time putting it into the box. "I think we could find a better place." At his snort of laughter, she narrowed her eyes. "I didn't mean that. Now, will you let go?"

"In a minute. Remember when we went out to dinner the other night?"

"Yes, I remember. Cliff—" She turned her head and saw that the two men were still there, still watching. Now the woman had joined them. "This really isn't funny."

"Thing is," he continued easily, "we have this custom around here. I take you out to dinner, then you reciprocate."

Out of patience, she wriggled against him and found that only made her blood pressure rise. "I haven't the time to go out to dinner right now. I'll get back to you in a few weeks."

"I'll take potluck."

"Potluck?" she repeated. "At *my* house?"

"Good idea."

"Wait a minute. I didn't say—"

"Unless you can't cook."

"Of course I can cook," she tossed back.

"Fine. Seven o'clock?"

She aimed her most deadly, most regal stare. "I'm hanging wallpaper tonight."

"You have to eat sometime." Before she could comment, he kissed her, briefly but firmly enough to make a point. "See you at seven," he said, then strolled over to his truck. "And Maggie," he added through the open window, "nothing fancy. I'm not fussy."

"You——" she began, but the roar of the truck's engine drowned her out. She was left standing alone, fuming, in the center of the parking lot. Knowing there were at least a dozen pair of eyes on her, Maggie kept her head high as she climbed into her own car.

She cursed Cliff repeatedly, and expertly, on the three-mile drive back to her house.

Maggie expected the men from Cliff's crew to be there when she returned. The discreet black car at the end of her driveway, however, was unexpected. She discovered as she pulled alongside it that she wasn't in the mood for visitors, not for neighbors calling to pay their respects or for curiosity-seekers. She wanted to be alone with the sander she'd rented from George Cooper.

As she stepped from the car, she spotted the rangy man with the salt-and-pepper hair crossing her front yard from the direction of the gully. And she recognized him.

"Miss Fitzgerald."

"Good morning. Lieutenant Reiker, isn't it?"

"Yes, ma'am."

What was the accepted etiquette, Maggie wondered, when you came home and found a homicide detective on your door-step? Maggie decided on the practical, marginally friendly approach. "Is there something I can do for you?"

"I'm going to have to ask for your cooperation, Miss Fitzgerald." The lieutenant kept his weight on one foot, as if his hips were troubling him. "I'm sure you'd like to get on with all your landscaping plans, but we want you to hold off on the pond a while longer."

"I see." She was afraid she did. "Can you tell me why?"

"We've received the medical examiner's preliminary report. We'll be investigating."

It might've been easier not to ask, not to know. Maggie wasn't certain she could live with herself if she took the coward's way out that she was obviously being offered. "Lieutenant, I'm not sure how much you're at liberty to tell me, but I do think I have a right to know certain things. This is my property."

"You won't be involved to any real extent, Miss Fitzgerald. This business goes back a long way."

"As long as my land's part of it, I'm involved." She caught herself worrying the strap of her bag, much as Joyce had done on her visit. She forced her hands to be still. "It'd be easier for me, Lieutenant, if I knew what was going on."

Reiker rubbed his hand over his face. The investigation was barely under way, and he already had a bad taste in his mouth. Maybe things that'd been dead and buried for ten years should just stay buried. Some things, he decided grimly. Yes, some things.

"The medical examiner determined that the remains belonged to a Caucasian male in his early fifties."

Maggie swallowed. That made it too real. Much too real. "How long—" she began, but had to swallow again. "How long had he been there?"

"The examiner puts it at about ten years."

"As long as the house has been empty," she murmured. She brought herself back, telling herself that it wasn't personal. Logically, practically, it had nothing to do with her. "I don't suppose they could determine how he died?"

"Shot," Reiker said flatly, and watched the horror fill her eyes. "Appears to've been a thirty-gauge shotgun, probably at close range."

"Good God." Murder. Yet hadn't she known it, sensed it almost from the first instant? Maggie stared out into the woods and watched two squirrels race up the trunk of a tree. How could it have happened here? "After so many years—" she began, but had to swallow yet again. "After so many years, wouldn't it be virtually impossible to identify the—him?"

"He was identified this morning." Reiker watched as she turned to him, pale, her eyes almost opaque. It gave him a bad feeling. He told himself it was because, like every other man in the country, he'd had a fantasy love affair with her mother twenty years before. He told himself it was because she was young enough to be his daughter. At times like this, he wished he'd chosen any other line of work.

"We found a ring, too, an old ring with a lot of fancy carving and three small diamond chips. An hour ago, Joyce Agee identified it as her father's. William Morgan was murdered and buried in that gully."

But that was wrong. Maggie dragged a hand through her hair and tried to think. No matter how bluntly, how practically, Reiker put it, it was wrong. "That can't be. I was told that William Morgan had an accident—something about a car accident."

"Ten years ago, his car went through the guardrail of the bridge crossing into West Virginia. His car was dragged out of the Potomac, but not his body. His body was never found...until a few days ago."

Through the rail, into the water, Maggie thought numbly. Like Jerry. They hadn't found Jerry's body, either, not for nearly a week. She'd lived through every kind of hell during that week. As she stood, staring straight ahead, she felt as though she were two people in two separate times. "What will you do now?"

"There'll be an official investigation. It has nothing to do with you, Miss Fitzgerald, other than we need for you to keep that section of your property clear. There'll be a team here this afternoon to start going over it again, just in case we missed something."

"All right. If you don't need anything else—"

"No, ma'am."

"I'll be inside."

As she walked across the lawn toward the house, she told herself that something that had happened ten years before had nothing to do with her. Ten years before, she'd been dealing with her own tragedy, the loss of her parents. Unable to resist, she looked back over her shoulder at the gully as she climbed the steps to the porch.

Joyce Agee's father, Maggie thought with a shudder. Joyce had sold her the house without knowing what would be discovered. She thought of the pretty, tense young woman who had been grateful for a simple kindness to her mother. Compelled, Maggie went to the pad scrawled with names and numbers beside the phone. Without hesitating, she called the number for Joyce Agee. The voice that answered was soft, hardly more than a whisper. Maggie felt a stab of sympathy.

"Mrs. Agee—Joyce, this is Maggie Fitzgerald."

"Oh... Yes, hello."

"I don't want to intrude." Now what? Maggie asked herself. She had no part of this, no link other than a plot of land that had lain neglected for a decade. "I just wanted you to know that I'm terribly sorry, and if there's anything I can do...I'd like to help."

"Thank you, there's nothing." Her voice hitched, then faltered. "It's been such a shock. We always thought—"

"Yes, I know. Please, don't think you have to talk to me or be polite. I only called because somehow—" She broke off, passing a hand over her hair. "I don't know. I feel as though I've set it all off."

"It's better to know the truth." Joyce's voice became suddenly calm. "It's always better to know. I worry about Mother."

"Is she all right?"

"I'm not— I'm not sure." Maggie sensed fatigue now, rather than tears. She understood that form of grief, as well. "She's here now. The doctor's with her."

"I won't keep you, then. Joyce, I understand we hardly know each other, but I would like to help. Please let me know if I can."

"I will. Thank you for calling."

Maggie replaced the receiver. That accomplished nothing, she reflected. It accomplished nothing, because she didn't know Joyce Agee. When you grieved, you needed someone you knew, the way she'd needed Jerry when her parents had been killed. Though she knew Joyce had a husband, Maggie thought of Cliff and the way he'd taken the woman's hands, the look of concern on his face, when he'd spoken to her. He'd be there for her, Maggie mused, and wished she knew what they meant to each other.

To give her excess energy an outlet, she switched on the rented sander.

The sun was low, the sky rosy with it, when Cliff drove toward the old Morgan property. His mind was full of questions. William Morgan murdered. He'd been shot, buried on his own property; then someone had covered the trail by sending his car into the river.

Cliff was close enough to the Morgans and to the people of Morganville to know that every other person in town might've wished William Morgan dead. He'd been a hard man, a cold man, with a genius for making money and enemies. But could someone who Cliff knew, someone he'd talk to on the street any day of the week, have actually murdered him?

In truth, he didn't give a damn about the old man, but he worried about Louella and Joyce—especially Joyce. He didn't like to see her the way she'd been that afternoon, so calm, so detached, with nerves snagged at the edge. She meant more to him than any other woman he'd known, yet there seemed to be no way to help her now. That was for Stan, Cliff thought, downshifting as he came to a corner.

God knew if the police would ever come up with anything viable. He didn't have much faith in that after ten years. That meant Joyce would have to live with knowing that her father had been murdered and that his murderer still walked free. Would she, Cliff mused, look at her neighbors and wonder?

Swearing, Cliff turned onto the lane that led to the Morgan place. There was someone else he worried about, he thought grimly, though he didn't have the excuse of a long, close friendship with this woman.

Damned if he wanted to worry about Maggie Fitzgerald. She was a woman from another place, who liked glittery parties and opening nights. Where he'd choose solitude, she'd choose crowds. She'd want champagne; he, cold beer. She'd prefer trips to Europe; he, a quiet ride down the river. She was the last person he needed to worry about.

She'd been married to a performer who'd flamed like a comet and who'd burned out just as quickly. Her escorts had been among the princes of the celebrity world. Tuxedos, silk scarves and diamond cufflinks, he thought derisively. What the hell was she doing in the middle of a mess like this? And what the hell, he asked himself, was she doing in his life?

He pulled up behind her car and stared broodingly at her house. Maybe with all that was going on she'd decide to go back west. He'd prefer it that way. Damned if he didn't want to believe he would. She had no business crashing into his thoughts the way she had lately. That music. He let out a long stream of curses as he remembered it. That night music. Cliff knew he wanted her the way he'd wanted no woman before. It was something he couldn't overcome. Something he could barely control.

So why was he here? Why had he pushed his way into a meeting she hadn't wanted? Because, he admitted, when he thought of the way it had been between them, he didn't want to overcome it. Tonight he didn't want control.

As he walked toward the front door, he reminded himself that he was dealing with a woman who was different from any he'd known. Approach with caution, he told himself, then knocked at the front door.

From the other side, Maggie gripped the knob with both hands and tugged. It took two tries before she opened the door, and by that time Killer was barking nonstop.

"You should have Bog take care of that," Cliff suggested. He bent down to ruffle the dog's fur. Killer flopped on his back, offering his belly.

"Yeah." She was glad to see him. Maggie told herself she would've been glad to see anyone, but when she looked at him, she knew it was a lie. All through the afternoon she'd waited. "I keep meaning to."

He saw tension in the way she stood, in the way one hand

still gripped the doorknob. Deliberately, he gave her a cocky smile. "So, what's for dinner?"

She let out a quick laugh as some of the nerves escaped. "Hamburgers."

"Hamburgers?"

"You did invite yourself," she reminded him. "And you did say not to fuss."

"So I did." He gave Killer a last scratch behind the ears, then rose.

"Well, since it's my first dinner party, I thought I'd stick with my speciality. It was either that or canned soup and cold sandwiches."

"If that's been your staple since you moved in, it's no wonder you're thin."

Frowning, Maggie glanced down at herself. "Do you realize you make a habit of criticizing?"

"I didn't say I didn't like thin women."

"That's not the point. You can come back and complain while I cook the hamburgers."

As they walked down the hall, Cliff noticed a few bare spots where she'd removed strips of wallpaper. Apparently she was serious about taking on the overwhelming job of redoing the house. When they passed the music room, he glanced in at her piano and wondered why. She was in the position of being able to hire a fleet of decorators and craftsmen. The job could be done in weeks, rather than the months, even years, it promised to take this way. The freshly sanded floor in the kitchen caught his eye.

"Nice job." Automatically, he crouched down to run his fingers over the floor's surface. The dog took this as an invitation to lick his face.

Maggie lifted a brow. "Well, thank you."

Catching the tone, he looked up at her. He couldn't deny that he'd been giving her a hard time from the outset. He had his reasons. The primary one as Cliff saw it now was her effect on him. "The question is," he said, rising again, "why you're doing it."

"The floor needed it." She turned to the counter to begin making patties.

"I meant why *you're* doing it."

"It's my house."

He wandered over to stand beside her. Again, he found himself watching her hands. "Did you sand your own floors in California?"

"No." Annoyed, she set the patties under the broiler. "How many can you eat?"

"One'll do. Why are you sanding floors and hanging wallpaper?"

"Because it's my house." Maggie grabbed a head of lettuce from the refrigerator and began to shred it for salad.

"It was your house in California, too."

"Not the way this is." She dropped the lettuce and faced him. Impatience, annoyance, frustration—the emotions were plainly on the surface for him to see. "Look, I don't expect you to understand. I don't *care* if you understand. This house is special. Even after everything that's happened, it's special."

No, he didn't understand, but he discovered he wanted to. "The police have contacted you, then."

"Yes." She began to shred lettuce with a vengeance. "That investigator, Lieutenant Reiker, was here this morning." Her fingers dug into the cold, wet leaves. "Damn it, Cliff, I feel gruesome. I called Joyce and felt like an idiot, an intruder. There was nothing I could say."

"Did you?" he murmured. Strange that Joyce hadn't said anything about it, he thought. Then again, Joyce had said very little to him. "There isn't anything for you to say." He put his hands on her shoulders and felt the tension ripple. "This is something Joyce and her mother and the police have to deal with. It's nothing to do with you."

"I tell myself that," she said quietly. "Intellectually, I know it's true, but—" She turned, because she needed someone. Because, she admitted, she needed him. "It happened right outside. I'm involved, connected, whether I want to be or not. A man was murdered a few yards from my house. He was killed in a spot where I'd planned to put a nice quiet pond, and now—''

"And now," Cliff said, interrupting, "it's ten years later."

"Why should that matter?" she demanded. "My parents were killed ten years ago— Time doesn't make any difference."

"That," he countered, less gently than he'd intended, "had everything to do with you."

With a sigh, she allowed herself the weakness of resting her head against him. "I know how Joyce is feeling now. Everywhere I look, something draws me into this."

The more Maggie talked of Joyce, the less Cliff thought of the quiet brunette, and the more he thought of Maggie. His fingers tangled in her hair. It wasn't desire he felt now, but an almost fierce, protective urge he'd never expected. Perhaps there was something he could do, he decided, drawing her away.

"You didn't know William Morgan."

"No, but—"

"I did. He was a cold, ruthless man who didn't believe in words like compassion or generosity." Deliberately, he set Maggie aside and tended to the meat under the broiler himself. "Half the town would've cheered ten years ago if it hadn't been for Louella. She loved the old man. Joyce loved him, too, but both of them feared him every bit as much. The police won't have an easy time proving who killed him, and the town won't care. I detested him myself, for a lot of reasons."

She didn't like knowing that he could speak of a man's murder so calmly, so coldly. But then, as she'd told him herself before, they really didn't understand each other. To keep her hands busy, Maggie went back to the salad. "Joyce?" she asked casually.

He glanced at her sharply, then leaned on the counter again. "Yeah, for one. Morgan believed in discipline. Old-fashioned discipline. Joyce was like my kid sister. When I caught Morgan going at her with a belt when she was sixteen, I threatened to kill him myself."

He said it so casually Maggie's blood froze. He saw the doubts and the questions in her eyes when she looked at him.

"And so," Cliff added, "as the stories go, did half the population of Morganville. No one grieved when they fished William Morgan's car out of the river."

"No one has the right to take a life," Maggie said in a shaky voice. "Not their own or anyone else's."

He remembered that they had fished her husband's car out of the water, too. He remembered that the final verdict had been suicide. "You'd be better off not making comparisons," he said roughly.

"They seem to make themselves."

"What happened to Jerry Browning was a tragic waste of a life and of a talent. Do you plan on taking the blame for that, too?"

"I never took the blame," Maggie said wearily.

"Did you love him?"

Her eyes were eloquent, but her voice was steady. "Not enough."

"Enough to be faithful to him for six years," Cliff countered.

She smiled as her own words came back to her. "Yes, enough for that. Still, there's more to love than loyalty, isn't there?"

His hand was gentle again when he touched her face. "You said you hadn't taken the blame."

"Responsibility and blame are different things."

"No." He shook his head. "There's no responsibility or blame this time, either. Don't you think it's the height of egotism to feel responsible for someone else's actions?"

She started to snap at him, but the words hit home. "Maybe. Maybe it is." It wasn't easy, but she shook off the mood and smiled. "I think the hamburgers are done. Let's eat."

Chapter 7

Maggie found the kitchen cozy with the smell of hot food and the patter of raindrops that had just begun to strike the windows. When she thought of it, she decided she'd never really experienced coziness before. Her parents had lived on a grand scale; huge, elegant rooms and huge, elegant parties, boisterous, eccentric friends. With her own home in Beverly Hills, Maggie had followed the same pattern. Extravagance might've been what she needed during that phase of her life, or it might've been a habit. She wasn't sure when it had begun to wear on her, any more than she was certain if she'd ever been as relaxed as she was at that moment, eating in her half-finished kitchen with a man she wasn't quite sure of.

He was strong, she mused. Perhaps she'd never allowed a strong man into her life. Her father had been strong, Maggie remembered. He'd been the type of man who could do and get precisely what he wanted simply because he wanted it. The strength hadn't been a physical one, but one of personality and will. But then, her mother had matched him with her own combination of grit and exuberance. Maggie had never seen a more perfect relationship than theirs.

Theirs had been an all-consuming, enduring love, with qualities of practicality, compassion and fire. They'd never competed, never envied each other's success. Support, she thought. Perhaps that had been the real key to the quality and lasting power of their relationship. Unquestioning mutual support. She hadn't found that in her own marriage, and she'd come to think her parents had been unique.

Something had happened to the balance in her relationship with Jerry. As he'd grown weaker, she'd grown stronger. Eventually, they'd come to a point where all the support had been on her side and all the need on his. Yet she'd stayed, because it had been impossible to forget that they'd been friends. Friends don't break promises.

She wondered, as she studied Cliff, what sort of friend he would be. And she wondered, though she tried not to, what he would be like as a lover.

"What're you thinking of?"

The question came so abruptly that Maggie almost overturned her glass. Quickly, she sorted out her thoughts and chose the least personal. She could hardly tell him what had been the last thing on her mind. "I was thinking," she began, picking up her wine again, "how cozy it is eating here in the kitchen. I'll probably demote the dining room to the last thing on my list."

"That's what you were thinking?" By the way he held her gaze, she knew he sensed there'd been other things.

"More or less." A woman who'd been interviewed and questioned all her life knew how to evade and dodge. Lifting the bottle, she filled Cliff's glass again. "The Bordeaux's another present from my agent. Or another bribe," she added.

"Bribe?"

"He wants me to give up this mad scheme of camping out in the wilderness and come back to civilization."

"He thinks he can persuade you with puppies and French wine?"

With a bubbling laugh, Maggie sipped. "If I weren't so attached to this place, either one might've worked."

"Is that what you are?" Cliff asked thoughtfully. "Attached?"

At the question, her eyes stopped laughing, and her soft,

wide mouth sobered. "In your business you should know that some things root quickly."

"Some do," he agreed. "And some that do can't acclimate to the new territory."

She tapped the side of her glass with a fingertip, wishing she understood why his doubts dug at her so deeply. "You don't have much faith in me, do you?"

"Maybe not." He shrugged as if to lighten a subject he wasn't so certain of any longer. "In any case, I'm finding it interesting to watch you make the adjustments."

She decided to go with his mood. "How'm I doing?"

"Better than I'd thought." He lifted his glass in a half toast. "But it's early yet."

She laughed, because arguing seemed like a waste of time. "Were you born cynical, Cliff, or did you take lessons?"

"Were you born an optimist?"

Both brows lifted to disappear under the fringe of sable bangs. *"Touché,"* Maggie said. No longer interested in the meal, she studied him, finding that while his face was very much to her liking, she still couldn't judge him by his eyes. Too much control, she thought. A person would only get inside his head if he or she was invited. "You know," she began slowly, "after I'd stopped being annoyed, I decided I was glad you were coming by this evening." Now she grinned. "I don't know when I might've opened the wine otherwise."

This time he grinned. "I annoy you?"

"I think you're well aware of that," Maggie returned dryly. "And that for your own personal reasons it pleases you to do so."

Cliff tasted the wine again. It was warm and rich, reminding him of her mouth. "Actually, I do."

He said it so easily that Maggie laughed again. "Is it just me, or is annoying people a hobby of yours?"

"Just you." Over the rim of his glass, he studied her. She'd pinned her hair up in a loose Gibson style that accentuated her delicate, old-fashioned features. She wore some dark contouring shadow that made her eyes seem even larger, but her mouth was naked. This was a woman, Cliff thought, who knew how to accentuate her own looks to the best advantage, subtly, so that a man would be caught before he analysed what was Maggie and what was illusion. "I like your reactions," Cliff continued after a moment. "You don't like to lose your temper."

"So you like to provoke me until I do."

"Yeah." He smiled again. "That about sizes it up."

"Why?" she demanded in a voice filled with exasperated amusement.

"I'm not immune to you," Cliff said, so quietly her fingers tightened on the stem of her glass. "I wouldn't like to think you were immune to me."

She sat for a moment, stirred and baffled. Before her emotions could rise any closer to the surface, she stood and began to clear the table. "No, I'm not. Would you like more wine or some coffee?"

His hands closed over hers on the dishes. Slowly, he rose, his gaze fixed on her face. Maggie felt as though the kitchen had shrunk in size. Like Alice in the rabbit hole, she thought confusedly, unsure whether to sample that tempting little bottle or not. The patter of rain outside seemed to grow to a roar.

"I want to make love with you."

She wasn't a child, Maggie told herself. She was an adult, and men had wanted her before. She'd resisted temptations before. But had any ever been quite so alluring? "We've already been through this."

His hands tightened on hers when she tried to turn away. "But we never resolved it."

No, she couldn't turn away, or run away, from a man like this, Maggie realized. She'd have to stand her ground. "I was sure we had. Perhaps coffee would be best, since you have to drive this evening and I have to work."

Cliff took the dishes and set them back on the table. With her hands empty, Maggie found herself at a loss. She folded her arms under her breasts, a habit Cliff had discovered she used whenever she was upset or disturbed. At the moment, he didn't care which she was, as long as she wasn't unmoved.

"We haven't resolved it," he repeated, and plucked a pin from her hair. "We haven't begun to resolve it."

Though her eyes remained steady, she backed up when he stepped closer. It made him feel as though he were stalking her, an odd and thrilling sensation. "I really thought I'd made myself clear," Maggie managed, in what sounded to her like a firm, dismissive tone.

"It's clear when I touch you." Cliff backed her up against the counter, then pulled another pin from her hair. "It's clear when you look at me like you're looking at me now."

Maggie's heart began to pound at the base of her throat. She was weakening; she felt it in the heaviness of her limbs, the lightness in her head. Desire was temptation, and temptation a seduction in itself. "I didn't say I didn't want you—"

"No, you didn't," Cliff interrupted. When he drew out the next pin, her hair fell heavily to her shoulders and lay there, dark and tousled. "I don't think lying comes easily to you."

How could she have been so relaxed a few moments before and so tense now? Every muscle in her body was taut in the effort to combat what seemed to be inevitable. "No, I don't lie." Her voice was lower, huskier. "I said I didn't know you. I said you didn't understand me."

Something flashed into him. Perhaps it was rage; perhaps it was need. "I don't give a damn how little we know each other or how little we understand each other. I know I want you." He gathered her hair in one hand. "I only have to touch you to know you want me."

Her eyes grew darker. Why did it always seem her desire was mixed with anger and, though she detested it, a certain weakness she couldn't control? "Can you really believe it's that simple?"

He had to. For the sake of his own survival, Cliff knew, he had to keep whatever was between them purely physical. They'd make love through the night until they were exhausted. In the morning, the need and the bond would be gone. He had to believe it. Otherwise... He didn't want to dwell on otherwise. "Why should it be complicated?" he countered.

The anger and the longing flowed through her. "Why indeed?" Maggie murmured.

The room had lost its cozy ambience. Now she felt she'd suffocate if she didn't escape it. Her eyes were stormy, his almost brutally calm, but she kept her gaze level on his while her thoughts raged. Why should she feel the need to rationalize, to romanticize? she asked herself. She wasn't an innocent young girl with misty dreams, but an adult, a widow, a professional woman who'd learned to live with reality. In reality, people took what they wanted, then dealt with the consequences. Now so would she.

"The bedroom's upstairs," she told him, and, brushing by him, walked out of the kitchen.

Disturbed, Cliff frowned after her. This was what he wanted, he thought. The lack of complications. Yet her abrupt acceptance had been so unexpected, so cool. No, he realized as he started after her, that wasn't what he wanted.

Maggie was at the base of the steps before he caught up with her. When she looked over her shoulder, he saw the fury in her eyes. The moment he took her arm, he felt the tension. This, he discovered, was what he wanted. He didn't want her cool, emotionless agreement or a careless acquiescence. He wanted to build that fury and tension until the passion that spawned them broke through. Before the night was over, he'd draw it all from her and purge himself, as well.

In silence, they climbed the stairs to the second floor.

The rain fell, strong and steady, against the windows and the newly seeded earth below. The sound made Maggie think of the subtle rhythmic percussion she'd imagined in the arrangement of the song she'd just completed. There was no moon to guide the way, so she moved from memory. Darkness was deep and without shadows. She didn't look when she entered the bedroom, but she knew Cliff was still beside her.

What now? she thought with sudden panic. What was she doing, bringing him here, to the single spot she considered purely private? He might learn more than she wanted before he left again, yet she might learn nothing more than she already knew. They wanted each other; it was unexplainable. It was undeniable.

As her nerves stretched tighter, Maggie was grateful for the dark. She didn't want him to see the doubts that would be clear on her face. As the need grew stronger, she knew she wouldn't have been able to conceal that, either. Darkness was better, she told herself, because it was anonymous. When he touched her, her body went rigid with a dozen conflicting emotions.

Feeling it, Cliff ran his hands over the slope of her shoulders, down to her lower back. He found he didn't want her to be too relaxed, to be too yielding. Not yet. He wanted to know she struggled against something deeper, something unnamed, even as he did.

"You don't want to give in to this," Cliff said quietly. "Or to me."

"No." Yet she felt the tremor, not fear but pleasure, course through her body when he slipped his hands under her thin wool sweater. "No, I don't."

"What choice is there?"

She could see his face through the gloom of darkness, close, very close, to hers. "Damn you," she whispered. "There's none at all."

He slid his hands up her naked back, through the neck opening of her sweater, until his fingers found her hair. "No, not for either of us."

His body was firm against hers. His voice, soft and low, was faintly edged with anger. She caught the scent of soap, sharp, unrepentantly male, that lingered on his skin. His face was mysterious, indistinct in the darkness. He might've been anyone. As Maggie felt the next fierce pull of desire, she almost wished he was.

"Make love with me," she demanded. A decision made quickly, freely, would leave no room for regrets. "Take me now. It's all either of us wants."

Was it? The question had barely formed in his mind when his mouth was on hers. Then there were no questions, just flame and flash and power. Understanding, if there had been any before, dimmed. Reason vanished. Sensation, and only sensation, ruled. While perhaps both of them had expected it, they were caught in a maelstrom in which neither of them had any control. Racked by it, they fell together onto the bed and let the fire rage.

He could find no gentleness to give her, but it seemed she neither demanded nor expected any. He wanted her naked but not vulnerable, soft but not yielding. If he had spoken the needs aloud, she could have been no more what he'd asked for. As she arched against him, her lips clung in a wild, urgent kiss that was only a prelude to passion. He pulled at her clothes, forgetting finesse, then caught his breath when, in an equal frenzy, she began to strip him.

Clothes were tossed aside as if they were meaningless. Her scent rose up from her skin, from her hair, clouding whatever logic he might have tried to regain. The mattress swayed and dipped as they rolled over it, mindless now of the rain, of the dark, of time and place.

Then they were naked, heated flesh to heated flesh. The desperation grew in each to have all there could be of the other. Whispered demands, labored breathing, moans and sighs of pleasure, drowned out the sound of falling rain. Her body was small and supple and surprisingly strong. All three aspects combined to drive him mad.

This was what it meant to be consumed. Maggie knew it as his hands skimmed over her, inciting thrill after thrill. She hungered, no, starved, for each new demand. Greedy for what pleasure he would give and what pleasure she would take, she allowed him whatever he wanted. She felt no shame, no hesitation, in tasting, in touching, in asking for more or in taking it.

If his body had been designed to her wish, it could have been no more perfect. She reveled in the leanness, the cords of muscle, the long, narrow bones that ran along his hips. Wherever, whenever, she touched, she could almost feel the blood throb under his skin.

She wanted to know he had no more control than she. She wanted to know they were both victims of their own combined power. The fuse that had been lit between them with a look was burning quickly. Desire was madness, and if the words she'd written were true, she'd cast aside her reason for it.

With a savageness they both craved, they came together, fighting to prolong an outrageous passion, greedy to capture that final flash of pleasure. She thought of whirlpools and high winds and the bellow of thunder. She felt the spin, the speed, and heard the roar. Then both her mind and body shuddered from the last violent surge.

Love? Maggie thought some dim time later, when her thoughts began to clear again. If this was making love, she'd been innocent all her life. Could something with so gentle a name have such a violent effect on the body? Hers was pulsing and throbbing as if she'd raced up one side of a mountain and fallen off the other. She'd written songs about love, songs about passion, yet she'd never fully understood her own words until now.

Until now, she thought, when the man who lay beside her had dared her to live her own fantasies. With him she'd found the answer to the dark, driving needs that gave the grit, or the wistfulness, to most of her music. She understood, but understanding opened the door to dozens of questions.

Maggie ran a hand up her own body, astonished at the lingering sense of power and of wonder. How long had she been waiting for this night to come? Perhaps it was possible for passion to lay dormant, unexplored, until it was triggered by a certain person at a certain time.

Maggie thought of the film her music would score. It had been that way for the female character. She'd been content with life, almost smug, until one day a man had entered it, a man she'd shared little common ground with, a man who'd ignited a spark that had changed everything. It hadn't mattered that the woman was intelligent, successful, independent. The man, merely by existing, had altered the scope and pattern of her life.

If the same thing was happening to her, there was still time to stop it before she, too, became so consumed by needs, so ruled by desire, that nothing would ever be the same again.

In the film, the relationship had spawned violence. Instinct told her that there was something between her and Cliff that could do the same. There was little moderation in either of them. It was extremes, she knew, that played havoc with human nature.

Maybe fate had brought her to this serene little plot of land with its undertones of violence. The same fate might have brought her to this taciturn, physical man who seemed connected with both the tranquillity and the danger. The question now was whether she was strong enough to deal with the consequences of each.

What, Maggie asked herself while she stared into the darkness, would happen next?

Because nothing was as he'd expected it, Cliff was silent. He'd wanted passion, but he'd never imagined the scope of it. He'd wanted what her song had whispered of, but the reality had been much more dramatic than any words or any melody. He'd been certain that once the tension between them had been released, once the lure had been accepted, the needs would lessen.

It was true his body was sated with a pleasure more intense than anything he'd known, but his mind— Cliff closed his eyes, wishing his mind would rest as easy. But it was too full of her. So full that he knew even a touch would set his body raging again. That kind of need was a shade too close to dependence for comfort. They had nothing to offer each other, he reminded himself, nothing but outrageous mutual desire.

And suddenly he remembered a line from her song. "Desire is madness."

If he could have stopped himself, he wouldn't have touched her again. He was already reaching for her.

"You're cold," he murmured, automatically drawing her against him to warm her.

"A bit." There was an awkwardness she didn't know how to alleviate and a need she didn't know how to explain.

"Here." He tugged the tangled spread over her, then pulled her close again. "Better?"

"Yes." Her body relaxed against his, even as her thoughts continued to race.

They lapsed into silence again, neither knowing quite how to deal with what had flared between them. Cliff listened to the rain beat against the window glass, adding to the sense of isolation. Even on a clear night, he knew, you would see no light from a neighboring house. "Are you having trouble staying out here alone?"

"Trouble?" Maggie hedged. She wanted to stay exactly as she was, wrapped close around him, warm and safe and untroubled. She didn't want to think now of staying in the big house alone, of sleeping alone.

"This place is more isolated than most around here." How soft she was, he thought. It brought him an odd sort of contentment to feel her hair lie against his shoulder. "A lot of people, even if they were raised here, would have trouble being this far back and alone, especially after everything that's happened."

No, she didn't want to talk about it. Maggie closed her eyes, reminding herself that she'd come here determined to take care of herself, to deal with whatever came. She drew a deep breath, but when she started to shift away, Cliff held her still.

"You are having trouble."

"No. No, not really." Her biggest problem at the moment was to keep her mind and body from wanting more of him. Opening her eyes again, she stared at the rain-drenched window. "I'll admit I've had a couple of restless nights since— well, since we started to dig the pond. It isn't easy knowing what happened in that gully ten years ago, and I have a very active imagination."

"Part of the job?" He turned toward her a bit more, so that her leg slid casually between his. Her skin was smooth as polished glass.

"I suppose." She laughed, but he thought he detected nerves in it. "One night I was certain I heard someone in the house."

He stopped stroking her hair, drawing her back far enough to see her eyes. "In the house?"

"Just my imagination," she said with a shrug. "Boards creaking in the attic, stealthy footsteps on the stairs, doors opening and closing. I worked myself up into quite a state."

He didn't like the sound of it, even in her dismissive tone of voice. "Don't you have a phone in this room?" Cliff demanded.

"Well, yes, but—"

"Why didn't you call the police?"

Maggie sighed and wished she'd never mentioned anything about it. He sounded like a cranky older brother scolding his scatterbrained sister. "Because I'd left the kitchen extension off the hook. I'd been trying to work that afternoon, and—" The word scatterbrained flowed back into her head. Embarrassed, she trailed off. "Anyway, it's better that I didn't call. I felt like an idiot in the morning in any case."

Imagination or not, Cliff reflected, she was still a woman alone, isolated, and everyone in a ten-mile radius knew it. "Are you locking your doors?"

"Cliff—"

"Maggie." He rolled until she was on her back and he was looking down at her. "Are you locking your doors?"

"I wasn't," she said, annoyed. "But after the sheriff came by, I—"

"Stan was here?"

A breath hissed out between her teeth. "Damn it, do you know how often you cut me off in the middle of a sentence?"

"Yes. When did Stan come by?"

"The day after the state police were here. He wanted to reassure me." She wasn't cold now, not with the way his body was pressed against hers. Desire began to stir again, not too quiet, not too slow. "He seems to know his job."

"He's been a good sheriff."

"But?" Maggie prompted, sensing more.

"Just a personal thing," Cliff murmured, shifting away again. Maggie felt the chill return immediately.

"Joyce," she said flatly, and started to rise. Cliff's arm came out to pin her down.

"You have a habit of saying little and implying a lot." His voice was cool now, his hold firm. "It's quite a talent."

"It seems we have little to say to each other."

"I don't have to explain myself to you."

She lay stiff and still. "I'm not asking you to."

"The hell you aren't." Angry, he sat up, drawing her with him so that the cover dropped away. Her skin was pale, her hair like a flood of night over her shoulders. Despite a strong will and a keen sense of privacy, he felt compelled to clarify. "Joyce's been like my sister. When she married Stan, I gave her away. I'm godfather to her oldest girl. It might be difficult for you to understand that kind of friendship."

It wasn't. It had been like that between herself and Jerry. The friendship had gradually deteriorated during marriage, because the marriage had been a mistake. "No, I understand it," Maggie said quietly. "I don't understand why you seem so concerned about her."

"That's my business."

"It certainly is."

He swore again. "Look, Joyce has been going through a difficult time. She never wanted to stay in Morganville. When she was a kid, she'd had ideas about going to the city and studying to be an actress."

"She wanted to act?"

"Pipe dreams, maybe." Cliff moved his shoulders. "Maybe not. She let them go when she married Stan, but she's never been happy staying in Morganville. One of the reasons she sold the house was so they'd have enough money to move. Stan won't budge."

"They could compromise."

"Stan doesn't understand how important it is to her to get away from here. She was eighteen when she married. Then she had three children over the next five years. She spent the first part of her life following her father's rules, the second caring for her children and her mother. A woman like you wouldn't understand that."

"I'm sick of that!" Maggie exploded, jerking away from him. "I'm sick to death of you putting me in some category. Pampered celebrity with no conception of how real people feel or live." Anger rocketed through her, so quick and powerful she never thought to repress it. "What kind of man are you, going to bed with a woman you haven't an ounce of respect for?"

Stunned by the sudden, passionate outburst, he watched her spring from the bed. "Wait a minute."

"No, I've made enough mistakes for one evening." She began to search for her clothes among those scattered on the floor. "You had your dinner and your sex," she said in a brittle tone. "Now get out."

Fury rose so that he had to fight it back. She was right, Cliff told himself. He'd come to take her to bed; that was all. Intimacy didn't always equal closeness. He wasn't interested in being close to her or in becoming involved with anything more than her body. Even as he thought it, the emptiness of it washed over him. The contentment he'd felt so briefly vanished. He could hear her unsteady breathing as she pulled on her sweater. Reaching for his clothes, he tried to concentrate on the sound of the rain instead.

"We're not finished, you and I," he murmured.

"Aren't we?" Enraged, aching, Maggie turned. She could feel the tears well in her eyes, but felt secure in the darkness. The sweater skimmed her thighs, leaving the length of her legs naked. She knew what he thought of her, and this time would give him the satisfaction of believing he was right. "We went to bed, and it was good for both of us," she said easily. "Not all one-night stands are as successful. You get a high rating as a lover, Cliff, if that helps your ego."

This time there was no controlling the temper that roared into him. Grabbing both her arms, he pulled her toward him. "Damn you, Maggie."

"Why?" she tossed back. "Because I said it first? Go home and curl up with your double standard, Cliff. I don't need it."

Everything she said hit home, and hit hard. If he stayed, he wasn't certain what he might do. Throttle her? It was tempting. Drag her back to bed and purge himself of the angry desire that pounded in him? More temptation. As he held her, he wasn't sure if it was he who was shaking or her, but he knew if he stayed, something volatile, perhaps irrevocable, would burst.

Dropping his hands, he walked from the room. "Lock your doors," he called out, and cursed her as he strode down the stairs.

Maggie wrapped her arms around herself and let the tears overflow. It was much too late for locks, she thought.

Chapter 8

For the next few days, Maggie worked like a Trojan. Her kitchen floor was sealed, making it her first fully and successfully completed project. She added three fresh strips of wallpaper to her bedroom, found a rug for the music room and cleaned the trim in the downstairs hall.

In the evenings, she worked at her piano until she was too tired to see the keys or hear her own music. She kept her phone off the hook. All in all, she decided, the life of a recluse had its advantages. She was productive, and no one interfered with the flow of her days. It became almost possible to believe that was what she wanted and no more.

Perhaps she was pushing herself. She might admit that, but she wouldn't admit she did so to prevent herself from thinking about her night with Cliff. That had been a mistake. It wasn't wise to dwell on mistakes.

She saw no one, spoke to no one, and told herself she was content to go on that way indefinitely.

But of course complete solitude lasts only so long. Maggie was painting the window trim in the music room when she heard the sound of an approaching car. She debated whether she might just ignore the caller until he or she went away again. As a beginning recluse, it was certainly her right. Then she recognized the old Lincoln. Setting the paint bucket on the drop cloth at her feet, Maggie went to the front door to meet Louella Morgan.

She looked even more frail this time, Maggie mused. Her skin seemed almost translucent against the tidy white hair. It was an odd, somewhat eerie combination of youth and age. As Maggie watched, Louella looked over toward the gully. For a moment she seemed like a statue, unmoving, unblinking, unbreathing. When Maggie saw her take a step toward the fenced-off section, she walked outside.

"Good morning, Mrs. Morgan."

Louella glanced up, her eyes focusing slowly. The hand she lifted to pat at her hair shook lightly. "I wanted to come."

"Of course." Maggie smiled and hoped she was doing the right thing. "Please come in. I was about to fix some coffee."

Louella walked up the sagging steps Maggie had yet to contact Bog about. "You've made some changes."

Unsure which route to take, she decided on light, cheerful chatter. "Yes, inside and out. The landscapers work faster than I do." Killer stood in the doorway, snarling and backing up. Maggie hushed him as they went inside.

"This wallpaper was here when we moved in," Louella murmured, looking around the hall. "I always meant to change it."

"Did you?" Maggie led her gently toward the living room as she spoke. "Perhaps you could give me some suggestions. I haven't quite made up my mind yet."

"Something warm," Louella said softly. "Something warm, with subtle color, so people would feel welcome. That's what I wanted."

"Yes, I'm sure that's just what it needs." She wanted to put her arm around the woman and tell her she understood. Perhaps it was kinder not to.

"A house like this should smell of lemon oil and flowers."

"It will," Maggie told her, wishing she could change the scent of dust and paint.

"I always felt it should be filled with children." She gazed around the room with the kind of misty concentration that made Maggie think she was seeing it as it had been more than twenty years before. "Children give a house its personality, you know, more than its decorating. They leave their mark on it."

"You have grandchildren, don't you?" Maggie steered her toward the sofa.

"Yes, Joyce's children. The baby's in school now. Time goes so quickly for the young. You've looked at the pictures?" Louella asked suddenly.

"The pictures?" Maggie's brow creased, then cleared. "Oh, yes, I've really only had a chance to glance at them. I've been a bit tied up." Remembering, she walked to the mantel and retrieved the envelope. "Your roses looked beautiful. I'm not sure I'd have that kind of talent."

Louella took the envelope and stared down at it. "Roses need love and discipline. Like children."

Maggie decided against another offer of coffee. Instead, she sat down beside Louella. "Perhaps if we looked at them together it would help."

"Old pictures." Louella opened the flap and drew them out. "There's so much to see in old pictures if you know where to look. Early spring," she murmured, looking down at the first snapshot. "You see, the hyacinths are blooming, and the daffodils."

Maggie studied the square, pristine black and white, but it was the man and small girl who caught her attention rather than the flowers. He was tall, broad in the chest, with a sharp-boned, lantern-jawed face. The suit he wore was severe and proper. Beside him, the little girl wore a frilly dress, ribboned at the waist with black strap shoes and a flowered bonnet.

It must've been Easter, Maggie concluded. The little girl smiled determinedly at the camera. Joyce would've been around four then, Maggie calculated, and perhaps a bit uncomfortable in the organdy and flounces. William Morgan didn't look cruel, she thought as she studied his set, unreadable face. He simply looked untouchable. She fought back a shudder and spoke lightly.

"I want to plant some bulbs myself. Things should be a little more settled by fall."

Louella said nothing as she turned over the next picture. This time Maggie was looking at a young Louella. The style of hair and dress told her the picture was more than twenty years old. The lopsided angle of the shot made her suspect that Joyce had taken it as a child.

"The roses," Louella murmured, running a finger over the picture where they grew in profusion. "Gone now, with no one to care for them."

"Do you have a garden now?"

"Joyce does." Louella set the picture aside and took up another. "I tend it now and then, but it isn't the same as having your own."

"No, it's not, but Joyce must be grateful for your help."

"She's never been easy in town," Louella said, half to herself. "Never easy. A pity she took after me rather than her father."

"She's lovely," Maggie told her, searching for something to say. "I hope to see more of her. Her husband mentioned that we have dinner."

"Stan's a good man. Solid. He's always loved her." The sad, elusive smile touched her lips. "He's been kind to me."

When she turned over the next picture, Maggie felt her stiffen. She saw the smile freeze rather than fade. Looking down, she saw William Morgan and a young, perhaps teen-aged Stan Agee. This more recent photo was in color, and the trees in the background were vibrant with fall. The two men were dressed in flannel shirts and caps, and each wore a drab-colored vest with what looked to Maggie like small weights around the hem. Each carried a shotgun.

Shells, not weights, Maggie realized as she looked at the vests again. They must've been hunting. And they stood, she noted, near the slope of the gully. Disturbed, she looked at the trees again, at the tapestry she wanted to see for herself.

"Joyce would've taken this," Louella murmured. "She hunted with her father. He taught her how to handle guns before she was twelve. It didn't matter that she hated them; she learned to please him. William looks pleased," Louella continued, though Maggie couldn't see it. "He liked to hunt this land. Now we know he died here. Here,'' she repeated, placing a palm over the picture. "Not three miles away, in the river. He never left his land. Somehow I think I always knew.''

"Mrs. Morgan." Maggie set the pictures aside and laid a hand on her arm. "I know this must be difficult for you; it must be like going through it all over again. I wish there was something I could do.''

Turning her head, Louella fixed Maggie with a long, unsmiling stare. "Put in your pond," she said flatly. "Plant your flowers. That's as it should be. The rest is over.''

When she started to rise, Maggie found herself more disturbed by the emotionless reply than she would've been with a bout of tears. "Your pictures," she began helplessly.

"Keep them." Louella walked to the doorway before she turned. "I've no need for them anymore.''

Should she have been depressed? Maggie wondered as she listened to the car drive away. Was her reaction normal empathy for another's tragedy, or was she allowing herself to become personally involved again? Over the last few days, she'd nearly convinced herself that the Morgan business had nothing to do with her. Now, after one brief contact, it was beginning again.

Yet it was more than a sense of involvement, Maggie admitted as she rubbed her arms to bring back warmth. There'd been something eerie in the way Louella had looked at the pictures. As if, Maggie reflected, she'd been putting the people in them to rest, though only one was dead.

Imagination again, she scolded herself. An overactive one. Yet hadn't there been something odd in the way Louella had studied that last snapshot? It had been as if she'd been searching for details, looking for something. With a frown, Maggie walked over and sifted through the pictures herself, stopping when she came to the color print.

There was William Morgan again, his hair a bit thinner, his eyes a bit sterner than they'd been in the Easter photo. Sheriff Agee stood beside him, hardly more than a boy, his build not quite filled out, his hair a little shaggy. He'd looked even more like a beachcomber in his youth, Maggie decided, though he held the gun as if he were very familiar with firearms. Looking at him, Maggie could easily see why Joyce had fallen for him hard enough to give up dreams of fame and fortune. He was young, handsome, with a trace of cocky sexuality around his mouth.

She could understand, too, why Joyce had feared and obeyed and struggled to please the man beside him. William Morgan looked straight at the camera, legs spread, the gun held in both hands. Cliff had described him as a hard, cold man. Maggie had no trouble believing him, but it didn't explain why Louella had been so disturbed by this one picture. Or why, Maggie added, she herself became uneasy when she looked at it.

Annoyed by her own susceptibility, she started to study the picture more closely when the rumble outside warned of another approaching vehicle.

When it rains it pours, she thought bad-temperedly. Tossing the picture carelessly on top of the others, she walked to the window. When Cliff's pickup came into view, the flare of excitement left her shaken. *Oh, no,* Maggie warned herself. *Not again. A woman who makes the same mistake twice deserves what she gets.* Determined, she picked up her brush and began to paint in long, hard strokes. Let him knock all he wanted, she thought with an angry toss of her head. She had work to do.

Minutes passed, but he didn't come to her door. Maggie continued to paint, telling herself it didn't matter to her what he was doing outside. When she tried to lean closer to the window to look through, paint smeared from the sill to her jeans. Swearing, she wiped at it and made it worse.

She didn't give a damn about Cliff Delaney, Maggie told herself. But she did care about having people wander around on her land. It was her right to go out and see what he was up to and order him away, she told herself as she set down her brush. If he were only checking on how her grass was growing, she fumed as she headed for the door, he should still have the courtesy to announce himself. By not announcing himself, he was denying her the satisfaction of ignoring him.

She yanked open the door but didn't, as she'd expected, see him bending over the little green sprouts that had begun to shoot up through the topsoil. Neither was he looking out over the plugs of phlox or the juniper shrubs on her front bank. Perhaps, Maggie thought with a frown, he'd gone around to check on the last project to be completed, the crown vetch on her eroding rear bank.

Annoyed that she hadn't thought of that in the first place, she started to turn back into the house when a movement near the gully caught her eye. For an instant, basic, primitive fear that slept in her awoke. She thought of ghouls and phantoms and legends of shades that never rest. In the next instant she recognized Cliff. As infuriated as she was embarrassed by her own reaction, she went to confront him.

As she drew closer, Maggie saw the willow, slender, small and tenderly green. Cliff was setting the ball of roots into a hole he'd dug out of the rocky soil with a pick and shovel. He stood perhaps six feet from the slope of the gully, his shirt tossed carelessly on the ground. She could see the muscles in his back ripple as he began to shovel dirt back into the hole. The twinge of her stomach told her that her reaction to him was no less powerful now than it had been before they'd made love.

Maggie straightened her shoulders and angled her chin. "What're you doing?"

Because he continued to shovel without breaking rhythm, she decided he'd known she was coming. "Planting a tree," Cliff said easily.

Her eyes narrowed dangerously. "I can see that. As far as I remember, I didn't order a willow from you."

"No." He knelt down to mound and smooth the dirt at the base of the tree. She watched his hands, knowing now what they could do on her body. It seemed he had the same talent with soil. "No charge."

Impatient with his nonanswers and with her own growing

arousal, she folded her arms. "Why are you planting a tree I didn't buy?"

Satisfied that the willow was secure, he rose. Leaning casually on the shovel, he studied her. No, he hadn't gotten her out of his system, Cliff decided. Seeing her again didn't relieve the knots of tension he'd been living with for days. Somehow he'd known it wouldn't, but he'd had to try. "Some people might call it a peace offering," he told her at length, then watched her mouth open and close again.

Maggie looked at the tree. It was so young, so fragile, but one day she would see it in full sweep, spreading over her pond, and— She stopped, realizing that it was the first time she'd thought of going through with the pond since the discovery. He must have known that, just as he'd known the willow might be enough to make her see the beauty and serenity again. Most of her anger had drained before she remembered to hold on to any of it.

"A peace offering," she repeated, running a finger down one delicate leaf. "Is that what you call it?"

Her voice had been cool, but he saw that her eyes had already started to warm. He wondered how many strong men she'd slain with that one look. "Maybe." He sliced the shovel into the ground where it stood, tilting slightly to the left. "Got anything cold in there to drink?"

It was an apology, Maggie decided, perhaps the only kind a man like him could give. It only took her five seconds to decide to accept it. "Maybe," she said in an equal tone, then turned to walk back toward the house. A smile curved her lips when he fell into step beside her. "Your men did an excellent job," she continued while they circled around toward the rear of the house. "I'm anxious to see how the stuff over the retaining wall's going to look."

"Crown vetch," Cliff supplied before he stopped to check the job, as she'd suspected he would. "You should see something come through in four or five more days. It'll spread fast enough to cover this bank before summer's over." He kept his hands in his back pockets as he studied the work his men had done and thought of the woman beside him. "You've been busy?"

Maggie lifted a brow. "I suppose so. The house needs a lot of attention."

"Seen the paper?"

"No," she said, puzzled. "Why?"

Cliff shrugged, then walked ahead to the screen door to open it. "There was a big story on finding William Morgan buried on his old land. Land," he continued when Maggie moved by him into the kitchen, "recently purchased by a celebrated songwriter."

She turned sharply. "They had my name?"

"Yeah, it was mentioned—several times."

"Damn," she whispered, and, forgetting he'd asked for a drink, she dropped into a chair. "I'd wanted to avoid that." Half hopefully, she glanced up. "The local paper?"

Helping himself, Cliff went to the refrigerator and searched out a soda. "Morganville doesn't have a paper. There were stories in the *Frederick Post* and the *Herald Mail.*" As he twisted off the top, he nodded toward the phone sitting off the hook. "If you hadn't done that, you'd have already answered a flood of calls from reporters." And from himself, Cliff thought silently. In the past twenty-four hours, he'd called her a dozen times. He'd vacillated between being frantic and furious every time he'd gotten a busy signal. What kind of woman left her phone off the hook for hours at a time? One who was independent of the outside world, he mused, or one who was hiding from it. Lifting the bottle, he drank. "That your escape route these days?"

In defense, Maggie rose and slammed the receiver back in place. "I don't need to escape from anything. You said yourself that this whole business doesn't have anything to do with me."

"So I did." He examined the liquid left in the bottle. "Maybe you were escaping from something else." He shifted his gaze until it locked on hers. "Were you hiding from me, Maggie?"

"Certainly not." She swept over to the sink and began to

scrub the paint splatters from her hands. "I told you, I've been busy."

"Too busy to answer the phone?"

"The phone's a distraction. If you want to start an argument, Cliff, you can just take your peace offering and—" The phone shrilled behind her so that she ended her suggestion with an oath. Before she could answer it herself, Cliff had picked up the phone.

"Yes?" He watched the fury spring into her eyes as he leaned on the counter. He'd missed that, he discovered, just as he'd missed the subtle sexiness of the scent she wore. "No, I'm sorry, Miss Fitzgerald isn't available for comment." He replaced the receiver while Maggie wiped her damp hands on her jeans.

"I can screen my own calls, thank you. When I want a liaison, I'll let you know."

He drank from the bottle again. "Just saving you some aggravation."

"I don't want you or anyone to save me aggravation," she fumed. "It's my aggravation, and I'll do whatever I want with it." He grinned, but before she could think of any retaliation, the phone rang again. "Don't you dare," she warned. Shoving him aside, she answered herself.

"Hello."

"Damn it, Maggie, you've been leaving the phone off the hook again."

She let out a huff of breath. A reporter might've been easier to deal with. "Hello, C.J. How are you?"

"I'll tell you how I am!"

Maggie drew the phone back from her ear and scowled at Cliff. "There's no need for you to hang around."

He took another long sip from the bottle before he settled back comfortably. "I don't mind."

"Maggie!" C.J.'s voice vibrated in her ear. "Who the hell are you talking to?"

"Nobody," she mumbled, deliberately turning her back on Cliff. "You were going to tell me how you were."

"For the past twenty-four hours I've been frantic trying to

get through to you. Maggie, it's irresponsible to leave your phone off the hook when people're trying to reach you.''

There was a bag of cookies on the counter. Maggie dug into it, then bit into one with a vengeance. ''Obviously I left it off the hook so I couldn't be reached.''

''If I hadn't gotten you this time, I was going to send a telegram, and I'm not even sure they deliver telegrams in that place. What the hell have you been doing?''

''I've been working,'' she said between her teeth. ''I can't work when the phone's ringing off the wall and people are forever coming by. I moved out here to be alone. I'm still waiting for that to happen.''

''That's a nice attitude,'' he tossed back. In Los Angeles, C.J. searched through his desk drawer for a roll of antacids. ''You've got people all over the country worried about you.''

''Damn it, people all over the country don't have to worry about me. I'm fine!''

''You sound fine.''

With an effort, Maggie controlled her precarious temper. When she lost it with C.J., she invariably lost the bout, as well. ''I'm sorry I snapped at you, C.J., but I'm tired of being criticized for doing what I want to do.''

''I'm not criticizing you,'' he grumbled over the peppermint-flavored pill. ''It's just natural concern. For God's sake, Maggie, who wouldn't be concerned after that business in the paper?''

She tensed and, without thinking, turned back to face Cliff. He was watching her intently, the neck of the bottle held loosely in his fingers. ''What business in the paper?''

''About that man's—ah, what was left of that man being dug up on your property. Good God, Maggie, I nearly had a heart attack when I read it. Then, not being able to reach you—''

''I'm sorry.'' She dragged a hand through her hair. ''I'm really sorry, C.J. I didn't think it would hit the papers, at least not out there.''

''So what I didn't know wouldn't hurt me?''

She smiled at the offended tone of voice. ''Yes, something

like that. I'd've called you with the details if I'd realized the
news would get that far."

"Get this far?" he retorted, unappeased. "Maggie, you
know that anything with your name in it's going to hit the
press on both sides of the Atlantic."

She began to rub one finger slowly up and down her right
temple. "And you know that was one of the reasons I wanted
to get out."

"Where you live isn't going to change that."

She sighed. "Apparently not."

"Besides, that doesn't have anything to do with what's happened now," C.J. argued. He pressed a hand to his nervous
stomach and wondered if a glass of Perrier would calm him.
Maybe scotch would be a better idea.

"I haven't seen the paper," Maggie began in an even tone,
"but I'm sure the whole thing was blown out of proportion."

"Blown out of proportion?" Again, she had to move the
receiver back from her ear. A few steps away, Cliff heard
C.J.'s voice clearly. "Did you or did you not stumble over a
pile of—of bones?"

She grimaced at the image. "Not exactly." She had to concentrate harder on keeping her voice calm. "Actually, it was
the dog that found them. The police came right out and took
over. I really haven't been involved." She saw Cliff lift a
brow at her final statement but made no comment.

"Maggie, it said that man had been murdered and buried
right there, only yards from your house."

"Ten years ago." She pressed her fingers more firmly
against her temple.

"Maggie, come home."

She closed her eyes, because his voice held the kind of plea
that was hard to resist. "C.J., I am home."

"Damn it, how am I supposed to sleep at night thinking of
you alone out in the middle of nowhere? For God's sake,
you're one of the most successful, wealthiest, most celebrated
women in the world, and you're living in Dogpatch."

"If I'm successful, wealthy and celebrated, I can live wherever I want." She struggled against temper again. However

he phrased it, whatever his tone, the concern was real. It was better to concentrate on that. "Besides, C.J., I have the vicious guard dog you sent me." She looked down to where Killer was sleeping peacefully at Cliff's feet. When she lifted her gaze, she found herself smiling into Cliff's face. "I couldn't be safer."

"If you hired a bodyguard—"

Now she laughed. "You're being an old woman again. The last thing I need's a bodyguard. I'm fine," she went on quickly before he could comment. "I've finished the score, I've a dozen ideas for new songs running around in my head, and I'm even considering another musical. Why don't you tell me how brilliant the score was?"

"You know it's brilliant," he mumbled. "It's probably the best thing you've done."

"More," she insisted. "Tell me more. My ego's starving."

He sighed, recognizing defeat. "When I played it for the producers, they were ecstatic. It was suggested that you come out and supervise the recording."

"Forget it." She began to pace to the sink and back again.

"Damn it, we'd come to you, but there's no studio in Hicksville."

"Morganville," she corrected mildly. "You don't need me for the recording."

"They want you to do the title song."

"What?" Surprised, she stopped her restless pacing.

"Now listen to me before you say no." C.J. straightened in his chair and put on his best negotiator's voice. "I realize you've always refused to perform or record, and I've never pressed you. But this is something I really think you should consider. Maggie, that song's dynamite, absolute dynamite, and nobody's going to be able to put into it what you did. After I played the tape, everyone in the room needed a cold shower."

Though she laughed, Maggie couldn't quite put the idea aside. "I can think of a half-dozen artists who could deliver that number, C.J. You don't need me."

"I can think of a dozen who could deliver it," he countered. "But not like you. The song needs you, Maggie. At least you could think about it."

She told herself she'd already refused him enough for one day. "Okay, I'll think about it."

"You let me know in a week."

"C.J.—"

"Okay, okay, two weeks."

"All right. And I'm sorry about the phone."

"You could at least get one of those hateful answering machines."

"Maybe. Take care of yourself, C.J."

"I always do. Just take your own advice."

"I always do. Bye." She hung up, heaving a long sigh. "I feel like I've just been taken to task by the school principal."

Cliff watched her pick up a folded dish towel, crumple it, then set it down again. "You know how to handle him."

"I've had plenty of practice."

"What's C.J. stand for?"

"Constant Jitters," she murmured, then shook her head. "No, to tell you the truth, I haven't any idea."

"Does he always give you a hard time?"

"I suppose." She picked up the dish towel again. "It seems the news hit the papers on the Coast. Then, when he couldn't reach me..." She trailed off, frowning out the window.

"You're tense."

She dropped the cloth over the edge of the sink. "No."

"Yes," Cliff corrected. "I can see it." Reaching out, he ran his hand down the side of her neck to the curve of her shoulder. "I can feel it."

The brush of his fingers made her skin hum. Slowly, she turned her head. "I don't want you to do that."

Deliberately, he took his other hand on a like journey, so that he could knead at the tension in both of her shoulders. Was it her nerves he sought to soothe or his own? "To touch you?" he said quietly. "It's difficult not to."

Knowing she was already weakening, Maggie lifted her hands to his wrists. "Put some effort into it," she advised as she tried to push him aside.

"I have for the past few days." His fingers pressed into her skin and released, pressed and released, in a rhythm that caused her bones to liquefy. "I decided it was a misdirection of energy when I could put the same effort into making love to you."

Her mind was starting to haze, her breath beginning to tremble. "We've nothing to give each other."

"We both know better than that." He lowered his head so that his lips could brush along the temple he'd seen her stroke while on the phone.

A sigh escaped before she stopped it. This wasn't what she wanted—it was everything she wanted. "Sex is—"

"A necessary and enjoyable part of life," Cliff finished before he moved his lips down to tease hers.

So this was seduction, Maggie thought as her mind began to float. This was arousal without will. She knew she wasn't resisting, but yielding, melting, submitting, just as she knew that when surrender was complete, her bridges would be in flames behind her.

"We'll only be two people sharing a bed," she murmured. "There's nothing else."

Whether it was a question or a statement, Cliff tried to believe it was true. If there was more, it wouldn't end, and he'd find himself tangled around a woman he barely understood for the rest of his life. If there were only needs, he could relinquish his control and race with them. If there was only desire, he could take whatever he wanted with no consequences. When she was softening and heating in his arms, what did he care for consequences?

"Let me feel you," he murmured against her lips. "I want your skin under my hands, smooth and hot, your heart pounding."

Anything, she thought dizzily. She'd give him anything, as long as he stayed close like this, as long as his mouth continued that dark, desperate, delirious seduction of her senses. He tugged her T-shirt over her head, then ran his hands down her sides, up again, so that the friction had her nearly mad for more. His shirt scraped against her taut nipples until his hands came between them to possess.

He could feel her heart beat now, and she could hear it pounding in her own head. Her thighs pressed against his with only two layers of thin, soft denim between. She could remember every slope and plane of his body, how it had felt warm and urgent and naked on hers.

He smelled of work and the outdoors, traces of sweat and turned earth. As the scent raced through her senses, she took her lips over his face and throat to draw in the taste.

Uncivilized, like the land that held them both. Alluring and not quite tamed, like the thick woods that surrounded them. If she thought at all, this is how she thought of the need that burned between them. There was danger in both, and pleasure and wonder. Throwing aside all reason, Maggie gave herself to it.

"Now," she demanded huskily. "I want you now."

With no sense of time or place, no hesitation, they lowered onto the floor. The struggle with clothes only added to the aura of desperation and unrelenting desire that sprang back whenever they touched. Warmth against warmth, they found each other.

When the phone shrilled on the wall beside them, neither heard. Whether it was by choice or the will of fate, there was nothing for either of them but each other.

A tremble, a moan, a rough caress, the scent and fury of passion; that was their world. Urgently and more urgently, they sought the taste and touch of each other, as if the hunger would never abate, as if neither would allow it to. The floor was hard and smooth beneath them. They rolled over it as if it were layered with feathers. Sunlight streamed in, falling over them. They explored all the secrets of the night.

Man for woman, woman for man—time had no place and place no meaning. Hot and open, his mouth found hers, and finding it, he burned with the need to possess her completely. His fingers dug into her hips as he shifted her on top of him so that her skin slid tantalizingly over his. He felt her throb, just as he felt the flood of passion beat against the weakened dam of his control. At the moment of joining, her body arched back in stunned pleasure. The pace was frenetic, leaving them both helpless and raging. On and on they drove each other, mercilessly, ruthlessly.

Through half-closed eyes, Cliff saw her shudder with the speed of the crest. Then he was swept up with her in the power of the ultimate heat dance.

Chapter 9

Had hours passed, or was his sense of time still distorted? Cliff tried to gauge the hour by the slant of the sun through the window, but couldn't be sure. He felt more than rested; he felt vitalized. Turning his head, he watched Maggie as she slept beside him. Though his own actions were vague in his mind, like a half dream that blurs on awakening, he could remember carrying her upstairs where they'd tumbled into bed. Wrapped around each other, they'd fallen into an exhausted sleep. Yes, that part was vague, he mused, but the rest—

On the kitchen floor. He ran a hand over his face, uncertain if he was pleased or astonished. Cliff discovered he was both.

He'd made love to her on the kitchen floor like a frantic teenager in the first spin of desire. By the time a man of experience had reached his thirties, he should be able to show a bit more control, use a bit more finesse. Yet he'd had neither both times he'd made love with her. Cliff wasn't certain that would change if he'd loved her a hundred times. She had some power over him that went deep and triggered frenzy rather than style. And yet... Because she was asleep and unaware, he brushed the hair from her cheek so that he could see more of her face. Looking at her was becoming a habit he wasn't sure could be easily broken. Yet when they lay quiet

like this, he was overwhelmed by a sense of protective tenderness. As far as he could remember, no other woman had
elicited either response from him before. The knowledge
wasn't comfortable.

Perhaps it was because when she slept as she did now, she
looked frail, defenseless, small. He'd never been able to resist
fragility. When she was in his arms, she was all fire and flare,
with a power so potent she seemed indestructible. Challenges
were something else he'd never been able to resist.

Just who was Maggie Fitzgerald? Cliff wondered while he
traced the shape of her mouth with a fingertip. He wouldn't
have said she was beautiful, yet her face had the power to
both stun and haunt a man. He hadn't expected her to be kind
or compassionate, yet he'd seen the qualities in her. He hadn't
expected her to be self-sufficient, yet she was proving to be
just that under an uneasy set of circumstances.

He frowned and unconsciously drew her closer. Maggie
murmured but slept on. Though he'd told her that she had no
connection with what had happened there ten years before,
Cliff didn't like knowing she was alone in the big, remote
house. Knowing Morganville was a quiet, settled town didn't
change that. Even the quiet, the settled, had undercurrents.
That had been made plain in the past two weeks.

Whoever had killed William Morgan had gone unpunished
for a decade. Whoever had murdered him had probably
walked the streets of town, chatted outside the bank, cheered
at Little League games. It wasn't a pleasant thought. Nor was
it pleasant to conclude that whoever had killed once might do
anything necessary to go on living a quiet, settled life in a
town where everyone knew your name and your history. It
might be a cliché about the murderer returning to the scene
of the crime, but—

She woke up alone, her mind still disoriented. Was it morning? she wondered groggily. When she shifted, lifting both
hands to push back her hair, she felt the sweet heaviness in
her limbs that came from lovemaking. Abruptly awake, she
looked over to see the bed beside her empty.

Perhaps she'd been dreaming. But when she felt the sheets

beside her, they were still warm, and when she turned her face into the pillow, his scent lingered on the case.

They'd made love on the kitchen floor, she remembered with a reaction that directly paralleled Cliff's. But she also remembered quite clearly the sensation of being carried up the stairs, gently, as if she'd been something precious. It was a warm memory, different from the erotic scene that had preceded it. A memory like that was something she could hold on to during some long, restless night in the future.

But he'd left, saying nothing.

Grow up, Maggie, she ordered herself. *Be sensible.* From the beginning she'd known this wasn't romance but desire. The only thing she'd gain from dwelling on the first was pain. Romance was for the impractical, the vulnerable, the naive. Hadn't she spent a great deal of her time training herself to be none of those things?

He didn't love her; she didn't love him. There was a twinge in her stomach at the second denial that had her biting her lip. No, she insisted, she didn't love him. She couldn't afford to.

He was a hard man, though she'd seen some softer aspects of him. He was intolerant, impatient and more often rude than not. A woman didn't need to fix her heart on a man like that. In any case, he'd made it clear that he wanted her body, and her body only. Twice she'd made the decision to give it to him, so she had no right to regrets, even though he'd left without a word.

Maggie flung her arms over her eyes and refused to acknowledge the growing fear that she'd already given him more than her body, without either of them being aware of it.

Then she heard it, the soft creak directly overhead. Slowly, she lowered her arms, then lay still. When it came the second time, the panic fluttered in her throat. She was awake, it was midafternoon, and the sounds came from the attic, not her imagination.

Though she was shaking, she climbed quietly out of bed. This time she wouldn't cower in her room while someone invaded her home. This time, she thought, moistening her lips as she slipped into her T-shirt, she'd find out who it was and what they wanted. Cold and clearheaded, she took the poker from the fireplace and slipped into the hallway.

The attic stairs were to her right. When she saw that the door at the top was open, fear sliced through her again. It hadn't been opened since she'd moved in. Shaking, determined, she took a firmer grip on the poker and started up the stairs.

At the doorway, she paused, hearing the faint whisper of movement inside. She pressed her lips together, swallowed, then stepped inside.

"Damn it, Maggie, you could hurt someone with that thing."

She jumped back, banging smartly into the doorjamb. "What are you doing up here?" she demanded as Cliff scowled back at her.

"Just checking. When's the last time you were up here?"

She expelled a breath, releasing pent-up tension. "Never. It's far down on my lists of priorities, so I haven't been up since I moved in."

He nodded, taking another glance around. "Someone has."

For the first time, she looked into the room. As she'd suspected, it contained little more than dust and cobwebs. It was high enough that Cliff could stand upright with an inch or so to spare, though at the sides it sloped down with the pitch of the roof. There was an old rocker that might prove interesting after refinishing, a sofa that was hopeless, two lamps without shades and a large upright traveling chest.

"It doesn't look as though anyone's been up here for years."

"More like a week," Cliff corrected. "Take a look at this."

He walked toward the chest, and making a face at the layer of dust on the floor, Maggie padded after him in her bare feet. "So?" she demanded. "Joyce mentioned that there were some things up here she didn't have any use for. I told her not to bother with them, that I'd take care of hauling them out when I was ready."

"I'd say someone already took something out." Cliff crouched in front of the dust-covered chest, then pointed.

Annoyed, stifling the urge to sneeze, Maggie bent toward the dust-covered chest. Then she saw it. Just near the lock, and very faint, was the imprint of a hand. "But—"

Cliff grabbed her wrist before she could touch the imprint herself. "I wouldn't."

"Someone was here," she murmured. "I didn't imagine it." Struggling for calm, she looked back at Cliff. "But what could anyone have wanted up here, in this thing?"

"Good question." He straightened, but kept her hand in his.

She wanted to play it light. "How about a good answer?"

"I think we might see what the sheriff thinks."

"You think it has something to do with—the other thing." Her voice was steady enough, but with his fingers on her wrist, he knew her pulse wasn't. "I think it's odd that everything's happening at once. Coincidences are curious things. You wouldn't be smart to let this one go."

"No." This wasn't ten years ago, she thought. This was now. "I'll call the sheriff."

"I'll do it."

She stopped in the doorway, bristling. "It's my house," she began.

"It certainly is," Cliff agreed mildly, then stunned her by running both hands up her naked thighs to her hips. "I don't mind looking at you half dressed, but it's bound to distract Stan."

"Very funny."

"No, very beautiful." While she stared, wide-eyed, he lowered his head and kissed her with the first true gentleness he'd shown. She didn't move or speak when he lifted his head again. Her eyes were still open. "I'll call the sheriff," Cliff said roughly. "You get some pants on."

Without waiting for her reply, he was heading down the steps, leaving her staring after him. Dazed, Maggie lifted a finger to trace over her own lips. That, she decided, had been as unexpected and as difficult to explain as anything else that had happened between them.

Utterly confused, Maggie left the poker tilted against the door and went back to her room. She couldn't have known he could kiss like that—tenderly, exquisitely. If she couldn't have known that, she couldn't have known that her heart could stop beating and her lungs could choke up. The totally different kiss had brought on a totally different reaction. This reaction, she knew, had left her without any form of defense.

A passionate, aggressive demand she could meet with passion and aggression of her own. There they were equal, and if she had no control, neither did he. Urgency would be met with urgency, fire with fire, but tenderness... What would she do if he kissed her like that again? And how long would she have to wait until he did? A woman could fall in love with a man who kissed like that.

Maggie caught herself. Some women, she corrected, hastily dragging on her jeans. Not her. She wasn't going to fall in love with Cliff Delaney. He wasn't for her. He wanted no more than—

Then she remembered that he hadn't left without a word. He hadn't left at all.

"Maggie!"

The voice from the bottom of the stairs had her jolting. "Yes." She answered him while she stared at her own astonished face in the mirror.

"Stan's on his way."

"All right, I'm coming down." In a minute, she added silently, in just a minute. Moving like someone who wasn't sure her legs could be trusted, she sat on the bed.

If she was falling in love with him, she'd better admit it now, while there was still time to do something about it. Was there still time? It washed over her that her time had been up days before, perhaps longer. Perhaps it had been up the moment he'd stepped out of his truck onto her land.

Now what? she asked herself. She'd let herself fall for a man she hardly knew, barely understood and wasn't altogether sure she liked a great deal of the time. He certainly didn't understand her and didn't appear to want to.

Yet he'd planted a willow in her yard. Perhaps he understood more than either of them realized. Of course, there couldn't be anything between them, really, she reminded herself hastily. They were poles apart in attitude. Still, for the moment, she had no choice but to follow her heart and hope that her mind would keep her somewhat level. As she rose, Maggie remembered fatalistically that it never had before.

It was quiet downstairs, but as soon as she came to the landing, she smelled coffee. She stood there a moment, wondering if she should be annoyed or pleased that Cliff was making himself at home. Unable to decide, she walked back to the kitchen.

"Want a cup?" Cliff asked as she entered. He was already leaning against the counter in his habitual position, drinking one of his own.

Maggie lifted a brow. "As a matter of fact, I would. Have any trouble finding what you needed?"

He ignored the sarcasm and reached in a cupboard for another cup. "Nope. You haven't eaten lunch."

"I generally don't." She came up behind him to pour the cup herself.

"I do," he said simply. With a naturalness Maggie thought bordered on arrogance, he opened the refrigerator and began to search through it.

"Just help yourself," she muttered before she scalded her tongue on the coffee.

"You'd better learn to stock up," Cliff told her when he found her supplies discouragingly slim. "It isn't unusual to get snowed in on a back road like this for a week at a time in the winter."

"I'll keep that in mind."

"You eat this stuff?" he asked, pushing aside a carton of yogurt.

"I happen to like it." She strode over, intending to slam the refrigerator door whether his hand was inside or not. Cliff outmaneuvered her by plucking out a single chicken leg, then stepping aside. "I'd just like to mention you're eating my dinner."

"Want a bite?" Apparently all amiability, he held out the drumstick. Maggie concentrated on keeping her lips from curving.

"No."

"Funny." Cliff took a bite and chewed thoughtfully. "Just coming into this kitchen seems to work up my appetite."

She shot him a look, well aware that she was now standing on the spot where they'd made wild love only a short time before. If he was trying to get a rise out of her, he was succeeding. If he was trying to distract her from what they'd discovered in the attic, he was succeeding, as well. Either way, Maggie found she couldn't resist him.

Deliberately, she took a step closer, running her hands slowly up his chest. It was time, she decided, to give him back a bit of his own. "Maybe I'm hungry, after all," she murmured, and, rising on her toes, brushed her lips teasingly over his.

Because he hadn't expected the move from her, Cliff did nothing. From the start he'd stalked and seduced. She was the lady, the crown princess with the wanton passion men often fantasize about on long, dark nights. Now, looking into those deep, velvet eyes, he thought her more of a witch. And who, he wondered as his blood began to swim, had been stalked and seduced?

She took his breath away—just the scent of her. She made his reason cloud—just the touch of her. When she looked at him like this, her eyes knowing, her lips parted and close, she was the only woman he wanted, the only woman he knew. At times like this, he wanted her with a fire that promised never to be banked. Quite suddenly and quite clearly, she terrified him.

"Maggie." He put a hand up to ward her off, to draw her closer; he'd never know, for the dog began to bark, and the rumble of a car laboring up the lane sounded from outside. Cliff dropped the hand to his side again. "That'll be Stan."

"Yes." She studied him with an open curiosity he wasn't ready to deal with.

"You'd better get the door."

"All right." She kept her gaze direct on his for another moment, rather pleased with the uncertainty she saw there. "You coming?"

"Yeah. In a minute." He waited until she had gone, then let out a long, uneasy breath. That had been too close for comfort. Too close to what, he wasn't certain, but he was certain he didn't like it. With his appetite strangely vanished, Cliff abandoned the drumstick and picked up his coffee. When he noticed his hands weren't quite steady, he downed the contents in one swallow.

Well, she certainly had enough to think about, Maggie mused as she walked down the hall. The sheriff was at her door again, Cliff was standing in her kitchen looking as though he'd been struck with a blunt instrument, and her own head was so light from a sense of—was it power?—that she didn't know what might happen next. Her move to the country certainly hadn't been quiet. She'd never been more stimulated in her life.

"Miss Fitzgerald."

"Sheriff." Maggie scooped Killer up in one arm to quiet his barking.

"Quite a beast you've got there," he commented. Then, holding out a hand, he allowed the puppy to sniff it cautiously. "Cliff gave me a call," he continued. "Said it looked like somebody's broken in the house."

"That seems to be the only explanation." Maggie stepped back to struggle with both the puppy and the door. "Although it doesn't make any sense to me. Apparently someone was in the attic last week."

"Last week?" Stan took care of the door himself, then rested his hand lightly, it seemed negligently, on the butt of his gun. "Why didn't you call before?"

Feeling foolish, Maggie set the dog down, giving him an impatient nudge on the rear that sent him scampering into the music room. "I woke up sometime in the middle of the night and heard noises. I admit it panicked me at the time, but in the morning..." She trailed off and shrugged. "In the morning, I thought it'd been my imagination, so I more or less forgot the whole thing."

Stan listened, and his nod was both understanding and prompting. "And now?"

"I happened to mention it to Cliff this...ah...this morning," she finished. "He was curious enough to go up into the attic."

"I see." Maggie had the feeling he saw everything, very well.

"Stan." Cliff strode down the hall from the kitchen, looking perfectly at ease. "Thanks for coming by."

I should've said that, Maggie thought, but before she could open her mouth again, the men were talking around her.

"Just part of the job," Stan stated. "You're doing quite a job yourself on the grounds outside."

"They're coming along."

Stan gave him a crooked, appealing smile. "You always liked a challenge."

They knew each other well enough that Cliff understood he referred to the woman, as well as her land. "Things would be dull without them," he said mildly.

"Heard you found something in the attic."

"Enough to make me think someone's been poking around."

"I'd better have a look."

"I'll show you," Maggie said flatly, then, sending Cliff a telling look, led the way upstairs.

When they came to the attic door, Stan glanced down at the poker still leaning against it. "Somebody could trip over that," he said mildly.

"I must have left it there before." Ignoring Cliff's grin, she picked it up and held it behind her back.

"Doesn't look like anyone's been up here in a long time," Stan commented as he brushed a cobweb away from his face.

"I haven't been up at all until today." Maggie shivered as a large black spider crawled sedately up the wall to her left.

She hadn't admitted to anyone yet that the prospect of insects and mice was primarily what had kept her out. "There's been so much else to do in the house." Deliberately, she stepped farther away from the wall.

"Not much up here." Stan rubbed a hand over his chin. "Joyce and I cleared out everything we were interested in when she first inherited. Louella already had everything she wanted. If you haven't been up," he continued, peering slowly around, "how do you know anything's missing?"

"I don't. It's this." For the second time, Maggie crossed the dusty floor to the trunk. This time it was she who crouched down and pointed.

Stan bent down over her, close enough that she could smell the simple department-store aftershave he wore. She recognized it and, on a wave of nostalgia, remembered her mother's driver had worn it, too. For no other reason, her sense of trust in him was confirmed.

"That's curious," Stan murmured, careful not to smear the faint outline. "Did you open this?"

"Neither of us touched it," Cliff said from behind.

With another nod, Stan pushed the button on the latch. His other hand came up automatically, stopping just short of gripping the trunk in the same spot the handprint was. "Looks like somebody did." Cautiously, he put his hand on the closure and tugged. "Locked." Sitting back on his haunches, he frowned at the trunk. "Damn if I can remember what's in this thing or if there's a key. Joyce might know—more'n likely Louella, though. Still..." With a shake of his head, he straightened. "It doesn't make much sense for somebody to break in and take something out of this old trunk, especially now that the house is occupied for the first time in ten years." He looked back at Maggie. "Are you sure nothing's missing from downstairs?"

"No—that is, I don't think so. Almost everything I shipped out's still in crates."

"Wouldn't hurt to take a good look."

"All right." She started back toward the second floor, realizing she hoped something would be missing. That would make sense; that would be tangible. The faint handprint on the trunk and no explanation gave her a queasy feeling in the stomach. A cut-and-dried burglary would only make her angry.

With the two men following, she went into her bedroom, checking her jewelry first. Everything was exactly as it should've been. In the next bedroom were crates that at a glance she could see were untouched and unopened.

"That's all up here. There's more crates downstairs and some paintings I haven't had reframed yet."

"Let's take a look."

Going with the sheriff's suggestion, Maggie headed for the stairs again.

"I don't like it," Cliff said to Stan in an undertone. "And you don't think she's going to find anything missing downstairs."

"Only thing that makes sense is a burglary, Cliff."

"A lot of things haven't made sense since we started digging in that gully."

Stan let out a quiet breath, watching Maggie's back as she descended the steps. "I know, and a lot of times there just aren't any answers."

"Are you going to tell Joyce about this?"

"I might have to." Stan stopped at the base of the stairs, running a hand over the back of his neck as though there were tension or weariness there. "She's a strong woman, Cliff. I guess I didn't know just how strong until this business started. I know when we first got married, a lot of people thought I did it for her inheritance."

"Not anyone who knew you."

Stan shrugged. "Anyway, that died down after a while, died completely after I became sheriff. I guess there were times I wondered whether Joyce ever thought it."

"She'd have told me if she had," Cliff said bluntly.

With a half laugh, Stan turned to him. "Yes, she would've at that."

Maggie came back into the hall from the music room.

"There's nothing missing in there, either. I've a few things in the living room, but—"

"Might as well be thorough," Stan told her, then strode across the hall and over the threshold. "Doing some painting?" he asked when he noticed the can and brush by the window.

"I'd planned to have all the trim done in here today," she said absently as she examined a few more packing boxes, "but then Mrs. Morgan stopped by, and—"

"Louella," Stan interrupted.

Because he was frowning, Maggie began to smooth it over. "Yes, though she didn't stay very long. We just looked over the pictures she'd lent me." Distracted, she picked up the stack. "Actually, I'd wanted to show these to you, Cliff. I wondered if you could tell me how to deal with getting some climbing roses like these started."

With the men flanking her, Maggie flipped through the snapshots.

"Louella certainly had a feel for making flowers look like they'd grown up on their own," she murmured. "I don't know if I have the talent for it."

"She always loved this place," Stan said. "She—" Then he stopped when she flipped to the color shot of himself and Morgan. "I'd forgotten about that one," he said after a moment. "Joyce took that the first day of deer season."

"Louella mentioned that she hunted."

"She did," Cliff put in, "because he wanted her to. Morgan had an—affection for guns."

And died by one, Maggie thought with a shudder. She turned the pictures facedown. "There's nothing missing anywhere that I can see, Sheriff."

He stared down at the pile of photos. "Well, then, I'll do a check of the doors and windows, see if anything's been forced."

"You can look," Maggie said with a sigh, "but I don't know if the doors were locked, and half the windows at least were open."

He gave her the look parents give children when they do

something foolish and expected. "I'll just poke around, anyway. Never can tell."

When he'd gone out, Maggie flopped down on the sofa and lapsed into silence. As if he had nothing better to do, Cliff wandered to the clock on the mantel and began to wind it. Killer came out from under the sofa and began to dance around his legs. The tension in the room was palpable. Maggie had almost given up wondering if it would ever be resolved.

Why would anyone break into an old trunk that had been neglected for years? Why had Cliff been in on the discovery, just as he'd been in on the discovery in the gully? What had caused her to fall in love with him, and would this need between them fade, as flash fires had a habit of doing? If she could understand any of it, perhaps the rest would fall into place and she'd know what move to make.

"There doesn't seem to be any forced entry," Stan said as he came back into the room. "I'll go into town, file a formal report and get to work on this, but—" He shook his head at Maggie. "I can't promise anything. I'd suggest you keep your doors locked and give some more thought to those dead bolts."

"I'll be staying here for the next few days," Cliff announced, throwing Stan and Maggie into surprised silence. He continued as if he hadn't noticed the reaction his statement caused. "Maggie won't be alone, though it would seem that whatever was wanted in the house was taken."

"Yeah." Stan scratched his nose, almost concealing a grin. "I'd better get back. I'll just let myself out."

Maggie didn't rouse herself to say goodbye but stared at Cliff until the front door shut. "Just what do you mean, you'll be staying here?"

"We'll have to do some grocery shopping first. I can't live off what you keep in that kitchen."

"Nobody asked you to live off it," she said, springing to her feet. "And nobody asked you to stay here. I don't understand why I have to keep reminding you whose house and land this is."

"Neither do I."

"You told *him*," she continued. "You just as good as announced to the town in general that you and I—"

"Are exactly what we are," Cliff finished easily. "You'd better get some shoes on, if we're going to town."

"I'm not going to town, and you're not staying here."

He moved so quickly she was caught completely off guard. His hands closed over both her arms. "I'm not letting you stay here alone until we know exactly what's going on."

"I've told you before I can take care of myself."

"Maybe you can, but we're not putting it to the test right now. I'm staying."

She gave him a long stare. The truth was, she didn't want to be alone. The truth was, she wanted him, perhaps too much for her own good. Yet he was the one insisting, she thought as her temper began to cool. Since he was insisting, perhaps he cared more than he was willing to admit. Maybe it was time she took a gamble on that.

"If I let you stay…" she began.

"I am staying."

"If I let you stay," she repeated coolly, "you have to cook dinner tonight."

He lifted a brow, and the grip on her arms relaxed slightly. "After sampling your cooking, you won't get any argument."

Refusing to be insulted, she nodded. "Fine. I'll get my shoes."

"Later." Before she knew what he was up to, they were tumbling back onto the sofa. "We've got all day."

Chapter 10

Maggie considered it ironic that she'd just begun to become accustomed to living alone and she was no longer living alone. Cliff made the transition unobtrusively. No fuss, no bother. A brisk, rather subtle sense of organization seemed to be a part of his makeup. She'd always respected organized people—from a safe distance.

He left early each morning, long before she considered it decent for a person to be out of his bed. He was quiet and efficient and never woke her. Occasionally, when she groped her way downstairs later in the morning, she'd find a scrawled note next to the coffeepot.

"Phone was off the hook again," it might say. Or "Milk's low. I'll pick some up."

Not exactly love letters, Maggie thought wryly. A man like Cliff wouldn't put his feelings down on paper the way she was compelled to. It was just one more area of opposition between them.

In any case, Maggie wasn't certain Cliff had any feelings about her other than impatience and an occasional bout of intolerance. Though there were times she suspected she touched some of his softer edges, he didn't act much like a lover. He brought her no flowers, but she remembered he'd planted a willow tree. He gave her no smooth, clever phrases, but she remembered the look she'd sometimes catch in his eyes. He wasn't a poet, he wasn't a romantic, but that look, that one long, intense look, said more than most women ever heard.

Perhaps, despite both of them, she was beginning to understand him. The more she understood, the more difficult it became to control a steadily growing love. He wasn't a man whose emotions could be pushed or channeled. She was a woman who, once her feelings were touched, ran with them in whatever direction they went.

Though she'd lived in the house outside of Morganville for only a month, Maggie understood a few basics of small-town life. Whatever she did became common knowledge almost before she'd done it. Whatever it was she did would draw a variety of opinions that would lead to a general consensus. There were a few key people whose opinion could sway that consensus. Cliff, she knew, was one of them, if he chose to bother. Stan Agee and the postmistress were others. It didn't take her long to discover that Bog was another whose opinion was sought and carefully weighed.

The politics in Morganville might've been on a smaller scale than those in southern California's music industry, but Maggie saw that they ran in the same vein. In L.A., however, she'd been second-generation royalty, while here she was an outsider. An outsider, she knew, whose notoriety could be either scorned or accepted. To date, she'd been fortunate, because most of the key people had decided to accept. Thinking of small, close-knit towns, she realized she'd taken a chance on that acceptance by living with Cliff.

Not living with, Maggie corrected as she spread adhesive on her newly stripped bathroom floor. He wasn't living with her; he was staying with her. There was a world of difference between the two. He hadn't moved in, bag and baggage, nor had there been any discussion about the length of his stay. It was, she decided, a bit like having a guest whom you didn't feel obligated to entertain or impress.

Unnecessarily, and through his own choice, he'd opted to be her bodyguard. And at night, when the sun went down and the woods were quiet, her body was his. He accepted her passion, her hungers and desires. Perhaps, just perhaps, one day he might accept her emotions, which raged just as hot, and just as high. First he had to come to understand her as she was beginning to understand him. Without that, and the respect that went with it, emotions and desires would wither and die.

Maggie set the next square of tile into position, then sat back to judge the outcome. The stone-patterned ceramic was rustic and would leave her free to use an infinite range of color combinations. She wanted nothing in her home to be too restricted or regimented, just as she wanted to do most of the changes and improvements herself.

Looking at the six pieces of tile she'd installed, Maggie nodded. She was becoming quite handy these days. Though her pansies had never recovered, they were her only major failure.

Pleased and ready for more, Maggie debated whether to mix up another batch of adhesive or to start the next wall of paper in her bedroom. There was only a wall and a half left to cover, she remembered; then it would be time to make a decision on curtains. Priscillas, cafés, Cape Cods... Nothing monumental, most people would say, she mused, but then she'd always left such things up to decorators before. Now, if something didn't work, she had no one to blame but herself.

With a laugh, she reached into the box of tiles again, swearing halfheartedly as she scraped her finger against a sharp edge. The price of being your own handyman, Maggie decided, going to the sink to run water over the cut. Maybe it was time to turn in the tiles for wallpaper and paste.

When the dog began to bark, she knew that either project would have to wait. Resigned, she turned off the tap just as the sound of a car reached her. Going to the tiny latticed window, she watched Lieutenant Reiker pull around the last curve.

Why was he back? she wondered, frowning. There couldn't possibly be any more information she could give him. When he didn't approach the house immediately, Maggie stayed where she was. He walked along the path of flagstone Cliff's crew had set just that week. When he reached the end, he didn't turn toward the porch, but looked out over the gully. Slowly, he drew out a cigarette, then lit it with a short wooden match. For several moments he just stood there, smoking and watching the dirt and rocks as if they had the answers he wanted. Then, before she could react, he turned and looked directly up at the window where she stood. Feeling like an idiot, she started down to meet him.

"Lieutenant." Maggie went cautiously down the porch steps and onto the sturdy new flagstone.

"Miss Fitzgerald." He flipped the cigarette stub into the tangle of brush near the gully. "Your place is coming along. Hard to believe what it looked like a few weeks ago."

"Thank you." He looked so harmless, so pleasant. She wondered if he carried a gun in a shoulder holster under his jacket.

"Noticed you planted a willow over there." But he looked at her, not at the gully. "It shouldn't be much longer before you can have your pond put in."

Like Reiker, Maggie didn't look toward the gully. "Does that mean the investigation's almost over?"

Reiker scratched along the side of his jaw. "I don't know if I'd say that. We're working on it."

She bit back a sigh. "Are you going to search the gully again?"

"I don't think it's going to come to that. We've been through it twice now. Thing is—" He stopped, shifting his weight to ease his hip. "I don't like loose ends. The more we look into this thing, the more we find. It's hard to tie up ends that've been dangling for ten years."

Was this a social call or an official one? she wondered, trying not to be annoyed. Maggie could remember how embarrassed he'd been when he'd asked for her autograph. At the moment, she didn't need a fan. "Lieutenant, is there something I can do?"

"I wondered if you'd had anyone coming around, someone you know, maybe someone you don't know."

"Coming around?"

"The murder happened here, Miss Fitzgerald, and the more we dig, the more people we find who had reason to kill Morgan. A lot of them still live in town."

She folded her arms under her breasts. "If you're trying to make me uneasy, Lieutenant, you're doing a good job."

"I don't want to do that, but I don't want to keep you in the dark, either." He hesitated, then decided to go with his instincts. "We discovered that Morgan withdrew twenty-five thousand cash from his bank account on the day he disappeared. His car was found, now his body's been found, but the money's never showed up."

"Twenty-five thousand," Maggie murmured. A tidy sum, even tidier ten years ago. "You're telling me you think the money was the motive for murder?"

"Money's always a motive for murder, and it's a loose end. We're checking a lot of people out, but it takes time. So far, nobody around here's ever flashed that kind of money." He started to reach for another cigarette, then apparently changed his mind. "I've got a couple of theories..."

She might've smiled if her head wasn't beginning to ache. "And you'd like to tell me?"

"Whoever killed Morgan was smart enough to cover his tracks. He might've been smart enough to know that coming up with twenty-five thousand dollars wouldn't go unnoticed in a town like this. Maybe, just maybe, he panicked and got rid of the money. Or maybe he hid it so he could wait a good long time, until any rumors about Morgan had died down; then it'd just be waiting for him."

"Ten years is a very long time, Lieutenant."

"Some people're more patient than others." He shrugged. "It's just a theory."

But it made her think. The attic, and the trunk and the handprint. "The other night—" she began, then stopped.

"Something happen the other night?" he prompted.

It was foolish not to tell him, to feel as though, if she did, she would be forging another link in the chain that bound her to everything that had happened. He was, after all, in charge of the investigation. "Well, it seems someone broke in and took something out of a trunk in the attic. I didn't realize it until days later; then I reported it to Sheriff Agee."

"That was the thing to do." His gaze lifted to the dormer window. "He come up with anything?"

"Not really. He did find a key. That is, his wife found one somewhere. He came back and opened the trunk, but it was empty."

"Would you mind if I had a look myself?"

She wanted it over, yet it seemed every step she took brought her in deeper. "No, I don't mind." Resigned, Maggie turned to lead him into the house. "It seems odd that anyone would hide money in the attic, then wait until someone was living here to claim it."

"You bought the place almost as soon as the sign was posted," Reiker reminded her.

"But it was nearly a month before I'd moved in."

"I heard Mrs. Agee kept quiet about the sale. Her husband didn't like the idea."

"You hear a lot of things, Lieutenant."

He gave her the slow, half-embarrassed smile he'd given her when he'd asked for her autograph. "I'm supposed to."

Maggie lapsed into silence until they reached the second floor. "The attic's up here. For what it's worth, I haven't found anything missing in the house."

"How'd they get in?" he asked as he began to climb the steeper, more narrow staircase.

"I don't know," she mumbled. "I wasn't locking my doors."

"But you are now?" He looked back over his shoulder.

"Yes, I'm locking them."

"Good." He went directly to the trunk, and, crouching down, studied the lock. The handprint had faded back to dust. "You say Mrs. Agee had the key?"

"Yes, or one of them. It seems this trunk belonged to the last people who rented the house, an old couple. The woman left it here after her husband died. Apparently there were at least two keys, but Joyce could only find one of them."

"Hmm." Reiker opened the now-unlocked trunk and peered inside, much as he'd peered into the gully. And it, Maggie thought, was just as empty now.

"Lieutenant, you don't really think there's a connection between this and—what you're investigating?"

"I don't like coincidences," he muttered, echoing Cliff's earlier statement. "You say the sheriff's looking into it?"

"Yes."

"I'll talk to him before I head back. Twenty-five thousand doesn't take up much room," he said. "It's a big trunk."

"I don't understand why anyone would let it sit in one for ten years."

"People're funny." He straightened, grunting a little with the effort. "Of course, it's just a theory. Another is that Morgan's mistress took the money and ran."

"His mistress?" Maggie repeated blankly.

"Alice Delaney," Reiker said easily. "She'd been having an affair with Morgan for five or six years. Funny how people'll talk once you get them started."

"Delaney?" Maggie said it quietly, hoping she'd heard incorrectly.

"That's right. As a matter of fact, it's her son who's been doing your landscaping. Coincidences," he repeated. "This business is full of them."

Somehow she managed to remain composed as they walked back downstairs. She spoke politely when he told her again how much he admired her music. Maybe she even smiled when she closed the door on him. When she was alone, Maggie felt her blood turn to ice, then drain.

Cliff's mother had been Morgan's mistress for years; then she'd disappeared, right after his death? Cliff would've known. Everyone would've known, she thought, and covered her face with both hands. What had she fallen into, and how would she ever get out again?

Maybe he was going crazy, but Cliff was beginning to think of the long, winding drive up the hill as going home. He'd never have believed he could consider the old Morgan place as home. Not with the way he'd always felt about William Morgan. Nor would he have believed the woman who lived there could make him think that way. It seemed a great deal was happening that he could neither stop nor harness. Yet staying with Maggie had been his own choice, just as leaving again would be—when he was ready. From time to time he found he needed to remind himself that he could and would leave again.

Yet when she laughed, the house was so warm. When she was angry, it was so full of life. When she sang—when she worked in the music room in the evening, Cliff thought. When the woods were quiet, before the moon had risen, she'd play. She'd sing snatches of words, sentences, phrases, as she composed. Long before she'd finished, he'd find himself in a frenzy of need. He wondered how she worked hour after hour, day after day, with such passion and feeling driving her.

It was the discipline, Cliff decided. He'd never expected her to be so disciplined about her music. The talent he'd admired all along, but in the few days he'd lived with her, he'd learned that she drove herself hard in the hours she worked.

A contrast, Cliff decided. It was an implausible contrast to the woman who jumped sporadically from one project to another in that big, dusty house. She left walls half papered, ceilings half painted. There were crates and boxes everywhere, most of which hadn't been touched. Rolls of supplies were tucked into every corner. He'd say her work on the house was precise, even creative, to the point where she'd leave off for something new.

She wasn't like anyone he'd ever known, and he realized that somewhere along the way he'd begun to understand her. It had been easier when he could dismiss her as a spoiled Hollywood princess who'd bought a dilapidated country house on a whim or for a publicity stunt. He knew now that she'd bought the house for no other reason than she'd loved it.

Perhaps she was a bit spoiled. She tended to give orders a little too casually. When she didn't get her own way, she tended to bristle or to freeze up. Cliff grinned. The same could be said of himself, he admitted.

To give Maggie her due, she hadn't run from the trouble or unpleasantness that had begun so shortly after she'd moved in. If he'd seen another woman stick as Maggie was sticking, he'd have said she'd indeed taken root. Cliff still had his doubts. Perhaps he fostered them purposely, because if he believed Maggie Fitzgerald would stay in Morganville, he might have to admit he wanted her to. He might have to admit that coming home every night to a woman who made him laugh and fume and throb wasn't something he'd give up without a fight.

He drove the last few yards, then stopped at the edge of the drive. The phlox was blooming on the bank. The new grass was like a green shadow over the soil. Maggie's petunias were a splash of color.

They'd both put part of themselves into the land already, he realized. Perhaps that in itself was a bond that would be difficult to break. Even as he stepped out of the truck, he wanted her, just the scent, just the softness of her. There was nothing he could do to change it.

There was no music. Cliff frowned as he slowly climbed the front steps. Maggie was always at her piano at this time of day. There were times he'd come back earlier and work on the yard himself. He'd know it was five o'clock, because that's when the music would begin, and it would continue for no less than an hour, often longer. Cliff looked at his watch: 5:35. Uneasy, he turned the knob on the front door.

Of course it was unlocked, he thought, annoyed. He'd left her a note that morning, telling her none of his crew would be there that day and to keep the doors locked. Senseless woman, he thought as he shoved the door open. Why couldn't she get it through her head that she was completely isolated here? Too many things had happened, and simply by living in this house, she was in the center of them.

Quiet. Too damn quiet, Cliff realized as annoyance began to fade into anxiety. The dog wasn't barking. The house had that echoing, empty feeling almost everyone can sense but can't explain. Though instinct told him no one was there, he began to go from room to room, calling her. Her name bounced back off the walls in his own voice and taunted him.

Where the hell was she, Cliff demanded as he took the stairs two at a time to check the second floor. He didn't like to admit that he could feel panic at nothing more than coming home to an empty house, but panic was exactly what he felt. Every day that week he'd been sure he'd had a crew, or part of one, working outside until he'd been there. He hadn't wanted her left alone, but because he couldn't explain it, Cliff had broken the ritual that day. And now he couldn't find her.

"Maggie!" Desperately, he searched the second floor, not even certain what he expected, or wanted, to find. He'd never experienced this kind of raw, basic fear. He only knew the house was empty and his woman was gone. A pair of her shoes sat carelessly in the center of the bedroom rug. A blouse was tossed negligently over a chair. The earrings he'd watched her take off the night before still lay on the dresser, beside a silver-backed brush engraved with her mother's initials. The room held her scent; it always did.

When he saw the new tiles in the bathroom, he tried to calm himself. In her helter-skelter way, she'd started a new project. But where in the hell—

Then, in the bowl of the sink, he saw something that stopped his heart. Against the pristine white porcelain were three drops of blood. He stared while panic swirled through him, making his head swim and his skin ice.

From somewhere outside, the dog began to bark frantically. Cliff was racing down the steps, not even aware that he called her name again and again.

He saw her as soon as he burst through the back door. She was coming slowly through the woods to the east, the dog dancing around her legs, leaping and nipping. She had her hands in the pockets, her head down. His mind took in every detail while the combination of fear and relief made his legs weak.

He ran toward her, seeing her head lift as he called her again. Then he had her in his arms, holding tight, closing his eyes and just feeling her, warm and whole and safe. He was too overcome with emotions that had no precedent to notice that she stood stiff and unyielding against him.

He buried his face in the soft luxury of her hair. ''Maggie, where've you been?''

This was the man she'd thought she was beginning to understand. This was the man she was beginning to love. Maggie stared straight ahead over his shoulder to the house beyond. ''I went for a walk.''

''Alone?'' he demanded irrationally, drawing her back. ''You went out alone?''

Everything turned cold; her skin, her manner, her eyes. ''It's my land, Cliff. Why shouldn't I go out alone?''

He caught himself before he could rage that she should've left him a note. What was happening to him? ''There was blood in the sink upstairs.''

''I cut my finger on a tile.''

He found he wanted to rage at her for that. She had no business hurting herself. ''You're usually playing this time of day,'' he managed.

''I'm not locked into a routine any more than I'm locked into the house. If you want a placid little female who's waiting to fall at your feet every night when you come home, you'd better look somewhere else.'' Leaving him staring, she broke away and went into the house.

Calmer but more confused, Cliff went into the kitchen to see her pouring a drink. Scotch, he noted, another first. With his mind a bit clearer, he could see that the normal color was absent from her cheeks and that her shoulders were stiff with tension. This time he didn't go to her or touch her.

''What's happened?''

Maggie swirled the scotch once before she swallowed.

She found it too warm, too strong, but she sipped again. ''I don't know what you mean.'' The kitchen was too small. Maggie took the glass and went out. The air was warm and soft. Outside there were no walls or ceilings to make her feel closed in. Circling around, she sat down on the spread of new grass. She'd sit here in the summer, Maggie thought, and read—Byron, if that was her mood. She'd let the sun fall over her, the silence cloak her, and read until she slept. Maggie continued to look out over the woods when Cliff's shadow slanted over her.

"Maggie, what's wrong with you?"

"I'm having a mood," she said flatly. "You'd expect spoiled celebrities to have moods, wouldn't you?"

Keeping his temper in check, Cliff sat down beside her, then took her chin in his hand. He waited until their eyes had met and held. "What?"

She'd known she'd have to tell him. It was the not knowing what there would be afterward that left her insides cold and knotted. "Lieutenant Reiker was here today," she began, but carefully removed Cliff's hand from her face.

Cliff swore, cursing himself for leaving her alone. "What'd he want?"

Maggie shrugged and sipped at the scotch again. "He's a man who doesn't like loose ends. Apparently he's been finding quite a number. It seems William Morgan withdrew twenty-five thousand dollars from his bank account on the day he was murdered."

"Twenty-five thousand?"

He sounded surprised, Maggie noted. Genuinely surprised. She recognized his expression, that thoughtful, narrow-eyed look that meant he was considering all the details and angles. How could she be certain of anything any longer? "The money was never recovered. One of Reiker's theories is that the murderer hid it away, patiently waiting until people forgot about Morgan."

Cliff's eyes sharpened. Automatically, he turned his head and looked back to the house. "Here?"

"Possibly."

"Ten years is a damn long time to sit on twenty-five thousand," Cliff muttered. Still, he didn't care for loose ends, either. "Did you tell him about the trunk in the attic?"

"Yes, he had a look at it himself."

He touched her shoulder, just his fingertips, so lightly that the touch offered whatever support she might want to take.

"It's upset you." Maggie said nothing, nor did she look at him. Tension began to work at his own muscles. "There's more."

"There's always more," Maggie said quietly. Now she looked at him; she had to. "He mentioned that Morgan's mistress had disappeared right after his death." She felt Cliff's fingers tighten convulsively on her shoulders just as she felt the waves of anger.

"She wasn't his mistress," Cliff said tightly. "My mother might've been foolish enough to fall in love with a man like Morgan, she might've been unwise enough to sleep with him, but she wasn't his mistress."

"Why didn't you tell me before?" Maggie demanded. "Why did you wait until I found out this way?"

"It doesn't have anything to do with you or with anything that's happened here." As restless anger swarmed in him, he rose.

"Coincidences," Maggie said quietly, but Cliff turned and stared down at her. "Weren't you the one who said not to trust coincidences?"

He was trapped, by an old anger and by a pair of depthless brown eyes. Again he found himself compelled to explain what he'd never explained before. "My mother was lonely and very vulnerable after my father died. Morgan knew how to exploit that. I was living outside of D.C. at the time. If I'd been here, I might've stopped it." Resentment welled up and was controlled. "He knew how to play on weaknesses, and he played on my mother's. When I found out they were lovers, I wanted to kill him."

He said it as he had once before, coldly, calmly. Maggie swallowed on a dry throat. "She was already too involved for anything to be done, deluded into believing she loved him, or maybe she did love him. Other intelligent women had. She'd been friends with Louella for years, but that didn't matter. When they found his car in the river, she snapped."

It was painful to look back on it, but Maggie's solemn brown eyes insisted he go on. "She didn't disappear; she came to me. She was frantic, and for the first time since she'd become involved with Morgan, she was seeing clearly again. Shame affects different people in different ways. My mother broke all ties with Morganville and everyone in it. She knew her relationship with Morgan wasn't a secret, and now that it was over, she simply couldn't face the gossip. She's still in D.C. She has a new life, and I don't want any of this to touch her.''

Was he always so unflaggingly protective of the women in his life? Maggie wondered. Joyce, his mother... Where, she wondered, did she fit in? "Cliff, I understand how you feel. My mother was one of the most precious people in my life, too. But there might not be anything you can do about it. They're reconstructing what happened ten years ago, and your mother has a part in it.''

But that wasn't all she was thinking, Cliff realized. Deliberately, he sat down beside her, struggling to keep the tension from his fingers when he took her shoulders. "You're wondering how much a part I might've had in it.''

"Don't." She tried to stand, but he held her still.

"It's possible that I could've shot Morgan to end a destructive relationship with my mother.''

"You hated him.''

"Yes.''

Her eyes never left his. They looked deep, searching. Logic might implicate him; his own temperament might make him suspect. Maggie stared into the smoky gray of his eyes and believed what she saw. "No," she murmured, drawing him against her. "No, I understand you too well.''

Her faith—the warm flood of it—almost destroyed him. "Do you?''

"Maybe too well," she murmured. "I was so frightened before.'' Closing her eyes, she drew in the familiar scent of him. He was real, he was solid, and for as long as she could hold on, he was hers. "Not now, not now that you're here.''

He could feel the pull, that slow, gentle pull. If he wasn't careful, he'd soon forget there was anything or anyone but her in his life. "Maggie.'' His fingers were already tangling in her hair. "You shouldn't trust without questions.''

"It isn't trust with questions," she countered. She wanted it to be only the two of them, with the rest of the world locked out, forgotten. Framing his face with her hands, she drew his mouth down to hers.

She'd expected fire, aggression, but his lips were soft and sweet. Confused, moved, Maggie drew back to stare at him. The eyes that had fascinated her from the beginning held hers as seconds edged closer to a minute. She was lost in the mists and the smoke. Without a word, he brought her close again.

With his eyes on hers, he lightly traced the shape of her face with a fingertip. This, he discovered, was the only face he ever needed to see again. Lightly, he outlined the shape of her lips. These, he knew, were the only lips he'd ever need to taste. With a gentleness he'd shown to no other lover, he lay her back. This was the only body he ever wanted to possess.

Tenderness left her stunned, weak. His mouth lingered on hers, but with such poignancy, the kiss alone made her bones liquefy. The grass was cool beneath her, the sun warm. Swimming in emotion, Maggie closed her eyes while his lips traveled over her face.

Had she ever been touched like this before? As if she were spun glass, his hands stroked over her. As if she were the rarest of delicacies, his lips tasted. And she was helplessly caught in the silken web that was more love than passion.

"Cliff—"

She might've told him, if his lips hadn't captured hers with a sweetness that left her speechless.

He'd never felt a stronger need to savor. It was as if each moment could be stretched to an hour as long as they lay together in the fragrant spring grass. The color in her cheeks was delicate; the sunlight combed through her hair. The look in her eyes was one no man could resist. It told him as clearly as words that she was his. He had only to claim. Knowing it, he moved only more slowly and touched only more reverently.

He undressed her while his kisses continued to hold her in the honey-steeped prison of pleasure. When she was naked, he watched how the sun streamed over her skin. Her large, expressive eyes were half closed. He could feel the pliancy in her body when, with a sigh, she lifted her hands to help him undress.

The raw, primitive need she so often incited in him didn't rise up. Instead, she drew out the softer emotions he normally held back. He wanted only to please her.

Gently, he lowered his mouth to her breast. He could hear her heartbeat increase in pace as he lingered there with his tongue tracing, his teeth nibbling. The tip grew taut, so that when he drew it into his mouth, he heard her breath shudder out, then catch again. Her hand moved through his hair as she lay back, saturated with sensation.

Her body was like a treasure to be discovered and admired before possession. Slowly, almost leisurely, he took those moist kisses and gentle hands over it, stopping, lingering, when he felt her shuddering response. He knew she was steeped in that dim, heavy world where passions hover around the edges and desires lick temptingly, like tiny tongues of fire. He wanted to keep her there for hours or days or years.

Her thighs were slender and long and pearl white. He loitered there, nudging them both closer, still closer to the edge. But not yet.

She'd forgotten where she was. Though her eyes were half opened, she saw nothing but mists and dreams. She could feel, oh, yes, she could feel each stroke of his hand, each warm brush of lips. She could hear gentle murmurs, quiet sighs that might've been his or hers. There was no reason to ever feel or hear anything else. She was slowly, inevitably, being drawn through the sweetness and into the heat. She began to crave it.

He felt the change in her body, heard the change in the breaths that whispered through her lips. He swept his mouth farther up her thigh, but still he didn't hurry. She would have all he had to give before they were finished.

She arched, catapulted with the sudden intensity of pleasure. She crested, quickly, shatteringly, with an abandonment of self and will. He wanted, demanded, just that. Before she could settle, he drove her up again until the madness once more began to creep into both of them. Cliff held it off, almost delirious with the knowledge that he could give her what a woman might only dream of. Her body was alive with sensations only he could bring to her. Her mind was swirling with thoughts of only him.

Knowing it, reveling in it, he slipped into her, taking her with a tenderness that lasted and lasted and lasted.

Chapter 11

Saturday morning, Maggie decided she could lie there, half dozing, until it was Saturday afternoon. She could feel the weight of Cliff's arm across her waist, his warm breath fluttering over her cheek. Without opening her eyes, she snuggled closer, wallowing in lazy contentment.

If she'd been certain he could be so gentle, she'd have fallen in love with him willingly. But how satisfying it was to have discovered it after her heart had already been lost. He had such emotion in him. Perhaps he was cautious with it, but she could love him much more comfortably knowing it was there and that now and again, unexpectedly, it would reach out to her.

No, it wasn't flowery phrases she wanted, but his stability. She didn't need smooth charm. When a woman found a man who was capable of such passion and such tenderness, she'd be a fool to want to change him in any way. Maggie Fitzgerald, she thought with a little satisfied smile, was no fool.

"What're you smiling at?"

Opening her eyes, Maggie looked directly into Cliff's. Because his were alert and direct, she knew he'd been awake for some time. She tried to blink away the mists and smiled again. "It feels good," she murmured, snuggling even closer. "You feel good."

He ran a hand down her back, over her hip and thigh. Yes, it felt very good. "Soft," Cliff said quietly. "So soft and smooth." He wondered how he'd gone so many years without being able to touch her like this, when she was lazy and warm and naked. He felt no tension in her, none of the subtle little signs he'd grown so adept at spotting. The need was very strong in him to keep that tension away for as long as he could. She'd walked unwittingly into a whirlpool, and somehow he was connected with it. If it was only for a day, he'd keep the problems at bay.

He rolled, pressed her down into the mattress so that she laughingly murmured a complaint. "Are you going to cook breakfast?" he demanded.

Maggie pillowed her head on her hands, giving him arrogant look for arrogant look. "You don't like my cooking."

"I've decided to be tolerant this morning."

"Have you?" She arched a brow. "How lucky for me."

"Floppy bacon and sloppy eggs," he told her before he nuzzled at her neck.

She shifted, enjoying the rough feel of the night's growth of beard against her skin. "What?"

"I don't like my bacon too crisp"—he nipped at the pulse in her throat—"or my eggs too set."

With a sigh, she closed her eyes again. She wanted to bottle this moment, so that she could take it out again whenever she needed to feel content. "I like my bacon so crisp it crumbles, and I don't like eggs at all."

"They're good for you." Cliff took his lips up her throat to nibble at her ear. "Might put some meat on you." As he spoke, he took his hand down her side again.

"Complaining?"

"Uh-uh." He ran his hand back up again so that his fingers brushed the side of her breast. "Though you do tend toward the lean side. We could build you up with three square meals a day and some exercise."

"No one needs three meals a day," she began, a bit huffily. "And as for exercise—"

"Do you like to dance?"

"Yes, but I—"

"Not much muscle," he noted, pinching her arm. "How's your endurance?"

She gave him a saucy look. "You should know."

With a laugh, he pressed his lips to hers. "You've a very quick, very wicked mind."

"Thanks."

"Now, about dancing. Ever been in a contre line?"

"A what?"

"I thought so." He shook his head, then shifted so that he could look down at her with pity. "Country dancing, Maggie."

Her brows drew together. "Square dancing?"

"No." It was time to educate the lady, Cliff decided, and drew her up to a sitting position. Her hair flowed wildly over her shoulders, the way he liked it best. "Square dancing's more formal, more regimented, than country dancing, but there'd be traditional music and a caller."

Maggie ran a finger up his chest. "Swing your partner and do-si-do?"

He felt the little thrill inch along his skin behind the trail of her finger. Did she know it? he wondered. From the smile that hovered on her lips, he thought she knew it very well. "Among other things."

Maggie linked her hands around his neck and let her head fall back so that she could look at him from beneath lowered lashes. "I'm sure it's all very fascinating, but I don't know why we're doing all this talking when you could be kissing me."

For an answer he gave her a long, searing kiss that left her breathless and pleased. "Because," he said, and nipped at her ear, "I want to go dancing with you."

Sighing, content, Maggie enjoyed the sensation of feeling her own blood begin to sizzle. "Where and when?"

"Tonight, in the park outside of town."

"Tonight?" She opened one eye. "Dancing in the park?"

"It's a tradition." He lay her back again but kept himself propped up so that his hand was free to skim her body. "A sort of Founder's Day celebration combined with rites of spring. Most of the town'll show. There'll be dancing till midnight, then a potluck supper. Then...'' He cupped her breast, enjoying the way her eyes clouded when he brushed a fingertip over the point. ''There's dancing till dawn for anybody who can handle it.''

''Until dawn?'' Intrigued and already hopelessly aroused, Maggie arched under him.

''You've danced until dawn before, I imagine.''

He'd said the wrong thing or used the wrong tone, because her body stiffened. No, he didn't want to bring up their differences now. At the moment, he could hardly recognize them. He lay down beside her and cradled her in his arms. ''We could watch the sun come up,'' he murmured. ''And the stars go out.''

She lay against him, but her mind was clear now. The doubts had returned. ''You never mentioned this to me before.''

''I didn't think you'd be much interested in country dances and potluck suppers. I guess I realized I was wrong.''

It was another kind of apology. Maggie accepted this one as easily as she had the first. Smiling again, she tilted her head back from him. ''Are you asking me for a date?''

He liked it when her eyes held that half-teasing, half-challenging light. ''Looks like it.''

''I'd love to.''

''Okay.'' Her hair fell onto his shoulder. Absently, he twisted the end around his finger. ''Now, about breakfast.''

She grinned, lowering her mouth to his. ''We'll have it for lunch.''

She didn't know what she expected, but Maggie looked forward to an evening out, away from the house, an evening to spend with other people. After her brief stab at being a hermit, she'd discovered that she could indeed take total command of her own needs. Being able to live with herself for long periods of time simply showed her that she didn't always have to in order to prove her independence. Perhaps she hadn't been attempting to learn anything with the dramatic change in her lifestyle, but she'd learned something, anyway. She could take charge of the tiny details of day-to-day living that she'd always left to others, but she didn't have to cut herself off from everyone to do it.

No, she didn't know what to expect, perhaps a quaint little festival with tinny music and warm lemonade in paper cups. She didn't expect to be particularly impressed. She certainly didn't expect to be enchanted.

The line of cars that sloped down the winding drive to the park surprised her. She'd thought most of the people in town would simply walk. When she mentioned it to Cliff, he shrugged and negotiated his pickup into a spot behind a yellow van.

"They come from all over the county, and from as far away as D.C. and Pennsylvania."

"Really?" Pursing her lips, she climbed out of the truck into the warm, clear night. There'd be a full moon, though the sun was just beginning to set. She wondered if the town had planned it that way or if it had been the luck of the draw. Either way, it was one more thing to be enjoyed. Putting her hand in Cliff's, she began to walk with him to the crest of the hill.

As she watched, the sun dropped lower behind the mountains in the west. She'd seen the sun sink gloriously into the sea and been awed by the colors and brilliance of sunsets in the snow-covered Alps. She'd seen the desert vibrate with color at dusk and cities glow with twilight. Somehow, watching the gold and mauve and pink layer over what were hardly more than foothills of a great range, she was more deeply affected. Perhaps it was foolish, perhaps it was fanciful, but she felt more a part of this place, more involved with the coming of this night, than she'd been of any other. On impulse, she threw her arms around Cliff's neck and held on.

Laughing, he put his hands on her hips. "What's this for?"

"It feels good," she said, echoing her morning words.

Then with a bang that shattered the silence, the music burst out. As a musician, she recognized each individual instrument—violin, banjo, guitar, piano. As a music lover, she felt her excitement leap.

"It's fabulous!" she exclaimed, drawing quickly away. "Absolutely fabulous. Hurry, I have to see." Maggie grabbed his hand and raced the rest of the way up the hill.

Her first impression was of a maze of people, two hundred, perhaps two hundred fifty, crowded together in a covered pavilion. Then she saw they were in lines, six, no, eight, she realized after a quick count. There would be a line of men facing a line of women, and so on, until they simply ran out of room. And they were moving to the music in a system that looked both confusing and fluid.

Some of the women wore skirts that flared out as they dipped, swayed or spun. Others wore jeans. Men's attire was no more consistent and no more formal than the women's. Some of the dancers wore sneakers, while a great many more wore what seemed to be old-fashioned black leather shoes that tied and had thick, sturdy heels. Still others wore what looked like oriental slippers with a single strap across the instep. It didn't seem to matter what was worn; everyone moved. Petticoats flashed, heels stomped, laughter rang out.

A woman stood at the edge of a small wooden stage in front of the band and belted out instructions in a singsong voice. Maggie might not have understood most of the words, but she understood rhythm. Already she was itching to try it herself.

"But how do they know what do to?" she shouted over the music. "How do they understand her?"

"It's a sequence of moves repeated over and over," Cliff told her. "Once you've got the sequence down, you don't even need a caller; she just adds to it."

A sequence, Maggie mused, and tried to find it. At first, she only saw bodies moving in what seemed a helter-skelter pattern, but gradually she began to see the repetition. Counting off the beats, she concentrated on one couple while trying to anticipate their next move. It pleased her to be able to find the sequence, just as the music pleased her ear and the swirling colors pleased her eye. She could smell a mixture of colognes, men's and women's, and the bursting fragrance of the spring flowers that skirted the pavilion.

As the sun dropped lower, the lights, strung overhead, spilled over the dancers. The floor vibrated under her feet so that she felt she was already dancing herself. With Cliff's arm around her, she watched with the undiluted fascination of discovering something new and exciting. She recognized the postmistress. The rather severe-looking middle-aged woman spun by like a dervish and flirted like a young girl.

Flirtation was part of it, Maggie realized as she began to watch faces instead of feet and bodies. Eye contact was essential, as were the saucy smiles she noted and the quick head tosses. It was, as perhaps dances had always been, a kind of mating ritual.

He hadn't thought she'd be fascinated or excited, but he recognized both in the look in her eyes. It gave Cliff overwhelming pleasure to know he'd brought that to her. Her face was flushed, her body already moving to the beat, and her eyes were everywhere at once. She didn't make him think of Maggie Fitzgerald, star baby and glamorous celebrity, but of Maggie, a woman he could hold on to and dance with until the sun came up again.

When the music ended, Maggie burst into raucous applause with everyone else. Laughing, her face tilted back, she grabbed his hand. "I have to try the next one, even if I make a fool of myself."

"Just listen to the calls and follow the music," he said simply as the lines began to form again. "They always run through the dance once before the music starts."

She listened as the next dance sequence was explained by the caller. Though she didn't understand half of the terms, Maggie tried to link them in her mind with the moves that followed. As Cliff guided her slowly through the paces, she enjoyed the sense of camaraderie and the lack of inhibitions around her.

Though she could sense that she was being watched with speculation and interest, Maggie refused to be perturbed by it. They had a right to look, she decided. It was, after all, the first time she'd participated in a town function, and she was being partnered by a man everyone seemed to know.

"This one's called, 'Whiskey before Breakfast,'" the caller sang out. "If you've tried it, you know it ain't as good for you as dancing." She stomped her foot on the platform, one, two, three, and the music began.

The dance was fast and exuberant. Maggie was caught up in the moves before she'd fully registered them. Right, then left; join left hands with your corner and turn around twice. Pass through. Balance and swing.

The first time Cliff whirled her around, she felt the rush of air on her face and laughed.

"Watch my eyes," he warned. "Or you'll be too dizzy to stand up."

"I like it!" she tossed back, then "Whoops!" as she botched the next step and hurried to keep up with the rest of the line.

She didn't mind the sense of confusion or the crowd. Shoulders bumped, feet tangled, her waist was gripped, and she was whirled around by people she'd never met. Teenagers danced with grandmothers. Ladies in frilly dresses swirled with men in jeans with bandannas in their back pockets. Obviously anyone was welcome to line up and dance, and Maggie had already noticed that women picked men for partners just as often as men picked women. It was a free-for-all, and the rules were loose.

As the steps became more repetitive and more instinctive, she began to enjoy it even more. Her steps became more animated, her concentration less focused on the moves and more on the music. She could see why it drove people to dance. Feet couldn't be still with that rhythm jangling out. She knew, as Cliff grabbed her and swung her in fast circles, that she could've danced for hours.

"That's it," he said, laughing as she clung to him.

"Already?" She was breathless but not nearly finished. "It was wonderful, but too short. When do we do another?"

"Any time you like."

"Now," she told him, sliding in as new lines formed.

She was fitting in as if she'd been to country dances in rural parks all her life. Perhaps he shouldn't have been surprised; she'd proved him wrong time and time again in his preconception of her. Yet in other ways, Cliff mused, he'd been right. She had an elegance that was too ingrained to be missed, whether she was scraping linoleum or lying in his arms. There was a polish that came from affluence and classy schools that set her apart from the other women around her. For days he'd been telling himself that it was that difference that attracted him as much as it put his back up. He couldn't explain the reason for either. He couldn't explain now, as he watched her begin the next dance as if she'd been moving to the call all her life, why she made him uneasy.

Circumstances, he told himself, and turned her back and around in a butterfly swing. The circumstances almost from the moment they'd met had been uneasy. That was bound to affect the way he felt when he looked at her—when he thought of her. And he thought of her, Cliff admitted, more often than he should; he looked at her less often than he wanted to.

Living with her for the past few days had given him the odd sensation of having something he hadn't known he'd wanted. There was something just a little too appealing about waking each morning with her warm beside him, about coming home to Maggie and her music. It would be wiser, much wiser, if he remembered those differences between them. No real common ground, he told himself again. But when she whirled into his arms, laughing, it was as though he'd been waiting for her.

The first few dances were a blur of color and sound and music. Maggie let herself go, realizing it had been weeks since she'd felt this free of tension and trouble. She'd danced in trendy clubs with celebrities, twirled in ballrooms with royalty, but she knew she'd never had as much simple fun as she was having now, following the caller and the fiddle.

As she turned to her next partner, she found her hand gripped by Stan Agee. Without his badge and gun, he might've been an attractive athlete in his prime. For a reason Maggie couldn't analyze, she tensed immediately on contact.

"Glad to see you're out, Miss Fitzgerald."

"Thank you." Determined not to give in to the mood, she smiled, lifting a hand to his shoulder as he began the spin. She caught his scent, the familiar department-store cologne, but it didn't soothe her.

"You catch on fast."

"It's wonderful. I can't believe I've missed it all my life." Out of the corner of her eye, she saw Cliff spinning with Joyce. The tension wouldn't dissolve.

"Save out a dance for me," he ordered before they whirled back to their original partners for the next step.

The moment he touched her, Cliff felt the rigidity of her muscles. "What's wrong?"

"Nothing." It was nothing, Maggie told herself, because she couldn't explain it. But now, as she swirled and turned from one pair of arms to another, it came to her that each time she danced with someone, she might be dancing with a murderer. How was she to know? It could be anyone—the real estate agent who'd sold her the house, the butcher who'd recommended the pork chops only the day before, the post-mistress, the bank teller. How was she to know?

Maggie's mind began to whirl. For an instant, her eyes locked on Lieutenant Reiker's as he stood on the sidelines, watching. Why here, she asked herself as she was snatched up and spun again. Why would he come here? Perhaps he was watching her—but why? Protecting her—from what?

Then she was in Cliff's arms again, grateful that her feet could follow the mindless repetition of the dance while her thoughts raced in dozens of directions. Hadn't Cliff said people came from all over to this all-night festival? Maybe Reiker was a country-dance enthusiast. More likely, she thought grimly, he'd wanted to see all the townspeople together, observe, dissect. She shuddered. It was his job, she reminded herself. He was only doing his job. But how she wished he'd go away.

There was Louella, seeming to float through the dance.

Rather than verve, she had a restrained dignity in her movements that was both lovely and uncomfortable to watch.
Lovely, Maggie realized, because Louella had the grace of a
natural dancer. Uncomfortable—though she wasn't able to put
her finger on it, Maggie sensed there was something beneath
the restraint that struggled for release.

Fanciful, she berated herself. She was being foolish and
fanciful, imagining things that weren't there. But the feeling
of discomfort was persistent. She was being watched, she
knew. By Reiker? Stan Agee, Joyce, Louella? By everyone,
Maggie thought. They all knew one another; they'd all known
William Morgan. She was the outsider who'd uncovered what
had been dead and buried for a decade. Logic indicated that
at least one of them would resent her for that—perhaps all of
them.

Suddenly, the music was too loud, the steps were too fast
and the air was too full of scent.

Then she was caught up in Bog's short, wiry arms and spun
at a breathless pace. "You're a good spinner, Miss Maggie,"
he told her, grinning and showing several gaps instead of
teeth. "One helluva spinner."

Looking down into his homely, wrinkled face, she broke
into a grin of her own. She was being ridiculous. No one
resented her. Why should they? She wasn't involved in a tragedy that was ten years old. It was time she stopped looking
beneath the surface and accepted things as she saw them. "I
love to spin!" she shouted to Bog, leaning back into it. "I
could spin for hours."

He gave a cackling laugh and released her for the next
sequence. The music built, but it no longer seemed too loud.
The tempo increased, but she could've danced faster and faster. When it was over, she had her hands linked around Cliff's
neck and was laughing.

There was no tension in her now, but there had been. He
thought he understood the reason. Deliberately, he steered her
away from the Agees and Louella. "I could use a beer."

"Sounds perfect. I'd like to watch another one, anyway.
It's the best show in town."

"You want a beer?"

Maggie glanced up, brow lifted. "Aren't I allowed?"

He shrugged and passed a man in overalls a dollar. "You just don't look like the beer type."

"You type too easily," Maggie countered, watching as beer was tapped from a wooden keg into paper cups.

"Maybe," he murmured as she sipped at the froth. "You're having a good time?"

"Yes." She laughed over the rim. The beer was lukewarm, but it was wet. Her foot was already tapping. They'd added a mandolin, she noticed. The sound was sweet and old-fashioned. "Didn't you think I would?"

"I thought you'd enjoy the music." He leaned against the wall so that he could see her with the dancers at her back. "I thought you needed to get out. But I didn't expect you to take to all this as if you'd been born doing it."

She lowered her half-empty cup and gave him a solemn smile. "When are you going to stop putting me in that shiny glass cage, Cliff? I'm not a delicate hothouse flower or a spoiled Hollywood bitch. I'm Maggie Fitzgerald, and I write music."

The look held for a long time while the music pulsed around them. "I think I know who you are." Lifting a hand, he ran the back of it down her cheek. "I think I know Maggie Fitzgerald. It might've been safer for both of us with you in that glass cage."

She felt the heat rise. It only took a touch. "We'll have to see, won't we?" With one brow still lifted in question, she touched her cup to his. "To new understanding?"

"All right." He cradled her chin in his hand before he kissed her. "We'll give it a shot."

"Miss Fitzgerald?"

Maggie turned to see a short man in his early twenties running a felt hat around and around in his hands. Until that moment, she'd been so intent on Cliff that she hadn't noticed the music had stopped. "You're the piano player." Her eyes lit, and the smile that could stun so unexpectedly curved on her lips. "You're wonderful."

He'd been nervous before; now he was overwhelmed. "I just— Thank you," he managed, staring at her with his soul in his eyes.

She doesn't even know it, Cliff realized. She wasn't aware that she could make a man want to grovel. Sipping his beer, he watched the piano player try to find his voice again.

"I couldn't believe it when I heard you were here."

"I live here," she told him simply.

The way she said it, so matter-of-factly, had Cliff looking at her again. She'd said it before, countless times in countless ways, but he realized now he hadn't listened. Yes, she lived here. She'd chosen to live here just as he had. It hardly mattered where she'd lived or how she'd lived before. She was here now because she'd chosen to be. And she was staying. For the first time, he fully believed it.

"Miss Fitzgerald…" The piano player crushed the brim of his hat in his fingers, torn between pleasure and anxiety. "I just wanted you to know it's great having you here. We don't want to push you into anything, but if you'd like to play anything, anything at all—"

"Are you asking?" she interrupted.

The boy stumbled over uncertain ground. "We just wanted you to know that if you'd like—"

"I don't know any of the songs," she told him, taking a last sip of beer. "Do you trust me to improvise?"

His mouth dropped open. "Are you kidding?"

She laughed and handed her cup to Cliff. "Hang on to this."

He shook his head, leaning back against the wall as she walked to the stage with the piano player. She had a habit of giving orders, he mused. Then he thought of the look of stunned admiration in the boy's eyes. Maybe it was worth it.

She played for an hour. It was, she discovered, as much fun making the music as it was dancing to it. She enjoyed the challenge of the unfamiliar music and the freewheeling style. Before she'd gone through the second number, Maggie had decided to write one of her own.

From the vantage point of the stage, she could see the dancers. She saw Louella again, partnered by Stan. Automatically, she searched the crowd for Joyce and found her, facing Cliff. As if she'd known he'd be there, her gaze was drawn to the left. Reiker leaned against a post, smoking, watching the dancers.

Who? Maggie wondered. Who is he watching? As the lines merged and shifted, she couldn't be sure, only that the direction of his gaze rested on where Stan danced with Louella and Cliff with Joyce.

If he saw one of them as a murderer, it didn't show in his eyes. They were calm and steady and made Maggie's stomach queasy. Deliberately, she turned her head and concentrated on the music.

"I didn't expect to lose my partner to a piano," Cliff said when the music paused again.

Maggie sent him an arch look. "You didn't appear to lack for any."

"A lone man's easy prey around here." Grabbing her hand, he drew her to her feet. "Hungry?"

"Is it midnight already?" Maggie pressed a hand to her stomach. "I'm starving."

They piled their plates high, though the light was so dim it was impossible to tell what they were eating until it was tasted. They sat on the grass under a tree and chatted easily to the people who passed by. It was easy, Maggie thought. They were just people drawn to one place by music. Again she felt a sense of camaraderie and connection. Leaning back, Maggie scanned the crowd.

"I don't see Louella."

"Stan would've taken her home," Cliff said between bites. "She never stays past midnight. He'll come back."

"Mmm." Maggie sampled what turned out to be Waldorf salad.

"Miss Fitzgerald."

Maggie set down her fork as Reiker crouched down beside her. "Lieutenant."

"I enjoyed your playing." He gave her the quiet smile that

had her cursing her reaction to him. "I've listened to your music for years, but I never expected to be able to hear you play."

"I'm glad you liked it." She knew she should leave it at that, but felt compelled to go on. "I haven't noticed you dancing."

"Me?" The smile turned sheepish. "No, I don't dance. My wife, now, she likes to come."

Maggie felt herself relax. So the explanation had been a simple one, an innocent one. "Most people who appreciate music like to dance."

"I'd like to. My feet don't." His gaze shifted to Cliff. "I want to thank you for your cooperation. It might help us tie up a few loose ends."

"Whatever I can do," Cliff said briskly. "We'd all like this business tied up."

Reiker nodded, then, with some effort, rose. "I hope you'll play some more before the night's over, Miss Fitzgerald. It's a real pleasure listening to you."

When he was gone, Maggie let out a long breath. "It isn't fair that he makes me uncomfortable. He's only doing his job." She began to pick at her food again when Cliff remained silent. "What did he mean by cooperation?"

"I contacted my mother. She's coming up Monday to give a statement."

"I see. That must be difficult for her."

"No." Cliff shrugged it off. "It was ten years ago. It's behind her. It's behind all of us," he added quietly, "but one."

Maggie closed her eyes on a shudder. She wouldn't think of it now, not tonight. "Dance with me again," she insisted when the musicians began to tune. "There are hours yet before dawn."

She never tired, even after the moon began to set. The music and the movement gave her the release she needed for nervous energy. Some dancers faded; others became only more exuberant as the night grew later. The music never stopped.

As the sky began to lighten, there were no more than a hundred dancers left on their feet. There was something mystical, something powerful, in watching the sun rise from behind the mountains while the music poured onto the air. As the light grew rosy with the new day, the last waltz was called.

Cliff folded Maggie in his arms and circled the floor. He could feel the life vibrate from her—exciting, strong. Once she'd stopped, he thought as he gathered her closer, she'd sleep for hours.

She moved with him, snug against him. Her heartbeat was steady, her hair soft. He watched the colors spread over the mountains to the east. Then she tilted back her head and smiled at him.

And when he realized he was in love with her, Cliff was stunned and speechless.

Chapter 12

Maggie might've noticed Cliff's abrupt withdrawal if she hadn't been so full of the night and the music. "I can't believe it's over. I've hours more dancing in me."

"You'll be asleep before you're home," Cliff told her, but made certain he wasn't touching her. He must be crazy, falling in love with a woman like her. She couldn't decide whether to hang wallpaper or lay tile. She gave orders. She wore silk under her jeans. He must be crazy.

But she could dance with him through the night. There was a ridge of strength and courage under the delicate features. She made music that was part heaven and part sin. Hadn't he known, and hadn't he fought so hard, because he'd known almost from the first that she was a woman he'd never get out of his mind?

Now she was climbing into the cab of his pickup and resting her head against his shoulder as if it belonged there. It did belong there. Though the acceptance didn't come easily to him, Cliff put his arm around her, drawing her closer. She belonged there.

"I don't know when I've had such a good time." The energy was draining out of her swiftly. Through sheer will, Maggie kept her eyes open.

"The music's still running around in your head."

She tilted her head so that she could see his profile. "I think you are beginning to understand me."

"Some."

"Some's enough." She yawned hugely. "It was fun playing tonight. You know, I've always avoided performing, mainly because I knew it would only open the door for more comparisons. But tonight…"

Cliff frowned, not certain if he liked the drift. "You're thinking of performing?"

"No, not on a regular basis. If I'd had a drive to do it, I'd have done it long before this." She shifted into a more comfortable position. "But I've decided to take C.J.'s advice and do the title song for *Heat Dance*. It's a compromise, a recording rather than a performance. And I do feel rather personally toward that song."

"You decided this tonight?"

"I've been leaning toward it for quite a while. It seems foolish to live by rules so strict you can't do something you really want to do. I really want to do that song." As her head began to droop, she noticed they were turning into her lane. "It'll mean flying back to L.A. for a few days for the taping, which'll thrill C.J." She gave a sleepy laugh. "He'll pull out every trick in the book to keep me from coming back."

Cliff felt the panic in his chest. He pulled the truck up at the end of the drive and set the brake. "I want you to marry me."

"What?" Half asleep, Maggie shook her head, certain she'd misunderstood.

"I want you to marry me," Cliff repeated, but this time he took her shoulders so that she wasn't slumped down in the seat any longer. "I don't care if you record a dozen songs. You're going to marry me before you go back to California."

To say she was stunned would've been an immeasurable understatement. Maggie stared at him as if one of them had lost his mind. "I must be a little foggy at the moment," she said slowly. "Are you saying you want to marry me?"

"You know damn well what I'm saying." It was too much to know the fear of losing her just when he'd realized he

Night Moves

couldn't live without her. He couldn't be calm; he couldn't be rational; he couldn't let her go without a pledge that she'd come back. "You're not going to California until you marry me."

Trying to clear her mind, Maggie drew back. "Are you talking about my doing a recording, or are we talking marriage? One has to do with my business, the other with my life."

Frustrated that she was calm when he couldn't be, Cliff dragged her back. "From now on, your life is my business."

"No." That sounded too familiar. "No, I don't want someone looking out for me, if that's what you mean. I won't take that kind of responsibility again, or that kind of guilt."

"I don't know what the hell you're talking about," Cliff exploded. "I'm telling you you're going to marry me."

"That's just it—you can't *tell* me!" She jerked away from him, and the sleepiness in her eyes had turned to fire. "Jerry told me we were getting married, and I went along because it seemed like the thing to do. He was my best friend. He'd helped me get over the death of my parents, encouraged me to write again. He wanted to take care of me." Maggie dragged a hand through her hair. "And I let him, until things started going downhill and he couldn't even take care of himself. I couldn't help him then. The pattern had been set, and I couldn't help him. Not again, Cliff. I won't be put in that glass cage again."

"This has nothing to do with your first marriage and nothing to do with cages," Cliff tossed back. "You can damn well take care of yourself, but you're going to marry me."

Her eyes narrowed into slits as she held down her own uncertain temper. "Why?"

"Because I'm telling you."

"Wrong answer." With a toss of her head, she was out of the truck and had slammed the door. "You can go cool off or go sleep it off or whatever you want," she told him coldly. "I'm going to bed." Turning on her heel, she strode up the shaky front steps to the door. As she turned the handle, she heard the sound of his truck descending the hill. *Let him go,* Maggie told herself before she could turn around and call him back. *You can't let yourself be pushed around that way.* When a man thinks he can order a woman to marry him, he deserves exactly what she'd given him, Maggie decided. A good swift kick in the ego. Imagine bringing up marriage out of the blue that way, she thought as she shoved open the front door. Marriage, not love. He dangled marriage at her as though it were a carrot at the end of a stick. She wasn't biting. If he wanted her, really wanted her, he'd have to do a hell of a lot better.

I love you. She leaned her head against the door and told herself she wouldn't cry. That's all it would've taken; that's all he'd needed to say. Understanding. No, she decided as she straightened again, they were still a long way from understanding each other.

Why wasn't the dog barking, she wondered grumpily as she pushed the door shut again. Terrific watchdog he'd turned out to be. Annoyed, she turned toward the steps, planning on a hot bath and a long sleep, when a scent stopped her. Candle wax, Maggie thought, puzzled. Roses? Odd, she thought. Her imagination was good, but not good enough to conjure up scents. She crossed toward the living room and stopped in the doorway.

Louella sat very straight and very prim in a high-backed chair. Her hands were neatly folded in the lap of the same misty-gray dress she'd worn for dancing. Her skin was so pale that the shadows under her eyes looked like bruises. The eyes themselves seemed to stare straight through Maggie. On the table beside her there were candles burning, the tapers hardly more than stubs now, with the wax pooled heavily on the base of the holders. A vase of fresh roses sat nearby, so that the breeze through the open window carried the scent through the room.

After the first shock, Maggie tried to bring her thoughts to order. It had been obvious from the first that Louella wasn't completely well. She'd have to be handled gently, Maggie thought, and so she approached her as one might a wounded bird.

"Mrs. Morgan," she said quietly, then cautiously touched a hand to her shoulder.

"I've always liked candlelight." Louella spoke in her calm, soft voice. "So much prettier than a lamp. I'd often burn candles in the evening."

"They're lovely." Maggie kept her tone gentle as she knelt beside her. "But it's morning now."

"Yes." Louella looked blankly at the sun-filled window. "I often sit up through the night. I like the sounds. The woods make such music at night."

Perhaps if she'd thought it through, Maggie wouldn't have questioned. She would simply have led Louella out to her car and driven her home. But she didn't think it through. "Do you often come here at night, Mrs. Morgan?"

"Sometimes I'll drive," she said dreamily. "Sometimes, if the night's as clear and warm as this, I'll walk. I used to walk a great deal as a girl. Joyce used to love to toddle on the paths in the woods when she was just a baby."

Maggie moistened her lips. "Do you come back here often, Mrs. Morgan, at night?"

"I know I should stay away. Joyce has told me so all along. But—" Louella sighed, and the small, sad smile touched her mouth. "She has Stan. Such a good man—they take care of each other. That's what marriage is, you know, loving and taking care of each other."

"Yes." Helplessly, Maggie watched as Louella's hands grew agitated in her lap.

"William wasn't a loving man. He just wasn't made that way. I wanted Joyce to have a loving man, like Stan." She lapsed into silence, closing her eyes and breathing shallowly so that Maggie thought she slept. Deciding it was best to call the Agees, she started to rise, when Louella's hand closed over hers.

"I followed him here that night," she whispered. Now her eyes were intense, fully focused. Maggie's mouth went dry.

"Followed him?"

"I didn't want anything to happen. Joyce loved him so."

Maggie struggled to keep her voice low and even, her eyes steady. "You followed your husband here?"

"William was here," Louella told her. "He was here, and he had the money. I knew he was going to do something dreadful, something he'd have gotten away with because of who he was. There had to be an end to it." Her fingers tightened convulsively on Maggie's, then relaxed just as abruptly as her head fell back. "Of course, the money couldn't be buried with him. I thought, no, if they find him, they shouldn't find the money. So I hid it."

"Here," Maggie managed. "In the attic."

"In the old trunk. I forgot all about it," Louella said as fatigue washed through her voice. "Forgot until a few weeks ago, when they dug in the gully. I came and took the money out and burned it, as I should've burned it ten years ago."

Maggie looked down at the hand that lay limply on hers. It was frail, the blue veins showing sharply against the thin ivory skin. Could that hand have pulled a trigger, sending a bullet into a man? Maggie shifted her gaze to Louella's face and saw it was now serene in sleep.

What do I do? Maggie asked herself as she laid Louella's hand carefully back in her lap. Call the police? Maggie looked at the peacefully sleeping, fragile figure in the chair. No, she couldn't; she didn't have the steel for it. She'd call Joyce.

She went to the phone and asked the operator for Joyce's number. There was no answer at the Agee house. Maggie sighed and glanced over her shoulder into the living room at Louella, who was still sleeping. She hated to do it, but she had to call Lieutenant Reiker. When she couldn't get hold of him, either, she left a message with his office.

Coming back into the living room, Maggie gasped as a figure moved toward her. "Oh, you frightened me."

"Sorry." Stan looked with concern from Maggie to his mother-in-law. "I came in the back. The dog's sleeping pretty heavily in the kitchen. Looks like Louella might've given him part of a sleeping pill to keep him quiet."

"Oh." Maggie made an instinctive move toward the kitchen.

"He's all right," Stan assured her. "He'll just be a little groggy when he wakes up."

"Sheriff—Stan," she decided, hoping the lack of formality would make it easier for him. "I was just about to call you. I think Louella's been here most of the night."

"I'm sorry." He rubbed his own sleep-starved eyes. "She's been getting steadily worse since this business started. Joyce and I don't want to put her in a home."

"No." Concerned, she touched his arm. "But she told me she wanders at night, and—" Maggie broke off and circled the room. Could she tell him what Louella had said? He was her son-in-law, but he was still the sheriff. The badge and the gun he wore reminded her.

"I heard what she told you, Maggie."

She turned, her eyes filled with compassion and concern. "What should we do? She's so fragile. I can't bear to be a part of having her punished for something that happened so long ago. And yet, if she killed..." With her conscience tearing her in different directions, she turned again.

"I don't know." Stan looked at Louella while he rubbed the back of his neck. "What she told you doesn't have to be true."

"But it makes sense," Maggie insisted. "She knew about the money. If she'd hid it in the trunk, then forgotten about it, blocked it out because it reminded her—" Maggie shook her head and forced herself to continue. "Stan, it's the only explanation for the break-in here." She covered her face with her hands as her sense of right and wrong battled. "She needs help," Maggie said abruptly. "She doesn't need police or lawyers. She needs a doctor."

Relief ran over Stan's face. "She'll get one. The best one Joyce and I can find."

Shaky, uncertain, Maggie rested a hand on the table. "She's devoted to you," she murmured. "She always speaks so highly of you, of how you love Joyce. I think she'd do anything she could to keep both of you happy."

As she spoke, Maggie's gaze was drawn down to where her palm rested—on the color snapshot of Morgan and Stan, near the gully. It would all be laid to rest now, she thought as she stared down at the photo. Louella had suffered enough, been punished enough for—

Distracted, she narrowed her eyes and looked closer. Why it came to her now, Maggie would never know, but she remembered Reiker's words. "We found a ring, too, an old ring with a lot of fancy carving and three small diamond chips...Joyce Agee identified it as her father's."

But in the picture William Morgan wasn't wearing the ring. Stan Agee was.

She looked up, her eyes dry and clear with the knowledge.

He didn't have to look at the picture under her hand. He'd already seen. "You should've let it go, Maggie."

She didn't stop to think, to reason; she only reacted. In a dead run, she headed for the front door. The move was so unexpected, she was into the hall with her hand on the knob before he'd taken the first step. As the door stuck, she cursed it, cursed her own inefficiency for not having it seen to weeks before. As she started to tug a second time, Stan's hand closed over her arm.

"Don't." His voice was low and strained. "I don't want to hurt you. I have to think this through."

With her back to the door, Maggie stared at him. She was alone in the house with a murderer. Alone, she thought desperately, except for a fragile old woman who loved him enough to have shielded him for ten years. Maggie watched him rest his hand on the butt of his gun.

"We'd better sit down."

Cliff drank his second cup of coffee and wished it was bourbon. If he'd tried to make a fool of himself over a woman, he could've done no better. Drinking in the strong, bitter taste, he scowled down at the laminated counter in the café. The scent of frying eggs and sausage did nothing for his appetite.

How could he have botched it so badly? What woman in her right mind, he asked himself, would respond favorably to a shouted, angry proposal? Maggie had given him the heave-ho, and now that he'd cooled off a bit, he couldn't blame her.

Still, he wasn't one of the fancy crowd she'd run with in L.A., he reminded himself. He wasn't going to change his manners for her any more than he expected her to change for him. She'd chosen to change her life before he'd been a part of it.

Chosen, Cliff thought again, cursing himself. She'd chosen her home, and he'd never seen anyone put down roots so quickly. He shouldn't have panicked at the mention of the recording in L.A. She'd be back. The land was as important to her as it was to him. Perhaps that had been their first bond, though they both insisted they'd had no common ground.

She'd be back, Cliff told himself again. He'd been an idiot to think bullying her into marriage would assure that. Maggie wouldn't be bullied, and she was here to stay. Those were two of the reasons he loved her.

He should have told her that, he thought, pushing the unwanted coffee aside. He could have found the words to tell her he'd been in love with her for weeks and that at dawn, with the morning light spilling over her face, he'd realized it. It had taken his breath away, stolen his senses, made him weak. He could've found the words to tell her.

Straightening from the counter, he checked his watch. She'd had an hour's sleep. Cliff decided a woman didn't need any more than that for a proper proposal of marriage. He tossed the money on the counter and began to whistle.

He continued to whistle as he took the road through town, until Joyce dashed into the street and frantically hailed him.

"Oh, Cliff!"

Though he'd stopped the car in the middle of the street, he was halfway out of it as he spoke. "What is it, one of the kids?"

"No, no." Struggling for calm, Joyce gripped his arms. She, too, hadn't changed from the dance, but the hair she'd worn up was now escaping its pins and falling in clumps. "It's my mother," she managed after a moment. "She hasn't been in bed all night—and Stan, I can't find Stan anywhere."

"We'll find Louella." Cliff brushed the hair from her face as he'd done since she'd been a child. "She might have been restless and gone for a walk. With the excitement last night—''

"Cliff." Joyce gripped his arms tighter. "I think she went out to the old place. I'm dead sure of it; it wouldn't be the first time."

He thought of Maggie with a little ripple of unease. "Maggie's home," he said soothingly. "She'll look out for her."

"She's been getting worse." Joyce's breath began to shudder. "Oh, Cliff, I thought I was doing the right thing, the only thing."

"What're you talking about?"

"I lied to the police. I lied before I'd thought it through, but I know I'd do the same thing again." She pressed her fingers to her eyes briefly, then dropped them. When she looked at Cliff now, she looked at him with a surface calm that was deadly. "I know who killed my father. I've known for weeks. Mother—it seems Mother's known for ten years."

"Get in," he ordered. He was thinking of Maggie now, of Maggie alone in the house, surrounded by woods. "Tell me while we drive."

Maggie's back was stiff and straight as she sat on a low bench. Moving only her eyes, she watched Stan pace the room. She wanted to believe he wouldn't hurt her. But he'd killed once, ten years before. Now he'd have to deal with her or pay for it.

"I never wanted Joyce to sell this house." He paced to the window, then back to the center of the room. "I never wanted it. The money meant nothing to me. Her money—her father's money—never has. How could I've guessed she'd get it into her head to put it on the market when I was out of town?"

He ran a hand over his shirt and left faint streaks. He's sweating, Maggie noted. It didn't help her nerves.

"She lied to the police about the ring."

Maggie moistened her lips. "She loves you."

"She didn't know—I'd never told her all these years. Then, when I finally had to, she stood by me. A man can't ask for more than that." He paced again, so that the soles of his shoes hitting hardwood and rug were the only sounds. "I didn't murder him," Stan said flatly. When he looked at Maggie, his eyes were glazed with fatigue. "It was an accident."

She gripped that, clung to that. "Then if you go to the police and explain—"

"Explain?" Stan cut her off. "Explain that I killed a man, buried him and drove his car into the river?" He rubbed the heels of his hands over his face. "I was only twenty," he began. "Joyce and I'd been in love for two years. Morgan had already made it clear that there couldn't be anything between us, so we saw each other in secret. When Joyce found out she was pregnant, there couldn't be any more secrets."

He leaned against the window and stared into the room. "We should've known there was something wrong when he took it so well, but we were both so relieved, both so thrilled at the idea of being married and starting a family, that we never caught on. He told us to keep it quiet for a few weeks while he arranged for the wedding."

Maggie remembered the stern face from the photograph. "But he didn't mean it."

"No, both of us were too wrapped up in each other to remember what kind of man he was." Stan kept moving in the same line, to the window, back to the center of the room, to the window again. "He said he was having trouble with groundhogs up at his old place. I was young and eager to do anything to keep on the right side of him. I told him I'd bring my shotgun one evening after work and take care of them."

He saw Maggie shudder and glance at the pistol on his hip. "It was dusk when he drove up. I didn't expect him. When he got out of the car, I remember thinking he looked like an undertaker, all in black with shiny shoes. He was carrying a little metal box that he set down on the stump of a tree near the gully. He didn't waste any time," Stan continued. "He told me outright that he'd never let a small-town nobody like me marry his daughter. He said he was going to send her away. Sweden or somewhere. She'd have the baby and give it away. He didn't expect me to keep quiet for nothing. He told me he had twenty-five thousand in the box. I was to take it and disappear.''

So the twenty-five thousand had been payoff money, blackmail. Yes, she could believe that the man in the photo had thought money would ensure anything.

''I got frantic. I couldn't believe he was threatening to take away everything I'd ever wanted. He could've done it, too.'' Stan wiped at the sweat that beaded on his upper lip. ''He would've done it without a second thought. I shouted at him. I told him he wasn't going to take Joyce and our baby away from me. I told him we'd go away, we didn't need his filthy money. He opened the cash box and showed me all those bills, as if it would tempt me. I knocked it out of his hands.''

His breath was coming quickly now, heavily, as if he were reliving that moment—the anger, the despair. Maggie felt her pity well up to tangle with her fear.

''He never lost his temper. Never once. He just bent down and scooped the money back in the box. He thought I wanted more. He never understood, wasn't capable of understanding. When it got to the point where he saw I wasn't going to take the money and go away, he picked up my gun just as calmly as he'd picked up the box. I knew, as sure as I'd ever know anything, that he'd kill me where I stood and he'd get away with it. Somehow he'd get away with it. All I could think was that I'd never see Joyce again, never hold our baby. I grabbed for the gun—it went off over my shoulder. We started struggling.''

He was panting now, his eyes glazed. Maggie could visualize the struggle between man and boy as clearly as if it were happening in front of her eyes. She shut them. Then she saw the scene in the film she'd scored in which overpowering need had erupted into irrevocable violence. But this was real and needed no music to spark the drama.

''He was strong—that old man was strong. I knew I'd be dead if I didn't get the gun away. Somehow—'' Stan dragged both his hands up his face and into his hair. ''Somehow I had it in my hands and was falling back. I'll never forget—it was like a dream, a nightmare. I was falling back, and the gun went off.''

She could picture it, all too clearly. Both sympathetic and afraid, Maggie dared to speak. "But it was an accident, self-defense.''

He shook his head as his hands dropped back to his side, back, she noted with a tremor, near the gun on his hip. "I was twenty, scraping pennies. I'd just killed the most important man in town, and there was twenty-five thousand dollars in a box next to his body. Who'd have believed me? Maybe I panicked, maybe I did the only sensible thing, but I buried him and his money in the gully, then sent his car into the river.''

"Louella..." Maggie began.

"I didn't know she'd followed me. I guess she knew Morgan better than anyone and understood he'd never let me marry Joyce. I didn't know she'd watched everything from the woods. Maybe if I had, things would've been different. It seemed she never really came out of the shock of losing her husband; now I understand better. She'd seen it all—then, for some reason of her own, she'd dug out the cash box and hidden it in the house. I guess she was protecting me all these years.''

"And Joyce?''

"She never knew.'' Stan shook his head and tugged at the collar of his shirt as if it were too tight. "I never told her. You have to understand. I love Joyce. I've loved her since she was a girl. There's nothing I wouldn't do for her if I could. If I'd told her everything, everything he'd threatened to do and what had happened, she might have thought—she might not have believed it was an accident. I couldn't have lived with that. For years I've done everything I could to make up for what happened in that gully. I dedicated myself to the law, to the town. I've been the best father, the best husband, I know how to be.''

He picked up the color snapshot and crushed it in his hand. "That damn picture. Damn ring. I was so wired up I didn't notice I'd lost it until days afterward. My grandfather's ring.''

He rubbed a hand over his temple. "Ten years later it's dug up with Morgan. Do you know how I felt when I learned that Joyce had identified it as her father's? She knew," he said passionately. "She knew it was mine, but she stood behind me. She never questioned me, and when I told her everything, she never doubted me. All these years—I've lived with it all these years."

"You don't have to live with it anymore." Maggie spoke calmly, though her heart was in her throat. He was strung so tight she couldn't gauge when he might snap or what he might do. "People respect you, know you. Louella saw everything. She'd testify."

"Louella's on the edge of a complete breakdown. Who knows if she'd be capable of making a coherent sentence if all this comes out? I have to think of Joyce, of my family, of my reputation." A muscle began to jerk in his cheek as he stared at Maggie. "There's so much at stake," he whispered. "So much to protect."

She watched his hand hover over the butt of his gun.

Cliff started up the steep lane at full speed, spitting gravel. Joyce's breathless story told him one vital thing. Maggie was caught in the middle of violence and passion that had simmered underground for ten years. If it erupted today, she'd be alone—alone because he'd been a fool. As he rounded the top curve, a man stepped into the path of the car, forcing him to brake. Swearing, Cliff stormed out of the car.

"Mr. Delaney," Reiker said mildly. "Mrs. Agee."

"Where's Maggie?" Cliff demanded, and would've moved past him if Reiker hadn't stopped him with a surprisingly strong grip.

"She's inside. At the moment, she's fine. Let's keep it that way."

"I'm going up."

"Not yet." He gave Cliff a long, steely look before he turned to Joyce. "Your mother's inside, Mrs. Agee. She's fine, sleeping. Your husband's in there, too."

"Stan." Joyce looked toward the house, taking an instinctive step forward.

"I've been keeping a close eye on things. Your husband told Miss Fitzgerald everything."

Cliff's blood iced. "Damn it, why haven't you gotten her out?"

"We're going to get her out. We're going to get them all out. Quietly."

"How do you know he won't hurt her?"

"I don't—if he's pushed. I want your help, Mrs. Agee. If your husband loves you as much as he says, you're the key." He looked toward the house. "He'd have heard the car. Better let him know you're here."

Inside the house, Stan had Maggie by the arm, holding her close as he stood at the window. She could feel his muscles jumping, hear his breath whistling. As terror washed over her, she closed her eyes and thought of Cliff. If he'd come back, everything would be all right. If he came back, the nightmare would end.

"Someone's out there." Stan jerked his head toward the open window, and his free hand opened and closed on the butt of his gun. "I can't let you talk to anyone. You have to understand. I can't risk it."

"I won't." His fingers dug into her arm so that the pain kept her head clear. "Stan, I want to help you. I swear I only want to help. If you hurt me, it'll never be over."

"Ten years," he muttered, straining to see any movement outside. "Ten years and he's still trying to ruin my life. I can't let him."

"Your life will be ruined if you do anything to me." *Be logical,* Maggie told herself as waves of panic threatened to overtake her. *Be calm.* "It wouldn't be an accident this time, Stan. This time you'd be a murderer. You'd never make Joyce understand."

His fingers tightened until she had to dig her teeth into her lower lip to keep from crying out. "Joyce stood behind me."

"She loves you. She believes in you. But if you hurt me, everything would change."

She felt him tremble. The grip on her arm loosened fractionally. As Maggie watched, Joyce walked up over the rise toward the house. At first, she thought she was hallucinating; then she heard Stan's breath catch. He saw her, too.

"Stan." Joyce's hand moved on her throat, as if she could make her voice stronger. "Stan, please come out."

"I don't want you involved in this." Stan's fingers were like iron on Maggie's arm again.

"I am involved. I've always been involved. I know everything you did you did for me."

"Damn it." He pressed his face against the window glass, pounding one fist steadily against the frame. "He can't ruin everything we've built."

"No, he can't." Joyce came closer to the house, measuring each step. In all the years she'd known her husband, she'd never heard despair in his voice. "Stan, he can't touch us now. We're together. We'll always be together."

"They'll take me away from you. The law." He squeezed his eyes tighter. "I've done my best by the law."

"Everyone knows that. Stan, I'll be with you. I love you. You're everything to me, my whole life. Please, please, don't do anything I'd be ashamed of."

Maggie felt him tense as he straightened from the window. The muscle was still working in his cheek. There was a line of sweat over his lip he no longer bothered to wipe away. He stared out the window, at Joyce, then over at the gully.

"Ten years," he whispered. "But it's still not over."

His fingers worked sporadically on Maggie's arm. Numb with fear, she watched as he drew the gun out of its holster. His eyes met hers, cold, clear blue, without expression. Perhaps she would've begged for her life, but she knew, as any prey knows, that mercy comes at the hunter's whim.

His expression never changed as he set the gun down on the sill and released her arm. Maggie felt her blood begin to pump again, fast and hot. "I'm going outside," Stan said flatly, "to my wife."

Weak with relief, Maggie sank down on the piano stool.

Without even the energy to weep, she buried her face in her hands.

"Oh, Maggie." Then Cliff's arms were around her, and she could feel the hard, fast beat of his heart. "That was the longest ten minutes of my life," he murmured as he began to run wild kisses over her face. "The longest."

She didn't want explanations. He was here; that was enough. "I kept telling myself you'd come. It kept me sane."

"I shouldn't have left you alone." He buried his face in her hair and drew in the scent.

She held him tighter. "I told you I could take care of myself."

He laughed, because she was in his arms and nothing had changed. "Yes, you did. It's over now." He framed her face in his hands so that he could study it. Pale, he noticed. The eyes were shadowed but steady. His Maggie was a woman who could take care of herself. "Reiker was outside, long enough to get the drift of what was going on. He's taking all three of them."

She thought of Louella's pale face, Stan's anguished eyes, Joyce's trembling voice. "They've been punished enough."

"Maybe." He ran his hands up her arms, just to assure himself she was whole and safe. "If he'd hurt you—"

"He wouldn't have." She shook her head and clung again. "He couldn't have. I want the pond, Cliff," she said fiercely. "I want you to put in the pond quickly, and I want to see the willow draping over it."

"You'll have it." He drew her back again. "And me? Will you have me, Maggie?"

She took a deep breath, letting his fingers rest on her face again. Again, she thought. She would try again and see if he understood. "Why should I?"

His brows drew together, but he managed to swallow the oath that came to mind. Instead, he kissed her, hard and long. "Because I love you."

She let out a trembling breath. She was indeed home. "That was the right answer."

* * * * *

**The Wolfe twins' stories—
together in one fantastic volume!**

USA TODAY **bestselling author**

JOAN HOHL

Double WOLFE

The emotional story of Matilda Wolfe plus an original short story about Matilda's twin sister, Lisa. The twins have followed different paths...but each leads to true love!

Look for DOUBLE WOLFE in January 2004.

"A compelling storyteller who weaves her tales with verve, passion and style."
—*New York Times* **bestselling author Nora Roberts**

Silhouette®

Where love comes alive™